'*What the Body Remembers* will surely be hailed as one of the most important and original novels about Indian history'

KEVIN BALDEOSINGH, CHAIRPERSON OF CARIBBEAN AND CANADA JUDGING PANEL FOR THE COMMONWEALTH WRITERS PRIZE

'Taking as its subject the huge and complicated canvas of pre- and post-Indian independence from 1937–47, *What the Body Remembers* is set in a Punjab seething with political unrest; but its themes and emotional heart are ancient ones of love, jealousy, infertility and religious fury, cunningly dovetailed into the saga of one Sikh family . . . the individual stories and complex religious and philosophical divisions are woven into the larger picture with supreme confidence and a poetic intensity. The characters shimmer with life, their predicaments grab the reader by the throat, their fate has the reader on the edge of the seat, their individual psychological journeys are instantly recognisable . . . offers a glimpse of humanity that is both intimate and universal . . . enthralling'

ELIZABETH BUCHAN, *THE TIMES*

'A sumptuous tour of that rich and poor a̶n̶d̶ ̶ nd chaotic country . . . a sweeping story . . . Baldwin offers us a moving and c̶ century India's most troubl

RON CARLSON, ̶w

'My favourite of all these excursions into the past . . . Baldwin plots the tale of India's violent partition as seen through the eyes of Roop, a Sikh girl born in Punjab . . . the charge of passion unspent gives the book its force'

NATASHA WALTER, *VOGUE*

'Its scope as a novel is as Victorian as Seth's *A Suitable Boy*; her focus on the eve of Indian independence and Pakistan's birth in August 1947 echoes Rushdie . . . an impressive first novel'

LORNA JACKSON, *QUILL & QUIRE*

'A captivating jewel of a novel by a seasoned and sophisticated writer . . . beyond being a compelling tale of individuals, *What the Body Remembers* offers a gimlet-eyed view of a pluralistic society's disintegration into factionalism and anarchy'

BELLA STANDER, *WASHINGTON POST*

'Complex characterisation is matched by the author's evocation of place . . . "cinematic" is the word for the sweep and urgency of this writing as it depicts escalating violence and impending doom . . . unique and unforgettable'

PATRICIA O'CONNELL, *SAN DIEGO UNION TRIBUNE*

'Imbued with the character of the land and the people . . . sensual on one level and political on another'

SUCHITRA BEHAL, *THE HINDU*

Shauna Singh Baldwin was born in Montreal and grew up in India. The author of *English Lessons and Other Stories* and the co-author of *A Foreign Visitor's Survival Guide to America*, her short stories have been published widely and she has won numerous prestigious literary prizes in Canada and India. She lives in Milwaukee with her Irish-American husband.

WHAT THE BODY REMEMBERS

Shauna Singh Baldwin

TRANSWORLD PUBLISHERS
61–63 Uxbridge Road, London W5 5SA
A division of The Random House Group Ltd.

RANDOM HOUSE AUSTRALIA (PTY) LTD
20 Alfred Street, Milsons Point, NSW 2061, Australia

RANDOM HOUSE NEW ZEALAND LTD
18 Poland Road, Glenfield, Auckland, New Zealand

RANDOM HOUSE (PTY) LTD
Endulini, 5a Jubilee Road, Parktown 2193, South Africa

This paperback edition published 2000 by Anchor,
a division of Transworld Publishers

First published in Great Britain by Doubleday, 1999

10 9 8 7 6 5 4 3 2 1

A catalogue record for this book is available from the British Library

ISBN 1862 30077 1

Typeset in Adobe Caslon by Falcon Oast Graphic Art
Printed in Great Britain by Clays Ltd, St Ives plc

For Amir,
Alexander Arjan, Sheila-Anne Jaya,
Piya, Ria and Toya,
Anyshka and Pravir; and Ameera

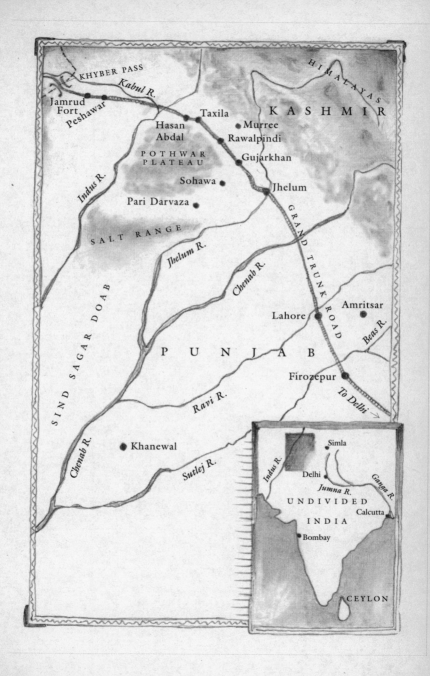

PROLOGUE

*I have grey eyes in this lifetime and they are wide open as I
    am
severed from my mother's womb. The futility of tears is for
    those
who have not, as I have, rolled the dice a few times.*

*If the circle that is your body falls on a ladder inscribed on
the game board of time, you climb. If it lands on a snake,
you slip–slide back. Resume your journey again.*

*And if you do not learn what you were meant to learn from
your past lives, you are condemned to repeat them.*

This is karma.

*So I do not cry, but I shriek and I curse and I rail as the
    midwife wraps me.*

*The midwife knows as I do already, testing the kick in my legs,
that I am not a boy. Against all odds, against every pandit's*

promise, despite a whole life of worship and expiation, I have slid down the snake's tail and for all the money and temple offerings I lavished on pandits the last time round, here I am again . . . born a woman.

All I have in the life I live now is my kismat: my wits and my will conjoined with my stars.

So angry am I, my eyes are open wide – never open your eyes in
a new life without forgetting your past ones. The midwife rolls me this way and that; she hopes it will soothe me. A girl who comes into this world with her eyes wide open will never lower them before a man.

If I find any of those pandits, I'll tear their hearts out.

Send their djinns to become insects again.

ONE

1937

1. Rawalpindi, Undivided India, 1937

Satya's heart is black and dense as a stone within her. She tells herself she pities Roop, but hears laughter answering her – how difficult it is to deceive yourself when you have known yourself a full forty-two years.

She has a servant summon Roop to her sitting room in the afternoon, when Sardarji has gone to a canal engineers' meeting. When she comes before her, Satya does not speak, but rises from the divan and takes Roop's chunni from her shoulders, as if in welcome, so she can study the girl. She takes Roop's chin and raises her face to the afternoon sun, willing it to blind her, but it will do her no such service. She studies Roop's features, her Pothwari skin, smooth as a new apricot beckoning from the limb of a tall tree, her wide, heavily lashed brown eyes. Unlike Satya's grey ones, they are demurely lowered, innocent.

A man could tell those eyes anything and they would believe him, a man could kiss those red lips for hours and they would look fuller and more luscious for the bruising.

Roop's hair is long, to her thighs, softened by amla and

scented with coconut. Unlike Satya's, it has no need yet for henna. Satya lifts Roop's plait around her shoulder and examines the tip – too few split ends; it has felt the scissors once at least, if not more.

Roop is a new Sikh, then, an uncomprehending carrier of the orthodoxy resurging in them all. Hindus, Sikhs, Muslims, they are like the three strands of her hair, a strong rope against the British, but separate nevertheless.

She unbinds Roop's hair. It falls, a moonlit river, down the valley of her spine.

She examines Roop's teeth and finds all of them whole, the back ones barely visible. She hopes that as they come they will bring pain. Roop's tongue is soft and a healthy pink and from it a man will hear no truths he cannot explain away. She presses her fingers to Roop's cheekbones, they are high, like her own. Some remnant of Afghan blood in their past; in other circumstances she might have been Roop's aunt or cousin.

Satya's hands drop to Roop's neck and encircle it lightly, for she is not trying to frighten her. And she sees Sardarji has given her a kantha necklace, one of her own. She knows the gold of this one well; she ordered it from the goldsmith herself, she knows every link in it and the sheen of its red enamel. She wore it last to a party full of Europeans. Its brilliance and its weight had comforted her, compensation for her tongue-tied state; the European ladies ignored her once they found she spoke no English.

She sees her kantha now, covering the hollow at Roop's neck and she wants to press her thumbnail in that hollow till Roop's red blood spurts and drips over them both.

She wants this.

She moves her hands, with no sign she recognizes the kantha, no hint she knows that Roop standing before her is a silent thief.

With such a tremulous placating smile.

Satya examines Roop's brow. Time is ploughing her own in three horizontal furrows, deepening by the day, but Roop's is still smooth. She pulls Roop's hair back over her ears and sees her own earrings. They are the ones Sardarji gave Satya, after her first pilgrimage to the first ineffectual sant, pleading for prayers. Satya knows these earrings well: three tiers of Burmese rubies surrounded by diamonds – real diamonds, not white sapphires – red-hearted flower shapes ending in large Basra teardrop pearls.

And Roop is wearing them.

Satya wants to tear them from the girl's ears, watch as Roop's tender lobes elongate and rip apart, wants to take back what is hers, rightfully hers.

But she moves her hands away.

'Come lie with me in the afternoons. You are alone on your side of the house, I am alone on my side. My pukkhawalla is better – he's from my village, our men are strong.'

Roop stands, uncomprehending. If she had been a blood-niece, or a cousin-sister, Satya would shout at her to stay away, to turn now and run before she gets hurt. And if Satya had been Roop's mother, Roop would be her daughter and none of this would have been necessary.

'Come,' she says again. 'It is useless for me to fight Sardarji's will; he is my husband, he has married you. Somehow I must accept that – and you.'

Roop's face lights up like a diya at Diwali.

'Oh, Bhainji.'

Sister.

Satya does not feel sisterly at all.

'Oh, Bhainji,' Roop says. 'I'm so glad. I told Sardarji, I will be no trouble, I will be just like a younger sister.'

And her silly tears fall on Satya's hand as she leads the girl to the bed.

Satya places herself in the path of the light from the inner courtyard, dismissing the servants hovering in attendance on the gallery that runs past her rooms. She lowers the reed chics past the casement till the sitting room, cool and dark, holds the sun at bay. The jute sack covering the block of ice in the corner slips to the floor. Exposed, the ice absorbs afternoon heat, weeps a dark puddle over the polished wood.

On the gallery, a pukkhawalla spits a red stream of paan, squats, his back to the wall. With a rope over one shoulder, he leans into pulling rhythm.

Back and forth, back and forth.

The rope worms through the wall and over a pulley near the ceiling, sets the huge wing of silk above the two women creaking.

Back and forth, back and forth.

The breeze from the pukkha moves from Satya to Roop and back again, doing nothing to cool Satya. She is white-hot inside, though if she could speak it out loud, it would be better to call it hurt or pain.

'Come, lie down,' Satya says.

She leads Roop from the sitting room to her bedroom and places a soft pillow beneath Roop's head to cradle her ruby earrings. She hears Roop's jutis plop to the floor behind her as the young girl draws her feet up, kundalini-snake on Satya's bed. She leans over Roop the way Sardarji leaned over Satya the years she cried for children, brushing tears from Roop's heavy lashes with her lips. She strokes her head as a mother would, says, 'Sleep, little one, we are together now.'

And Roop sleeps, overcome by the afternoon heat.

While Satya watches her.

So trusting, so very stupid.

On Roop's arm, thrown back over her head, are Satya's gold bangles, and on her fingers, Satya's rings. Her feet are small and narrow for her height. Around her ankles she wears Satya's gold panjebs. On her toes, Satya's toe rings.

Satya could unfasten them from Roop while she sleeps, but thievery has never been a trait in her family.

Why is Roop so trusting? How can she be so confident she will produce a child? How can Roop not look at her, Satya, and think, 'This is what I might become?' How can she not see danger in blundering deep into the tigress's den to steal her chance of ever bearing a cub?

Had Satya been like her once? Had she ever been so witless and yet so charming?

Young women these days think they are invincible, that they have only to smile and good things will happen to them.

Look at me, she wants to tell her. Barren, but still useful; she manages Sardarji's whole estate. Does Roop think it an easy task? Does Roop think it means just giving orders?

'No, little "sister",' she will say, 'Sardarji's mukhtiar,

Manager Abdul Aziz, does my bidding because he respects my judgment, he knows he cannot cheat me, I am too watchful. Not a pai of Sardarji's money is spent on mere ornamentation or given to the undeserving.'

The money she gave to the sants, though . . . that was a contribution to their future.

Perhaps Sardarji felt she gave the holy men too much – then he had only to say one word! One word in her ear and she would not have spent another pai on intercessors, but would have prayed to Vaheguru herself.

Only, she has never felt that Vaheguru listens to a woman's prayers.

When Sardarji's sister, Toshi – that *churail!* that witch! – when she began her insinuations that Sardarji should marry again, Satya laughed. Said, 'Yes, what a good idea!'

And she said she would find a good Sikh girl herself, a woman for her husband.

She said this for ten years while her heart sank lower and lower and her body betrayed her every moon-month with its bleeding. And in that time, the man who could best protect her, her father, lost his power. Thin, maudlin, lazy – that is not a man. When the British turned land rights to paper, he could prove nothing, not even fitness for working! He lost the land. Never even knew it until he tried renewing his land pledges for more liquor, more opium, then more liquor. By then it was too late. In the end he locked himself in a room with all the British-supplied gin he could muster and drank himself to death – one gulp, one drink, next drink, next gulp.

When he was gone, Satya's only brother sold the last of the land to buy a lorry and sent their mother, practical, accepting old Bebeji, to live with a cousin. He lived in that lorry only three days before a band of dacoits drove him from it and left his robbed, bleeding corpse half hidden in a wheat field by the roadside. A Sikh tenant-farmer's wheat field, not even some high-up landowner's wheat field! What a way to die: young, and for no reason. Not even a martyr's death, or a soldier's. Just a useless, meaningless death.

Satya will not die that way.

No, when she dies there will be a reason.

With her brother's death, her doom wrote itself into the lines of her hands. The palmists said they saw a daughter or a long-lost sister in her hand. They said it in the 'could-be' tone of men who trade the kindness of lies for the wisdom of truth; they have to make a living.

Still Satya found no woman ugly enough for Sardarji to marry.

In all the Sind-Sagar doab, that land that lies between the Indus and its sister river, the Jhelum, where women are raised to bend like saplings with every wind so long as it speaks with a voice of authority, Satya found no woman pliant enough for her husband. Though she was far from schooled, she found no woman schooled enough to match him. Though she could speak no English, she declared his new mate must know the git-mit, git-mit talk and be raised to sit on chairs. And as the times changed and women began to walk in the streets and even in protest marches, she declared all of them unworthy to come into her presence, let alone his.

When she was forty years old, she read her fate in Toshi's eyes, saw it in the way she and her husband, Sardar Kushal Singh, ignored her when they came to visit, and no longer asked about her when Sardarji stopped to visit at their home. She went to the sants then and asked them for curses. They told her they were men devoted to God and that she must be self-effacing, humble, grateful for her undiminished status, the magnanimity of her husband, her continued unharmed existence. And she was so angry she began to accuse Sardarji of slighting her when he had done nothing. They would fight so the loving was sweeter, and she would argue so his long absences inspecting canal improvements were easier to bear. And Sardarji sent her to Toshi for child-inducing potions and pippal fruit; but such was her state of fear she took none of them in case Toshi was trying to poison her, to make way for a new wife.

Bebeji came to visit with the sowing season and reasoned with Satya. She said women have been heard of who can have children even till the age of sixty.

Satya said, 'I don't have time to wait till then.'

Bebeji saw that fear had tied Satya's hands and feet, pinned her body to the bed, and she saw how it drained her, like a well that fills by night and exhausts itself by day. She saw how Satya had almost reverted to the old custom of purdah, and she laughed at her daughter for seeking the sanctuary of what she had once decried in Muslim women around her.

Bebeji made sure no one noticed any difference in the daily management of Sardarji's household affairs – many wise men took birth in Bebeji's family.

But how do you talk to a mother about the things that happen between a husband and a wife in the dark? How could Satya speak of the pain of his touch, so gentle, so forbearing, so kind – when she could not repay it with children? What right had she to share his bed and bring nothing from the coupling?

'A man is pleasured,' Bebeji said, 'you can see it afterwards. But,' she shelled a Kashmiri pistachio between her strong back teeth, 'a woman is merely cracked open for seeding like the earth before the force of the plough. If she is fertile, good for the farmer, if not, bad for her.'

Bebeji came from an honest family.

When Sardarji stopped coming for pleasure, Satya kept it a secret, even from Bebeji. And she asked Bebeji questions – levers slanting under trap doors – prodding her obliquely to name the men in their family who could and would come to her assistance if she should need it. There were a few – Satya's family was not completely powerless, but Sardarji was un-arguably one of the most powerful in the tacit brotherhood of high-up Sikh men. Any protest from men of Satya's kin would be heard and tolerated, but in the end she would be a fleet and lissome kakar petrified before a tiger; and if the tiger is hungry, the barking-deer must die.

Hai, to die!

For she cannot bear more remembering.

She knows his body so well, so many years of holding each other in times of tiredness, in times of hope, in times of debt and of loss. Can a young woman know him this way? Can a young woman ever know his friends and laugh with them in the rueful way of those who've learned from living? How will a young woman know that he breathes deeply when he thinks too much, that he wipes his forehead in the cold heart of winter when the British settlement officer approaches to collect his yearly taxes? How can a young woman know how to manage his flour mill while he is hunting kakar with his English 'superiors'? How will she know how to give orders that sound as if she is a mere mouth for his words? How will she know that his voice is angry with the servants only when he is tired or hungry? How can she understand that all his talk of logic and discipline in the English people's corridors and his writing in brown paper files about the great boons of irrigation engineering brought by the conquerors are belied by his donations to the freedom-fighting Akali Party?

These thoughts fill Satya as she gazes at Roop's sleeping figure and she remembers the day she could no longer continue her pretence that she was looking for a second wife for her husband.

That day, calling to her serving woman, Mani Mai, to join her, Satya left her sitting room, walked down the gallery overlooking the open central courtyard of Sardarji's haveli, and moved through the narrow passageway leading to the servants' wing. Servants' children ran knock-kneed before her as she swept past the unpainted mosquito havens that were their parents' quarters. In awed silence, the children melted into the wells of staircases, some clambering to the third and fourth storeys, some as high as the terrace, to watch Satya lean over the second-storey-gallery wall. Her grey eyes swept the scrap of courtyard below, framed on all sides by narrow verandas and whitewashed storerooms. No silk pukkhas fanned the air within any servant family's room in this wing.

Satya's shouts, in Urdu and Punjabi, prodded an ant-line of men entering the courtyard below. From bent heads and backs, they heaved sacks bubbled by apricots, picked from Sardarji's orchards, to the stone floor of the courtyard. Then they shuffled outside the haveli for more.

With Mani Mai following behind, Satya descended the steep staircase to enter the sorting room on the ground floor. Now the servants rolled the apricots out before her on gunny sacks, the heavy sweet scent of the fruit mixing with the smell of wet coir. She sat on a reed stool or paced the sorting room, supervising. Damaged ones, even those with small bruises, were to be set aside for poor relatives or beggars, the unblemished ones to be sent to higher-ups or kept for Sardarji's table. She felt their skins and looked for any sign of rot – rotten ones can spoil a whole basketful overnight.

Satya scolded Sardarji's valet who, protesting this menial work assigned him, placed a darkening apricot in a sorting basket of fruit for Sardarji's table. It was then that Satya's own serving woman, Mani Mai, let out an insolent cackle.

'Dehna Singh was only doing what he sees happening in this home,' she said.

Satya did not let Mani Mai see she had been hurt.

Instead she took the overripe fruit in her hand and dug her teeth in its softening hide. It was oversweet, pleading to be liked. Its slackening fermenting flesh came away readily, squelching. She told herself it was good and ate some more. Mani Mai watched, eyes narrowing with amusement. Satya ate the whole apricot and sucked at its pit. She tasted the tiny, dry, wrinkled stone in her mouth.

She swallowed it, willing it to travel all the way to her womb.

Felt no pain as it scraped the tender lining of her throat, caught like a stopper in her gullet.

Mani Mai didn't hasten to help Satya. Didn't pat her back, didn't run for a tumbler of water.

Just watched. Motionless, her amusement fading, but no solicitude rushing to take its place, as Satya's lungs sucked for air, as she hacked, choked, coughed.

That moment, Satya knew she had lost the one ally every woman should have, if she can afford it, a faithful maidservant.

When Satya finally spat the stone out, all Mani Mai did was call on her god, '*Allah!* Every woman has her kismat.'

Mani Mai's family had lost all its land two generations ago, but she retained the talent of the high-born to moralize over the less fortunate.

The next day Satya sent Mani Mai away to her village, twelve miles north of Rawalpindi, saying surely Mani Mai must want to visit her family, was it not many years since she had done so?

And then Satya sent for the munshi. Reclining on a long-legged, uncomfortable European sofa in the centre courtyard in the main wing of the haveli, she made the munshi write a letter for her. 'Sit close,' she said, 'I have lost my voice,' and she dictated to him in a slow metallic rasp, a pathetic shadow of her usual haughty tone.

When he was finished, she pressed the ball of her thumb to the blue chunk of the ink pad, and then to paper, wet ink seeping into the furrows of her thumbprint. No one could make that swirled oval but she; no second wife could duplicate that mark.

She paid the munshi well — but not too much lest he become suspicious — and she sent the letter to the only woman who owed her anything, her cousin-sister Mumta.

Mumta would not deny her, Mumta would come.

In memory of a night of tears and pain twenty years ago when their hands together sent a small red-silk-covered bier afloat down the Indus, Mumta would come. In memory of three salwars soaked in a baby's blood, in memory of marigolds unable to perfume a furtive death, Mumta would come. In memory of that baby that was Mumta's first, her dropped one, that baby that could not be born before marriage, in memory of that birth that became non-birth and that small atma denied its given body on this rotation of the wheel, in memory of Mumta's hands held tightly and of her screams silenced against Satya's breast, Mumta would come.

Satya called Mumta to her side, twenty years after that night by the Indus, her letter innocent, gracious, innocuous.

'Come and stay a while.'

Because Satya realized, late but well, that all secrets have their uses.

Mumta came and did not ask why Satya suggested that she sleep in Satya's bedroom at night; she understood there was no longer a chance Sardarji would visit.

Mumta's sons were grown and her position secure by now, but crescent-shaped shadows clung beneath her eyes. Her breath came short, laboured and shallow, as if already tethered by the noose of Dharmraj, green-skinned regent of the netherworld.

Satya and Mumta spoke little; there was not much to say, even if Mumta had had breath to speak. And when a servant brought the news that Sardarji had married a young girl, surreptitiously, without telling Satya, Mumta was there to hold Satya through the night and wipe her tears as if Satya were her secret baby, grown now, wounded once again.

Mumta knew how it would be for Satya, that she would not be able to face her afterwards, just as Mumta had not found it possible to face Satya for twenty years after that night by the Indus.

It would be so for Satya as well.

So in the morning Mumta was gone and Bebeji arrived, clucking like an indignant hen – 'Perhaps it is not news but rumours! You listen to people in the bazaar, this is what I taught you? Go, find a sant who will sleep with you for money, get a son that way – you have been foolish! Do I have to teach you everything?'

But Satya was still with grieving.

She remembered their first times – when Sardarji would abandon the rough wool of his English suits for the soft white Peshawari kurta-salwar and stand at her back, removing first her jamavar shawl, then her jewellery. And their first years of planning, the way they had been partners from the time they met anew on the seventh anniversary of their wedding, after his return from England. And she remembered later years when he began moving up because England-educated Indians were scarce and the British preferred people from the smaller quoms – people like Sikhs, Parsis or Muslims – from whom elevation in His Majesty's government would bring more gratitude than the largest quom, the Hindus, could muster. Recent years, when she would tell him to go alone to garden parties, horse shows, Gymkhana Club polo balls and dinner dances, times when she asked why would he not bring his office-wallas home, and he did, and they mistook her for a serving woman like Mani Mai, just because she did not speak English.

When evening came and Bebeji fell asleep, Satya hid her face behind a coarse black burqa, the kind Muslim women wear in the bazaar, and ordered a spirited mare hitched to her personal pink tonga. Alighting at Sardar Kushal Singh's home, she found her husband inside but no sign of the girl. She discarded her disguise, and she threatened and raged and wheedled for hours.

'I still have life to give, why do you throw me away?'

Sardarji roared, 'I do not throw you away, I tell you! You will have all izzat, all respect; you will be looked after.'

'You will throw me away – I know it. If not now, then later.'

'Satya, you should know me better.'

'Please, let's not pretend we know each other any more. Yes, I know you, know you better than you know yourself.'

'I know you very well, too – you have a tongue sharper than Kakeyi's. I tell you, I'm so tired of your shouting.'

'Tired of my shouting? You don't want me because I tell you what you have become. I tell you what I see inside you, that's why you throw me away.'

Sardar Kushal Singh raised his voice. 'Collect your wits, Satya! You have brought this upon yourself with your quarrelling.'

Then Satya screamed so loud the djinns might hear. '*Aaaaaaaaeeeeeeeeeeeeeiiiiiiiiii!!!*'

But jo hoya, so hoya – what is done is done.

Eventually, she pulled the tattered remains of her dignity about her, took the coarse cotton burqa from Toshi – that *churail!* – and hid her tearstained face beneath its blackness. She climbed back into her pink tonga and returned to her private sitting room to sit by a dying fire. And she talked to the shadows and cried for herself because she had not wanted all that he wanted, because she would not forget her past lives just because the British people say there are none but this, because she wished she did not come from an honest family and that her name was not Satya – Truth – so she could get away from the truth, take refuge in self-pity, take comfort in lies.

And so she prayed Sardarji had found a girl willing to become everything he wanted her to be.

Satya looks at Roop's sleeping figure, slender and innocent. She is taller than Satya so at least she cannot wear Satya's clothes. She looks healthy enough; she should be able to give Sardarji sons.

What if she cannot? She could not bear it if Sardarji were disappointed again. Roop must bear him sons. Satya will see to it. She will teach her. She will tell her how to be with him.

No.

Never!

Why has Roop been married by her family to a man so much her senior?

Twenty-five years.

There must be something wrong with her – or wrong with her family.

Mani Mai said Roop has no mother – that must be why she is so trusting. A mother would have taught her to beware of other women, especially of first wives.

Roop stirs. Satya rolls over and away. And so they sleep, backs to one another.

And Satya dreams.

Sardarji is beside me again, his snoring lending rhythm to the moonlight silvering the courtyard. Roop lies between us, her body pale and hairless, limbs supple and careless. And from between Roop's legs there sprout apricot buds ready to open into flowers.

And Sardarji plucks these, one by one, and gives them to me.

TWO

1928-1937

2

When the wind-god, Vayu, bearer of perfume, god of all the Northwest of India, blows through the Suleimans, he snakes his way through the Khyber Pass to Punjab. There he crosses the Indus and chases his shadow across the city in the bowl at the base of the Margalla Hills. When angry he brings dust storms, when sad he brings rain, watering the cracked lips of the land, setting Persian-wheels creaking.

Blowing east, Vayu gnaws at the plateau called Pothwar till it falls away beneath him to plains beyond Jhelum. He blows dry past the Salt Range, over lush rolling hills where the silvery ribbons of the Jhelum, the Chenab, the Ravi and its canals seek the Indus. Then he climbs the watershed between Lahore and Amritsar. Stooping low for a blessing at the feet of the Himalayas, he whisks canals streaming from the Sutlej and the Beas, sweeps unobstructed across the river plain of the Ganga and rises to sear the heart of India. When he returns, circling over the Arabian Sea, hauling monsoon clouds into position, he sleeps a weary sleep on the breast of the Indus.

And he believes his gifts are all Punjabis need to make them happy.

Oh, foolish Vayu!

In the ages since he first inhaled, before India was ever called India, Vayu has guided army after army through the mountain passes to Punjab. The English circulate a story that a race of tall, blond, blue-eyed Aryans invaded first, from the Caucasus, Vayu ushering them forward, to lord it over darker people, drive them south, but Vayu, oblivious to bloodline, remembers only that he caught music from migrants over the passes, melded it to language. Then Vayu guided invaders whose traces still remain – Persians; Alexander the Great astride his Bucephalus; Hun raiders and traders from Afghanistan; Mahmud of Ghazni, the idol-breaking raider from Turkestan; fugitives and refugees from the Mongols. Vayu's winds stirred war cries from the horsemen of the first Mughal, Babar of Samarkand, then he brought news of successions of Mughal emperors, father to son, father to son.

In the ages since he first inhaled, before India was ever called India, Vayu invited animist gods to join him in the Aryan Hindu pantheon, even as animists themselves were falling to the level of menials. It was Vayu who swept the ground before Mahavira Jain, heard the first lessons of non-violence. He listened in awe as Gautama Buddha taught Buddhism's eightfold path, saved Buddha's ideas, puffing them out of reach of Hinduism, to sanctuary in the Himalayas and Tibet. Then, when Islam first sank its roots in Punjab, Vayu shifted direction, bringing the Prophet Muhammad's revelations of Allah to sway the hearts of raja and menials alike, melding languages again – Prakrit and Persian to Urdu.

Ages later, Vayu saw a boy, Nanak, refuse the ritual black thread of his Hindu ancestors, commune with Muslim Sufis, then walk his own path. He saw Nanak lead the first Sikhs to a single faceless God, and gather into the Sikh quom those who would seek the divine with him. Vayu's winds felt Guru Nanak's spirit enter nine more Gurus' lives, and later it was Vayu who rustled between the pages of the Guru Granth Sahib, when the rapturous poems of all ten Gurus became the Sikh quom's remaining guide.

It was Vayu who rode in the manes of horses when the Persians and Afghans sacked Lahore and snatched away its women; it was he who stirred the pennants of Sikh chiefs wresting control from the Afghans, slaying in vengeance, bereaving more women. And when the English pressed north-west, it could have been Vayu who led their forces to slaughter in Afghanistan. Later, his breezes rode across Punjab at the shoulders of the Sikh warriors of Maharaj Ranjit Singh, and when those warriors fell in battle against the British it was Vayu, as always, who brought word to their widows.

When Vayu skirts the doorway of the fairies at Pari Darvaza, small village of mud and brick scooped from the soil, he finds few Hindus there to call his name; those who once did were driven south or converted, generations ago, from Hinduism to Islam. Instead, in Pari Darvaza, he finds Sikhs celebrating harvest festivals and the anniversary days of their ten Gurus' lives, and Muslims who mark the passage of the day by the muezzin's call to prayer. Other villages in Punjab have Hindus living side by side with Muslims, but Pari Darvaza belongs to a Sikh, and every farmer here occupies and tills the land around the crumbling village walls at Sardarji's pleasure.

Pari Darvaza, April 1928

A young Sikh boy swings back his black mane of hair and dives, going for his sister's ankles, trying to pull her under the surface. A waterfall arches above them, harsh to the lips, brittle white as an old woman's long hair.

Soft sand meets Roop's toes as she paddles to keep her nose above water in the pool beneath the fall. A cotton kameez clings from her neck to below her knees, and she is squealing, laughing. She peers in the muddy water, glimpses blurred white – Jeevan's cotton shorts – and quickly rolls her bare legs up to her chest. He brushes by, skin on skin. Spray studs the blue of the sky as he surfaces. They laugh together as the serving woman calls them. Hot rotis and curries, unpacked from a brass tiffin carrier, await Roop's appetite.

Her mama's phulkari-embroidered red shawl envelops

Roop, as if it were winter instead of ripening to the full blaze of summer. Sheltering Roop behind it, Gujri holds out a clean dry cotton kachcha just like Jeevan's. Roop hops, putting one leg through, then the other. Gujri ties the cord of the kachcha below Roop's navel. Then, still behind the shawl, she holds out the baggy legs of a white salwar and when Roop steps into it, pulls its string tight at Roop's waist. A dry cotton kameez blindfolds Roop for a second as Gujri pulls it over her head, then past her knees. Both salwar and kameez belong to Roop's mama too, but are made down to Roop's size. Then the softness of Mama's white muslin chunni settles over Roop's head and across her shoulders, frames her Pothwari skin, smooth as a new apricot beckoning from the limb of a tall tree, her wide, heavily lashed brown eyes.

'Roop can have my share of the pickle,' says her elder sister, rabbit teeth sucking on lower lip.

But Roop shakes her head. She doesn't want lemon pickle, even if giving it makes Madani look selfless. She shrugs off Mama's shawl and joins Jeevan, imitating his puffing – squatting, standing, squatting – before they sit together on the blanket.

'So you think you're going to march in the army, too?' There is mock admiration in Jeevan's voice. He reaches for a wheat roti with an arm browner than his torso. Around his wrist, a thin steel circle, the kara his father bought for him at the Golden Temple in Amritsar, catches the sunshine, 'I get double the rotis since I'm double your age.'

'Hanji!' Roop agrees happily. 'You have to eat fourteen! I could eat seven rotis today, I'm so hungry.'

'I can't eat nine,' complains Madani.

Jeevan states the bet: 'If you eat seven rotis I'll take you to Lahore and get you an English ribbon – a bright pink one for your hair instead of this cheap-cheez.' He reaches over, pulls Roop's single wet plait with its tassel of red silk.

Roop twists away from Jeevan. She tears a wedge from a wheat roti and reaches into the tiffin bowl, but her hand meets a slap from Gujri – 'Ay, Roop-bi! No eggs for you – the egg-bhurji is for Jeevan.'

Roop moves her wedge of roti to the next tiffin bowl, but

Gujri pushes her hand away there too. 'That's chicken, for Jeevan,' she says. 'Take some daal.'

Jeevan offers his plate, 'Achcha, just a small bite, here's some chicken.'

'Eggs and meat for a girl? No, don't waste them,' says Gujri, 'Very risky. Already she has too much Mangal in her stars; makes her quarrelsome. Roop, you have the daal.' Pointing to the lentils. 'And I made savayan for you. See,' she tips the container of sweet milk-boiled noodles at Roop, 'afterwards.'

Roop dips the roti in the lentils and stuffs it in her mouth, chewing carefully; a last baby tooth is about to fall.

'Young lady, have you been practising your boxing lately?' Jeevan asks, imitating his headmaster's voice. He doesn't need to distract her. Roop is old enough, she understands – she doesn't *need* the egg-bhurji; he does. He's going to join the army.

'No, sir,' she says, brown eyes twinkling.

Gujri shakes her head at them. 'Leave it, Jeevan, eat now.'

'Put up your fists, then, come on.' He jumps up and prances round her.

Goaded, Roop scrambles up and plants her bare feet squarely in the grass, balls her small fist and flings it at his upheld palms.

Smack!

Jeevan's hands remain steady.

'Knuckles up, don't show me your girly wrists. Come on. Harder, Harder!'

She hits again, laughing. This time the punch is deft and well placed, her weight behind it, as Jeevan himself might punch.

He reels back; can he be hurt? No. The glance he throws in her direction is one of surprise.

'Enough. Let's eat,' he says.

Abrupt. Disapproving.

What has she done? She watches Jeevan's face for clues. She should have been less strong, that was it.

She gives Jeevan an inquiring smile. He smiles back. All is well again.

Gujri counts out rotis. 'I'd get so tired if I made as many rotis as I have years.'

'How old are you, Gujri?' Roop asks, chewing carefully because of her loose tooth.

'*Huh!* I am as old as I am, I live till I die, then again it starts. What to tell you,' she says.

Gujri knows things as if they are cut into her, and through the transparence of her white chunni, Roop, standing, can see the sun-browned welt that is the centre parting of her hair. Gujri is a plainswoman, darker than any Pothwari. She came barefoot behind the men bearing Mama's palanquin all the way to Pari Darvaza – this was before her too-small feet hurt her all the time. She was a gift to the bride's family, like Mama's dowry pots and pans. Widowed at Roop's age, just seven, Gujri says her whole village thought her unlucky after her husband died, even though she'd never seen him, never, ever, and in those days her elders advised she should not marry again lest she kill another husband. So Gujri's father brought her to Roop's grandmother in Kuntrila and folded his hands before Nani. And Nani took Gujri in, raised her as a Sikh, and had her trained to cook and spin and care for the family when they were sick.

Gujri knows the whole Guru Granth Sahib by heart, can tell the *Ramayan* story, the *Mahabharat*, and the janam-sakhis and can sing 'Heer' in her high reedy voice. Though she doesn't know the namaaz prayers that Muslims learn, she knows the waterfall here can give them a strong stomach and that swimming in the pool below is good for their eyes. She knows tulsi leaves are good for the throat, and neem twigs are good for cleaning Roop's teeth, and every night she takes Madani's head in the crook of her arm to press her thumb against Madani's protruding gums so Madani'll find a husband.

Despite her bet with Jeevan, Roop can't eat more than two rotis and a little taste of savayan, and like pythons they are all overcome by sleep afterwards, Roop's head on Gujri's lap, Madani covering her mouth with her chunni even while sleeping, Jeevan on his stomach, unbound hair spread across his back to dry in the sun.

The earth-beat of galloping hooves shakes them awake.

There is a whinny and a 'Whoa, boy.'

Jeevan stands up and quickly winds his hair to a topknot.

Even without his turban, he looks strong and fearless.

A deep voice says some words in a rough strange language. 'What are you doing here, boy?' Roop has never seen a ghost-man before. She giggles with sudden nervousness. Jeevan frowns at her and turns to face the horseman.

The horseman's sandy brows meet over slitty transparent eyes. Beardless as a girl, his tone of command makes it clear it is a man. Jodhpurs balloon from knee to waist, above brick-brown boots. A green velvet riding jacket squares his shoulders over a white sweat-damp shirt. A black velvet hat hides most of his ginger hair. One white-gloved hand reins the prancing brown gelding in, the other flicks at it with the crop assisted by a pair of sharp-wheeled spurs, mixed messages that keep it under control.

'Ji, Sahib,' answers her brother. It is the extent of Jeevan's English.

In broken Punjabi, the horseman demands to know where they are from.

Gujri draws her chunni across the lower half of her face. Her strong hands clasp first Madani's and then Roop's shoulders, to turn their curious eyes away.

'Pari Darvaza.'

'Bap ka naam?' Roop, hearing with the back of her head. Why does he want to know her father's name?

'Dipty Bachan Singh,' she hears Jeevan say.

The ghostman looks them over, then turns the horse's head, and still looking over his shoulder at them with those trans-parent eyes, spurs his horse to a trot. Roop sees him stand and sit in the stirrups in rhythm with the horse's trot. He looks so funny she mimics his bounce for Gujri's benefit, but Gujri isn't laughing.

Jeevan says, a bit too valiantly, 'Not to worry – Papaji is lambardar, number one in Pari Darvaza. That's why English people call him Dipty, Dipty Bachan Singh.'

Men like Bachan Singh work hard to remain unnoticed; this encounter is unusual enough to be ominous.

The picnic is over.

Gujri says to Jeevan, 'Your Papaji will be angry, he might say I put Madani and Roop in the way of outside men.'

Quickly, she spreads a mustard-coloured cloth and stacks the tiffin bowls. They are grooved to fit perfectly, one above the other, like sisters ranked in order of birth. She pulls the opposite corners of the cloth to meet in the middle, knotting them, north to south, east to west, the tiffin carrier secure at the centre. Jeevan coaxes the camel to its knobbly front knees. Gujri ties the tiffin bundle to the rope dangling from the cushion-saddle. Roop slips her feet into her jutis and scrambles on first. Then Madani sits behind Roop, before the camel's hump, careful to adjust her baggy salwar to cover her ankles. Jeevan drapes his body across the second half of the saddle behind the girls, holding his turban with one hand and groaning he is wounded from a battle against the Afghans and could they please drop him off for an amputation at the mission hospital?

Gujri walks before the camel slowly, wincing a little. The thick-necked camel leaves the roar of the waterfall behind and descends the craggy tufted hills back to Pari Darvaza with heavy sure feet, picking its way past trees shedding their leaves in readiness for searing summer.

'Papaji's land ends there,' Jeevan says proudly. Sitting up, he points the same way Papaji does when the patwari visits to record land boundaries before the monsoon. It isn't really Papaji's land; all of this belongs to Sardarji, the jagirdar, but Papaji holds it and will leave Jeevan his right to farm it someday.

Roop, like Madani, is Papaji and Jeevan's guest for a while, just till her marriage.

The camel towers above the flat roof of the post office. Here, a footpath, packed firm by the bare feet of many poor women walking slowly, branches from the wide dirt road and winds up a slope to the brick-lined lanes of the village.

Now the camel slows, adjusting its gait, passing a long line of women walking again in the steps of their forebears on the footpath.

The women's hips sway past the bright blue post office door like the leaf boats Roop and her friends sail down the centre drain of Pari Darvaza's narrow lanes. From her undulating perch above the sag of the camel's neck, Roop looks down on bundles of firewood or red-brown narrow-mouthed pitchers of water from the Muslim well, balanced on the crowns of each woman's head. The border of a chunni pulls close to erase a smile, sometimes a whole face.

Not for me the things these women have to bear. I'll not carry firewood, nor any pitchers of water.

Gujri leads the camel down the brick-lined lanes. The four or five shops of the bazaar are almost empty; it is Friday afternoon and several Muslim men are at juma prayers.

Now the gates leading to the three-domed mosque at the end of the street are open. The faithful emerge.

A tall youth with intelligent eyes runs up to the camel. 'Jeevan!'

Jeevan jumps off the back of the camel with a thud and embraces his friend. They are off to play a few rounds of kabaddi near the Mughal tombs at the far end of the village.

But Roop must go home with Gujri and Madani.

The camel stalks between clusters of walled compounds with a highbrow air, rocking onward through ever-narrower lanes, Gujri walking before it, avoiding the centre drain.

And so they come to the tunnel.

Between two facing three-storey havelis, a weathered carved archway shades the length of the lane, joining the two inner-most, largest havelis in Pari Darvaza — Roop's father's home, and that of his half-brother — at the level of their second-storey windows.

Where the lane enters the tunnel, a blind man with matted hair falling to his ochre rags sits, bows his old head and looks within himself. He doesn't beg, Roop's mama always says; he simply gives you the opportunity to be generous.

Madani nudges Roop and Roop leans from the camel. The blind man looks up at her with pearl-sheathed eyes. 'Here,' she says, dropping her leftover rotis in his cupped hands.

Cool air meets Roop's hot cheeks like Mama's touch, soft and familiar; the camel has entered gloom, keeping to the left of the centre drain.

The lane widens.

Two storeys above Roop's head, the weathered-grey carved arch joins the two identical facing three-storey havelis. The mud-plastered brick face of her father's haveli rises to Roop's right, her clean side, and mirroring it, her half-uncle's haveli rises on her unclean side. The tunnel widens further at its waist, making it easier to load and unload camels. Inside each haveli, single oblong courtyards open to sun and rain are framed on all sides by covered galleries, pocketed by cool whitewashed rooms.

Traders from the plains beyond Jhelum are loading camel and donkey caravans with dried chilies, grain and salt to be bartered or sold in Rawalpindi, Murree, Peshawar, Lahore and Delhi – all the places Jeevan has promised to take Roop someday. The traders lead their camels and donkeys around a knot of labourers squatting around a wooden instrument almost as large as its battery – a wireless Bachan Singh took as payment from an Afghan trader, for Jeevan, now become village property. A turbaned trader turns knobs and dials, squatting a little apart from the Muslim traders pulling on and then passing the mouthpiece of a bubbling chillum around their semicircle. Impassioned debate crosses and recrosses the chillum arm – where do the voices really come from?

As the camel lurches to a stop before her father's haveli door, Roop thinks, she, Roop, is different.

I am Dipty Bachan Singh's daughter and I have good kismat. I'll never need to wait for someone's generosity like the blind man.

Papaji is not in the tunnel supervising the loading. More and more since Mama's illness, he's been leaving the details to Shyam Chacha, his half-brother.

The Sikh trader who takes his camel's reins from Gujri and orders it to its knees has cheeks burned dark by the sun.

'He's from the plains,' Madani giggles. 'Look how he ties it,' she whispers.

The trader turns his back, averting his gaze, so Bachan Singh's daughters can alight in modesty and Roop sees he ties his turban smaller, tighter and rounder than Papaji or Jeevan and there is no safa-cloth trailing from its base down his back.

Roop is first to dismount.

The camel jiggles its lower lip and dribbles. Reaching on tiptoe, Roop pats its pompous nose, then jumps the centre drain and crosses the street. Standing on the wide semicircular doorstep, before the flower-carved door of Papaji's haveli, she hefts the engraved metal padlock to her shoulder and backs quickly away so it thuds against the brass-studded grey-brown timber, echoing densely in the courtyard behind.

Though she can hear Revati Bhua approaching, Roop kicks her juti impatiently against the base of the door.

Bachan Singh's eldest cousin-sister, Revati Bhua, has been visiting the family for two years now and no one takes her seriously when she says she'll cut her visit short 'fut-a-fut,' very soon. Whenever Revati Bhua says that, Bachan Singh hastens to respond that everything has a vaqt, a time, and comes and goes when it is ready, in its season, like wheat, like maize, like cherries from Kashmir, and guests who are always welcome. And whenever Bachan Singh says that, Revati Bhua sighs with relief; an unmarried woman, she has no sons to look after her in her old age and she has never been truly welcome in any other relative's home. But Bachan Singh says a cousin-sister, even a distant one, is just the same as a sister, no difference at all, and no man should manufacture differences where there are none. In the two years since she came to stay in Bachan Singh's haveli with just her small tachey case, Revati Bhua has become bhua to every man, woman and child in Pari Darvaza by listening well to all their woes, and is no longer aunt just to Roop, Madani and Jeevan.

As Revati Bhua unlatches the timber door to the haveli from the inside, Madani hisses behind Roop, 'Roop, we should pay our respects to Shyam Chacha and Chachi!' Shyam Chacha is Papaji's half-brother, owner of the mirror haveli across the tunnel and Chachi, his wife.

Roop has seen that Chachi's chunni-covered head leans from their second-storey window, but she pretends she doesn't, continuing through the scalloped doorway to bury her face in Revati Bhua's bulky kameez for a quick embrace. Roop knows very well she should love Shyam Chacha, but she can't help thinking, *Let Madani go and visit them. Shyam Chacha will embrace her and ask how is Mama, when everyone knows he will do some treachery as soon as Papaji's back is turned.*

And Roop is off, running across the sun-roasted courtyard to see her mama.

Mama lies flat on her manji in the front room because it is coolest here and it's the only room on the ground floor that has a doorway wide enough for the rope-bed to be carried from the haveli into the tunnel, Mama upon it. From this room, she can see and hear and advise about all that happens in the inner courtyard – her advice is either, 'Whatever Vaheguru's will,' or 'Share with each other' or 'Give to those who need.' When she feels very sick, four trusted menservants lift the whole frame of the manji and carry it through the doorway for Mama to enter her curtained, carved palanquin, the same that first brought her from Kuntrila to Papaji's home. And in the palanquin, she can be carried in full purdah to the railway station for yet another trip to Rawalpindi or Lahore to see one more well-reputed hakim.

Roop, Madani and Jeevan sleep on any manji they happen to be sitting on when sleep comes, but Mama has a special manji. Her body is so light now, despite the baby mounded inside, that the rope mesh of her manji stretches tight and flat across its wooden frame and never needs tightening.

The noodles are still sweet on Roop's tongue. The pungent scent of camel sweat clings to her baggy white salwar. Her eyes adjust to cool shadow. Papaji sits on a reed stool by Mama's side, in her grandmother's usual spot. His white turban leans close, obscuring Mama's face. He's patting Mama's hand but stops as soon as Roop enters.

Papaji strokes his flowing moustache and pulls his curly grey-brown beard down across his chest as if he does not know what to try next.

Nani must be annoyed with Papaji if she is not at Mama's side.

Nani arrived last Lorhi, when all of Pari Darvaza was lit by bonfires, and the whoops and yells of hooch-inspired bhangra-dancers soared over the drums of the festival, 'Baley! Baley!' With only a bareback pad between her and an old mare's extended trot, she rode all the way from Kuntrila 'to look after your mama.' So old her every order is law to the servants, to Roop and Madani, Nani can even sometimes order Jeevan with one glance of her fierce eyes.

Roop can't remember Mama ever ordering anyone around

– she only remembers her mama being too sick to do more than lie there, the instep of one foot resting on the ankle of the other as she caresses Roop's face. Mama listens as Roop sings her shabads. She sometimes says her life in this body will soon be over, but no one believes her; she isn't *that* sick.

'Deputy,' Bachan Singh corrects Roop when she tells him about the English man. 'Jeevan should have said Deputy, not Dipty.' Bachan Singh's limited English is the best in the village, and though he cannot read or write it, he uses it when necessary for important matters, caring little if his listener understands or not. He writes Punjabi well, however, in both Persian and Gurmukhi scripts.

Papaji sighs, like a camel assuming a familiar weight. 'Must have been the district magistrate. Someone in Pari Darvaza must have been reported for making his own salt from the soil and I'll have to pay the fine for it again or cut it out of his rent.'

Pari Darvaza, doorway of the fairies, is also doorway to salt lick and salt marshes burrowing their way from the Pothwar plateau to rise at the Salt Range. A camel-load of salt made from the soil and sold on the sly can help the tenant-farmers around Pari Darvaza avoid salt imported from England, then double-priced to meet His Majesty's desire for taxes.

But first, Papaji says, he is going to take Mama to Lahore to see an English-medicine doctor at Mayo Hospital because all the local hakims are unable to help her.

A hospital! That's where you go to die.

But Nani stands rigid in the doorway. Brown-toothed, wrinkled as a dried date, she has heard Papaji. Covering her head respectfully but firmly, she tells Papaji right to his face, 'No, she will not go. Am I dead that you have to take her to the hospital and show her body to strange men? Is it not bad enough that my granddaughter' – pointing to Madani who has come in from the tunnel – 'is nine years old and still goes about unveiled so every sweeper knows the colour of her skin? You are not a small man, you are the lambardar. You must set a good example. My daughter will stay here and bring this house another son.'

Roop's eyes dart to the sun-drenched courtyard; will Revati

Bhua waddle in? But Revati Bhua is just a poor relation, a woman whose kismat left her unmarried, a guest in Papaji's house. Like Roop and Madani till their weddings. Roop sees Revati Bhua dash at her eyes with the corner of her chunni and turn away.

Papaji shakes his head, but does not challenge Nani, eldest of his inner courtyard, further.

And Mama stays.

Roop squats just inside the open door of Bachan Singh's haveli, the wispy end of her single plait sweeping the wide semicircular doorstep. Madani and Huma sit, knees tucked beneath their chins, and Roop's eyes follow the flying hands of the two older girls, tossing stones.

Roop's small hands have not yet mastered even the first round of the five-stone game: tossing a pebble in the air, picking up another while catching the first before it hits the ground. She squats, practising, her unclean hand helping her right hand, but she cannot snatch a single stone without disturbing the rest.

'Not like that. One hand only!' Madani reaches over and slaps Roop's hand.

Huma raises doe eyes, says kindly, 'See? Like this.' Slowly, carefully, she throws a pebble in the air, waiting till the very last for it to descend, before catching it overhanded in her palm.

Glass bangles tinkle beneath the sleeves of a new peridot-green cotton kameez Huma's ami sewed for her; Roop will ask her mama to make her a kameez just like that.

Not now; when Mama gets well.

Roop throws her pebble in the air again, but there are shouts at the far end of the tunnel.

'Har! Har!'

Roop's pebble bounces and clacks on the doorstep.

The cries rise from the knot of men gathered where the back of the tunnel opens onto fields. There Deputy Bachan Singh is matching his prized black partridges against the brown partridges of Abu Ibrahim, Huma's father.

Roop looks up in time to see Papaji's turban and Abu Ibrahim's round cap uncovering their partridge cages. There is a desperate fluttering as cage doors open just enough to let a strong hand enfold partridge wings. The partridge hens press against their cages to watch and worry, their cries of alarm, *ti-lo! ti-lo!*, drowned by the bet-making around them; the louder they squeal, the higher they raise the stakes on the courage of their mates.

Papaji and Abu Ibrahim place their partridges eye to eye at the centre of the circle of men, breast to breast, till partridge fear heats to anger.

'Fight! Fight!' shout the onlookers. By the rules of the game, they cannot touch the two birds once they are released into the circle, but they can hiss and poke at the partridge hens, ruffle their feathers, frighten them till they raise a piteous call for their mates' protection.

Ti-lo! Ti-lo!

The partridges claw forward as soon as they hear their hens' cry, unsheath their sharp talons, feathers fluffing to menace. Vayu carries the gamy scent of desperation down the tunnel to Roop.

This morning's crowd includes some of Abu Ibrahim's followers from towns around Pari Darvaza. Muslims come to pay their respects to the holy pir whose fame rises from his Sufi ancestors at rest in their tombs since the time of the Mughals at the far end of Pari Darvaza. They give the Abu Ibrahim anything they can muster – wheat, barley, rupees, annas or just pais – for a blessing for a sick camel, for his amulets and spells against the evil eye. On Thursdays, Muslim women come to him with hopes for their sons or for their men's welfare; on Fridays, his words seed in men in the mosque, and each week he waters them anew. Today his followers have stayed to place bets on the pir's partridges – this pir doesn't object to gambling, so it must be permitted.

The oval silhouette of Jeevan's turban identifies Papaji's side of the crowd – he's shouting too, goading the black partridges. But Jeevan's arm rests across the shoulders of Ibrahim, Huma's older brother, the tall youth with intelligent eyes cheering for the brown partridge. The brown partridge's beak is now covered with blood, its feathers splashed red, a slash running from its wary eye to its still-puffed breast.

Abu Ibrahim has been known as 'father of Ibrahim' ever since Ibrahim's birth and now his real name is forgotten by all. He is a stocky man whose brush moustache and neatly trimmed beard are a tribute to the daily ministrations of the village barber. His place of greatest comfort is in the sanctum of the three-domed mosque at the end of the bazaar, teaching Muslim boys and men the ninety-nine names of Allah, describing the uncleanness of pork and promising them curvaceous houris with bedroom eyes awaiting them in paradise. Usually he is a cautious man, ordering the weaver-tailor to cut his salwar two inches above his ankles to be ready all year round for monsoon floods, tying black flags to his tonga wheels against the evil eye, but today a gambling fever grasps his tongue.

Abu Ibrahim pokes a stick through the cage of the brown partridge hen and shouts to his partridge, 'Fight! Fight like Babar the Great!'

Bachan Singh goads his black fighter-bird, 'Ay, listen to me, partridge! Fight like a Sikh!'

'*Hein?*' Abu Ibrahim feigns indignation.

'My partridges,' Bachan Singh jests to his side of the crowd, 'avenge each Guru beheaded at the hands of the Mughals!'

Sikhs in the crowd agree cheerily. 'Ah-ho!'

Abu Ibrahim returns, 'Mine will make yours return every inch of marble your Maharaja Ranjit Singh stripped from the tombs of our emperors!'

Muslims standing behind the pir laugh uneasily.

Burdened by such expectations, the partridges clash again and again in a great fluttering dust cloud. A tense silence knits the watching crowd. Whoops, whistles and catcalls encourage the birds, but it is over in just a few minutes, when one of the partridges turns tail and flies out of the circle, leaving his hen to the victor.

Another round, pairing a new set of partridges.

The birds squawk and flutter, bloodying the dust again. Men who lost in the last round cheer wildly in hope that they will win in this one.

At the end, winners in the crowd are paid, bloodied and ruffled bird-feathers are smoothed by now gentle hands, and the warriors are returned to their cages. Their hens will comfort them now and their owners will treat them with herbs that will close their wounds, restore their mettle.

The crowd thins, exchanging predictions for future battles – the next fight is always bloodier, always more violent.

Labourers return to the fields, traders tend their camels.

A white-turbaned man with a long, curly grey-brown beard, and a round-capped Muslim with a neatly trimmed beard linger – Bachan Singh and Abu Ibrahim discussing village council matters.

Abu Ibrahim calls to Huma on his way out of the tunnel; her hand stops in mid-air. Pebbles roll to the doorstep as Huma rises, runs without farewell to her father's side. Madani sucks her lip, disappointed. Abu Ibrahim carries his partridge cage in one hand and Roop sees the fingers of the other tighten around Huma's arm, a signal for her to drape her chunni across her face before walking through the bazaar with her father.

I'm not like Huma. Papaji doesn't make me learn namaaz prayers or cover my whole face with a chunni or a burqa as Muslim girls do.

Roop tucks her chunni behind her ears and returns in earnest to her five-stone game.

Madani flicks a pebble into the air, playing against herself now.

Roop balances on the slat of the front-room threshold, knees to her chest. She wears another of Mama's kameezes made down first to Madani's size, then to hers, and Mama's long white chunni over her head and shoulders. The high-pitched whine of circling mosquitoes fills her ears. Since early dawn, each scream from her mama has brought Roop new tears. What did Mama do to deserve this torment that tears at her insides, spewing blood, leaving her eyes glazed?

Mama lies on her back on the manji, surrounded by Nani,

Revati Bhua, Gujri and Madani. The bald moon-mounds of Mama's knees are bent the way she sits in her palanquin.

'The baby has not turned in her belly,' Khanma says tensely. 'It will come feet first.'

She exchanges an anxious glance with Gujri, and the room grows closer, hotter.

Now Mama moans only a little, sandalwood skin turning dark, shining.

Roop takes her chunni off, ties it about her head to restrain her sweat. But though it belongs to Mama, the chunni is too short to be a turban; soon it slouches over Roop's eyes.

The weaver-tailor's wife, Khanma, has turned midwife tonight. She smooths black hair over greying temples, pulls it back, winds it over her clean hand, into a sleek bun. Tight, so tight her hair oil glistens in the glow of the wick lantern. She drops to her haunches and pokes thoughtfully at the fire smouldering at the heart of the clay stove in the corner.

'Ay, learn,' says Nani, cuffing the back of Roop's head so she almost falls into the room, 'learn what we women are for!'

The rough cotton of Gujri's chunni wipes Roop's cheeks. Gujri reassures her gently, 'Learning is just remembering slowly, like simmer coming to boil.'

'Hanji!' Revati Bhua nods, with one eye on Nani for approval. 'Learn now.' Obediently, Roop moves to stand next to Madani. She pries at her loose tooth with her tongue, it hangs by a thread.

Khanma places the end of a rope in Mama's hand. Mama musters her strength, pulls just a little at the rope.

Khanma encourages, 'Now! Push!'

Mama pushes till her skin is wet-sand dark as Khanma's.

Screams dwindle to sharp gasps of pain.

The gasps come faster.

Roop bites down on the end of her chunni to stop herself from crying out with Mama.

It is taking so long, how can Mama stand so much pain?

Madani whispers, 'This is how it happens, every time.'

'But how do you know?' whispers Roop.

'I know.'

Sometimes Madani's infuriating certainty can be oddly consoling.

Khanma's mouth is puckered, blowing, 'Sl-phoo, sl-phoo!' so the burning coals can heat the shiny hammered-metal pan of water. She wears no bangles; unclean work is being done.

A sharp cry pulls air into the new baby's lungs. Madani shifts her weight beside Roop, sticking her hip out, as she did for Roop to ride her till Roop became too tall. Roop follows her movement, preparing.

Her turn now.

But the small bloody thing taken from between Mama's knees won't be riding Roop's hip very soon. Khanma works deftly, cutting the baby from Mama's cord, wiping it clean, wrapping it in an old clean turban. 'It's a boy!' she announces triumphantly, almost as if making him is her achievement, rather than Mama's.

Hearing this, Nani takes him and rocks him, welcoming. Then her shape on the wall grows small as she lays the boy-baby on Mama's breast. There he'll begin forgetting his past lives.

But Gujri sees that he is barely breathing. Quickly, she places three bricks in the dying coals. From Mama's wedding trunk in the corner of the room, she removes an old brown chunni and tears it to rags. So serious is Gujri's face, Nani seems to forget she should scold Gujri for using her mistress's clothes. When the bricks are warm, Gujri removes them with tongs and puts them down on the strips of the chunni, wrapping them. Then she places the baby between them on the floor. Just his small brown nose peeks through his wrapping.

Nani and Gujri have forgotten Mama now that she has done what women are for. Khanma puts the bloody rags, the after-birth and the great length of the boy-baby's lifeline to Mama into a pitcher.

'Bury it deep,' Nani commands Khanma. 'Let it burrow beneath the earth and bring this house another son.'

Revati Bhua wipes Mama's pale face. Mama pulls her phulkari-embroidered red shawl close and shivers as if it is cold. She breathes through flared nostrils like Papaji's favourite horse, Nirvair. Roop moves towards Mama, but Nani takes her arm in a vice-like grip and pushes her outside.

Then Madani.

Exhausted, Madani and Roop surrender to sleep in the watery moonlight of the courtyard. Knee to knee, so one breathes in when the other breathes out, taking only what they need from the night.

In the morning, Gujri sponges Mama with cloths dipped in cold water from the Hindu well, trying to reduce her fever.

By noon, she calls Papaji, who sends a field labourer running to nearby Sohawa, for that village's best hakim. He comes, a gnarled bandy-legged man armed with the heirloom herbs his family has grafted and watered over centuries, spells against djinns, and juniper branches he places carefully in the centre of the courtyard and lights so Mama can inhale their healing smoke. He dances round the smouldering fire calling all the fairies around Pari Darvaza to take pity and make her well.

But Mama grows hotter than the relentless afternoon.

When the light above the courtyard begins to dwindle, Nani rises from Mama's side to close the Guru Granth Sahib in the small prayer room, putting the Guru to bed for the night. The muezzin's call for evening prayers resonates from the mosque calling to all the Muslims in Pari Darvaza. Roop climbs onto the manji with Mama, gently slips an arm under her neck and holds her bony shoulders.

No one stops her this time. Her new baby brother lies beside Mama, too.

Listless.

'Sing me a shabad, Roop,' Mama says through parched, uncomplaining lips.

Roop begins singing, words from the Guru Granth Sahib, ear to Mama's breast, listening to her heart beat time for the song. Her clear young voice rises, circles the room, 'Mera vaid Guru Gobinda' – the Guru is my healer. After the first verse, Mama takes the shabad from Roop, in a voice old before its time, a voice that falters, fades, rises, falters, fades.

The sun sweeps the doorway with its last rays, slinks away from Pari Darvaza.

The singer has become the song. Mama's vaqt, her time, has come.

The baby whimpers.

Gujri comes into the room and picks up the baby; she takes one look at Mama and Roop and runs from the room crying out for Nani and Papaji. Madani comes, climbs into Mama's bed too; she and Roop hold Mama from either side, silently, so Mama will not be alone as her atma leaves them.

Nani comes shrieking. 'Like some churail from the past,' says Papaji, his voice like shifting stones. Roop reaches up to touch his beard. Wet, salt wet.

Jeevan comes, sombre for once. He doesn't pull Roop's plait, but stands at the door, broad hands swinging slowly at his sides, as if he does not know who to fight.

Gujri takes over, calling Khanma to prepare Mama for her journey, while Nani's cries fill the air.

Revati Bhua rocks and weeps.

Papaji crosses the tunnel and tells Shyam Chacha to inform the village elders first, then others; he sends Jeevan to bring marigold garlands and a seamless cloth from Khanma's husband.

Madani puts her arm around Roop and leads her to sit on a manji in the courtyard. She looks straight ahead, eyes dry – her atma must have felt such loss before. Rope winding round the wood frame of the manji digs through Roop's salwar to her thighs, hurts her palms, so Roop knows she, Roop, is still alive.

The door to Mama's front room is closed all night; Roop and Madani hold each other, dozing fitfully on the manji in the courtyard. One breathing in as the other breathes out.

Nani wakes up the Guru. She opens the Guru Granth Sahib to read the Kirtan Sohila from the holy book again and again, loudly, accusingly at Vaheguru, all the way to morning, when Mama's feet and head are Himalaya and Nilgiri peaks under the white sheet and Papaji and Jeevan carry her out.

For the last time, four strong men in white, colour of sadness, colour of mourning, roll back the sleeves of their kurtas, lift Roop's mama to their shoulders and move forward.

Madani stops at the door of the haveli, but Roop covers her head and presses on behind Papaji and Jeevan, following her mama's body.

At the mouth of the tunnel, Papaji turns to her and says, 'Go back. Go home.'

Roop looks up at him, confused.

Papaji says in English, so very serious is he, 'This is men's work – not for you.'

Mama will be burned, and Roop cannot be with her. Only Papaji and Jeevan can be present; they are men. Then when Mama is nothing but ashes, Papaji and Jeevan will take her all the way to Hardwar to float away upon the Ganga – why can Roop not be with Mama to hold her hand and say farewell?

Roop looks to Jeevan for support, but he doesn't see her. He stares ahead, stone-faced but for the tremble at the corner of his mouth.

Stopped, Roop stands at the mouth of the tunnel and watches till Mama's body is just a small white dot squeezed between the walls of the village.

The taste of blood fills her mouth; her last baby tooth has come away from her gum.

The white kurtas of the men turn the corner, and Roop's mama vanishes into a tan haze of dust.

'Hai! Hai!'

It seems that almost all the women in Pari Darvaza fill Papaji's sitting room, as well as some from towns around. Crowded into the room where men usually sit before Papaji's worn low desk to air their anxieties and discuss the plummeting prices of wheat and barley, now sit the women, white-garbed and cross-legged on the threadbare carpet. They beat their breasts, rocking, crying, lamenting with one voice – will they ever stop? They cry from their wombs, they pant and howl out all the pain in this life and their past ones, they give tongue to the silent sorrow of men too manly to cry.

It is a siapa.

Nani leads the siapa, full-throated, eyes closed, rocking before them as she questions, 'Who is there left of my blood? Who is left to care for me? Old age is come; I am left alone.'

'Nobody,' they agree.

'My husband is gone, my sons killed in a war far away. This was my last daughter; she is gone. Who is there left of my blood?'

'No one,' the women moan as one.

'What is a woman without children?'

'Nothing,' agree the women, one-voiced. 'No one.'

Roop turns to Gujri clanking her pots and pans upon the clay stove in the rasoi across the courtyard, for comfort.

'Your Papaji will not like this,' says Gujri. 'He says only Hindus hold siapas now.'

Papaji and Jeevan will be back from Hardwar soon; a skinny rubbed-raw tonga horse will clip-clop down the tree-lined road from Gujarkhan Station and Papaji will see Nani has disobeyed him and held the old siapa ceremony, though he's told her kindly but firmly there is 'no need.' Revati Bhua is mourning as loudly as Nani, just stopping for breath more often.

The wailing continues, sobs and shrieks rising from the throats of the mourners. Gujri sniffs, pointing her ladle at two women whose buttocks spill over the threshold of Bachan Singh's sitting room, close to the jutis and sandals the women inside have discarded like small boats washed up against the shore. Madani sits puffy-eyed and lost on one of the manjis strewn about the courtyard, her hands smoothing wrinkles from Mama's kameezes just off the clothesline.

'That one,' Gujri says to Roop because she happens to be listening. 'That one's husband went ahead and joined the Anjuman-i-Islamia society.' The Muslim society, ably assisted by Abu Ibrahim, has recruited a few members in Pari Darvaza. 'And ever since, she's started calling her Sikh neighbours kafirs, unbelievers! What to tell you – even merely devout Muslims look like heretics to those people.

'The one beside her,' Gujri skewers a green chili deftly, adds it to the wide-mouthed pot rocking on the clay stove, 'your mama said I should grind wheat and chickpeas for her when she had her last child but these days her husband says Sikhs like your papaji lick the boots of the British.'

Roop wanders into the front room, where Mama lay so long. Mama's wedding trunks remain, their backs to the far wall, and her flat oblong empty manji.

Will Mama feel the burning? The blazing heat from the flames all around her? Madani and I should be with her now, just to hold her hand.

Roop wanders back into Gujri's cookroom, wiping her nose on her chunni.

'This is why,' says Gujri, stirring spicy brown beads of 'Pindi cholas in the pot, 'This is why these women cry. Not for your mama, but for your Papaji's second son, for those who are left behind in this life.'

Nani shrieks.

Roop runs from the rasoi to the door of Papaji's sitting room. She looks for Nani's white chunni-clad head across a sea of bobbing white chunni-clad heads.

There is Nani, facing Roop and all the other women. Tears course down Nani's cheeks. Fists thump her chest like oval hammers.

Now Roop is making up for tears unshed in her past lives, crying more for Nani than for herself – she is young, Nani is old.

Nani flings her chunni aside and her white straggly hair comes loose.

Cloth rips; Nani's chest lies bare.

Nani shakes her white mane wildly and raises her hands, hands that hold the huge iron lock from the door of the haveli. It catches the light for a moment, hanging in the air above the mourning women before it descends, smiting Nani between her sagging, wrinkled breasts.

There is blood. Roop cannot move.

The massive iron lock rises again – where does Nani find the strength to lift it?

It falls.

Again it rises, again it falls.

The bloody gash in Nani's breast widens. Blood spatters the women closest to her. No one notices. Not one stops her wailing, each lost in her own sorrows. Roop wants to run to her, to cry, 'Stop!' but the room is full of egg-shaped women, swaying and rocking in pain. She cannot reach her. She looks for Madani; Madani sits listless, eyes turned inward. Where is Gujri? She looks towards the rasoi. It is empty.

Revati Bhua? Revati Bhua is nowhere to be seen.

Now the wound in Nani's chest has become a furrow and her cries dwindle to moans of pain. A hush creeps over the room and still no one stops her as the heavy iron lock plunges in and out of that burning chasm. Finally, it falls from her bloody hands and lands with a muted thump on the stone floor. Nani slips sideways, grunting as her shoulder hits the ground.

Gujri suddenly appears. Gently, she covers Nani's head, half carries her away.

By the time Papaji and Jeevan return travel-weary from Hardwar, where they left Mama's ashes in the Ganga, Nani lies flat on a manji in a cool darkened room upstairs. Jeevan is at Shyam Chacha's house, paying his respects, but Roop runs immediately to Bachan Singh to tell what has happened to Nani and all about the siapa. They go upstairs. Roop stands quietly beside her father as he chews a corner of his moustache and looks down at Nani and her bloody bandage lying on the manji before him. Madani, sitting beside Revati Bhua on a low divan in the corner, begins muttering the Sukhmani so no one can ask her any questions. Revati Bhua's eyes squint in deep concentration; she holds a white chunni, hemstitching at arm's length in the fading light from the small window.

Papaji says simply, 'This is what happens to a woman who doesn't listen.'

Revati Bhua nods her agreement. 'Hanji!'

Revati Bhua always agrees with Papaji.

'Nani listens,' Roop assures him, defending her grand-mother.

'But she doesn't obey,' he says. 'There should be no difference between one and the other.'

Nani has been mouse-quiet upstairs in her room on the second storey of the haveli. Roop sits with Madani and Revati Bhua on a manji pulled to a wedge of shade in the gallery framing the courtyard, helping shell peas for the evening meal. She and Madani have collected the tiniest and sweetest peas in the laps of their kameezes; these are for Jeevan, when he comes home, on foot from the Vernacular Middle School in Sohawa.

Papaji strides into the inner courtyard, tight-lipped, his eyes narrowed to slits.

He announces, 'From this day forward no one in this family will go any more to the Hindu temple.'

Revati Bhua cups chubby hands over her ears, 'Don't say such things!' The temple to Lakshmi is her evening delight and she takes Roop and Madani with her to listen to Pandit Dinanath read the *Ramayan*. By now, Roop has heard many times how Ram was exiled by wish of his stepmother Kakeyi, how the ten-headed demon Ravan tricked good-good sweet-sweet obedient Sita out of her circle and stole her away with him to Sri Lanka, and then how Ram went to Sri Lanka to bring back his wife with the help of the monkey god, Hanuman, and the monkey army. She knows the Aarti and the Sandhya, expects many of the slow deliberate gestures in Pandit Dinanath's ceremonies, loves the chink of cymbals, the bells that wake Lakshmi's undivided attention.

'No, Revatiji, I say no more temple and,' picking up Roop's plait and thrusting it under Revati's nose with such force it jerks Roop's head, 'no more cutting of anyone's hair.'

Roop yowls, more surprised than pained. Revati Bhua hangs her chunni-clad head; she took her sewing scissors to the end of Roop's black plait just yesterday, trimming off split ends.

Papaji paces the courtyard, voice rising. 'From now on,' he shouts at the huddle of women sitting cross-legged on the manji, 'we will keep all five Ks the Guru said to keep. Properly, as we should have. I departed from my father's oath – all my troubles have come of this.'

All his troubles: Mama gone, Nani wounded and in-consolable, two daughters to marry off, and one of them, Roop, born on Tuesday, when the Mangal star is at peak strength. Past Papaji, Gujri squats at the door of the rasoi, trying, with a finger dipped in milk, to feed the baby – two weeks old and still no bigger than when he came.

Roop's left hand twists her steel kara about her clean wrist.

I do observe the five Ks, my kara, anyway. Kes — my hair is long, isn't it, even if Revati Bhua trimmed it a little. And I wear a clean cotton kachcha every day. Jeevan says he wears his steel kirpan just for me — Madani doesn't wear a kirpan either. And I do use Jeevan's sandalwood kanga, sometimes, to comb my hair.

'Leave Roop, what has she done?' says Revati Bhua, taking Roop's head over the rim of her bosom and rubbing it more roughly than Papaji's hair-pulling, so Roop wriggles away. 'What happened, ji?'

Papaji pulls up another manji, sits down heavily.

'*Hai!* Blood!' squeaks Madani, surprised into baring her teeth.

Bloodstains rust on Papaji's grey-brown beard and the sleeves of his kurta.

'Arya Samaj Hindus,' Papaji says at length, shaking his turbaned head.

The group draws close. Fundamentalists of the Arya Samaj, preaching the infallibility of the Vedas, have never been the centre of such attention in Bachan Singh's haveli till now.

'I was in Gujarkhan — Gujarkhan! Only two villages from here! Arya Samaj followers took that retired miltry-man's son, you know, that young boy who was going off to join the Sikh Regiment, like his father, next week. They took him, hobbled like a goat, but still bellowing, through Gujarkhan and stopped in the bazaar so everyone could see him and then they went to the temple where everything was prepared — the holy fire, the waiting pandit. There they tore off his turban, undid his knot of hair, and *cut it off.* All of it! Returned him to shuddhi, they said.'

He sees only Revati Bhua understands the word.

'That's their Sanskrit word for impure.'

Why do they think we're impure?

'*Hai, ni!*' Revati Bhua's hand presses against her breast, concerned for Papaji. 'Where were you?'

'I came too late.' Brown knotty hands cover his face. 'I went to meet that Baluchi camel-walla about some carpet wool — I wanted a better price. Something was wrong, though. The bazaar was unusually deserted as I made my way back, but there was an uproar near the tonga stand. As I drew near, I saw the young man stagger from the temple holding an unravelled turban in his bloody hands. Then he fell to the ground, moaning.'

'Then?' Revati Bhua urges.

'I ran to his side,' says Papaji. 'He looked up at me and cried, 'Don't touch me! Leave me!' He had tried to protect his hair with his hands and they were slashed, bleeding.

'But I helped him up and embraced him, comforted him as if he were my own son. And with my kirpan drawn, at the ready, we walked through the bazaar to his home. No one dared raise their eyes before us, they kept them lowered where they saw the flash of the blade and the sharp point at the tip of its arc.

'We walked together all the way to the door of his father's home, and there I left him, poor boy. Such humiliation.'

'But why, Papaji?' Roop asks.

'They believe we are strayed Hindus, fallen away.' Bachan Singh lifts his turban from his head and Revati Bhua and Roop move apart on their manji, to make room for it. A jab from Madani's elbow prods Roop to uncross her legs and dangle her feet off the manji, so they are as far as possible from the turban.

Bachan Singh's underturban clings wetly to his forehead though the full heat of summer is not yet upon them. His top-knot sags beneath it.

'But you didn't stray – you weren't ever a Hindu.' Roop jumps off the manji and sidles into her niche between papaji's knees.

'Oh, I? No, I was made a Sikh by my father.' He assumes an explaining tone. 'My papaji, your dada, had taken three wives and still found himself without a son. So he went to a very wise holy man, a sant – you know a sant? – and he said, 'Santji, tell me what must I do?' The sant told him he must take a bachan before the Guru Granth Sahib, and so my papaji gave his word in the presence of the Guru, that if he was blessed with a son, he would make me a Sikh and call me Bachan.

'But not all Sikhs are like me. Others – even some high-up people – changed from being Hindus because the Sikh Gurus spoke to their hearts. No Arya Samaji Hindu can do anything about that.'

'Then why isn't Shyam Chacha a Sikh, too?' asks Roop.

'Because my papaji only promised that *I* would be a Sikh, so when your Shyam Chacha was born to his fourth wife, there was no need for any change, so he let him grow up a Hindu.'

'It's all the English people's fault,' Revati Bhua shifts from one buttock to the other; the rope mesh of the manji groans. Her father, Papaji's older cousin-brother, was a Hindu, too. '*Our* Arya Samajis here are not like that – Pandit Dinanath, our goldsmith, our barber. The Arya Samajis who come to our temple say everything should be simple-simple, not praying for show. Must be too-too many Christian padris holding their prayer meetings in Gujarkhan. People get afraid they are losing Hindus.'

'No,' says Papaji, 'this is not a made-in-England matter. These Arya Samaji Hindus were misguided, misled right here, in Punjab.'

Roop takes a peapod from Revati Bhua and squeezes till it cracks, pushing her thumbnail down the open crease. Jade beads spurt into the brass bowl, joining the others.

'With his hair cut off,' Papaji continues, 'that boy won't be allowed to join the Sikh Regiment – the British tell us now who is a Sikh and who isn't – but mostly, it's our own problem.' Strong hands pull Roop onto his knee. 'You remember. No more temple for you, you go to the gurdwara instead. No more Hindu superstitions and ceremonies – you study the Guru Granth Sahib's words. Revatiji, no chillum, no tobacco in this house, not even in your paan.'

A stricken look crosses Revati Bhua's face, but Papaji goes on, 'None of your brass idols in this house, Revatiji, no Hindu ceremonies, no Aarti, no Sandhya, no offerings to that tulsi tree on the terrace. I don't want to hear a single bell – understand? Gujri, no more Muslim meat is to enter this house, not even if Abu Ibrahim sends goat meat he slaughters for our labourers at Sadqa; the Guru forbids killing animals slowly and painfully.'

He smooths first one side of his moustache, then the other.

'Tomorrow we'll begin an Akhand Paath. Three days of reading the Guru's words should purify this house and bring us back to mindfulness – Revatiji, you see to it.'

'But . . .'

Papaji's face assumes a look of amazed insult.

Revati Bhua's voice trails away.

Her mouth opens again; her hand rises immediately, covering it.

Papaji looks directly at Revati Bhua but does not seem to see her.

It is to immobile, mute Lakshmi that Revati Bhua always tells her story; Roop has never seen her talk to Vaheguru, just to Lakshmi. Revati Bhua tells Lakshmi how it became too late, how she got too old for any family of good caste to give her a mangalsutra pendant that might have hung about her neck, telling the world she had been taken in marriage. How can Papaji ask Revati Bhua to leave Lakshmi and talk to the Guru? The Guru is not an idol, like Lakshmi. You can't put vermilion powder on the Guru Granth Sahib, you can't bathe it either. You can only wake the holy book in the morning, put it to bed at night, garland it with marigolds, dress it, gold-bordered silk rippling from between its pages, offer it sticky-sweet parshaad, then pretend it has eaten.

Papaji does not seem to see that Revati Bhua is choking back tears, though she sits directly before him.

'Baat khatam!'

The matter is ended; no one speaks.

When Papaji has returned to the fields Revati takes to her manji, crying till there are three pairs of lips on her face. Roop and Madani try all afternoon to comfort her. Gujri explains to Roop, 'Papaji did not see, because he sees Revati Bhua the way all men see their women, from the corner of each eye. That is just how they see.'

Revati Bhua sighs, 'Yes, it's not their fault; that's how they see.'

'I have been blind,' Papaji tells Jeevan that night.

The sky is curdled. Cloud patches obscure the stars, smudge the open anklet of the moon. Revati Bhua slumbers on a manji beside Roop's. Madani's mouth is open. Gujri is a coiled bundle on the ground, next to the baby's manji. The whole family sleeps on the terrace to catch the slightest breath of breeze. All except Nani, who, Gujri says, 'Won't take my medicine, won't let Papaji call a hakim, what to say about going to the hospital.'

'Tolerance, ha!' says Papaji. 'I have let my family walk the border between one faith and another, I have let you all practise this one in the morning, that one in the evening. The holy sant who advised my father said I would be born a girl unless my father agreed to make me a Sikh. My father kept his promise – but what have I done? Here I am slowly breaking his promise, like a woman who turns her face towards any man's voice. So the wheat grew stunted last season, and so did the maize, even with so much rain. So your mama is gone and Nani cannot find peace. But today I had my warning and I would be witless not to heed it.'

His voice resumes its characteristic brusqueness. 'We are Singhs. Remember this.'

Jeevan says, low and serious, no joking at all, 'I will remember.'

Roop struggles to keep her eyes open, squints up at the Mangal star.

Bachan Singh says, after a while, 'When I went to Amritsar, I saw the lane where General Dyer told Indians they must crawl because an English missionary woman got beaten up there by ruffians. When he gave the crawling order, there was a picket at each end of the lane that no one could pass. A teacher who lived there pulled up his kurta and showed me his ribs; still he has scars from the army boots that kicked him along, making him crawl like a worm at bayonet point all the way down the lane. To his own home.'

Jeevan gives a sympathetic grunt, props himself on one elbow.

'Then,' says Papaji, 'I went to see Jallianwala Bagh – you know Jallianwala Bagh, of course.'

'Hanji,' prompts Jeevan.

Roop is half listening.

'It's very close to the Golden Temple – a big clearing surrounded by the back walls of haveli compounds, so parts of the wall are very high and other parts are just one storey. I didn't think it would be so large. I went through the passage into Jallianwala Bagh, you know which passage I mean, na? I tell you, it was hardly one camel-length wide – a little more than seven feet. General Dyer said he marched his Gurkhas through there because it was *too narrow* to drive an armoured car. Imagine that – he was going to bring an armoured car against the people gathered there!'

Walking the site of General Dyer's massacre of civilians nine years ago has deepened the event in Bachan Singh as if it had happened just yesterday.

'I thought of those people, some talking, laughing, playing cards, telling stories, some listening to speeches. Not even hearing the soldiers' boots in the passageway, then looking up and seeing rifles pointed in their faces. I stood where he had stood and ordered the Gurkhas to fire on the crowd because they would not disperse. How could he miss? Where were those poor people to go? A carpenter who saw the slaughter from his terrace overlooking Jallianwala Bagh said there could have been fifteen thousand, there might have been fifty thousand, some were just sitting, minding the shoes of people who had gone to pay their respects at the Golden Temple. Some were there because their homes were too small to fit all the family members who had arrived for the fair. He said when they sank to the ground crying and bleeding, women lying on top of children, men pulling dead bodies over themselves, he swore he heard an Englishman shout, 'Fire low!' And then he said General Dyer's Gurkhas really fired low, reloaded and fired again – volley after volley. Fifty men. And sixteen hundred and fifty rounds, they fired. I saw a few bullet marks in the walls where those poor people tried to climb over, get away. And the carpenter showed me where a bullet hit his home below the window he was watching from. No, most of the bullets found their mark.'

'Why did the Gurkhas fire?' asks Jeevan. 'Why didn't they put their guns away?'

'Who knows?! What love should a Gurkha soldier have for

people from the plains? They must have been afraid; any man who refused could have been shot right there on the spot, they could have been court-martialled, they could have been hanged. Very loyal, the British call them, when they mean 'afraid to die.' You, you learn how they fight these days, so no one can make you afraid – understand?'

'My teacher said General Dyer didn't know there was no other way for people to get out,' says Jeevan.

'*Hein?!* If they were English people, you think he would have fired? Only Indian lives are so worthless to them. I met an old man who said they left his son and grandchildren there for hours,' Papaji says. 'Those people were almost all Sikhs who had come for the Baisakhi fair. It must be as big as the cattle fair in Lahore, I think, though I've never attended. So it was April; hot speeches for hot weather. The General said he had forbidden people to meet – how he did his forbidding, who knows? If he wrote it down on his leaflets, does that mean everyone knew it? No. How many people are there in this world who know how to read?'

Papaji is asking questions of the sky, questions to which Jeevan and Roop have no answers.

'Did you see the well?' asks Jeevan. The well at Jallianwala Bagh had filled with the bodies of men, women and children trying to escape General Dyer's bullets.

'I saw the well.' Papaji's voice deepens. 'I could not see the bottom. It's so wide, too. The old man lost his only son and his two small grandsons in the massacre and now he comes and sits there every day – he told me almost two thousand bodies were recovered.'

'From that well?'

'No, don't be stupid as an owl, that well could only drown a few hundred people. Some were crushed to death, some suffocated, body piling upon body. Two thousand bodies were carried away from the compound. For days the funeral pyres blazed! I could smell death in that garden, where the old man's tears fell. The djinns of the dead haunt it forever.'

He clears his throat, noisily.

'The English magistrate who comes here told me less than four hundred people died – he lies; it cannot be. These

English don't think we know or understand – of course we know, of course we understand.'

Why does Papaji tell Jeevan this story? Roop wonders. Whenever Gujri tells Roop a story, she reminds Roop that stories are not told for the telling, but for the teaching.

'What I'm saying is, it was after that garden filled with bodies of Sikhs that everyone – Gandhi, Jinnah and our own brave Master Tara Singh – fully understood the true nature of those ten-faced Ravans.' Roop knows he means the British.

'Sikh martyrs. Aam-log. Ki kende ne? – what do you say in English? – ordinary Sikhs. Like you and me, not high-up Sikhs, gave their lives so that our leaders and all of India could learn what these Europeans really are. That they are not here to help India, not here for our progress, they are here to feed their greed by taxing us – taxes on everything, even the salt a man needs to cook food in his rasoi. Did they come here because we were poor? No. We were rich when they came and took Maharaj Ranjit Singh's kingdom and kidnapped his son. How do you think we became poor and getting poorer all the time? And after Jallianwala Bagh, Gandhiji and his Indian National Congress fighting for freedom from the British didn't say, 'These martyrs follow the ten Gurus, we will not claim their long-haired dead as our martyrs,' did they? No. Nine years ago, I remember very well Gandhiji protested the crawling order and the firing, and the deaths of the Sikhs who died there, just as he has protested other deaths since. But now? It is a different time, now. These Arya Samajis in Gujarkhan are trying to convert one Sikh at a time, back to being Hindus! Gandhiji should stop them, tell them they must understand that everyone should be allowed to follow the Guru and God of his choice.'

Papaji forgets to remember that he no longer allows Revati Bhua to follow the God of her choice. Gujri is right, Roop thinks, men only see women from the corners of their eyes. Their eyes are like horses' eyes: they do not see what lies directly before them.

'Why doesn't Gandhiji stop them?' asks Jeevan.

'Sometimes you are stupid as an owl – get a little wisdom, understand? Because after Jallianwala Bagh, the British had to agree that each religion, each community, should be represented in the legislature of each province according to the numbers of its people. So now, Muslims need more Muslims, Hindus need more Hindus, and we Sikhs need more Sikhs. Mahatma Gandhi is a Hindu. He doesn't need to stop the Arya Samaj movement – he just needs more Sikhs to cut their hair and say they are Hindus next time the census people ask.' He pauses for breath. 'Master Tara Singh and the Akali Party are very correct, very right. We Sikhs must keep all five Ks as the Guru said, keep our kes long, wear it under a turban even if we're dodging bullets in the army, change our cotton kachchas every day, wear sandalwood kangas, steel karas and kirpans. How else can we know who is a Sikh, or who *says* he is a Sikh just to please his landlord, or who just wants to get a seat in the place where the landowners chatter?'

Revati Bhua turns on her side on the manji beside Roop and sighs.

'What about Christians?' asks Jeevan.

'Christians, huh! They're always looking for more Indians to call them Father this and Mother that. I'm not saying the padris and nuns are insincere, understand? They are most sincere, but they want our izzat – what do you say in English? Honour, yes? – to sit in the palm of their hands.' After a moment he adds, 'You, you go to the mission school soon, you learn to speak English, so you learn how they think – understand?'

Bachan Singh's partridges flutter in their cages and the baby boy issues a feeble cry. At once, Gujri comes awake, rises, and takes him in her arms.

Gujri hums, lulling the baby back to sleep.

'General Dyer died last year,' Bachan Singh says.

Gujri's soft humming compels Roop's almond eyes to close.

'The old man who sits in Jallianwala Bagh every day, he told me the governor of Punjab, the man who controlled General Dyer, Sir Michael O'Dwyer, is still telling Englishmen to this day – nine years since Jallianwala Bagh! – that General Dyer killed Punjabis that day to prevent another mutiny. To save India for the English. Understand, will you! These legislatures we Indian people are struggling and fighting to be represented in are just for show – only the higher-ups sit in them and vote, people like our Sardarji, those who are landlords. And you – don't think for one mint-skint that these Englishmen will leave India in my this-life or yours; they will not. Understand? It will never happen.'

'Understood.'

The Mangal star shines radiant, powerful above Roop. She turns, lying on her stomach now. She tucks her arms beneath her to thwart mosquitoes and buries her nose in Mama's shawl. The men's voices deepen and fade as Roop reassures herself, drifting into sleep. She is an observing Sikh now – Mangal's power can't touch her.

Can it?

Roop sits cross-legged on the wide doorstep, chin resting on her palm-heel, waiting for the bangle seller to enter the tunnel, because Gujri says she has more than enough chopping and mending and stirring to do without Roop's sad brown eyes following her around, getting in her way.

Across the tunnel, Shyam Chacha's hand rests on the shoulder of the patwari making his usual round before the rains, to record land boundaries. His Gandhi cap leans close to the shorter man's ear, till his greasy black short hair and the patwari's are level. Gujri said once that Shyam Chacha and Papaji were so unlike, she could not believe they came from the same father. Papaji is the kind of man, she said, who is happy with the daal and wheaten rotis Vaheguru's bounty places before him, and all he asks is to dine with dignity. But Shyam Chacha – if he is served daal, he will complain with his customary dourness that he has no roti, and having no roti will spoil his whole enjoyment of hot daal. If he is served roti, he will say he doesn't have enough daal to go with it – that not having enough daal will spoil his enjoyment of hot rotis. But, she said, no one can predict how much daal and how much roti Shyam Chacha really needs before he can be happy. So, he will always be hungry. And Gujri should know; she served Shyam Chacha daal and roti when Papaji and Shyam Chacha still ate together in the courtyard of the haveli they happened to be in when hunger came.

Shyam Chacha's larynx bobs in his indiarubber neck.

Now a clinking; coins change hands.

At the far end of the tunnel, near the stable and the cow-compound where the brick-lined tunnel meets field patches, Khanma's twig broom is at work, stirring the odour of camel dung.

Chachi's chunni-clad head leans from the second-storey window. 'Ay, kuti! Hurry up, na!' Her curses prod Khanma's twig broom. Chachi, a sweet-sweet woman, is never shrill with Roop, or Madani or Jeevan – or any high-up person – just with Khanma.

It has been almost a month since Bachan Singh came home from Gujarkhan and told Roop she must stop being a Hindu and be only a Sikh. Now it seems so long ago to Roop – though maybe it was only a little before the rains came – that Mama left Pari Darvaza in search of a new body somewhere, and Nani's wound began.

Revati Bhua polished her brass Lakshmi and her Ganesh for the last time, wrapped them in her never-used wedding saris and locked them away – one, two, just like that – in her tachey case with the silver-belled anklets she would have worn at her wedding if she'd ever had one.

This morning she took Roop and Madani, one in each hand, and led them to the small village gurdwara for the Japji at dawn. When they passed Pandit Dinanath reciting the *Ramayan*, telling how Ram went to rescue Sita from ten-headed Ravan, Revati Bhua stopped for a moment as if to check that her chunni still covered her head, then sighed and moved on. Roop knows Revati Bhua still waters the tulsi plant on the terrace, but Revati Bhua no longer makes the water an offering.

Bachan Singh's home was purified by three days and nights of reading from the Guru Granth Sahib. The granthi and his wife came from the local gurdwara to join Bachan Singh, Revati Bhua, Jeevan and Madani, directing them on the right way to take turns between them. They read all night in the small prayer room by lantern-light, while monsoon rain gusts swirled like djinns in the courtyard. Nani just lay on the floor before the Guru Granth Sahib during the prayers – all three days, all two nights, listening, moaning only a few times when she thought no one would hear.

When Papaji's voice became tired, it was Jeevan's turn. His voice joined Papaji's as he seated himself behind the Guru Granth Sahib, carefully so Vaheguru wouldn't notice a second's pause as its name was praised. Roop made sure Jeevan didn't fall asleep while reading at night; if his turban nodded forward, she poked him gently with the wooden handle of a yak-hair flywhisk. Roop wanted to help them read, for Revati Bhua and Madani have begun teaching her, but the holy book, body of the Guru, is printed all in one word, with no spaces, and Madani said Roop could make a mistake.

Madani could at least have let her try, though. For when the last lines were spoken into silence, they all stood before the holy book as Papaji apologized humbly to Vaheguru for all their mistakes.

If Madani knew from the beginning that Papaji was going to ask forgiveness, why couldn't she let me make a few mistakes? I could talk to Vaheguru that way, ask it does my mama miss me? Did the flames catch her long hair? Did she ignite from within? Does she know how much I wanted to be with her?

Then Bachan Singh read the Ardaas from a small book of prayers he bought on his pilgrimage to the Golden Temple in Amritsar. The Ardaas reminded them of the first five beloveds: the first Singhs; the forty Sikhs who stood by the tenth Guru at his last battle against a Mughal tyrant; Sikhs cut limb from limb by Muslim tyrants; two sons of the tenth Guru bricked up alive in a wall for their refusal to convert to Islam; martyrs whose scalps were removed; men who were tied to wheels and their bodies broken to pieces; men and women who were cut by saws and flayed alive by Mughal emperors for their faith, but did not convert to Islam.

Then Roop extended a cupped pair of hands for the granthi to fill with hot sticky-sweet parshaad, parshaad Madani helped Gujri cook that morning. But the granthi only gave Roop a small-small . . .

The bangle seller has entered the tunnel, waking Roop from her musing.

He carries two jute bundles, dingy brown, with the promise of sparkle inside. They oscillate from three ropes tied to each end of a long stick with its fulcrum on his shoulders, supporting the fragile hidden circles of bright coloured glass. Rolled tight under his arm, a reed prayer mat awaits his need to kneel before his Allah.

He rests his bundles on the floor of the tunnel and squats. With a practised flourish, he unties the first bundle before Roop.

Colour prisms splash, shoot and shimmer on the haveli's mud-plastered walls.

'Gujri!'

Gujri comes, wiping her hands on a corner of her chunni. Seeing the bangle seller, she returns with three small bruised bananas and lays them on the ground before him. 'Give her a dozen bangles,' she orders, then returns to her rasoi.

Roop cannot find any bangles that lift her heart.

She shakes her head. 'I don't need any bangles.'

The bangle seller says nothing, but opens his second bundle.

Vermilion reds, mustard golds, purples and green glass. Red glass, pink glass, glass that has passed through fire, melted, then spun down a wood cone to Roop's size, cooled, till it formed a hot skin that could bear the touch of a paintbrush tip, dotting it with gold, threading it with silver.

Such tinkling, shimmering fragility, doesn't she want a few?

But even new bangles fail to bring a smile to Roop's eyes. 'Take the bananas,' she says, remembering Mama said she must be generous. 'I don't *need* any bangles.'

The bangle seller eyes the bananas and spits, considering.

Then he shifts closer on his haunches. 'Tattoo?' he suggests helpfully, being a man who has no aim to receive without giving something in return.

Revati Bhua has one, so does Nani. So Roop clenches her fist at the end of her outstretched arm and nods. She scrunches her eyes and commands, 'Write my name.' The bangle seller holds the needle poised above the light brown skin on her unclean side.

'Qya naam?'

'Roop,' she says.

Roop, temporary vessel of God. Small body, just a shape. Feeling gone.

Roop was only to be her temporary name, just till Papaji had enough time and money for her naming ceremony. She might have had a real name if her little brother had lived. Papaji might have named her when his son's name was chosen before the Guru. One, two, just like that.

But the last of Mama's body died quietly like three – or maybe it was four? – other brothers before him, and before his fortieth day, so, like Roop, he remained unnamed by the Guru.

The bangle seller grips her arm. The tattoo needle hurts. But very little, just pinpricks. It punctures; blue stain seeps beneath her skin like Mama's smell. Skin turns to canvas. Ink spreads across the vulnerable softness of her inner wrist, giving shape to the sound of her name.

The tattoo is complete.

Roop examines her left arm with startled dismay. She had expected him to write in the Guru's script, Gurmukhi. Instead, he started from the right, and wrote her name in Persian script, as if he were writing in Urdu.

Papaji, Gujri, everyone will be angry. Urdu is a language only Muslims use.

Oh, but I will smile at Papaji and he will forget anger, I will climb on his knee and he will say, 'Achcha, fer na karin.' Don't do it again.

There is pain now in Roop's wrist, pain that has cause, cause she can see.

The pain of her heart is invisible; no one cries for that kind of pain.

Cradling her now throbbing arm, she thanks the bangle seller and returns inside the haveli. She avoids everyone in the centre courtyard by climbing the narrow steep staircase past the second storey to the terrace. There she rests her elbows on the wall near Papaji's fighter partridges straining and fluttering in their bamboo cages. Chin resting upon her knuckles, she looks out over Pari Darvaza.

Immediately below is the carved rounded wooden roof of the tunnel attaching Papaji's home to Shyam Chacha's. She cannot see the matted locks of the blind man, but he must be there, motionless, at its mouth. Nirvair and Papaji's three other horses have a stable near the cow compound at the other end of the tunnel, and Roop can just see a water carrier's head bobbing over the stream flowing from his goatskin to the water trough for Papaji's bullocks and cows.

No one in Pari Darvaza but my Papaji has a separate stable or cow compound.

Roop has started with better kismat from her previous lives than the blind man from his, but next time she may slip down the ladder – she may have caused Mama to die by letting Revati Bhua take scissors to the end of her long plait and by praying to Revati Bhua's brass idols when she was Hindu and Sikh all at once. And because her body wouldn't move at the siapa, she wasn't able to stop Nani from making her wound that doesn't heal. And maybe she hasn't been loving enough, or grateful enough, or giving enough, and the boy-baby found this out and died – Madani always says she isn't giving enough.

She places her hand, tattoo up, on the terrace wall and traces its outline with a finger. If she continues this way, she'll be a dog in her next life.

Or I might have to come back as a girl again.

Past the blind man there are more clusters of compounds, each home sharing walls with its neighbour, impenetrable without invitation. She can see Huma's father's compound, past the small bazaar where Khanma's husband, the weaver-tailor, sits sewing in his shop, near the three onion-shaped domes of the mosque. Most of the Muslim homes in the village cluster around their pir's home, where Huma lives with her abu.

Papaji and Abu Ibrahim haven't matched their partridges again for a long time. Maybe because Mama became so sick or because Shyam Chacha frowned so much.

Big-bellied Pandit Dinanath lives in the compound attached to the triangular dome of the Hindu temple, with most of the village's other Hindus in their compounds around. Roop hasn't played hopscotch with the pandit's daughters for a long time now, because Revati Bhua no longer takes her to the temple to hear the *Ramayan*.

The Sikh gurdwara in Pari Darvaza is larger than the temple, long and low with a single rounded plaster dome. Inside, the granthi, overfull of his midday meal, sleeps as he guards the Guru Granth Sahib.

On the edge of the village overlooking the fields lie two Muslim tombs surrounded by a walled compound – Sufi saints from Mughal times, Abu Ibrahim's ancestors. Beyond the compound that encloses them is an open patch scuffed bald by round after round of Jeevan and Ibrahim's endless games of kabaddi.

Near the crumbling remains of the village walls lies the ruined archway that gives Pari Darvaza its name, doorway of the fairies. The fairies should have come to help Mama, through that archway, when the hakim called them.

But they didn't.

North, past the mud and brick walls of Pari Darvaza, past the irregular patches of rain-fed fields and dusty roads, past Sohawa and Kuntrila, Roop knows the Grand Trunk Road runs hard, white and straight. There the traders' camel caravans turn west for Gujarkhan, Rawalpindi and the Storytellers' Bazaar in Peshawar, or east to the city of Jhelum and the capital of the whole of Punjab province: Lahore.

Why do Roop's thoughts fill with other places today? Mama and the new baby brother who was to ride her hip are gone on to their next life and Roop was not even allowed to be present to say goodbye.

Why does Roop still walk and talk and remember and plan when they cannot?

In the blue distance, two diamond-shaped paper kites hover and swoop above earth-crags and date palms: a red kite, with a smaller blue one riding its wake.

Rise! soar!

The fragile kites pitch and yaw, tugging at twine.

Now they catch a breath of wind; swoop, dive and surge on their way.

Roop's eyes brim and overflow. She prays: *May kind, loving, caring hands be waiting to break their fall.*

3. Pari Darvaza, August 1928

The sickness comes upon them after the monsoon has greened the land.

Typhoid!

It rises from stagnant hollows between hot dusty rows of maize, from puddles collected in ruts that follow wheels of bullock carts, and it goes looking for children in every haveli. Carried in food and by water, it fells them, Allah-fearing Muslim children like Huma and Ibrahim, God-appeasing Hindu children like Pandit Dinanath's daughters and lastly, the God-praising Sikhs. First Jeevan, then Madani, writhe and sweat in a half-dream time, and now it is Roop's fever that knits Bachan Singh's eyebrows over worried eyes.

Only Gujri continues unaffected, serene, bringing warm onion poultices to place on their stomachs, ladles full of whole black peppers to be chewed and swallowed without protest, despite the tears streaming down their faces. She administers carom seeds cleverly disguised in her flat round rotis, and the unsalted water remaining from boiling lentils. It does little good – Roop can't keep any of it in her, but she takes Gujri's remedies on the promise of a translucent lump of raw sugar to sweeten her mouth.

At the untouchables' entrance at the back of the haveli, Khanma sways, praying equally to her Allah and to Sitala, big mother, goddess of smallpox, to spare Deputy Bachan Singh's children. Khanma delivered the boy-baby who died; her kismat in this village cannot stand more death.

Gujri tells her Sitala has not visited them, that this is typhoid, not smallpox, but Khanma prays anyway, bringing them amulets blessed by Abu Ibrahim and threads blessed by the Hindu astrologer.

'Evil eye,' she wails.

'No one is blaming you, no one will send you away.' Refuse has begun piling up and Gujri wants Khanma to put her twig broom to work and take it away; no one in Bachan Singh's family is born to this work. So she says, soothingly, 'This is all karma.'

But Khanma's Allah doesn't offer her the promise of a next life, and so she wails, 'Someone will!' Untouchables, even if they turn Muslim like Khanma, always get blamed for anything unpleasant in life.

All the while, Nani moans in her room. 'Mai mar javan.' Roop has heard beggars before, but they do not beg to die. Nani's wound has lips that will not close, a tongue that will not still, blood that will not congeal to scar. It continues, turning within to gnaw upon itself, cries without sound, screams with no solace.

Gujri says, 'No woman should outlive her children, no mother should wash a dead child.' And her lips move in silent prayer but, to Roop's surprise, though she tends Nani, she will not comfort her, nor will she cry with her. 'A husbandless, childless woman; such terrible kismat . . . what she must have done in her past life!'

But with Roop, Madani and Jeevan, she is tender and firm, rough palms grazing Roop's cheek as she looks for any signs that the disease is stealing her beauty. Pimples like Madani's or brown spots or mustard-yellow eyes like the goldsmith's daughter got from her sickness last year – they would ruin her chances. Revati Bhua says the goldsmith's daughter didn't get yellow eyes from sickness; she just looked too closely at her father's gold in his workshop and her eyes have reflected it ever since.

Roop, too, wants to examine her face, but Gujri forbids her the mirror — her face might stay the way it saw itself or might lose the last of its beauty; mirrors are greedy. The thought of losing her complexion, smooth as a new apricot beckoning from the limb of a tall tree, or the soft sheen of her long dark hair! What if her almond-shaped eyes changed from their warm shiny brown to glassy transparent blue like the Englishman they saw the day of the picnic? She might become like Madani, in whom service and loyalty must take the place of beauty, a woman of average kismat and no power to change it.

'You two look at each other in the mirror,' Revati Bhua suggests as a compromise. 'Girls need mirrors to see each other. Then you can tell each other how you look.'

Madani looks in the mirror and her eyes meet Roop's. 'You are so beautiful, little bhain,' says Madani, wistfully.

'You are more beautiful,' Roop lies, before Madani's rabbit teeth in the mirror.

Gujri leans over Roop. A wrinkle line cuts into Gujri's cinnamon skin, from the nose ring nestled in the curve of her nostril to the turned-down corner of her mouth. Above her slim nose a single frown line stays between her eyes, from scolding. Gujri must be as old as Mama and have only a few years to live; Roop pushes Gujri's hands away. She is so afraid to love Gujri, she says, 'I don't like to be touched by a servant.'

Gujri's shoulders stiffen as if bracing against a new wind. Her brows draw close for a second. Then she moves to Madani and lets Roop lie in her sweat until Roop calls for her, angry and afraid she might die, with or without beauty.

A caregiving woman has her uses, too.

When the fever abates, Roop stretches on a manji in the courtyard, feeling the warmth of the morning sun on her cheeks, revelling in the quickening in her limbs. On her index finger, she wears Mama's sapphire ring, three sapphires and two smaller round diamonds, and the red shawl that still smells of her.

Ginger whiffs past her nose – Gujri waving a ladle at her from the rasoi. 'Ay, you'll get dark. No one will marry you if you lie in the sun.' Roop stays on the manji anyway, looking up at the cloudless blue oblong framed by mud-plastered brick. It is an ocean of milk that she will return to and it will take her to Mama. Her eyes are closing; she tries to remember how it felt to die.

Revati Bhua wakes her with a slap. 'Ay, take off that ring, I tell you for your own good. Sapphires are so unlucky, they make girls quarrelsome, they make them give trouble.'

But Roop won't give Revati the ring. She makes a fist of her hand and pretends her ears don't speak to her.

'Stubborn girl,' said Revati. 'Bad things will happen to you! Your mama never wore that ring; she knew better.' And Roop's ear rings and stings as it encounters the flat of Revati's palm.

Roop stuffs the sapphire ring in the turned-up toe of her juti.

Mama is gone and all sweetness, all fire, gone with her. Papaji didn't let Roop say goodbye. No one allowed Roop to carry her mama away, help lift her to the funeral pyre, no one let Roop hold her mama's hand as the flames took her away.

Roop will be generous like Mama, she will be kind and everyone will love her.

But she doesn't want to die like her, never having seen the street or the bazaar, never going out without purdah. She won't marry a village lambardar like Papaji – she is as beautiful as Mama and can marry a man higher than a headman. Maybe a miltry man, a trading, money-lending sahukar, a landowning jagirdar.

Maybe a raja.

Papaji says so, not to Roop, but to Nani, who, days after Roop has grown strong again, still lies on a manji in the courtyard, letting flies buzz about her wound. He tells Nani what the astrologer, Jyotshi Sundar Chand, said of each of them (and Jyotshi Sundar Chand should know – he predicted the last war that scattered Sikhs, Hindus and Muslims across the black water to fight for England). He said Madani will bring fortune to her in-laws, that Jeevan will be a fighting man. And of Roop he said she has good kismat – that is, for a girl born on Tuesday under the strong-strong influence of the Mangal star.

After the second rain of the day comes the scent of earth, pale brown as Mama. Drawing in large gulps of air, Roop tries to hold Mama within but she can't breathe deep enough to breathe her out again, fully formed, smiling.

Roop and Madani are taking turns playing kikli with big-eyed, long-legged Huma on a dry spot near the stables at the far end of the tunnel. A moment ago, Huma's soft hands were in Roop's, now it's Madani's turn to chant all in one breath –

> *Kikli kaleer di*
> *Pug mere vir di*
> *Dupatta merey bhai da*
> *Phphittey muhn javai da*

Arms crossed at the elbow, Madani and Huma hold hands and twirl, keeping their large eyes fixed on one another as the world moves past them. They blur. They laugh, they stagger.

Roop's feet are still and no one holds her hands. Even so, the fields and the expanse of the clear blue sky spin around her and she falls at the same moment as they.

The singing stops.

Roop lies, face half buried in mud, with Mama's white chunni spread about her like the wings of a bird felled in flight. She lies without laughter; her ribs press into earth.

With my body will I protect her, mother-smelling earth; then Mama can form herself again from this soil of Punjab.

But the earth stays hard, unyielding.

Madani, hand cupped over mouth, bends over Roop.

She shouts to Roop.

No sound.

Madani's hand falls away from her mouth.

Her mouth moves.

But Roop hears no sound.

Roop lifts her head from the wet coldness of mud, answers Madani.

Madani's mouth is open. Her lips move. From them come words without sound.

For a long moment, Madani frowns down at Roop.

Then Huma jumps up, panting. 'I'm thirsty.'

Moving on shaky legs, Huma runs back into the tunnel. Madani follows, then Roop, still shaking her head and clutching Mama's chunni. Back in the courtyard, mud comes away from Roop's ear with a sucking pop, just in time to hear the air split with a shriek from the cookroom.

'You shameless girl! Don't you ever come into my rasoi again!' It is Gujri, rushing forward with a hand raised to slap Huma. '*Chi!* Dirty girl. Don't you let your shadow come near it! *Huh!*'

Huma backs away from Gujri, doe eyes round with shock.

Roop and Madani look from Gujri to Huma.

Madani takes a step towards Gujri, Roop towards Huma.

Huma backs away further, her eyes accusing all of them, a trembling hand to her chunni, ensuring it covers her before she stumbles out into the tunnel.

Roop should be able to hear the slam of the carved timber door or the slap of Huma's sandals in the tunnel, but she can't.

Roop tosses her head the way Nirvair tosses her mane; the tassel of red silk at the end of her plait whips around her shoulders.

Perhaps she has mud in her other ear, too. Perhaps it's been there for a while, because she never heard Gujri or Revati Bhua say Huma was untouchable, like Khanma.

Papaji touches Abu Ibrahim when they make their black partridges fight in the tunnel, or capture quail in winter.

But Abu Ibrahim only eats fruit or drinks tea with Papaji. Gujri has a separate copper thal to hold the pir's food if he should happen to accept, and separate copper tumblers, even though Abu Ibrahim is so holy he is known for miles around.

And Ibrahim?

Jeevan touches Ibrahim when they ride Nirvair or play kabaddi together.

But Ibrahim never stays to eat after riding, nor does Jeevan offer him food. And Gujri goes all the way to the Hindu well every morning to draw drinking water, carrying it back to the tunnel in a pitcher balanced on her head.

When Huma asked for water once before, Roop remembers, Gujri placed it before Huma on the ground the way she placed the bananas before the bangle seller. Huma picked it up, but Gujri's hand and Huma's never touched.

There was never such contamination, until now.

Roop and Madani retreat to the second-storey gallery. Nani lies in the room behind them, still moaning she wants to die.

'Don't you tell Nani,' Madani orders Roop. 'She'll say it's my fault because I didn't keep Huma outside.'

Roop leans over the gallery wall to hear Gujri and Revati Bhua talking.

'Bring cow's urine,' suggests Revati Bhua in the courtyard below. 'It has *great* power. Just one drop can purify the whole rasoi.'

So sacred is a cow.

Madani's arm suddenly reaches around Roop, stopping her from going head first over the mud-plastered brick of the gallery wall. 'I'll make you go to the cow compound to get the cow urine!' she threatens from behind.

'You go. I can't,' says Roop, backing away from the wall. She crooks her little finger in her ear and hops on one leg to bring back sound.

The two little girls watch the women below them sitting on their haunches outside the cookroom, immobilized by their dismay. Roop strains to hear, though Revati's and Gujri's mouths are clearly not whispering. One ear seems to have no trouble hearing everything they say, so Roop uses it, cocking her head under her chunni. She would tell Madani, but Madani is absorbed by the dilemma below.

'What about Ganga water?' says Revati Bhua. 'Pandit Dinanath went on a pilgrimage to Hardwar – he brought a full jar.' One hand rises above the other to demonstrate the height. 'His wife will have some left.'

Ganga water from so far away is precious. The pandit's wife will not be able to give any without permission. And the pandit, if he finds out why Ganga water is required, will suggest a purification ceremony.

A *Hindu* purification ceremony.

For a *Sikh* household.

No. The two women agree: It takes a man to ask another man for Ganga water.

The heat of women's discussion and debate cooks neither daal nor rotis. By nightfall when Bachan Singh and Jeevan return, hungry and weary from the fields, the growl of Roop's hunger and theirs is indistinguishable from the growl of any Muslim or Hindu or Christian hunger.

Papaji says there is 'no need' for the cow's urine or Ganga water or any purification ceremony. He reminds Gujri, 'Sikhs must not practise untouchability.'

His general statement is a personal rebuke.

'*Hein?*' says Gujri, surprised. She expected to be praised for her defence of Papaji's home, for her loyalty to the purity of his whole family.

'Even Gandhiji has learned this now from Guru Nanak. Gandhiji says people of no caste are just as clean as higher-ups.' Papaji sounds desperate to persuade her.

Even Roop knows Papaji is stretching the truth, for Jeevan said once that Mahatma Gandhi only began preaching against untouchability once he found out how it felt to be treated like an untouchable, while Guru Nanak, the first Sikh Guru, always preached against it, even though he was from a high-up family and never really felt what it is like. Jeevan knows these things because he says he's going to teach history some day. Roop wonders whether Mahatma Gandhi ever read Guru Nanak's words. But Papaji's words, true or false, are achieving the desired effect.

Gujri sniffs, shaking her head, but at last she reenters the cookroom, lights the fire under the clay stove and begins knuckling water into wheat flour for rotis. It is late at night by the time everyone's hunger is appeased and calm is restored.

The next time Roop and Madani leave the tunnel and walk through the little bazaar, kebab-hot in the afternoon, to get Huma and play kikli, Huma's ami opens the door in the wall of Abu Ibrahim's compound just a crack.

'Huma is saying namaaz,' her mother says.

Closes the door.

And the next time, Huma's cousin-sister says the same thing.

And the time after that, all that Roop can see of Huma are eyes shining lacquer-black, then the heavy woollen socks peeping out under the hem of her new black burqa. Huma says, 'My abu says I'm too old to play kikli with you any more. If you want to play, he says you must come to our house.'

Roop hears Huma's words with only one ear. Roop hears Huma's words, but she does not like what they say.

Nani stops her moaning and instead begins her prayers. She leans on two canes and moves her decaying body slowly to Papaji's prayer room where she sits all day, reading from the holy book, not as Roop has always seen her, chanting it like a mantra to ward off sickness, death and all the things that lie in wait for everyone, but slowly, line by line, as if trying for the first time to understand the words.

Recovered from her typhoid fever, Roop joins Nani in the prayer room for the Rehraas in the evening. Nani stops chanting every few minutes to think about the Guru's words, trying to find out if they are meant for her too. 'Rahau,' she says. The Guru is telling her to pause, but Nani pauses for a very long reflective time. All ten Gurus speak as 'Nanak,' the first Guru of the ten, so Roop cannot tell, until she says 'Mahala' and the number of the Guru, which body of Nanak has spoken.

'You don't need to know which body of Nanak is speaking,' Nani wheezes, slowly, gently undressing the holy book, wrapping it in white silk to attire it for the night. 'You just praise. The Gurus have merely left us their poetry to honour Vaheguru.'

She says the words the Gurus wrote are powerful, so powerful that few people read them any more; faction fights faction in each gurdwara till only the purest Sikhs – long-haired, following all ten Gurus – find themselves welcome at worship. Today, she says, people only worship and admire the Gurus' words like pre-Vedic ciphers scattered across the sacred pages. Words that often turned against their authors to martyr them, poor words that now stand alone without their authors to defend them.

Roop says the Guru Granth Sahib's words with Nani carefully, testing them. And soon she feels them, too. Practical words. Telling her the Guru's rules are simple – work hard, share with your neighbour, repeat the name of God. That worship at graves is not for Sikhs, that worship before Hindu idols is not for Sikhs. That kirpans must leave their scabbards in defence of the weak and of truth, that if injustice can no longer be fought with words, Sikhs must fight well.

Telling her that living can taste bitter, can taste salty, can taste sour, but can taste sweet like the greasy-sweet taste of the Guru's parshaad.

Telling her she has one good ear, and the other just needs cleaning.

But Nani cannot find the Guru's words that will give her hope. The bloody bandage across her chest swells and then stinks but she will allow no one to change it.

'I have no one to live for. The men of my blood are all gone now.'

Roop doesn't want to be like Nani, giving herself wounds that do not heal. She says, 'Papaji'll look after you, Naniji, you can live with us.'

'And take from a daughter's family?' Nani says in a contemptuous hiss. 'What, you think I am so shameless? I would not stay here one mint-skint except that I am too weak to go home, now. No. I have no one.'

The night Nani asks to be lowered to the ground to die and the cotton wick of the oil lamp beside her burns low, she calls for Roop and Madani. 'Listen and obey your father.'

There should be no difference between one and the other.

'And your brother.'

Nani is fighting for breath. She lies back, exhausted. Roop takes her hand.

'Bachanji!' Nani wheezes. Bachan Singh rushes to her side. 'You promise me – give me your bachan – promise me you will always look after Gujri. She is a widow, she has no one. I promised her father . . .'

'I give my bachan,' Papaji assures her. 'You know I will keep it.'

The smell of death swirls in the tiny close room. And now it is Gujri whose shadow shakes, sways and trembles most in the gold lantern light.

When dawn lights the void of the sky above the courtyard, Nani opens her eyes. 'Bachanji!' she says, in a wheezing whisper.

When he comes close, she opens her lined brown fist, revealing her solid gold anklets. She places them in his hand, closes his hand about them, her payment for having lived in a married daughter's home.

4. Pari Darvaza, January–June 1929

Roop wakes to the *coo-hoo, coo-hoo* of a koel laying its eggs in a jackdaw's nest. A wide white moon is setting in the translucent sky over the courtyard, and Revati Bhua, Madani and Jeevan are still asleep on their manjis beside her. It will soon be time to go to the gurdwara for the morning Japji prayer.

Already, Roop can hear villagers passing through the lane behind the haveli, trudging to the fields to relieve themselves.

Her lashes flutter.

She burrows back under her quilt.

Roop doesn't have to go to the fields like other girls in the village, for Papaji has a latrine that Khanma has to clean every day. Papaji had the latrine built for Mama because she had always been in purdah. But he has told Madani and Roop they must continue to use it even though they will not be in purdah, because they are getting older and who knows what could happen to young girls going alone to the fields, no man to protect them – any man could carry Roop or Madani away and then, he smiles his slow smile, what would he do, left all alone with no one to look after him?

But now men's voices leap and burrow behind the flower-carved timber door to the tunnel, two voices so similar it is as if a man spoke and answered himself.

Roop leaves the warmth of her lumpy cotton quilt and ventures to the door, nudges it open a crack and listens.

One ear hears Papaji and Shyam Chacha, fighting again. Their words in her other ear come and go. But – no blood, no visible wound, no trouble.

'When the kaan mailiya comes to the village, get her ears cleaned,' Papaji ordered Gujri. The ear-cleaning man plies his trade through Rawalpindi area. Armed with tweezers and wood splints, he peers and probes his customers' ears for wax and dirt.

But Pari Darvaza is small. The ear-cleaning man finds more people who need him in larger villages, people who will pay a few annas more for his diligence and skill.

Roop has no need to add to Revati Bhua's or Gujri's worries. And Madani? Madani will only say it is Roop's fault and slap her. And Jeevan? Jeevan, studying history each night by lantern-light so he can teach it some day, does not notice Roop's ear. Jeevan has inherited his eyes from Papaji. Like all men, he sees like a horse, blind to things that lie directly before him.

'If I cannot pay you next harvest, you will have three more acres to farm, I am giving you my word,' Papaji is saying. 'But now, you please fill my share, I'm requesting. If I have to borrow again from the 'Pindi sahukar ...'

In Punjab, the English government is only a hundred years old and has had less time to seep beneath each man's skin, to trap him in self-loathing, than elsewhere in India, but still every man in the province knows deep in the bone that he owns nothing truly, wholly, that possession of the land is one hundred per cent of the law. Each crop belongs first to his overlord – chaudhary, jagirdar, raja or settlement officer – and Bachan Singh knows it is his kismat to be satisfied with the remains. The jagirdar's share is set at a third of the grain, but when the weighing scales belong to Sardarji's brother-in-law, the sahukar, it is the sahukar who tells Bachan Singh how much he may keep to eat and to sell.

'You haven't returned any grain you took last year, why should I believe you'll return this?' sneers Shyam Chacha. 'How many years must I wait? Don't I have mouths to feed?' The words glaze the cold morning air between him and Papaji.

Shyam Chacha's three sons, Hindus like their father, cut their hair. They don't wear a kirpan to defend anyone who is wronged. Jeevan says he doesn't think they even change their cotton kachchas each day as the Guru bid Sikhs – but maybe they do.

Papaji reminds Shyam Chacha in the same tone he uses to explain to Roop, 'Shyam-bhai, the cooperative society loan is due, I want to send Jeevan to the mission school in Murree this year so he may learn English. I have two daughters to marry, you have only sons. You are my brother; you must help me.'

'You may be older, but maybe we are not brothers. You're a wastrel, unworthy of our father's trust. Who knows where your mother came by your seed?'

'I am asking you with folded hands,' says Papaji, ignoring the insult. It's a very big insult, because Papaji is older than Shyam Chacha and Shyam Chacha should be obeying everything Papaji says.

'Fold your hands in the temple, then will I know we are brothers,' says Shyam Chacha.

Bachan Singh's half-brother has been attending Arya Samaj Hindu reform meetings in Gujarkhan lately, and since he was told that Mahatma Gandhi thinks a turban 'dirty,' would rather Bachan Singh wore a white homespun Gandhi cap instead.

'I cannot do that, by our father's oath.'

'Then grow tobacco next season, on a little bit of land, as I do – Sardarji and the sahukar don't have to know.'

Papaji shakes his head. 'Even the Guru's horse would balk at the edge of my field,' he said. 'I cannot do that.'

'Then you have bad kismat. There is nothing I can do.'

Shyam Chacha tosses his shawl over his shoulder, turns away. Roop sees Papaji waiting for a long while, as if hoping for a change of heart. She returns to her manji and the still-warm cocoon of her quilt, waiting.

The haveli door creaks open, then shut.

Roop forgets their argument as Pari Darvaza stirs into morning, pauses briefly at midday, stirs again through the sunny brisk afternoon.

But their words return when the breeze turns warm and summer scorches the earth khaki once again.

Field labourers' sickles hack at the tall swaying wheat in the fields around Pari Darvaza as Roop sits on the doorstep of Bachan Singh's haveli, listening to camel traders' stories. She watches men carry sheaves of felled grain through the tunnel for days.

When the harvest is done, Bachan Singh goes to the road to meet the bullock carts sent by the sahukar to bring all of Papaji's grain to his weighing scales.

'It's just like when we go to the gurdwara,' Madani explains to Roop as they watch Papaji hoist Jeevan up onto the lead cart with a chit addressed to Sardar Kushal Singh, sahukar. 'You make parshaad as hot and sweet and fresh as you can and you take it to the gurdwara as your offering. And at the gurdwara, the granthi takes *all* of it from you and puts it in his big brass bowl. Then he gives you back only as much as he thinks you need. And you must be very very grateful for what you get.'

Jeevan will ride all the way to Rawalpindi on the bullock cart so Papaji can explain his tiny crop of silky light brown grain, the colour of Mama's soft skin, and ask Sardar Kushal Singh, the sahukar, to ask Sardarji, the jagirdar, to ask the British to take just a little less from him this year.

'I know,' says Roop. 'You and Gujri keep making more parshaad for the gurdwara because you think if you make more, the granthi will leave you more. But he's much-much cleverer than you. He always puts the same size little-little bit in your hands.'

'So? Still I'm grateful, not like you,' says Madani, virtuously.

Roop crosses her eyes like a djinn-woman, scaring Madani into horrified silence.

'Nothing to worry,' Papaji says to Jeevan as he motions the lead cart forward.

And it does seem there isn't anything to worry about.

When afternoon gives way to the sudden pallor of evening, Gujri brings wheat rotis as usual for the casteless Sikh and Muslim threshers and she waddles painfully between the labourers who squat in two lines in the tunnel. She bends, scoops potato curry from the copper bucket to broad leaf-plates in their outstretched hands. She feeds them liberally, as if she were serving full-caste Sikhs, or as if they were in the free cookroom in the village gurdwara. She even makes lemon pickle for them and offers it a second time, careful to break its clay jar when they leave, so that no one in Papaji's house can be defiled by their touch.

5. Lahore, April 1930

It is the Baisakhi Festival, and Papaji said he must go to the cattle fair in Lahore to personally supervise the loading and hauling of an English piano. Jeevan said he wouldn't let Papaji go alone, but how could he go without his poochal, his tail, little Roop? Then Roop, letting loyalty conquer her aching curiosity to see Lahore, capital of the whole province of Punjab, said she couldn't go without Madani. Then Madani dutifully said she couldn't go anywhere without Revati Bhua.

So now they are all in Lahore, though it did seem Roop, Revati Bhua and Madani waited a very long time in the ladies' waiting room in Gujarkhan's train station listening to the cries from tea stalls: 'Hindu chai!' 'Muslim chai!' as Papaji counted out his precious silver rupees at the ticket counter. There were two water spouts in the station, one saying Hindus Only and another saying Muslims Only, and Papaji said the water came from the same-same source under the spouts, but if it would make Revati Bhua feel better, they could all drink from the

Hindu one, because no one has yet provided a third one for all the people who are neither.

At the cattle fair, Jeevan buys Roop the bright pink English ribbon he promised her two years ago. She ties the ribbon in her single plait, clutching her old tassel of red silk till she meets a legless beggar and drops it into his hand. Roop peers into the side of a kaleidoscope cart till her eyes dazzle and spin. She almost falls off her perch in the stand as she imitates tent-peggers leaning sideways from their saddles to drive wooden tent pegs into the ground. She holds Jeevan's hand tight as a bull jumps a thin small tonga horse with fear-deadened eyes. Amazement slackens her jaw as a tightrope walker holds a fire-brand in each hand and scales a high wire tied to the top of a telegraph pole. She scrambles into the camel cart beside the muzzled pianoforte flat on its back, bound for 'Pindi, and when the camel sets the cart rolling, she yelps for Jeevan or Papaji to help her off it.

At the entrance to Bano Bazaar, Bachan Singh takes Roop's hand in his. In the other hand, he carries a small square cloth bundle. 'Roop will come with me,' he says, ignoring the way her yearning brown eyes linger on bright bands of cloth that the shopkeepers unfurl before her. Jeevan, excluded from the tortuous narrow lanes of the bazaar reserved for only women to shop, just because he is a boy, stands waiting and waiting for Revati Bhua and Madani.

'Salwar-kameez? Lehnga?' the shopkeepers call behind her as her arm is pulled along. She skips to keep up with Papaji till he gets to the corner of Ewing Street.

There the red brick of Mayo Hospital, Lord Mayo's hospital, looms before her.

Roop's little body tenses. She begins pulling and slanting back-wards and by the time Papaji has walked from the corner of Ewing Street to the red brick roundabout before the hospital, her small bottom is scraping the road and the heels of her sandals are ploughing the dirt.

She is sobbing that she is not like Nani, she doesn't want to die yet.

Papaji puts his cloth bundle down on the gravel, and dhaaps Roop a big dhaap with the flat of his hand. 'This is for your own good,' he says. So Roop stands up, stops pulling and listens sullenly as he explains to the form-filling man sitting in the centre of the roundabout, 'I just want her ears cleaned, there is nothing really wrong with this daughter of mine.'

Clutching the form filled out in English, Bachan Singh and Roop progress to the hospital veranda. There Bachan Singh drops Roop's hand to open the cloth bundle.

'What is that?' asks Roop.

'It's our kursi nashin certificate signed by the district magistrate himself.'

Bachan Singh allows Roop to touch it. The certificate, issued to Bachan Singh's father, certifies he and members of his family are permitted to sit in a chair when waiting or calling on an English gentleman. Bachan Singh has brought it with him as a precaution, to give himself confidence to sit on the bench outside Mayo Hospital.

Father and daughter wait, sitting carefully at the edge of the bench, avoiding the stares of common labourers squatting before them on the veranda.

The English doctor, a ghostman with a white coat and a pink silk handkerchief that loops from his breast pocket, makes Roop sit on a wooden chair, under the dome of a white electric light. His whiskers tickle her cheek. He makes her say only sounds in the English language, though there are many more sounds in the world. And her good ear can tell her about all of them and her tongue can repeat all of them, even if she does not know what some of them mean.

But her other ear is 'gone.' It has no 'bol' in it; it no longer speaks to Roop. It lives in the world of silence, alone; no wonder Roop is only half listening all the time.

'Typhoid, I suppose? Typhoid fever can do that, my lovely,' says the doctor.

Outside the gates of Mayo Hospital, Papaji gives a street vendor two whole pais from his kurta pocket for a sticky bar of pomegranate ice. Sweet red juice chills Roop's lips as Papaji swings his square bundle in one hand, pulls her by the arm with the other, all the way down The Mall Road.

Bachan Singh strides along, in the grip of thoughts that assail him from inside. Past Malika Victoria's haughty statue at

Charing Cross, past the pink sandstone High Court, past the red brick Secretariat building and at last he enters Lawrence Gardens. Here the city sound fades; and only Vayu rushes through the leafy fullness of ancient trees; Bachan Singh has come here so he may hear himself think.

Roop takes off her jutis. Red flagstones are fiery hot beneath her tired small feet. Stepping in a fountain, she feels the water lick its way around her ankles. She balances on the narrow divide between two reflecting pools, setting one foot before the other like the tightrope walker at the cattle fair. A pomegranate smile floats on the water's brown surface above a parrot-green salwar-kameez and in the single long plait under Mama's white muslin chunni twines the new pink English ribbon Jeevan bought her at last.

Papaji says, 'Beti, not to tell anyone, achcha? People will talk. Why give them something to talk about?'

Roop stands with her toes just wet, as the fountains rise into the dwindling day. Papaji sits beneath an Arjan tree holding his head in shaking hands, 'Who will take you now?' he says. 'I do not have enough to change your kismat.'

The pomegranate smile on the face in the water trembles, fades.

Roop crouches before Papaji, pulls at his hands, 'My kismat is still good, don't worry, Papaji. Jyotshi Sundar Chand said I have good kismat. Didn't he say I'll marry a rich man?'

'Marry a rich man? Now? What rich man will marry a girl with one ear?'

Roop's heart sinks.

'You must make me a bachan, all right?' He is so serious; she feels as chilled as the pomegranate ice, though she stands before the mighty fire of Lahore's summer heat.

'Of course, Papaji.' Any promise to please her Papaji.

'No one must know this, understand? No one.'

'Not even Jeevan?'

'Not even Jeevan.'

'Not even Madani, or Gujri or Revati Bhua?'

Not one of them.

'You tell them your ear got cleaned,' says Papaji.

She puts her hand in his. The bachan is made. When they

leave Lawrence Gardens to meet Jeevan, Madani and Revati, the pomegranate smile floats again.

Uncertainly, just on the surface.

When they return to Bano Bazaar, Jeevan has gone to find a tonga. The street is growing crowded with a press of white-clad Gandhi-capped Hindus, round-capped Muslims and black-turbaned Sikhs, angry about something.

'Jeevan said he'll meet us at Lahori Gate.' Revati Bhua points down the street to the gate in the wall of the Old City. She turns back to the shopkeeper behind his shallow baskets of Darjeeling and Assam tea leaves. 'Now tell me. You are the *only* tea dealer I shop from in all of Lahore – what price will you give for me?'

Though it is quite clear from Revati Bhua's Pothwari Punjabi accent that she is not native to Lahore, the shop-keeper begins the game, by calling her a good-good woman. 'For *you*, bibi . . .'

Madani holds a jar of carrot pickle she bought at Anarkali Bazaar in one hand. Papaji gives Roop's hand into Madani's free hand.

'Wait here, I think I see Jeevan.'

He strides away.

Roop slips her hand from Madani's grasp and joins the moving crowd.

She loses a juti in a puddle, feels mud squelch between her toes. Madani, holding the jar of carrot pickle, shouts 'Stop!' in a dust-choked croak, but now Roop is caught like a fish in a net, and she is swept along with the tide towards the Lahori Gate.

Her chunni – Mama's white chunni – drops to her shoulders, her head is bare and her ear is ringing with slogans: '*Inquilab zindabad!*' '*Toady-bacha, hai, hai!*' She wriggles through the other side of the crowd and runs past walking chanting men, until they stop. She cannot see what for.

Around her there are only men in white kurtas and the occasional weskit. No girls, no women. These men smell different from her Papaji, the raw unfinished smell of anger.

She must get to the front and find out what they are listening to. She wriggles sideways, between the press of men.

No one stops her, though she is tall for nine, so rapt are they. Now she can see.

There are a few women at the front, one whose fist hammers air. Others stand behind her with banners tied to poles covered with English writing. Roop has never seen men stand and listen while women talk in the open street. The woman is talking about clothes – Roop likes clothes.

'On behalf of the Ladies' Picketing Board I inform all Indians that the very cloth your clothes are made from is made by people not of our quom.' She says it is made by British people, people who call themselves Europeans so Indians will think they are rajas of more than one tiny island. They make the cloth from Indian silk and cotton thread – the kind Khanma's husband, the weaver-tailor, spins from bales brought by camels to the tunnel haveli – and these people sell it back to us, so they can grow rich. She looks as kind and generous as Mama, but determined; there is no softness in the planes of her earth-brown face.

Sunset swaths of blue and orange tint the rapt crowd. Black turbans, Gandhi caps, furry karakuli caps and round caps nod. Cries of assent fill the air.

What the woman says must be true, if the men agree.

Now the determined woman urges the people in the crowd to burn all their foreign clothes and says she will be the first to do so. A bonfire is built before her and the crowd backs away as its flames grow strong and leap as high as Jeevan said Mama's funeral pyre had flamed. But Roop is afraid for this woman, this determined woman who speaks so loud in the street, away from her own home, who must be attracted to flames like a moth to a candle. She waits for the woman to walk into the fire, as Sita did, when Ram tested her in the *Ramayan*.

But the woman does not.

Instead she lets her chunni slip from its place around her head. A white chunni, colour of sadness, colour of mourning. She takes her white chunni from her shoulders and holds it up for all to see. She carries her head so proudly that no one notices

94

the absence of her chunni. Her words have persuaded the crowd to see it on her though she has removed it, her words more important than her modesty.

Now the determined woman throws her white chunni on the bonfire, and the flames attack it.

This is what Mama's body must have looked like, on the pyre.

Roop shivers slightly, looks around.

The crowd is roaring approval, and there is a great sound of men removing weskits and kurtas. Some women have brought bundles of saris, some men have brought European suits and ties. They tear and hurl garments onto the blaze.

The determined woman's white chunni is being smothered. Curling and browning in the heart of the flames.

Alone, like Mama's body on the pyre.

Roop feels her hands pull at her own throat till it is naked, and then she is walking towards the fire, carrying a length of muslin across her arms, like a dead woman.

And Roop throws her own white chunni into the flames, Mama's white chunni, watches it burn.

It is not proof against fire. Nor was my mama.

Madani catches up with Roop, breath ragged, eyes flashing, orange pickle oil splattered over her kameez. Roop feels the sting of Madani's palm against her cheek, and when Papaji comes, sitting with Jeevan and the driver facing front in the tonga, and learns about her escapade, she feels his palm too, twice as hard as Madani's and twice as humiliating.

'Don't you follow outside men. You don't even know what they were saying! You could have been taken, you could have been raped, anything could have happened!'

Everyone scolds and shouts as if to prove they care. It's all since Mama left.

Roop sits in the tonga between Revati Bhua and Madani, heels drumming against the boards under the back seat.

'If my mama was here . . .'

Papaji, facing front, the back of his turban to Roop, says it is Revati Bhua's fault, she did not look after Roop 'like a mother,' teach her the great importance of her chunni, her modesty, the dangers of unknown men, and the importance of obedience 'for her own good.'

Revati Bhua's double chin trembles. Big terrified tears flow all the way home in the train and the tonga to Pari Darvaza, till the whites of her eyes look like cracked eggs. Roop tries to explain it isn't Revati Bhua's fault, that she'd run off with the protesters herself. She wants to tell Papaji she placed Mama on the pyre, saw her chance to tell Mama goodbye.

Roop falls silent when Madani orders her to give her new pink English ribbon back to Jeevan, as punishment; the pink English ribbon she's waited for him to buy her for two whole years.

Jeevan puts it in the breast pocket of his kurta; it loops out like the English doctor's handkerchief. He doesn't smile at Roop, but talks to Papaji about cricketers and cricket scores.

All are agreed. This running away is a warning: Roop must be controlled or worse things could happen.

Roop was going to forget to remember her bachan to Papaji and was going to tell Jeevan and Madani about her bad ear, but if they don't want her to speak, she'll just keep her bachan, pretend she's listening and obeying like a good-good sweet-sweet girl with two working ears and who will ever know the difference?

Lajo Bhua is an older cousin-sister of Papaji's, in Firozepur. Roop and Madani will attend the local Sikh girls' school attached to the gurdwara there because Papaji doesn't trust Revati Bhua with his daughters any more. Pari Darvaza is too small to have a girls' school, even if anyone besides Papaji had wanted one. Abu Ibrahim says Papaji will be sorry one day that he is educating Roop and Madani, because 'what do they need it for?' But Papaji doesn't want his daughters learning any more stories about Hindu gods and goddesses from Pandit Dinanath or Revati Bhua or learning Muslim prayers like Huma. They will live with Lajo Bhua at her husband's home and she will look after them like-a-mother.

Lajo Bhua is a slight woman of about forty-five, who was never rich enough to be in purdah like Mama. Her own children – two girls, no sons – are long gone, married into families in other towns. Her husband's two-room home hides itself in a lane off a tumultuous bazaar, at the point where the lane obligingly curves around an old mango tree. A narrow wooden balcony on the second storey leans over the lane, and from it hangs Lajo Bhua's great indulgence, a carved wide wooden raft-swing.

Inside, she places a single manji in the dank-smelling windowless rasoi for Roop and Madani to sleep and study. Shelves lined with old issues of Punjabi newspapers in the rasoi hold pots and pans, brass trays and bowls, jam jars long emptied of jam and shortbread biscuit tins long emptied of biscuits. Lajo Bhua spends all day cross-legged on a mat on the floor of the adjoining room squinting over sequins as she embroiders in the slotted rays from the barred window.

In the evenings she crouches to make tea and then brings her copper tumbler to the raft-swing in the veranda. Between sips, as the swing squeaks and creaks, she dispenses the rules to Roop and Madani.

'Rule number one: You want to make a good marriage; you must be more graceful, more pleasing to your elders. I want to hear only "achchaji", "hanji", and "yes-ji" from you. Never "nahinji" or "no-ji".'

Lajo Bhua says Roop has been overindulged, given too many expectations. Roop doesn't like plain wheat roti, she wants Lajo Bhua to make it the way Gujri did, crumbling it with brown sugar. She won't eat a banana unless it is cut up and placed on a thali before her. Roop wants to wear a fresh clean kameez every day; Lajo Bhua has to wash it for her. Roop doesn't want to sleep on a mat on the floor; she wants to sleep with Lajo Bhua on a manji, wants Lajo Bhua to tell her stories till she falls asleep. She doesn't understand that Lajo Bhua is always so tired from embroidering. So many expectations, says Lajo Bhua, may be all right now; she's not complaining for herself, of course, but says it only for Roop – who knows what kind of family Roop will have to adjust to. At least she should be taught gratitude for Papaji's lenience now.

Every time Lajo Bhua yells, 'Rule number two: Speak softly, always softly!' Roop giggles. Even Madani has to bite her lower lip for composure.

Bhua's big, burly husband has a shop in the bazaar where he sits all day making sweet-sweet things to sell to passersby. But in the evening he comes home and unloads his bitter tongue at Lajo Bhua's failure and his misfortune, 'Useless woman, I have paid two dowries for marrying you, no sons you brought me.'

When he has gone to bet upon his nightly games of cards, Lajo Bhua wipes her tears and reveals the most important rule of all, rule number three: 'Never feel angry, never, never. No matter what happens, or what your husband says, never feel angry. You might be hurt, but never ever feel angry,' she whispers to Madani and Roop.

Now the cinema has come to Firozepur, and Lajo Bhua brings Roop and Madani all the way to the hall in a tonga, and she jostles at the women's ticket window for their tickets, as if Roop and Madani were her own children.

The cinema has black and white people, crackly, larger than any Roop has ever seen, and an actress as beautiful as Mama. 'Her name is Sulochana,' says all-knowing Madani.

On the scrap of stage before the screen, a tabla patters, a harmonium wheezes, and a violin wails tireless background music for the tale to unfold before Roop, the musicians unhindered by any conception of harmony. Sometimes the musicians deliver the actors' speeches in Urdu, sometimes in Punjabi. And when the title cards appear, the musicians leap to their feet and shout their meaning to all in the Punjabi-speaking audience who cannot read, or cannot read English, Gujarati, Hindi or Urdu.

Then, for a while, everyone falls quiet, sharing the story.

Roop speaks softly to herself in the secret dark, to see if anyone will notice she is abiding by rule number two.

No one notices.

Madani and Lajo Bhua recede, till Roop is stranded on a dark island of panic.

She reaches for Madani's hand.

And Madani finds Mama's sapphire ring on Roop's hand and hisses at her to take it off.

Roop wants to ball her hand into a fist and poke it in Madani's side, but she doesn't, because Lajo Bhua says

Madani is older and has to be respected, and because of rule number three.

Instead Roop says, 'Achchaji,' as directed by rule number one.

By the end of the long-long story, Roop can see the very large people are not black or white or even brown, but mostly shades of grey. Coming out of the picture hall, Roop walks tall with her thighs brushing together and flicks her almond eyes so much like Sulochana in the picture, that Bhua slaps her.

'Look more humble, like Madani. Can't you be a good girl, for-your-own-good?'

The next day, her first at the Sikh girls' school, Roop sits cross-legged in the row beside Madani, and scrawls on a whitewashed slate. Paper is expensive; it comes from England.

After three days, she begs and wheedles Lajo Bhua to write a paper letter to Papaji: 'Tell him, please come and get me. This is not the right school for me,' she orders Lajo Bhua. 'I want to go to a school with chairs.'

Madani finds out what Roop has written and is upset almost to tears. 'This is the most inexpensive school for us, Roop. How could Lajo Bhua write this for you? You want too much. And how selfish you are, asking like that!'

'Why can't I go to a school with chairs?' says Roop. 'How will I live in a rich man's house if all I know how to do is sit on the ground like a dihaati?'

Sitting on the ground like a peasant is the worst thing Roop can yet imagine.

'Papaji has less money now, you will have to make do with less.'

'Why does he have less money?'

'Less land means less money.'

'Why does he have less land?'

'Because Mama was sick and he needed money. So he borrowed from Shyam Chacha.'

'So the crops will come and he can give it back to Chacha.'

But things that look simple never are.

Shyam Chacha has told the patwari who records land holdings that it is his holding, not Papaji's. 'Maybe a little money changed hands, who knows?' says Madani.

All Papaji's loans from Shyam Chacha have been recorded as land transfers, and little by little, Shyam Chacha has taken away almost half of Papaji's inheritance.

'This is what happens,' says Madani, rabbit-faced sage, 'when a man doesn't care if he has to cheat his own half-brother to get land.'

So Roop sits on the ground under a banyan tree with all the children of the poor and says, 'Punj-chowke-vee, punj-punje-punji . . .' When she doesn't speak the multiplication tables in chorus, the teacher-ni tells Roop that girls who don't say words the way all the other girls say them should be sent home, all the way to Pari Darvaza, in shame.

Madani weeps and pleads till the teacher-ni relents – Roop can stay because Madani must be rewarded for such selfless and humble requesting.

'If you are sent home,' Madani tells her, 'your shame will be mine – everyone of the same blood is affected forever by one person's mistake. Understand, Roop!'

She says she weeps because she loves Roop, but Roop can see she weeps for herself, fear of shame shining on the rims of her surma-blackened eyes. There is something smug about Madani now, something confident, pitying, in the way she talks to Roop, the confidence of a woman whose future is secure, whose path is clear. A little rocky, perhaps, but clear, in a way that her pursed rabbit mouth, twisting first left, then right, suggests Roop's will not be. Perhaps she talks this way because Roop is born under the star of Mangal, perhaps it is because Roop won't stop wearing Mama's sapphire ring.

Papaji arrives at Lajo Bhua's husband's home one morning, having taken a third-class seat on the night train to save money, bringing Gujri's sweet peththas wrapped in a British-made handkerchief.

He has a new plan: Madani and Roop will attend a boarding school for Sikh girls, Bhai Takht Singh's school, a place with walls twelve feet high so they'll be insulated from all the anger brewing in Punjab, and so Roop can't run away on any more protest marches.

'Now see what you've done,' says Madani. 'He must have taken a new loan from the sahukar in 'Pindi just because *you* want to go to a school with chairs. If this continues, he'll have no dowry left for you.'

Roop says, heart sinking, 'I don't believe you.'

But Bachan Singh goes to the boarding school and admits them, one, two, just like that.

And Lajo Bhua, who was supposed to be 'like a mother,' is relieved.

Then Roop and Madani stand on the platform with Lajo Bhua and her husband and watch a soot-smirched Ganga-blue turban lean from the train and blend into hot sky as the train pulls Papaji away from the station. Roop weeps huge dis-believing tears that rise as though from a hole at the base of her tummy, till Madani and Lajo Bhua threaten to leave her all alone on the platform.

It is the night before Roop and Madani are to leave for board-ing school; a new wooden trunk and two bulging bedding rolls are packed, ready for the short tonga ride to Bhai Takht Singh's Sikh Girls' School with chairs for Roop and walls twelve feet high. Madani and Bhua sit on the swing together, and Roop listens from her perch in the rough, steady arms of the mango tree.

'Why doesn't your Papaji take your mama's family land?' says Bhua. 'Twenty acres in Kuntrila, and there's a road being built to make it even better.'

'Everyone in that family died. We don't take unlucky people's money.'

'Then who will get it?' says Lajo Bhua.

Madani gives the blameless ground a hard push with her foot and sets the swing moving gently, 'Some cousin-brother can take it. We don't need it.'

But less land means less money. Papaji isn't helping his kismat at all. And if his kismat turns bad, Roop now knows her kismat, because she is younger, because she has one bad ear and because she is born under the Mangal star, is turning worse than Madani's.

And Jeevan?

Jeevan will have good kismat; he is a boy.

A clay diya sputters, sucking the last drop of oil from its wick, extinguishing itself. Night, dense and full of the singing of crickets, like a mirror-inlaid shawl, pulls itself over Bhai Takht Singh's boarding school. A jackal stretches his neck, howling for a small piece of the moon.

Madani sleeps beside Roop in the dormitory, plaits wound round her throat for warmth. Roop has Mama's phulkari-embroidered red shawl from home, under her cheek. Her cotton quilt smells of Revati Bhua's hands wiped on it after eating parshaad at the gurdwara, and of the day Jeevan used a corner of it to clean a .303 Papaji had bought in Peshawar.

Mama's sapphire ring cuts into Roop's cheek. She showed it to the twin orphan girls, Mandeep and Tandeep, who don't have a wooden trunk like theirs at the foot of their bed. Mind-Lit-by-God's-Light and Body-Lit-by-God's-Light, both of them lie fast asleep beside her, as if God's light is unable to penetrate this velvet dark. Tandeep gave Roop some sound advice, 'If they don't treat you nicely here, tell them you'll become a Christian. Then they give you three round toasts with your milk at breakfast instead of two.'

But even if you become a Christian, without a father you can end up a servant somewhere. Madani says if they lose Papaji, they'll end up unlucky as Mandeep and Tandeep and have to cook and clean in a gurdwara or in some poor Sikh family's home because there won't be any family willing to take them.

Roop doesn't want to be anyone's servant, like Khanma or Gujri. Ever.

She'll tell Papaji and he'll take her back to the fairies in Pari Darvaza.

Treacherous fairies, fairies who should have come through the ruined archway to help Mama, but didn't.

Given paper, in letter-writing class, she writes to Jeevan, whom Papaji has sent to Rawalpindi to live with a cousin-brother there. She writes, 'I don't want to help in the kitchen here, like a servant. Please can you send three rupees a month for me, so the school won't make me do this?' Roop remembers Gujri's face streaming tears over the purple entrails of onions. Cooking should be learned by women who need it in place of beauty.

She isn't that kind of woman.

She will have servants.

The teacher-ni, gaunt, cat's-eye spectacled, reads Jeevan's reply. He says he can't send her money because he has to bribe a teacher to tutor him in English so he can do what Papaji wants him to: go to Murree, high in the Margalla Hills above Rawalpindi, to study at the mission school.

He says if he doesn't pay for English tutoring his 'marks will suffer,' but he promises to take Roop to Murree one day.

The teacher-ni, whose dark complexion and excessive desire for education has left her still unmarried at nineteen (though her family has tried very hard to get her a good match many times), makes Roop stand in the corner with both her stick-thin arms in the air until every muscle burns and her palms fill with prickling needles. Not because she doesn't want to learn cooking, but for *saying* she doesn't want to learn it.

Roop thinks of Jeevan's suffering marks, marks that shrivel and drop, shrivel and die, so her brother becomes a no-future man who cannot protect her at all, and she cries for Jeevan's marks, till the teacher-ni thinks she's had pain enough.

Roop takes revenge, flattening every roti she makes in the ghee-smelling school kitchen into maps of India, lumpy topheavy triangles riddled with the gaping holes of princely kingdoms. The teacher-ni gives up, seeing no reason to waste flour on Roop.

In April when the heat in Firozepur threatens to char the grain right on the stalks in the fields, Roop and Madani go home to Pari Darvaza where Papaji and Shyam Chacha no longer speak to one another and Revati Bhua still visits indefinitely.

Soon Jeevan comes back to Pari Darvaza for the summer, too, leaner, serious, his soft beard now mixed with acne, his voice deepening to authority, but joking and teasing Roop as always.

'Was the monsoon good enough that I may buy a second-hand bicycle?' he asks. If he gets a bicycle, he can cycle instead of walk every morning to school.

'Bilkul! Of course!' Papaji says.

Bachan Singh can only read and write in Persian and Gurmukhi script, and his daughters only need to learn Gurmukhi to write their Punjabi, but Jeevan must learn to speak, read and write English.

Gujri cooks a tall stack of wheat rotis and fills a whole brass bucket with steaming potato curry to feed the harvesters. The men sit in rows in the tunnel just as they have always done and take their water from an earthen pitcher so no one will have to touch them, but this year Gujri is not generous. In fact, she is careful and stingy as she has never been before, filling her ladle to half its capacity for each man. There are surprised grumbles and murmured curses from the sweat-lathered Muslims and Sikhs, but they cannot take back their labour, nor can they safely ask for more.

Roop stuffs Mama's sapphire ring away in the turned-up toe of her juti. Her mouth cannot remember the pomegranate smile that floated on the surface of the reflecting pool.

6. Pari Darvaza, 1933

The third torrid summer Roop and Madani return from Bhai Takht Singh's school to Pari Darvaza, Madani begins to bleed.

Gentle hints from Gujri, Revati Bhua and Khanma turn to murmurs that take flight beyond the tunnel and through people of common caste past Pari Darvaza from Kuntrila to Sohawa to Jhelum and 'Pindi. 'The child is a woman and is no longer to be kept in our trust. Find a family, find a boy.' Soon Madani is being summoned to Papaji's sitting room for viewing by visiting prospective mothers-in-law and aunts and is making sweet savayan every day to show off her cooking.

While they have been at Bhai Takht Singh's, learning the Gurus' shabads and embroidery, so many events have passed them by. Mahatma Gandhi walked two hundred and forty miles to pick up a lump of salt and refused to pay the British tax on it. Freedom fighter Bhagat Singh climbed the gallows and swung for tossing a bomb into the legislative assembly to make the deaf hear; his Sikh friends and relatives say the Mahatma stood by as if he were deaf himself and, in the name of non-violence, just let the British kill him. The Mahatma raised the national flag of a free India and it did not have a strip of deep Sikh blue as he promised; across Punjab, Sikhs mutter the reason – the Mahatma doesn't care for meat-eaters. A famous pir gave a speech in Jhelum and he told Abu Ibrahim to give all of Pari Darvaza's donations at his mosque to the All-India Muslim League. Sikh demonstrators led by Master Tara Singh protested when the British gunned down Pathan Muslims in Peshawar; they were beaten senseless by the police just north of Pari Darvaza on the Grand Trunk Road. Now freedom fighter Subas Chandra Bose has been arrested for appealing to the Sikhs of Punjab to produce more men like Bhagat Singh, and has been deported to Europe. And foreign-made chunnis are still needed for burning, if independence is to be won.

But Roop and Madani were in a school with walls twelve feet high, and all this passed them by.

'Is Papaji marrying you to a rich man or to a poor man?' Roop asks one evening, turning up the wick in the lantern beside Madani.

Madani looks up from the pansies and butterflies, spread across the manji. 'I don't know.' She has dissuaded Papaji from buying the more expensive sheets and pillowcases with the Manchester embroidery for her dowry; she will embroider them herself. She sits, cross-legged, hunched over for days now.

There are so many kameezes and chunnis and shawls to embroider; at such a pace, they are never going to anyone's haveli till next Diwali.

'Didn't you ask? If they didn't say anything, he must be poor,' Roop says. 'If he was rich, you wouldn't still be embroidering flowers all day and you wouldn't still be cooking with Gujri. You'd be practising how to say "How do you do?" and "Delighted to meet you."'

'So, are you practising "How do you do?" and "Delighted to meet you"? And when do you think you're going to use it?'

'Papaji is going to find me a rich man,' Roop declares. She pulls a corner of Madani's work onto her knee and examines the neat, even stitches.

Madani's hand curves like a small cave over the pansies. 'Every woman has her own kismat. Don't disappoint him.'

'I won't disappoint him,' Roop says carefully. She has kept her bad ear secret by sensing and adjusting her position in relation to each person's voice in a room, always watching when they speak. Her secret, kept so far even from Madani, shows she is not like other women – she can be ambitious even though she was born on a Tuesday under the strong-strong influence of the Mangal star.

Madani examines herself in the mirror. Catching Roop's eye, she asks, 'If I don't smile, do you think they will notice my teeth?'

'No, they won't. Why do you think I'm going to disappoint Papaji?'

'I don't, Roop. I'm just warning you because you can be so ungrateful sometimes.'

'I'm not ungrateful.'

'No, but be less stubborn, be a sweet-sweet girl. If Mama were here, that's what she would tell you.'

Roop is quiet – for about a minute.

'So, how did you stop the bleeding?'

'I put rags and it stopped.'

'How long did it take?'

'Two or three days.'

'You might have died, like Mama.' Roop feels tears coming.

'No, you foolish girl, it was just bad blood and it needed to come out. Women don't die of pain – it turns into children, remember I told you? Don't cry. It makes you look ugly, like this, see?' She rolls a scrap of pale pink cotton into a ball and opens her hand to show the crumpled result.

Roop wipes her cheeks immediately. 'I can't bear pain,' she gulps.

'You will have pain.'

'I won't. I'll marry a rich man, you'll see.'

'Achcha, you marry a rich man – now, go away and let me finish this.'

'What is his name?'

'Who?'

'Your about-to-be husband.'

'I don't know. Papaji knows, Revati Bhua knows. Why do I also need to know his name?'

'Did his papa choose his name from the Guru Granth Sahib?'

'I don't know.'

'You don't know *anything*.'

'So? Am I going to pickle his name, or what? Am I going to call him by his name, right to his face? Huh, I'm not so shameless.'

'I just want to hear if it sounds handsome or not,' Roop says, threading a needle with red silk for her sister. 'What will you call him if you can't say his name?'

'I'll say, "Ayji!" like Mama always said to Papaji. Now you go away, chui.'

And Madani pulls her chunni forward, like a shutter closing.

In the courtyard, Jeevan is training Ibrahim for the army. Grass reeds knot at the base of Ibrahim's salwar and a khaki bandage winds about his right ankle to assist him in knowing left from right. The two boys march to Jeevan's shout, 'Ghass . . . ghass . . . ghass, puttee, ghass!'

Papaji, standing in the veranda gallery outside his sitting room, watching with a hand shading his eyes from the sunset, says, 'What are you doing, Jeevan, why don't you march forward?'

'Left . . . left . . . left, right, left!' shouts Jeevan, switching to English. 'We're marking time, Papaji.'

'Marking time? Time cannot be marked, how are you marking time?'

'Papaji, we're just practising.'

'Why don't you move forward, Jeevan?'

'Marching in the same place, Papaji.'

'*Ooloo!* Enough left, right, left. Move forward! I say, what is the use of stepping like that in the same place, Jeevan? No Sikh soldier-saint marches at the same spot for so long, understand?'

Bachan Singh believes ridicule, generously applied, will toughen Jeevan into a man. Jeevan is quiet, though Roop can feel his need to say something.

But even if Papaji is wrong, Roop knows Jeevan can't shame him by arguing in front of Ibrahim.

'Forward march!' Jeevan shouts, instead.

Roop settles herself cross-legged on a manji, watching, but not watching.

She has to study Jeevan's wedding, then Madani's, very carefully. Roop's wedding will be bigger and much more expensive. She will have a palanquin made in London and perhaps her husband-to-be will come for her in a wedding procession with an English bagpipe and drum band, instead of an Indian shehnai and dhol-drum band. She'll tell Papaji to ask her husband to bring trumpets – she likes trumpets – they'll play 'Nikka Mota Bajra' just for her.

Sometimes, Roop thinks, Madani doesn't notice her any more. She's always up on the terrace, humming to Papaji's black partridges. Roop will be different when she gets married; she will ask Papaji if the orphans, Mandeep and Tandeep, can come to Pari Darvaza for her wedding.

Roop reaches up and grasps the iron handles of the new stand-up swing Papaji has installed in the doorway of the haveli for Jeevan, to prepare him for his army tests now that he's passed college. She tries to pull her legs up to waist level as Jeevan does, but Gujri comes out of the cookroom, slaps at her and says, 'Get down immediately! What will people say, boys' things happening in a girl's body? Enough, you're too old for this.'

Roop lowers her knees a little, 'Make me churi if I get down?' Gujri's fingers can crumble roti with brown sugar and butter to make churi with a touch that might have been Mama's.

But Gujri slaps at Roop again.

Hard enough that Roop's feet drop to the ground and her brown eyes fill in surprise.

'Roop! Boys' things happening in a girl's body. I tell you for-your-own-good – people will say you are too ziddi, understand?'

But Roop doesn't feel quarrelsome, just confused. She wriggles away from Gujri easily, bare feet slapping the dusty courtyard, and runs up the steep brick staircase to the terrace. Out of Gujri's reach.

It will be a double wedding; Jeevan first, because he is oldest and then, a week later, Madani will marry a Sikh from Sargodha. Madani's husband-to-be is from a family of horse-breeders, who turned colonists after his father was given a reward grant of canal colony land for service in the last British war.

Roop's turn is not yet, at least not before fourteen, maybe even fifteen, says Papaji, because of a new English law. Roop sits before Papaji's low desk in the sitting room and reminds Papaji that Mama came to his parents' home at twelve, but Papaji merely says, 'This is a new zamana,' and returns to his ledger.

New times.

'Marriage,' says Gujri, 'is expensive – a double wedding may be less, some ceremonies and all the gatherings being one time instead of two. But still expensive.'

Madani still does her hair in two plaits with light blue ribbons from her school uniform, though no one would object now if she wore a bun. She still sings her shabads while Roop tries to learn 'Suhe ve churre valia' to sing at the women's celebrations.

Jeevan buys four batteries from the new shop in Jhelum and strings electric lights through the tunnel where Madani's husband-to-be will ride in on his white horse and he and all the members of his family will meet Papaji, Jeevan and Shyam Chacha the night before the wedding. Gujri shakes her head, grumbling because the lights will ensure that the revelry of the milni ceremony will continue well past sundown and Madani's groom and his family plan to stay with them seven nights. 'A three-day stay is quite honourable, why do these people have to bankrupt their new daughter-in-law's family?' she demands.

Papaji shrugs and sighs.

My poor Papaji, we are such a terrible burden to him.

How can Madani be so calm with her wedding approaching? They have rupees in their pockets for once, rupees Papaji took from behind four bricks in the wall of his sitting room, rupees to buy wedding kameezes of red and turquoise silk, lehnga skirts and the ivory bangles Madani will wear for a year after marriage. Still she haggles over every penny. Revati Bhua assures her Papaji will never ask for an account, but Madani replies, 'If we spend too much we'll find the buggy unusable for a while until there is money to repair a wheel or we'll find him wearing a patched salwar.' Madani notices things like that.

Roop tells everyone who comes to the tunnel the details of Madani's wedding. The word spreads rapidly until Gujri tells her to stop – Papaji will have too many people to feed. Gujri chooses what the men in the wedding procession will be fed, saying, 'They should be fed well, but not so well that they think Madanji's dowry is too little.'

Roop amuses herself by ordering Khanma around until poor old Khanma doesn't know which command to obey first. She tells Khanma to quench the new lights Jeevan has just strung in the tunnel, then she and Madani creep behind Khanma, bursting into peals of laughter as Khanma blows her cheeks out like a shehnai player and flaps her chunni at the electric bulbs.

'In your new home, will you have 'lectric lights, Madani?' Roop asks when they can laugh no more.

'You'll have 'lectric lights in your home, Roop,' Madani says, putting her arm around Roop's waist. They lean against one another. Madani pulls away first. Nowadays, an invisible mirror seems to accompany her everywhere, she checks herself against it any chance she gets. 'Come, let's see the palanquin.'

In the tunnel, three carpenters are refurbishing the palanquin that brought Roop's mama, sanding the creaky box that will bring Jeevan's bride, Kusum, to Bachan Singh's home, reattaching its long, carved handles. Fearing blame from Bachan Singh or Jeevan, they cannot be persuaded to let the girls climb into the palanquin before the wedding, much less allow Roop to recline in it and play at being abducted by Afghans.

Madani will be carried in the palanquin for just a short distance, because Sargodha is so far away you need a train to get there.

'Who will carry you?' Roop asks. 'You're too heavy for just Jeevan and Papaji, and Shyam Chacha is so short – it'll look lopsided and you'll have to hold on inside to keep from slipping.'

Madani sounds annoyed. 'I'll be crying. I won't notice.'

'Why will you be crying?' Roop asks.

'Because I will be sad.'

'Are you sad now?'

'No, but I will be then.'

'Why?'

'Because I'll be leaving home forever, chui. You'll be crying too, when you leave. All brides are sad.' Unlike Jeevan, Madani only calls Roop 'mouse' when she doesn't want Roop to bother her.

'But you can come back . . . ?' She looks at Madani, but Madani's eyes are fixed on some distant horizon.

'No, I can't come back, not to live here, just to visit for a few days sometimes or when I have a child.'

'Why not?'

'*Ttt!* Because I'm to be *married.*'

Then Madani relents, puts her arms around Roop. 'Don't spoil your face by crying. You have to look very pretty in my wedding so we can find you a good match and then you'll leave Papaji's house, too, and go to your real family's home.'

'You don't want to come back?' Roop is still in tears, though she knows it makes her look ugly.

Madani puts on her explaining voice, 'When you go to your real home you'll get beautiful clothes and jewellery, you'll be like a little rani with a raja who'll be as handsome as Guru Gobind Singh, and you'll see, you'll have a much bigger wedding than mine.'

But she doesn't mean it. Roop can tell from her tone, even with only one ear.

* * *

The marigold and jasmine garlands Madani will exchange with her groom arrive in shallow reed baskets and it is Roop's duty to remind Khanma to water them occasionally so they will last till the ceremony. Madani will be married in the centre courtyard of Papaji's haveli, circling her father's prized new copy of the Guru Granth Sahib he bought at the Golden Temple bazaar in Amritsar. Then the musicians will sing their shabads and Sant Puran Singh will make them promise God to have many children. And then Papaji will tie a knot between Madani's chunni and her new husband's silk shawl and they will all eat Gujri's hot parshaad and Gujri's special makki rotis and spinach saag and lots of sweet savayan.

No wedding in Papaji's family can be complete without Sant Puran Singh, a fair-skinned old man who ties his large white turban with a Rawalpindi shamla-fan on the side as if permanently in celebration, and a very long safa trailing down his back. His pure white beard falls to a wisp at the kirpan belt round his waist and he walks with his hands clasped before him as if permanently in prayer. This is no ordinary man, but the very sant to whom Papaji's father had prayed for a son, one who had renounced the world at fourteen, overcome by remorse for having killed a doe. He had said, 'I cannot make a doe,' and he had vowed to be a sant and devote himself to God for ever after.

First he will marry Jeevan to shy, dimpled Kusum from Kusum's father's home in the next village, Chakwal.

Roop knows Kusum.

Kusum's father sometimes brought Kusum with him when he came to visit Papaji. And whenever he came, he'd tell Kusum in a meant-to-be-overheard voice that Papaji's home was her real home and that Roop and Madani were Kusum's real sisters. Which, when she was younger, made Roop believe Kusum had been born into a fairy family.

And Kusum's father would tell Papaji how good-good sweet-sweet Kusum was becoming every day, reminding Papaji that his Kusum was promised to Jeevan since before she was born, all because Kusum's mother and Mama were friends.

Kusum was always the one who could hopscotch the best of them all, never once losing her balance or hopping into the wrong square. She could sidestep every puddle in monsoons when Roop and even Madani came home with salwars muddied and wet. If she were blindfolded she would still be able to cook Jeevan's favourite chicken curry and egg bhurji.

Now Kusum has grown taller than Madani and even more bosomy. Dark hair wisps escape from her bun and her eyes glow whenever Jeevan is near; that's why her father told Papaji, 'Now is the right time.'

So Papaji, true to the name Bachan as always, will fulfil Mama's promise to take Kusum from her father's family even though Kusum's father can no longer give Kusum any dowry at all. Papaji says he doesn't need any dowry when a good-good sweet-sweet Lakshmi is coming to live in his home.

After Jeevan's wedding comes Madani's. Nights will resound with the gulp-gulp beat of wedding drums and the high-pitched voices of girls singing 'Suhe ve churre valia main kehni an' after the ivory bangle ceremony. And Madani won't take off her ivory bangles for a whole year, not even at night, or the evil eye might fall upon her husband. She will wear Mama's lehnga skirt on her wedding day, Mama's gold jhumkas in her ears, Nani's gold hoop-nathli fastened to her nose, its weight supported by a gold chain pinned high in the parting of her hair. Nani's gold panjebs will meet around her ankles. Madani says Roop can't have henna painted on her palms or feet till her own wedding, but the bangle seller comes to filigree hers with the brown paste. When it dries and cracks it leaves Madani's hands stained like soft orange flowers.

Roop hitches up her new pink silk salwar and kameez − not really new, but Mama's made down to her size for the occasion − and perches before Jeevan in the saddle. Over Revati Bhua's counsel and Gujri's dire predictions, Bachan Singh has indulged his younger daughter by allowing her to take the place a younger brother would have taken in Jeevan's wedding. Jeevan and Roop are more accustomed to riding Nirvair bareback up the rolling crags to the waterfall than at this slow high-stepping walk all the way to Chakwal for Jeevan's wedding.

The bay is so good-natured that, contrary to Bachan Singh's forebodings, her every step is well controlled, even in the press of the wedding procession and with the ruckus of wailing shehnai and drums right behind her.

Roop pats her at every step and watches every twitch of her curly ears to ensure her good behaviour. Nirvair isn't pure-bred Kathiawari or her ears would meet in the middle, so Papaji has bought her for less, but no one would ever know it from her fine head; she holds it high and proud as Alexander the Great's Bucephalus. Jeevan's white-brocade-clad arms tighten around Roop whenever the bay tosses her head, if it seems she might rear. A special shamla-fan rises above the crown of his red silk turban today, and he looks as if he could scoop Kusum up with one arm, throw her across the back of the bay and gallop home. His cheeks, his moustache and even his beard glisten with sweat behind marigold and rose garlands swinging from the peak of his turban.

'Nervous?' Roop teases.

'Quiet, *shudai!*' he hisses in return. 'Wait till your bride-groom comes dressed like this on his horse, then you can tease him.'

Papaji is on foot, somewhere in the procession of rose turbans leading the mare as she clops from the haveli through the tunnel and past the mosque where Abu Ibrahim does his Islamic duty by frowning at the musicians, though his own son Ibrahim shows his friendship with Papaji and Jeevan by dancing right along with them. They pass through the small Hindu area, not even large enough to be called a neighbourhood. As Jeevan rides through Pari Darvaza, the shriek of the shehnai brings people and more people out of their compounds – Muslims, Sikhs, Hindus, the caste and the casteless – to give Deputy Bachan Singh and Roop's handsome big brother their blessing, to join the wedding procession with their tongas and ekka-carts or just to take an open-throated swallow from an upheld pitcher of bhang.

Shyam Chacha wore his new white homespun Gandhi cap, stood at his doorstep, and watched the wedding procession leave Papaji's haveli. He too frowned like Abu Ibrahim and glowered lizard eyes. And didn't join in.

Jeevan shrugged. 'Pity Shyam Chacha. No reason to live but for money.'

No one will ever match Jeevan in generosity or in courage. And he is my protector, Madani's and mine – every year we will remind him with the gold thread of a rakhri tied around his wrist and every year he will renew his promise.

Roop settles back in Jeevan's embrace. The torches of the wedding procession bleach the indigo night.

Jeevan's wedding procession stays at Kusum's father's home in Chakwal for four days. On the fifth morning, when Roop has grown weary of the cheek-pinching of her elders and Kusum has thrown rice over her shoulders for next year's harvest, Papaji departs for home in the two-wheeled buggy; traders are bringing carpets from Kashmir today. Madani is consoling Kusum's mother in their courtyard when Roop announces to Gujri she will ride Nirvair home, taking a shortcut over the sandy scrub so Jeevan can walk before his new bride's palanquin.

'It isn't far,' Roop protests. She burns to do something her-self, without Madani or Gujri or Jeevan there to tell her how, show her why, predict her failure, assist with everything.

'Your Papaji will have the skin right off my back,' Gujri predicts, her eyes concentric circles of alarm. 'How will it look, an almost-woman riding alone all the way, five miles?'

'Then what's it to me?' Roop is heartless.

Gujri looks ready to weep.

'Tell Papaji it's my fault, I told you I'd take the horse myself.'

No answer.

'Achcha, I won't ride, I'll walk her home. Ja, na!' She orders Gujri in exasperation. And Gujri says, 'Achcha, go then, but be careful' and she stands watching Roop loop the reins over one arm and saunter away with the bay mare.

Roop knows the way well. She and Jeevan have ridden along the winding trail many times, but she notices things while walking that she'd never have noticed from atop the bay

– buffalo-dung droppings somehow missed by fuel-collecting women, and a few small whitewashed shrines, no higher than her knee.

Trees she cannot name embrace above her and hold in the muggy warmth. Mynahs cock their gold beaks and fly at her approach. The Kathiawari pulls at a bush, snorting gently and swishing her long black tail, till Roop coaxes her away. A brown partridge scuttles away in the undergrowth. Roop tightens her grip on the reins in case the mare should be alarmed by a vulture or a rabbit, but Nirvair ambles along, undisturbed. Roop talks to her as they walk, hums a shabad to keep her spirits up and remind all ten Gurus to watch over her.

A small tomb points towards Mecca just a little off the path, an incense stick burned to the quick before it. It's baby-size; the little brother who was to ride her hip might have had one like it if he'd taken birth as a Muslim.

Roop stops to say the first pauri of the Japji Sahib over it, careful not to let the mare's hooves come close to it. Then she checks the quilted base of her baggy salwar. It's a little muddy, but not too much; Khanma can wash it for her.

The afternoon sun slants through the trees and her wedding finery begins to itch. Soon she is sweating into her pink silk kameez; Gujri will be so annoyed.

The thin soles of her fine embroidered jutis with their turned-up toes have twice been pierced by thistles and Roop debates breaking her promise and mounting the bay, but she knows that would merit a slap. Besides, Jeevan is not with her to help her mount and she can see no boulder large enough to stand on.

There is a clearing ahead, she reminds herself, where women rest their pitchers of well water and where everyone stops to talk. She will ask one of them to soak a corner of her chunni in water to wipe her face – their water might pollute her if she drank from it – and from there perhaps she will be able to see Pari Darvaza and the tunnel haveli.

The women must already have gone home for the day, for the clearing is empty. Sand in the clearing is hot and soft under Roop's feet and the sun has found its way to shine directly above her. Her brass anklets and glass bangles begin to burn against her skin.

She calls out for anyone sleeping in the shade who might show him or herself, but no one answers.

She is alone.

She has never been alone before. Alone without her people.

It is a bereft feeling, a lost feeling.

It is a fear and an ache so deep it can only have come from the sorrows of her previous lives. It is a feeling of distance, such distance from anyone of her blood that none of them would hear her if she called, no one will help if she is hurt and no one would know if she died. This aloneness, this void is how Mama must feel, this distance is how far Mama is from Roop.

She tells Nirvair home is not far away, and that Papaji will be waiting for them, that Madani and Jeevan will have started home by now and could be worrying about her, but the aloneness persists as if she were mourning the loss of everything she has ever known. Her throat is tight with fear. Mama's sapphire ring is still on her index finger, but her hands are cold and clammy.

If she does not see people she has seen before, how is she to know that she is not dead and already in the next life? Nirvair stamps and snorts, but her presence is no comfort. She needs to see *people*, people of her blood. She needs to smell them, come close to them, touch them.

She stops and puts her arms around the horse's great strong neck. Nirvair's heart beats normally in her wide chest as Roop's races in fear. She takes deep breaths like a yogi and the horse nuzzles her. She turns her back on the empty clearing, looks back the way she's come.

A woman walks slowly into the clearing. A sob of thanks and a cry of recognition breaks from Roop, 'Gujri!'

On the cracked rinds of her too-small feet, Gujri has followed Roop, walking the painful five-mile trail from Kusum's parents' home in Chakwal, watching her, protecting her, doing her duty, staying a bend behind on the path, careful not to let Roop see her.

Gujri takes Roop in her arms. They lead the mare home together.

'I was all *alone*, Gujri.'

'Roop-bi, you're so ziddi that if you're not careful everyone will say: "Let her be alone."'

Roop promises she will be less wilful, more respectful, more grateful, more obedient – whatever it takes to be included in the realm of the living.

'If you're not careful, everyone will say: "Let her be alone."'

Gujri's words return to Roop as if Gujri had spoken into her ear, only Gujri is busy helping Madani's wedding guests roll up their bedding in preparation for Madani's departure to her new home in Sargodha three days' journey away. Madani sits in the middle of the courtyard of the home she is about to leave, looking all alone in all her red and gold finery, surrounded by her dowry: her new family, her real family, has requested it be displayed before they leave. The wedding guests move between rows of laden manjis, examining what the bride has brought for them. 'How many gold necklaces has the Deputy Bachan Singh, lambardar of Pari Darvaza, given for Madani's unmarried sisters-in-law?' come matronly whispers. 'How many salwar-kameez lengths for her new mother-in-law?' They make scornful faces and sigh jadedly as their fingers feel fabrics to know if they are silk or merely cotton.

The brass and copper pots and pans are so many it takes one manji just to hold their shine, though Revati Bhua says Madani will live with her new husband's parents and will never use them. Gujri predicts they'll be given away to the groom's sisters for their dowries.

The new relations barely glance at Madani's embroidery work; they probably think it was machine-made in Manchester.

The gold border of Madani's chunni falls past her mouth to her chin, veiling her face, but Roop can see from the set of her head she is proud of the display; there is nothing to apologize for.

But Bachan Singh is apologizing anyway, as though his life depended upon his humility.

He is bowing over his folded hands in a back corner of the

courtyard before Madani's new father-in-law, the Risaldar-Major, a tall burly man with a chestful of British war medals and a white too-small turban tied in rigid sweeps above a three-day frown. Roop goes to Papaji's side and places her soft hand in Papaji's cold unsteady one. He does not notice her as he continues his excuses. 'These past rains were very bad, was it not so in Sargodha? Ah, but of course you have canals to give water to your fields, there.'

Madani's father-in-law does not change expression, his brows draw closer and he gazes meaningfully at Madani's dowry spread about her. 'We did not expect to be insulted in this way,' he says. 'Is this all we can show our neighbours and relatives? Such a good Dipty's family, we told everyone. We said we are bringing back a Kohinoor for our son.'

The threat is in his voice; the little Kohinoor wrapped in all her finery sitting in the centre of her father's courtyard may find herself rejected, left behind.

Which is more terrible, being left behind or being left alone?

Roop cannot tell any difference between the two.

She shudders for Madani.

Papaji seems to shrink.

Then his hands rise, adjusting his turban more firmly on his head. 'Please wait here,' he tells Madani's father-in-law. And he goes into his sitting room in search of his most honoured guest, Sardar Kushal Singh, the sahukar.

Sardar Kushal Singh is a man who does not need to tell anyone his business. Everyone from 'Pindi to Pari Darvaza knows it the way a bullock knows the scent of the man who brings it fodder at dawn and whips it in the sultry afternoon. In Sardar Kushal Singh's wood cabinets lie the meticulous accounts of all Bachan Singh's doings, along with everyone else's. Loans taken for doctors, deaths and dowries, land pledged and redeemed. Sardar Kushal Singh knows every pai made in Pari Darvaza and can project its whereabouts within range of a cattle fair or two. In his head lie genealogies of Muslims, Hindus and Sikhs alike – predictors of his risk. In his trunks lie the gold mohur-coins, men's loi shawls, fine gold-bordered lehngas and the gold jewellery of those whose lineage failed them when it came to holding land. In his courtyard stand buffaloes exchanged by farmers in years the rains came too late, or came early, gave too much or gave too little. He takes the measure of a man in rupees and he knows a man's soft spots the way an archer knows to aim – cards, liquor, women-of-the-night.

Sardar Kushal Singh's name fits him better today than ever before – he is a comfortable man. When he married a woman in 'Pindi with a large land dowry, he justified his father-in-law's confidence, being no leech of a son-in-law, but a man who moves on every opportunity, changeable as circumstance. He has the good sense, though, to ward off jelsy – or jealousy, Jeevan would correct Roop – with a humbleness that insinuates him into every home in Pari Darvaza. He visits them, not everyone, to be sure, but certainly the more well-to-do if he is merely passing by, and says, 'Hanji,' 'Achchaji,' 'Ah-hoji,' or even 'Ji, huzoor,' to them as though he were their servant, and not the other way around. Thus he thwarts the attention of jelsy, the usual penalty paid by moneyed men. And so Sardar Kushal Singh has become an almost-member of many families in Pari Darvaza, including Abu Ibrahim's – who finds in his Koran a violent loathing of all men of usury – and Deputy Bachan Singh's.

This is the man Papaji brings to add his deep whisper to Papaji's and Madani's father-in-law. Roop is banished to Gujri's side while Madani's price is renegotiated.

Madani sits still through all of this, mouth closed so her new family won't notice her protruding teeth. Her new husband is nowhere in evidence.

Soon the three men emerge from the corner of the courtyard and Sardar Kushal Singh and Madani's father-in-law are smiling. Madani's father-in-law throws an arm around Papaji and boxes his arm playfully.

Sardar Kushal Singh rubs his hands gently and smooths his droopy moustache with the money-feeling fingers of his right hand. He says to Papaji he is so glad to have been of service. 'Jo hukum,' whatever you command me, he says, his eyes closed piously, warding away any lurking jelsy.

Madani's dowry has been increased.

Papaji says of Madani's father-in-law, in the tone of a man who speaks a fervent wish as if it were already realized, 'He is a most sincere man.'

Madani's honour is saved.

But will Papaji now have enough for Roop's dowry? If not, what will he do? She isn't deserving and good and careful like Madani. And she was born on Tuesday under the very-very strong influence of the Mangal star. And she has only one good ear. She doesn't know how to do embroidery like Madani or cook like Gujri, nor does she want to know how. Perhaps she doesn't deserve a dowry big enough to marry a man from a good family.

If there isn't enough left for Roop after Madani's dowry, she might have to stay unmarried. Then she'd be like Revati Bhua and have to just live with Papaji in Pari Darvaza and be religious all day long. That would be like being an orphan servant – do girls like Tandeep and Mandeep get invited to weddings like this one? No, they don't. See: Tandeep and Mandeep are far away in Firozepur right now.

Roop helps Gujri fold away the display of Madani's salwar-kameezes and saris and pack them in two wedding chests. She helps Madani lock them. Roop wishes she were older than Madani and had to be married first, but she helps her sister into the palanquin. Then she and her new sister-in-law, Kusum, stand at the now lockless carved timber door of the haveli, as Jeevan and Papaji shoulder Madani's palanquin. Roop can't tell if Madani is crying. Madani won't look back as she throws rice, that would be bad luck for anyone left behind. Then Papaji and Jeevan stop at the mouth of the tunnel and let the strange men of Madani's new family take Madani away from Roop.

Now Madani's kismat must take care of her.

Returning through the scalloped archway, Jeevan pulls Roop's plait a little to comfort her, but he is looking at Kusum's dimpled simpering round face and the tightness of Kusum's kameez across her breasts in a way that leaves Roop alone even though she is right here with them.

Jeevan is leaving soon, too, leaving to join the Indian Military Academy in Dehradun after the rains, in August. He has long forgotten when he was all knees and elbows, as Roop still is, and when his bones hurt from growing past Papaji, past the regulation six feet required to join the Sikh Regiment. He has long forgotten the day he said he just couldn't pass the

English examination. Now he explains rather than complains to Roop that though the British want more Indians in the Indian army, they want them all to speak English. Papaji doesn't know anyone who owes him a favour any more; he's borrowed money and favours from everyone he knows to get Jeevan first to the mission school in Murree, then to English-medium college, and now to the Indian Military Academy.

Jeevan has worked on everything it takes to get into the Indian Military Academy; Bachan Singh had to buy Jeevan many pairs of new shoes to improve his hockey and cricket at clubs in 'Pindi. Jeevan has given up riding ticketless on the train to Lahore so he and Ibrahim could sleep at the caravan serai, given up listening in chai stalls to the re-remembering of General Dyer's massacre at Jallianwala Bagh. He has given up betting on hockey matches and cricket, given up wrestling and kabaddi and the company of any friends who call themselves 'socialists,' and whom Bachan Singh calls 'very wrong sort of people.'

And he has given up wanting to teach history because Bachan Singh shouted, 'You want to teach history in a school? *Ooloo!* – what for do you need to learn history today? Is history a useful subject, tell me? English sikho!'

Learn English!

And now because Jeevan has become obedient, Bachan Singh has rewarded him with a new windup gramophone. And given the weaver-tailor, Fazl Karim, extra grain so he will make Jeevan a white dinner jacket for the Indian Military Academy.

Kusum smooths her chunni over her shoulder, blushes. The Indian Military Academy doesn't like its Indian officers-in-training to be married; Kusum will stay in Pari Darvaza. Papaji says there's 'no need' for Jeevan to tell the English officers at the IMA of his marriage; they can't understand, they'll think him married far too young.

Jeevan leads Kusum upstairs to his rooms on the second storey, leaving Roop at the threshold, the dark yawn of the tunnel opening before her.

Really alone.

7. Pari Darvaza, 1937

'Your mama wants you to be married,' says Revati Bhua.

Roop looks up from a Bhai Vir Singh novel about a good-good sweet-sweet Sikh woman abducted time and again by Muslim tyrants, a woman whose honour nevertheless always stayed intact because valiant Sikh men rode to her rescue. Bhai Vir Singh's heroine helped Sikh men fight the Afghan tyrants two hundred years ago, in the days when the Sikhs were driven into the jungles, when the Sikhs were starving but survived by their wits and their kirpans, never converting to Islam. And when the Sikh men didn't need her any more, Roop is reading, the Sikh woman returned to being good-good, sweet-sweet, and dying undaunted, gave a rousing martyr's speech upon ever-smiling lips.

Punjabi novels about the Sikhs are all Bachan Singh allows Roop to read; even newspapers are not for good-good Sikh girls these days. Fewer traders load their camels in the tunnel now, and the camels of those that do seem leaner. Those who come bring news of more hunger strikes and sit-ins, more protest marches and rallies. But Bachan Singh says Roop is too old now to sit by their hubbling, bubbling chillums and hear their stories, because of 'what people will say.'

Revati Bhua sits on the ground, sucking lips over clenched teeth, fingers skimming the blur of Jeevan's old bicycle wheel rim, reborn, with a little adjustment, as her spinning wheel. She is trying to follow Mahatma Gandhi instead of Lakshmi in the temple, but so far her following extends only to spinning.

There has been nothing to do every summer since Madani left four years ago but to sit with Revati Bhua or Kusum and wait for the crops to grow. While Papaji will not accuse his half-brother in public court before the English district magistrate, he allows no coming-going between the two havelis, so Roop could not cross the tunnel to visit Shyam Chacha or Chachi even if she wanted to.

Roop passed the tenth standard by applying herself at the end of the school year just before the examinations, filling her waking memory rapidly, emptying it to the page, then forgetting – why remember things she will never need to do what a woman is for? A too-smart woman can be left unmarried and remain without children for her old age.

Roop has forgotten the taste of eggs and chicken. She is no longer quarrelsome; she knows when to be quiet. She expects only the things she truly needs. She is no longer adventurous, having learned the fear of unrelated men from Gujri, Revati Bhua and Kusum. Though she has avoided learning how to cook, she is not the same Roop who laughed under the water- fall; she has learned at last to please Bachan Singh as Madani did, as Kusum does in turn, covering her head, being silent and obedient.

But though Roop has learned that to listen is to obey, Bachan Singh has made no move to arrange her marriage. There are no Sikhs in Pari Darvaza whose sons are equal to Deputy Bachan Singh in birth, and no offers have come for her from caste-Sikh families in villages around, beauty or no beauty.

Jeevan's two fat-cheeked baby boys are fast becoming a reproach. Roop plays with them every day, telling them the same things Kusum tells them: how handsome they are, how strong, how brave, how generous they will be to their mother when they are grown. She serves them the way Kusum does, peeling and unseeding grapes for their small mouths, her palm smacking the ground to chide the earth when it scrapes against their knees, defending them from Papaji's least frown.

But she does give them gladly to Khanma when it is time to clean their chi-chi pi-pi.

She wants her own boys.

As Kusum, nodding pityingly in Revati Bhua's direction, said once, 'A woman who has sons will never be alone in her old age.'

But first, a marriage has to be arranged by someone.

Kusum is too shy to arrange anything for Roop – she doesn't know *any*one but poor casteless Sikhs for whom she makes daal and roti in the village gurdwara's free kitchen each day. She moves slower and slower as her belly grows bigger, expecting her third child.

Papaji said, a few days ago, that Kusum is Lakshmi incarnate and Roop should follow everything she does, learn from her example. When Kusum brought Papaji his evening tumbler of tea and crouched by his manji to massage his tired legs, he said, 'Understand, Roop. A daughter leaves her father's home, goes to another family's home, but a daughter-in-law like Kusum has come to her real home, na? Can't you learn to make tea as sweet and 'Pindi cholas as fiery as Kusum's?'

Roop doesn't have any jelsy of Kusum, and there is nothing Kusum does that Roop wants to do – Kusum just waits for Jeevan's visits and letters and helps Gujri in the cookroom, weeping over onions, grinding chilies, or slowly stirring fiery dark brown 'Pindi cholas in the wide mouth of the pan rocking on the clay stove.

Bachan Singh's hand rested on his Kusum's head in blessing as he chided Roop, 'You want your in-laws to love you just like another daughter, no?'

She does, of course she does.

But Roop's in-laws will love Roop without cooking, for they will have servants. Roop is sure there is no need for her to learn cooking, no matter how patiently Kusum promises to teach her.

Roop's in-laws won't live in a little village like Pari Darvaza. Her husband will take her away and show her what Jeevan and the traders speak of – The Mall Road in Murree, a fisherman casting his delicate net in the Indus, the mountain paths of Hunza. Even the capital of all India – Delhi.

But when?

Huma's wedding was last year and she is long gone from Pari Darvaza, married into a family in Lahore. Bachan Singh allowed his Roop to attend only the girls' gatherings and the women's celebrations, where her sweet voice could not be heard by ineligible Muslim men. Revati Bhua went with Roop as chaperone, though Huma's home is not more than a short walk from the mouth of the tunnel. Like Madani, Huma said she didn't know her husband's name and this very moment Huma is calling her husband 'Ayji' or 'mia' or just 'Him.'

Bachan Singh says there is 'no need' for Roop to go as far as the post office, no more than a hundred yards from the tunnel haveli, and so she has not been even that far since her return from Bhai Takht Singh's school in Firozepur.

The last excitement Roop had was Pandit Dinanath's daughters' weddings and that was before the last rains and now even the pandit's daughters are gone.

Only Roop is left here.

Unmarried.

So when Revati Bhua says, 'Your mother wants you to be married,' Roop eagerly asks, 'How do you know?'

'She came last night in my dream.'

Mama appears only in Revati Bhua's dreams – and only when she wants something done. Roop has tried often to reach Mama with her own dreams and explain that she is trying to be good-good, sweet-sweet and obedient as Sita so everyone will love her just the way they loved Mama, but she doesn't really want to be like her mama and never see anything beyond Pari Darvaza. Mama's face was veiled so often before she became sick that Roop cannot remember her the way Revati Bhua does, unveiled and radiant, but can only remember dull eyes, almond-shaped, like her own.

She is becoming so much like Mama, though.

She absorbs Bachan Singh's fears, just as her mama did while confined in purdah, and ripens them to fullness. For Roop's heart has become a storeroom where Bachan Singh hoards the full measure of her giving. That young heart presses like a coiled steel spring against her breast. Heart that does not venture outside the haveli for fear of Bachan Singh's displeasure, heart afraid to glance at or speak to an unrelated man in the village unless he be a small boy or a white-bearded elder for fear of what-people-will-say. Heart that beats hard and fast as a tabla in her chest if her chunni falls but once, for a moment, to her shoulders, lest a man be smitten because Roop tempted him.

By now, Bachan Singh, Gujri, Revati and Kusum have done their duty well: Roop has learned shame.

Roop has come to dread what-people-will-say.

It is a dread Roop shares with other girls in Pari Darvaza – Sikh, Hindu or Muslim – fear of her own body, that lurer of lust from the eyes of unrelated men. But in Roop that dread runs much deeper than in many other girls, runs deep into bone, for Bachan Singh's love is a love stronger than any father's in the village. So his fear of other men looms larger.

The deeper Bachan Singh's dread, the tighter the lunge-rein that holds Roop to his haveli. And the tighter and shorter that lunge-rein grows, the tighter coils the spring of Roop's giving, pent up within her, waiting for a man to call husband.

And Mama wants her to get married!

Roop urges Revati Bhua, 'Tell. Tell, *na*!'

'I had milk after dinner because I was worried about you and it always gives me a pain in my stomach to worry. So I had the milk and slept, always thinking of you, never of myself, and I dreamed I was flying all the way to Kuntrila, so many kos from here I flew. In a mint-skint, in the blink of an eye. I looked down and there were only women in the fields – maybe the men were gone fighting somewhere. The air was full of their crooning and comforting as they tended the newly sown seeds, talked to them, admired them, persuaded them to stand tall and face the sun.'

Revati Bhua rubs cotton between her thumb and forefinger, drawing the thread longer and longer. She will give the thread to Khanma, who weaves dung-smelling cloth on the loom in her windowless hut for her husband, Fazl Karim, to sew kameezes.

'Then one of them stood up and called to me so I flew closer. It was your mama. She looked just as she was when she was first married. Then she was ten, eleven, who knows how old – but smooth-skinned, so full of hope. She held out her arms to me and we embraced. Hanji, I felt her young chest touch my breasts here and here.' Revati Bhua dabs at her formidable front.

'So her love for you flowed to me and she whispered in my ear – tell Roop it is time, tell my husband, it is time she was married.'

Roop sighs; Revati Bhua doesn't need to persuade her.

Hai! To be married and free of Papaji's endless restrictions and policing! It seems Kusum has been brought as Jeevan's wife just to be Roop's kotwal, or if not her gaoler, then at least her chaperone. Revati Bhua is no better – if Roop climbs to the terrace, Revati Bhua puffs her way up the narrow staircase behind her. Roop longs to ride Nirvair as she has each summer, the mare's still-willing old hooves throwing sand in the eyes of the sun, but Papaji has decreed Roop can no longer ride, even chaperoned by Jeevan, for fear she will have no blood on the sheets when she marries.

If Mama were alive, the matter would be settled by now. Mothers arrange such things, not men. They check antecedents, talk about tendencies in the lineage, ask the questions to which fathers want answers. Mama arranged Jeevan's marriage to Kusum long before dying, why could she not have done the same for Roop – right away, at birth? Now Mama had caused a problem for Papaji and for Roop, but mostly for Roop.

Roop puts her book away; reading is for defeated girls, girls who can't be married.

Revati Bhua says, 'Do some embroidery.' Her spinning bicycle wheel moves slowly at first, then faster and faster.

I must trust Papaji and not lose hope.

Perhaps she will try something ambitious: a crewel-pattern against white cushion covers.

'How do you do?' she whispers to herself. She takes up her needle and threads it with blue wool, then green. 'Delighted to meet you.'

Sardar Kushal Singh comes to visit Papaji in the afternoon, a few days later, when he knows the heat will have driven everyone indoors. In the time it takes him to plod up the road from the post office, emerald-green turban bobbing above a starched white kurta, hands clasped behind his back, a young goatherd has run to Bachan Singh bringing word he can expect an important guest. Sardar Kushal Singh walks the labyrinth of the village's high-walled narrow lanes with a sure and practised step.

He nods to Abu Ibrahim, who sits upon the steps to the gate of the mosque reading aloud from the Urdu newspaper to the postman, the tanner, the nightwatchman, the water-carrier and the butcher. Stopping for a moment only, Sardar Kushal Singh folds his hands, saying, 'Ram, Ram' to Pandit Dinanath, cross-legged behind his open wooden lockbox in the temple, counting donations. Walking through the bazaar, he eyes the jalebis in the sweetmaker's small case of wood and glass; black flies pick their way across their sweet orange surface. He takes just enough time at the small gurdwara for a quick touch of his humble head before the marigold-garlanded Guru Granth Sahib. And only then does he come to the door of Bachan Singh's side of the tunnel haveli and ask, in his extremely polite voice, if he may be admitted.

Revati Bhua and Roop sit on each end of Mama's old manji and take turns fanning themselves with a twirling hand-pukkhi as Papaji ushers Sardar Kushal Singh into his sitting room. Hands still clasped behind him, Sardar Kushal Singh picks his way across the white sheet spread to cover the holes scuffed in Papaji's dhurrie, like a large white rooster. Kusum has taken a trader's camel and her sons to bathe at the waterfall; the haveli is strangely quiet without the usual shouts of Jeevan's boys.

Grateful for the unexpected excitement, Roop listens through the thick henna curtains hanging in the doorway between the two rooms.

When Papaji says it is not his home but belongs to his guest, it is now true, because the soft voice is the owner of many slips of paper with Deputy Bachan Singh's name signed at the corner.

The divan creaks as Sardar Kushal Singh eases himself down low upon it, and Papaji shouts to Gujri for tea, 'Gujri! Chai!'

Gujri serves copper tumblers of chai almost before the words have left his mouth, her head covered before the sahukar, eyes following Sardar Kushal Singh warily. She returns to the cook-room and in a moment comes the sound of her stone chakki, grinding flour, a familiar sound that usually comes in Roop's ear in the mornings.

Sardar Kushal Singh asks after Papaji's health, asks how Jeevan is progressing at the Indian Military Academy, asks if all is well in Sargodha among Madani's family.

Bachan Singh knows the sahukar wants something he has in his power to give; the marigold tucked in the crown of Sardar Kushal Singh's turban tells him the moneylender stopped at the village gurdwara first. And the shamla-fan rising from his turban says the sahukar is celebrating something. But Bachan Singh owes Sardar Kushal Singh too much already to want the sahukar even to remember his name, let alone come to his home.

'All is well,' says Papaji, raising his voice over Gujri's chakki. 'Her father-in-law sent a telegram to say another son has happened.'

'And still they are happy with her dowry?'

'Ji, huzoor – yes, yes. Thanks to your generosity.'

'Very good, very good.' Sardar Kushal Singh does not bother to correct Bachan Singh, but of course he is charging him his full thirty-seven per cent interest on this act of generosity.

Through the centre chink in the henna curtains, Roop sees Sardar Kushal Singh stroke his beard. He looks at Papaji now, as if just remembering.

'You have another daughter,' he says.

Roop and Revati Bhua clutch each other in excitement. This is an auspicious day! Sardar Kushal Singh has three sons. It could be the eldest, but he has a wife. No, not even the middle one, he too is married. Perhaps it is the youngest? Yes, maybe the youngest.

Revati Bhua almost crushes Roop, leaning close and informing her ear in a slurping whisper – 'The oldest will inherit his father's business, the middle one is now in the Gourmint Service, he was so very bright. The youngest must be in the miltry. Yes, must be the miltry, Pandit Dinanath's wife will know.'

'Ji, huzoor,' says Papaji. Roop wishes he wouldn't be so deferential to Sardar Kushal Singh.

There is a pause. 'She is beautiful,' Sardar Kushal Singh says. 'I remember people in your older daughter's wedding procession saying they should have asked for the younger one.'

'She was too young, then,' Papaji says, 'not even twelve.'

'It is this new zamana,' says Sardar Kushal Singh, shaking his head.

'Ji, huzoor.'

The two share a moment of silent sorrow for the passing of the old zamana, the old times. The law, only a generation old, says that any man who marries or marries off a too-young girl – and now a 'too-young girl' might be as old as fourteen – can be put in prison. Both Bachan Singh and Sardar Kushal Singh are quite sure that the law is foreign-inspired; they feel that it gives the interfering British just one more flimsy pretext to clap an Indian in prison for up to a month for the crime of 'child-marriage,' which most Punjabi fathers would call just doing their duty, providing a girl the protection of two families, instead of just one. This new zamana, their moment of sorrow observes, is why Roop is still sitting at home doing crewel embroidery.

Sardar Kushal Singh cannot say what he thinks of this law, because he, like most moneylenders, depends on British laws for his living.

Instead he strokes his beard and says, 'Good, good.'

After a pause, 'She can read and write?'

'She has passed class ten, so not too much.'

'Some education is good, and if her husband likes more, he can teach her.'

Papaji says, 'That is always true.'

'Now, bhai, we have known each other many years—'

Papaji nods.

'We are people who think the same-same way, so you must know what I am thinking.'

Again Papaji says, 'Ji, huzoor.'

'I have come myself – I could have sent the village barber like everyone else does, I could have asked the granthi at the gurdwara to ask you so that I did not have to trouble myself, but no, I have come myself to ask: I would like a rishta, a marriage relationship, with your family.'

Papaji's voice lifts and sings like song spooling from Jeevan's windup gramophone, in his eagerness to discharge his duty.

Any son of Sardar Kushal Singh is a man of prospects.

'Ji, huzoor!'

'Then it's agreed?' Sardar Kushal Singh insists. He is watching Papaji's face carefully.

Gujri's stone chakki slows, then starts its rhythmic grinding again.

'But of course. Everything I have is yours. There is no need even to ask.' Bachan Singh is so eager, he cannot believe his Roop's good kismat. A relationship by marriage with Sardar Kushal Singh's family! A family of moneylending sahukars, landowning jagirdars – Sikhs blessed with land grants going all the way back to before the British, to Maharaj Ranjit Singh's time.

The stone chakki slows again. Gujri takes to a louder pounding in the mortar; the scent of garlic laces the heat.

'I have your word? Your bachan?' Sardar Kushal Singh's moustache is stained with tea, he seems anxious to leave now.

'Bilkul. No question,' says Papaji emphatically. 'My very name is Bachan.'

Sardar Kushal Singh rises.

'Huzoor?' says Papaji, as his guest is almost to the door of the sitting room. Sardar Kushal Singh turns. 'Which of your sons is this rishta for?'

Sardar Kushal Singh smiles. 'No, Bachan Singhji. Not for one of my sons.' He is laughing, and Roop can see his eyes now that she is standing on tiptoe at the chink in the curtain. They seem wide, sincere.

'Then . . . ?' Papaji's eyebrows meet above his nose immediately.

Sardar Kushal Singh comes to embrace Papaji, holds Papaji's shoulders so hard his knuckles pale. 'No, no, this rishta is for my brother-in-law. You know – Sardarji, the jagirdar himself. Vaheguru's blessings are with you; your family has never seen such good fortune.'

Gujri begins grinding again. Round, and again round.

Papaji is quiet. His brown turban slumps forward a little.

Roop's heart is beating hard against her ribs. Why is Papaji so silent? Why does he not exult as Roop is ready to do?

'I think – ' says Papaji. 'I think he is older, quite a bit older, no?'

'Just a little more than forty years old. Healthy, like a tiger. An engineer. But you know this.' Sardar Kushal Singh sounds impatient.

'And it is true he has one wife?' says Papaji. His brown turban sinks lower.

Is that so bad? Roop wonders. *Papaji's father had four wives. That's how Shyam Chacha and he are half-brothers.*

'Only one,' says Sardar Kushal Singh, comfortingly. 'And childless.'

Hai, poor woman, what kismat!

Why doesn't Papaji embrace Sardar Kushal Singh in return? The henna curtain trembles with Roop's eagerness. She wants to tear it apart, say yes herself, as if it were she who had been asked.

Tear it apart just to open the world a little wider.

Just in case Sardar Kushal Singh takes Papaji's silence for refusal. Just in case, so she won't be left unmarried.

Gujri gives the chakki a long groaning grind and stops.

Papaji raises his turban a little, and his eyes dart left, right, as if the walls of his sitting room have become unfamiliar. 'My father had four wives; always they were fighting. Even now, my half-brother and I . . .'

His voice trails away.

Deputy Bachan Singh has hoped for many things for his Roop, not all of which are possible. He has indulged her all this time in case her kismat brings her a husband who will not be kind. He has sent her to school against all advice, in keeping with the Guru's teachings on women's equality. He has kept her bad ear a secret, he has been quiet about her being born under the influence of Mangal. Now he must weigh the honour she brings him from this rishta, this marriage relationship, against the price of refusal.

Sardar Kushal Singh says reassuringly, pointedly, 'Sardarji is also a modern man; he does not require any dowry.' And then he lets a meaningful silence lengthen, widen, deepen and remind. No words are required.

Gujri returns to pounding.

Eventually Papaji says, 'I gave you my word.'

'Yes, indeed,' says Sardar Kushal Singh. 'Yes, you did.'

Roop can no longer see or hear them through the henna curtain; Papaji and Sardar Kushal Singh have left the sitting room. She watches from the wide doorway of the front room till a green turban and a brown turban pass beneath the scalloped archway and into the tunnel. She thinks the brown turban is nodding. Then she turns back to Revati Bhua who sits glum and expressionless until she can see Papaji and know from his face what she is expected to think.

When Papaji returns at last, Roop is waiting in the court-yard, hands smoothing her kameez, excitement dancing in her eyes.

Oh, to be married, to be married!

To have a family ask for her before she turns seventeen and people in the village start their chattering. And to Sardar Kushal Singh's brother-in-law! Sardarji, a jagirdar, lord of any number of villages the size of Pari Darvaza. She is saved, saved from living the rest of her days in Pari Darvaza like her mama, saved from being a guest like Revati Bhua in Papaji's home forever.

Papaji returns and shouts at Gujri because it is convenient to shout at her; Gujri stops her pounding at last. Revati Bhua has nodded off, trusting someone will let her know, eventually, whether this is an occasion for mourning or celebration.

Papaji sits cross-legged in his sitting room behind his desk, with Roop before him. He puts on his explaining voice and describes Sardar Kushal Singh's visit to her, as if he didn't know she and Revati Bhua were behind the henna curtain all along. Because the telling helps him remember the things he cannot escape: first his dharam, his duty, to arrange a marriage for Roop. Second, his bachan, his promise to Sardar Kushal Singh.

Since Bachan Singh cannot refuse by going back on his word, there are only two possibilities.

'I can tell him that the horoscopes do not match, or I can say the girl has said no.' He looks at Roop, turning his head like a horse to see her truly, instead of the way he has always seen her before this day, no different from the way most Punjabi men have always seen their women, from the corner of his eye. And it is only when he turns his head this way that he sees her for the first time as she is, not just a good-good sweet-sweet obedient daughter, but as Roop: ambitious, slightly vain, lazily intelligent. Disturbed, he turns his head again, and she returns to the way he remembers her always: a pretty little girl with one long plait in a parrot-green salwar-kameez who balanced on the narrow divide between two reflecting pools, setting one foot before the other, like the tightrope walker at the cattle fair.

Now Roop says, 'Will I have servants?'

'Yes, beti, many servants. At least fifty servants in his home in 'Pindi. But . . .'

Roop interrupts, 'Nice clothes?' She is half listening, as usual. She likes clothes.

'Yes, nice clothes. But . . .'

Revati Bhua chides, 'Yes, tell her, she does not understand. Explain to her . . .'

'Beta, he has one wife already.' He calls her *beta* – my son – to show her she is no less precious than a son to him, this is how much he esteems her. Then, 'Of course, she is childless.'

Naturally, a man who has a childless wife will look for another.

Roop, long legs folded beneath her like a fresh-dropped filly, leans an elbow on Papaji's low desk. 'Then what is one more woman in a house where there are fifty people? And no other families have asked for me.' She drums slender fingers on the well-scratched shisham. 'Papaji, you can tell Sardar Kushal Singh I say yes.'

Papaji exchanges a glance with Revati Bhua. He takes a partridge-feather quill in hand, sharpens it.

Hesitates.

Roop makes a writing motion to encourage the quill. Bachan Singh dips it in the inkwell sunk into his desk and begins writing a chit to Sardar Kushal Singh, asking for Sardarji's horoscope. At the end of the letter he adds a request for Sardarji's photograph, saying, 'It will help the girl decide.'

'He is', says Jyotshi Sundar Chand, summoned from his customary spot before the Lakshmi temple to squat on his flat broad feet in Papaji's sitting room, 'born on the cusp of Vayu and the sign of the Bull. You can see here,' he pokes his finger at the astrological chart he unrolls and holds between two yellow-nailed big toes, 'and here, and maybe a little here; now at this moment he has a lot of mangli inside, he is under the influence of Mangal. Let me see . . . yes. He was born on Tuesday, see? Here. A very strong planet, Mangal is, you know, especially if he was born on Tuesday.

'Now, you take the little Lakshmi's chart and compare . . .' He unrolls Roop's chart. Sixteen years old, it is unlined. He holds it under Bachan Singh's nose, underscoring Bachan Singh's inability to understand it. Five generations or more in Bachan Singh's family have been unable to understand astrological charts prepared by five generations or more of Jyotshi Sundar Chand's, but that is immaterial; Bachan Singh wouldn't hurt the astrologer's feelings by not consulting him.

Roop, the 'little Lakshmi,' whom he is speaking of as if she were already miles away in Rawalpindi, sits with Kusum beside Papaji. She strains over his desk to see her future husband's astrological chart. The photograph she was shown was useless in forming a picture of him in her mind, just a black smudge in the centre of a grey square – probably the location of his beard. Staring at his chart might bring her a better image, but it is so old and crumbling.

Kusum's tug on the sleeve of her kameez pulls Roop back.

'See, hers is smooth, nothing straying into areas it shouldn't be seen in, nothing out of place, a little mischief here and there, but that is like a playfulness that can be restrained under good influences, good guidance. She, too, is born under the influence of Mangal.

'Bachan Singhji, take this rishta, take this relationship right now. If you wait longer you will not find it easy to find the little Lakshmi a good match. A Manglik girl. Bad luck for her husband, you know. A non-Manglik man could come to an early death. But these,' his shaven head wobbles left, then right, with such certainty that Papaji's beard also begins to sway, 'these are compatible charts. He is born on Tuesday, she is born on Tuesday. Her Mangal influence will be good for his Mangal; she will be fruitful where the other has failed.'

Roop pinches Kusum's arm in sudden understanding. Jyotshi Sundar Chand has the key, how is it he has never told Papaji this before? The influence of the Mangal star on Roop can be vanquished by finding a husband with strong Mangal influence in *his* stars.

Bachan Singh reaches into the kurta pocket that rides over his heart and places a whole silver rupee in the jyotshi's palm. 'May you be blessed if you are right, Jyotshiji.'

So Roop will be good for this man, fruitful, compatible. Of course, Deputy Bachan Singh does not think to ask: will this man or his Mangal be good for Roop?

Jyotshi Sundar Chand has just said, 'Ram, Ram!' and passed into the tunnel when the postman ambles in with a letter addressed to Deputy Bachan Singh.

The news has already travelled three days' journey away to Sargodha, as if Vayu had blown it clear across Punjab.

Papaji, Revati Bhua, Kusum, Gujri and Roop have told no one, 'not even your partridges,' says Revati Bhua, fearfully. Yet the letter is from Madani, a letter with congratulations: she and her husband will come for Roop's wedding. And she says she expects another child.

'Sardar Kushal Singh told me to hurry the wedding preparations as Sardarji must go to Khanewal and take up the posting the government has given him there.' Papaji strokes his beard. 'But even so I think Sardarji's family is too anxious, too hasty.'

Maybe anxious, maybe smart.

It no longer matters whether Jyotshi Sundar Chand found

their charts compatible. Roop's name has been spoken in the same breath with Sardarji's.

Deputy Bachan Singh's izzat, his family honour, decrees there is no going back now.

Roop waits. Days. And nights.

She waits for Papaji to give Kusum or Revati Bhua money to buy Roop new salwar-kameezes in the market at Jhelum, but no money comes. She waits for Gujri and Revati Bhua and Kusum or even Khanma to spread the word in the village – Come to our Roop's wedding! – but the women are silent, as if nothing were going to happen. She waits for Papaji to take rupees from the loose bricks in his sitting-room wall, send a labourer to call the goldsmith, order new jewellery, but the goldsmith does not come. She waits for Papaji to send a labourer to call the sweetmaker, and to order sweet jalebis to be served to Roop's bridegroom's wedding procession, but the sweetmaker does not come.

Roop stops waiting.

She will be married. But there will be no band, no wailing shehnai. No trumpets. And none of her friends from Bhai Takht Singh's Sikh Girls' School will be invited to sing 'Suhe ve churre valia main kehni an' at a girls-only sangeet night. She will wear Mama's hand ornaments and Mama's ruby tikka on her forehead and the spiralled gold chain that came in Mama's dowry – these are all that remain after Madani's dowry, the rest melted in the goldsmith's forge in the past few years.

Jeevan, now a first lieutenant ICO – Indian Commissioned Officer – in the British Indian Army, stops at Pari Darvaza on his way to Jamrud Fort on the frontier between British India and the tribal areas. So handsome in his khaki turban, two crowns on his shoulder, he goes to his next posting. 'Alpha Company of the Two-eight Punjabis.' His teasing stirs the mid-morning air, bringing the scent of the Himalayan foothills and an energy Roop had almost forgotten to the still-ness that besets the courtyard.

When Papaji leaves for Sohawa with a camel-load of

timber, Kusum, Revati Bhua, Jeevan and Roop take their places cross-legged upon a cloth spread upon a reed mat in the centre of the courtyard. Gujri brings them daal and chili-hot brown Rawalpindi cholas.

'You know I wanted to come to your pipping ceremony, Virji.' For a moment Roop's palm cups the roughness of the hairnetted beard rolled and tied beneath her brother's chin. 'But Papaji said there were too many boys; he said you never know who might misbehave.'

'He was worried about what-people-might-say,' Kusum hastens to explain. She rests her copper thali on her protruding stomach. 'And Revati Bhua couldn't go because Roop and I couldn't be left all alone here.'

Jeevan's commanding officer still has no idea of Kusum's existence, of Jeevan's married state. Bachan Singh says Jeevan can tell him after this visit, say he got married in two days to save money.

'Huh, all that way you can't go when a baby is happening,' says Revati Bhua.

'I'll be allotted a bungalow in the cantonment soon,' says Jeevan, comfortingly. 'With servants and all. So I'll take you away soon.'

'And leave Papaji alone?' Kusum's face clouds.

'He won't be alone,' Jeevan says. 'Revati Bhua is here, Gujri is here to cook for him. There are dozens of people coming and going. . .'

'No, no. I mean – Papaji will not leave here, and so how can I leave him alone and just go with you to the army bungalow? You can ask him if he will leave Pari Darvaza and come with us, but I think he will say no.'

'I'll ask him,' Jeevan promises.

'And if he will not go, I think I should stay here a little longer. No reason to separate the children from him yet, na?'

'All right, all right!' Jeevan takes a large wedge of roti and fills it with daal.

'Tell about your pipping ceremony, Jeevan,' says Roop, deflecting any hint of tension.

'Papaji was so disappointed I wasn't assigned to the Sikh Regiment,' Jeevan recounts. 'Do you know, I wrote five letters to persuade him to come to Dehradun for the ceremony.'

Of course Bachan Singh has not mentioned five letters of persuasion to Roop or Kusum.

'How did you persuade him?' asks Roop, smiling.

'Last time I came home for leave I said, "You should be happy I'm in the Punjab Regiment, Papaji," and I told him, "We're all Punjabis – Sikhs, Hindus, Muslims – there's no difference, Papaji."'

'Then what did he say?'

'*Huh!* "No difference!"' Jeevan imitates Bachan Singh imitating Jeevan. '"There are big differences. The Guru said, 'Na hum Hindu, na Musalmaan' – what did he mean? He meant we are not Hindus, we are not Muslims."'

'And what did you say?' Roop is enjoying his performance.

'I said, "Yes, Papaji, but we're all Punjabis, aren't we?"' says Jeevan. 'And I said, "*You* are the one who always says that no one should manufacture differences where there are none."'

Laughter sprinkles like salt upon everyone's daal and roti.

'I said, "What should I have done, Papaji, should I have *refused* to be in the Punjab Regiment?"'

'*Haw!* Right to his face you said that?' Roop admires his audacity. 'What did he say then?'

'He said, "Did I say that? Of course I didn't say that!"' And Jeevan begins describing his pipping ceremony.

Vayu could tell it better, though, tell that within Jeevan's description of the splendid pageantry of his midnight pipping ceremony hides the scene that Vayu saw, when, thus coaxed, Bachan Singh took a tiffin carrier filled by Gujri, and a bedding roll, changed three trains and rode third class for two days all the way to the Indian Military Academy at Dehradun. And there he wandered Dehradun's bazaars – very careful to ask the names of streets where an Indian man such as himself, dressed in kurta-salwar, might not be permitted by English law. A little before midnight, the shamla-fan of a starched white turban lifting his head high, Bachan Singh showed his pass and braved the sentries at the gates of the Indian Military Academy to take his seat in a straight-backed chair in the enclosure bearing the sign Family Members of Indian Gentlemen Cadets. He sat, hunched, hands clasped between his knees, beside high-up, qualified Indians, sat and listened to bagpipes play 'Auld Lang Syne' for Jeevan, listened to all the English speeches as if he understood every word, instead of one in fifty. And after the ceremony, he returned to Pari Darvaza, duty done, legs crossing gratefully into lotus position again, behind his own desk in his own sitting room.

Jeevan is promising Roop, 'Don't worry, chui, I'll be here for your wedding.' He uses her nickname and Roop feels her spirits lift. 'I'll challenge that new husband of yours to a wrestling match before he takes you away.'

After the meal, Gujri pours water from an earthen jar for Revati Bhua, Jeevan, then Kusum and Roop to rinse their hands over a rain drain in the corner of the courtyard. Not a drop will be wasted; the water will flow down the centre drain in the tunnel to nourish the fields.

Then Jeevan escorts Roop to old Fazl Karim's shop in the bazaar just past the tunnel, and looks on protectively.

One wedding lehnga, that's all Roop can order. The grey-haired, stubble-faced weaver-tailor stands before Roop and holds his ragged tape measure up between. He estimates the angle he should use to stitch darts in her kameez, then the length of her arms, the cinch to her waist, the spread of her hips, respectful and careful never to touch her. If he were Hindu, like Jyotshi Sundar Chand, anyone might think he was measuring her astral body.

Roop and Jeevan walk back to the tunnel, Jeevan dropping a coin in the lap of the blind man at the corner. The blind man shakes his matted head in thanks, returns to looking within.

The fairy doorway in Pari Darvaza is wide open, with fairies smiling.

Jeevan leaves that evening, equipped with enough rupees from behind the loose bricks in Papaji's sitting room to buy a polo pony for himself, in Rawalpindi. Ibrahim goes with him to be his bearer and stand behind his chair at the officers' mess, and so Abu Ibrahim gives each young man a parting gift: an amulet to keep away the djinns. Jeevan ties his upon his clean wrist, where it joins its power to the cool strength of his kara's steel, and the sister-love glinting in the gold thread of the last rakhris Roop and Madani tied there. He takes a long time saying his farewells to Kusum, then he's off to Jamrud Fort on the Northwest Frontier.

And Papaji's tunnel haveli is woman-quiet again.

The sameness of each hour has fallen about Roop again a few days later. She is so tired of sewing and embroidering and refusing Gujri's every offer to teach her cooking.

'Sardar Kushal Singh has sent word, yesterday,' says Papaji. It is early morning and he has just woken the Guru Granth Sahib, said his morning prayers and dressed the book in fresh red silk cloths. 'The boy's side will meet us at Punja Sahib Gurdwara.'

A sudden shock races through Roop. She will not be married from her father's home, but miles away at Punja Sahib Gurdwara? And Papaji looks relieved?

Bachan Singh can no longer afford to host a whole wedding procession for even one night. Punja Sahib Gurdwara – the place where Guru Nanak left his handprint in stone – will be a compromise.

Guru Nanak, on his wanderings in search of understanding, stopped at the base of a hill near the town of Hasan Abdal, close to Taxila. There he sent his Muslim disciple to the top of the hill to ask the pir, Wali Kandhari, for some water. Furious at being disturbed, the Muslim pir hurled a great rock down the slope at Guru Nanak. Guru Nanak held up his hand, and his punja, his palm, stayed the rock, and a spring burst from its base. The gurdwara built around the Guru's handprint in the rock is beautiful, famous, almost as holy as the Golden Temple in Amritsar, but . . .

This won't be like Madani's wedding at all. There will be parshaad, but there won't be any spinach saag, or makki rotis. And no sweet milk-boiled savayan noodles.

Just donated daal and wheat rotis, cooked by volunteers in the Guru's cookroom.

Roop takes the news across the courtyard to Revati Bhua, plump spider spinning cotton from her bicycle wheel.

'Punja Sahib is close to Jamrud Fort.' Revati Bhua offers

comfort in geography; Jeevan will find it easy to attend.

But it is a marriage of a poor man's daughter. Papaji has certainly fallen far.

'Will there be marigolds?' she asks Revati Bhua.

'Yes, beti, there will be marigolds.'

There will be marigolds. But no friends.

'No,' says Papaji, as he leaves for the fields. 'There is no need for Mandeep or Tandeep to come.'

Kusum will be in Chakwal at her parents' home, recovering from another baby by then, and she will not be able to come home in time for Roop's wedding.

Lajo Bhua cannot come all the way from Firozepur and leave her husband without a woman to cook for him, but she sends a wedding chunni with a cousin-brother passing within a village or two of Pari Darvaza. It is a chunni of scarlet georgette encrusted with her delicate gold salma-sitara embroidery. With this, Papaji's gloom seems to lift just a little; he will not need to buy one from Rawalpindi or Jhelum.

Now Fazl Karim comes to deliver Roop's lehnga, and it must be perfect at the first fitting – there is no time for alterations – and so the old fellow has peered through his thick spectacles day and night to sew Roop's lehnga within the mere two weeks allowed by the date Sardarji set for the wedding. Roop tries on her new red-and-gold silk kameez and twirls, the full skirt of the lehnga billowing beneath her. And over it, she wears the scarlet chunni embroidered by Lajo Bhua.

Fazl Karim beams.

Papaji says, 'Vah!' to compliment the tailor.

But later, when Roop wanders into the stable to bid Nirvair goodbye, she finds her gone. All that remains is the smell of manure and saddle leather. Fresh hoofprints lead past Roop on the dirt floor. Roop runs from the stable, runs back into the tunnel, back to the courtyard.

'*Hai!* Gujri!'

At Roop's stricken cry, Gujri comes to the door of her rasoi, brown fingers coated green with the bitter juice of the karela plants she is slicing for the evening meal.

'Your Papaji has sold her to a tonga man in Gujarkhan,' Gujri informs Roop, as if these things happen every day, every day.

Not Nirvair, not a tonga horse!

Roop screams and cries as if Mama had gone from her again.

Roop can see the arms of the tonga descending. She is glad only one ear can hear the weight of the leather traces descending to buckle Nirvair into the stiff open embrace. She is glad her bad ear cannot hear the surprised nicker low in Nirvair's throat as the harness tightens and an unbending bit is thrust between her teeth. She can see the chafing begin as the beautiful black-brown fur rubs away to the skin, oozes pink pus. Roop's eyes fill for the almost-pure Kathiawari bay who held her head so high and pranced in Jeevan's wedding procession.

How could Papaji have sold her?

Gujri takes to making peththas as if readying herself to feed the entire 8th Punjabi Regiment.

Revati Bhua listens and then scolds, '*Hut!* What is the use of tears?'

She waddles over to her battered old tachey case and takes her silver-belled anklets from it, the same she might have worn for her wedding, if she had had one.

'*Chup!* Stop crying right now – you wear these for your wedding.'

Touched, Roop gives Revati Bhua a weak smile and tries to wear it through the day. She will teeter on the edge of desperation from now until she leaves the tunnel home. Papaji's rupees have dwindled more than she had ever imagined.

Who knows, if Sardarji is as rich as they say, maybe he can help Papaji – but no, Papaji will never take anything from a married daughter's family.

A sticky-soft ball presses into Roop's hand.

'Have a peththa,' says Gujri, as if Roop were seven years old again, and sweet tastes could still cure all pain.

'Don't say anything – don't reproach your Papaji. He is sad for Nirvair too. Her kismat must protect her, now. What to tell you?'

8. Hasan Abdal, October, 1937

Roop's marriage party arrives at Punja Sahib Gurdwara just as twilight brings the barefoot worshippers to their feet to recite the daily Ardaas in remembrance of all the Gurus and martyrs from Mughal times.

Sooty, dusty from the long tonga ride to Hasan Abdal village from the two-room rail-stop, Roop, following Revati Bhua, Gujri, Madani and her husband and Jeevan in turn, gives her sandals to a volunteer at the gurdwara gate-house. The others go ahead, but Roop waits as Papaji arranges with a granthi to rent two adjoining rooms in the pilgrims' quarters. Then she follows him to join the queue of the faithful.

Roop descends three white marble steps till the water gushing from the base of the holy stone mutes the tinkle of Revati Bhua's silver anklets. She leans into the scalloped arch and places her small slender right hand in the deep large handprint of Guru Nanak. The stone is warm, as if the Guru had brought it to rest just a moment ago.

If Vaheguru has doubts, this is the time to tell Bachan Singh, or even Roop.

But there is no sign. No sign at all.

Roop climbs the three white marble steps on the opposite side, up to Papaji, to make room for the other pilgrims jostling behind her.

The Rehraas chant rises into the October night, quelling the cawing of crows. The sky above the gurdwara tints itself a shadow-laden blue and deepens to display the brilliance of Mangal. Strolling round the gurdwara, the better to see the plaster leaves that cup its large white dome, Roop, Revati Bhua, Madani and her husband read the dedications in Punjabi carved into marble flagstones in the gurdwara walls and platform in Gurmukhi script. Papaji and Jeevan can also read the Punjabi carved in Persian script, but only Jeevan can read the two or three carvings in English. He reads aloud for Papaji's pleasure.

Gujri can't read any of them. Gujri says, 'Those who need to tell why or how much they gave here have too much haumai.'

Too much self-ness.

'Not good for their karma.'

The Rehraas over, Bachan Singh leaves his women in the care of the Guru. He introduces himself to the Head Granthi and explains that Sant Puran Singh will arrive tomorrow morning to perform the wedding, for without the Sant's blessing there can be no marriage in his family.

'Has anyone from the boy's wedding party arrived yet?' he asks. 'We should start the milni ceremony soon – all are tired.'

A milni ceremony can take hours, the men of the groom's family formally meeting the men of the bride's family.

The Head Granthi points to two rose-coloured silk turbans above European suits sitting cross-legged on the marble platform skirting the great domed building. There is Sardar Kushal Singh and his brother-in-law, the 'boy' in this wedding, forty-two-year-old Sardarji. And beside them, a tall, turbanless, head-kerchiefed figure in a pale green silk garb of a kind Bachan Singh has never seen. There are just three men in this wedding procession. Bachan Singh's capability to host more is suspect.

Bachan Singh swallows hard; this milni ceremony will not take very long.

Jeevan and Madani's husband join him now. They walk solemnly across the marble.

The men in European suits rise to their feet.

Bachan Singh, Jeevan and Madani's husband in his turn, representing all the men in Roop's family, embrace Sardar Kushal Singh.

The man in the pale green silk garb is introduced as Sardarji's loyal mukhtiar, Manager Abdul Aziz. Sardar Kushal Singh, less polite and holy today, sniggers in Bachan Singh's ear, 'Sardarji told Manager Abdul Aziz he must get a lounge suit or an evening suit of silk for the wedding and what does he do but tell a tailor to make him a nightsuit out of silk. So he came wearing the nightsuit, because he was afraid to let Sardarji's gift go to waste.'

Manager Abdul Aziz, a lean careworn man, wears the pale green silk nightsuit and the ill-fitting handkerchief like a crane flapping by the bank of a strange jheel, but embraces Bachan Singh and Jeevan with enthusiasm.

His mistake is one Bachan Singh could have made too. Lounge suit. Evening suit. Night suit. How many suits are there? Why is there a difference?

Sardarji does not need to be introduced. Bachan Singh embraces him. His new son-in-law's long beard is tied and tucked beneath his chin and set with fixo and has but a single streak of grey. Unlike Bachan Singh, Sardarji is a man who has never needed to pray for rain or gamble his seed to land where it may.

* * *

The next morning, the coir matting is dry and rough beneath Roop's bare newly hennaed feet as she enters Punja Sahib Gurdwara from the open doorway to the east, with Papaji, Jeevan, Madani, Gujri and Revati Bhua all at her side. The four doors of the gurdwara are open to all castes and the four corners of the world the way the Guru says they should be.

The spring called forth by Guru Nanak's hand bubbles past as if it has caught Roop's excitement.

She carries a marigold garland in hands where henna swirls for the first time. She falls to her knees, touches her forehead before the Guru. Rises.

A man in an English suit, with a turban like a full-blown rose above falcon eyes and a black beard with a single streak of grey, stands beside her. The shamla-fan of his celebration turban stands high and proud. From the base of his neck where the rose turban meets his grey English suit comes a safa of silk that must be at least the length of his hidden hair. She bows her head before him, raises her arms and places her marigold garland about his neck. Now she feels his hands at her shoulders, hears the rustle of silk in her ear, inhales marigold perfume as his garland settles around her neck in exchange.

Roop bows her head again before the Guru, sure that her Papaji has done his best.

Through the red blur of Lajo Bhua's chunni Roop senses the Guru Granth Sahib spread on its low pedestal, the kindly face of Sant Puran Singh above it, his pale hands smoothing its yellowed pages, his white beard bobbing forward and back, ready to recite the Lavaan. Her upper arm brushes the arm of the man to whom she has been given as she takes her place by his side and sits cross-legged before the Guru.

About Roop's neck spirals the comforting weight of Mama's gold chain. Mama's ruby tikka is warm upon her forehead. She rests her palms down in her lap so Mama's hand ornaments show, gold chains flowing from each ring to the gold bangle at her wrist.

'Keep that tattoo covered,' Gujri had advised. 'Sardarji's family are not new Sikhs like us – they will not like it that you had it written in Persian script, like some Muslim.'

But on Roop's right hand, again, against all Revati's counselling and admonitions, and so carefully that Gujri has not noticed, there is Mama's sapphire ring.

So sure is Roop that unlucky things happen only to other girls.

She keeps her eyes lowered, as Madani had. And as Mama must have when she married Papaji. But she flicks her eyes like Sulochana did in the pictures, just once, sideways, to see him.

She can see only his cuff.

A *frayed* cuff.

A chill creeps through the small room of the gurdwara and enters the buttery smell of stale parshaad.

Could Papaji and Sardar Kushal Singh have married her to a poor man? An odour of silent beseeching clings to the pilgrims who crowd behind her, as Roop's wedding begins.

If they have, what can she do?

Another sidelong glance.

Relief.

She shouldn't have doubted Papaji or Sardar Kushal Singh.

The cuff is frayed, but her new husband wears an emerald cuff-link.

She straightens her spine, lowers her head a little further.

Another sidelong glance.

Veins flow river-blue beneath light skin on the foot that almost touches her knee; his feet must rarely feel the sun. And there is a corn on the side of his big toe; he must wear closed European shoes all the time.

Another sidelong glance.

The weight of a large diamond stretches his earlobe just below the line of his rose silk turban.

Yes, indeed, she should not have doubted Papaji.

The musicians sing with their eyes closed. Everyone sings with their eyes closed. After she has walked three circles behind him, her eyes fixed upon the pale soft skin of his heels, she walks the last circle before him, the Guru's reminder to his Sikhs that all brides are princesses.

Rose petals fill the air.

Marigolds perfume the air with their promise of love.

Marigolds – the bud of fertility that wishes her children, the flame of the earth, ever-present reminder of summer.

Afterwards, Papaji, Roop, Jeevan, Revati Bhua and Gujri stand on the balcony and watch the pilgrims stepping down to the water, wading and bathing in the lap of the spring-fed stream.

Gujri whispers, 'Roop-bi, remember if you are ziddi, everyone will say let-her-be-alone.'

They lick the greasy, sweet parshaad from their fingers.

Sardarji offers Bachan Singh a large white handkerchief. Bachan Singh holds it carefully by its corners, folds it and gives it back. Then he rubs his hands on his beard so as not to waste a single drop of the Guru's favour.

The wedding party takes its place in rows on the floor of the gurdwara's kitchen. When volunteers have ladled food on their copper thals, Sardarji raises Roop's chunni just till it reveals her brown almond eyes. A half smile lifts his black mustachios, but he soon regains his stern exterior.

Revati Bhua says, 'Oh, Virji, I have raised her for this day,' and bursts into tears. Sardarji seems somewhat taken aback, but 'vir' – brother – is the right word for Revati Bhua to use.

Gujri crosses her legs and presses her too-small feet in the crooks of her knees; those feet always hurt if she has to leave her domain, the tunnel home in Pari Darvaza. Now she faces Sardarji's mukhtiar, Abdul Aziz. They sit just a little apart from the two families joined by the marriage, though in the same rows. Manager Abdul Aziz is served from the same daal bucket as Gujri, and because it is the Guru's kitchen and not Deputy Bachan Singh's rasoi and because Manager Abdul Aziz is Sardarji's guest, Gujri has to accept it. But she refuses water from the volunteer's pitcher, simply because Abdul Aziz has been served from it.

Sardarji takes a piece of roti and its fill of daal, so that his hand may feed Roop. Now Roop's turn. When his lips enclose the tips of her fingers, she does not dare raise her half-closed eyes to his, because brides must be shy. With her veil lowered again, the round of her thali on the ground, the wheat roti and daal on the flat copper are all she can see. Her hennaed right hand, Mama's gold ornament covering her wrist and the tattoo with her name, moves over the food to her mouth.

Her new husband tells a joke and laughs at it, a belly laugh, his head thrown back, white teeth flashing in his dark beard, enjoying the moment. Roop is reassured. A man who laughs like that – straight out, with no snickering hesitation in case anyone who might be offended is listening – that is a man of power, a man in control, a man who can make a woman's life easy.

Manager Abdul Aziz leaves the group to walk down the streets of Hasan Abdal, climb the mountain path, and pay his respects at the Muslim pir's memorial. Jeevan embraces Roop and leaves, stammering slightly as he says 'Sat Sri Akal' to Sardarji – and without challenging his new brother-in-law, even teasingly, to that wrestling match he'd threatened. Soon Madani's husband leads Madani out of the gurdwara compound and she is gone.

Since there is no dowry to lay out on manjis and no relatives to show it to if there were one, Revati Bhua and Gujri open bedding rolls for their second night in the pilgrims' rooms around the gurdwara.

Roop loves Gujri's stories about other people, other places, other times that really have nothing to do with girls of good kismat like Roop. She listens, head resting on Gujri's comfortable lap, lulled despite her excitement. But this night, after only one story, Gujri explains to Roop, quickly, practically, what part of a man's body goes where and how she must expect it to hurt – 'Now you need to know.'

Suddenly Roop's head jerks from Gujri's firm pull on her plait. '*Ay!* Are you listening? There must – ' Gujri glares down at her ' – there *must* be blood on the sheets or you'll see: everyone will say let-her-be-alone.'

All the way from Punja Sahib Gurdwara the next morning, Roop listens in silence as Sardarji drives the motor car he has brought to carry her away, instead of a palanquin as Mama, Madani and Kusum had. His hand is lighter in complexion than hers, square-fingered, with short, clean nails, and a steel kara that shines against its dark curly hair.

'This is a DeSoto,' he says. 'You know, each motor car feels different. This one has a more finely tuned engine than scores of others, so I like it, yes, like it very much. I ordered it all the way from America and it came to Bombay by sea – Americans call this colour chocolate brown.'

Roop has never seen chocolate to know what chocolate brown might mean. The last time she moved so fast was on the train to and from Bhai Takht Singh's Sikh Girls' School in Firozepur, but this motion is different, faster than a full gallop on Nirvair. Fields, kikar trees, forts, roadside shops, villages, all blur as the motor car responds to his touch.

He is reassuring her, telling her an older sister waits for her, but – 'Don't worry if Satya does not love you right away. She has suffered many years, her kismat is not good, she is to be pitied but never disrespected in any way. No one must say I was ungenerous.'

Sardarji has planned it all. 'We will not wait in Rawalpindi for people's tongues to begin their chatter. We will leave very soon for my posting to Khanewal. By the time we come back, in one-two years, talk will have died down.'

She is glad he sits on the side of her good ear or she might be discovered and sent home immediately, damaged goods. Her breath comes jagged and uneven from her mouth and she does not know whether it is the unaccustomed motor car leaping beneath her on the Grand Trunk Road or the fear of what is to come that makes her stomach churn and her womb cramp within her. Even in boarding school, she was never without a blood relative near or beside her.

They drive for a while in silence. The October sun strengthens above the motor car.

A traffic constable dances a strange dance, one hand held up like the handprint at Punja Sahib Gurdwara, the other beckoning.

Roop tenses, leans back as if she could stop the car.

'He is signalling to clear the road,' says Sardarji. 'When he beckons, the traffic will clear and the DeSoto can move past.'

The traffic clears.

Sardarji was right.

Roop relaxes, settles into her well-padded seat.

With his protection, surely the road is clear from here to my next life.

As they cross the Leh River and enter Rawalpindi, the news Vayu brings from Lahore and Delhi to the fields of Punjab says that moderates of the three-religion coalition have turned away from moderation.

That the coalition party in Punjab Province has made a pact with Mr Jinnah, the suited and monocled leader of the Muslim League, 'England-returned' only two years ago, to claim leadership of every Muslim in India.

And that the Sikh leader, Master Tara Singh, has therefore declared that his Akali Party will tie the fortunes of every Sikh to the multi-godded Hindus and their Indian National Congress spread through all of India in the freedom struggle against the British. Now his rhetoric at every chest-thumping political rally reminds Sikhs of the Gurus who were martyred two hundred years ago by order of the Mughals, the same whose descendants – Muslims like Abu Ibrahim, Ibrahim, Huma and her ami – the Sikhs live among and between in Punjab Province today.

Democracy rubs its hands in the wings and smiles its most benign smile. If the British leave India to the independence she is fighting for, Democracy will be ready to throw the dice and play its sorry games of numbers with India's leaders across the unveiled face of India. Only once before, long before Kaliyug, this age of misfortune, in the days of which the *Mahabharat* tells, was there such a game of dice as begins in India today – in that game, played with ivory dice by god-kings, Draupadi, that good-good, sweet-sweet obedient wife of five gods, was staked.

And lost.

Along with all her five husbands.

Today, in the India desired by the Indian National Congress – though Mahatma Gandhi and Nehru say often that they fight for a secular India, so that the holy days of all religions shall be proclaimed gazetted holidays – Muslims fear that Hindus will make their raj in the very image of this British raj, claiming to be the origin of all ideas, claiming all knowing, categorizing each man by blood, caste and skin, auctioning opportunity to the privileged few, controlling protest by blows of hard bamboo sticks, by torture and prisons, and by guns.

And their fear is rising.

Once Hindus forget to remember the word 'secular,' Muslim men throughout India know they will be forced – along with Sikh men, Christians, Buddhists, Jains, Jews, Parsis, tribals and animists – to accept the whims of many gods not of their choosing. Men foretell one another's actions by their very own, and Muslims know deep in the bone that Hindus have not forgotten the Mughal raj. And so Muslims scattered far away through the subcontinent began first to whisper, then to shout pleas to brother-Muslims clustered strong and safe from Lahore to the Khyber in the west; from Kashmir to Karachi on the Arabian Sea; through Bengal Province in the east; in Delhi; and even to faraway Muslim students in England: 'Do not forget us, you must protect us, protect all Muslims, against the coming Hindu raj.'

Even poets of hope have begun to discern the dangers of unity – Muhammad Iqbal fuels his fountain pen with ink of Islamic green; his verses now proclaim the imperative: an Islamic nation.

All this is churning in Punjab.

In Rawalpindi, such news buzzes from the cantonment and the Rawalpindi Club, where Europeans foxtrot to the remembered rhythms of England, to the lanes that cross and loop through Rajah Bazaar.

But in Roop's good ear there are only Papaji's parting words, 'Above all, give no trouble.'

THREE

1937–1940

9

Sardarji's mind is not on Roop.

Wedding accomplished, a beautiful bride. He won't tell Satya about Roop just yet; she's bound to find out for herself. A little unpleasantness ahead in that department, but then she'll be grateful, then he'll have sons, and all with a minimum of fuss.

Right now, he prefers to enjoy this morning after his second wedding. He barely remembers his first wedding, three weeks before leaving for England; he was only sixteen. The twenty-six years with Satya might be considered an unforeseen detour, but this second marriage will correct that, set life flowing down the right channels again.

Next item on the programme.

Cunningham.

Mr Cunningham, his English-gentleman-inside, again demands an explanation.

He came by Cunningham many years ago when Sardarji had persuaded his father to send him to England, telling him he would learn English technology for India.

'Why England?' the Chaudhary asked. 'What is there so important to learn that you need to cross the black water?'

'Examinations are held only in England,' he explained to the Chaudhary, government services being open, in theory, to Indians, but closed unless an Indian mustered the gall and the rupees to undertake a passage to England.

'If you have to go, become a lawyer, then,' his father snapped. 'Why engineering? No son of mine should work with his hands!'

But, Sardarji told him, if Indians could conceive the zero, build the stately Golden Temple, the Rohtas Fort, Moenjodaro, the rustless ageless Ashoka pillar and the marble Taj Mahal, are they not equipped from birth to understand buttresses and stresses?

If his father had listened Sardarji might have explained it this way: to know your adversary, you enter his mind and see from his eyes. You eat his food and feel the way it must feel to him, going down fireless, settling complacently in his stomach. Beef – yes, beef – Wellington, fish and chips, Brussels sprouts, baked vegetables and mincemeat puddings. You watch his mentors and understand the qualities he admires, you walk in his cities, learn the names of the places he yearns for as if they were holy: Trafalgar Square, Fortnum and Mason, the Inns of Court, Oxford, Cambridge and that holy Ganga of the English man, the River Thames.

In England, Sardarji had made mental notes of the cosy aphorisms of British nannies – it is always good to know the teachings your opponent has been raised with so you can quote them, *in extremis* – he'd made a study of the Bible, the Bhagavadgita, the *Ramayan* and Koran for the same reasons, concluding privately that the Guru Granth Sahib was definitely more progressive, more suited to the needs of modern men. In England too, Sardarji memorized all the scientific statements made in the Guru Granth Sahib by the ten Gurus, should any English man ever challenge him on the subject.

And he'd lived the British caste system, so the English could never again pretend that they have none. He'd heard the accents of Glasgow and Surrey and Lancashire and found there were many ways English could be spoken, and that the hardness of d's and t's that clung to his own tongue like curry was no measure of the mind that mouthed them. Like an actor in a play, he donned the suit and pants and made them believe he was just like them – only with a turban.

And he has shown himself flexible and reasonable and adaptable, able to absorb the scientific method.

That was so many years ago.

By the time he had done the sensible thing about Kitty and returned from Balliol in 1918, he had acquired Cunningham, his own personal English-gentleman-inside.

Cunningham.

Cunningham still saddles Sardarji's mind, hoary phantom remnant of his years in England. And now Sardarji cannot remember how he thought before he learned to think with Cunningham. Cunningham, grafted so long ago, does the watching now and argues less and less as long as Sardarji asks only the questions Cunningham approves of, walks and talks the way Cunningham has taught. Cunningham can edit paragraphs in Sardarji's mind before releasing them for utterance, and now that he has trained Sardarji on what is Done and Simply Not Done, generally stays within the bounds of reasonable discourse. If Cunningham becomes overpowering, Sardarji can silence him with land revenue and octroi estimates, gurus Cunningham reveres more than Christ. Cunningham's voice at the back of Sardarji's mind is a small price to pay for the cachet of an English education, the immediate offer of a topnotch position in the slowly-Indianizing 'Indian' Service of Engineers, with the opportunity to pay off all the debts his elder brother had incurred with his father's blessing and guarantees. His elder brother, pious poet, opening the doors of the flour mill every time there was a famine, telling the poor – come, take what you need.

Such a foolish chap.

What remains from those lonely years at Balliol is a feeling of gratitude that he is no longer outside, nose to the glass of the laboratory.

He has been allowed a toehold on the crowded threshold of the inner sanctum where the real chess game is played.

And he has discovered that in the setting up of what is to be measured, in the establishment of perimeter and the positioning of the observer to the observed, lies a certain measure of freedom. To him who defines the terms, supplies the explanations and marks the space go the petty compensations of British categorization.

Even so, he still keeps from Cunningham what he calls his 'ten per cent,' his turban, his faith, the untranslated, untranslatable residue of his being.

Sardarji has become that strange rare being, the contradiction and exception to the rule of Indian inferiority, a convenient oddity providing hope of advancement to Indians, convincing his British masters – particularly his superior in the department, Mr Timothy Farquharson – of their magnanimity.

He has worked – so hard he has worked – to educate his English superiors that there is infinite variation in shades of brown. Brown skins beyond the colour of tuppence, mud huts and parched leaves; in-between browns like the muddy water gushing from the headworks of a dam, browns the colour of bridges and barrages and medicine bottles. Some lighter browns, khaki browns like his own, closer to their Aryan skin tone than others – so Cunningham says. And around the time his British seniors had been forced to acknowledge these varying shades of brownness and had, as with all things, created categories for each – such as Maratha, Gurkha, Sikh – that could be called to mind by image or by Kipling's rhyme, Cunningham began to tell Sardarji his own people look 'all alike.'

So, since his return from England, Sardarji has called his own people 'Indians' and 'them,' as Cunningham does, forgetting when he knew 'them' to be 'us.'

All of which makes it of great importance to have a son – many sons. Very important, he says to Cunningham, now. Because without sons to remind the world of its doer, a man's work dies at the same instant as a man's body.

Cunningham says, 'A credible theory.'

'No, try to understand,' he tells Cunningham. 'My sons will start a clean race, their blood uncontaminated by the past. A new race from the Best of Both Worlds. They will be progressive Indians, Indians with no Mr Cunninghams-inside, able to cope with all the Mr Timothy Farquharsons of this world.'

It is simply not done to point out the obvious to Cunningham: ever since the British came to India, the time-honoured tradition of adopting a son has been the shortest path to losing a whole kingdom or jagir, be it state or mere estate – consider what happened to Maharaj Ranjit Singh's kingdom, or, in Sardarji's own lifetime, to Maharaj Nabha; perfectly normal adoptions by both Maharajas went 'unrecognized' and became excuses for the British to snatch whole kingdoms away. What was their legal-sounding appellation for land-pilferage? Lapse. Yes, they once called it the Doctrine of Lapse – still it happens.

Sardarji is not of that class of people for whom there are no consequences because they have nothing to lose. No. He must do as his role in 'Pindi dictates. He has great responsibilities; many people depend on him. He cannot simply do as he pleases.

Now he gives Cunningham that part of his motive that he thinks Cunningham can comprehend; it's just so much easier. He says to Cunningham, 'It is important for me – just as it is for you English men – that my sons come from a girl I know has not been used before.'

'Oh, come now, sir,' says Cunningham.

'Cooperate, would you, Cunningham?'

Cunningham subsides for a while.

Sardarji's thoughts turn to his father and the futility of explanations. The Chaudhary died angry with his younger son, wounded by what he called Sardarji's growing selfishness, for Sardarji had become unwilling to help his relatives – especially distant ones – having learned a new word, *nepotism*. The Chaudhary would say, 'Then who will come to your help in times of war, or when you are old, or sick, or poor? This paap you call "nepotism" is what I call *duty*. You cannot even see that much.'

That was before Sardarji could find the words to explain any of this. Before he'd even thought it through as any rational, objective man should. His mother would have listened but plague took her when Sardarji was still in England. Sardarji held his sorrow inside him a whole year past her death; his elder brother's debts and the oceans between them made Sardarji's return for her funeral impossible.

And so Sardarji thinks and drives, slowing as he enters Rawalpindi to let street urchins fling their small bodies at the running board of the motor car to welcome him home.

'Baksheesh, Sardarji!' come their hopeful cries.

Roop laughs with him, the chains from her rings to the tight gold bangle encircling her wrist catching sunlight aging past midday.

She drops her chunni past her face.

The way a good-good, sweet-sweet wife should.

Sardarji leans out of his DeSoto and flings several annas in the dust.

Rawalpindi, October 1937

Roop should appreciate her good fortune. She has been married, despite Papaji's misfortunes, despite having no mother to arrange her marriage, despite being born under the very strong influence of the Mangal star, despite having one bad ear.

She should be joyful, unafraid.

Except that she is locked in the deepening gloom of a small storeroom at the ground level of Sardar Kushal Singh's three-storey haveli, still dressed in her red-gold wedding lehnga. All three doors are locked, not just the door to the courtyard. There is a strong smell of horses and bullocks behind the wooden door to her left, her unclean side, while Sardarji's voice thunders and wheedles in the sitting room past the wooden door. It is her wedding night and when Sardarji turned the slender black wheel of the motor car and said, 'We will go to Sardar Kushal Singh's home, that way there will be no trouble,' she didn't ask why.

Sardarji said, like Revati Bhua holding up a brass Lakshmi, 'She is so good, a real bibi.'

Sardarji's sister Toshiji's face is broad and square, her dark brown eyes alert, careful. Though some might say her nose is too large or her behind a little too broad and complacent, she is quite unremarkable.

She embraced Roop like a mother and ushered her into this storeroom. She spoke rapidly, like one unaccustomed to being heard. 'You must be tired from your marriage and your long journey.'

Then Toshiji left, locking the door behind her.

Roop is sixteen years old; she is not tired.

Toshiji must have locked the door to the courtyard from habit, all the other rooms on the ground level appear to be storerooms too, except for Sardar Kushal Singh's sitting room. She must not have realized the other two doors were locked, too.

A red-black tartan blanket and one flat pillow on a sagging European-style bed.

The pillow cannot block the sound of a woman crying in the distance. It comes in her good ear, like the sound of a wounded animal.

A china jug of water, a basin and a glass on a corner table; perhaps her temporary keeping has been planned.

Her wooden trunk, the same that she and Madani took to Bhai Takht Singh's school, stands half empty at the foot of the bed, latches closed like the Guru's eyes, leather handles pressed flat against its sides, Mama's phulkari-embroidered red shawl within.

Through the bars of the storeroom window she sees her new elder sister, raging like some churail in the courtyard outside.

'Did I not tell you I – I, myself – would find you a woman?'

Even in anger, Satya is beautiful. Small-built, slender, with feline grey eyes. Honey-brown arms circled with gold armlets flail Sardarji's chest till he holds her wrists to stop her. Her hair parts sleek, black as a jackdaw's wings, about the oval of her face.

A woman who looks beautiful even when she is in tears.

Sardarji pulls Satya into Sardar Kushal Singh's sitting room, which adjoins the storeroom, and Roop moves to the keyhole in the door between them. Fine carpets of forest green and lapis blue sprawl between low divans and ripple up and down the walls. Sardar Kushal Singh sits behind a low desk – like Papaji's, only less battered. At the far end of the room, fire pulses behind a wrought iron grate and releases the scent of sandalwood incense. Satya stalks Sardarji as he moves to stand before the fire. Roop's eye takes in Satya's black silk kameez bordered in gold, the voluminous silk folds of her baggy pink salwar, a pink and black printed chunni fallen about her shoulders. Roop has never heard a woman raise her voice to her husband before another man or stand before a man with her head uncovered.

'I still have life to give, why do you throw me away?'

And Sardarji's roar, 'I do not throw you away, I tell you! You will have all izzat, all respect, you will be looked after.'

'You will throw me away – I know it. If not now, then later.'

'Satya, you should know me better.'

'Please, let's not pretend we know each other any more. Yes, I know you, know you better than you know yourself.'

'I know you very well, too – you have a tongue sharper than Kakeyi's. I tell you, I'm so tired of your shouting.'

'Tired of my shouting? You don't want me, because I tell you what you have become. I tell you what I see inside you, that's why you throw me away.'

Now Sardar Kushal Singh raises his voice, too. 'Collect your wits, Satya! You have brought this upon yourself with your quarrelling.'

And this brings a great scream from Satya, as though one woman could take in the pain of the world and give it back in sound.

'*Aaaaaaaaeeeeeeeeeeeeeiiiiiiiiii!!!*'

Roop retreats from the keyhole and flings herself in the supine palm of the sagging bed.

She shakes her head.

Such a scream! Though it moves in an instant into the past, it lingers in every crevice of Roop's skull.

Her breath comes fast. Bewildered.

How is it no one has taught Satya to say 'Hanji, achchaji, yes-ji?' and to speak softly, always softly? How generous is my new husband! How kind indeed to keep a woman who rages so, when he could throw her out on the street with nowhere to go.

Roop covers her ear with a cupped hand so she can no longer hear the terrible things Satya is saying to their husband. She props herself on one elbow, ear still covered, and, with a hennaed fingertip, traces lifelines that intersect in the palm of the red-black tartan.

She does not try the door to the courtyard again, or the door to the sitting room, but as the light fades, moves to the back window instead. Past the flat roofs of Rawalpindi, a silver fog drops its net gently across the purple-blue folds of the Margalla Hills. She rubs at the window pane as if rubbing could erase it − Sardarji and Satya facing one another in Sardar Kushal Singh's sitting room, the fire contained in its fireplace, smouldering between them.

Sun swells over the tops of the Margalla Hills, shooting exploratory rays over valleys it abandoned the night before. Waking in the dust-moted light, Roop slips her hennaed feet into her gold-embroidered jutis and tries the door to the courtyard.

This time she finds it unlocked.

She uses the tiny crouch-toilet across the courtyard, washes her hands and feet in the water trough and returns to the storeroom.

In a few minutes the sun flashes into the room as Toshiji enters, a glass of hot tea cupped in a corner of her chunni.

'Have you washed?' Toshiji eyes the still-full jug on the corner table.

'Yes, I washed.' Roop nods at the water-trough outside.

Toshiji's nose wrinkles. She places the tea on the night-stand. She leaves the door slightly ajar.

Roop goes back to waiting, grateful for the hot sweet tea − she has not eaten since the food Sardarji put in her mouth at Punja Sahib Gurdwara.

She imagines the day half gone − at least, it would be in Pari Darvaza, and by now she has said the Japji five times, the Sukhmani twice, because she has never been alone so long − when Sardarji returns. He leads her from the storeroom, gently, as though he carries hope flowering on his arm. 'Narain Singh!' he calls as they emerge from Sardar Kushal Singh's home into the busy street.

The young driver beside the DeSoto snaps to attention and opens the back door of the motor car. He joins his hands before Roop in greeting, he will drive them to Sardarji's ancestral haveli now. Sardar Kushal Singh and Toshiji embrace Roop and she gets in the car. Sardarji gets in before Roop can stammer her question, has her wedding trunk been placed in the car? Mama's phulkari-embroidered red shawl is in it.

No, it hasn't. The car stops. Narain Singh is sent back for the trunk, the trunk placed in the dickey of the car.

Sardarji waits with a small smile that says Roop is a child who must be indulged. Of course, Sardarji has no need of any possessions she may have brought with her.

Roop settles back in the car.

I must have imagined the door was locked.

When the road narrows to a labyrinth of lanes, the DeSoto stops at Banni Chowk in Rajah Bazaar and Sardarji leads Roop on foot through Saidpuri Gate to his ancestral neighbourhood, a neighbourhood full of homes within shops and shops within homes, some no larger than a thin man's seated frame, some cavernous narrow halls where the price of everything is known only in terms of some other thing. Springing from the patronage and needs of his clan over seven generations, these shops, whether rented or owned, have passed from father to son, and, in some sad cases, out of a family to a daughter's husband. In all that time, only the master has changed, from the Mughals to Maharaj Ranjit Singh to the British.

Here is a man who spends his days repeating the ninety-nine names of Allah, there a man who spends his days repeating the thousand names of Vishnu. Here a man sways behind a clay chillum, there a man hiccups over his tenth bottle of English beer. A court pleader leans his wigged head from his book-lined chamber to watch a roadside dentist plant his knee on the drum-wide chest of a wrestler and pull till tooth and bellow and blood spring from the open mouth. Here a bangle seller wraps a dozen glass bangles and a subtle inquiry of matrimonial interest in the crumbling softness of a Punjabi newspaper.

From the sweetmaker's shop comes the aroma of potato pakoras sizzling in a massive iron bowl of hot oil. Skinned chickens and lamb shanks swing from the awnings of a butcher shop, glistening a rich pink. A goldsmith holds his delicate copper scale before the mesh-masked glittering eyes of burqa-clad women and a tailor treadles his sewing machine to make evening suits, lounge suits and night suits. Here is a cobbler so humble he knows himself unworthy to look at the sky; there a turban-dyer so brash he paints the sky new colours with his customers' turbans. Here the dented kettle of the chai seller spouts resolutions for All-India Muslim League rallies as little boys pitch cricket balls in a dead-end lane. Here a goat, hobbled and tied to a hitching post, sinks to its knees and bleats for the promise of refuse, there five sleepy laden donkeys stand and wait and wait and wait.

There is no need for such people to see even the colour of his new wife's skin, and Sardarji is pleased to see Roop wears her chunni forward now almost to her chin and keeps her eyes upon his feet.

At the heart of the labyrinthine jumble of shops, a ten-foot-high wrought iron gate stops the adventurous, forbids entry. Sardarji calls to the watchman, 'Kholo, bhai!' Before the words leave his lips, the gate is opened for him and Roop to enter.

Inside, the clamour of the bazaar falls abruptly silent. The smells of pakoras, goats, donkeys, of chillums and stale beer, of sweat and survival, halt their onslaught. Horses nicker a welcome from a stable beside the gate.

The two-man, one-elephant narrow lane has broadened to a brick-lined street as it enters a huge walled courtyard domed by the overhead sun. Now two halves of a great four-storey haveli straddle the street. So large, the great havelis contain courtyards upon courtyards, family wings, servants' wings and guest wings. Two main entrances face one another across the street, their scalloped arches and brass-studded, finely carved doors leaning towards one another in dignified greeting. One, stunted, decaying, where his elder brother lived out his pious, unambitious life, and the other, Sardarji's half, well watered by an underground stream, its subterranean godowns full of grain and gold, where the only need is of sons to inherit his thirteen villages and the new India. Standing in the doorway, Sardarji motions to Roop to raise her chunni so she can see: level with the top of the doorways, terrace gardens glow green, a fountain arcs in greeting. A white peacock considers Roop with a garnet-red eye, unfurls its tail and dances before them.

Roop's jewellery jingles, a clap of delight.

Sardarji points, showing Roop the two-hundred-year-old banyan that grows out of and back into his haveli's brick walls, shading its centre courtyard within and the terrace garden without. And he says this haveli is where he carries out his dharam, his duty, to insulate the whole mohalla – all the people who live in this area, qualified or illiterate, Sikh, Hindu or Muslim – from the whims of its ultimate master, while working toward modernizing India.

'Indeed?' says ever-present Cunningham. 'That's a bit rich. I mean, considering you just popped out and added a second wife when you've been giving us all the impression you're above that sort of thing? It's simply not done these days, old chap.'

'I repeat, Cunningham, this is a very ancient custom,' says Sardarji.

Cunningham snorts. 'Next you'll backslide to eating raw meat,' he says.

'Well, then,' Sardarji retorts. 'I do it because I can.'

There should be ceremony before a wife enters her real home, a few pauris of prayer before a step over a new threshold. But Sardarji simply ushers Roop across his threshold till she stands just inside the haveli, at the corner of the largest court-yard she has ever seen, tiled in marble. The banyan's leaves wave three storeys above her, offering shade. A European sofa, up-holstered in purple velvet, stands at its centre. Sardarji leads Roop up a dark stone spiral staircase to a carved teakwood gallery that overlooks the courtyard and runs past Roop's new chambers: four teakwood-floored rooms linked by three round-arched doorframes fitted with blue-and-gold stained glass.

Though the ropes from the blue-and-gold raw silk pukkhas hanging from their ceilings dangle into the gallery, ready for pukkhawallas to pull in rhythm, only the smallest has any furniture at present. A heavy wrought iron fourposter stands on a crimson-and-sapphire Tabriz carpet and drops its veil of champagne lace past a two-drawer nightstand.

A blue-and-white porcelain clock edged in gold stands upon the nightstand. Sardarji jokes its hands are joined together in greeting just for Roop. 'It's saying Sat Sri Akal,' he says, laughing.

Roop smiles. Sardarji nods his approval.

A Tuscany tapestry hangs on the wall behind the bed – a gentleman in heeled shoes, stockings and plus-fours bowing as he presents a rose to a pale woman with a very tiny waist above her hoop skirt. A long ostrich feather sprouts from her hat and her expression is one of charmed delighted thankfulness.

A kidney-shaped grey-painted Queen Anne dressing table, with a three-panel mirror, lends its curves to the starkness where two white walls meet. A silver-backed brush and comb set rests, bristles down, on its lace doily. Powdered surma and surmi lie in small brass vials, ready to mix and accentuate the almond shape of Roop's eyes.

And beside them, a black velvet box.

'Open it,' he says. And observes her face light up like a diya at Diwali as she spies the gold kantha necklace inside, and holds it up to admire the sheen of its red enamel. Now another box. In it are earrings: three tiers of Burmese rubies surrounded by diamonds – real diamonds, not white sapphires – red-hearted flower shapes ending in large Basra teardrop pearls. Sardarji's heart stirs. He watches Roop's eyes sparkle as she reaches beneath her chunni to her tender young earlobes before the Queen Anne mirror and turns her head to look.

Right, left.

And a third box, this one oblong. Roop presses her hennaed fingers to the clasp. 'Panjeban!' she cries. She unscrews the posts of her tawdry silver ones, hitches her lehnga just a little above her ankles and arches her feet to show his gold ones in their stead.

Cunningham says, 'We'd have to be sixteen again, I should think, to feel such an extravagance of delight.'

Kitty was delightable just this way.

Catharine – Kate. Daughter of a working man, a woman of no nobility, no refinement. Kitty. When he first met her in his landlady's drawing room he thought she was the one for whom the song was written,

> *Kitty, isn't it a pity*
> *in the city*
> *you work so hard?*

Kitty was nearly married when her beau was called up for the army. Sardarji forgave her this, as he forgave her skirts above the ankles, hands hard and strong from plugging telephone connections into the switchboard, lipstick applied in a red gash across her pale face. He forgave all this for her primrose complexion. Ghost-pale, fair-haired as Guinevere.

She was two years his senior and given to improving her mind. There were evenings when their minds met and played, neither of them conscious of being clothed differently, of looking different. On afternoon walks in Hyde Park – chance meetings, he called them – he forgot sometimes that she was only a small-brained woman, so analytical was her mind, so fresh her perspective.

It came, sad to say, of her being a working-class woman, a supporter of the Labour Party. To be a true critic of Empire, he now realizes, was an impossibility from any other vantage; it was what made her side with Indians, see past his turban and his skin to treat him the way she wished to be treated by her own people.

But he had not done her that favour in return. When he left England, sealing his promises to write with the kisses Kitty'd taught him to give her, he never planned to teach first Satya, and now a village girl like Roop, to kiss like a European.

At that time, he'd told Kitty he'd write, that he'd send for her, that some day he'd marry her and they'd progress past holding hands in cinema halls.

But when he returned, she returned, in his mind, to the amorphous mass of 'the English,' smudged and blurred into her quom.

What could he have written anyway? That he'd met Satya on his return, wife of seven years, as if for the first time? That, for all his posturing as a proud landowner's son, he'd come home to debt? That plague had taken his mother? How would Kitty have understood these things, the effects of his own peculiar karma? He wrote letters he consigned to the dustbin, for a letter is not truly written till it is posted.

'This girl will make me feel sixteen again,' he says to Cunningham.

Sardarji shows Roop where to press the switch for the brass sconce lights. She stands there for a while, turning them on, then off, on, then off.

He opens the door to the tiled bathroom with its mahogany-seated enamel commode and clawfoot bathtub, points out the door the sweeper uses to enter and clean the room.

In the bedroom again, Sardarji demonstrates the tasselled tapestry bell pull by which she can call her personal maid-servant, Mani Mai.

When he pulls it, however, Atma Singh, the cook, appears instead. His pupils remain constricted as he peers at Sardarji with opium-serened eyes suited to looking at the sun. A luxuriant silver beard cascades from fine-lined leather-brown cheeks. The padded shoulders of Sardarji's livery, a white button-front linen coat, broadens his thin shoulders, and a blue brocade cummerbund adds girth to his frame. Beneath the coat, narrow starched white pyjama trousers elongate short, slightly bandy legs bequeathed by the Hun blood tinging Atma Singh's ancestry. A partridge-beige turban with a fringe of blue silk adds four inches to his stature. Well trained by Satya to read Sardarji's every gesture and know his needs, in his many years of service Atma Singh has learned the art of appearing absent while present in a room, a quality some servants never achieve, and for which many are apprenticed to him in Sardarji's home.

'Bari-Sardarniji has sent Mani Mai to her village for a few days,' he says. 'She will be back tomorrow morning.'

Sardarji knows who has sent Mani Mai to her village. Satya, interfering so soon.

His eyebrows meet over falcon eyes. Best to ignore it. Now he must wait for Mani Mai to return – Roop must be made clean before . . . well, before. Village girls can be carriers of germs and disease – yes, he will have to wait so that Mani Mai will see to it for him.

'I – I am sure I have no need,' breathes Roop. She is quite overawed.

'Mani Mai will help you before you meet Satya,' says Sardarji.

'Oh, Sardarji, I will be no trouble. I will be just like a younger sister.'

Sardarji's full lips part for a second beneath his moustache. Then he thinks better of it, stretches himself to full height and leads the way. 'The rest of these rooms,' he explains, matter-of-factly, closed European shoes echoing in the high-ceilinged emptiness, 'are for the children.'

That night, Roop lies on her back in the fourposter bed with the lace curtains drawn back and tied with a velvet bow, and she listens to the unaccustomed carving and measuring of the circumference of time.

Tick tick, tick tick.

Above her, the polished wood ceiling is inlaid with ivory flowers.

Tick tick, tick tick.

She turns the clock's face away. She muffles the blue-and-white porcelain with the pillow.

Tick tick, tick tick.

She puts the clock and the pillow under the bed and sleeps an easy deep sleep on her good ear.

Mani Mai comes in at first light and has to shake her to wake her. Roop sits up quickly, her eyes on Mani Mai's mouth; she must learn quickly to read people in Sardarji's home or her secret will be found out and she sent home.

Mani Mai says, 'Chota hazri.' A plate of unbruised apricots, toast and chai.

Or rather, chai ingredients to be assembled to make tea. The milk has been kept apart until the last moment, and the tea must be poured from the fat china teapot through a silver strainer to a small cup instead of a brass tumbler. Crystals of white sugar pour from a small china bowl to a teaspoon and the teaspoon adds them to the tea. By the time Mani Mai finally gives Roop her tea, it is cold and tasteless.

Roop takes the toast from the tray and dips it in the tea.

Mani Mai says, 'Ji, don't do that.'

'No?' Anxious to please.

'No.' Mani Mai takes the toast from Roop's hand, lays it back on the tray. 'No need for worry, I will help you, inshallah. I was a man's third wife once till he cast me away, peace be upon him.'

Mynah eyes an inch from Roop's, Mani Mai's dark hand caresses her cheek, like a mother's.

Suddenly a wailing sound penetrates the haveli, a sound that fills the room like Satya's screams. The timber floors tremble, the rafters resonate with its wail. Roop covers her good ear with one hand. A second later, her other ear.

But Mani Mai says calmly, unfolding the new salwar-kameezes Sardarji has thoughtfully provided, already sewn as though he had taken her measure before ever laying eyes on her, 'No need for worry – it's the siren from the cantonment. It tells men it is time to go to work at Sardarji's flour mill or the brewery, the ordnance factory or the government offices. They don't have pretty clocks like this one,' nodding at the porcelain clock. 'In the city men have to leave their homes to work. This is the new zamana.' Her tongue clicks, sorrowing over the new times.

She places a kameez – red silk with solid gold buttons, crusted with sequinned embroidery – on the bed for Roop to admire. Such a kameez would take Lajo Bhua three months to embroider. And Sardarji has provided a brassiere-bunyaan and panties instead of a kachcha for her – like the ones English women wear. Mani Mai demonstrates how she should cover her small breasts with the brassiere's cones and twist her arms behind her back to fasten it.

Mani Mai calls, 'Azhar Sheikh!'

A small dark man creeps carefully along the outside wall of the haveli. Through the sweeper's door, he brings a brass bucket of hot water and another of cold and places them on the wooden grille set in the clawfoot bathtub, never raising his eyes.

The commode is high and cold beneath her thighs, but Mani Mai says this is the way to use it. In the bathtub, Roop mixes hot and cold water in the small brass pitcher before pouring it over her limbs. Mani Mai squats in a corner of the bathroom supervising her just as Gujri and Revati Bhua used to. 'Wash down there. Clean properly. Yes, with soap.'

She softens her hair with amla and Mani Mai massages it with coconut oil and brushes it for her with the silver-backed brush before the curvy dressing table in the corner.

Roop wants to run down the spiral stone staircase and explore the rest of Sardarji's haveli, courtyards that open to other courtyards, many times larger than Papaji's haveli.

Shaandaar!

Opulent.

But Mani Mai says there is 'no need.' Instead, she leads Roop through the door, past the pukkhawalla pulling at his rope, to the gallery overlooking the courtyard.

Says, 'Bari-Sardarni's rooms are opposite,' as if that is all Roop needs to know.

Bari means larger.

But Roop has seen that Satya is shorter.

'Bari-Sardarni,' repeats Roop, realizing Mani Mai means Satya is senior.

And Mani Mai calls Roop 'Choti-Sardarni.'

Little Sardarni.

Something within Roop shrinks a little to meet the junior title.

At least she is the wife of a Sardar and can be called Sardarni. If she hadn't pressed Papaji to accept this rishta she might still be Roop-bi back in Pari Darvaza.

A rapid clattering comes from the ground floor. Roop gives

Mani Mai a questioning glance. Mani Mai holds her hands out before her and makes a pecking motion.

Roop is still mystified.

Mani Mai points to the ground floor and now Roop sees Sardarji seated at an English desk, index fingers poking at a clattering machine. The back wall of the room he sits in is filled with shelves upon shelves of books.

'Taip-writer,' says Mani Mai.

'Taip-writer,' repeats Roop.

They return to Roop's room in silence and wait.

When the porcelain clock says one o'clock, Atma Singh knocks on Roop's door with lunch on a silver tray. Instead of just daal and roti as in Papaji's home, a glass of sweet lassi, chicken reshmi-kebabs, lamb chapli-kebabs and mint raita are placed before Roop. Chicken! Lamb! In all her life, Roop has never before been offered meat.

'Ahista!'

Mani Mai wants her to chew slowly.

Roop slows.

There are even saunf seeds to scent her breath afterwards.

Mani Mai takes the tray away. The pukkhawalla leans into his pulling rhythm on the gallery, setting the silk pukkha above Roop swinging back and forth, back and forth.

Sardarji's hand turns the knob of her bedroom door. He saunters in, thumb inserted jauntily at the waist of his grey flannel trousers, the chain of his timepiece resting lightly on his matching grey waistcoat. He removes his turban and tie and lies down next to her with a contented sigh, closes his eyes.

He makes no move towards her.

Roop sits nervously at the edge of the bed clinging to its heavy metal post. Should she call Mani Mai? Ask for her chaperoning mynah eyes to follow her like Gujri's, Revati Bhua's and Kusum's? Should she call her?

No, this is all right.

This kind of being alone with a man, this is permitted. This one man, her husband, has been permitted.

He seems to be sleeping.

She has had no opportunity to study his face; it is, she

decides, stealing glances at him, a great deal more handsome than the smudgy photo, eyebrows heavy and dark, long lashes, a full moustache above well-formed lips. A long dark beard with a silver streak rolled and tied sleekly beneath his chin. He must hold it pressed behind a thatha-cloth every morning to set it so close to his cheeks. A different scent from anyone she has ever known; sandalwood, mixed with something strange. A high forehead crowned with a topknot of still-dark silky hair – still thick too, considering he is so old he is already past forty.

Dark curly chest hair shows where the white of his shirt meets bronze.

Sardarji's eyes open, sad brown eyes of a seeking man. He reaches for her, pulls the scarlet georgette of her chunni slowly from her head. It falls to the floor.

Strong hands grip her upper arms, she lowers her eyes before his.

He fumbles at the gold buttons of her new red kameez.

Hai, he's going to tear it!

His mouth covers hers like a man long hungry, it makes a strange sucking sound. A hand tugs the cord of her salwar. She gasps, jerks away as it searches and caresses the warm hollow between her legs.

He stops.

Rises, removes his waistcoat, unbuttons his trousers, removes his kachcha. Then his warmth returns to her side as he caresses her, strokes her, croons to her as if to a child, lifting her kameez. She sees herself reflected in his eyes, eyes that spark with approval as his fingers meet her new brassiere-bunyaan. His warmth is about her as he moves to free her breasts, the brassiere releases her; she breathes a deep breath of relief.

Curiosity moves her closer to him, moves her to touch him.

She feels him tense, the hardness and leanness of his body demanding hers be tuned to his. And hers, ever-tuned now to demand of voice or gesture, responding. She goes past his sandalwood perfume to learn his unique scent, feels him explore curve and line and swell of her limbs. She matches her breath to his in quickening rhythm, his big hands grip her hips, her body remembering like simmer coming to boil what goes where and why.

His weight is upon her.

A shard of pain divides her; she clenches her teeth not to scream.

Women's pain turns into sons. Vaheguru, let there be blood on the sheets!

His weight crushes air from her lungs.

Her black hair and his flow loose and combine.

Vaheguru, let there be blood on the sheets!

He thrusts within her to a place her body does not remember owning. Hidden place, locked-away place, sealed place, imprisoned place, place that waited so long for one man given the key.

Fragile place, so tender and giving.

Hai!

All the giving pent up within her, pierced at last.

He occupies her.

Skin boundaries dissolve; she cannot sense where she ends, he begins.

Her giving, that great giving, gives itself to the one man permitted.

Loving and warm, it flows from her like tears drawn from an interior core.

A thought chases itself away from her mind –

This, too, is what women are for.

He hums a strange tune as he dresses, an English-sounding song, and when he leaves, she notices the porcelain clock has stilled, its hands stopped at three o'clock.

It stands like the traffic constable signalling for her to move now, move while the road is still clear.

But Roop puts it back on the nightstand, fingers caressing the elegance of its fired veneer.

Gujri never told me it was so painful, but then Gujri was never a bride, only a widow. Kusum never told me either. One of them should have told me, someone should have told me...

From between her legs a bloody rose blooms upon the white linen sheet.

Now no one can say: 'Let her be alone.'

10

It has been a few days since Satya summoned Roop to her private sitting room, only a few days since Satya examined her, studied her features, her Pothwari skin, smooth as a new apricot beckoning from the limb of a tall tree, her wide, heavily lashed brown eyes, so demurely lowered, innocent. Since that first afternoon, Satya has ordered Roop to sleep beside her every afternoon, to prevent her from tempting Sardarji into visiting her. Roop has maintained a respectful downcast silence, but only after Satya, with an unkindness uncharacteristic of her family, told Roop her wanton smiles were not welcome in Satya's presence.

'No matter,' Satya tells herself. 'Though she is raised to sit on chairs and can read and write village Punjabi, she cannot speak or read the git-mit, git-mit talk.'

And now, after the wedding come wedding photographs in the studio.

Both Roop and Satya are dressed in new wedding finery. Satya's wedding lehnga had grown too short many years ago, and she ordered this one herself.

'In celebration of your marriage,' she said to Sardarji.

His pleased smile still rankles within her.

The lehnga's voluminous crimson skirt is topped with a form-fitting silk choli that leaves Satya's midriff bare. Covering her choli completely, a crimson brocade kameez falls to her wrists and below her knees, restraining her lehnga's gathered fullness. A gold pin fastens a chunni of crimson georgette at the centre parting of her henna-dark hair.

Roop wears Sardar Kushal Singh and Toshi's wedding gift, a more expensive, more ornate red lehnga, to replace the one Bachan Singh bought from the weaver-tailor Fazl Karim. She wears her mama's gold chain and hand ornaments, her mama's ruby tikka on her forehead and the first gifts Sardarji gave her – the kantha necklace, the ruby earrings. On her ankles, Satya's gold panjebs, on her fingers and toes, Satya's rings.

Sardarji is waiting for them, four horses jingling in harness before him in the victoria. Satya climbs in first, Roop second. She wants Roop to sit before them and stare at Sardarji and herself all the way. But Sardarji's reputation must be considered and Satya and Roop must sit together, side by side, as if this dowryless village woman were her equal.

Sardarji is eating almonds Atma Singh has soaked in milk to loosen their skins. He holds out his hand to Satya, offering them. Her fingers close about one, just brushing his. She rubs it between her palms and it splits cleanly. She places one half in her mouth, crushes it.

It's bitter!

Satya leans forward, pits her mouth against Vayu's cool breeze, spits it away, *thoo!*

She says, 'Every almond on the tree that came from is bitter too, yet its owner knowingly added it to almonds from superior trees in the hope no one would taste the difference.'

But Sardarji is raising his walking stick in greeting to the men in the bazaar who stand almost in the gutter as the victoria takes up the street.

'Milavat,' says Satya, to the safa-cloth trailing down Sardarji's back.

Adulteration.

Of the high-up with the low.

What good can come of this?

Roop's face is hidden by her chunni. Past the traffic constable, Sardarji crosses his hands over the head of his walking stick and they rock in the well-sprung sateen seats down The Mall Road to the Empress of India Photo Studio.

The photographer is an obsequious man, because his customers love obsequiousness. He arranges Roop and Satya in the lap of a giant red butterfly, his most intricately carved and gilded settee. He moves left of the camera on its tripod and tells Roop to face him. And she, still veiled, moves her knees till they point in the direction of his voice. He walks a step to the right of the camera and tells Satya to move as well.

Their knees touch.

Then he asks with folded hands and bowed head that Sardarji take his place behind the settee.

When the photographer ducks under his black cloth like a Nepali dragon dancer, Sardarji's hand moves to Roop's shoulder.

He flicks a finger; she raises her chunni.

Then a light burst that freezes them to paper for the silver frame on Sardarji's desk. No picture will be replaced by this one, for no camera ever recorded Sardarji's wedding to Satya. Can Satya prove she was married to him before Roop? Surely there are a few people alive today who remember her wedding, but there are no photographs, no papers she can use to bring her wedding to Sardarji's mind, if he should choose to forget it.

But what can a photo say? Satya will not need this photo to remember what it will not tell, the how-they-got-there, one, two, just like that in the victoria, or the bitter-almond taste that remains on her tongue and will seep into all the coming years.

Before she lowers her chunni again, Satya sees Roop's eyes dart to him.

She watches the coy lift of Roop's mouth.

In answer, a twirl of his mustachio.

How to bear this?

She lowers her eyes to hide tears, lowers them to the second half of the almond she still holds in the tan leaf-shape of her strong hand.

That hand clenches around it.

A dozen thin twenty-four-carat bangles and a gold Omega watch Sardarji bought her to replace the ornaments he gave to Roop shine up at her, bribe for her acquiescence, mark of his continued generosity.

11. Rawalpindi, November, 1937

Sardarji's household is moving to southeast Punjab in procession to take up residence at the Irrigation Department's
canal colony bungalow in Khanewal. Sardarji visited there
before his promotion when he was just a canal engineer, but
now he goes after building a few dams, planning a few canal
systems, as Executive Engineer. The royal-blue Austin
Princess leads, with Manager Abdul Aziz and Sardarji's steno
in the front seat with the driver, and Dehna Singh, Sardarji's
valet, beside him. Then Roop with Satya – seething beneath
her veil – in the back seat of the DeSoto with Narain Singh.

Roop's face is unveiled as it was before her marriage in Pari
Darvaza, since Sardarji has not asked her to cover it again since
the day in the photographer's studio. Almond eyes strain wide
to take in everything from coloured-paper kite shops to fruit
stalls, fishmongers and butcher shops as they bump and
meander through the main arteries of the bazaar that embraces
Sardarji's haveli.

She has been married only two weeks and already there are

too many things to remember. Sardarji was very busy preparing for his new posting, but Roop was not forgotten; he ordered Mani Mai to see that Atma Singh gave her lessons.

Atma Singh has trained many a junior rani for his former master, the Maharaj of Nabha. When the British dethroned the maharaja to seize his kingdom, they allowed him only a few servants in exile and so, Atma Singh explained, it was no reflection on his loyalty – that was never ever in question – when he and his son, now driver Narain Singh, came to Sardarji. He would, Roop thought, have been gentle, patient and respectful even if Mani Mai had not been watching like a baleful hawk from her squat on the floor. Careful not to touch her, Atma Singh also called her Choti-Sardarni as he demonstrated the angle of incline by which her head should indicate to a bearer that he must remove her plate. He moved hollow-chested at her elbow, with the silver tray held to her left to serve, removed from her right. Then he held a silver fork and demonstrated how it must stab the roundness of peas, accurately, elegantly.

'Fork in left, knife in right.' The English, she learned, eat with their unclean hand. 'Close your mouth, Choti-Sardarniji. Sit straight. Cover your head.'

Mani Mai also gave Roop many things to remember. 'No bindi on your forehead; Sardarji says that's a Hindu custom. No vermilion powder in the parting of your hair – he doesn't like it. No mangal-sutra pendant will be given to you to be worn about your neck; Sardarji says that is a Hindu custom, too. No nose rings, those are for Hindus, or Muslims like me.' And she taught Roop to brush her teeth with toothpaste and a brush in place of neem, because Sardarji prefers women's gums pale.

When Roop told her, 'I do not know how to cook,' and hastened to add, 'but I will be glad to learn if Sardarji really wants me to,' a great cackle burst from Mani Mai.

'Don't worry. Cooking is not what women like you are for.'

Satya shifts in her seat. She would order Roop to stop her humming if they were completely alone, but Roop hums a shabad and it would look impious to stop her. She holds a handkerchief scented with night queen uttar to her nose to keep Roop's smell away and clenches her other hand in her lap.

She cannot feel as joyful as Sardarji about this posting or his new rank. And she told him so when it was announced in his department, just before this secret marriage, and Sardarji came home shouting, 'Satya! Satya! I have been promoted!' all the way up the stairs to her sitting room.

After hearing his news, Satya had said quietly, 'This posting and your new position are another bone the British can throw before Mahatma Gandhi and Nehru, hoping to appease the non-cooperators and all the self-rule agitators, justify the blood spilled and pain endured by protesters.'

'Are you really suggesting I do not merit this?' he growled.

'I say only that you may be excellent at engineering, but you may not be worthy of the freedom fighters' sacrifices.'

As she saw joy fade from his face, Satya cursed her own tongue that would not be still, saw him turn away.

His secret marriage to Roop was not long thereafter.

Behind the DeSoto are two Bedford lorries full of cooking utensils and supplies, bedding and bicycles. An Irrigation Department fleet of cycle-messengers will follow after they have sacrificed and distributed goat meat for their Sadqa. Atma Singh and some of the Hindu servants will take the train, third class.

Now they hum past the cricket ground on the smooth road to 'Pindi cantonment. Instead of centre drains in the streets there are now ditches on each side. Here the bougainvillaea-clad compound walls of the Viceroy Commissioned Officers keep their distance from the thoroughfare and the metalled double carriageway of The Mall becomes the Grand Trunk Road.

Now the Grand Trunk Road, carrier of every conquering invader's horde into the heart of India, punches straight and definite out of the heart of 'Pindi, carrying Satya fermenting agony to anger under her veil and Roop fizzing like soda water for Sardarji's evening whisky.

And so they sit, bottled together in the chocolate-brown DeSoto.

So fast does Vayu carry word, mouth to mouth through Punjab, that by the time Sardarji's cavalcade arrives in Khanewal on the banks of the silty, swaggering Ravi, every canal colony resident knows of Sardarji's secret marriage to his unveiled beauty.

The Irrigation Department's canal bungalow and its guest houses sprawl on an unnecessary hill in the treeless dust of the Punjab plain. The main bungalow is newly whitewashed and waiting, in a walled compound broken only by a wood-slat gate, a gate half open, half closed, rusting at the hinges. Eight cylindrical white columns support seven palladian arches and the well-pruned aspirations of money vines. Flagstone verandas gird the bungalow, deep and wide, to hold Sardarji and Cunningham on a platform above their supplicants; four steps where light lies down for them to walk on as they ascend. White-painted wicker chairs with beige chintz cushions huddle about a wicker table, backs to the sunlight pouring through the veranda arches. A great expanse of watered green edged with flower beds spreads about the bungalow like a bordered lehnga. Mulberry and papaya trees drop their fruit before the bungalow and long-fingered date palms encircle it to sweep the clouds from the sky.

And Sardarji, Cunningham often reminds him, is the first Sikh, indeed the first Indian, to occupy it.

The clay, brick and lean-to home-shops at the base of the hill radiate from the canal colony bungalow and its surrounding guest houses in a Union Jack plan. The colony exists to serve the Irrigation Department, and every man, woman and child in it is working to ensure that the countryside stays green, so more water octroi fees can be collected by the British.

Curiosity, as much as the need to be seen saluting the Executive Engineer, brings every labourer, trolley-man and surveyor to add his salaam to the welcome committee crowded in the arc of the pebble-strewn driveway as the Austin Princess leads the DeSoto to a stop before the bungalow. What's done is done, and Sardarji's marriage is like the steep grade of a gorge that cuts past all the layers of soil and reaches for bedrock, proving that an Indian who climbs so high is still a brother.

Now Satya alights, her chunni not merely covering her head as Roop's does, but pulled past her face to her shoulders, virtuous hauteur displacing the hoped-for spectacle of her suffering. Her veil draws attention to Roop's exposed Pothwari skin as she emerges next from the car.

An appreciative murmur rises till Sardarji's eyebrows draw together.

It stops. Mid-murmur.

All eyes are now lowered to the level of Roop's hennaed feet. Her gold-embroidered jutis crunch the pebbled driveway as Sardarji leads her to her room in the sprawling bungalow and consigns her to the care of Mani Mai. Roop senses Satya has gone in a different direction. She does not notice how far they have to walk to her room or how small it is, barely larger than the storeroom in which she spent her wedding night. Or how it juts from the back of the house like an afterthought.

But here is something in the room that Roop has not seen before; an electric table fan on a ledge before one window. She stands in the way of its coolness, letting it lift her kameez away from her hot skin. Her eyes try to follow just one blade of its three as the fan turns, but the one blurs as it joins the dance of its mates, becoming indistinguishable.

Delight.

She slides the shutters up and down. Where the veranda passes Roop's room, a planter's chair reaches long broad arms past the glass-faced oval of a carved shisham-wood table to a small pliable wicker chair.

Across the green, cactus marks the border where snap-dragons and gladioli surround purple-hearted lemon pansies in their beds against the whitewashed compound wall. A round-capped mali squat-walks slowly, weeding patiently.

Roop's bed is large and hard, not as giving as a rope-manji or soft as the fourposter bed. On the tip-mirror dressing table lies a half-sphere of glass. A paperweight, Mani Mai explains. It is there just to hold down trifling things that could take flight on a single gust from the table fan. Its smooth cool hardness enlarges the henna patterns that swirl on her palms.

She holds it to the light, compares the delicate lemon of the flowers waving without to the pansy immured in the glass; not so different, but this one has been set apart from all the rest, placed where its beauty can be admired.

That evening a liveried bearer sounds the gong in the dining room and Roop finds Sardarji at the head of the polished expanse of Kashmiri walnut, Satya at its foot. She takes a chair midway down the length of the dining table and listens as closely as she can, as Sardarji and Satya talk of friends they know and places they have visited together.

Dark brown Rawalpindi cholas bring Roop's tongue the only familiar taste in the meal and remind her of Kusum stirring a rocking wide-mouthed pot on a clay stove so patiently, hours and hours. She misses Gujri's sweet peththas, yearns to sit on a manji and lean against Revati Bhua's comfortable largeness.

She remembers to eat with her mouth closed, and Satya smiles encouragement as Roop douses the lace tablemat with most of the water from her finger bowl.

Khanewal, February 1938

Three moon-months past their arrival at Khanewal, the rhythm of Roop's menses has broken. With clean strips torn from old sheets, she waits for her monthly pain and finds herself freed of it.

Sardarji stands on the bungalow veranda like a raja holding court, every morning. Here, over steaming tea, he takes chota hazri from a bearer's tray, the small offering before his main breakfast. Crunching toast blackened with Marmite, he stands in the foreground of the shushing flow sound of the canal, clad in a kurta-pyjama and a pashmina-wool shawl, as farmers bring him water disputes and supplications, ask him for advice. Manager Abdul Aziz brings him telegrams reporting water levels, remodellings and masonry repairs of falls and junctions. Before he calls for Dehna Singh to help him dress for the day in European suit and tie, his steno is at his elbow to take letters.

Today, Mani Mai brings him word.

Roop is with child, or as Sardarji conveys it to Manager Abdul Aziz, bringing his hands together, raising them high, with a nod of his turban to the infinite, 'in a family way.'

Dictating, he speaks slowly, carefully, enjoying the sound of his voice.

12. Khanewal, June, 1938

Satya stands on the veranda, fanning herself with a hand-pukkhi. A bearer bends over the glass-topped table behind her, serves the pinni sweets Satya made with her own hands for Sardarji's afternoon tea – sweet-sweet, soft honey-gold as a hill-woman's skin. And in case any Europeans happen to drop in, Satya is prepared; the bearer will offer them pistachio biscuits ordered all the way from Faletti's Hotel in Lahore.

The white cakey squares remind her of the Afghan who trudged up to the canal colony bungalow yesterday with eyes darting to the western horizon as if his beloved Suleiman Mountains might at any moment come into view. His red beard was dusty, his Peshawari sandals were falling to pieces on his feet, the cloth bag slung from his shoulder was empty. He said, in Urdu spattered with Pashto, that he'd spent his last four annas on food that had given him a great stomach-ache and made him froth at the mouth – Mani Mai took the white cake and the remains of its wrapping to Sardarji so it could be read.

'Sunlight soap,' Sardarji said, throwing back his turban and releasing his great belly laugh. 'Give him lots of water and some food.'

But the Afghan would take nothing as charity. So Satya ordered Mani Mai to serve him kava tea, daal and roti outside the kitchen on the servants' veranda, in exchange for the jezail he must have smuggled, bullets and all, past the British India border checkpoint at Jamrud.

Now Satya brings the gun to the veranda from her room to test it, to learn its curves and feel its weight against her silk-clad shoulder. She runs her fingers over its engraved stock, caresses the curve of its black barrel.

She has watched Roop turning ripe and full. Roop moves without haste, with a full-bottomed deliberateness, and when she stops, she is a top slowing and bobbing to rest. She holds her stomach before her with a waiting smile as if a baby's temporary residence within her were a licence to enforce her will on any relative within miles. Before now she kept her gaze lowered before Satya and Sardarji, but in these days of waiting, when her craving for the tart taste of mulberry sends Sardarji shouting for a servant to climb the tree shadowing the main drawing room, she even goes without her chunni occasionally, and her body seems unapologetically on fire. Her surma-rimmed eyes have attached themselves to Sardarji. Her tongue seems to have grown too big for her mouth; she has developed a childish lisp, and with it, she tests her power over them all.

At Sardarji's orders, the canal colony's Indian doctor-ji comes every Sunday. Ingratiating, sweaty either from concern or from the exertion of cycling up the hill to the canal colony bungalow, he disappears into Roop's room with his worn brown satchel and the ten brown bottles he rotates as medicine. He is in her room for up to an hour at a time.

Teaching her ujjai-breathing to help deliver a boy, he says. *Huh!*

Satya watches carefully. Mani Mai is always present as chaperone, but Satya hopes Roop will make just one mistake.

It is amazing; Roop has not noticed one ratti of Satya's pain or her anger. Roop doesn't compete with Satya, Roop doesn't even know she is hurting her. Most days, Roop doesn't even think of her.

Roop must be made to think of her. Satya will *make* Roop think of her.

She will make Sardarji think of her. How dare he slight her when she is not a nobody like Roop, but comes from a family famous for its bravery?

Sardarji is unconscious of being unkind; he is such a busy man.

The bearer straightens, surveys the table, stands back. Satya sits in one of the chintz-covered chairs with the jezail's weight across her knees.

Sardarji and Roop emerge from the bungalow. He leads her to a chair, places a cushion at the small of her back and takes his seat opposite Satya. Relaxing, he lifts his turban a little away from his forehead, lets it drop. The bearer brings him the five o'clock telegram – a sudden rise of canal water levels on the upper gauges. Sardarji calls for Manager Abdul Aziz, deliberates, then gives his orders.

Manager Abdul Aziz lopes away.

Coyly, Roop says, 'Hai, please na, I have a craving for the last pinni sweet, if you're not eating it?'

And Sardarji beams like a rising sun, just at her asking.

The soft hair on Satya's arms lifts in revulsion. She pulls her chunni forward. Her index finger pushes soft muslin past her lips, till the chunni is clenched between her teeth.

How can Roop take anything Sardarji gives, even the last pinni sweet on his plate, as evidence of his love? Satya cannot receive that way and feel gratitude; she wants food made for her alone, a shared bed, not a corner Sardarji isn't using. And they are not his pinni sweets to give. Satya made them today, made them herself, without Atma Singh's help; they are grooved with the imprint of her own hands. Why does he claim them without making them himself? What gives him the right to betray the work of her body into Roop's freshly hennaed hands?

It is clear, Satya will have to show Roop an example. Examples create fear, fear keeps control. That's how Sardarji's mother kept Satya during all the years he was in England.

Distance contracts between another time and this, memory bringing before her all the actions she repeats in this life – oh,

Satya never learns, never improves her karma. Sardarji's mother was the one who noticed first just how bad Satya is, made Satya watch her own thoughts twisting, told Satya where all this loving and wanting would lead her.

To this, to this.

Weakened first by influenza, that sour old thing cursed Satya every day, every day that Satya washed her mouldering body, even as she knew the plague could swell Satya's throat and kill her too. Black death, they called it – servants ran from its name. Satya could not run – she did not come from a family of cowards and she told herself she had overcome plague once before, in a previous life. The Chaudhary, Sardarji's father, moved to his elder son's side of the house immediately, leaving Satya alone, sixteen years old, alone to clean her mother-in-law's vomit, her chi-chi, pi-pi, lift her swollen limbs, cook and feed her spoonfuls of soggy rice-lentil khichri.

Watch her shrivel up.

Die.

Who else was there to do it? Toshi – that *churail!* – had small sons then, and her own mother-in-law to look after. Servants should never see a high-up family member without dignity, never. No, there was only Satya, sixteen years old, with feet wanting to run home to Bebeji and fingers yearning to caress a dilruba's strings, lose herself in its music. Only the shadow people to listen to the melancholy ghazals rising from her young throat, only the shadow people to watch her wipe her own tears, take her in their larger memories, frighten her with their stories of other girls who knew worse, much worse than she.

Did Sardarji know this?

Perhaps.

On his return from England he cried so much for his mother, but never for Satya's hands, turned hard, turned capable in his absence. He did not ask who tended her or who was there to lift her head and give her water. He did not ask and so he did not know. He did not wish to see, so he did not see, even from the corner of his eye, how the muscles of her back and arms had turned strong, solid.

All he saw were debts that were written on paper.

Why should Roop have things so easy? Roop should be cowed and careful as a servant who knows one misstep can lose a whole family's livelihood.

But not too much.

Satya still needs Roop for what Roop's body can do.

She lifts the jezail to show him, tells him about the Afghan, so far from home, wandering, hungry, but unable to receive another's charity without suspicion. 'Very interesting,' he says. 'Why did you want the weapon, my dear?'

My dear.

She wants to tear at him. *No no no, not him, surely not her husband, surely she didn't want to tear at his face, make him hurt the way he was hurting her, no, no. Never think these thoughts, wipe them out, no no no.*

'I thought I'd try some target practice,' she says instead.

'Achcha?' He takes the gun, raises it to his shoulder, sighting along the narrow barrel.

Gives it back to her, indulgent, genial.

She raises the gun, cocks it, points it at a papaya tree.

Sardarji, his cup halfway to his lips says, 'Satya, not a tree.'

Fire cracks from the jezail.

Missed.

Satya loads again, cocks it, points.

'Satya!'

Satya shoots. *Tha!* The sound echoes again.

Missed again.

Doors slam, servants run, shouting, 'Kya hua? Kya hua?'

Satya loads again, cocks it, points, taking her time.

Shoots. *Tha!*

A papaya opens like two cupped hands, delivering its black seeds. They ooze from pale gold flesh.

Roop blanches, a nervous giggle escapes her.

Sardarji puts his cup down with a clatter. 'Satya!' His voice is sharp, shocked. 'Didn't I say "not a tree"? How could you? What did it do to you?'

'Nothing,' she says. *Nothing but bear fruit.*

Roop says, 'I don't feel well.'

'Oh, yes, go to bed, bhain,' Satya says, sisterly and

solicitous. She can go back now, go back to being piteous and wronged and long-suffering, now she can stand it a while longer, tell herself again that she desires only Sardarji's happiness, only his welfare.

Roop goes to bed early, like a child.

Sardarji goes past Satya's room to Roop's that night and probably whispers, 'Never mind, Roop, you look after our son.'

13. Khanewal, July 1938

At sunset, as farmers' sons prod their cows and bullocks homewards, Roop, in a new bright green cotton kameez and baggy purple salwar walks with Sardarji on the dirt road by the weedy canal. Sardarji walks deliberately as usual, stopping at intervals for Roop – distended, heavy, uncomfortable – to catch up. His navy blue turban matches his tie. The victoria driver, uniformed in Sardarji's Sikh colours of gold and royal blue, clicks to the team of four matched greys and stays a discreet distance behind.

Sardarji inspects the canal and the fields as he walks, so he can decide if he wishes to stop its flowing soon.

'The canals are elegant, Roop. Well then, beautiful. Come *on*, then, come along. . . Beautiful because they fulfil their function well,' he explains. He adds under his breath, in English, 'I try to teach Mr Farquharson this, but there is so little in India that he judges beautiful.'

A few yards away, a new canal trench widens, gouged by pickaxes that arc and fall an arm's length from lean dark backs agleam with sweat. Village women with metal bowls of earth balanced on their heads walk barefoot up the steep grade from the trench.

Past the clink and thud of pickaxes, Sardarji says, 'Satya has been terribly upset again.'

Roop steals a glance at him, uncertain.

What does he expect me to say?

Canal colonist farmers – Hindus, Sikhs and Muslims alike – stop to fold their hands before Sardarji; their land is nothing without canal-brought fingers of cool water that soothe the dry furrows in their fields. He raises his walking stick in acknowledgment.

'I thought she would be upset for a while, but that she might soon grow to love you. Especially when she saw you were in a family way. But,' he rotates a large hand about his wrist in puzzlement, 'even now she feels neglected.'

They walk further.

Mustard leaves wave, their green reminding her of Gujri's steaming spinach saag served with makki rotis. Fat green ring-necked parrots shift their weight from foot to foot on telegraph lines, like Revati Bhua. A warm breeze threatens to separate Roop's chunni from her hair.

She wonders what Kusum is dimpling at right now, whether Jeevan's older son is learning to play kabaddi like his father, whether his younger son still sucks his thumb, and whether Papaji misses Roop. Papaji's last letter said only that Jyotshi Sundar Chand says a war is coming the like of which the British have never seen.

Jeevan has written to her only once, to send her his usual eleven rupees for the rakhri of woven gold thread she had made and sent to him. Did he wear it around his wrist and did it remind him of his promise to protect her? But he is busy now, training sepoys in Sialkot, a garrison town in southern Punjab. He says being in the army is teaching him there are so many kinds of Indians, not just Hindus, Sikhs and Muslims, but people whose languages are all their own, unmixed by any invasions. Some areas of India, he writes, have never been called colony, and are still ruled by rajas. And as he moves from posting to posting and teaches them to fight, he says he has learned it is not only, as the English believe, Sikhs, Gurkhas and Marathas who can fight, but all men whose bodies remember humiliation and anger from this and past lives.

'Yesterday,' Sardarji is saying, 'I tried to explain to Satya for a long time. She was weeping, she was weeping.'

Roop's brow knits with worry.

'She says she loves you, you know. She says it was your kismat to come to this home.' Sardarji is nodding as if urging, yes, believe this.

So Roop smiles at him.

'She said she wishes you had come to her as a daughter. Not as her saukan, her co-wife.'

Why does he tell me this? Sardarji is a man who speaks when he has a reason.

By now Roop knows she must do as others do, listen carefully for Sardarji's every wish.

'Women need babies,' he says, discovery resonating in his tone. 'They grow sick and quarrelsome without children to look after. They become shrill and loud. They threaten terrible things. They might even curse. They become quite truly unbearable.'

He turns on the path, blocking Roop. The victoria driver pulls back on the reins. 'Roop, I must satisfy her.'

'Satisfy her?' says Roop. A bright green parrot cocks its head on the telegraph line.

'Yes, satisfy her.'

And now Sardarji is suggesting, in his most problem-solving voice, that she give Satya a baby. This baby that lies within her and pushes at her stomach like a fish in the Ganga.

Give her 'sister' her baby.

But I like babies. I want my own. I know how to look after them – I looked after Jeevan's little boys. I love their soft cheeks, their tiny feet. I love the way they look at their mothers. Who knows, this child I carry may be the atma my mother carried, the little brother who was to ride my hip – perhaps that atma comes now through me.

Roop's throat constricts into silence.

Please, don't ask this.

Can she say no?

Roop waits for him to ask her so she might say it, but he does not ask at all, he assumes she will want what he wants. Sardarji's suggestion is to assist her in learning his wishes, every woman is a Sita to her Ram, and what Ram wants, Sita will enjoy doing.

She opens her mouth to speak, but Sardarji turns back to the path, walks on. For a moment she thinks he has forgotten the subject as he pokes at the masonry of the canal, the silver handle of his walking stick flashing like a kirpan tempered by the sun. But now, turning back to her, he takes her arm and tucks it in his, pats her hand as if they were completely alone. Blood rises in her cheeks, she is conscious of the victoria driver's curious eyes.

'You will feel the joy of sacrifice, the happiness of giving. And don't worry, we will have another child. See how your sister's grey eyes are sad, see how she longs for what you have.' He gestures to her distended stomach. 'Roop, if I give her this son, she will not bother me at all.'

Roop looks away.

A few months ago there was a Roop who might have protested, a Roop who had no fear because she could imagine no harm, no consequences. A few years ago there was a Roop who could have stood before many a man and known herself his better by blood. But that Roop is gone and in her place stands a woman who has climbed beyond her father's kin, and now must hold fast to the gains of fortune.

If she refuses, she can be sent home a failure, a burden to Papaji. Tongues will flap in the village. Papaji's izzat will be dragged in the mud – Abu Ibrahim will tell Papaji, 'What can you expect from sending a girl to school, she becomes quarrelsome, she gives trouble.'

Her submission is all Sardarji requires. She wonders, is that so difficult? What does it cost her? And surely, if she really wants to keep this child, Sardarji who has given her jewels, new clothes, even a new lehnga and a room with an electric fan, surely he will indulge her again. And if it will make Satya happy, poor woman, will it not smooth the way for Roop?

But no, *no* – this child is hers, don't give him to Satya. Take the next one, not this one she has carried and crooned to these many months.

Can she ask him this? Sweat crawls at her temples.

It is a test. Not an end-of-the-year examination test, such as the one Roop gave at Bhai Takht Singh's Sikh Girls' School in Firozepur, but a test all the same. This is a fire test, the kind of test Ram asked Sita to take when he became unsure that Sita was worthy to be his queen.

Roop's test is not like Sita's – Sardarji does not ask for an agnipariksha, a walk through fire. But, unlike Sita, who was a goddess and so pure she could not fail, Roop is only mortal and not even allowed to believe in Ram or Sita because she is no longer a Hindu, but a Sikh. Roop could fail this test because she isn't good-good sweet-sweet as Sita; she isn't generous enough to let Satya have a child.

She steals a glance at Sardarji's set face and trembles almost to falling.

If Sardarji does not come to visit her in the afternoons, who will come to visit her?

Satya has not invited Roop to lie with her in the afternoons since Roop began carrying this child, but, Roop thinks, it could be because Satya has been so busy unpacking the crates and jute sacks, supervising Atma Singh and the other servants in the cookhouse and the mali on the lawns.

This morning Roop watched from her room as Satya stood in the sun on the back lawn, arms akimbo, before two servant boys beating dust from carpets with long bamboo sticks, shouting directions in Urdu. She pointed, gave a sharp command, and the boys took a rust-red silk Kerman carpet, with its cascading tree-of-life, by its cream-fringed corners and heaved a section of it into a long low brass basin. 'Bring water!' Satya shouted. The boys ran to the tap in the cookhouse and each filled a brass bucket of water. They returned, each with an arm extended to balance the water's weight. Then they added Sunlight soap, and stepped in, wading to the ankle in the basin, kneading the carpet clean with their toes, in sections. And Satya stood there, directing when they should stop, wash another section, when they should run and get clean water. She watched with an eagle eye as they moved the carpet to the veranda and their feet scraped water from the fine silk. Then her voice rang out again, directing them to the shade where the bungalow veranda passed Roop's room. The boys staggered under the sodden carpet roll, carrying it to dry beside the planter's chair, the oval glass table and the small wicker chair on the veranda.

Roop saw that Satya noticed her standing, watching from her window, and Satya could have said to Roop as she had in Rawalpindi, a few days after Roop's wedding, 'Come lie with me in the afternoons. . .' but Satya's gaze dropped to Roop's roundness and she turned away. The invitation Roop eagerly awaited did not come.

If no one comes to see Roop in the afternoons – or at any time of the day – surely she will feel alone, abandoned. She remembers that feeling, she knows its terror.

How big a sacrifice can it be?

If she refuses, perhaps Sardarji will allow her to stay with him and if he were very angry she could ask him to please marry yet another wife and just give her pocket money to live.

Papaji's words sound in her ear as if he were standing right beside her – 'Above all, give no trouble.'

'Good girl, I'm glad that's settled. I knew you would be sensible.' Sardarji interrupts her thoughts. He holds his hand out to help her into the victoria.

The driver gathers the reins. '*Tlt, tlt.*'

The four matched grey horses jingle their polished harness and toss their heads in disbelief.

14

I am laughter, I am light, and she runs in pursuit till we reach the tunnel. I am in first, my eyes adjusting quickly to the echoing darkness. I hide from her behind a kneeling camel laden with gunny sacks before the heavy wooden door to my uncle's haveli. I look back and she is silhouetted against the bright disc at the mouth, her face in shadow. A turquoise chunni bordered in woven gold arches above her shoulders and the mouth of the tunnel repeats her shape.

'Roop!' she calls. The camel shifts his weight and rolls an indifferent eye in my direction.

'Chup!' I warn, pressing a finger to my lips. I sink to my haunches.

Coarse grains of black pepper seeping through the gunny sack and the tickle of camel hair assault my nose. And in a moment our hide-and-seek is ended by a sneeze that throws my small body out of hiding.

The camel closes his eyes, unmoved. I wait for her to find me, envelop me in her smell, wait for her arms to hold me.

I look up at the light and she is gone.

'Mama!' I cry.

Shyam Chacha's Gandhi cap leans from his doorway and tells me to stop my wailing.

I step across the drain. My fists pound the door of Papaji's haveli.

'Kholo, na! Open!'

But no one opens the door to me.

'Kholo, Papaji!' I cry again, pounding my fists on the door.

Brass studs shine from the door in the half light. The flowers carved into the weatherbeaten wood are sharp; their petals cut my hands.

Looking up, I see a huge brass padlock through the latch at the top of the door. It is not our old ornamental padlock, the one my Nani used to smite her breast and die.

This one has bloody fingerprints dried into its grey metal surface and it tells me I cannot go home.

15. Khanewal, September 1938

It is a girl.

Despite the whole canal colony's fervent expectations, hopes, blessings and prayers, despite all Mani Mai's prayers to her Allah, her charms and amulets, the womb-world has prepared and sent Roop a girl who took twenty hours to be born, so reluctant was she to take birth again.

Roop sits alone in her room, legs propped apart on cushions, a soft silk quilt over her stretched hip bones and she writes the sad news in a telegram to Papaji.

Her jaws are stiff from biting down on a towel all through the night. Her limbs are heavy and ache all over. She is sore from the ripping and gouging of her flesh down there. Her mouth is dry as if it played nest to a legion of moths.

'Mani Mai!' she calls, when the telegram is written.

Mani Mai comes soon, but not, Roop imagines, as soon as she is called. She will take Roop's letter to the telegraph man's one-room shack at the foot of the hill and he will translate it first into English and then Morse code, so it tip-tips from under his fingers all the way to Pari Darvaza and there it will be translated back to English and then reborn again in Punjabi. Along the way so many things can happen that no one can predict, not even Jyotshi Sundar Chand.

If she had not borne Sardarji's child, she could have gone home to give birth, the way Kusum went home to her parents in Chakwal for each of Jeevan's three boys. But Roop, if she had been lucky, could have been carrying Sardarji's son and so she has been attended by a nurse who came by train all the way from Mayo Hospital in Lahore, the Indian doctor-ji and a red-faced Dr Barlow, who left for Bombay just as soon as the girl was born, being 'ever so anxious to sail home for leave.' But Mani Mai did the most, being there to cut the cord with a sickle and offer it to the care of the soil beneath the pansies, to clean and wash for the new mother and child.

And Bhainji, her sister Satya, came into the room every few hours to warn that Sardarji would expect a perfect son; there must be no damage as Roop worked to separate the child from her body.

Mani Mai takes the telegram, leaves.

Roop is weak but grateful; at least she has done what women are for. There is a baby in the cot that swings from the ceiling beside her, girl though it be.

She switches on the electric fan, watches as one blade joins the spin of its mates, becomes indistinguishable.

Outside, past the veranda, the mali squat-walks the length of the lawn with a scythe. His arm rises above his round cap, then descends, hacking the grass neatly at its base. Again his arm rises, descends. So practised is he, the lawn in his wake is close-cropped, even and smooth as a Tabriz carpet.

Mani Mai returns and sits at the foot of Roop's bed, massaging her aching legs. 'Bari-Sardarni says you have bad kismat. She says you have brought too much of Mangal's influence to this and it will not allow you to make boys.'

Roop's tears come easily. 'No one in my family ever said I have bad kismat. No one. Everyone always said I have good kismat.'

Mani Mai shrugs. 'Who knows how good kismat may have changed to bad? Only Allah.' She leaves Roop to cry alone while she calls to Atma Singh for a cup of tea.

Soon a gong sounds to tell them Atma Singh has placed the tea on the dining-room table.

But when Mani Mai brings her tea, Roop takes one sip and spits it in the saucer, *thoo!*

There is salt in the tea instead of sugar.

'*Hein?*' says Mani Mai. 'Atma Singh would never put salt in tea!' A brown finger dips in the teacup. A drop moves to her mouth.

A pause.

'Roopji, this is Bari-Sardarni.'

Roop tastes salt again as more tears surface, flow down her soft cheeks. Bhainji, her sister Satya, should show concern for her like a mother, but . . .

I deserve this. I made a girl.

A day later as Sardarji and the Superintending Engineer, Mr Timothy Farquharson, newly arrived from Lahore, clink their whisky sodas on the veranda, the postman brings Sardarji a telegram from Papaji: Jyotshi Sundar Chand says it is written in Roop's stars – did he not say it before? – one girl, then not one but *two* boys.

Mani Mai reports Sardarji said merely, 'That is most interesting, most interesting.' She leaves Roop alone again and goes to Satya to tell her, triumph shining in her mynah eyes.

Roop lies back in relief, holding her emptied stomach, looking at the small bundle beside her.

Who is there to teach Roop how to read this baby's little body, to know if it cries for milk or from discomfort or for the sorrows of leaving its former life? Gujri, Revati Bhua, Kusum are all far away in Pari Darvaza. And Roop does not even know the direction of Madani's home from Khanewal. Why hadn't she paid more attention when they cared for Jeevan's sons? She tries to remember how it was possible for Kusum to labour all day cooking Papaji's favourite curries, all the cups of tea Papaji ever asked for, and still take care of Jeevan's boys. Who can tell Roop how to feed this baby, bathe her, hold her? What if Roop drops her, chokes her or rolls over her in her sleep? Who is there to prevent these terrors from happening?

She feels so foolish – no mother to guide her.

What can Roop use from the teaching she received at Bhai Takht Singh's school? The poetry of the Guru Granth Sahib? Cooking? Embroidery?

When Mani Mai returns, Roop says, 'Please, can you get me some pink wool and knitting needles?'

She will purl a pastel shell to hold her daughter: a cardigan with mother-of-pearl buttons, and a crocheted cap to fit her daughter's dark feathery head. Pink, auspicious pink, just watered-down red, iridescent with silent warnings, petal pink, trusting, crushable pink.

Memory needs its little props, insertions from the past, the silent evidence of other times to bring old selves crowding to the fore, casting their shadows across the floor of the waking mind. As Mani Mai takes the telegram to Roop, Sardarji, sitting on the veranda, whisky soda in hand, watches his department superior, the Indian-born English man Mr Timothy Farquharson, stroking his old school tie, portable reminder of his public school days in England. Britishers would exude unconcealed disdain and call him 'country-born,' but the stripes on that tie redeem him to a place about on par with Sardarji, Sardarji with his Balliol degree in engineering but lower birth as an Indian.

Mr Farquharson is a tall but narrow man who wears a narrow tie, narrow khaki pants and a solar topee that fits his narrow head. He owes his fitness to tennis at the English-only clubs and his bachelorhood to the absence of a wife too faint of heart to make more than one visit to India several years ago (being far too sensitive to endure the sight of Indians' poverty, but not sensitive enough to forgo an iota of the comfort made possible by Mr Farquharson's remittances).

Mr Farquharson's features are sharp, Sardarji will allow, quite aquiline. But he has narrow feet, narrow hands and a face elongated past handsomeness. He is short-sighted but entirely too vain to wear spectacles, and so his eyes are always narrowed to a look of permanent suspicion. A little stooped, he walks beneath the weight of unacknowledged assumptions.

He would prefer, Sardarji is amused to find, that Sardarji were a little more reassuringly different from himself, but Sardarji presses his advantage in this regard.

His hip flask is usually empty of cognac by noon. Not that Sardarji is, like Mr Jinnah or Mahatma Gandhi, religiously or morally opposed to alcohol. Far from it – indeed, when negotiating, he is hesitant to trust a man who doesn't drink. But Farquharson downs fiery joyless gulps as if he requires VSOP to reignite enthusiasm for each day.

Today he seems less sozzled than usual, so Sardarji is anxious to ask him.

Mr Farquharson, Cunningham assures him, treasures his English public school years, all five of them, before his return to India and Bishop Cotton's School in Simla. It was at the English public school, after all, that he learned to elocute in the plummy tones of Empire instead of the haw-haw imitation of the India-born crowd. Then, perhaps because his father died, Mr Farquharson had made do with Roorkee College of Engineering – Cunningham says it is simply not done to remind Mr Farquharson he'd attended an Indian college of engineering, because everyone, especially Mr Farquharson, knows it isn't quite the same thing as Balliol. And it is also, Cunningham says, simply not done to remind Mr Farquharson that Sardarji had trained him when Mr Farquharson was just a beginning canal engineer, and sozzled only after sundown.

'Twenty years ago,' says Mr Farquharson, 'these plains were but sand dunes and salt. One day all those Indians in Lahore now shouting "*Inquilab zindabad!*" – I can't even pronounce it. "Long live protest" – and asking for their bloody independence before they are ready for it, will look back and thank us, Sardarji.' He opens the clasp of a long, slim pocket diary and writes quickly, a slanted script. The diary is preparation for a memoir that will settle his score with India and tell how fitting should be the emotion of gratitude, even if Indians like Sardarji cannot quite bring themselves to feel it.

'See what the Dutch have done in the Dutch East Indies. I draw your attention to the cruelty of the Frenchman, the Belgian in the Congo. But the English man – always the gentleman! It's our undoing. Education, uplift, banning of that awful habit women have here – what's it called? Self-immolation on their husband's funeral pyres. Yes, suttee – the railroads, the telegraph, these canals.' Mr Farquharson's arm sweeps the horizon. 'And what do we get? "*Inquilab zindabad!*" Positively *ridiculous*. Protest for protest's sake. Troublemakers all, enjoying the trouble they create.'

Sardarji bites into a cucumber sandwich. There is no reason why Mr Farquharson cannot get his tongue around Indian words, having lived in India most of his life, but Mr Farquharson lives for the preservation of his incomprehension.

'Our very presence in the desolation of their lives should give them pause.'

He has heard this from Mr Farquharson before: there are so many other places he could have chosen to be – Nigeria, Kenya, South Africa, the British West Indies, Canada. But no, he'd said in his application to the Foreign Office he was 'particularly interested in a post in His Majesty's Empire in India.'

And England has appreciated Mr Farquharson. It has, and one must give England credit. You don't rise to Superintending Engineer by magic. No, you rise in a progressive manner, over the heads of Indians like Sardarji, even if they are older and educated in England.

Merit speaks for itself, yes. Speaks for itself.

'All these years in India, Sardarji, they are wearing me out,' says Mr Farquharson. 'I admit it at last,' he says. 'It will take more than civil engineering to civilize these people.' Sardarji listens, nods – it is all he is expected to do. Mr Farquharson will go back, eventually. They all do, once they've made their fortunes. He can see him now: retired, with the trophies of his travels and perhaps a faithful bearer or two, comfortably ensconced in a Tudor in Knightsbridge. Perhaps Mr Farquharson will be a little different from the rest, being India-born and having worked with Indians like Sardarji. Perhaps he will stay on in Lahore after retirement, build a high-walled home close to the Gymkhana Club, have as many prostitutes as the Hira Mandi area can supply. Perhaps Mr Farquharson will take up watercolours or etching to illustrate his memoirs, waiting for the day he is ready to be buried beside his parents. In that cemetery in Simla, where Britishers lay claim to India even in death, one plot at a time.

There are a number of years to wait for that to happen, however: twenty years. Whereas Sardarji at forty-three has only twelve to go before retirement, only twelve years left in which to leave his mark on India, bring her into the future. Twelve years – ergo, Sardarji is highly likely to stay at the level of Executive Engineer – it's as high as he can go, as Mr Farquharson has no reason to oblige him by stepping aside. From there to Chief Engineer of Punjab . . .

'Not bloody likely,' says Cunningham.

'A few years ago it wasn't bloody likely I'd make it this far, Cunningham,' Sardarji reminds him. He would not have made it this far, but for a karmic coincidence of circumstances: when the Indian Service of Engineers, decimated by losses at the Somme and Ypres, began accepting qualified Indians, Sardarji was there, Oxford-stamped new diploma in hand. And Sardarji was back in British India, a junior engineer, when reforms were declared after the massacre at Jallianwala Bagh. He presented his qualifications, was accepted.

'But, naturally,' Cunningham said.

Now Sardarji's inner clock is ticking again; it's time to move higher.

Sardarji has, he thinks, found a place in the Irrigation Department where he can move higher than Mr Farquharson, and Mr Farquharson doesn't have to step aside for him. It is an excellent idea, and Sardarji's spirits are high – he can see no reason for denial.

If Sardarji were Consulting Engineer to the Central Design Division, he might adjust British thinking, modify British models to fit the unique requirements of India, explain to his British superiors that designs that work in England do not always work in India; that because of India's heat, metal buckles faster here than in England; that the gears in the silt ejectors on canals can grind themselves to hot pulp in half the time here than in wet, chilly England; explain that earth must be carried fistful by fistful here to give work to many. He would make them understand that digging in Punjab often excavates fossil cities like Moenjodaro and Harappa, lost rivers, five-thousand-year-old artifacts, the graves and pyres of djinns – superstitions, perhaps, but superstitions he can overcome for them.

Diplomatically, by explaining to Indians.

At the Central Design Division, Sardarji could renew his acquaintance with British plans for the largest earthen dam in the world, Bhakra Dam, a dam to irrigate and power all of Northern India, prevent famines for all time, bring light to every village, every city. Bhakra, to be built across the Sutlej in a narrow gorge a Britisher noted was 'made by God for storage,' has been on the drafting table since Sardarji returned from England, and he has checked its progress year by year by prodding Mr Farquharson and others frequently on the subject. In his mind, he has already constructed Bhakra's coffer dams, building it so much higher than the original plan of 390 feet, impounding far more than its projected two-and-a-half-million acre-feet of water, planning each link in its network of canals to be cut into the Punjab plains far east of Khanewal.

Bhakra.

But first he must be assigned to the Central Design Division where he can study the plans for Bhakra, correct them, use his special knowledge of old and new to bridge the distance between India and England faster. Advocate the latest designs, argue strongly against implementation in India of British engineers' discarded debris. Prevent India from repeating English mistakes, take advantage of English history.

'Cunningham,' he says, 'he who evaluates alternative designs, selects and sets the standards makes a difference for all time, can influence centuries.'

'You might as well have a shot at it, then,' says Cunningham.

Sardarji clears his throat, turns to Mr Farquharson and says, 'As you are here, there is something I would like to discuss, something I have not mentioned earlier, because I did not wish to impose. My next posting is due in a year and I wished to ask you to put in a good word for a transfer to the Central Design Division. I would like to be part of the setting of standards for the Irrigation Department.'

Mr Farquharson narrows his eyes further and looks down

the lawn to the wood-slat gate of the bungalow. Half open, half closed, rusting at the hinges.

'I don't think it would be advisable, my dear chap. Not at this time. There's just too much unrest. If you ask me, Mr Gandhi should stick to religion and stay out of politics.'

Sardarji leans forward, places his elbows on his knees, listening carefully. He has a great distaste for *asking* and it is remarkably unfortunate that he had to ask Mr Farquharson for what should be his by merit, by right, by seniority – by caste. And he wonders, what can Mr Gandhi and politics have to do with his posting?

'In fact, I am of the opinion that you should stay an extra term right here,' Mr Farquharson pronounces.

Sardarji straightens. 'Good lord, sir, you can't possibly mean that!' Falcon eyes sweep the flatness of the plains. Why, his entire education would be wasted in this backwater. This promotion is a stepping stone to better things, and he is the first Indian to achieve it, but to be posted here for two terms! The planning centres for modernization in irrigation engineering are Lahore or Delhi – any place but here.

It dawns on Sardarji: Mr Farquharson's purpose in posting him to Khanewal may be precisely to keep Sardarji away from the centre.

But no, why would Mr Farquharson do that to a qualified man?

A waste, surely.

'Oh, I'm quite serious, dear boy, quite serious. As a practical matter,' says Mr Farquharson, in an explaining voice. 'You must face the fact that Indian engineers are simply incapable of anything but assembly. Little boys playing with Meccano sets purchased for them by the Central Design Division.'

Sardarji struggles with Cunningham, who is holding a muzzle before his lips and saying, 'Be silent, sir, subside!' but who finally lets him say, 'But I hope you will at least look into it.'

'We shall see,' Mr Farquharson says, his face impassive.

Exactly who is 'we'?

The bland taste of cucumber is in Sardarji's mouth. He swallows hard. Feels it, slimy and green, going down.

It is from such humiliations that larger resistance comes. Far from being engaged with Mr Farquharson in a joint endeavour to bring the boons of engineering to India, Sardarji knows now that Mr Farquharson finds him no different from any other Indian, no better, no worse.

Was Satya right in saying this prime posting and Sardarji's new rank are but a sop, a happy statistic to be dangled before Mahatma Gandhi's non-cooperation movement, before self-rule agitators and the blood and pain of protesters?

'Now, let's not get carried away,' says Cunningham. 'Fair play and all that.'

Sardarji can see he will simply need to train this Englishman further.

A great fatigue comes over him, an old fatigue he knows too well.

Why do I have to educate one European at a time? Why does it fall to me?

Mr Farquharson, he tells Cunningham, is no gentleman.

'I wouldn't say that, if I were you,' says Cunningham. 'It's simply not done.'

When Roop is no longer unclean, eight days after the girl's birth, Sardarji comes to see her. He stops at the foot of her bed in the afternoon, jolting her awake. She rises immediately, reaches into the cot swinging beside her to lift the little one, put the girl-baby in his arms – can he refuse her? Eyes still closed and head still peaked and soft from her voyage through Roop's life canal. Little ball of life made from sperm and woman's pain. How can any man not be moved to treasure this new life? Was it this baby who chose her girlhood or has Roop herself been at fault, her body betraying her will, sculpting the form it remembers best, a woman's, forgetting to add the weight of a small toto to the baby's little pelvis, a weight to bear the responsibility of Sardarji's line?

Sardarji takes the baby, an unwanted gift, in the crook of his arm. He looks at Roop, barely glancing at the little girl's face and he reaches in his pocket.

A single silver rupee drops to the bedspread. Roop looks at it, then at him.

'Tell Mani Mai to call the tailor; wear some prettier clothes.' He is brusque, like a gaoler speaking to a prisoner. 'Scientifically,' he says, looking down at the little bundle, 'we can eliminate the hypothesis that my having children is an impossibility.'

Roop doesn't understand his English words. She wants him to stay, hold her, commiserate over the pain she has borne for his sake.

But there is something different between them now. She has passed a fire test, Sita's agnipariksha.

He gives the child back to her with a brief 'We'll try again soon,' and she knows he means to be reassuring.

She smiles, coquettish, but gets no response. She has moved from child woman to woman-with-child. There is no going back.

'Sardar Kushal Singh and Toshi will come and stay to celebrate Diwali – and to see the girl, of course. Meanwhile, I have told Satya to tell Atma Singh we will feed the poor tomorrow.' He turns at the door of her room, says, 'I told Satya, feed the poor as if she were a boy.'

He is so generous, so generous.

For forty days and nights Roop has a daughter.

For forty days and nights Roop lies beside the nameless little white bundle, ravelling and unravelling her to marvel at her perfect hands and feet, nails small as lentil seeds, lashes long and dark against the wheat tones of her skin. This is life she made within her, turning her blood to flesh and then to milk. She touches the little girl's soft arms and knows some day they will grow and hold her grandchildren, touches the pale roses of her nipples and knows some day this child will hold a child to them as Roop has held her to hers. She feels her daughter's toothless gums, suckling, draining the fullness brimming in her, taking, taking, giving back only smiles, yawns, threads of drool and spittle.

'This is my smell,' she tells the baby. 'Remember it. This is the taste of my body. Remember it. This is the touch of my hands, feel it. This is my tongue, suck from it all the words it should have spoken, the words it wants to say.'

Say them for me.

The baby laughs and kicks and sleeps again. How will she learn without Roop? Will Roop be there to tell her that her little sorrows are not tragedy, that life can be lived through and in spite of heartbreak? Can Satya become a mother without the pain of bringing this child to daylight? No, this baby will be motherless, the way Roop was motherless. So she will repeat Roop's life – *can there be no other way?*

'Listen, but do not obey everything,' she tells the baby, and begins to pour into her tiny ears all she might tell her in ten, twenty, fifty years. 'Always speak. Never be silent. Respect your elders, but don't be too generous . . . say what you want.'

Don't be like me.

The baby yawns.

Roop lies awake late into the night, afraid to sleep. Things can be taken from you when you sleep, things from inside, parts others need more than you, why stop at a baby? When she nods off, a scent like wet leaves enters her sleep; the wrapped bundle in the swing-cot beside her needs her. No one has ever needed her before. To this baby, she is neither guest nor burden, but the giver of life, like the canal waters rushing in her ear.

She would swallow her little girl back within her. Or, if she could, she would take her into her womb again. But this baby is no longer hers, not now.

To love this baby I am about to lose is folly. Useless. Stop love now, lest it grow. Stop it now, lest it show in glance or touch. Stop it at the quick.

In the darkness, Roop's fingers clench about Mama's ring. She threads it on a black string about the girl-baby's neck and its three sapphires and two smaller round diamonds wink at her.

'Wear this for me,' she breathes into the sleeping baby's ear. 'It will make you quarrelsome and then my sister will have to send you back to me.'

* * *

The day comes. A fine dust hangs in the air; the canal sound is still. The October sun is high and bright. For once it is not too hot, it is not too cold – it seems there is nothing wrong anywhere in the whole world.

Roop wraps Mama's phulkari-embroidered shawl about her girl-baby so only her little brown nose and jet-black eyes are exposed. She encircles the baby's wrist with another black thread to ward off the evil eye and checks again: Mama's sapphire ring hangs about the baby's neck.

A small quiet room in the canal bungalow has been converted to a prayer room for the duration of Sardarji's posting in Khanewal. The Guru Granth Sahib lies closed upon a solid silver pedestal, and today the holy book is dressed in Sardarji's colours of blue and gold. Marigold and rose garlands cling to the scalloped canopy above the Guru. Sardar Kushal Singh, rose turban tied with a shamla-fan today, takes his seat behind the holy book and reads from it as if he does not hear himself speak, as if his ears are closed to the meaning of the Guru's words.

Then Toshiji takes his place, rolling on her large behind as she pulls her ankles up beneath her. She closes the book, bows her long nose over it in prayer and opens it so the first letter of the baby's name is given by the Guru from the top left-hand corner of a random page.

It is the letter 'pappa,' so Sardarji says, indifferently, 'Pavan.' Little breeze. Because he is Aries, born on the cusp of Vayu and the sign of the Bull, and she, his daughter.

Then he nods at Roop. Sardar Kushal Singh nods his shamla-fan at Roop. Toshi follows their lead. An expectant Satya sits beside Sardarji, confident Roop will meet her need.

So Roop holds her just-named baby girl out to her 'sister' and lays her in those cold proud arms. How is it her breath comes jagged and forced, as if she would breathe for her girl-baby as well? She trembles now as if her atma felt winter gust through the small room. Her breastbone is cracking from a pain ripping to her centre chakra.

Forgive me, little one. I have no way to keep you.

'Give no trouble,' Roop says aloud to Pavan as her fingers leave the baby and she cannot hold back the tears. 'Above all, give no trouble.'

All rise to their feet for the Ardaas to remember other Sikh martyrs, the five beloved ones, the forty martyrs. There were women, the prayer chant reminds, who gave so much more than Roop gives today. One mother, wife of the tenth Guru, Mata Sundari, watched her two sons, Zorawar and Jhujjar, bricked up alive rather than convert to Islam, there were women who saw their men cut to pieces limb from limb by Muslim tyrants, women who saw their sons' skulls removed, men who were tied to wheels and their bodies broken to pieces, men and women who were cut by saws, who were flayed alive by Afghan or Mughal tyrants for their faith, but did not convert.

For their faith. What has this giving to do with my faith? No, don't doubt. Don't think this. Mama always said give to those who need. Satya needs this baby more than I.

The Ardaas comes to an end. 'Vaheguruji da Khalsa. Vaheguruji ki fateh!' And all lower their foreheads to touch the ground before the Guru Granth Sahib.

And Pavan, sensing unfamiliar arms, losing her mother's scent, shrieks and screams for both of them, opening the pink hole of her mouth, wrinkling her face till she looks like Nani doing siapa.

This is our dharma, our duty, little one. Some, like you, learn it early.

Now Roop is alone, cross-legged on the floor of the small prayer room after the others are gone, gazing disbelievingly at her empty lap. She knows now how a mountain must feel as a tree is torn away; she knows how it must feel as the bark is knifed and the sharp blade of a saw rocks the tree from its bearings. In her ear come the creaking and straining, the *dhar-*sound as the tree falls away from its root. This is how numb a mountain must feel when wind and rain lash its exposed surface.

She can hear the family in the dining room, collecting around the polished table. The scent of Satya's celebration – sweet parshaad and fried puris – wafts its way to her while she sits immobile and hollow as that mountain when the tree is hauled away and its stump is all that remains. This must be how it feels.

She does not join them at the table for the midday meal. She goes within to lie in her darkened room and wait Sardarji's further will. There is no need for decision or uncertainty; she has been good as Sita for her lord.

But though she lies waiting, the promised joy of sacrifice does not come.

That evening Sardarji brings her three new pretty-pretty kameezes with salma-sitara embroidery to celebrate the first anniversary of their wedding. A little early, but a celebration, nonetheless.

'I know you like pretty clothes,' he says, holding them up before her.

Roop's breasts are milk-filled and tender, sore, weighted and painful. And at the base of her tummy is a hole that cannot be embroidered away. She has grown a face upon her face, skin that congeals over skin. Sardarji has brought her Yardley's lavender powder to give the finishing touches.

'Don't worry,' he says. 'The next one will be a boy.'

16. Rawalpindi, December 1938

A white shawl of snow lies upon the breast of the Margalla Hills where Pothwari kikar gives way to regal pine. The train steaming into Rawalpindi station stops to unload Europeans from their tinted glass coupés, and then the rest of India, including Satya's new Bengali Muslim maidservant, Jorimon, an orphan, saddle-brown of face, dark limbs lithe under a plainswoman's bordered sari, carrying baby Pavan. Then it puffs and clangs its way slowly through the filigree-walled tunnel, little more than an archway, that serves as the women's platform. There Satya and other high-caste women, veiled to varying degrees, alight away from the curious eyes of unrelated men.

A telegram from Manager Abdul Aziz will have summoned servants to help her. Satya's eyes sweep the crowd.

Men of all faiths mill as usual on the platform, and this morning most are Muslim men on their way to Lahore for another Muslim League political rally – Pathan tribesmen, devout Sunnis, less-orthodox Shias, Ismailis, Ahmadiyas, the degree of their faith in Islam opaque to the eye, their style of dress or headdress a guide only to the regions they call home.

Turbans of Sikh men from different regions, sects, orthodoxy and caste stand out in the crowd: a beaked printed turban of an ordinary Sikh from 'Pindi; a horizontally tied white turban of a Namdhari Sikh; a steel kara glinting on the wrist of a shorn Sikh, a Sahajdhari; an untouchable Sikh man plying his father's sweeper trade; the cobalt-blue turban, long sword and spear of a Nihang Sikh.

The only place all Sikh men can believe themselves equal to Sardarji is in the gurdwara.

Past the crowd, Sardarji's victoria driver has brought Satya's pink tonga. Behind him, a camel-mounted servant stands waiting.

Satya draws herself up in stiff-necked, affronted, haughty silence until the crowd of men parts, allowing her, then Jorimon with baby Pavan, through.

The victoria driver hugs a shawl about his chest and the camel sowar stamps his feet. The epaulettes on the camel sowar's kurta lift in surprise; Satya has brought little for the camel to carry – did she imagine it or had he looked at her just a little too long before dropping his eyes? If he wasn't careful, she might just forget to order his uniform next season.

But perhaps the camel sowar noticed the difference in her. The confidence that has returned from having Sardarji place his first child in her arms. That little helpless thing depends on her now – not Roop – for its every breath. Needs her – not Roop – for its very survival. It needs Satya the way a woman needs a father, a husband or a brother: for her protection.

Once the laden camel has risen from its knees and the camel sowar has kicked it to a walk, Satya motions to the victoria driver to join Jorimon and the baby in the back seat of the tonga. Then she takes her place in the driver's seat. Takes the reins.

Pink tonga wheels roll forward, the mare breaks into a steady trot.

There is no reason for me to stay any longer in Khanewal – what is there for me to do while Sardarji travels on inspection tours or goes away to meetings in Lahore or in Delhi?

In 'Pindi there are women besides Toshi – that *churail!* – to whom she wishes to show her prize, a child in her lap, a trophy for her years of loyal and frugal service. Besides, she must manage Sardarji's accounts for the flour mill, availing herself of the munshi's writing ability, manage repairs to the old haveli and designate elders as arbitrators for the never-ending disputes among Sardarji's tenants. In a few months there will be sacks of apricots from Sardarji's orchards to be sorted and sent to higher-ups, to petty officials, and to rising freedom fighters in the Congress Party – all on Sardarji's behalf.

Huh, I'd like to see if Roop could help Sardarji this way.

She doesn't enjoy helping Sardarji send the apricots each year. He pretends not to hear her, his face going blank, his eyes looking past her when she describes his actions as she sees them – 'You send fruit every year to the higher-ups just to keep all of them happy, just to do the unrequested favours that will bind them to you now in case you need them later. Why don't you take a stand, either say you're for independence and join the protesters or say you're a puppet of the British so people can respect you or revile you, but at least know what you feel?'

But the years in England taught Sardarji to think without feeling. England took the passion from his heart and replaced it with a seeking that spans lifetimes, a cold seeking that showed itself in his eyes. Once he'd paid off his brother's debts. Once he'd moved higher up in the world.

Once he stopped coming to Satya's bed.

He has steeled himself against passion of all kinds – anger, love, tenderness – meeting them all with logic and ambition. Today he talks about bringing India into the modern world instead of making India free and he will work for anyone who will help him in that goal, no matter what they ask of him. He does not need to work at all, he could live lavishly on the income from his mill and his land, so there is some prod that goads him from within, pricks him forward as the puny rod of a mahout moves a mighty elephant to its bidding.

Strong, gentle creatures, elephants. One leg chained to a tree at birth, for training, each elephant feels the weight of that chain even when it is removed, and works patiently for its fill of fodder or a single shout of approval.

And Satya?

His sycophancy is corrupting her too.

But I do it for my husband, only for him.

The thought brings no comfort, only self-loathing.

Satya glances over her shoulder to baby Pavan in Jorimon's lap.

Satya has not examined the child carefully, it is enough that it is here, and Jorimon is hired to feed and bathe and touch the things upper-caste and British women do not touch, the chi-chi pi-pi of their infants.

A tiny hand uncoils, reaches toward Satya.

Satya's heart lifts inexplicably. Now, now they have a child, will he not see the future as she does, a future without Europeans trampling his spirit?

Of course he will. He is a Sikh – and he'll change when people of his quom need him, because what choice will he have then?

Mr Jinnah changed when his Muslim quom needed him. Did he not return from England, more than sixty years old, clad like Sardarji in the European monkey-suit and tie, and did he not begin to be heard by Hindus in the Indian National Congress?

All of us change, even I, delivered from barrenness by this child.

And now she has Jorimon to help her, a woman who needs to work with her hands for her living, touch and clean strange people's babies and their bodies, so no cooking. A necessary woman, like Mani Mai, with wrinkles already supple and dense about her dark eyes, cabbage-faced Jorimon is a long way from the orphanage in Bengal that sent her into the world. Her skilful hands have tended Christian, Muslim, Hindu and Sikh babies across India as she was given, passed bodily, from household to household. And Satya too, will rid herself of Jorimon just as soon as she can – orphans can bring bad luck once they have lost their usefulness.

Pink tonga wheels creak and bump across the streets of Rawalpindi, then occupy the lane as they trace the labyrinth of Saidpur Bazaar. Subtle movements of muscle and bone carry meaning from Satya's hands, through the reins to the mare's mouth. The scent of leather, the clip-clop of the mare's hooves and the rolling of tonga wheels on the brick-lined lane are more vivid in Satya's thoughts than any of the early-morning hawkers calling their wares to her through the bazaar.

Satya glances at Jorimon in the back seat – Sardarji's compass could duplicate the shape of that face, repeat that blankness. Round wistful eyes promise Satya loyalty, a nose that does not greatly exceed Jorimon's tiny button mouth promises quietness, docility.

The tonga mare halts.

Satya alights, sweeps through the carved scalloped archways, up the stone stairway to her apartments, Jorimon hurrying behind her with baby Pavan.

17. Khanewal, December 1938

The stars have not yet begun to pale, but Roop stands on the front veranda, a blanket about her shoulders, to wave Sardarji goodbye.

Sardarji is wearing a Saxon-blue turban, his black velvet hunting jacket, a white oxford shirt and Saxon-blue cravat over jodhpurs. He has taken his kirpan to his side and is going pig-sticking with Mr Farquharson. December is a little early to find a really meaty boar, but, Sardarji says to Roop from the saddle, 'the sport will be just the ticket.'

His words steam into the cold dawn; Roop smiles as if she understands. The hunters set off, lances sharp, the pennants of their accompanying grooms flying high, horses nodding at the bit.

There was a time Roop would have loved to ride with them for the scent of dust and horse-sweat and the rise and fall of galloping hooves beneath her, a time she would have liked to ride with the chase, crashing through field, scrub and thorn. Where is Nirvair now, and does her tonga driver feed her lumps of brown sugar and put his arms about her great strong neck?

Perhaps Sardarji thinks I am still weak. It is only three months.

Muscles in her legs yearn to tense about a horse's bare back, feel herself moving forward in the lift and fall of canter, then full gallop. But here in the canal colony bungalow, the very air is still, closed, musty as the underchamber of a Muslim tomb.

Mani Mai serves Roop's morning tea on the back veranda shaded by a mango tree. The mali places a vase on the glass-topped oval: a single purple-hearted lemon pansy.

I am not good-good enough for all he has done for me. If I am not careful, everyone will say let her be alone.

She should have given her daughter freely, willingly, with no hesitation. 'Be generous,' Mama would have said.

And was I generous? No.

Roop held her daughter to her as if Pavan were hers alone. If Sardarji had not expressed his will, she would not have shared her daughter with Satya, so selfish and ungrateful had she become.

What is the use of having even one ear to listen if not to obey? There should be no difference between one and the other.

Because Roop cannot listen and obey like other women, she also has trouble remembering. Though she sits with her good ear turned towards him always, it is so difficult to remember the things he wants her to remember. New names of things – there are so many more things around her now, each with its own special purpose. New names of people – all the English names of men in his department. New names of places – how far she is from Papaji's home. And now it is difficult also to remember before she came to Sardarji's house, the fear smell of Revati Bhua's conciliation, the charm of Jeevan's teasing. Was Shyam Chacha's scowl really so discontented, was Papaji's face quite as worried as she remembers? Kusum dimpling over her youngest son's quips as she braided his dark hair, the sweet taste of Gujri's peththas . . . all receding.

Instead, two soft small arms, tiny feet and toes brush her dampening kameez. . .

A child laughs in a distant room, she thinks she hears it with her good ear. That laugh is Roop's laugh, the same that

Jeevan once drew from her by the tickle of his lithe fingers.

'Pavan,' she whispers. 'Pavan.'

So far away ... will my daughter laugh like me, mimicking me from the sounds she heard coiled within my belly or will she sound like Satya, sharp-tongued, peremptory?

Can Roop walk by the canal without Sardarji's protection or does he expect her to keep some purdah like Mama and Satya? Can she ask for a tonga to drive her to the train station without his permission, and return to 'Pindi? She does not know. If she ran from Sardarji's home where could her feet take her? She has never been to a bazaar alone, always she had someone older with her. Madani, Revati Bhua, Gujri, Kusum, Jeevan or Papaji. She has never bought a cup of tea in the bazaar, alone. Always she had someone older with her.

A cup of chai, I will say. The chai-walla will set his eyes on me, wondering why, noting how it was asked, and watching till I leave.

She was never so uncertain when she was small, only now. Were Roop's the legs that had gripped Nirvair's furry brown skin as she galloped dirt trails with Jeevan, kicking silver sand in the eyes of the sun? Were Roop's the heels that had urged Nirvair up the sides of scrubby hillocks? Were Roop's the hands that held Nirvair's reins and jumped log and brush? Such fearlessness comes from being unable to imagine consequence.

Now Sardarji's every movement has consequence, every shift in glance, every twitch of a muscle has meaning beyond meaning. Roop makes more rules for herself than Lajo Bhua ever specified. She makes her rules from the lift of Sardarji's eyebrow, manufactures adages from the curl of his moustache, stitches whole yarns of potential calamity from the flick of his wrist as he checks the time on his Omega.

He is cause and she effect.

She measures the distance she can walk to stay within earshot of his call, loud though it is. She is a mass of taut strings, awaiting the sweep of his bow.

She, who once rode Nirvair bareback across silver sand, cannot tell how 'Roop' came to mean mother-ness without child-ness and yes-ness without no-ness, like a word reversing meaning as it passes from mouth to mouth.

Could it have been otherwise? What if Papaji had become a Hindu as Shyam Chacha wanted him to be, instead of a Sikh? What if Roop had not been born under the influence of Mangal? What if she had both ears? Could she then have married a wifeless man? Could she have kept her little daughter?

Every woman has her own kismat. Mine is so much better than most.

In the rambling canal colony house there are many rooms, she has not explored them all. She is not sure she should, but there is nothing else to do. Sardar Kushal Singh and Toshiji have departed, there is no one who would dare arrive uninvited.

Leaving her tea untouched, Roop twirls the mali's gift between cold fingers and wanders through the canal bungalow, avoiding the small prayer room. She walks in rooms whose light and air are gifts from the seesaw panes of roshandaans above, some she has been led to or shown by Sardarji or Mani Mai. Withdrawing rooms within drawing rooms where well-upholstered chairs face matching sofas, where meetings within meetings can be held, and where people are received in accordance with their standing. The library full of books in English, books she cannot read. Sardarji's office – he has a European desk with pigeon-holes, not one you can sit at cross-legged like Papaji's or Sardar Kushal Singh's – filled with books, notebooks and files where Department men have recorded canal levels in the Lower Bari Doab area every day since the European century began and never asked the river why it gives men power, why it flows at all when it knows the harnesses and restraints that lie in wait downstream.

In another room there is only a long table with green felt stretched over it and a large light above, the way the ear doctor's office was in Lord Mayo's hospital. Long sticks are ranged against the wall and above them photographs of pale solar-topeed men with dangling shotguns, their boots planted on the stilled ribs of tigers.

Then a room lined with glass-front cabinets where china plates and crystal bowls – all packed in crates and brought from

'Pindi – are placed to delight his eye. Some china plates, Atma Singh says, Wedgwood queen's-ware, for instance, are used just a few times a year for special occasions and placed on the topmost shelves, out of reach.

There are a few small rooms close to the cookhouse where her voice, saying the Sukhmani as she goes, becomes softer, softer. When she stands in the smallest, a room so small she can only stand within it and watch the world beyond its threshold, she is Sita in her man-inscribed circle.

Her voice, now just a whisper.

Idol in her niche.

She stands there for hours, silent, diffused into the cold dense air like a coin palmed by a magician's nimble fingers, here and not here, come and not come, gone and not gone, all together.

This way she can give no trouble.

If he needs her, he can call. She will come. She stands alone with the scent of her sweat and the sound of her heart.

Dhak-dhak. Dhak-dhak.

Sardarji and Mr Farquharson leave the lazy sway of the Ravi. Molten silver, it winds its way west to swell first the Chenab, then the Indus. They have ridden north three hours or more and the softness of canal-irrigated fields beneath their horses' hooves has changed to hard-packed scrubland. Wavy golden grass reaches past the tops of their boots. Most of the way they have been silent beneath the fading stars, enjoying the clink of tack and the occasional prance of a too-anxious mare. Each man is experienced in hunting boar, but this is the first time they have hunted together. The rules of the chase are simple, they extend back before the quoms of either man believed themselves civilized – the boar's-head trophy goes to the man who first runs it to the ground and lances it.

Nearby, a yogi with matted hair joins his palms above his head and lifts his ribcage, beginning suryanamaskar, his salutation to the sun. He inhales, lowering his fingertips to touch the earth, folding his body in two. He exhales, touching his palms to the earth. He lunges back, balancing on his toes and palms, lowers his head to the ground before the sun.

The sun rises warm upon the shoulders of the horsemen. They rise on the balls of their feet in the stirrups and trot through the arid grassland. Canal labourers, and villagers engaged as beaters of the scrubby grass – Sikh and Hindu men who will not mind that they intend to kill a pig for food – fan out before them, trampling the coarse grass under the hard pads of their bare feet and shouting 'Harrr! Harrrr!' They beat and hack at the tall grass before them and now their cries change to shouts: a snuffling, grunting black boar is rooting and running before the two lances.

Sardarji is closest as the tusker breaks cover and points its snout at a tangle of kikar trees in the distance.

Instantly, he digs his heels into the mare's sides and is off, right hand gripping the lance horizontal to the ground, at the ready.

His knees are welded to the thoroughbred's saddle, he anticipates her every stride, lifting her between his legs to jump tussock, rock and tuft. The drumming of her hooves accelerates, her steady snort speeds to a pant. An electric charge flows between his mind and hers, guiding her so she cannot misstep.

Mr Farquharson and the mounted grooms are left behind; Sardarji chases alone.

Eyes flash white as the mare picks up the scent of the boar. The blue-black squealing mass vanishes and the mare slows to a canter, looking left, right. Her nostrils flare. He lets leather slip through his left hand to her butter-soft young mouth, feels her take it; she has found a ravine camouflaged by the kikar trees and now, a path wide enough to descend in pursuit. He shifts the weight of his torso to her hindquarters, she angles down into the undergrowth. At the bottom of the ravine, he touches his crop to her side, feels her bound forward again. For a moment, Sardarji thinks he has lost the boar, then the mare proves she can see better than he in the dappled green gloom. He can hear Mr Farquharson above him, shouting, 'Tally-ho, Sardarji!'

'Tally-ho!' he shouts back, to let Mr Farquharson know his

position. He has to trust the mare now, let her lead him into the darkness. The crumbled gold ravine-sides blur as the mare extends her stride. He leans forward, his weight off the saddle, the lance firm in his grip.

A log blocks the way. The boar scuttles over it, squealing. It looks back for an instant; small squinty eyes. Huge dagger-sharp tusks.

Sardarji leans forward for the jump. The log is not much taller than a brush jump at a steeplechase. The mare strides, one, two, *hup*.

She takes the jump higher than she needs, her forelegs landing well clear of the small log. Puzzled, he takes his eyes off the boar to glance back and see what she has saved him from – a king cobra sways its deadly hood, then subsides, hissing in disappointment.

But now the sides of the ravine rise before the boar and corner it so it turns to fight. The mare halts, hooves ploughing the ground, pushing back on her haunches. Sardarji leans forward as she wheels. Holding her tight between his knees, he thrusts the point of his lance into the rough bluish-black hide, the full weight of his body behind it.

'*Cheeargh!*' The tusker bellows its pain.

The mare rears as Sardarji pulls his lance out, blood-tipped. As her hooves descend, Sardarji goes for the deadly snout. He is cool, rational as ever. Jolted, his turban leaves his hair, and his topknot loosens. As the lance in his hand jars against bone, his long black hair tumbles about his shoulders.

This time a gargle of blood rushes from the boar.

It staggers.

Blood blackens, soaking the earth.

Within minutes, the boar is no longer an adversary; it quivers, then lies still, a miserable carcass.

Sardarji answers a shout from above him, 'Here!'

Mr Farquharson urges his horse down into the ravine. He trots over to Sardarji, who has dismounted and is tying first his hair-knot and then his Saxon-blue turban.

'What a tusker! He gave a surprisingly good chase!' Sardarji says, one end of his turban clenched between smiling lips. But instead of admiring the boar, Mr Farquharson halts and watches Sardarji tying his turban, with academic interest, as if a rare animal cavorted in a cage before him.

Sardarji's normal deftness slows. He looks around; what is Mr Farquharson watching? Mr Farquharson is watching him, there is no one else. Unless his still-heaving grazing mare or the boar could be considered possibilities for observation. He becomes conscious of his turban as if it were separate from him, conscious of his sweat-stained dishevelled state and the fact that he is a little bald in the middle of his hair-knot. A consciousness dawns, that his belly is just a little wider than the waist of his britches and that Mr Farquharson is merely thirty-five and looks quite definitely natty.

And so he is off guard as Mr Farquharson says, 'I say, Sardarji, that's awfully nice of you. I'm just pleased as punch, actually. Imagine the faces of the chaps at the Gymkhana Club when they see this picture.'

Mr Farquharson's arm arches to beckon his groom to his stirrup. 'Camera lao!'

The groom runs back to his horse. Reaching in the saddle-bag, he brings forth a leather cube. He pulls the flap up and in his hand rests a Kodak camera. This he gives to Mr Farquharson, dismounted by now and standing with his foot squarely on the black carcass.

'You know how to work one of these damn things, don't you? Right, right, well then. Click away, sir, click away.'

'This is preposterous,' Sardarji says to Cunningham. And Cunningham informs him it would be simply not done to point out to Mr Farquharson that he has changed all the rules of pigsticking just as Sardarji was about to claim his trophy.

'But this is quite unsportsmanlike,' Sardarji says.

'Quite so, old boy. Shocking bad form. Pen him a nasty note, why don't you?' Cunningham says, with his usual sang-froid.

'I can't do that, Cunningham.'

'Well, then . . . ?' And there the matter will have to rest.

Sardarji looks at Mr Farquharson upside down in the Kodak's reflective lens. Mr Farquharson attempts to look fierce for the photo, the shutter whirrs and snaps. Sardarji winds the film forward with more force in his wrist than strictly necessary.

The grooms take the sahibs' lances. Two beaters gut the boar and tie its legs together. A pole run between the legs rises and rests on their shoulders.

Sardarji pats his mare with a cupped hand; a hollow sound.

He vaults into her saddle and joins Mr Farquharson for the long ride back to Khanewal.

Mr Farquharson is pleased, genial.

Sardarji rides slightly behind the Superintending Engineer, now. The mare deepens her gait to comfort him, but by the time they climb the hill to the canal colony bungalow, the English saddle has chafed through his britches and rubbed his inner thigh raw. His legs are stiff, as if carved into position.

The only time Sardarji ever feels tired is when he has no trophy to show for his pains.

In the distance, the yogi changes his stance. He lunges forward on his right foot, his left straight out behind him. He joins his palms above his head and inhales till his ribs press taut against his shiny dark skin.

He has moved into warrior position.

The yogi holds the position as Sardarji faces forward, touches his heels to his mare's sides and urges her forward to catch up with Mr Farquharson.

18. Rawalpindi, January 1939

Past the circle of light in Satya's private sitting room, shadow people embrace and dissolve, changing the texture of darkness. Cabbage-faced Jorimon – *so lazy these Bengali Muslims are* – nods before the leaping fire, a taut rope between her big toe and the girl-child's cradle moving in time to a rabab playing somewhere below in Saidpur Bazaar.

The girl-baby sleeps. Ever since Satya brought her to 'Pindi she sleeps all day and cries all night; she is too ugly to show visitors, cow's milk is not good enough for her; she has wet her nappies several times today, she is hungry, needy.

Insatiable. Just like her mother, just like Roop. Low-class hunger is in this girl's blood.

Once Sardarji told Satya a tale – perhaps he has forgotten it now – a tale about a man who persuaded a woman to elope with him, taking her father's camel. Crossing a stream, the camel sat down in the water, soaking all their belongings.

The corner of Satya's mouth lifts, remembering.

The lovers dismounted and the man began to beat the

camel, but the woman stopped him, saying, 'Don't beat her, my love! This camel's mother used to do the same every time she crossed a stream.'

'Is that so?' said the man. 'Then I say: get back on the camel and I will take you back to your father, for I have no wish for my daughter to elope as her mother-to-be does today.'

Sardarji should remember that story; he thinks his bloodline is strong enough to counter Roop's.

Huh! Already this girl-child shows all the signs of Roop's neediness, Roop's grasping nature, Roop's sharp eye for other women's ornaments – see how Pavan follows the clinking of Jorimon's bangles and grabs at the silver chain dangling from Jorimon's neck as the woman changes her nappy. She will be just like her mother's father, impractical, spendthrift – it is in her blood, how can this poor child help it?

The shadow people dance on the walls. Satya stretches her compact limbs on her divan, watches.

She knows these djinns.

Not all the dead are wise; some are cheaters and liars, some crippled and angry, others just sad. But Satya speaks with them all, they have met her ancestors.

Now they speak with one voice, jeering.

'This is his gift? A girl-child? He gave you his refuse, then. A gift of no value; it cost him nothing to give it.'

And they withhold their blessings, refusing to arch their shadows as far as Pavan's cradle. The nappy changed, small grunts come from the cradle and Jorimon returns to her seat on the floor.

Satya moves to the side of the cradle. Logs glow red, sparks fly up the chimney. The black hair on the girl's head is soft.

'Ooo-er.' Small fingers close about Satya's finger.

Satya's fingers trail the girl-baby's cheek.

Only love can melt me now.

Stop, don't love yet!

She must not allow herself to love. Even as her heart warms at the baby's touch, Satya tells herself she feels only revulsion for Roop's girl. Yes, a disgust so deep she must have met Pavan in a past life. When the child raises her soft arms towards Satya, that disgust rises in her till she trembles for fear she might hurt the child.

That little gurgle. So innocent.

But, Satya thinks, are children really innocent? Choosing the moment of their birth, they come into the world already informed by the community that spawned them, informed to love and hate the way their religion and their family say is fit. They come conscious of the level of their birth, they come guilty with all the unresolved vices of their past lives and the vices of their blood.

No, no child is an innocent.

Especially not a girl-child. Why, men of every colour and creed find blame in girls for rains that come or don't come, but mostly, men blame girls for living.

The shadow people are right; a girl-child is not sufficient. She will tell Sardarji as soon as he comes to Rawalpindi: Roop must make a boy for Sardarji and Satya will raise him well.

For Sardarji's sake.

19. Khanewal, August 1939

Night, and Sardarji's weight is upon Roop again, and his desire is a leech-like thing that sucks and pulls and wants and wants and wants, demands and asks and implores her for give-ness and fullness and unself-ness to heal itself and grow. Some nights it wins and takes all of her till she is hollow and hungry and hurting from head to toe, drained as if muscle and bone were pulped and pipped without regard for the remains required to face the daylight. Skin, folding over itself weakly, misshapen, her body a bag of air and water for its pleasure.

Sardarji says he hates to sleep; there are too many things to be done, too many responsibilities and he might miss one of them and then all the Mr Farquharsons of this world will say, 'What can one expect? He is an Indian.'

But many nights, when it is over, he says, 'Sleep next to me, little brown koel.' And Roop stays, saying she is afraid – so afraid – of the dark. Then Sardarji keeps the lamp lit so she does not miss a word he says.

'I do not dream while sleeping,' he tells her. 'But all my waking dreams are for India.'

Often, when his weight lifts from her and his arms are about her, Roop feels the slight shudder his hands can draw from her.

Sardarji thinks she yearns for that uncontrollable instant of pleasure, for he laughs afterwards, 'You village girls!' bringing a hot flush of shame to Roop's cheeks, reviving her fear of her own body.

But it is really his closeness, the holding, the touching, that Roop needs.

In his arms, her hair mingling with his on the pillow, she feels less alone.

Afterwards, she can return to her room, moon-shadow crawling like a lowly untouchable along his bungalow walls.

20. Khanewal, October 1939

Such a pretty sweet thing, so playful, so loving.

Sardarji feels just like a sharpened kirpan, after Roop has satisfied him; it's his most creative time.

Sometimes, as now, he makes his way to the library to put his feet up on an ottoman and memorize a few quotations, just for mental exercise.

Quotations, he has discovered, are the way to Mr Farquharson's approbation – they convince him, if he needs further convincing, that Sardarji has no thoughts of his own but those of occidental thinkers. A part of Sardarji's library moves with him on every posting, hallmark of his gentleman-hood, each book pre-approved by Cunningham, except for a few Punjabi and Persian volumes and the Guru Granth Sahib.

He orders his books from England, from a musty little book-shop owned by a retired India hand, a former colonel, who, seeing Sardarji's turban hesitating outside the shop window one misty morning in Oxford, came out to inquire if he could read English. 'Yes, sir,' Sardarji told the colonel, proudly. 'I began teaching myself English aboard ship, on my way here to England. I am studying to be an engineer.'

So lonely he was, in those days, so speechless, so unsure of his prospects, being a younger son.

But full of fight.

Yes, full of fight – how spirited were those debates with the colonel! How quickly he had learned to joust and wrestle with words, how sure he'd been that he was the one who could turn English and logic against the English!

That, the colonel reminded him often, was the Sikh way. 'Ah, Sikhs, Gurkhas, the best, the only good fighters. A little thick-headed, my lad, but you need to be, shall we say, a little thick in the head to be brave, to be loyal.'

The colonel died last year, his executor sent Sardarji a last shipment, books he had not ordered. Here they are: Ernest Trumpp's contemptuous translation of the Guru Granth Sahib, and Joseph Davey Cunningham's *History of the Sikhs*.

Mr Cunningham, British resident within Sardarji says, 'A topping gift, that was.'

'The colonel's parting shot. Reinforcement for you,' Sardarji retorts. 'You're beginning to need some, actually.'

'Backsliding a tad, what? Simply not done, old chap.'

'Oh, *do* be still, Cunningham.'

Sardarji uses the teak stepstool to bring himself level with the top shelf. Here the most revered of authors speak from the past. He prides himself on his selection, his good taste. He browses the shelves, dissatisfaction rising, burgeoning to anxiety – he will need more books. He has not enough for so long a stay in this cul-de-sac posting.

Rai Alam Khan will be visiting soon, from Lahore. He will ask Rai Alam which books he may have received lately from London.

Rai Alam Khan is a qualified man, a government man. Like Sardarji he is a member of the suited set, the heaven-born, the Indian Civil Service, and like Sardarji he has enough land that he need never work, but sees his civic duty in governance. He is a Cambridge man – Sardarji doesn't hold that against him – for he is an ICS accountant and a trusted old friend ever since Sardarji needed a negotiator between himself and the

Muslims working in his flour mill in 'Pindi. They met soon after Sardarji's return from England, when Rai Alam founded the Tuesday Lunch Club for qualified gentlemen to dine together. It was the fashion of the times, what people in those days called Khilafat, the harmony movement between Hindus and Muslims.

Whenever Sardarji has work in Lahore, he arranges his schedule to enjoy the audacity of the Tuesday Lunch Club, to join Alamji in his subtle discrediting of what is, after all, a Hindu superstition. Sardarji's attendance at the Tuesday Lunch Club is a thumbed nose at the dominant influence of Mangal in Sardarji's stars – for on Tuesday, Mangal's influence is very strong, so the Lunch Club issues its challenge to the star week after week. But even if Sardarji does not believe in the influence of Mangal, attending the Tuesday Lunch Club still demonstrates that enlightened, qualified, well-read Indians, landlords all, can partake of food together in hotel restaurants where no one inquires too closely into a cook's religion, and can overcome their religious scruples, rise above native superstitions.

As he descends from the stepstool, it occurs to Sardarji that he has never asked Rai Alam Khan if he too happened to take birth under the influence of Mangal; it is not a question one can drop casually into conversation.

'I should jolly well say not,' says Cunningham. 'It would betray a certain predisposition to believe in such nonsense.'

'*My* attendance at Tuesday luncheons doubles the challenge to Mangal,' Sardarji tells him, stoutly.

Seating himself in his wingback chair, Sardarji puts his feet up on the ottoman and cracks a leather-bound volume of G.K. Chesterton's essays.

Still anxious. For really, he has not brought enough books from 'Pindi for a second term in Khanewal.

Rai Alam's library is quite as extensive as Sardarji's, but Sardarji suspects Alamji has not read every book in it as Sardarji has in his, closely, absorbing the fine logic of Socrates, Plato, Aristotle and Descartes. Alamji's library is full of the great Urdu poets, Mir Taqi Mir, Ghalib and a few volumes of that new poet, Muhammad Iqbal. Too melancholy by far, those Urdu poets, preferring to sorrow over unattainable loves instead of appreciating Vaheguru's infinite bounty of beautiful women, but he can agree with Alamji on Rumi, the Turkish Sufi poet – both can quote Jalal-ud-din Rumi; Rumi is Sardarji's bridge to Rai Alam's mind. Beyond poetry, however, Rai Alam's interests run more to the study of contemporary politics and economics, so his presence is always enlightening.

A few years ago, when he last visited Rai Alam Khan in Simla where the central government had moved for the summer, they'd had a vigorous debate over British investment in India – Sardarji said the canals and railways and the postal service the British had given India were bringing a commercial revolution. Rai Alam said most of the money for that revolution came right from the 'crippling' revenue that landowners and farmers paid to the British, not out of British people's pockets. And he talked of how capital transfers had been far exceeded by land revenue payments, for so many years.

Sardarji, prompted nicely by Cunningham, said, 'Indians are born complaining about land revenue. Don't you complain about it? And the sources of your statistics are not verifiable.'

Perhaps we should revisit that debate some time. I may attempt to take the other side, now.

Just for the sport of course, Cunningham, just for sport.

But all in all, Sardarji listens when Alamji talks because Alamji listens when Sardarji talks.

Roop listens.

Sardarji felt Roop's brown eyes following his lips tonight, drinking in his every word.

Quite pleasurable.

Satya never listens to me this way.

Once, he'd been explaining how his careful analysis of water levels for a season showed him an anomaly in flow that the Department could turn to great pecuniary advantage with another barrage and a few canals. And he recounted how he'd told Mr Farquharson so, suggested it gently until Mr Farquharson actually believed it to be his own idea. The sons of those peasants would never know what he'd done for them, of course, but he'd tell his own sons someday.

And that eyebrow of Satya's had risen, 'You did it for them, na?'

'Yes, of course, for them.'

'*Hein?*'

'Don't say *hein*, Satya,' he corrected. 'It's rude; simply not done.'

'What should I say? Tell me. Feed me the words you want to hear, so I can say them to you.'

'You should say, "Really, is that so?" if you disagree,' he told her.

'So you want me to say, "Really, is that so?" instead of telling you to your face when you are making excuses for yourself.' And she had painstakingly learned those four English words, so her every repetition dripped sarcasm.

'I treat you just the way the Guru said to, like a princess,' he said to her soothingly, before his marriage to Roop, when a visit to Sardar Kushal Singh and Toshi had enraged her beyond speech. 'But nothing satisfies you.'

'Really, is that so?' she'd said.

No, Satya hasn't listened to him for a long time. She takes everything Sardarji says and follows it with her own explanatory titles, as if composing one of those silent movies he and Kitty used to watch in London.

She's become so wilful.

He can see he will have to put his foot down some day; overcome his natural kindness.

But Roop – she is his comfort for taking birth in India.

21. Khanewal, October 1939

Though the pain of her girl-child has not yet passed and the bad blood has not built within her enough so the moon can move her menses once again, Roop feels the quickening of life. This time she welcomes it warily; it is an old friend now, who knows just where to hurt her. Her stomach churns with fear – she could die as young as Mama, so painful it is to do what women are for.

Ever watchful, Mani Mai tells Sardarji that Roop is again 'in a family way.'

At the news, the canal colony house fills with more servants and supplicants. Mani Mai orders a tailor-master to set up a new Singer sewing machine on the back veranda outside Roop's room and he treadles away every morning, sewing Roop new large and roomy kameezes; Sardarji says she is too thin, she must gain weight.

When Roop is past her morning retching, Mani Mai spreads a white tablecloth upon the mahogany dinner table, and lays the table for four with gilt-edged rose-rimmed queen's-ware – Mr Farquharson and Rai Alam Khan are invited to dinner.

'No pork,' Mani Mai reminds Atma Singh sharply, retiring to her place in the cookhouse. 'And Rai Alam Khan will be fasting; he won't eat at all.' The thirty days of Ramazan are making Mani Mai grumpy, though she rises to eat a few wheat rotis, every day before dawn.

Sardarji beckons Roop with a forefinger, so Roop joins him, excitement raising her spirits, even as she yearns for Pavan.

Liveried bearers stand attentively behind each chair. In Roop's ear comes the rustle of starched lace serviettes on the tablecloth, the clink and tinkle of silver forks and spoons in soup tureens, the clatter and scrape of metal on china as the butter dish passes and then toast, upright, cooling rapidly between the silver bars of a toast-holder.

Rai Alam Khan, the new addition to Sardarji's table, a debonair, brush-moustached, karakuli-capped Peshawari Muslim, flashes a magnificent leer at Roop. Mani Mai said he has three wives, and is working his way to the four allowed by his reading of the Koran. But they are not with him – they must be living in his ancestral home in strict seclusion while he is posted to Lahore.

'You must bring your beautiful new wife to Simla, Sardarji,' says Rai Alam Khan, smoothing the sleeves of his navy blue blazer. 'She will enjoy the mountain air. I rent a cottage there every summer. Come and stay.'

Rai Alam Khan tips his bowl of chicken soup; he is not fasting for Ramazan, as Mani Mai said he would be.

Safely through the watery soup, Roop lifts the outside fork in her unclean hand as Atma Singh, watching from the window in the pantry door, taught her. Beneath the thick white sauce on her plate, she smells fish, knows she must eat whatever unfamiliar thing is before her, without even touching it first with her fingers. She cuts a piece, raises it to her mouth.

It smells strange.

She lowers her fork.

Atma Singh nods and waves from behind the pantry door.

She raises the white-sauce-smothered fish to her mouth.

The smell!

She lowers the fork again.

Atma Singh's turban is bobbing up and down now.

Roop raises a gold-braceleted hand to her pert little nose, pinches it tight between thumb and forefinger, and swallows the fish.

Atma Singh's turban vanishes abruptly from the window.

'*Roo-oo-oop!*' Sardarji bellows from the head of the table.

Roop's fork clatters to the plate. Her eyes fill in seconds. Her ear sings and stings as if it had felt the dhaap of a giant slap; big things don't seem to mean as much as the small things in Sardarji's home.

Sardarji snaps his fingers at a bearer. 'Take it away.'

Then to Mr Farquharson, 'She doesn't quite appreciate fish yet.'

And to Roop. 'No tears, young lady, thank you very much, no tears now.'

Roop wipes her eyes and then her nose on the serviette and offers Sardarji her most pacifying smile. Atma Singh's turban appears in the window again, his eyes pointedly closed like the Guru's. She can feel his supporting message as if he were at her elbow.

Be calm, Choti-Sardarni, be calm.

She takes a deep ujjai-breath, the way the Indian doctor-ji taught her.

Sardarji's jovial, bearded face and Mr Farquharson's ruddy clean-shaven one are smiling at her reassuringly.

The conversation bounces past Roop and around her, in the polished English prose of men who acknowledge one another's rank.

How would my Papaji look, seated at this table?

She does not know they speak of a man called Hitler and the need for all in His Majesty's Empire to stand united against him in war.

'It's a just war, a war against evil,' Mr Farquharson says, un-usually sober. The Christian theological construct is lost upon his audience. 'I, for one, shall be eager to serve.'

'But he just *proclaimed* that India will participate.' Rai Alam

Khan is speaking of the Viceroy. His diction is thespian, elegant as Sardarji's.

'It was constitutionally correct,' says Mr Farquharson sincerely.

Sardarji clarifies for him, 'Yes, my dear sir, but it was quite unwise not to consult the Indian National Congress. It was quite predictable that they would resign from all provincial ministries.'

The resignation of Congress ministers has paralysed the government.

'Did the broadcast say whether the Viceroy consulted Mr Jinnah – or any other member of the Muslim League?'

Mr Farquharson dismisses Rai Alam Khan's question with a wave. 'Not to worry – the governors of the provinces are fine upstanding fellows. A little direct rule and we'll have the whole country stiffened up, ready to stomach a little war.'

Sardarji bristles at the implied insult. 'I was in England during the Great War, I was at Balliol, then. Now that was a *war*. Sixty thousand Indians died for Britain in that war. This one will be just a skirmish by contrast, bound to be over soon.'

'The Indian ministers were doing nothing of importance, after all,' says Mr Farquharson.

'Really? Is that so?' says Rai Alam Khan, deadpan.

Sardarji studies his baked vegetables, pauses, remembering. 'Do you know, during that war, I met Princess Bamba, the daughter of Maharaj Dalip Singh. Maharaj Dalip Singh was the son of Maharaj Ranjit Singh.'

Roop looks up at the mention of Maharaj Ranjit Singh, the same who Papaji told her ruled all of Punjab before the British.

'Dalip Singh – the same who presented the Kohinoor to Queen Victoria?' says Mr Farquharson, chewing slowly.

'The same. Though, of course, presented is not the word I would use, sir. From what his daughter told me, the British suggested to him that he make a gift of it in person to the Queen.'

'It was part of the treaty Ranjit Singh signed,' Mr Farquharson corrects soothingly, as if willing to forgive his host a slight social blunder. 'The boy merely presented it personally.' His eyes narrow further, evaluating.

'Well, what should an eleven-year-old boy have done? So far from home, alone without people of his own about him, all his personal possessions considered a part of the spoils. He was even converted to Christianity. Refusal was simply not an option. Such a sad story.' Something seems to compel Sardarji to his subject, as if he wants Mr Farquharson to feel responsible for the actions of his quom.

But if Mr Farquharson feels responsible, he shows no sign of it; it is only members of vanquished races who feel responsible for all the actions of their quoms.

'But even so, his daughter, Princess Bamba, became a nurse and saved many British lives,' continues Sardarji. He is triumphant, as if her achievement were his own, and Mr Farquharson should acknowledge the magnanimity of the Sikh maharaja's tribe.

But only the vanquished are really interested in history; only the vanquished yearn to be seen and heard within it.

Keeping his eye on Sardarji, Mr Farquharson takes a pipe and safety matches from the pocket of his white dinner jacket.

Roop looks from one to the other, waits for Sardarji to stop him.

But Sardarji has for once fallen strangely quiet. He, who just bellowed at Roop for holding her nose, is quiet before Mr Farquharson.

Mr Farquharson strikes a match, cradles the pipe in both hands. The musty scent of burning tobacco wrinkles Roop's nose as he blows tobacco smoke before Sardarji's face. The trader's chillums in the tunnel at Pari Darvaza never smelled quite as pungent.

Understanding glimmers in Roop: Mr Farquharson is the man who draws the circle beyond which Sardarji cannot go. The canal bungalow belongs to the British government; Sardarji occupies it at their pleasure. He cannot forbid Mr Farquharson to light his pipe, even at his own dining table, and Mr Farquharson has lit his pipe, though he knows it offends all Sikhs, especially those from old families, like Sardarji.

Still Sardarji says nothing about the pipe. Instead, he

changes the subject. 'Alamji, what have you been reading lately? I recommend *The Decline and Fall of the Roman Empire*. I've been rereading it lately and have found it most instructive.'

Rai Alam Khan laughs, '*Oy*, Sardarji, I too have a beautiful new wife; I don't reread old books these days. You must hide this one away from young men, you know what they say about old men who get too trusting. Does she sing?'

Sardarji says proudly, 'Oh, yes. She sings shabads beautifully. I call her my little brown koel.'

Rai Alam's face hardens a little. 'Shabads,' he repeats.

Mr Farquharson gives Sardarji a puzzled look.

'Our hymns.' A little annoyed. 'Surely you know what shabads are.'

Mr Farquharson leans back in his chair, 'Oh,' he says scornfully, 'yes, perhaps I do remember now.' He pulls on the pipe again. 'Sardarji, why don't you teach her to sing Muslim hymns as well?'

Mr Farquharson would pull a tiger's tail, then wonder why it mauls him.

'I think not,' Sardarji says through his teeth.

'We don't have hymns,' Rai Alam seems to repeat an explanation he has given before. 'Just the Kalima.' He refers to the Muslim affirmation of faith, that which makes a convert just by the speaking of words. No Sikh would want any woman who said those words. Rai Alam Khan knows that – his tongue wads in his cheek, his eyes twinkle at Sardarji.

But Sardarji has a policy never to laugh at jokes not of his own making. Instead, he searches for common ground. 'You have the poetry of the Sufi saints,' he says. 'Most Muslims considered Guru Nanak was one of them. In fact, my great-grandfather four times removed was called Lachcha *Khan* – so he was a Muslim, perhaps a Pathan from the far Northwest. Who became a Sikh.'

'That's not something you Sikhs tend to remember nowadays, is it?' Rai Alam Khan sounds serious now, too serious.

'Quite so!' says Mr Farquharson. Then he leans forward, voice planing to monotone, 'Sardarji, I recommend you reread *The Causes and Course of the French Revolution*. I think you will find it quite enlightening.'

The smoke from Mr Farquharson's pipe rises to the chandeliers. Sardarji's brow clouds and his eyes narrow. Mr Farquharson's words put the matter in perspective. He has reminded Sardarji: what stands between him and the Muslims in his mill and on his land is His Majesty's British raj.

Sardarji raises his champagne glass for another change of subject. 'Gentlemen, my *lady* wife!'

'How do you do?' Roop says in a great rush, bringing the words she has practised and waited to use these many years, to her lips. 'Delighted to meet you.'

Her enthusiasm breaks the tension.

'Delighted to meet you,' Mr Farquharson says gallantly. He gulps the contents of his glass, holds it out to the bearer behind his chair, for immediate refill.

Sardarji beams.

Roop sits straighter. Though her ache for Pavan is eating a hole within her that cannot be embroidered away, the caress of their admiring gazes on her young expectant face feels so *nice*.

22. Rawalpindi, April 1940

Satya unlatches her octagonal paandaan, raises its lid. Sardarji doesn't like her to eat paan, calls it a dirty Indian habit, but Sardarji is not here in her private sitting room in Rawalpindi. The nine compartments of the paandaan send her their aromas and invite her to blend them. Zarda, chuna, cinnamon, anise, fennel, cardamom, tamarind, and her own addition to the usual ingredients, black cumin.

Her mouth waters.

The core of the paandaan, the centre, lies empty but for half a bitter almond — this Satya has saved.

But not for today.

She places a fresh green paan leaf in her hand. Considers. She daubs the paan leaf with chuna paste, preparing.

She sees Roop in her mind; Roop, loosening the cord of her salwar a little more each day as her great belly grows. Sardarji and Roop together in Khanewal with his coming son, and Satya can feel Roop eat and grow, eat and grow, like a papaya again ready to burst forth a thousand black seeds.

She places seeds of black cumin, so dear, so rare, black cumin seeds at the centre of the paan leaf.

Sardarji wrote to say this baby is all in front and lower than the first time, and several astrologers who stopped at the canal bungalow have predicted it must be a boy.

Now sweet betel wood to garnish the cumin, dark as blood clots, barely silvered with virk.

And now she almost hears Sardarji order Roop to take milk and almonds. She sees him with her, asking so gently, 'Are you hungry for sweet rice kheer or imli chutney?'

Where is the imli? Let tamarind sourness seep into the cumin. She smears brown sticky tamarind paste on the green paan leaf. So gently, so gently.

Who can refuse a woman glowing as Roop must be? All things that enter are joined to her body, absorbed and lost, un-differentiated.

She folds the paan leaf over more spices, wraps it into a triangular wad.

'Lie down here,' she hears him say to Roop. And, 'Put your feet up, my dear.'

The whole household in the Khanewal canal colony must be dancing about Roop, hope in their eyes. This time an heir, this time a son.

Slowly, Satya opens her mouth, places the paan within.

Then she bites down sudden and hard.

Sweet betel juice oozes to her tongue, tamarind souring the cumin, cinnamon bittering the chuna, anise strengthening fennel, cardamom scenting the zarda, and black cumin seeds tingeing them all with the taste of ground sorrow.

When Roop first came to Sardarji's home, Toshi – that *churail!* – said, 'Time will heal you.'

She said that this is how you feel when your saukan, your co-wife, first enters your home, but time will heal.

How would Toshi know?

Ever since Sardarji's family and Sardar Kushal Singh cemented their friendship with Toshi's dowry, Toshi has known that, sons or no sons, respect in her husband's family could drain away overnight without Sardarji's protection. But no one has even suggested to Toshi that Sardar Kushal Singh take another wife, so how can she presume to know how it feels?

Rai Alam Khan's seniormost begum, yes, she understood a little – for it happened to her for the second time, just a few months before it happened to Satya. Same-to-same way – secretly, Alamji went to some village and took a young village girl as his third wife. Begum Khan's letter to Satya arrived with Jorimon, her parting gift. It said, 'I kept my izzat, my dignity. I said I will go and live with my eldest son in Karachi.'

If Satya had a son, perhaps she too could have made such a choice.

But, to leave Sardarji?

No.

Never.

When women like Toshi say time will heal, they mean that time will heal not so the wound bleeds any less, but so the bleeding becomes my habitual companion, and only if it stops one day will I notice its absence.

Next time she makes a paan this way, with black cumin seeds, betel and tamarind, it will be for Roop.

'Sukhi rahen,' May they remain happy. That's what she said to Sardar Kushal Singh when he came to inquire after Satya's health, representing Sardarji as always. May they remain happy, is what she said when he, slyly watching her face for her reaction, revealed the hard stone hidden in his polite solicitations: that Sardarji, far from leaving Roop alone and travelling to Lahore and Delhi, had been conducting his affairs from Khanewal, spending months with the temptress. And when she said 'sukhi rahen,' Sardar Kushal Singh's cheeks beamed red above his beard, taking credit for happiness in all. Satya could just see it as he told her: Sardarji's large square forefinger fitting itself in the dial of the telephone while a clerk brought him tea, and Satya could just hear him shouting at Sardar Kushal Singh, roaring into the black mouthpiece, that it must be a boy, it is 'so active' in Roop's stomach, Sardarji can see him kicking to be let out.

Now the lid of her paandaan shields its contents, and she latches it. Caresses the design embossed upon its silver surface.

'Sukhi rahen' is what she says to Toshi, who has grown so fearful of speaking to Satya now, afraid of losing her brother's favour, afraid, afraid – why do women like her spend their whole lives *afraid*?

Satya does not come from a family of people who are afraid. *No.*

I must overcome my natural kindness to do what must be done.

She wipes red betel juice from the corners of her mouth. Sardarji would say, '*Aiiikh!* you look like Kali,' forgetting that the Goddess of Death is essential to life.

Satya will go to Khanewal in May for the birth of Sardarji's heir.

She lifts the paandaan in both hands, places it carefully on a shelf in the sandalwood-panelled cupboard in her sitting room. Closes the cupboard door on it.

For the moment.

I must go, for Sardarji's sake.

Khanewal, May 1940

Around the canal bungalow, a shimmering blanket of heat oppresses the plains and the canal water rushes daily to slake the great thirst of the land. Roop is eighteen, almost nineteen, but with Sardarji gone to America, she knows the terror of aloneness as if she were twelve years old and walking into the clearing with Nirvair again. Every night she reaches up to latch her bedroom door, dread rising. Only unrelated men and servants are here to protect her now.

The day Satya arrived in Khanewal, Sardarji said with delighted surprise, 'Your sister has come all the way from 'Pindi to look after you in your confinement.'

Roop's heart beat faster then, but the taste of disappointment came, brutal and immediate.

Satya left little Pavan, baby Pavan, in Rawalpindi with Jorimon.

The Yardley's lavender talcum could not hide Roop's tears, but Sardarji reassured her every day till the very day he left, saying there was no need to worry. He said Jorimon would look after Pavan 'like a mother,' and he didn't want to see any more of Roop's tears or hear any more about it.

Roop no longer knows what 'like a mother' means or could mean or why men say it to her. So many women are described this way that like-a-mother brings no image to meet the word-sound. Is Revati Bhua, who could only weep fearful tears before Papaji, 'like a mother'? Or is Lajo Bhua, who was so relieved when Roop and Madani were taken from her and sent to boarding school, 'like a mother'? Roop has begun to think no like-a-mother woman is like-a-mother except in the wishes of the men who say it.

A few days ago the postman brought a letter from Sardarji enclosing a postcard snapshot. He could read the label 'Boulder Dam' on the picture, but Sardarji's English was beyond his capability. So Satya summoned Manager Abdul Aziz to the front veranda to read it.

Evening had spread, a soothing poultice across the pus-boil sun. Manager Abdul Aziz kept his distance on the driveway, his boat-shaped furry karakuli cap rocking with his almost-shout as he read Sardarji's letter at Satya and Roop together, reading it first in English, then translating to Punjabi. The letter was addressed only to Satya, but Roop was allowed to listen.

Sardarji had packed his European shoes in a felt bag on one side of a tachey case and his turbans on the other, as far apart as possible, and, British Indian passport in hand, took an ocean liner from Bombay. He is on a tour to study the construction in progress on the Grand Coulee Dam. Now he says the evening Rehraas when Roop says her morning Japji, and the Japji when Roop says her Rehraas. He wrote that he walked the streets of New York to admire the steel skeletons supporting the Chrysler and Empire State Buildings.

I found their skins of concrete, decorated with un-ornamented metal, quite attractive, functional. Indians spend too much effort on decoration and not enough on building. But equally, I felt a great anxiety: how far India has to go! How will we catch up with this? India is not progressing fast enough; all that Indians consider large is so small by comparison with American dams and powerhouses. Yet Mr Gandhi and the Congress Party would evict the Empire completely, take us back to village life.

Our hosts are well-qualified men, but quite unsophisticated. Having few or no servants, they suffer from the childlike conceit that any uneducated labourer can be raised and moulded to be as qualified as themselves. I advised them that such words should be spoken carefully, only among those who understand it as a laudable objective; otherwise they will raise expectations that a poor labourer cannot possibly fulfil in one lifetime.

Even so, the poorest man here is a king in contrast to the poor I left in Bombay when I embarked. Satya, one day, mark my words, Punjab's canals and dams will make it possible to feed all our people, notwithstanding Mr Malthus's theories.

Our hosts presented us each with a gilt-framed copy of their Declaration of Independence, though I conjecture they have not perused it carefully in some time, for their former slaves, the Negroes, are as our untouchables. My companion is well qualified, from a good Kshatriya family from Rajasthan, but he is substantially darker than I. Well advised by our hosts that he could be turned away from the dining room, I have escorted him every evening so we are known, by my turban, to be foreign. I explained to the manager at some length that we are of Aryan descent, but few Americans have ever met a Sikh, or any others with turbans, except as circus performers.

I long for England, where such ignorance is less conspicuous than in my student days. We return to London tomorrow, and none too soon.

Of all Sardarji's words, Roop understands only that he feels Indians spend too much effort on decoration. But his words do not seem to match the makeup of his mind – Mani Mai says Roop must decorate herself always, always, with jewels and ornaments. 'That,' she said, 'is the surest way for you to carve your place of respect in Sardarji's life, and for people to know how much he respects you. And,' Mani Mai adds, 'there's no need for the Bari-Sardarni to know what he gives you.'

Following Sardarji's orders, Roop is moved to Satya's larger, cooler apartments in the canal bungalow for the birth of his son. When Roop's waters break, Satya directs Dr Barlow to sit in Sardarji's leather wingback armchair in the library. Satya will call him if he is needed.

So now Dr Barlow sits and reads *Ozymandias*, mopping the large pores of his red face with a monogrammed handkerchief. Satya has sent the Indian doctor-ji home on his bicycle because his presence was not auspicious last time. Dr Barlow asks Satya, 'Are you quite well, dear madam?' and Satya's lips smile.

In spite of the May heat, Satya has the servants light a fire in her apartments to heat water. Woodsmoke mingles with the fragrance of agarbathi incense in the breathless room.

Shadow people leap from the hot roaring fire and dance across the walls.

Wisps of hair in Roop's mouth, the watery salt taste of blood. Pain. Wave after wave, and she is gasping, choking, biting down. Wet sheets. Lungs gulping air. Muscles that stretch and rip. Bones shifting within her.

And hours later a child erupts, hot, lava-slippery, past the tunnel of her larger lips, purple weight that separates from her at last.

Is it a boy? Is it a boy?

Lying on her side, emerging from the haze of pain, Roop can see Satya's unsmiling lips close to Mani Mai's ear. So fast they move, she cannot read them. Roop's good ear is turned to the pillow, she cannot hear Satya's directions.

Her limbs are again heavy, so heavy.

Is it a boy? Is it a boy?

It must be a boy – the child came with no hesitation, giving a single announcing cry. But it could just be that her body remembered it had given birth before.

Where is the baby?

Mani Mai's hands wipe the baby, strong fingers loop around the cord. Cutting quick, sharply. Severing, as she had done once before.

But this time she turns away and as Roop watches, paralysed, feeds the whole length of the severed birth-cord to the open fire.

Roop should scream now, scream loud as a hurt animal. But Satya's oval face is above her. Eyes, darkened to haematite, hard as gun-metal, impale her. A towel gags her mouth.

Sound dies in her throat.

Then, only then, does Mani Mai place the baby at Roop's side and shout to all, 'It is a boy!'

Almond eyes follow Mani Mai – *How can you let this happen to me? Stop her!*

The cord that joined Roop's son to his birth mother will not burrow beneath the soil in the flower beds, it cannot grow again or take further nourishment from her. The odour of charring human flesh fills the room and tells Roop this boy is not her protection – no.

He is Satya's.

It is almost midday, but Roop lies curled like a conch shell on the floor in the corner of her room. She wears bridal scarlet, the colour of anguish, but no tears come. She, once the gift, has become gift-giver who keeps on giving: one girl-baby, now she is to give a boy.

Five small pounds.

Too late she knows she was married for this, her obligatory altruism. Too late, she knows her ambition has overtaken her kismat.

Why cry now, did she not marry knowing another woman's rights preceded her own? Did she not choose this life in desperation, afraid she might know the great shame, the stigma of women like Revati Bhua who are left unmarried? Why does she now weep and wail when Satya only asserts her right, why does she want to crawl to her on bended knees and ask for mercy? If she had the words, who could she ask to spare her this one achievement in a world that says this is all that women are for?

Spare me this, spare me just this son, just a little longer. I give no trouble.

She would stay away from Satya, with her son as her protection. Satya can always ask Sardarji to get another wife who will not be weak as Roop. So long she dreamed of some woman who would be like a mother, but Satya is not the one, not the one.

In the same swing-cot Pavan left so quickly lies her son. Look, he recognizes her – after only ten days he calls his mother with an imperious cry, beckons her with the crook of his tiny fingers, asks that she give her blue-white milk to his lips as she gave her body to his father, lightly, believing in her good kismat, with no heed for consequences.

Such joy to be needed, but how long and how much and how many times will Roop be expected to give? Can she not keep him just till she can explain his mother was a person once, perhaps even, she must acknowledge, with desires and ambition, before she became but a vessel bringing him to life?

Roop has been watching her son's every breath; in his survival lies her future.

Five small pounds.

She knows the danger, remembers the little body that was her brother once, and how that nameless little body died. If her son should die, she will have failed. If he should die, what can stop Sardarji from sending her home in disgrace? Where a man has tried two women for the perpetuation of his tribe, why not try a third? A fourth? What is there to stop him?

Will her milk be enough for this child's insatiable, jagiri hunger? She touches herself where her breasts are full and tender.

Now Mani Mai squats on the floor beside her and her strong hand grips Roop's arm. Her glittering eyes come close to Roop's. In one hand she waves a tortoiseshell-handled, crocodile-skin purse.

'What is this way of sleeping? *Hut!* On the floor?' she scolds. 'I came to tell you Sardarji has returned.' Roop is quiet. 'I said you were resting, so you will have time to dry those tears. Make yourself beautiful. See, this is what he brought you. You must carry it to dinner.'

Mani Mai has brought a message from Sardarji, newly inspired from his trip abroad, 'He says he wants a modern baby. There is no need for you to feed the boy.'

She helps Roop to her feet and pulls her over to the mirror. Roop's eyes are dull, red, puffy. 'Look here, this is a good mirror, see yourself as he will see you. Then remember you are his sheesh mahal!'

Mani Mai's hands grip Roop's shoulders and shake her, 'Make yourself beautiful again – now!'

Her voice is urgent, but Roop makes no answer.

Mani Mai unbinds Roop's plait and begins brushing her long black hair, snapping Roop's head back.

'*Hai, Allah!* Don't listen to me, then! Who am I to tell you, I'm no one, just a stupid old woman who is trying to help a great Sardarni like you. What do you care that I have been your servant ever since you came to Sardarji's home, or that I brought two of your children into this world, what right have I to speak, ji?'

She cocks her head behind Roop's in the mirror, till their eyes meet; it's the only way Mani Mai can truly see Roop. 'You have made a son now. Do you think you have to stay in Bari-Sardarni's shadow much longer? Take courage, Roopji!'

But a woman's advice or praise is of such low value that Roop feels little gratitude.

'You are angry with me,' Mani Mai says in a coaxing tone.

'You are still loyal to Satyaji. With no hesitation you did as she ordered.' Roop's voice trembles.

Mani Mai shrugs, 'If I had refused, I could have had nowhere to go. You know how far my village is from here? I'm not so lucky as you, to have a husband who keeps me like a jewel in velvet.'

Roop sighs, relenting – Mani Mai is right. She must not expect from her what is beyond the poor woman's capacity to give. She puts her arms around the old woman and rests her head on Mani Mai's shoulder, as if Mani Mai were Gujri.

'Don't leave me alone,' she whispers.

Mani Mai pats her arm.

Who can she ask for help? Not Dr Barlow, who, Satya laughed, ran in terror from Sardarji's study after the boy was born, saying he was sure he had been bitten by a female anopheles mosquito. And the Indian doctor-ji's ten brown bottles are surely not the answer.

Mani Mai brings chickpea paste to rub on Roop's face, rings Roop's red eyes with surma and prepares her like a papier-mâché puppet doll about to play her part.

When she is ready, Mani Mai pries her away from looking at her son in the crib, takes her hand and says, 'Come, I'll show you what has come for your son.' She leads Roop to where the veranda passes the pantry. On this side of the bungalow there are no columns supporting arches, just wooden posts and lattices sustaining a few heat-shrivelled tomato vines. Mani Mai leads her down the trellised passage from the pantry to the cookhouse, and Roop follows, curious in spite of her worries.

A white cow with gentle black old-soul eyes stands chewing thoughtfully, near the leaning bricks of the servants' quarters opposite the cookhouse. Tent-haunched, low-necked, imperturbable.

Mani Mai thrusts a lump of brown sugar into Roop's hands. 'Feed her. See, she will feed the boy, make him grow strong.'

The cow's lips are soft as Nirvair's as it takes the lump from Roop's hand, leaves a sticky brown dribble on her fingers.

Satya joins them on the cookhouse veranda, stands with her arms folded across her breasts, and sniffs in contempt. 'Dirty beast, no wonder Hindus worship it – they are so weak they worship everything.' She glances at Roop, reminding: Roop is not from an old Sikh family, Roop has Hindu blood. And she adds, with a touch of triumph, 'Sardarji says he doesn't believe in cow-worship – he even ate beef in England.'

Roop remembers Revati Bhua, for whom a drop of a cow's urine was sacred enough to cleanse a whole cookroom. Poor Revati Bhua who had no choice but to wrap her idols away in her tachey case and who still gave her unused silver anklets to Roop as comfort. Or born-Hindu Gujri, who was raised a Sikh, and who cared for her when she had the typhoid, and followed her, walking five miles on the cracked rinds of her too-small feet just so Roop wouldn't be alone. And Pandit Dinanath's daughters with whom she played hopscotch by the temple, and silver-tongued Pandit Dinanath himself, who told Roop and Madani the story of the *Ramayan* though he knew them to be Sikhs. And she remembers Jyotshi Sundar Chand whose Hindu astrology told how the influence of Mangal on Roop's life could be vanquished by a man also under Mangal's influence. And there is Papaji's half-brother, Shyam Chacha, whom she must love because he is linked to her by blood.

These memories struggle within her, but Roop closes her heart to them and wishes desperately that she were from a pure and old Sikh family.

She pats the cow's nose.

'She is beautiful,' she says to Mani Mai, and turns away. As she passes through the airless cookhouse, the back of Atma Singh's turban is to her. He fans hot coals at the base of the clay stove. Sweat pours down his kurta.

She stops.

Mani Mai remains on the veranda with Satya, as sunshine streams through the open door. In the corner, five sweeper-men crouch over brass vessels, their polishing hands grey with ash. A washerman is counting and sorting clothing he will wash in canal water and return to the bungalow. Another fills his iron with hot coals, Sardarji's newspaper ready beside him, to be pressed carefully.

Atma Singh has taught her to eat with fork and knife – what more advice can she ask of so poor a man as he? She stands looking at him till the kitchen warms further with her fevered thoughts and at last he turns his turban away from the tandoor, notices her. He rises immediately, hands folded before her. 'Choti-Sardarniji?' He draws a cane stool close for her and squats before her. So close, he must see her red eyes brimming.

'Sardarji's baba is only five pounds.' Suddenly, she is shaking.

'Hein? Five pounds?' Atma Singh strokes his white beard. He does not need to be told the consequences if the boy were to die – Roop is not the first choti-sardarni in the world. There have been co-wives and junior ranis, temporary wives and concubines for centuries before her. But Roop knows by now not to ask help or compassion for herself. The only appeal that Atma Singh's loyalty to Sardarji's clan will understand is one for her son.

'What . . . what should I do?'

There is a long silence.

Atma Singh rests his arms straight before him on his knees. He looks through the doorway where Satya's shape stops the sun, haughty nose jutting from the rounded arch of her covered head. Advice is not to be rushed, it has a vaqt, a time when it comes, like everything else, but Roop has so little time, so little time.

Eventually, Atma Singh purses his lips, sucks his teeth and says, 'I will do as you command, and prepare almond and cashew milk for him twice a day. I will do as you say and give him herbs; no opium, though, but raw eggs and ginger that will stir his blood to manhood better than a woman's milk.'

Roop has not commanded at all; it is Atma Singh who humbles himself so she will feel better in her position as choti-sardarni. If his student does not succeed, the teacher will have failed.

Every morning and evening his pestle squeezes herbs and almonds to a fine white paste and his fork whips sugar with a raw egg, and as soon as the baby can stomach it, he stands stoop-shouldered at the door of Roop's apartments, balancing a warmed baby bottle upon a silver salver.

Roop, Satya and Mani Mai tune themselves to anticipate the boy-baby's every demand, learn this cry is for pain, this one for anger, this shout is to exercise his lungs and that one says a nappy is full and reeking.

At one month, he has them trained.

The perambulator Sardarji bought in London from Carter's Infant Carriages of Portland Street arrives, its hood folded back like a harmonium ready to play. Four wheels, two large, two small. 'So Comfy!' He read the caption as he showed it to

Roop in the catalogue, 'with inclusive prices of over 50 charming models. Made by the pre-eminent firm of Invalid's Furniture Manufacturers. By Appointment to the Queen.'

Roop wheels the boy beneath the papaya trees, and the mali picks offerings of purple-hearted lemon pansies from the flower bed and places them on the lace-covered cushions lining the pram.

What of Pavan, her little Pavan, left in the big haveli in Jorimon's care? Does Jorimon wheel her about in such a pram? No, a pram like this is not in her little girl's kismat.

Though the boy grows stronger with Atma Singh's supplements of cashew and almond milk, Roop knows she will soon be parted from him.

No one has said so. No one needs to.

It is understood, as if every ear had listened to the same strange unwavering music spinning from Sardarji's Victrola.

Stop, don't love yet! Hold back love then, for love can only suffer. Hold back love and give him care as a nurse tends to a patient with a love that says, 'Tomorrow you and I must part, because I wish you well.'

Satya is sure of it – confidence rings in her voice as she orders Roop to wheel the baby to her side. Satya treats Roop as if she and Mani Mai came from the same family, as if Roop should consider herself lucky to get tea, two meals a day and a roof over her head.

'And what use are you as a wife if you cannot even cook?' she scolds.

Mani Mai says, 'Y'Allah!' wonderstruck at Satya's behaviour.

At night, Roop gentles Sardarji's baby son in her arms and rocks him to sleep. She marvels at his small feet, each toe a perfect miniature of a man's; she kisses their soft soles, so when he becomes a man, his body may remember the mark of this stolen moment. She has forty days again, before his naming, before she gives him into Satya's arms and swallows tears, stretches her lips in a giving smile, and says again, 'My child is now yours, treat him well.'

Heat crescendoes into June haze. 'Allah knows this is what we need,' says Mani Mai to Roop, who lies, still weak and tired from her labour, before the electric fan. 'The hotter it is now, the sweeter will the papayas be in their season.'

Roop has so little time, so little time.

She hears Sardarji singing, somewhere in the distance, but because of her bad ear, or perhaps because he sings in English, she cannot understand the words.

Sardarji is in his bathroom, singing; a full-throated bellow from the base of his lungs. His shoulders shrug like a bhangra dancer as he splashes cool water over them. He rubs his wet feet together and stamps them on the wood-slat platform. He dips a copper mug into the shiny bucket and pours hot water over his long silver-streaked hair. Sings –

> *Kitty, isn't it a pity,*
> *in the city*
> *you work so hard?*
> *Baley, Baley!*

The copper warms in his hand, prompting the thought that he, unlike poor Mr Farquharson, has no difficulty in reconciling his religion and science. All Sardarji needs to do is think of copper and ask himself what force it is that tells copper it must expand when hot, contract when cool, and he can understand the paeans of praise all ten Gurus lavish on the force that pervades the universe.

'Pantheism,' sniffs Cunningham.

'No, Cunningham. Energy, force. Pan-entheism, something that goes beyond entity.'

In less philosophical moments, however, and for facility in action, Sardarji is wont to do the same as qualified men of all faiths do, picturing his God not as the ten Gurus saw it, but in his own image; a rational maleness, whose high position demands that he dedicate himself to keeping the mainspring of the universe wound up and ticking.

A competent being, able to guide and speak for those beneath him, especially the incompetent.

Women, for instance – his mother excepted from the category, naturally.

Lathering his long hair now, Sardarji thinks that if his mother had been alive when he returned from England, she would have listened and forgiven him, to hear that the thought of cutting his kes and so never needing to tie a turban again *had* crossed his mind.

But only on one occasion.

Maybe two or three.

It happened on mornings in Oxford when the walk past staring faces to his tutor seemed particularly daunting, but he'd told himself sternly: any conversion, however small, dissipates energy. Lapsing to a Sahajdhari, shorn Sikh, would make Vaheguru's energy less available to him, lessen the power that drives him like an engine from within. Sardarji reminded himself that it is difference in energy that makes it possible to generate power. Without his turban – his difference, his specialness – it would be a tepid universe.

This is the reason, he would have liked to explain to the Chaudhary, his father, why India needs engineers, to take advantage of the different energies of Vaheguru, to catalyze creation.

Help Vaheguru along.

'Quite so,' Cunningham pipes up. 'Though it's simply not done to put it quite that way. Order being vastly superior to disorder, it's mastery over nature, sir, that's the ticket. Mastery over nature.'

Sardarji lathers his hair a second time with Sunlight soap.

So lavishly has he fed the poor it must surely cover his son's karma debts from all his past lives. His son will be a scientist like his father, and go to college in England. But before that he will send him to a better school to learn Latin, so that by knowing where words have come from, he may project where they are going. And of course, to learn to comport himself like a gentleman. He will send his son to Chief's College, Lahore, where the sons of maharajas will be his friends.

Sardarji has already sent Dehna Singh to Lahore by train – 'Go register him there,' he told him, 'put him on the waiting list.' The boy is only five pounds but the astrologers who have stopped by the canal colony bungalow with their charts and predictions are right: he will live. Sikh boys do not give up easily.

Cunningham warns him with stories of bad things that happen to boys in boarding schools, dangers of wasted seed and consequent insanity.

'But,' he tells Cunningham, 'these are bukvaas, the kind of fears you English bring up when you don't want Indians to have the advantages you have.'

That he once believed such stories is immaterial. What is the point of looking back?

Because when he does look back, there is Kitty.

Kitty is the story before Cunningham, the story he has never told Mr Farquharson. And so Mr Farquharson cannot speak it from his silence, colour it for him with his analogies, his metaphors and strange labels so any second telling is marred by comparison to the first.

Pretty Kitty.

And so, though it has been so many years, whenever he is truly happy – as he is now – he still sings:

> *Kitty, isn't it a pity,*
> *in the city*
> *you work so hard?*
> *Baley, Baley!*

He wonders sometimes if Kitty thinks of him.

23. Khanewal, July 1940

Before Roop's amazed eyes, Jorimon leads Pavan into Roop's room and places a knotted bundle of Pavan's few clothes, Mama's phulkari-embroidered red shawl and sapphire ring on Roop's bed. Jorimon says to Pavan, 'Jao – go to your mama.'

To Roop, she says, 'Bari-Sardarni is returning her – she says she does not need a girl now. Two children are too much to look after.'

It is a month since Sardarji's little son left Roop. He was removed to Satya's side of the canal colony house as soon as Roop placed him in Satya's arms, just as she had Pavan. It was done correctly, with all proper ceremony: Sardar Kushal Singh and Toshiji came all the way from 'Pindi and again Sardar Kushal Singh read from the Guru Granth Sahib before the child received a name: Devinder, from the Guru, and the nickname Timmy, in honour of Mr Timothy Farquharson.

This time, Sardarji invited many friends from Lahore, from 'Pindi, Delhi and Bombay for his son's naming ceremony. Punjabi men – Hindu, Sikh and Muslim together – filled the canal colony house for more than a month. They picnicked and argued politics by the banks of the canals, asking, 'Who is this Mr Jinnah and how can he say he speaks for all Muslims in India?' 'Who is this Master Tara Singh?' and 'Does the Akali Party speak for Sikhs like Sardarji and his tenant farmers and for casteless Sikhs, or do they just claim to do so?' And they pontificated and pondered the question, 'Should illiterate peasants be allowed to vote and the country given over to unqualified men?'

They rode the canals on motorboats, laughing as bathing horses and buffaloes showed them the whites of their eyes. In the evenings, the songs they sang around the bungalow's empty fireplace – ghazals and ballads, qawwalis and pub songs – the poems they recited – tappas and limericks, shairi and sonnets – rose over the rushing of the canal to fill Roop's ear.

Out of respect to Satya, knowing only Satya these many years, Sardarji's guests brought their highest-ranking wives, first wives who turned from Roop and would not speak to her, as if she had used her body shamelessly in some way. These women did not care that she was married before the Guru Granth Sahib or that the girl-baby and now her son were gone from her to Satya; they saw her as no better than a concubine. Roop could expect no advice from them, no solace. Nor was she asked to sit at the dining table; all that month, at Satya's orders, Atma Singh brought Roop's meals to her room on a tray.

Sardarji's friends left, eventually; even Mr Farquharson, who honoured them with a final appearance for dinner, so very flattered by Sardarji's son's new name that he didn't notice Roop's absence at the table. Perhaps he mistook Satya for Roop.

That night Vayu's monsoon winds broke through the vice of the brain-boiling heat and as soon as Mr Farquharson left, Satya shortened the boy's name to Timcu – Mani Mai told Roop Sardarji allowed it, not in words, but by silence.

And once again, Roop did not feel the promised rush of happiness that should have been hers from the giving.

Till now.

'Pavan!'

Pavan puts a hand in her mouth.

'Pavan!' coaxes Roop. 'Look at me.'

Every muscle asks Roop to move toward Pavan, but she will not. Is this another test of Roop, as Sita was tested by Ram in the *Ramayan*? Whose test is this – is it Pavan's? And if the little girl fails by opening her arms to Roop, will the wrath of Sardarji and Satya follow?

Roop looks to Jorimon for guidance and believes she sees contempt there, for is not Jorimon's face modelled upon Satya's like a goddess's second head and arms? An orphan's scant choices encourage fierce loyalty.

The maidservant makes no motion to stroke the little girl's head and instead disengages the folds of her sari from Pavan's tiny fists. What Jorimon says must be true, then, for a maidservant like her could only reject those big loving eyes if Satya had rejected them first.

Why ask why? Why ask how?

Roop feels as if her prayers have snatched Pavan before her uncertain toddle sent her over a cliff.

It was Mama's sapphire ring that made Pavan too quarrelsome for Satya to keep, and so she has been returned.

Pavan looks away.

Please, baby, aa ja, ni, take a step in my direction. I am your mother, know me, love me.

Pavan offers a shy pearly smile and hides her pointed chin in the folds of Jorimon's sari.

'Can you leave her?' asks Roop, still so uncertain about giving orders in Sardarji's house. She does it pleadingly rather than imperiously, and she knows Jorimon can tell the difference.

The maidservant melts away. She will return to Satya – with what report, Roop cannot guess.

Unbelieving still, though her daughter is returned, Roop feels as if she stands panting before an inscrutable Vaheguru in her accustomed asking pose. Pavan toddles past, small limbs swaying, and steadies herself against the dressing table. An inquiring finger reaches out to touch the half-sphere of glass that immures the purple-hearted lemon pansy. Roop sits on the stool behind her and marvels at the rich softness of Pavan's skin, as soft as her own used to be, marvels at Pavan's dark lashes fluttering shyly against her cheek.

Was Roop once so small, so confident, so unconstrained? Tasting shapes and colours, testing the possibility that sound will hold the meanings it is given? No, she cannot remember it.

'Pavan! Look at me, baby! Look at me,' she says again, turning the child to face her.

Pavan turns her head to the right, her eyes sidle left and she smiles happily.

Roop moves to Pavan's right. 'Dekh, Pavan, mehnu dekh!' she said again.

Pavan turns her head left, waves a soft small hand.

What has Satya taught her?

'Evil eye,' says Mani Mai, when summoned. Surely not. Who might have been praising Pavan lately, attracting the evil eye? Roop cannot imagine Satya praising her.

Mani Mai crouches by Pavan and turns her so the dressing-table mirror reflects her face, hoping to deflect the power of the evil eye back on itself. Pavan's eyes swing slowly up to the mirror, lock on Roop's and meet there.

Yes, she can see like a girl. We must both look in the mirror at the same time and find each other. But how is it that she seems also to see like a man?

Now Pavan strokes her own cheek, she runs her small fingers through jet black curls, she smiles at herself and presses her hand to the small rosette of her lips, then leans forward and kisses herself in the mirror.

Roop takes Pavan's shoulders and turns the small body at a right angle to the mirror. And still the child has to look away to see her mother. Because without turning her head, Pavan sees Roop the way men see their women, from the corners of their eyes.

And now in Roop there come all the warnings Nani and Gujri and Revati Bhua and Madani and Kusum and Lajo Bhua and her teacher-ni and Papaji and everyone ever said to her.

Gujri saying, 'Boys' things happening in a girl's body' and, 'Everyone will say let-her-be-alone.'

Think, think!

If her child sees like a girl and like a boy, there is something wrong with her. If there is something wrong with her, there is something wrong with Roop. With the body that made her, shaped her. And there could also be something wrong with Timcu. And then, if something is wrong with Timcu, Sardarji will be very angry indeed. And then he will shout at her. She hears his roar in her ear right now, a roar so loud Roop's good ear might go bad too, a roar so loud everyone will hear her shame.

And then she'll be sent home.

And then?

And then what will she do in Pari Darvaza but grow fat and old and sad, like Revati Bhua, musty-old and querulous.

And the children?

If they are not perfect, he can send them home too and never acknowledge them. Then both she and Pavan will be a burden to Papaji. No one will think less of Sardarji for it – everyone will be sorry for him that he was cheated so.

No, no.

Who will ever marry Pavan with such eyes? No one must think her daughter imperfect.

Roop will have to do something.

What?

What?

She will teach Pavan to hide her eyes, look downwards, look away.

It can be done.

Has Roop not learned how to live with one ear secretly silent? Yes, she has. Not even Mani Mai knows she has taught herself to read more than sound.

Pavan stumbles against a low wooden piri stool, and Roop's own shins cry out at the crack of it. She runs over to Pavan and examines her. Both Pavan's shins are grazed and dabbed red with mercurochrome.

Hasn't Satya noticed Pavan's eyes?

No, she must not have noticed. This is something only a blood mother must feel. A woman who is just 'like a mother' is not a mother. She will not have felt Pavan's pain in her bones.

But Pavan can be taught not to walk into things. Roop can

make her wear socks thick as Huma wore, socks that will protect her shins from the marks of constant injury that will surely come from this stumbling. No one must ever treat her daughter like the blind man before the tunnel. No!

Her daughter will never look within herself and cry, her daughter will never beg. Her love will see to it, enfold Pavan in pretence, cover her weak eyes with deceit, the way Papaji once told Roop to hide her bad ear. Sardarji will never guess – his eyes see only what he expects to see.

But this – boys' things happening in a girl's body.

She watches Pavan every day after that, as the little girl claps her delight in the warm afternoon rain, as Mani Mai chases her across the veranda to feed her, as the child's laughter fills Roop's tiny room with a happiness that would be perfect, if it were not for Timcu's absence and her daughter's strange eyes. At night she will not let Pavan use the swing-cot where Timcu lay but holds the little girl to her breast; the fragrance of Satya's night queen uttar fills her sleep, threatening to take this warm adoring little thing from her again. 'The evil eye has fallen on her,' says Mani Mai.

'My love can cure it,' says Roop.

'Inshallah,' agrees Mani Mai.

If Allah wills.

But as days pass, Roop's worry only grows, eating away at her inside till a constant pain rides within her and makes her prefer spiceless English food to curry. Sardarji says her taste is improving greatly, that Roop appreciates the finer things in life – he knew it all along. Atma Singh prescribes milk for Roop's pain, but Roop cannot bring herself to ask the old man his advice for Pavan.

Why does her daughter look at Roop like a man, from the corners of her eyes? Something in Pavan's karma has come to greet her in this life. Some remnant of a boy-life has come with Pavan to this one, something her body remembers from another existence as it toddles into piri stools and crashes into walls. She must be born equally boy and girl in this life, for if she were only boy, she would not see Roop at all except from the corner of her eye, would not see her as other girls see each other, in the dressing-table mirror.

'We shouldn't give her any eggs,' Roop suggests to Mani Mai. 'No meat, either.'

Mani Mai says, 'Bilkul nahin.'

None at all.

But still this boy-thing keeps happening in Pavan's girl-body.

And soon Roop remembers, like simmer coming to boil, what the people who loved her have been trying to teach her for years. That the greatest love-gift an elder can give a daughter is to hurt her lovingly, gently, for-her-own-good, before a cruel world brings longer lament. Before she becomes like Roop, a woman with too much ambition, too many expectations – a woman who gives trouble to men.

Pavan must be taught a lesson only a blood mother can teach. She must be taught to lower her eyes and hide this weakness, this defect. Or all of them – Roop, Pavan and Timcu – all of them can be sent home to Papaji.

So Roop draws back her hand, one day when Pavan blunders almost into the twirling arms of the heavy electric fan. She draws back the hand closest to the ear that does not hear and she closes her eyes and slaps Pavan, little Pavan, not yet two, and just come back to her.

Tha!

Like Nani's cuff to her head. 'Ay, learn what women are for!' Like Revati Bhua's slap for wearing Mama's sapphire ring, like so many dhaaps that women need every so often for-their-own-good.

Not very hard, but hard enough.

Even so, her good ear hears that *tha!* Her love hears the crack of it. Her fingers smart from the softness of Pavan's surprised cheek and Roop knows she has made a hole like her own within Pavan, a hole that cannot be embroidered away.

Big black eyes widen and fill.

A dam has risen in a moment, without a single handful of dirt or donkey-load of stone. A lake of fear that will stretch and lengthen between Roop and little Pavan, the way it does with any woman who enlightens her daughter early, for-her-own-good.

But still Pavan has to look away to really see Roop, as if

Roop were a monsoon raindrop clinging to the money vines climbing the front veranda columns; nearly invisible.

Roop is shaking, but she has done what needed to be done.

The canal sound has stopped. Soon the household will return to Rawalpindi – Sardarji says his 'exile' in Khanewal is over. When they return, she will show Pavan her apartments in Sardarji's ancestral home, and tell her the rewards that lie in store for little girls who learn rules number one, two and three.

Little Pavan takes refuge behind Mani Mai's shawl-clad seen-much-worse-than-this, felt-much-worse-than-this shoulders, and wails the question all little girls ask their mamas, if they have a mama to guide them, the question to which there is no answer – 'Mein ki kita?'

What did I do wrong?

FOUR

1940-1941

24. Rawalpindi, September 1940

Vayu rustles the banyan leaves above Satya. Sitting on the terrace garden, she crushes a piece of sugar cane between strong white teeth, swallows the cool sweetness and spits the fibrous husk in the rain-gutter.

The wavering.

There it is again, like a soot-plumed flame dancing within a kerosene lantern. First an incline towards decision, resolve thickening the way sugar cane juice boils down to molasses, resisting alternative, kinder ways of saying, Buss! Enough! or – as she wants Mr Farquharson and all his quom to say – 'Goodbye forever and thank you,' and then the reverse, a pulling back to the comfort of rhythms established for three years now.

Why can she and Roop not simply go on the way they are, comfortable in their separate apartments, in their different roles in his life, she the wife of his early years of struggle and of building, and Roop the wife for modern times, the one for English dinner parties with Sardarji's 'superiors' and for ornament?

If only Roop were a bazaar woman, predictably loose and coarse and grasping. Satya could say she'd ensnared Sardarji, used uttar and wine and bound his heart in the tendrils of her black hair. But no, she'd met his picture and his astrological chart, like any bride of good family. Her only crime is to have brought no dowry and to have no means of support but the fruitfulness of her young womb.

Sardarji is not in need, like many in Punjab. The war the British had to join and fight because they call themselves Europeans is already a year old. High-up people in India are making fortunes supplying it – Rai Alam Khan's first wife wrote to say her son is supplying khaki uniforms sewn by tailor-masters in Karachi, tent cloth, silk for their parachutes, spittoons of hammered metal for field hospitals. With Mr Farquharson suddenly called for miltry duty, Sardarji has been promoted to Superintending Engineer. No, they are not in need, they have plenty, they can be charitable and give shelter to a woman of lesser birth than she, a shallow village woman who can produce children but knows little else about life.

Doesn't it take a dirty anna to make sweet yoghurt from a bowl of milk?

I come from a family of kind people, people known for their generosity. But . . .

Yesterday a Kashmiri came to Sardarji's haveli gate with fine jamavar and shahtoosh shawls, and Roop and Satya sat together in the banyan-filtered sunlight in the courtyard as he took the bundle from his head and untied its knots, north from south, east from west, and showed the treasures within.

'The shawls choose their owners,' said the Kashmiri. 'I only ask a fair price for bringing them to their new homes. They guide me with whispers through the streets, giving me directions.'

And that day Satya believed him.

'How I wish we women could do as your shawls do,' she said.

Pavan played and Timcu gurgled nearby, under Mani Mai's watchful eye. And Roop, like a bird trying its wings, wrapped herself in the red and black swirls of a jamavar shawl and laughed for joy. She pouted and wheedled as she haggled, but the Kashmiri looked only at Satya, reclining on the European sofa, with whom he had matched wits many times over the years. Satya tested the shawl, spread it, examined each ambi for variations of colour and of texture, proof that two sets of hands might have brought it to wholeness, but there was none. Not a single colour stood out more than the others, not a stitch strayed from its pattern. She questioned him about the family it came from. How many good women did it have? Were their relations harmonious? To all her questions he answered well, and so Satya bought the shawl for Roop, knowing for whom she would wear it, even as her surprised and happy thanks took wings about the courtyard ...

Knowing.

If he went to a bazaar woman and paid her, Satya would not know. Men need prostitutes to cool the heat that comes upon them, time after time. But she cannot bear the sound of his slippers scuffing the gallery as he passes her room, the creak of the door as he enters Roop's room. The proof of his favour – Roop's body thickening to ripeness. Two children, proof of her fertility and Satya's failure.

Three years ago, he swore he needed her to have a son. Now he has one. Then why does he still go to her, night after night? Roop's weaknesses have become her coy excuses – one of the few English phrases she has learned and uses most is 'Oh-I-can't!' And every time she laughs how innocent and stupid she is, the more Sardarji must be petting her and cuddling her at night.

If Satya had chosen a second wife for Sardarji, she would at least have chosen a woman who could cook and speak the git-mit, git-mit talk.

But in Roop's every simpering mistake is cunning, so much cunning. This village girl is not quite as stupid as I thought.

What for do we need her, I will ask Sardarji. She has done the needful.

Send her home.

Still she wavers, kindness trying to overcome her better judgment. The longer Roop stays, the more she will become Sardarji's habit, instead of his release. The longer she stays, the more she will learn from Satya, for Satya teaches by example.

She will tell Sardarji they will faithfully discharge whatever promises he made to Roop's father. Perhaps they could be generous and keep her in some haveli in the bazaar. Satya will treat her fairly, as one treats a poor relation or a faithful servant; Roop will lose nothing.

No.

Send her home.

Day has aged to grey in Sardarji's haveli and Roop props herself on an elbow, holding Pavan to her heart in the fourposter bed. Pavan's black curls are gathered into a ponytail that scratches under Roop's chin, her temples are soft beneath Roop's fingers. Roop begins a rhythmic pat at Pavan's brow.

'Pavan, who am I?'

'Roop,' nods Pavan, for whom this is a game.

'No, no, say "Ma-ma."'

'Roop,' laughs two-year-old Pavan, tossing her curls, looking directly at Roop, without seeing her at all. 'Choti-Sardarni.' And then, with unconscious cruelty, 'Jorimon!'

And Pavan calls Satya 'Bari-Sardarni,' as Roop does.

Roop's tummy aches with the fear it will always be so; nothing will change. Why does Satya not yet love her like a sister? Even after Roop has given Satya two children, Satya's haughty face knows no peace. In those grey eyes there is only fear, fear turning to hate, hate that radiates to Roop.

Everyone loves me, Sardarji, Mani Mai, Atma Singh – even the white peacock dances for me when I walk across the terrace garden. But Satya, my sister, to whom I have given two children – she still cannot find love for me.

Would Madani ever treat Roop this way? No. Would Kusum, though not a blood sister, but a sister-in-law? No.

Little Pavan curls up against Roop as if she would roll herself into Roop's stomach again, coconut scenting her black curls, the weight of her head stopping the blood flowing through Roop's arm.

Roop tries to feel it again, Pavan in her stomach, the visceral hot pain of that unwilling birth. One day she will tell

Pavan, 'This is how it was, and one day you will feel it too, for there are no other ways little girls grow to women.'

Then pity comes for Satya, who has never earned the name Mother, has never felt split inside, never been two in a body that was one. Never felt slick blood gush from her belly, like canal water rushing to the fields. How can Roop feel anger for Satya?

Lajo Bhua's rule number three is always with her. Rule number three, whispered to Roop and to Madani, so long ago. 'Never feel angry, never, never. No matter what happens . . . never feel angry. You might be hurt, but never ever feel angry.'

After a while, in the dark on the fourposter bed, Roop whispers again, 'Pavan, baby, what is my name?'

But, lulled by Roop's patting hand, Pavan's butterfly lashes lie close against her cheeks and her breath comes deep and even.

There are afternoons when the shimmer-haze of resurging after-monsoon heat offers Roop a mirage to replace the hope of friendship or love between herself and Satya: a wary, thorny shrub mirage to tend – companionship. It is a mirage that comes again this afternoon when Satya summons Roop to her private sitting room and, dismissing the hovering servants, all except the pukkhawalla, lowers the reed chics, masking the sun.

Satya needs an audience today, Sardarji being away in Delhi, giving his considered opinion in meetings with the Central Design Division now that Mr Farquharson is away in Burma.

Mirage rising again before her, Roop enters Satya's rooms as summoned, taking her seat on a low piri close to Satya's divan. Satya steadies the gourd base of her dilruba against a bent knee, fingers its strings gently. Roop listens as her bow calls forth notes that soften the hard planes in that set oval face.

'Is not my dilruba better than any gramophone?' Satya's question seems to rise from some long-ago debate.

'Oh, Bhainji, yes!' breathes Roop, delighted to confirm it.

'I play differently for each listener,' Satya explains. 'Sardarji's gramophone can only play a song its one way, same-to-same, every time, till it winds down. That is not music.'

The bow glides across the dilruba's strings for some time. Then Satya says, as if she were talking to the reed-chic shadows playing upon the wall before her, 'Many years ago, I used to play for him in the evenings. That was when he had come back from London and he was so happy to be home, that everything Indian was beautiful.' She sighs. 'Now, Sardarji says my music sounds out of tune; he likes only the gramophone music. But I tell him so many times – these British people's music is different from ours – it cannot measure five, seven or twelve beats to a measure and it doesn't have as many notes. It is not *I* who am out of tune, but *they* who cannot hear beauty in my dilruba.'

'You play beautifully, Bhainji,' Roop assures her. 'Can you teach me also?'

Satya inclines her gaze to Roop's level. 'Teach you! *Huh!* What can you learn? Music like this is beyond women like you.'

After a while, she says, 'A few years after he came back from England, Sardarji bought me a pianoforte – I have it stored away, upstairs. I asked him, "What does this name mean, pianoforte?" He said it means "soft and loud." I said, "Only two ways, it plays? Soft and loud? Nothing in between?" He said, "What more do you need, but soft and loud, and see the keys are all tuned precisely so you cannot be out of tune." I said, "I cannot leave my dilruba; for its very name means the song of my heart."'

She begins a plaintive melody that grows rich with passion, tumultuous notes that trill and resonate to the ivory flowers inlaid in the ceiling, insist they be heard.

The silken pukkha above them stills as the pukkhawalla outside stops his pulling to listen.

Satya ends on a strong, deep note that vibrates through the warm room.

After a moment, she says in an amending way, 'What can I teach anyone? All of us need our own ideas, not foreign ideas;

this is what I tell Sardarji. But he – his mind is their colony also.' She laughs bitterly. 'I told him, "I too am a colony – your colony."'

Her hand grazes Roop's cheek. 'Now you. So . . . we sit here together. Birds in the same cage.'

The thought comes distilled from her ferment, the explanation given to herself as much as to Roop.

'Birds – this morning a bird-walla brought his birdcage to the haveli, did you see him? That dirty ragged man wheeling his bicycle, with so many sparrows in that one small cage tied to its carrier? He cried, "Allah will give you his blessing! Buy a sparrow, set it free. Allah will bless you!" Didn't you hear him?'

Roop shakes her head, hoping it was not her bad ear's fault that it had not heard the bird-walla's call, but encouraging Satya's story.

'It took a whole rupee to open his cage door for all the birds, and they all stopped their fluttering and pecking and flew,' says Satya. 'And I was so angry, so angry! I told him no one would have to buy them and set them free if he hadn't first trapped them in his cage, why should his Allah give any blessing?'

'What did he say?' Roop asks.

'He said, "Every man has a family to provide for – Allah will understand."'

Sympathetic strings vibrate beneath the melody drawn by Satya's bow.

'Birds, yes, that's what we are.'

She lays her bow beside her on the divan for a moment, for her hand to twirl about her wrist in puzzlement. 'That I should have become relative to you – this is a strange new zamana.' She lifts her bow, draws it across the dilruba again, shaking her head at the riddle of these new times.

For a moment, Roop thinks she sees an opening there to Satya's heart, thinks Satya can see her, Roop, without Sardarji as mirror, that for once there is no Bari-Sardarni, no Choti-Sardarni, just the two of them sitting, one woman making music, one listening to notes soaring, cascading into the sleepy steamy afternoon.

But when the banyan's leaf-shade lengthens across the

courtyard and it is time to raise the reed chics, Roop's mirage fades, too.

Mani Mai and Jorimon bring the children down into the courtyard after their nap, laying painted wooden toys before Timcu, a ball of pink wool before Pavan. Satya reclines on the European sofa so that Roop has either to stand or squat with Jorimon and Mani Mai.

Squat with the serving women.

No.

So Roop stands.

Dehna Singh serves tea on silver tea trays – spiced chai in a silver tumbler for Satya, a china teapot, teacup and saucer for Roop. Roop takes her teacup and stands beside Mani Mai to be sure Pavan keeps her eyes lowered and doesn't hurt her shins.

Little Timcu crawls a few paces across the courtyard to the women's encouraging cries, till he falls flat and cries, and Satya, Jorimon, Mani Mai and Roop are at his side together, soothing, 'Ah, mere bachey, na, na!'

Feeling Roop's love, smelling her scent, the little boy holds out his arms to Roop instead of Satya and Roop lifts him, rubbing his small back, with his bottom resting on her forearms, turning away to breathe in that moment, hold it forever in memory.

Satya circles Roop, and her long fingers steal about the little boy's tender ribcage. Timcu, trapped between them, looks from one to the other, wide-eyed, tear channels shining on his cheeks.

'*Dey!*' Satya orders Roop, tightening her grip on the boy.

'Ik mint,' pleads Roop, desperate for one minute with her son.

Satya's fingers tighten. Timcu's eyes fill again; a squeal fills Roop's ear.

Immediately, Roop holds Timcu out to Satya. 'Don't hurt him!' she whispers. 'See, by himself he was going to you. By himself.'

Satya takes the boy. 'So selfish, this stupid girl is,' she says to Jorimon.

Then to Roop, 'Get out of my sight. Mar ja kitey.'

Go, die somewhere.

At that, Roop bursts into tears and runs out of the courtyard.

She climbs to the terraced garden, confides her anguish to the white peacock.

The haveli casts its mighty shadow down upon the lawn.

'*Kyon?*' cries the peacock, prancing from one clawed foot to the other. '*Kyon?*' he fans his gold-flecked tail, as if asking why.

Roop tells him she doesn't know why.

The peacock can bring no tear to his garnet eye for Roop, and soon he gives a swish of his long tail, and perches on a raised flagstone with a ring at its centre, the entrance to the underground stream that supplies the whole haveli. Roop has seen servants climbing from that entrance, carrying gunny sacks of grain or water in goatskins and large earthen jars.

Curiosity rises, wipes Roop's tears with her chunni and demands that Roop investigate further.

'*Hut! Hut!*'

She shoos the peacock off the flagstone and tugs at the ring, heaving it away. A pair of pigeons flutters away, alarmed.

A staircase ripples down into darkness.

Roop intends no more than an amusing diversion, the square of blue at the top of the stairs growing smaller as she descends. At the bottom, the air is thick and cool, as if long untouched by the fierce sun above. When her eyes adjust to gloom, she is in a small stone chamber, perhaps ten paces long, echoing with the music of flowing water, notes sweet as any rendered by a dilruba's strings.

At the far end of the chamber, Roop discerns a wide metal spout affixed to the mouth of the underground stream scenting the core of Sardarji's haveli. At her feet, what Sardarji's haveli does not require disappears into a passage, to be channelled away to the bazaar and homes outside the great haveli.

Roop follows the bubbling stream into the passage, careful to keep her jutis dry. A few steps and it widens to reveal a godown speared by sunshine streaming from an air shaft in the stone roof. Here jute sacks full of grain and brass-trimmed wooden trunks of valuables are stacked or stored till needed. A second chamber opens off this one, and others beyond it.

Roop's eyes follow the great roots of the old banyan beginning from this stream, rising mossy-green all around her on its way up the stairs, to join the haveli walls.

Crunch!

The sound was behind and above her.

Roop rushes back through the passage in time to see the small square of hot blue sky above her disappear.

Thud!

Where the banyan's roots meet the surface, there rests the flagstone, covering the staircase.

A chill passes through Roop.

'*Kholo! Open Up!*'

She runs up the stairs, screaming.

But her voice bounces off the flagstone at the top of the stairs and returns to her ear.

She stops, waits.

Surely the someone outside must have heard?

Roop swallows hard.

She climbs to the third stair from the top, turns and doubles over till her head and shoulders are below the flagstone. Now she strains till her cotton kameez chafes at the back of her neck, and she calls.

'*Mani Mai! Mani Mai!*'

Strains at the stone, calls again –

'*Kholo! Kholo na!*'

The stone lifts a few inches, letting in air, but Roop is not strong enough to lift it completely away from the mouth of the entrance. To lift it completely, she would have to be standing outside on the terrace garden.

Sinking down on the step, she wipes sweat pouring down her face, with her chunni.

What should I do?

Warm, dank air rises about her as she presses her lips to the crack in the flagstone and cries out again and again. She slips her steel kara from her right wrist and uses it to rap on the heavy stone.

'*Mani Mai! Mani Mai!*'

She is alone.

That thought frightens her more than the darkness.

She tells herself that Atma Singh will send a dishwasher boy to fetch drinking water soon, someone to hear her.

There is a skittering sound.

A rat, twitching its whiskers at her from the base of the stairs.

'*Hut!*'

Roop takes off her juti, grips it tightly in her unclean hand, ready for the rat to come any closer.

She takes a deep ujjai-breath like a yogi, and begins saying the Sukhmani prayer to calm herself. Every few pauris, she raps the stone with her steel kara and cries out again.

'*Mani Mai! Mani Mai!*' and '*Kholo! Kholo na!*'

Hours later, Roop's voice has waned to whisper. Her steel kara is dented from its knocking against the stone. One end of her chunni is a crushed wet ball. Her single plait itches through her kameez, wet against her spine.

The Mangal star is so close, Roop could pluck it from the dark quilt of the sky, by the time there is a scraping sound and the flagstone lifts from the entrance to the chamber.

Warm hands grip Roop's cold fingers tight as Mani Mai scolds, 'Everywhere I was looking for you!' and she almost carries Roop back into the haveli.

As they cross the courtyard, Satya stands above, on the gallery outside her sitting room, and shouts, 'Did you find her? I told you there was no need to worry. Keep her in her room from now on, or she'll run away again. Who knows, perhaps she's meeting some strange man in the bazaar, then making up stories to explain why she was gone – shameless, she is.'

Mani Mai whispers, as she helps an exhausted Roop to bed, 'Choti-Sardarni, be careful.'

Roop's mirage, that wary, thorny shrub mirage, vanishes for ever.

And in its place grows fear.

Satya dreams.

I am Indus in whom the five beloved tributaries collide and flow south to the wrist of the sea. I burble and I leap from the

Hindu Kush, turning ripple to wave, dancing naked but for sunshine, gushing, effervescing, moulding sharp stones to smooth pebbles, rolling past wheat fields, taking the thirst from the tongues of wild beings and tame goats, nursing the eggs of fish and of fowl. Caressed to swollen ecstasy by monsoon breezes, too clever to be held, too wise to be tamed.

I am Indus.

Comes a wind I have never met before, Vayu from the sea, greedy, carrying the weight of a million unshed tears; he slows me with pity.

I call to him; perhaps I can help him. He sighs and comes northward to meet me, telling me he will be grateful if I cleanse the salt ocean when I reach it. And he lowers his mouth like the beasts and drinks from me, greedily, angrily, until I cry it must stop, 'Buss, na!'

But no, he will not, draining me with an unnatural unrelenting thirst, until I push him from me and persuade him he must move on.

Now, belatedly, this wind thinks to repay me so he builds me canals that flow from me like sparkling mukaish-embroidered chunnis laid out to dry across the desert. The canals feed the desert till it turns green, and now small wanderers stop at their banks — and they stay. Then the wind leaves, magnanimous and sated, and weakly, I babble my thanks, 'Shukriya!'

Left in my bed, I discover pain in each limb, weight in each joint. The raw, unlined canals stir my muddy water, bringing all that is buried and denied to the surface. I can hardly move, my thighs are stained white by the fine salt dust that extinguishes life in my valley.

I drag my way southwards, sluggish and slow, covered in this residue. My hollow breasts swing before me.

Moon phases mark my waiting.

Then comes a hakim, that courteous herbal healer who lives in the plains. Breathing solicitously and carefully on my sleeping shape, he takes a kirpan, hones its steel blade, cuts the salt from my thighs. Deep gashes, till I bleed so long and so much his brow knits in worry and repulsion. I bleed into cloths first and then into clay pots he places carefully at my side. Then into my canals flows my blood, so strong and so red, the salt dissolves.

She wakes.

Hot, flushed with new resolve.

Though the full meaning of her dream may lie concealed, a part of it suggests action.

The hakim's concern is like Sardarji's; when Sardarji returns from Delhi, she will play it like an instrument, sa-a, re-e-e, ga-a-a, wavering in word and action, matching his kindness with feigned anxiety for Roop, until he agrees with her that 'we will do what's best for all of us.'

Or she can take action, so the hakim need take none.

Action where action is required.

'Do the needful,' Sardarji always tells her, never needing to specify further. And Satya always has. Over the years, she has anticipated his wishes for all the things he does not wish to be known for – tenants to be evicted, rent collected, compromises advocated, festivals observed, 'superstitions' propitiated – beliefs and actions he does not wish to be his. This is just another needful. Of course, he *must* wish Roop gone.

She walks from the haveli into the blue-grey morning. The white peacock prances before her, the fountain arches to greet her. Sardarji's horses nicker and snort warnings about dreams whose full meanings are ignored and left to the future.

Satya's salwar brushes the sheen from Sardarji's terrace lawn, leaving dark blotches where she passes.

Rawalpindi, October 1940

It is Navratri; their Hindu neighbours are performing nine nights of ceremonies. All of 'Pindi hums in anticipation of the tenth day – Dusshera and the Ram-Lila.

Sardarji reads in his study as Satya, standing in the court-yard, directs the servants to bring labourers to carry a sofa on their backs and take it to John Company Bagh, a public garden half a day's walk away.

There Sardarji will sit in the shade of their special tent, as Ram rescues Sita from Ravan and carries her away from Sri Lanka, the mango-shaped island Sardarji showed her on his prized beige-brown globe. Hanuman's monkey soldiers will offer Ram their backs as their bridge, he will avenge Sita's abduction again, and they will all be there to relive it.

Satya comes to the door of the study. She needs to know whether Sardarji wants anything.

'Satya, do you know,' says Sardarji, inserting a forefinger in a bound volume with English writing, 'this Mr Darwin I am reading is the English man who made the discovery of Hanuman, the monkey god. He says Hanuman is the commander of his monkey soldiers and our species; we are all descended from him.' He is attempting to explain the natural order of life in terms Satya might understand.

'English sahibs discover things that are already known; that way they appear infallible.' Her gaze sweeps the room to confirm the servants have dusted. She adds, 'Hanuman is the son of Vayu, why doesn't Mr Darwin say we are all descended from Vayu?'

'You don't understand, Satya.'

'You always say, "You don't understand, Satya,"' comes her retort. 'I *do* understand. I understand only too well the things that begin as English ideas and are retold to me as if you were Muhammad hearing the Koran.'

'Why are you so concerned where an idea comes from as long as it is excellent?'

'How is it that all the ideas you think are excellent are English?'

'That is not so – English civilization has many excellent ideas that were born in India.'

'But do they say, do they ever acknowledge, that any of their ideas came from us?'

'The English have a knack, an understanding of how to improve upon ideas,' says Sardarji, evading Satya's question.

'So that they can sell them back to us.'

Satya draws her chunni over her head and goes to the door of the courtyard to see if the labourers have come.

Sardarji calls after her, 'No, so that excellent ideas can be used for a better future.'

'A better future for whom?' asks Satya, returning. The labourers have not come. 'Them or us?'

'Well – both, Satya. Both.'

'Do they pay Indians for their ideas?'

'I receive a salary, others receive wages – yes. Which ideas do you mean?'

'Old ideas, many ideas they rename and call their own. You used to say, before you went to England, that Indians invented the shunya, what they now call 'zero.' Well, did they pay us for it?'

'*Offo*! Satya, that was so long ago. Indians haven't had many good ideas since.'

'Sardarji, you say yourself no one knows which ideas are good or bad until they can be tested in the world, and you also know we cannot make even a nail or a match ourselves – everything has to come here from England. Then, if they cannot be tested, how can anyone know if Indian ideas are good or bad or somewhere in between? And,' she says, out-flanking her adversary, 'how much opium, gin and whisky have they sold us?' Her father's face returns from the edge of memory – one gulp, one drink, next drink, next gulp. 'I only see a better future when they leave. Then we can decide which ideas are better for us and which are better for them.'

'Indians can't decide anything.' Sardarji gives a great laugh. 'Without the British, the Indian National Congress will be arguing till the next century. How many committees and councils have I sat on where the Chief Engineer's veto or the Viceroy's veto was necessary to resolve the issues.'

'Then what? Instead of the Viceroy, can't an Indian man do this veto-sheeto? Won't that be better than what we have?' Her voice ricochets off marble tiles, the courtyard rings with her passion. 'Everywhere they tramp across our land, they see and remember only themselves.'

'So?' says Sardarji, with deadly calm. 'Is that any different from other invaders India has had? Would Indians not see and remember only themselves, as you so quaintly put it, if Indians were the invaders?'

'Yes, it *is* different. Other invaders became part of India – we gave, they gave. Can you tell now from looking at anyone's face today who is Muslim, who is Hindu? These people you work for though you need not work at all, these men only take, take, take. And the English women – *hai*, they are worse.' A hand rises to her neck, remembering. Her kantha necklace, now Roop's, and the party full of Europeans. How its brilliance and its weight had comforted her, compensation for her tongue-tied state, how the European ladies ignored her once they found she spoke no English. 'We are not like them, we do not invade.'

'Only because Indians have never had power and unity enough to do so, lately,' says Sardarji. As her mouth opens to respond, he adds, 'You are so quarrelsome.'

'I tell you the truth.'

'I know, but why so sharply?'

'You pretend everything English is perfect.'

'I certainly do not. See, I enjoy the Ram-Lila. Of course, I offer my patronage by my presence, and it most certainly does not imply I believe these Hindu tales.'

'They are not tales, they are history. Like your English people's Jesus story.'

Sardarji snorts.

'Our Gurus are history,' says Satya. 'We have their own words, only a little over four hundred years old. Not gospels and tales others have told.'

'That's different,' says Sardarji, returning to Mr Darwin.

Pigeons flutter and preen in the cornices above. Looking up, Satya sees Roop leaning over the edge of the gallery.

Eavesdropping as usual.

Satya looks at her hands, large and capable, palms pink and well-lined. Hands that can raise children – after all, what is there to do? Jorimon will dress them, feed them, clothe them, till they are sent to boarding school where they will learn to speak and read English, come back, and join Sardarji in lording it over the land.

Roop does not appear in the tableau fixed in Satya's mind.

Satya asks sweetly, innocently, 'Do you really wish for the whole family to be seen in public?'

'Mmm-hm,' says Sardarji, engrossed.

'The children, of course, but does Roop need to come? There will be English people attending, generals, the police commissioner, the district magistrate, the district commissioner, higher-ups in your department. And she really doesn't have the requisite dignity yet.'

'Do as you judge best,' he says, absently.

At Satya's bidding, the servants roll up a nine-by-twelve-foot carpet of Kerman design – she has selected the best – four hundred knots per inch, a carpet of turquoise and blue. It takes three men to carry it from the haveli to John Company Bagh.

Now two old fellows with rheumy eyes arrive. Satya directs them in Urdu, as she usually does with the Muslim servants, to carry a velvet-covered three-cushion sofa, which came by train from Lahore, to the fair grounds, and place it in the shamiana tent.

The old men bend their knobbly backs. Two servants load the sofa, tie it to their waists with an old turban, help them straighten and stagger from the courtyard.

'Shukriya, bhaijaan,' says Satya, thanking one of them in Urdu, calling him brother.

Satya will rely on Mani Mai's long old tongue, which she knows will take Roop the message that there is 'no need' for Roop to attend the Ram-Lila and also explain Satya's decision. Poor thing, to be so simple that all decisions require explanation – the girl-child will be just like her unless Satya intervenes now, early and firmly.

I will tell Sardarji he should be generous. When Roop is returned to her family, he can offer to keep the girl-child, even give her a dowry when the time comes.

But that village family . . . hai, so grasping. They will be sure to accept.

This is the difficulty with being too generous.

The boy will be like Sardarji. Straightforward, loving a good laugh, a good whisky, and the sport of good argument with men, but avoiding conflict with women; all this runs in his blood.

Back in her private sitting room, Satya calls Mani Mai before her and unlatches her paandaan. The nine compartments of the paandaan waft aromas to her nose and invite her to blend them. Cinnamon, anise, fennel, cardamom, imli and cumin. In the soft centre of the green paan leaf, she daubs betel-nut paste and sprinkles black cumin seeds, so dear, so rare. She garnishes the cumin with soft sweet betel wood, dark as blood clots, silvered with virk. She smears the sourness of sticky brown tamarind paste so gently, so gently.

And now she adds the second half of that bitter almond saved in her paandaan since that day at the photographer's studio, three years ago.

Mani Mai watches with deepening fear.

Satya folds the paan leaf over the bitterness of the almond and spices carefully. She says, 'Take this to Choti-Sardarni, it will help her appetite.' She holds it out to her, her face friendly and innocent.

What is this I do?

Somewhere my family must have been afflicted by a ten-headed Ravan's incarnation.

Mani Mai takes the paan and scuttles away and Satya laughs, actress without audience. There is nothing in that paan that will hurt anyone's stomach, but when is a gift just a gift, and when is it a message from one hand to another's?

Mani Mai will explain her gift to Roop, and Satya knows Mani Mai will do it well, mindful of stories Satya has told her about this life and her past ones. Mani Mai will make warning signs from her small gift of paan that Satya could not improve on. Mani Mai will tell Roop tales of other choti-sardarnis and junior ranis in Punjab taken suddenly, inexplicably ill, young girls just like Roop who never saw poison coming.

Mani Mai will tell Roop how very stupid were those women to trust their food.

She will remind Roop of a certain cup of salted tea, of a baby's birth cord fed to the fire, of a flagstone that lay heavy across the entrance to the underground stream.

Mani Mai will foretell, she will make predictions. She will open that paan before Roop and search its ingredients to find the unusual. And, testing first the black cumin seeds and then the punishing bitterness of the half-almond, she will prophesy calamity.

As for Roop – Satya thinks Roop has had more kismat than many village women, and should have been careful to remain useful, maybe even have learned the git-mit, git-mit talk.

Too late now.

Mani Mai comes to Satya's room the next day to tell her

Roop has refused her food at night and again in the morning.

'She must be pining for home, poor Roop,' says Satya. 'I will call a compounder to give her an injection.' But she doesn't, returning instead to her private sitting room. She stretches out on her divan and watches the huge wing of the silk pukkha swinging now towards Roop's side of the house, now back to hers.

There is really no need for violence, just the threat of it will do wonders.

The Ram-Lila stage is erected, the actors come naturally by their roles. The man everyone knows as a kalal becomes ten-headed Ravan; the kalal is already one whose silver is unholy, having earned it from liquor, so the choice is popular and the man carries his additional stigma well. A potter from Taxila becomes Sita because his hands know round gestures of shaping and the pleasure of wheels that turn full circle. A young Hindu is chosen to be Ram, tall and clear-eyed, with a beard just fuzzing at the edges of his cheeks. He looks to Satya like Sardarji, the way he was when Satya saw him when he returned from England – except Sardarji wore a turban and European attire neck to toe.

Everyone knows the story well and how it will end. Why then will they sit before the actors again this year?

Because each of us is changed by the roles we are given – the course of our change depends upon our pedigree and our past.

The audience comes not to answer the question why, but to learn a different how, on this and every Dusshera. And this day it is only Satya who sits beside Sardarji in the Austin Princess and alone with him on the three-seater velvet sofa, and it is only she who inclines her head over her folded hands, saying 'Sat Sri Akal' to the wives of his equals.

It is a pity there are not more here to see her, but Muslim and Sikh landowning families no longer attend Hindu festivals with the same enthusiasm as they did a few years ago. Muslim families, because Mr Jinnah has begun wearing an Indian-style shervani coat in place of his English suit, and is being called Quaid-e-Azam – father of a nation – and has made a great speech demanding to establish his majority-Muslim nation, a nation he calls Pakistan, place of the pure.

Can there be anyone or anything that can remain pure and survive?

Satya strives for purity; always it eludes her.

Sardarji says not to take Mr Jinnah seriously, for he is by no means an observant Muslim − he drinks, and Sardarji is re-assured by that (Mr Jinnah also smokes, a weakness that Sardarji does not find reassuring). But Sardarji's Muslim friends seem to be taking Mr Jinnah seriously, or there would be more of them here.

And many Sikh families are not attending today, because Mahatma Gandhi strongly condemned a Sikh who voyaged all the way to London to silence Sir Michael O'Dwyer, the former Governor of Punjab, with bullets, for proclaiming mass-murderer General Dyer a hero from 1919 till now. The Governor, who had been the highest English higher-up in Punjab at the time of the massacre at Jallianwala Bagh, told his English countrymen every chance he got that the General's order to fire upon Indians penned into Jallianwala Bagh and the massacre that followed had 'saved India.' If the assassin had not been a Sikh, Sardarji explains, Mahatma Gandhi might not have seen those bullets as 'insanity.'

When the Ram-Lila is over, the Austin Princess takes Sardarji and Satya back to the haveli. They alight for the walk through the bazaar to the haveli, with Jorimon and the children.

Sardarji strides away to his study as Mani Mai approaches Satya and the children, takes Pavan's hand from Jorimon's to return the little girl to Roop.

'Choti-Sardarni has refused food all day,' Mani Mai ventures to Satya.

Satya is unmoved.

'Fasting is good before a journey,' she tells Mani Mai.

'Journey?' Satya savours the rank smell of fear, though Mani Mai bows her head before her.

'A nice visit home for a while.'

At nightfall, Satya and Sardarji, Sardar Kushal Singh and Toshi gather on the terrace garden with their Hindu neigh-bours to welcome Lord Ram home with fireworks. Clay diyas flicker in every recess and window of the great haveli. Bets rise on gin rummy and canasta hands, laughter scatters across the lawn.

No one asked the actors to act the rest of the *Ramayan* story: the story that did not end with Ram's homecoming and the celebrations of Diwali – how Ram rejected Sita, innocent though she was, because a mere washerman suggested that in her time as Ravan's hostage, Sita might have become impure.

And how Sita shamed him for all time, outdoing him in performing her duty. But everyone knows the story . . . how Sita called upon the labia of the earth to open wide again, take her back within them, how Sita walked into the maw of the earth with her eyes wide open and her izzat intact, dying of her own will, the same way she was born.

Servants light the fuses; fireworks spin, crackle or sparkle, and dodge away. The fireworks flame saffron red, phosphor bluish-white, and Muslim green for Sardarji and his guests. The smell of burning sulphur fills the dark.

Satya's lips move at Sardarji's diamond-studded earlobe. She offers him crumbly pinni sweets impressed with the mark of her fingers. 'Such a pity Roop is unwell,' she whispers. 'How she would love this display.'

It could be true; Mani Mai says it is four days since Roop took food or water.

The children are with Satya again, this evening, and Jorimon is there to look after their needs. Excitable, unruly children, with that peasant-like pushy curiosity, so like their mother's. But just a look from Satya, or a slight pucker between Sardarji's eyebrows, is enough to still them at this early age; they will be manageable.

25

It is the fifth night that Roop lies on the fourposter bed, staring at the ceiling of polished wood inlaid with ivory. She has taken no food, she has drunk no water – even the water in the bathroom is polluted for her, for she once saw the Muslim sweeper, Azhar Sheikh, drinking from it. The usual fear pain in her belly has changed its dull ache to a fiery constant throbbing.

For four nights she tried to give no trouble, and instead sent Papaji and Jeevan one dream-message each. She crinkled her eyes tightly and asked Vaheguru to carry her words to them: 'Papaji, Jeevan. Think of me here, in this room, nineteen years old with no mother to guide me. Neither of you told me this is what I need to survive here, this constant vigilance. Think how my heart aches for words of concern, not for Sardarji's second wife or for the mother of his children, but for Roop. Papaji, my fear takes sustenance before I do. It nibbles at every roti, spills every tumbler of water on the tile floor in the bathroom to test its colour. It listens at my keyhole in case my 'sister' should lock me in, it clutches my throat so I will not complain and be sent home for ingratitude. Jeevan, I am your sister, remember your promise to protect me when I sent you the gold thread rakhri I made to tie about your wrist last monsoon? Think of your sister now.'

For four nights she tried to send them these dreams and every day she hoped for a sign that Papaji or Jeevan felt her mind touch theirs.

But Mani Mai said men can't imagine a woman's world, they have to be told of her pain in words or they live in oblivion.

On this night, her stomach gnaws like a wild thing within her. Closing her eyes, she can almost smell Gujri's special makki rotis. A pat of fresh-churned butter, white, gleaming, melting into the dark green of Gujri's spinach saag. She can almost feel the heat from the golden makki rotis, taste the tang of the mustard spinach ground for hours by Gujri's hands. And the milky sweetness of savayan noodles . . .

With the memory of Gujri's spinach saag comes a clarity only hunger strikers and freedom fighters know – Roop will have to send Bachan Singh a letter.

She rises; the room spins about her. She steadies herself against the bedpost for a moment, sinking her toes into the Tabriz carpet.

She tiptoes down the staircase to Sardarji's desk. She pulls the switch cord of his green-glass-shaded brass lamp, finds paper and a large heavy fountain pen in the paper stand behind the taip-writer.

She writes to Papaji, all the words she tried to say in her dream and more:

They are their father's children to do with them as he pleases. I who bore them am to be discarded, empty husk of no consequence now. They are his, not mine. His to give to her, his to care for, his to starve or shame or abandon.

Her fingers cramp round the fountain pen and move across foolscap, guiding the fragile steel of its nib. Ink scent fills her nostrils. There are other words within her that have no words.

Soundless things, they cry or clap or jeer without a voice to give them utterance. But they are hers and haunt the room she moves in, slipping between the cracks and fissures of dreams; they scheme behind her eyelids. Perhaps she should say them as she used to, chirping like a small brown koel, so sweetly and softly, no one will notice till the words have taken wing and gone past her lips. Then she could pretend they spoke themselves, just slipped out in mischief, and be called a good-good, sweet-sweet obedient girl again.

She uses Sardarji's blotter after writing, its solid arc steamrolling her words, crushing the outlines of her tears to star-splotches, faint blue on the lined paper. *Read between the lines, Papaji, read around them, past them, between them. In the spaces between the words is your daughter. In the unspoken, in the unwritten, there is Roop.* From the blurred edges of memory comes the taste of abandonment. There was Papaji at Firozepur railway station, dimming into distance, certain no man can raise two little girls without a wife. There was Papaji again at Punja Sahib Gurdwara, sending her to this, her real home, whispering in her ear, 'Above all, give no trouble.'

But now, will he protect her? *Can he?*

She signs her name in Gurmukhi script: the letters raising their stick-thin arms above their heads as if some teacher-ni has punished them for speaking out of chorus.

She folds it, takes an envelope from the paper stand – no one will notice its absence in this house of plenty – and in a moment she is climbing the dark spiral. She inches along the wooden gallery to her room – one creak and Satya could discover her, with what consequence she cannot imagine.

To whom should Roop give this letter for posting? If Satya finds out that Mani Mai posted this letter for Roop, might she dismiss Mani Mai, leaving the children no one but Jorimon?

What kind of woman is Jorimon?

Star streams dance before her eyes, the question is unanswerable. Roop and Jorimon have never exchanged more than a few words.

It is best not to endanger Mani Mai.

Roop cannot imagine walking through the bazaar unaccompanied by Mani Mai, to post the letter herself.

In the morning, when Azhar Sheikh enters through the second door of the bathroom, bearing copper buckets of hot water and of cold, Roop says his name so he raises his eyes as far as her ankles. The man who clears away other people's chi-chi from the commode is a man whom nothing can disgust and Azhar Sheikh is, she is sure, unable to read.

She puts the letter in his dark hand, along with a whole silver rupee from the crocodile-skin purse with the tortoise-shell clasp. Azhar Sheikh's eyes do not rise further, nor does he refuse her gentle request. For him Roop's every word is an order.

Then Roop returns to her bed and the growing pain of her hunger.

When Roop has become light-headed from her fear and fasting and her stomach has shrunk within her so it no longer cries for food, a postcard redolent of camels and black pepper arrives covered in Papaji's precise calligraphy. 'Beti,' he begins, calling her daughter, 'your Lajo Bhua's grandson's eldest cousin-sister is getting married and would be most upset if you do not attend.'

She takes the invitation to Sardarji, stops at the door of his study and waits the way the steno does, but leaning against the doorjamb for strength, until he looks up. The small cream-coloured patch trembles in her extended hand.

Sardarji reads it and says, 'Tell Narain Singh to take you.' Then he returns to his papers. 'I am leaving for Lahore and Delhi soon; it will take me a few months. It's impossible to get anything done in either city – Congress ministers are agitating and demonstrating instead of planning for the future of the country, and the higher-up officials who make the decisions only want to know if America has joined the war yet.'

I will write to him from my father's home, thinks Roop. When I am safe I can tell him what is in my heart. A paper shall hold the evidence. Perfumed by the rose uttar he loves between my breasts, it will describe my longing for the touch of his skin against mine, it

303

will rest in his hands, unresisting as I was and he will fold it after
reading it and put it in his inner coat pocket.

Mani Mai rolls a bedding roll for her with a few salwar-kameezes. '*Y'Allah*, what is there to worry about the children – am I dead or what? Jorimon is here, Bari-Sardarni is here. No – they are in no danger. Only you are in danger, especially if Sardarji is gone. So we must go – go *now*.'

Now Roop is on her way back to Pari Darvaza, with Mani Mai as chaperone so she will not be alone with Narain Singh – unrelated young men can misbehave anytime. Roop will alight at the doorway of the fairies, and Mani Mai will return to 'Pindi with Narain Singh – she being too old and not high-up enough to need a chaperone.

The driver and the two women jolt along in the DeSoto out of 'Pindi and onto the Grand Trunk Road, to Gujarkhan, to the tree-lined road through Sohawa and three hours later, Roop sees the familiar sight of labourers' bent backs in the fields, women carrying water, firewood, baskets of dung. The chocolate-brown DeSoto bumps around the tufted hillocks and noses into Pari Darvaza, a cloud of dust in its wake.

Pari Darvaza, November 1940

'Go back.' A pleading note Roop has heard only once before is in Papaji's voice, that pleading note with which he apologized for Madani's dowry.

Roop's head slumps over her knees on a manji in the court-yard. She wishes she had not listened to Mani Mai; wishes she had brought the children. The aroma of spinach saag and makki rotis fills the late morning air – Gujri is cooking Roop's favourite. The syncopated thump of cloth meeting stone comes to Roop's ear: Khanma washing clothes somewhere in the back of the haveli. A horse in the stable neighs, cowbells clink in the cow compound. Revati Bhua sits on her manji, peeling papayas for Jeevan's sons who will return at midday from the Vernacular Middle School and ask Roop again, where is their cousin-sister Pavan and their cousin-brother Timcu?

But with what excuse could I have brought the children?
Would the Bari-Sardarni have let me take them?

Without them, she is empty. So empty, anyone can fill her with his angry words.

Papaji continues his tirade, pacing the courtyard, swatting away muslin folds of bright green, turquoise and lemon-yellow starched turbans hanging on the clothesline.

'One bitter almond in a paan and you think it means the Bari-Sardarni will poison you? How many bitter almonds have I eaten in my life for you children – every camel-load that comes must have at least a maund of them. For this you come running home to disgrace your father? Such ingratitude I have only seen in churas and chamars.' Bachan Singh turns to English for emphasis. 'Understand? Only in sweepers – outcastes!'

He has shrunk within his skin in the three years since Roop left. His turban seems too big for his head, his beard cascades, all-grey now, over sunken cheeks, bushy eyebrows droop above his tired eyes.

He is very old, almost forty-four. I should not have returned, but where else could I have gone?

Roop's tears stream steadily.

'You did not say – Sardar Kushal Singh did not say – I would have to give Bari-Sardarniji one child and now even the boy.'

Papaji snorts, 'Then what is so terrible? She will look after them like-a-mother – no – better, because she will not give in to their every wish the way I did every day of your life. It is my fault all this has happened. I indulged you too much, now you think you can give everyone trouble.'

He spies Kusum, walking down the gallery with a copper thali full of birdseed in her hands, on her way up to the terrace to feed his partridges.

'What I'm asking is: does your sister-in-law give me trouble like this? No – Kusum always says "Achchaji" and "Yes-ji." Never "Nahinji" and "No-ji" like you. Did Kusum say, after having two children, "Bussji – enough-ji! I'm returning to my parents?" Does she leave her children with Gujri and Revati Bhua and run home whenever someone by *chance* says a harsh word? No. My Kusum doesn't drag my turban in the mud, but my own daughter – ha! From the day you were born, I have had nothing from you but trouble.'

'Papaji—'

'And,' he cuts in, 'did you ask if your children would be given to the Bari-Sardarni? No, all you wanted was to have pretty clothes and to sit on chairs in a rich man's home. I did not lie to you; I told you he is older. I told you he was married already to one woman. But you – all you wanted was pretty clothes.'

Almond eyes fill. Had Papaji ever mentioned the slight possibility that her children would be given to Satya?

If so, Roop cannot remember it.

Her eyes fall to the kameez she wears – papaya-gold with small black bandini-dots. Sardarji bought it for her when he visited the maharaja of Jaipur's state.

Pretty clothes – were they really all I wanted or all I knew to want?

Bachan Singh is right, but he forgets to remember he offered his Roop no other choice. He forgets to remember he shut her away in a school with walls twelve feet high. He forgets to remember how Roop's heart became a storeroom where he hoarded the full measure of her giving, how he constrained Roop in his haveli, so even Pari Darvaza's little post office a mere hundred yards away was too far for her to wander unchaperoned. Forgets to remember she could only attend the women's ceremonies at Huma's wedding. Forgets to remember she was forbidden to ride Nirvair for fear there would be no blood on the sheets. Forgets to remember that she absorbed his fears without even being confined in purdah till she was afraid to glance at an unrelated man in the village unless he was a small boy or a white-bearded elder for fear of what-people-will-say.

Forgets he gave her only one man, to accept or refuse.

Forgets that if she had said no, his bachan to Sardar Kushal Singh would have been broken and then what-would-people-say?

All Roop had wanted was to part the henna curtain just a little wider.

How small Pari Darvaza seems now, with just two wells, five or six shops in its bazaar and a few trees – barely enough to shade it. Even the tunnel is not as large as I remember, and Papaji's haveli is nothing beside Sardarji's. No wonder Pari Darvaza's dirt road reaches for the tarred road to the Grand Trunk Road in hope it might drag itself to the city. I could have remained here, yes, but then everyone would have pitied me and said I was left unmarried.

Revati Bhua, even greyer than Papaji now, and still visiting, agrees from her manji, 'True. Very true.' She smells mouldy, damp. The great rolls of her flesh have been wrapped in cobwebs while Roop has been to 'Pindi and to Khanewal.

Revati Bhua has not changed; and she is still kind – the day after Roop arrived, she called on Mahatma Gandhi to forgive her lapse and asked Papaji for a small bag of wheat for Fazl Karim in exchange for a whole skein of blue and green British wool for Roop to do crewel embroidery.

But now in Roop there comes a realization that takes her breath, mists her eyes.

My Papaji is no different from any other Punjabi man. He may be a God-praising Sikh, he may be lambardar, he may be dipty of all Pari Darvaza, but in the end, he is just a poor, ordinary Punjabi village man.

And with that understanding, her sobs echo through Papaji's haveli; she does not care who hears her.

The slap of cloth against stone continues without pause.

Bachan Singh changes strategy in mid-stride.

'Beti.' He assumes an explaining tone, calling her daughter. 'You should go back to him. You have been here since after Diwali, but you are staying too long; we will all be disgraced. Go back, before the eyes of the world are turned upon us, before men in the village council begin raising questions about you. No one in Pari Darvaza saw you married; if you return, they will say it was a lie, that you were some man's concubine. People remember only what their eyes have seen. Understand? What did not happen before their eyes – those things people cannot remember. You have come back without your children, and everyone in Pari Darvaza will say you are here without Sardarji's permission.'

Roop is so weary of everyone's explaining to her, they explain everything but their reasons for explaining.

Does Papaji have a reason for his explaining?

No, no! Papaji loves me, he cares only for my reputation.

Suddenly a look of alarm crosses Papaji's face. He glances at Revati Bhua – she is not looking at him – and then at Roop. He touches his ear in mute inquiry.

Roop shakes her head.

No, her treatment at Satya's hands is not because her secret is known. No, she has not been sent home as damaged goods.

The corner of Roop's chunni is a dark wet ball. She says, 'I could be with child, then no one would talk.'

'You are too thin. No one will believe you.'

Gujri has been plying Roop with savayan and peththas since she arrived, Gujri's solution to all life's problems, but Roop has not put on weight.

'What Papaji is saying,' Revati Bhua suggests from her manji, 'is that death should be preferable to dishonour for good-good Sikh girls.'

'Did I say that?' Papaji storms. 'No, I did not say that.'

A look of bewilderment crosses Revati Bhua's face. She subsides.

'Where is Jeevan?' Roop asks. Her heart beats violently. Why would people who have known her since she was as small as Pavan not believe her?

'He was posted to Amritsar, I know from his last letter. He said he could be promoted to major soon if he sees any action in Burma or Africa.' Bachan Singh's voice rings with pride. With British officers relocating, the war is helping Indians rise faster in the army than they ever could in peacetime. 'But these days, he is still a captain.'

His voice sharpens with worry, 'I have to wait until he writes to me again to know where he is posted now. I haven't heard from him in months.'

Roop feels her courage falter. She wants Timcu's soft body in her arms again, she wants to meet Pavan's eyes in the mirror, kiss her black curls.

How can my own Papaji have any doubt that I have been wronged? Any question that I was in danger? I have given him trouble by coming home, but can he not see I was so afraid I came without my children? Can Papaji not see, see even from the corner of his eye, that I was pressed beyond endurance?

A thumb rubs at the indelible blue of her tattoo as if she might erase it. *If I were small again, I could climb on his knee and smile a pretty smile at him and he would say, 'Achcha, fer na karin.'* Don't do it again.

Papaji knits his brown knotty fingers, rubs the heels of his palms together. Roop's wide eyes follow him, caroming back and forth across the courtyard.

Papaji halts his pacing.

'I'll write to him in Amritsar; I'm sure the letter will be forwarded. Jeevan must come home before we all feel Sardarji's wrath. But now I'm telling you, Rub da vasta – for God's sake – go back to 'Pindi immediately.'

Gujri comes forward and places a callused palm beneath Roop's elbow. She tells Papaji, right to his face, 'She will go back – she is a good girl – but not now. After a few days.'

And Roop understands now, like simmer coming to boil: Papaji will not protect her. His duty to Roop ended the day of her marriage, but his duty to Jeevan lasts to the day his body follows Mama's to cremation and beyond. Jeevan's inheritance is far, far more important to Papaji than Roop's life or children. And for that he stands within a circle inscribed by Sardarji.

If Bachan Singh complains of Roop's treatment, Sardarji can raise his claim on every harvest; he can ring the well, from which all Hindus and Sikhs draw their water, with strong-strong men, declare it closed to Roop's father. He could order Sardar Kushal Singh to request all his loans at once and, worst of all, Sardarji could refuse to allow Jeevan to farm his jagir after Papaji is gone.

Only Roop's kismat can help her now.

I have good kismat – everyone always said so.

Sapphires in Mama's ring wink up at her. Diamonds sparkle.

Slowly, she takes a deep breath, lifts her head.

'You write to Sardarji,' Papaji's gruffness allows no response, 'and say you will return after Guru Tegh Bahadur's martyrdom day. There is no need to tell him any poison stories.'

Bachan Singh's words are boring into the hole at the base of Roop's tummy, that hole that will not be embroidered away, a hole that widens each day as she finds herself alone in the world though a crowd of her quom might mill about her.

Despite her doing what women are for.

Pari Darvaza, December 1940

'You listen to Papaji *so* seriously. I don't understand why you can't hear his wishes and say "achchaji" and "yes-ji," and then do whatever you feel is right for the family.'

Six in the morning, and Revati Bhua, Kusum and Roop have already been to the gurdwara for the morning Japji. Revati Bhua is in the prayer-room now, waking up the Guru Granth Sahib for the day. A few sturdy hens cluck, pecking for crumbs around the cookroom.

But listening and obeying – Papaji always said there should be no difference between one and the other.

Kusum helped Gujri make rumble-tumble eggs for the boys and filled their tiffin carriers for school. Now she has parted her six-year-old son's hair horizontally across the back of his head with his sandalwood kanga. Head bent under a sleek black fall of hair, 'This-one' sits with his back to her on a manji as her quick fingers plait the lower half of his hair to a wisp.

Roop watches from her end of the manji, the younger boy's handkerchiefed topknot rubbing against her chin – 'That-one' is heavy on her knees, but reminds her so much of Timcu that she cannot bear to move for fear he will run away to play. Five years old now, he can be scared back to sucking his thumb only when Gujri threatens that the Afghans are coming. That-one doesn't know the last time the Afghans crumbled Pari Darvaza's walls was two centuries ago, or that no one in Pari Darvaza has felt the need to rebuild the village walls since then. But neither Kusum nor Revati Bhua have offered alternatives to the disciplining fear.

'But Papaji said I have to go back . . .'

'*Baba!* I know what he said. The whole mohalla, everyone, must have heard what he said. Jeevan also shouts, just like him, whenever he comes.' Lower plait completed, Kusum turns her son to face her, gathering his black fall of hair into her hands. 'Last time Jeevan came he was shouting as if I was marching behind him in his Alpha company. Shouting that This-one −' This-one held by his hair gives a wriggle and receives a cuff to his ears − 'This-one should be wearing a turban every day now. So Papaji said, "Yes, Kusum: make him wear his turban."'

'So then you should make him wear one, na? *So* handsome, he'll look.'

Kusum begins plaiting the upper half of This-one's hair, weaving the lower plait into it.

'In June Papaji said this, June. Imagine! So hot it was, then. And all the way This-one has to walk to Sohawa, for school. And then if it comes off while he's playing the other boys may not have respect for it, they might drag it in the mud or their shoes might touch it. And the Master-ji there is a Hindu, he won't know how to tie it for This-one. I think by the time Jeevan returns, he will be able to tie it himself, but not now.'

'*Hai*, did you say "no-ji" to Papaji, then?'

Kusum begins winding the plait to a topknot.

'No, *baba*! I said, "achchaji," and "yes-ji." Why give trouble saying "nahinji" or "no-ji" for little things?'

This is a new idea for Roop − for a woman to say yes-ji and not to obey immediately, perhaps continue doing whatever she needs to do.

'So you never say "no-ji"?'

'"No-ji" is only for big things. I don't say "no-ji," but I don't do everything fut-a-fut, immediately, sometimes. You also, you could wait a little longer before going back. By then Bari-Sardarni will be feeling sorry. I know − she must be missing her little sister Roop by now, just like your children must be missing you. But, no no no, don't say "nahinji" or "no-ji" − of course not. Why to make trouble for every little thing?'

'Poison is not a big thing, then?' Roop is trying to understand.

'It is a big thing for you – you think you're so important. For Papaji, izzat is bigger.'

Kusum assumes Roop's ambitions and her own are the same: to please Bachan Singh. But for Roop, pleasing her father is becoming less attractive every minute.

Kusum continues, 'Roop, your Papaji knows what is *right*. Not for one of us, two of us, but for all of us. You must understand, he knows from his heart what is right, not just what is good for *you*.'

She wants to tell Kusum it is not her own life that is so important; everyone comes back in a new life someday – but that she wants to feel Pavan's slender arms about her neck, kiss those butterfly-wing lashes, feel Timcu's soft cheeks against her own. She wants to be there to see Pavan and Timcu grow, to comfort them when the world can't meet their expectations.

Even if they never call her 'Mama.'

The words fill her throat but do not pass her lips; praise for a child tempts the evil eye.

Topknot completed, Kusum takes a clean black starched underturban from her side and places it over her son's forehead, bringing two corners together in a knot at the back of his head. Then the lower corners come up and knot above the topknot.

'And you see—' Kusum gestures at the completed underturban, absent a turban on This-one's head.

'So then, didn't Papaji get angry at you?'

Kusum dimples.

'No – he forgot all about it, just as I thought he would. Which man sees what women do right before their eyes?'

Roop takes a moment to ponder this. Should she tell Kusum about Pavan's eyes, so much like a man's, but also like a girl's?

No.

Pavan's secret is like Roop's secret, like Roop's bad ear.

Slowly, it comes to Roop: if men can't see what is right before their eyes, maybe Papaji won't notice if she is disobedient.

She must probe further.

'And Jeevan? Didn't he get angry?'

'I said to myself, by the time Jeevan comes back next time and gets angry, This-one will be old enough to tie his turban himself.'

So, now that Papaji has written to Jeevan, if Roop doesn't obey Papaji, perhaps he won't notice until after Jeevan comes home.

A hen stops pecking around the cookroom, fluffs her chest and clucks defiantly.

'Up!' Kusum shoos This-one.

The manji creaks as the two boys scramble off and run to Gujri, who stands beside two satchels at the door to the cook-room holding their small kirpan belts and water bottles.

Kusum and Roop lean against the carved scalloped door-way, waving as the taller one takes his little brother's hand, carrying both satchels and water bottles over his shoulder. The boys' steel kirpans bounce at their waists as they head down the tunnel past the blind man.

Kusum is folding her hands in greeting before Chachi's chunni-clad head, already in its usual place at the second-storey window across the lane. 'Sat Sri Akal!'

She turns back to Roop.

'Shyam Chacha asked me yesterday, "Has Sardarji sent Roop-bi home?"'

Roop's fear of what-people-will-say clutches within her.

'What did you tell him?'

'I told him you had been *very* sick after your last childbirth, and had come home *only* to rest *just* for a while.' Kusum's hands smooth her kameez over her thighs. 'I did the same, you know, one time.'

Kusum did stay at her parents' home in Chakwal a long time after her last childbirth, but not for the same reason as Roop, for the baby Kusum was to have while Roop was being married at Punja Sahib Gurdwara is not here. Kusum has never spoken of it to Roop, but then Roop has never been home to talk to Kusum about it, since her wedding to Sardarji.

Only This-one and That-one are left.

What words can Roop say that will comfort a mother who has lost a child to death? At least her Pavan and her Timcu are alive, even if they are not with her, nor call her 'Mama.' She remembers how afraid she was when Timcu was only five small pounds at birth – those fears for Timcu are fading as he grows stronger living in Satya's apartments, eating eggs and chicken every second day, getting the best of everything. How lucky she is, how lucky.

Roop's arm finds its way about Kusum's waist, and the two stand together, the way Roop and Madani – how many years ago it seems! – once stood and watched the carpenters sanding that creaky box, Mama's palanquin, which brought Kusum here, to her real home.

When they return to the courtyard, Revati Bhua has pulled a manji to the centre of the courtyard and is lying on her side under a cotton quilt, with her chunni drawn across her face.

'Are you sick?' Kusum's hand caresses Revati Bhua's brow.

'No, but I had a dream last night and it was so real, so real, I can't tell you how strangely real it was. This morning I went to pray, *still* I'm seeing this dream passing in front of my eyes.'

A chuckle bubbles in Roop, she knows what's coming next.

Sensing Roop, Revati Bhua rolls herself upright like a bedding roll, trussed and ready for travel. 'Your mama came to me in my dream.'

'She did?' Kusum winks at Roop.

Kusum and Roop sit at the foot of the manji. Roop remembers how she, hungry and desperate, tried to send Papaji and Jeevan one dream each, and how her dreams refused to journey. But even so, she says, 'Tell, na! What happened?' for Roop has believed Revati Bhua's dreams of Mama since she was small and wants very much to believe again, believe all the dreams Revati Bhua tells about Mama, for now especially she wishes Mama could advise her.

'Yes, believe this. She came in her palanquin, carried by four strong men. She looked just the way she looked every time she went home to Kuntrila or to someone's wedding covered up in purdah, only her lovely eyes showing. Such big-big eyes she had, Roop – just like yours. She was looking for you, she said. And her fingers curved around the curtain of the palanquin. I climbed in with her – suddenly I was thin as you or you. And the curtain fell back down and we were together in the hot darkness of the palanquin. Then your Mama raised her chunni. She was beautiful as I remembered her – skin smooth as a new apricot, the colour of pale-pale brown sugar. Just like you.

'And she leaned forward and whispered in my ear, such a whisper, I heard it all the way to my heart. She said, "Tell my Roop, tell her there is no need to obey Papaji just now, right away. Tell her she can wait a little, but only a few days more. But then, after that . . . then she must return to her real home."'

Revati Bhua pauses, hangs her head as if listening, looking within.

'Then?' prompts Kusum, a smothered smile dimpling her cheek.

'She said, "Tell her men forget women who do not stand before their eyes each day. . ."' Revati Bhua takes a deep breath, and the message is finally complete. '"Tell her she doesn't have to go right now, but soon."'

The old woman's eyes glisten, and she bites her lip.

Kusum strokes Revati Bhua's arm.

So Revati and Mama think Roop should delay.

They are right, thinks Roop, but only half right. Their advice is women's half-right advice, what any daughter-in-law or cousin-sister should say.

But saying 'achchaji' and 'yes-ji' to Papaji, going back to Sardarji now or going back later will only delay Roop's fate.

Delay will not answer her need to see her children again, or help her stay alive to do it.

Even so, Kusum and Revati's counsel, but particularly Kusum's, has piqued Roop's memory, to think of what Papaji forgets.

Papaji forgets I am not like other good-good, sweet-sweet Punjabi girls. I have one bad ear that does not listen.

So sometimes, it cannot obey.

26. Rawalpindi, February 1941

A gastric rumble afflicts the shifting ground beneath 'Pindi. Chill air stretches across the lap of the Margalla Hills. The banyan over the centre courtyard of Sardarji's haveli sucks at its roots and grows. Every brick in the three-storey haveli trembles.

Sardarji is accustomed to tremors of the earth in 'Pindi, but he stands now at the heart of Roop's room with a perplexed frown on his face.

It is four months since Sardarji gave his permission for the wedding Roop wished to attend. But entering the courtyard, his peacock-blue turban dusty with travel from dawn to midday, he found only Satya to greet him, grey eyes wide, ever concerned for his comfort. And in place of Roop, Dehna Singh bowed his white turban before him and extended a silver salver. On it, a letter, carefully folded, its rose-uttar scent bringing the soft breasts of his little brown koel to mind.

He opened it slowly, becoming aware of Satya's complacent silence, Dehna Singh's white gloves – usually motionless unless proffering something – spinning the salver compulsively.

The letter asked him to come to Pari Darvaza and speak to her father. He had forgotten the name of her village. And what was her father's name?

Bachan Singh, yes.

He quietly folded the letter, tucked it in his inner coat pocket.

Nothing else but silence, expanding now, filling Roop's room.

Arranged carefully on the lace doily of her grey-painted dressing-table, before the Queen Anne mirror, is a black velvet box, a gold kantha necklace within. His dusty fingers smudge the sheen of its red enamel. And another box with earrings: three tiers of Burmese rubies. And a third box, this one oblong. Hesitating, Sardarji opens it, sees gold anklets glinting, hears her voice again, sees her again, arching her foot, pressing her hennaed fingers to the clasp. 'Panjeban!' Roop's happy voice cries into that deafening silence.

But these are messages he understands, they inform the silence by their presence: a woman does not leave her husband's first gifts if she means to return in a few days or weeks. No, a woman who leaves her ornaments leaves that unmistakable, silent, accusing message that says 'I have been wronged.'

Perhaps it's true, then, what Satya yelled as he climbed the stairs and strode the gallery to Roop's room – Roop was pining for her childhood home, she could not adjust to life in so grand a haveli. Satya – that wife of his! – quarrelsome as ever after so many months of separation.

To think, little Roop causing all this trouble for nothing.

If she had only said once, 'I am suffering!' would he not have given her solace? He had given her full wifehood, circled the Guru Granth Sahib four times with her for the Guru's blessing as a planet circles the sun, satellite in wake. He did not just take her, as he could have if she were a bazaar woman of no bloodline.

'Such ingratitude,' says Cunningham, mocking him from a spot at the base of his turban. 'A common failing of Indians.'

'Cunningham, let me think.'

If she had complained, asked him but once, would he not have been generous? He was always generous – did she not know that by now? And how had she repaid his generosity?

With betrayal.

Sardarji prowls Roop's empty chamber with the gold bangles he'd bought in Delhi dangling from his fingers. He'd matched their size to a set of blue glass bangles she had worn to his chambers the last time he bedded her. She should know he would not forget to bring her a present. So why would she, knowing a present was coming to her, return to her father's home? Women have mysterious ways of saying things and none are comprehensible.

He pulls the tasselled tapestry bell pull for Mani Mai.

Women cause their own problems by not speaking up, by not asking for a man's help. They all need and want a man's help, but a man has to be asked, he cannot dream that somehow a woman's tender heart has been hurt. Besides, women's hearts are always getting hurt. A man has to tread so carefully with women. But if a man were to worry about the effect of his actions on women, why, he would never get anything done at all.

So now what to do?

Instead of Mani Mai, Narain Singh has come running to answer the bell. 'Mani Mai has gone to Choti-Sardarni's village,' says Narain Singh, and adds, throat bobbing up and down, 'to look after the children.'

'*Timcu?*' The words echo from Sardarji in a roar. Sardarji has not thought to look into the next room to see if his son was there, being accustomed to the child's most proper fear of him, the same fear Sardarji always felt of his own father.

Cunningham gives a great guffaw.

Sardarji does not ask or worry about his daughter; the girl is nothing.

How could Satya have allowed this?

The force of Sardarji's gaze forces Narain Singh to drop his eyes to the ground and squirm. A demanding silence follows, till Narain Singh can return to that gaze and stammer, 'Choti-Sardarni ordered that the children be brought to her, so Mani Mai and I took them to Pari Darvaza. She said there was another wedding in her family and it was her duty to show them, show their faces so that all would know your line.'

Choti-Sardarni, the little sardarni, his little brown koel, has given the best of excuses. Duty calls. The only greater force is a higher duty. Of course, Satya could not have refused to send the children. Roop is much cleverer than Sardarji has given her credit for.

But to go without his permission?

He releases Narain Singh by looking elsewhere and the driver vanishes gratefully.

Alone, Sardarji clenches both hands about the heavy wrought iron frame of the fourposter bed, the bed in which he took her that first time.

Suddenly, he pulls the frame inwards to his chest.

Biceps bulge, muscles strain away from his neck.

Still he pulls.

His dust-crusted peacock-blue turban warms at his fore-head. His lungs fill and hold till his eyes cloud.

He pulls harder.

The woman with the tiny waist smiles down at him from the Tuscany tapestry with her expression of delighted gratitude. The frame bends inward, but it does not break.

He releases the bed frame.

Pats it approvingly – well-designed, structurally sound.

'A momentary lapse,' he assures Cunningham.

He descends the spiral stone stairway and crosses the court-yard. He ignores Satya's anxious query, 'Ki hoya, ji?'

What has happened? she asks. Satya knows very well what-ever has happened. If he knows her, it's something she doesn't plan to tell him.

He ignores his Underwood calling him to work to make India green.

He walks into his dressing room and sits, hands on the wide haunches of a Chippendale sofa chair, like a mali with a trowel and water beside him and no garden to tend.

'*Ohai!*' he calls.

Dehna Singh appears. Sardarji stretches his legs out before him and the valet squats to untie his laces and remove his shiny black shoes and grey wool socks. Then his dark grey coat, matching waistcoat and the pocket watch. He holds out his arms for his emerald cuff links to be removed. Next the tie tack and the peacock-blue tie, the starched collar, the collar stays. Dehna Singh unbuttons and removes his black suspenders. When his shirt and dark grey woollen trousers are removed, all that remains is his white cotton Punjabi kachcha. And his peacock-blue turban with its safa trailing down his back.

'Going native so early in the day?' sniffs Cunningham.

'Be quiet, Cunningham.'

He dons the comfort of a white starched kurta and baggy salwar. His feet spread gratefully into a broad Peshawari sandal, and he leaves the haveli for a walk through Rajah Bazaar.

The bazaar always gives him ideas. It is where connections come to him between old and new, it is where he watches for similarities between men, similarities of purpose that can be woven into alliances, moulded towards cooperation, generalized as the norm. He goes to the bazaar when he needs its smells and its timelessness, when he needs advice from older men swaying behind hookahs and the respectful admiration of younger men or just the strength of its unabashed Punjabi acquisitiveness to goad his ambitions.

It is evening and the bazaar holds no ladies. There are no ladies whose hearts he may search for explanation. What would he ask? 'Why is it, do you think, that my younger wife has absconded without my permission, and taken my son?' No, only a courtesan may be found to listen to his question and how can such a woman know the answer? Poor women and bad women's lives move by different rules – they have no men to care about their reputation.

Sardarji is unaccustomed to finding himself bereft of explanation. Why, they come from England, Wales, Scotland, Ireland and sometimes America, imprisoned in their monolingual universes, and they turn to him, educated in their tongue, for translation, for mediation. And he delivers explanations of layers of invading influence upon influence throughout Punjab's history. But how to explain this behaviour from Roop, a woman to whom he has given every kindness?

How to explain it to Rai Alam Khan and his friends at the Tuesday Lunch Club, or to Sardar Kushal Singh?

This he asks himself as he strides along the narrow lanes of the bazaar, Narain Singh following at a respectful distance. He stops at shops along the way. Here a fruit-walla rises from his perch before a pyramid of guavas, supplicating his patronage. There a cobbler leaves his paidan to rise and touch Sardarji's feet. At the cloth shop, the owner comes into the street with a length of new wool suiting, just arrived from London. Sardarji gestures to Narain Singh to receive it. Manager Abdul Aziz will deliver a basket of dates in exchange; Sardarji has known the clothier far too long to offer him money.

And all the time he is greeting them with 'Salam Aleikum' or 'Sat Sri Akal' or 'Ram Ram' and asking about the health of these men's businesses, he thinks how men understand the principles of life. Giving and receiving, men understand these things. *Quid pro quo*, something for something. Good Latin words. He wishes he'd learned Latin at Khalsa High School – if you know where words come from you can sometimes tell where they are going – but he's made sure he knows enough to get by. *Quid pro quo* is one of those good British expressions. It is also one that men understand and women don't.

If Roop is going to get his protection, his name, and live like a little rani in his home, she is going to have to give something. Whatever possible. *Sons, for one thing. Not just one son, and that, too, a sickly little chap. Yes, sons. And loyalty. These are his rights. He is within his rights, by Jove, within his rights. Everyone can see that.*

But women don't see things. They just feel. The world would be better if only women were more objective; that is their basic problem. Lack of objectivity. They get too caught up in situations, feel too deeply, introduce too many variables and so their sense of judgment leaves their poor brains entirely. Now if they could be taught to see the whole, step back from looking at the veins of leaves on trees and see a whole forest, they would understand there are natural forces we all have to appreciate, such as the fact that some races of men are more capable than others, or that men are stronger than women, these are natural things.

For the first time since Kitty, Sardarji finds himself aware of them: women. He continues through the bazaar, feeling their eyes, a thousand strange women's eyes, their longing pushing against walls of brick and wood and mud till every carved jharokha-window bulges from its socket and leans over the crowded bazaar. Why has he never noticed women pressing into his space before?

Women, alchemists of men's seed.

Returning home, Sardarji sits in a wicker chair on the terrace lawn, right ankle on left knee, stroking his beard, thinking, till long past sunset. The white peacock sidles close to his motionless figure, lifts its fantail and considers him with its garnet eye. Sardarji does not move; he learned to ignore cramp and pain in his body a long time ago – it was irrelevant to his work. By his brain and reason he has always known that qualified men like himself can pull India and all the people below them into modernity, never mind Gandhi's archaic ideas.

It would not look well to leave immediately. To do so might look unmanly, as if a Sikh of his standing had jumped to obey a woman's summons – it would give the situation far more importance than it deserves. No one will dare to harm a hair on his son's head. No, the best course of action is to wait a few days and visit her village as if it were merely on his way somewhere else.

A man whose woman has returned his first gifts and taken his son without permission would be quite justified in taking a few servants with him, strong men, armed with bamboo sticks to scare her father into returning his woman and his children.

Fireflies pinprick the dark. The banyan sighs, squeezes the haveli tighter.

Perhaps Roop does not know what a hell he can make for her family in – what was her village's strange name? Pari Darvaza – Doorway of the Fairies. Its very name is fanciful, superstitious, backward. The first thing Indians should do if they get independence is to change the names of all these backward villages – give them numbers.

'Righto,' says Cunningham.

Except the Hindu villages – for Hindus, everything is holy, for them even numbers are worthy of worship.

Even so, numbers would be better, they have meaning, they stand for counted, dependable things. Sardarji always was comfortable working in equations and statistics; he finds them easy, it's words that are ambiguous. He enjoys his charts – hieroglyphics, Kitty called them – representations of reality. Symbol, number and counting. Frequency of occurrence dictates significance. Significance indicates congruence with theory, theory translated to words is the model for policy. Policy translated to strategy and regulation forces action. And lord knows, Indians have to be forced to take action against the problems of millennia.

But this disappearance of Roop with his children, without his permission, has no frequency of occurrence. It hasn't occurred in his life before, and certainly he has never heard of it in any other man's life. Roop should fear his wrath, if not the loss of his favour.

It is significant that she doesn't. She knows him too well, knows he cannot raise a finger against the tremulous sweetness of his little brown koel, mother of his son.

Audacious.

Roop's behaviour is just a symptom of the moral collapse happening everywhere. No one thinking of the country that could be after three hundred years of foreign rule. Just every man thinking his own quom, his own needs, are most important, while all of India falls further and further behind.

This is what the Guru calls haumai, too much self-ness.

'Cunningham, what Roop has done – we Sikhs call it haumai. It is what you call "simply not done".'

'I wouldn't dream of using force, if I were you,' Cunningham says. 'You're a gentleman and a negotiator – it's simply not done.'

And so Sardarji will go to Pari Darvaza and, using only words, will bring back Roop.

And his son.

* * *

Satya stands in Sardarji's study just to smell his sandalwood fixo and Brylcreem smell. She dusts his Underwood with a corner of her chunni, she touches the leather spines of books she cannot read, fingers the pages Sardarji turns with reverence, like a man touching dead skin.

What has he found in these books that has changed him so? Since reading them, he is nothing like the Sardarji I used to know.

He has time for these books, though he is a man who is always afraid of time, racing against it to some unknown destination.

She holds his well-thumbed Mr Darwin to her breast.

Those from the best families – gentlemen's families – we prevail in the end.

In the courtyard, the leaves of the banyan whisper in the wind. Vayu brings word of men tortured in jail for sedition, farmers marching off to serve in North Africa, of volunteers of the Indian National Congress who hand out Gandhi caps to Hindus, and of Muslim League volunteers who hand out round caps to Muslims. They speak of food that should have gone to Calcutta and all the people in the province of Bengal, diverted to British soldiers; they predict famines that follow surely as night follows day.

But Satya knows only that her Sardarji came back to her. For just a few days he returned to her bed, as a man who knows all his actions are pre-forgiven. Satya's heart leapt and she felt the way she had when she first saw him after his return from Balliol; frightened by the force of her own love, the pain of it.

Had he learned from Roop's absence what most men never learn: that one woman is much like another – except in fidelity?

A fickle selfish village girl like Roop, what can one expect?

Thus Satya forgets to remember a little girl taken, a certain cup of salted tea, a boy-child's birth cord fed to the fire, then a little boy taken, a flagstone that rested so heavy over a godown, a paan with a bitter almond sent as message from one hand to another's.

All Satya can feel is that her Sardarji came back, came back to Satya the way a trader returns to walk the streets of a city that raised him from boy to man. His hands re-remembering her body were sure, practised, economical in movement, and different – Roop has taught him the pleasure of giving pleasure.

But then, just when she was becoming accustomed to his weight beside her every night, just when she had begun sleeping through his roaring snore, just when he had begun to order his whisky soda served by the fire in her private sitting room in the evenings, just when she could almost believe Sardar Kushal Singh and Toshi – that *churail!* – had never put Roop in his way to tempt him, Sardarji left her again one day at dawn.

Of course Sardarji must not let his son learn Roop's low-class ways, of course he must bring his son back to Satya.

He did not need words; has she not felt his intentions in their loving?

Yes, she has.

Except for one moment.

It was the moment when his beard scratched her cheek and his falcon eyes looked directly down upon her, held her eyes until he must have seen how very small his face was, how very tiny, reflected in her grey eyes. And in that long, long moment, she knew Sardarji expected her to lower her eyes before him.

But she couldn't.

Just. Could. Not.

She was a woman who came into the world with her eyes wide open and so could never lower them before a man.

And when that moment had passed, Satya felt his disappointment, knew that he saw himself reflected small in her grey eyes. So very small that he could not bear the image of himself.

With a deep groan, he rolled away from her.

But that was only *one* moment, out of all the moments Satya has given him.

Yes, he has gone to tell Roop she has done what she was brought here to do. He will tell her she can remain in her village – what was its name? – Pari Darvaza.

Satya returns Mr Darwin to its slot in the bookcase.

Pari Darvaza, February 1941

Sardarji's Austin Princess comes to Pari Darvaza like a small steam engine, breathing dust. Narain Singh stops the motor car at the one-room post and telegraph office and pounds at the bright blue door. He shakes the postman awake, 'Take Sardarji to Dipty Bachan Singh's home. I must wait here to look after the motor car.'

Sardarji owns this land for miles around; wheat plumes roll in the wind under his protection, mustard flowers bloom at his will and by his favour, but it is his first time at the doorway of the fairies. Collecting the usual crowd of onlookers, children and goats, the abruptly wide-awake postman leads Sardarji through the narrow brick streets, advising him to hitch his trousers up to avoid the gutter carrying soapy water through their centre. Sardarji lowers his cobalt-blue turban and picks his way in his shiny black European shoes, avoiding gobar patties left by wandering buffaloes. He swings his swagger stick and the questioning eyes of women watch him from doors open just a crack.

It is a good thing he did not know just how small Roop's village truly was, and that the full strength of a wedding procession of a man of his standing had not tried to squeeze itself through the tiny lanes of this hamlet. Why, there is barely room for two to walk abreast in one of these lanes, and if two men but lean over their folded hands, to greet one another with a 'Sat Sri Akal,' they might knock turbans. If he were to brag, he might point out that the lanes of Rajah Bazaar around his own haveli are a little wider than these.

The mosque is larger than the gurdwara or the temple in this village, and he has never seen so many doors painted a forbidding, almost insulting, Islamic green. Jinnah is getting stronger. He continues to press his demands for Muslim representation to be guaranteed when India becomes self-governing after the war, but no one curbs him or appeases him with promises; the British are too busy fighting the Japanese and Germans, and Gandhi is too busy trying to take everyone back to some glorious conception of medieval India. This village with the gutter at its centre, this village of dung patties impressed with hand marks, patties drying on mud walls in the February sun – is this what Gandhi's Hindu raj and Pandit Nehru's socialism will bring? If this village were laid out scientifically the streets would be straight, broad enough for transport. The fields would be fields, not small strips fragmented by litigious tenants.

But the number of Muslims here! Sardarji feels the hair on the back of his neck begin to rise. All about him, round-capped men say 'Salaam Aleikum' quite loudly as he passes. There is not one voice that greets him, in deference to his faith, with: 'Sat Sri Akal.'

Perhaps he should have brought a few strong servants with him – Sardar Kushal Singh, arranger of his marriage, or Manager Abdul Aziz.

Both the Chaudhary, his father, and his brother knew all these men by name, a task Sardarji has delegated to Sardar Kushal Singh and Manager Abdul Aziz these many years. Heir to his brother's debts, Sardarji was never heir to the easy familiarity that pious poet had with these village people, has never felt them trust him the way they trusted his brother. But of course, if a man did as his elder brother had, opening the flour mill every time there was a famine and saying 'Take what you need,' that man will be popular, trusted – but not prosperous.

Sardarji feels his turban weighing heavy on his head, marking him among them, turning him to Stranger. And their eyes! Hostile stares seem fixed on his back. Farquharson's face is before him. 'Sardarji, I recommend you reread *The Causes and Course of the French Revolution*. I think you will find it quite enlightening.'

'You're being quite illogical, actually,' says Cunningham.

At the mouth of the tunnel, the postman, exhausted by his unaccustomed exertion, halts and ushers Sardarji forward into the dim gloom. Sardarji must knock at Deputy Bachan Singh's door himself. He raises his swagger stick to the flowers carved in the timber door.

Once. Twice.

Then waits beneath the scalloped archway. A man in a Gandhi cap comes to the door of the house across the gutter.

Men behind their chillums extend uneasy puzzled stares. Children stay at a safe distance, whispering, giggling. A woman's covered head appears in a second-floor window, watching silently.

A slap of sandals, a bolt draws back. For a second he stares down into his daughter's surma-rimmed eyes; they spark in adoration, drop shyly.

He brushes past her to Bachan Singh who comes hurrying to meet him, with 'Aao, huzoor! Ji, huzoor!' and folded hands that tremble ever so slightly as he ushers Sardarji to his sitting room and calls, 'Gujri, chai!'

By now, Sardarji is so grateful to see a turbaned head in this village, he embraces Bachan Singh with more affection and bonhomie than he planned to muster.

Bachan Singh vanishes for a moment and returns staggering beneath the weight of two European cane-mesh chairs so Sardarji may have his choice: the one with the frayed seat, or the one with the frayed back. For himself, Bachan Singh draws his ankles up behind his low desk and looks up at his son-in-law, beseechingly.

The sweetmaker comes to the courtyard door to ask if he should send sweets for the visitor – and stays. The weaver-tailor, the barber and the night watchman come in with no explanation. The pandit's well-oiled belly quivers as he asks if Gujri has enough milk for the jagirdar's appetite – and then stays. Abu Ibrahim leaves his shoes outside Papaji's sitting room and steps in and, hearing Bachan Singh's desperate silence, understands that he is needed, and stays. And then curious village men crowd in to see what the jagirdar might have to discuss with the lambardar.

For a moment, Sardarji considers shooing everyone out of the room, but that could cause trouble.

What if these men begin to believe he was conspiring with his father-in-law against Muslims?

Best to do everything in public, then at least we will all remember what was said.

Why do such concerns come to him these days?

It's all Jinnah's fault. He is everywhere, rabble-rousing, repeating his freshly minted word, Pakistan, letting the least-qualified

Muslims, like these men here, assign it whatever meaning they desire. Jinnah with his two-nation theory, as if Hindus and Muslims were the only rulers India had ever known before the British raj.

And now Captain Jeevan Singh, apprised by messages travelling mouth to ear, mouth to ear, steps into the courtyard, his lungs expanded so his muscles ripple taut beneath his kurta. He folds his hands, saying 'Sat Sri Akal' to Sardarji, but his golden turban barely bows, to show the minimum of respect. He stands between his father and his brother-in-law, fighting fit, arms crossed upon his chest, kirpan dangling at his hip.

'I am on leave for few days only,' says Jeevan. 'So I have come to see Papaji. Now I am here and you are here, it is very fortunate.' His English is India-learned, book-learned, a little stilted by contrast with Sardarji's, the words passing through Punjabi before release – but passable. Captain Jeevan does not mention Bachan Singh's urgent letter, forwarded from cantonment to cantonment till it reached him in the Thar, training in the desert for his next posting in North Africa, the letter that asked him to come back to Pari Darvaza, to remonstrate with Roop.

Kusum brings tea, serving Jeevan first, then Sardarji, then Bachan Singh.

It does not occur to Sardarji or Bachan Singh or anyone else to ask Roop to come in and speak, perhaps give her own explanation.

'Ah, yes,' says Sardarji. 'I too was just passing through.'

Everyone's health having been inquired about, Sardarji leans forward, 'Bachan Singhji, what has happened?'

Bachan Singh strokes his grey beard and looks miserable.

Jeevan, however, is ready.

'Sardarji, we must also ask you this very question,' he says, using English.

Sardarji is not expecting challenge to be met with challenge. He speaks to Bachan Singh again, in Punjabi. 'I can only say I am very surprised.'

And Jeevan replies for his father again, in English.

'We also are extremely surprised.'

'I could never believe a daughter of yours could do this –

what have I not given her?' Now Sardarji is using English, realizing his real opponent.

'We also could never believe you would do this.' Jeevan ignores Bachan Singh's restraining hand on his arm and the imploring looks of the older men, sensing stance and scent and tone, for they do not understand the English coursing like alternating current between Jeevan and Sardarji.

Ask what he wants, their eyes say. How much he wants, when he wants it. Give it to him, as we always do.

'Matlab?'

'Meaning,' says Jeevan, 'we gave you our best jewel, our Roop. The most beautiful girl in Pari Darvaza. She has given you a son. How is it you can send her home?'

'I?' Sardarji is startled, off balance. 'I did not send her home. She came for a wedding and stayed without my permission.' He switches to Punjabi, appealing to the audience to feel the extent of Roop's rebellion.

By this time Bachan Singh has grasped his son's strategy. He ventures, shaking his head, 'This is impossible. A girl or woman staying apne aap, without permission . . . this cannot be.'

'I tell you I had no idea,' said Sardarji, feeling himself getting a little hot under his starched collar. 'I had to come here myself, once I knew.' He translates for the audience, which shifts on its haunches, marvelling.

The jagirdar came himself. It was a big problem. He didn't send a chit, or a servant, or Sardar Kushal Singh – so much has he been inconvenienced. They shake their heads. He had to come *himself*.

Jeevan says, 'But she must have got the idea somewhere, from somewhere it came, no? Women don't just get ideas by themselves, from somewhere she is thinking you want to send her away.'

Sardarji leans back in the chair with the frayed back. He exudes power in waves so strong it rocks the audience back on their heels. His eyes snap, his turban seems to grow larger on his head. Still Jeevan stands beside his father, arms crossed, relaxed, a young sher confronting the king of the pride.

But Jeevan is not dealing with a farmer or a mere sahukar

like Sardar Kushal Singh. He is dealing with a man who has dug deep canals and built high dams. A man who may have misjudged the tactics required to tackle this small problem, but not a man who spends any length of time in learning. A man who can change his tactics as quickly as the occasion demands.

As Sardarji does now:

'I think,' he says, 'that she has been led astray. Completely misguided. It is a great pity.'

'Ji?' said Bachan Singh. 'It is not true that you wished to send her home?'

'Never think that, Bachan Singh! How could I send home the mother of my son?'

Bachan Singh translates for the audience – so that all the men hear Sardarji's affirmation of Roop's reputation, his acknowledgment of his son.

The audience murmurs appreciatively.

True, true. Who would send home the mother of a son?

Jeevan says, 'I am relieved to hear you say this.'

Bachan Singh begins to rise from his seat, but Jeevan has only paused for effect. He continues in Punjabi for the benefit of the audience, ignoring Bachan Singh's frown. 'Because if it were true that you had sent her home, you know I would have been left with no choice . . .'

The little audience waits, savouring the coming ultimatum. They know the tone of its delivery, they have seen it in squabble after squabble, over zan, zamin, zevar, the three things that bring the blood to boil in the Punjab. Women, land, gold.

Jeevan switches to English, to which every educated Indian's ears are ever open, and gives it quietly, firmly, the way only a trained warrior can give it, looking his brother-in-law, the jagirdar, his family's overlord these seven generations, in the eye.

'With all due respect, Sardarji, I would have to kill you.'

Bachan Singh lowers his turban as if he has just heard his own death sentence and whispers in Abu Ibrahim's ear, and soon all the men in the audience nod turbans, topis and beards. 'True, true.'

Sardarji places his cane in the crook of the chair and then

his hands on his knees. Slowly, his palms turn upwards.

'I understand.' And he does understand; he understands it with his ten per cent. To Cunningham he says, *Be still, sir. I will try and explain this to you later.*

Jeevan now hastens to add, 'It does not mean I do not respect you, you are like my older brother, but a matter of izzat is a matter of izzat.' He cannot find the word for izzat in English – 'honour' is far too weak.

Sardarji says in Punjabi to Bachan Singh, 'I understand.'

He lifts the tumbler Kusum placed at his side, stirs the sweet crystals that silt at its base.

Jeevan says, making amends, 'I think I know who has misguided Roop. She's a good girl, she does not think of such things by herself.'

Sardarji waits till the tea stops swirling and he can again see himself in its brown surface. 'Who?' he asks absently.

'It is Bari-Sardarni.'

'Bari-Sardarni?'

'Yes, Roop became sure you did not want her – who else but your senior wife could have told her this?'

Sardarji blinks, but waits.

'And,' says Jeevan dramatically, 'she asked for the children to come here because she thought someone was trying to poison them.'

'Poison my son?'

'Ah-hoji.' Jeevan nods. Neither Bachan Singh nor Jeevan know if Roop was ever afraid for the children – it is just a slight exaggeration.

'Never. This is impossible.'

Sardarji can hold ignorance as a pose for just so long. Now it has begun to appear wilful.

'This is cent-per-cent correct.' Bachan Singh suddenly finds his voice and the English words with which to make his protest. Neither Bachan Singh nor Jeevan find it important to mention Roop's fear of being poisoned herself. Timcu is far more important to Sardarji – and when bargaining, you phrase your reasons for the one whose ear they will fall on.

'And you think Bari-Sardarni, Satya, said this to Roop?' says Sardarji, in Punjabi, as if considering the possibility.

'How else could she have thought it?'

The three men and their audience all nod their agreement. How else could Roop have thought it but with the thoughts of an older woman?

Bachan Singh says peevishly, in Punjabi, 'Your Bari-Sardarniji is possessed of a djinn.' He is feeling more confident, ready now to give advice as a father-in-law should to a son-in-law. 'You should make her live somewhere else.'

'Correct,' says the sweetseller. 'Yeh correct hai,' says Abu Ibrahim. 'Very correct,' says Pandit Dinanath.

'Tell her she should separate now. She has had four years since your second marriage, still she has had no son.' He is pointing out the score, as if Roop and Satya had been in a race to produce sons. 'Tell her she should go now.' Bachan Singh is on the offensive, now, emboldened by Sardarji's quietness.

Jeevan, towering over Sardarji, his large, heavy hair-knot bobbing under his gold turban says, respectfully, 'It will save all of our izzat.'

Satya wouldn't harm his son in any way; she wouldn't dare. Her threats are those of a pitiful old adder who strikes an intruder though her poison sacs are empty. If Sardarji chose to cast her out with no support, she would simply have nowhere to go.

Ergo, she wouldn't dare.

But Satya has been interfering too much, she has gone too far. He will deal with her later.

But right now, Sardarji has a new and different concern. His walk through Pari Darvaza has shown him this is a village where most of his tenants are Muslim. This lambardar, Deputy Bachan Singh, appears to be one of the very few Sikhs – probably the sole support of the local gurdwara. It would undermine his authority as leader of the village council if Sardarji were to publicly disagree with him over a mere woman and it might pave the way for some pir or worse to take Bachan Singh's place. If Sardarji is as harsh as he feels justified in being after the excuse – and of course it is an excuse – that they have presented, the Muslims in this village will say, 'See, Sikh jagirdars are always harsh,' and the Sikhs in this village will not be able to deny it.

'Yes,' says Sardarji. 'Achchaji.' He drains the last of his tea, grimacing at its bitter dregs, places the glass in Kusum's hand. 'It will save all from embarrassment. I will tell her she will have to live separately now.'

'Alone,' urges Jeevan, pushing his advantage.

'Alone,' says Sardarji, with a sigh. Of course, Satya will have his name as her protection, but he will miss the comfort of her capable presence, her anticipation of his habits.

'I will bring Roop and the children to you myself,' offers Jeevan. 'When you have a separate household set up for her.'

The trump card has been held in Jeevan's hand all along – Sardarji cannot take his son away before all the men present in Pari Darvaza, and still keep his turban secure upon his head, and his head secure upon his shoulders.

'I am being posted to Lahore,' says Sardarji, sighing again. 'I have been promoted again – I have so many responsibilities.' Sardarji's way to Lahore has not been paved by Mr Farquharson, but by Mr Farquharson's absence. He looks around but as no one in the little audience can imagine responsibilities that go beyond the survival of a man and his family, no one seems ready to commiserate. 'Send Roop to me there. I will tell Satya that she must stay in 'Pindi with the children.'

But there is more.

'A mother and her children should not be separated,' Bachan Singh advises. He offers the general principle, an ethical reminder to be understood as a personal rebuke to his son-in-law.

Crafty old man.

Bachan Singh is about the same age as Sardarji, but the opinion of a man with the whiter beard is heard loudest in a village. And a promise made before an elder is a promise to be kept.

Sardarji is realizing rapidly that his full humility is required in making amends.

He nods in deference to his father-in-law.

'Yes, I misspoke. Forgive me – send both children, then.' The tongues of these men will work through all his villages and Sardarji would prefer, in these uncertain times, to be known for generosity.

Bachan Singh brightens and, all being settled, begins to discuss the wheat in harvest, the Akali Party's prospects.

Abu Ibrahim wants to know if Sardarji has met Mr Jinnah, touched his hand or feet.

No, and no, he replies.

And then there are smaller tenants whom he must greet, for who knows when he may pass this way again? And they ask him the question he has answered in villages time after time as the Irrigation Department progresses: 'How can it be, Sardarji, that canal water can be just as good as well water for the fields? All of us know that God-given electric power in the water is leached out by dams and machinery long before the canal water ever reaches the fields. . .'

And Sardarji holds forth, explaining.

He explains it very well . . . far better than his elder brother could have, that is certain, without sentimental poetry to further indulge their natural superstitions.

As soon as possible – which is a good three hours later, without sight or sound of Timcu or of Roop – Sardarji says 'Sat Sri Akal' to Bachan Singh and then all round 'Khuda hafiz' or 'Ram Ram' or 'Sat Sri Akal' to the small but determined audience, and takes his leave. And to prove he holds no grudge, he puts aside his distaste for nepotism and assures Bachan Singh he will put in a good word, and Captain Jeevan Singh will get a better posting – to Lahore, perhaps even to Delhi. He will see to it, and, he assures them, he will look after Roop as if she were a flower.

The village children try to imitate his swagger as he emerges from the tunnel. But now he holds his stick low at his side. The children whisper and giggle as he walks through the village and climbs into the Austin, a hand steadying his turban.

The dusty starter turns over once, twice, and then Narain Singh stops, waits. The postman's khaki uniform and then his round cap fill Sardarji's window. Then his arm and a hand grasping the handle of Bachan Singh's parting gift, a pair of perfectly matched black fighter partridges in a divided bamboo cage.

'Put them in the front seat,' says Sardarji, wearily. A game bird smell fills the motor car. He leans back, closes his eyes.

Cunningham, he thinks, *you were right all along. A poor lambardar's daughter. Huh, she is not grateful.*

What, he asks himself, *could he have done? Married a used woman – a widow? Why would a qualified man of his stature ask for a flower with petals browning and decaying, to grace his dinner table or his withdrawing room?*

Yes, Bachan Singh and Captain Jeevan Singh are clever. And it might be useful to have a well-disposed young brother-in-law in the army in these uncertain times.

It will be nice to get his little brown koel back – he's missed her at night, wished she'd been at the government rest house with him at the capital, Delhi – or rather, New Delhi. Where the ministers he taps for budget allocations for cranes and turbines have Galileo's theory confused: their sun still revolves about Lutyens, the New Delhi architect chap, and his impressive sandstone monuments.

But you have to give the English credit; New Delhi is impressive.

Roop would have been awestruck by the edifices of New Delhi – smooth-paved Kingsway with its statue of the late King George, the domed, colonnaded Viceroy's palace, the deep rounded arches of the Secretariat, the dignified opulence of the Chamber of Princes, the whitewashed elegance of Connaught Place showrooms – while Satya would have been sarcastic, mocking as he admired those edifices. Would have laughed when he called them emblems of a new era, extolled their excellent mix of Indian and English architecture, the power of Western science and civilization embodied in their diverse elements – she would have derided any architect who mixes cobra fountains with Britannic lions.

It is difficult to imagine Satya at his side, in a ballroom or the state dining room at the Viceroy's palace, difficult to imagine her ever understanding that those buildings brought work to the hands of millions of workers, their women and children.

Sardarji doubts Satya has great concern for the stonecutters and labourers who climb the Viceroy's palace ramparts on shaky bamboo ladders for eight annas, half a rupee per day (even women are paid six annas, boys four), but Satya would have mocked, 'From whom did your British friends take the money to build this one? Which maharaja's poor subjects paid for that one?' just because she cannot abide the British, or the English language she calls 'git-mit,' or the modern things they bring.

And Satya would not have missed the opportunity to remind him of the legend that haunts the capital: that any emperor so conceited and vain as to rebuild Delhi to suit his desires will lose her – so losing all of India – and mourn.

Yes, he chooses Roop over Satya, chooses to take Roop to Lahore.

Roop will listen to him admiringly, carefully, her eyes upon his mouth as if ropes of pearls fell from his lips, while Satya has never lowered her eyes before him and carries herself far too confidently.

Who knows what Satya has been teaching Roop in his absence? What might she have said to Roop about him?

Poor little Roop needs izzat and, unfortunately, he will have to put a stop to Satya's interfering. Satya doesn't have Roop's vulnerability; she can look after herself.

He does so hate women's silly quarrels; they always need a man at some point to put a stop to their bickering and draw a line that must not be crossed. Chatter, gossip, foolishness, lies – they're so childish.

'Now tell me, Cunningham, what choice do I have? I must divide my household or lose my dearly bought son.'

'A pity,' consoles Cunningham. 'Inevitable, convenient – still, definitely a pity.'

27. Rawalpindi, July 1941

The fragrance of warm mustard oil hovers over Satya. Henna-dark hair coils away from Jorimon's strong kneading thumbs pressing her shoulders into the soft divan. Though she is a bad-luck orphan, Jorimon does give excellent massages; her skill keeps Satya from giving Jorimon away.

It is several months now since Sardarji left her behind in 'Pindi with trusted but unrelated men, Manager Abdul Aziz and servants, including Dehna Singh and Jorimon, to tend her. Atma Singh went to Lahore, too, and Sardarji had a new cook brought into the old haveli for Satya before he left, a step that said this separation would be longer than any she had ever before endured.

At first, to her surprise, Satya found aloneness pleasurable.

The servants were no more than hands to do and feet to run when required, and Satya began to revel in quiet.

Alone, she ate when hungry, slept when tired, bathed when she felt it necessary to feel clean limbs. Alone, she spoke freely, spoke aloud to herself, spoke her mind as a woman much older would do – *What does it matter? No ears of consequence are here to hear me.*

In the sorting room, apricots brought from Sardarji's orchards ripened and fermented in the moist heat, their heavy sweet scent mixing with the smell of wet coir. This year, she will not send them to any of Sardarji's higher-ups – let them moulder and reek. Then, only then, will she allow the sweepers to roll up the matting, take them away.

Alone, she found the need to love herself and did it carefully, crimping her eyes shut as Jorimon's strong fingers worked amla and henna into her wet hair. But slowly, his absence began to fester like a wound that would not heal. Driving her pink tonga through the bazaar, Satya felt the pity of low-class people for her abandoned state – they know, they know. For servants talk, how can anyone stop them? She saw pity in the eyes of the bread man bearing his wooden trunk of loaves to sell, thought she heard poor men laugh at her in the bazaar beyond the gate. The snide speculations of low-class people floated over the haveli walls till the very banyan leaves snickered to every little breeze.

And Sardar Kushal Singh and Toshi. Neither one held Sardarji responsible, they reserved their blame for Satya, boycotting her as if she were a prostitute.

But Satya was no prostitute; she had married only once – once was enough for her.

But not for him.

She cannot deny it: she has been left here alone.

And this evening, when Jorimon's thumbs slip and circle deep between muscle and bone, bringing things that lie buried and denied to the surface, Satya becomes afraid Jorimon will notice the liquid shine of her eyes.

'*Buss!*' she says.

Jorimon's hands stop immediately. 'You Bengalis. So lazy!' Jorimon drops her gaze.

'Have you stopped your wailing, huh?' Satya asks.

'Wailing, Sardarniji?'

'You were crying yesterday because the new cook forgot to make rice for you. Did he make it today?'

'Ji-han, Sardarniji.'

'Good. Then look pleasant. And none of this "ji-han" – you speak Punjabi in this house, not Urdu or Hindi. Say "hanji" or "ah-ho."'

'Hanji, Sardarniji.'

Jorimon rises slowly from her knees and adjusts her sari palloo across her thin chest. She takes the brass bowl of mustard oil from Satya's side, covers her head and shuffles past the pukkhawalla rocking and pulling on the gallery.

Such slowness!

Jorimon is a non-cooperation movement of one.

Infuriating.

Alone, Satya massages each arm herself; she has been exploring her limbs more each day, learning, it seems for the first time, where they begin, where one flows into another, giving her body the attention that for so many years she had given exclusively to Sardarji.

Her breasts, still high and firm. Her stomach – poor unstretched stomach – flat, its navel well centred in its chakra. Her hips were always narrow, but not so narrow people would have been unwilling to believe she could have borne a small son, five pounds small, like Timcu – why should the truth be laid bare for all to see?

The only place her shield is broken is between her legs; that cannot be mended. But the rest of her is intact. Her inner thighs are taut. Her calves and ankles are still slender.

A toe she'd known only from above is shaped like a small hammer. It can grip tight, clench, and unclench like a fist. A ligament, sharp and tight, flexes her strong hard heel.

These days, Satya's body remembers for her and it tells her to be daring in ways she could never contemplate before.

A few days ago she called for a boxwalla to enter the scalloped archway of the haveli so she could finger the imported off-the-shoulder dresses he carried to those shameless English women in the cantonment. Yesterday she went without kameez or choli above her lehnga, letting her bare shoulders feel only the soft touch of a shahtoosh shawl, delicate as a cobweb.

Once, she even let it slip so a shoulder felt the warmth of sunlight!

She laughs aloud at the memory.

What does it matter?
My husband does not want me.

Satya wipes the oil from her limbs and dresses in a loose silk kameez, grey as her eyes. Beneath it, she ties the cord of a black salwar. She drapes a widow-white chunni over her head.

She leaves her sitting room and climbs the spiral staircase to the gallery that runs past Roop's chambers filled with that ungainly long-legged English furniture.

How Sardarji wasted his good money on that low-class woman.

Again and again she sees it – Sardarji coming into her sitting room on his return from Roop's village – Pari Darvaza, yes, she knows that name now. She feels the muscles of her abdomen tense again; she rose on her divan. Her feet searched in vain beneath the tasselled covering of the divan for the Kolhapuri sandals he'd bought her on his last trip to Bombay. She welcomed his scent again, scent of sandalwood fixo and Brylcreem. But his face was stern, his gaze coming to rest on the banyan leaves vying for the sun's attention past her sitting-room window.

And then Sardarji's mouth said in English, 'Satya, I have decided. When I take up my posting in Lahore, you will remain here. You will be looked after, you will want for nothing. But you cannot come to Lahore. You fight too much – I never get any peace.'

In English, so the words sounded rational to his ear, as though they named the only course of action he could take.

And then in Punjabi, for her to give meaning to the sounds – for her to truly understand.

And she, knowing there was nowhere to go but where he decreed, stood barefoot before him and said, with all the dignity she could muster, 'This cannot be.'

The acrid scent of her own sweat rose about her from the full horror of the slight – the very slightest – possibility she could join poor women fetching water, cooking, mending, in the back alleys of smelly bazaars, or become some other woman's servant the way Mani Mai had.

She asked him, sweetly, as softly as she could manage, 'Why do you treat me this way? You have a son. You gave him to me – why do you take him away?'

He shrugged, his hands spread wide.

'A mother and her children should never be separated,' he said slowly, halting as if the words were suggested by someone else.

But it is not true, not true. A mother and daughter are always separated, it is just that some are separated earlier than others – Satya has not seen Bebeji in almost four years, since the night Roop came; Bebeji being careful never to let it be said she takes from a married daughter's home. And a mother and her son are separated as soon as a son is old enough to be sent to boarding school – English mothers or Indian, if they are high-up enough.

But she could not say this to Sardarji. She could only shed silly woman-tears as he stalked about her sitting room, 'I *am* your son's mother; you gave me your son to raise. When you take your Timcu away you take away my very izzat!'

'You have too much anger!' he exploded.

Her knees buckled before that rage.

Did he hate her so much?

What had she done to him that was so wrong?

She had to sit down. 'All of 'Pindi will know you are abandoning me, if not now then as the time goes by. Please, don't do this to me, piara!'

And in English he said, 'Who taught you to raise your voice to your husband this way? It is jealousy, all jealousy. I tell you I won't countenance it.'

Oh, she understood the words, all right. There are some things that need no translation.

Satya leaves Roop's apartments and climbs the stone spiral staircase to the third storey.

Here, in guest apartments and sitting rooms are displayed the collected souvenirs of Sardarji's travels and the legacies of previous generations. Distinctive pieces, not to be found in Rawalpindi or Lahore; Sardarji calls them the result of refinement, of taste, travel, things selected, bought, and kept, not for their use but for their beauty.

Foreign things; useless things.

But could he not have kept her with him, like these useless things?

The dusty pianoforte stands upright in the corner.

Ebony men advance upon an ivory king in slow and purposeful battle. A grandfather clock chimes beside a Moroccan savonarola chair, a Limoges crystal bird alights upon an elephant-foot table. A bust of an Egyptian queen with sightless eyes perches upon an enamel-inlaid brass heater. A carved Chinese armoire gathers more years to itself.

Can a village woman like Roop appreciate such things? Never.

Satya returns to the stone stairs, remembering in a circle.

Climbing, climbing.

Memories have sedimented in her over the years, striped layers on her mind so one year and another are just shades apart. She has not realized how many years she lived in a state of readiness, anticipating Sardarji's every whim expressed in a movement, sometimes a sidelong glance, or a sigh of longing.

His absence is like the lifting of mosquito netting at dawn.

Protection gone, unstrained air enters her world.

A frightening world . . .

Her face sets, resolute.

Unless you come, as I do, from a bold and fighting family.

The stairwell narrows to a dark airless shaft past the third storey. Satya places one foot carefully before the other, rising slowly. Cool stone walls meet her fingers.

A recessed stone-filigree window throws faded diamonds on the stairs. She leans into its sill, eyes close to its mesh, like a woman trapped alive behind a stone burqa.

She tended Sardarji the one other time he came back to her, a time he'd left Roop in Khanewal and broken his journey on his way north to a meeting in Kashmir. Stopping to give her a new cook from Faletti's Hotel in Lahore, to meet Satya and that first baby, that girl-baby so like her mother, he was stricken for a week with a bout of indigestion he ascribed to this country, its filthy backwardness, its lack of planning, lack of rational foresight, all this religious mumbo-jumbo.

'Isabgol,' he said.

She administered Isabgol, and Eno's Fruit Salts. A cup of birada and cornflakes sodden with milk. The household was subjected to these for days; it would clear his stomach of things brought by the winds of change, Indian winds,

Gandhian winds, blowing just when he had made himself almost, but not quite, English.

'It must be the new cook's fault; it can't be Atma Singh's fault,' said Satya. 'So what if Atma Singh takes a little opium now and then; his puddings are superb, you say so yourself. His trifles and lemon soufflés are so delicate they would cause jelsy in every English man in the Rawalpindi Club if they had the chance to taste it. Someone has praised you too much – it's the evil eye.'

Sardarji looked at Satya witheringly, 'Only the Hindu mind is so superstitious,' he said, prostrate upon his rosewood bed.

Rebuked, she confined herself to plumping cushions. He continued, 'One trip back to England – just one. A glimpse of Wordsworth's golden daffodils along Hampstead Heath, *Hamlet* at the Shaftesbury Theatre, a dinner with the dons at Balliol.' That, he felt, was all it would take to cure him.

All.

As he lay upon his bed specially fitted with an imported mattress, his turban on the nightstand beside him in case of emergency, Sardarji yearned for England.

In this Satya could not help him. But then, neither could Roop.

'Too much thinking makes a man tired,' she had offered.

'They have made it us and them, now, Satya, us and them. Indians are a people without gratitude.'

Satya said, 'How long should we be grateful and how much? Are you blind to their true intentions, their relations with others? Yesterday Azhar Sheikh told me how his old father was beaten and jailed in Peshawar again and I gave him a full day's leave to go and plead for his release.'

'Indians are a disorderly people,' he moaned, clutching his stomach. 'The Hindus are doing it.'

'We are also doing it, we Sikhs,' said Satya. She was proud of their resistance.

'No, it is the Sahajdhari Sikhs.' The less orthodox Sikhs.

He sat up in bed, reaching for the enamel chamber-pot. 'They,' he said, letting loose a stream with a hollow echo, 'they cut their hair. It takes away their discipline, their objectivity.

We Singhs are the only Sikhs with that unshakeable firmness, that steadfast loyalty.'

'Mmm-hm,' she said, sceptically. 'Long hair,' she told him, stroking his on the pillow, 'does not guarantee a man will follow the Gurus in all ways. Guru Nanak had but one wife.' She put the chamber-pot beneath his bed – the sweeper, Azhar Sheikh, would collect it in the morning – and drew the curtains.

And though she knew he didn't want to hear it, she could not resist adding, 'It is not only Sahajdhari Sikhs protesting. There are qualified, intelligent, government-service Muslims too, people like Rai Alam Khan – Indian Civil Service gentlemen who donate to the Muslim League, the Congress, the Akali Party, chupke-chupke, under the table, as you do. And there are others. You know their names as well as I: your Indian friends from the Tuesday Lunch Club?'

'True. Qualified men should be counselling Jinnah, instead of letting him listen to poets like Muhammad Iqbal.'

'Poets get a hearing only once they are dead. If Iqbal were still alive, do you think Muslims would care what he said?'

'Tell the cook I will have just an omelette for dinner.'

'Sardarji, one day you will wish you had listened to me, prepared yourself. There is a Hindu raj coming when the English leave – Jinnah understands that.'

'The English will never completely leave, Satya – how you argue! Can a chemical reaction be run backwards? Indians can progress to a dominion, or a union, or a federation – never mind Mr Gandhi's speeches. But they need the English for their betterment, and the English will always need Indian labour. Mr Churchill will not countenance independence. You don't *understand* – India cannot go backwards, we'll all be Philistines.'

'Philistine-shilistine.' Satya mocked the idea she could not fathom. 'I *do* understand, better than you know. Perhaps I have seen this happen before, in some past life, who can say? But someday you will remember my words.'

She left his room, and gave his orders to the cook, but ordered Indian food for herself. His words made her desire the fiery heat of red chilies and the aroma of hot masala sizzling in a wide iron pot. She needed spices, she wanted spices – the very thing the British first came here for – perhaps she swallowed them daily just so they couldn't have all of them. She wanted the smell of coriander and the slow frying of cumin. She wanted the saturated stickiness of white rasogullahs crumbling between her fingers, the spit and hiss of white paneer balls swelling and bobbing in hot butter-ghee.

Satya emerges from the dark well of the stairs to a sky grey-pink as a pigeon's wing. She fills her lungs full of the warm open air, stretches her arms above her head to the shadows. The fragrance of her uttar, queen of the night, mingles with the spice-scent of kebab meat turning on spits in the bazaar. She is at the very top of the old haveli, past the highest leaf of the banyan. Rawalpindi stretches in all directions, like a child's painted wooden toys flung in the lap of the Margalla Hills.

Gandhiji says Indian men and women must stop their wanting, says it is the core of all trouble, the red-hot chili that spreads into food, turning words to curses in Indian mouths, setting Hindu and Sikh against Muslim. Like Buddha before him, he talks of the joys of renunciation, the happiness in self-denial, in celibacy and in hunger.

Celibacy, huh!

Satya has known celibacy.

Gandhi fasts almost to death, he chooses celibacy, his body shrivels. Why does he not die of unsatisfied desire? Where, he asks, will wanting end?

But she, Satya, she cannot stop her wanting.

Wanting cannot be stopped by will alone.

But, Satya thinks, unlike Mahatma Gandhi, she does not *pretend*, does not deny the presence of her desire like sweet, simple little Roop, whose almond eyes tell Sardarji she only wants *his* betterment, only wants *his* prestige, wants things for the children she may bear and not for herself, not for herself, but to look nice for him.

Satya cannot deny her love, but she will not flutter her eye-lashes like Roop and pretend stupidity and incompetence to win his love.

How can she pretend, she whose very name means Truth.

Once she raged to Sardarji –

'I want . . .

'I want your love, not your duty.

'I want your fidelity, not your generosity.

'I want, not for you, but for me, for myself. Because though I have failed to do what we women are for, I am still here, still your wife, still Satya.'

And, if he were here now I would say, 'In return let me share, as the Guru himself allows me, share your burdens, your obligations, your vulnerability. Let us face them, not you alone, or I alone, but you and I.'

But no no no, Satya cannot say any of these things.

If she were to see Sardarji now, this very minute, she would call him her love, her only love. Say, 'Come back to me, piara.'

When Sardarji comes back to me, who will dare to notice any resemblance in the boy to that cheap and vulgar woman?

Below her, on the roofs of the smaller havelis of Rajah Bazaar, boys and men tug and tangle the glass-encrusted strings of fragile paper squares of pink, purple, green and gold. Their kites engage in battle till only one remains to tell her story.

Just let Sardarji try to present Roop to his government friends at the Cosmopolitan Club in Lahore. Roop has made a son, but that is not *all* he needs now that he is stationed at the capital of Punjab. Roop may be able to sit on chairs, she may have learned to eat with knife and fork, but she – like Satya, it's true – cannot speak the git-mit, git-mit talk. But unlike Satya, she will not know how to mock the words she does not know and carry her ignorance like a badge of nationalist honour.

The shadow people tell her: Roop will be overawed by Lahore society; soon her vulgar village ways will bring Sardarji home to Satya. It is only a matter of time before he sees: leaving Satya behind in 'Pindi is wasteful.

Why, Roop cannot even cook!

At the far end of the neighbourhood, qawwali singers chorus. The steady beat of ankle bells *chumm-chumm* and the sweetish smell of opium ride the warm breeze. Muslims in the Muslim quarter; she does not know them.

They treat their women so badly, so badly, they cover them up in chadors and burqas.

FIVE

28. Lahore, July 1942

'Pani Lao!' The governess uses her scant Hindustani to ask for drinking water, and her strange accent still grates in Roop's ear after a year of hearing it.

The cord of a white linen sari petticoat presses tight about Roop's waist. Pink chiffon pools at her feet. She holds her forearms crossed before her, unaccustomed to the tightness of the choli baring her midriff in place of her loose kameez. Cricket match finals are in the offing; Sardarji has told Roop she will be at his side and should wear a sari like the wives of other civil servants. So Roop stands before a long tilting mirror in her dressing room, where she can catch Pavan's black eyes occasionally – how intently the little girl observes her in that mirror! Timcu's nappied bottom rests on a Bijar carpet and a clenched fist clutches a piece from the Meccano set Sardarji bought him.

'Boiled pani!' Boiled water.

'Ever since the teacher-ni arrived, Atma Singh has had to soak all the vegetables in pinky-pani,' Mani Mai says.

Sardarji approved the governess's precaution against germs.

The governess. Thin-lipped, wasp-waisted woman with sapphire eyes set deep in a pale-tomato face. Brown shoulder-short hair that ripples in the sunlight, disciplined nightly by Kirby grips that twist on her scalp. As soon as Miss Henrietta Barlow unpacked her hat box, her portmanteau and Bible in her apartments near the nursery in Sardarji's government home on Club Road, she began ordering Atma Singh and Mani Mai about as if born to command.

It is a small well-knit world at the peak of Punjabi society – maharajas, nawabs, civil servants – these Indian families patronize useful English people with good references. And Miss Barlow is none other than the sister of the red-faced Dr Barlow, come to India with him after his last home leave.

It was because Miss Barlow was shocked – completely shocked – by Dr Barlow's terrible, horrible stories of India and the tracts and pamphlets her Bible reading group gave her about Indian women, that she felt her dear departed mother's thwarted ambitions taking root in her own breast. And so, a few months before the war, she booked her cabin to India, port-out-starboard-home, determined to bring Indian women and their little brown babies to Christ, and certain that earlier missionaries failed precisely because they brought the Church in their suitcases, wore it on their sleeves. Miss Barlow, however, came well persuaded of her calling, but disguised in a governess costume.

Finding that her small inheritance went a great deal further in India – especially since the war began – and that she was much better off than women bombed, blitzed and struggling on rationing in England, Miss Barlow braved the Lahore heat for the creature comforts a woman of her means could never buy at home.

She is here because she wants to save the innocents – the women, the children.

But Roop is unaware of this, caring only that Timcu and Pavan are with her and that their laughter rings through Sardarji's bungalow.

Roop has her own apartments now, also just off the nursery. They are as large as any Satya ever had – a large bedroom, a private sitting room, her very own dressing room and store-room – a little large for her solitary wedding trunk. Before the mirror of her dressing table stands a black velvet box, a gold kantha necklace within. And a box with earrings: three tiers of Burmese rubies surrounded by diamonds. And a third box, this one oblong, with the gold panjebs Sardarji gave her for her ankles when she was just a young bride of sixteen.

Roop is twenty-one now and *so* much more sophisticated.

Mani Mai holds the gold-bordered pink chiffon before her lumpy figure, then repeats the movement before Roop's bare slim waist. '*Y'Allah!*' she chortles, 'you can see right through it. Choti-Sardarni, be careful that your Sardarji is the only one to admire you. Take a shawl – that beautiful Kashmiri one Bari-Sardarni gave you – and hold it,' she demonstrates with her white chunni, 'low, like this.' She loops the chunni around herself and takes its ends in the crooks of her elbows. 'Then no one can see any bare skin. But do it loosely, so his hand can come between it and your back. You must be careful to keep his favour.'

Jeevan had delivered her to Sardarji this time, and Roop's palanquin was not a DeSoto but a fifteen-hundred-weighter truck. Vayu's sand-laden loo wind abraded her cheeks as they sped past weeping willows trailing their boughs in the Upper Bari Doab Canal. Mani Mai held grimly to Timcu and Pavan, and soon the truck swept through a low gate and crunched to a halt outside Sardarji's newly allotted bungalow on Club Road.

Roop wore the red-and-gold lehnga old Fazl Karim had sewn for her three years before, the chunni with Lajo Bhua's salma-sitara embroidery, Mama's phulkari-embroidered red shawl folded upon her forearm, Mama's sapphire ring and a wide, charming, loving smile as her only protection against Sardarji's possible wrath.

And these were sufficient. Sardarji stood on the veranda with his arms open wide and stopped her as she knelt to touch his feet.

'Remember what I told you,' Jeevan whispered parting advice in her good ear. 'Learn English!' and then in Punjabi, 'English sikho!'

This whitewashed government bungalow is similar to the canal colony bungalow in Khanewal, only so much larger. Green-white chunnis of bougainvillaea adorn each of its eleven arches. And there are other civil servants' government-issue houses just as large and imposing on Club Road, their compound walls touching Sardarji's. The round-capped mali who draws water from the canal till the lawn shines green as malachite says the flowers he plants in earthen pots along the bungalow's drive are Prophet flowers.

Sardarji has corrected him several times.

'Its name is Guru-flower,' Sardarji says, emphatically.

The mali whacks his cow harder as he hitches it to the lawncutter, but does not challenge Sardarji to his face.

That day, returning Roop pushed Timcu before her and Sardarji's face became stern as he held out his hand for the skinny little toddler to shake. For a moment, his hand rested on Pavan's tight-plaited hair. He turned to Roop and – before Jeevan, so dashing in his Captain's uniform – ceremoniously presented her with the keys to the house and the pantry. As Jeevan drove away, Sardarji's hand cupped Roop's elbow and led her to her apartments.

And he said off-handedly, 'Don't worry, Satya shall not come near Timcu again.'

That night Roop wept with relief in Sardarji's arms, apologizing so prettily till his face softened, for having left him alone, and she promised never to do anything without his permission ever again.

And she asked him, good-good, sweet-sweet as a little brown koel, if he could find a teacher-ni for Timcu to learn English.

And the very next day Sardarji ordered an Anglo-Indian nanny in a white dress almost to her ankles, from Mayo Hospital. She spoke no Punjabi, no Urdu, no Hindi, because she thought she was English and might leave for England any day. But Sardarji said her English was also 'atrocious, absolutely atrocious.' Since the nanny was, Sardarji said, 'more than ten-per-cent unsatisfactory,' and caused Mani Mai to sulk and simmer with jelsy – jealousy, Jeevan would have corrected Roop – till the bungalow became quite unbearable,

Roop was introduced, one afternoon tea, to Miss Hetty Barlow.

Miss Barlow speaks excellent English and has a complexion, Sardarji said appreciatively at dinner, 'like English primroses.'

Mani Mai whispered the governess craves food that has been squashed or condensed into tins – meat, fish, even milk. Tins, and packets of Britannia digestive biscuits. Mani Mai saw the governess's hoard in her cupboard, enough to set up a government ration-shop. And the Miss-sahib hired her own cycle-mounted servant boy to bring her cigarettes from the bazaar. But, Mani Mai says, these English women are all same-to-same, all like *that*.

Roop has been managing Sardarji's home – been learning, anyway. Every morning she unlocks the cabinets in the pantry for Atma Singh, smiles a winning smile and says, 'So, Atma Singhji, what will you make today?'

And Atma Singh says, 'I will do as you command me and make . . .' and he names Sardarji's favourite dishes.

And every evening, Sardarji commends Roop on her selection from Atma Singh's repertoire and says how loving and graceful she looks, peeling mangoes and papaya for his sweet-dish after dinner.

Mani Mai has finished tucking the sari all the way around Roop's petticoat. Pink chiffon clings to Roop's hips, rises and curls across her bare midriff, lies lightly across her breasts and falls over her left shoulder till its gold border comes level with her hair, moonlit river that falls down the valley of her spine. She brings Roop the gold kantha from the black velvet box and places it about her neck, using a corner of her chunni to bring forth the sheen of its red enamel. Roop takes the earrings from Mani Mai's hand, three tiers of Burmese rubies surrounded by diamonds. Mani Mai opens the oblong box, and Roop arches her feet for the gold panjebs to be fastened about her ankles. Now Mani Mai crouches before her to pull each pleat even with the stone floor.

Roop's merry eyes meet Pavan's in the mirror as Mani Mai says, 'Kick the pleats a little with every step so it looks as if you just glide forward.'

* * *

Sardarji sits in a leather-upholstered blue chair with nail-studded trim. At a teak desk with a leather blotting pad. In his Lahore bungalow office on Club Road, lined with shelves that accommodate many books from his library in 'Pindi as if specially designed to receive them.

He is oblivious to the jackdaws cawing, clamouring at his window. The beauty of the hibiscus bushes swaying gently in the clear morning light outside goes unnoticed.

Finally posted to the capital of Punjab Province: Lahore, he has completed more than a year's service, constructing the barrage and canals near Bhakra, preparing for the building of that mighty dam.

His steno faces the opposite wall at a smaller wooden desk – minus the leather blotting pad – on which brown-paper files are stacked past the marble wainscot. He stretches fingers cramped from scratching with the two-inch remainder of a lead pencil in his copy book since early morning. The result: writing like Persian script, incomprehensible as astrology.

It would have been nice to share this first year in Lahore with Satya; she would have understood how long he worked to be posted here. But—

It is her own fault.

Perhaps in a few years if Satya comes to him ready to touch his feet, with eyes downcast, with the word 'sorry' repeating itself on her lips and a sweeter tongue, Sardarji might take her in and give her the keys of his household again. But let her come with reproach and recrimination and no man will ever call him weak enough to be her slave.

A wall clock chimes noon. Sardarji must finish his correspondence quickly. Today he will dine with the Tuesday Lunch Club at Faletti's Hotel with a select group of high-up, qualified men, Rai Alam Khan among them. Then he will continue to his office in the Secretariat where his new desk, commissioned from his own funds, is being delivered. Far more elegant than anything the absent Mr Farquharson would have ordered, Sardarji's desk is solid mahogany inlaid with mother-of-pearl flowers.

'Steno!'

The steno jumps to readiness at his elbow, pen poised above his notebook.

Sardarji dictates.

'Dear – Satya – comma – by Vaheguru's grace I write from Lahore – full stop – Your sister is managing the house quite well – full stop – Mother and son are well – full stop – I have engaged an English governess to teach Timcu English – full stop – Ask Abdul Aziz for anything you need – full stop.'

Nothing more to be said, so he ends with the Sikh greeting,

'Sat Sri Akal.'

God is great.

29. Rawalpindi, July 1942

i

In Sardarji's chair before his typewriter, Satya cracks the red seal on his first letter and, mistrusting her voice, proffers it mutely to Manager Abdul Aziz to read. He clears his throat, reads Sardarji's letter and translates.

It is short, and it does not begin with his respects.

There is a silence, perhaps of the manager's pity.

So Sardarji is with his renewed bride, my 'sister,' and still has not relented to say when I should join him in Lahore. Let him spurn me, I grow stronger. I dig within me and when I clear away weeds and leaves and loose earth, I hit bedrock, smooth as the truth I am named for, elegant. Heart-solid, extent unknown. This is mine, this simple hardness that moves from life to next life, impervious to any man's whims.

Because there is a higher law.

An English governess has been teaching *Timcu* English?

Satya knows better. Satya knows who must have requested a governess and who wants to learn English. If Roop learns the git-mit, git-mit talk, Satya will be replaceable. Satya, after all, cannot even read.

Sardarji must be waiting for her to apologize, waiting for her to beg him to return her izzat.

She will not.

Never!

He should be the one to apologize.

But will he?

Unlikely.

'Open the second letter,' she orders. Sharp-toned enough to kill Manager Abdul Aziz's pity. 'Why has it come so soon after the first?'

The second letter from Sardarji says: for the third time, Roop is 'in a family way.'

How to bear this?

Aloud she mutters, 'So Roop has called forth life again.'

Sardarji continues his dalliance with the temptress even after a son has been born. Then how can Satya lie to herself any more – there is no chance his heart will return to her. How can any man love and protect a woman he does not respect? She has lied to herself too long, her deeds running counter to her name.

Some men are not entitled to know truth.

'Leave me,' she says.

Manager Abdul Aziz vanishes.

She paces the study, a caged and wounded tigress. 'Know this, Sardarji, she can call forth life, but I – I can call forth Death. Know this!'

Are the aspects she despises in Roop the only ones she has left to use?

A dilruba has twenty-one strings – not because all of them are required at once, but only when called upon by the music. Often it remains silent, waiting its chance to accompany a singer worthy of its sophistication.

She picks at the cracked red wax seal. He must have held the wax stick to the fire till it dripped red tears onto this envelope, crushed it flat with a brass seal, then waited for it to cool and clot to hardness.

To Sardarji, standing tall and proud behind the red settee in the wedding photo on his desk she says, 'Oh, fear not for yourself, Sardarji, I still love you the way foolish Sita loved her Ram even after he spurned her.'

What can she do?

She can get older, managing his estate. She can go insane. She can turn to Vaheguru; she can open Sardarji's haveli doors to charity, enhance his reputation in the quom.

If Timcu had never been born, she would have known a single sorrow – that of barrenness. But this is beyond barrenness. This is indifference.

Can all the years, so many years together, mean so little?

Where from do her eyes bring their tears?

I am not wife, for my husband has abandoned me. I am not widow, for he still lives. I am not mother, for the son he gave me is taken away, I am not sister, for I have no brother. With no father, I am but daughter of my Bebeji.

And so I am no one.

Why was this body given to her, body that imprisons her? Why does it linger when all that is left here is shame? Body that does not know how to die, body that shrinks from death as if blinded by its infinite beauty.

I deserve this. I never learn, never improve my karma. Sardarji's mother was right, she who noticed first just how bad I am, made me watch my own thoughts twisting, told me where all this loving and wanting would lead me.

Clutch of fear, smoke of anger, ashes of rage – these are the only truths this body has learned in this life.

Where from do her eyes bring more tears?

I have learned only the actions of taking, the pleasures of snatching like a man. I, watcher of myself, know well that I blamed Roop only because she was the woman nearest to Sardarji, the man truly responsible for each minute of these five years.

And my karma has paid me for it – I have become all I hated in Roop – dependent, grasping, begging for the leftovers of his love.

Hai, that she were already beyond tears, beyond wanting, eating, washing, dressing, sleeping, loving, hurting, children and no-children, thought and no-thought, body and nobody.

Body and no-body.

That is the key.

She can release herself, yes.

She does not have to be trapped in matter. There is a place she can go by choice, her own choice. By her will, her own free will. Somewhere there may be life without fear, where she can begin again.

But not now, not here.

Go simply.

Burn away flesh, burn it away slowly.

Simply go.

Surrender to death, tempter of all martyrs.

Wake to that dignity that comes from refusal, refusal to live without izzat!

But . . .

No harm must come to Sardarji or his reputation, it is the situation that must be corrected, balance restored, harmony returned. Why yearn to live in the same household, sharing his attention with Roop – meek, incompetent beauty? Or live here, separated from him by his command; like a peacock that dances alone in a forest.

If she subtracts herself, it will solve the problem.

Water, blood, bone, fat, sinew, will go, go to the realm where no woman is old, where all women are beautiful, no matter how useless, where woman is a second sun, not sun-light, where she is a second moon, not moonlight.

But no one must suspect it.

Hai, for the peace of it, the freedom of it, consciousness returning to the great unconscious, *hai*, to become one with the shadows. Then can she close the book of this life in which she has been incapable of writing and wait for a better time, find Sardarji again.

Find Sardarji in some later time, when women like her, prickly as cactus, shall not be abandoned and ignored. Then she will feel again as new flesh meets her atma, taking it in like nourishment, taking Satya into each cell and remembering all she knows now, the thought, the un-thought. Forgetting nothing, not one good deed or one bad deed of her own, not one good deed or bad deed against her. Taking all her remembered lives from the great karmic memory, old actions leaving trace elements in baby-soft bones, shaping them like wet clay.

Surely there will come a time when just being can bring izzat in return, when a woman will be allowed to choose her owner, when a woman will not be owned, when love will be enough payment for marriage, children or no children, just because her shakti takes shape and walks the world again.

What she wants is really *that* simple.

30. Rawalpindi, July 1942

Simple.

Achieving simplicity isn't easy.

It takes time and planning to reach simplicity.

Satya has time.

And planning is a skill that runs in her family.

She calls for the munshi's talent again and writes once more to Mumta. The letter innocent, gracious, innocuous. 'Come and stay a while.'

And Mumta comes, in a tonga, with just a bundle of clothes resting on her knees. Thin – so thin now – already looking past Satya with the deep holes of faraway eyes to her next life.

Such altruism will Satya display, Sardarji will always be reminded of his guilt. Let silence reverberate forever with the absence of Satya, the knowledge that but for a little more love, she would still be. By her absence will she make her presence felt, till they will both long for her as devotees long to be reunited with the infinite.

What you have done now, Sardarji, is worse than the with-holding of love, of respect and attention. All these I could bear, but not indifference. Remember the untold story, Sardarji, that part of the Ramayan *story the Ram-Lila reenactments do not tell. No matter how perfidious was Ram, Sita outdid him in doing her duty, even at the cost of her life.*

Sita, too, gave Ram the gift of her absence, called upon the earth to open and swallow her, called upon death to wake Ram's remorse when she could not speak to it herself. Sita, too, walked into the earth's fiery core, clear-eyed and willing, offering the finest gift she could give to her lord. Sita, too, entered the soundless scream of the earth, withholding her presence at her husband's moment of triumph, countered all aspersions on her worthiness with absence.

But it must be done so Sardarji can always say to the world, 'It was inevitable, it was her kismat.'

This gift must be given so he never knows he was given it.

Rawalpindi, August 1942

When a jatha of pilgrims on their way to visit every gurdwara between Lahore and Peshawar stops to ask for water from a Sikh well, Satya tells Dehna Singh to bring them into the haveli. Nihang Sikhs, they wear the bright blue and saffron of the Defender Sikh sect, carrying long sharp steel talwars encased in sun-faded scabbards bouncing against their calves, in place of the usual shorter kirpans. On their turbans they wear the khanda; its crossed swords shine their willingness to fight for God and quom. Their spears are walking sticks; in this group of holy soldiers two women travellers will be well protected.

Satya orders that they be fed — all thirty-five of them — in rows in the centre courtyard. And then she bids them sleep in the centre courtyard for the night. If Sardarji had been present, he would never have allowed it; he would have said, 'Who knows what germs they might carry?' and made them sleep outside on the terrace garden.

Mumta, standing on the gallery above as the thirty-five

nihangs eat, coughing with a balled fist below her ribcage, says it herself, without prompting from Satya: 'How good it would be to go with them.'

And Satya says, 'That is my wish too.'

And she prepares to leave the next morning over Mumta's warnings. 'Hai! It's bad luck to begin a journey on Tuesday.'

Let Mangal do its worst. The worst is what I yearn for.

They leave on the day of Mangal with sturdy chappals on their feet, with two salwar-kameezes each. Without bedding rolls, or jewellery or even Jorimon to tend to their needs, and without a chocolate-brown DeSoto to drive them.

Just Satya and Mumta. Cousin-sisters, friends to one another, just for the bad times.

At the first gurdwara outside Rawalpindi, Satya joins the throng of chunni-clad women sitting on coir matting before the Guru Granth Sahib, and she rocks and murmurs Vaheguru's praises with them. The Gurus tell how to reach the divine but offer her no guidance for her pain.

What was it I sowed in the opaqueness of my karma that brings such bitter harvest?

In the Guru's cookroom that evening they sit together in rows with all the other pilgrims, and when Mumta coughs, doubled over, hacking, spitting into the corner of her chunni, Satya rubs her back. The knobs of Mumta's spine shift beneath her skin.

Mumta, give me this, let me share your pain, knowing it leads to the comfort of death. Mumta, I envy you this, the sentence that has removed you so long from the living, the violence of each breath breathed out.

'I would take your pain,' Satya tells her.

Mumta answers simply, 'It's my kismat. By Vaheguru's blessing, I am still alive.'

Meal completed, they wash their hands, wipe them on their chunnis and ask for admittance at the dharmsala for the night. They are given a place on a floor in the women's quarters with the other pilgrims, twelve to a room no bigger than a storeroom. Satya had forgotten the unwashed smell of poor women. Her sweat, their sweat, the odour is the same. The coir matting is harsh beneath her shoulder and hip. She rolls her chunni into a ball under her head and leaves an end loose to protect her face from mosquitoes and any possible stares of unrelated men.

Mumta lies next to her, her face turned away from Satya and to the wall. As the pilgrims drift into sleep, she begins hacking and spitting with a force that rocks her into sitting position. Her eyes are glazed. Satya sits before her, heels tucked beneath her buttocks, and rubs her shoulders and her stomach.

Give me this, Mumta.

If Satya dies of tuberculosis, no one will blame Sardarji. Then no one can say he is cruel, or that he was not generous. And if she lies dying of TB, pale-lipped, emaciated as Mumta, Sardarji might look after her again. He will come to her bedside full of concern and pain for her pain. He will hold her the way she holds Mumta now and when she dies he will, even though it be for the benefit of those around him, cry like the son she never bore.

How long will it take Satya to die? She cannot know. Some women like Mumta take years, others go in the time between seeding and harvest. There are tales of rich men who take to the hills, to sanatoriums in Murree and Simla and Darjeeling, and if they live like kings they can keep TB at bay. So it gets its name – raj-rog, disease of kings – only the rajas survive it.

Mumta grows afraid for Satya, turns away. She throws off Satya's touch, pretending now to do so in sleep. She coughs a hacking cough. Women in the tiny sleeping room bury their ears in the squares of upraised arms and sigh, trying to sleep. No one is foolish enough to complain aloud; what ails one today could ail the other tomorrow. Some sit up, go back to praying. Some leave to sit in the gurdwara instead.

Suffering, prayer. There are so few choices.

But not for Satya. Not for her these choices. She has found a way out. A way she can choose freely where no one can stop her.

Except Mumta.

She must bide her time, in case Mumta is scared away.

The next morning they leave the gurdwara and join the jatha again for the walk to Punja Sahib. There are more gurdwaras to rest at along the way, small gurdwaras where she sits close, sometimes full in the way of Mumta's breath.

But Mumta draws her chunni over her mouth, masking her breath.

Satya waits.

She waits for the jatha of pilgrims to get to Punja Sahib Gurdwara, at Hasan Abdal. Punja Sahib is where Sardarji married Roop. It is where his betrayal took place, secret betrayal, a marriage with no music, no relatives, no dowry.

Mock marriage.

Satya feels a quickening within her, certainty enfolds her now and she carries her head high, shoulders back.

Punja Sahib is where she will find her opportunity.

It is appropriate, it is right. The true Guru of Gurus, the Sacha-Padsha, Vaheguru, cannot deny her this revenge.

Vaheguru was not watching before, Vaheguru had more important things to do when Sardarji married Roop here. Let it turn away for an instant this time as well. Let there be events that dwarf Satya's small desires, events bigger than one woman's desire to die. Surely there will be something to distract Vaheguru again.

And then, in the interstice of Vaheguru's attention, she will strike.

Hasan Abdal, August 1942

A hesitant rain beads on Satya's face and neck and bosom as she walks. A light cooling rain on parched skin, on her eyelids, her cracked and swollen lips. It plays its tabla on the tin roof of village shacks they pass, layers a thin slippery skin over the dust of the Grand Trunk Road. As the two women enter Punja Sahib Gurdwara, dusty, footsore, carrying hunger low in their stomachs, the news is moving on Vayu's monsoon winds from the plains – Mahatma Gandhi told the British, 'Leave India in God's hands,' and so today the British have

367

imprisoned him, Nehru and all the other Congress freedom fighters for making trouble during their war. In protest at their imprisonment, riots have broken out outside police stations and government offices. And Indians are being sent to jail without trial, by the thousands.

Vaheguru will have to look away from Satya.

Satya's chance has come.

Cool running water from the Guru's spring within the gurdwara soothes the burning soles of Satya's feet. Crouching, she touches her forehead to each marble stair of the gurdwara. She follows Mumta past the pilgrims on the platform outside the gurdwara to the central chamber.

There the musicians sing with their eyes closed. Everyone sings with their eyes closed.

After listening a while, she and Mumta walk slowly, respectfully, to join the line of the faithful descending the three steps to touch the boulder, where Guru Nanak's handprint still rests embedded in stone.

The boulder is not as large as she remembers it from other times, times when Sardarji and a happy young woman called Satya came here to pay their respects together. She presses her tan palm to its blackness, searches, as Mumta did before her, for the groove of the Guru's miracle.

Guru Nanak stopped this boulder with one gesture, can the Supreme Guru he spoke for not stop me now?

Their fingers meet, searching, touch lightly on the hot black surface. Mumta pulls away.

But there is no sign.

Returning to the marble platform, they walk around to where steps lead down to Guru Nanak's spring. Mumta takes off her chunni, descends the steps and wades in, kameez bloating, staining dark, her black hair-knot sagging first, then bobbing on the water. She swims away from Satya, cups her hand to drink the holy water.

Satya removes her chunni, follows her, entrusts her body to the amniotic pull of the sun-warmed water.

Does she know my need? Has she felt it? Can she know what I want from her?

She must act soon. Here. At the place where Sardarji and Roop performed the very ceremony that Sardarji had performed with Satya, before he left for England to learn his modern excuses. Here, where Sardarji threw her away in full sight of his God. That God who, the Guru says, holds that women are princesses, each one as valuable as a man. That same God who did not stop Sardarji's marriage; there were so many other women who needed helping.

That afternoon in the pilgrims' quarters, Satya moves quickly to take a place on the matting close to the wall, forcing Mumta to lie with her back to the next woman in the room.

'Turn away from me, Satya,' she says.

Satya looks around. Two little girls giggle and gossip in the corner the way she and Mumta used to as children. A woman runs a comb through her hair; her hair parts where it always parts. A bindi-marked grandmother helps a young girl tie her sari. Two old women lean close and remember together, holding one another's bent knees, telling stories of much worse things that happen to poorer women, all the time, all the time.

'Don't worry, Mumta.' She moves closer to her so their thighs are separated only by the thin muslin of their salwars. She takes Mumta's chin, turns her face to her own.

She drinks it from Mumta's lips. Pleading, first, then fiercely, tasting the harshness of Mumta's shock, but permitting no pulling back. Not in Mumta. Not in herself.

She parts Mumta's lips, takes her poison by a European kiss, and she is thinking of Sardarji as her lips touch Mumta's, remembering how he taught her this when he returned from England, taught her to kiss.

It is the only way.

Tuberculosis, I am yours. Claim me.

Sardarji, I begin death from this moment. In the world's eyes. The world does not know I died five years ago.

Satya releases Mumta, a snake dropping its victim. The two little girls continue their giggling and gossiping in the corner just the way she and Mumta used to as children. The woman who was combing her hair now brings a half-braided black rope before her shoulder and weaves it to a plait with quick strong fingers. The bindi-marked grandmother continues tying the young girl's sari. And the old women continue their remembering of much worse things that poor women's bodies remember, all the time, through all time.

Satya has taken poison. Mumta knows it.

Mumta jerks away, her eyes wide with horror, a hand cupped over her mouth.

'Satya!' She covers her head. Her shoulders shake, she coughs and spits blood.

A smile of triumph stretches Satya's lips. She trembles with daring. There is a long, long moment till a mixture of pity, sorrow and understanding dawns in Mumta's eyes.

Satya turns away.

No pity. I want no pity. Not yours, not anyone's.

Soon Satya hears Mumta whispering urgently, 'Ik Onkar, Sat Gur prasad, Jai ghar kirat akhiai, karte ka hoe bicharo . . .'

She is saying the Kirtan Sohila, the prayer for the dead.

For both of them.

Outside the tiny women pilgrims' room, thunder rumbles in the hungry sky and to the wheat fields around the walled compound of the majestic old gurdwara comes the serrated kiss of lightning. Then comes the downpour from monsoon clouds so angry, dark and sudden, they burst past the might of the sun.

SIX

1943-1944

31. Rawalpindi, April 1943

Roop hurries to catch up with Sardarji's long stride, his new boy-baby in her arms. Sardarji's walking stick swings down the centre of the sunny trellised veranda, preceded by the quick steps of uniformed orderlies and nurses. Gauze screen doors set in the peeling yellowed wall of the TB ward fly open, Sardarji is shown inside, then Roop, with many salaams and namastes. They stay to stare as long as they can in silence until he waves his hand, dismissing all but one.

Bumping around bullock carts and camels on the Grand Trunk Road from Lahore in the Austin, Sardarji raised his nose from *The Statesman* long enough to say, 'I wrote and told her two months ago: she should have gone to the hospital sooner – this wife of mine just doesn't listen at all. She was always so ziddi, so ziddi.'

Stubborn.

Even after her operation Satya wouldn't *ask* Sardarji to come and see her. No, it was Bebeji, Satya's mother, who told Manager Abdul Aziz to tell Sardarji that Satya had had an operation and wanted to see him one last time. And since she said Satya wanted to see the new boy-baby, Sardarji has brought Roop and the nameless little bundle with him.

Sardarji wanted her to have a private room, but there are none to spare in the TB hospital. But he offered, and no one can say he has not been generous.

Roop follows Sardarji through the screen door, eyes adjusting to the halved sunlight. She shifts the weight of her baby to her other arm. Still flaccid from his birth, her stomach is weak at the prospect of meeting Satya once more, but where Sardarji leads, Roop must follow.

She stops just inside, though, and covers the baby's face with her chunni.

Satya lies flat on a white metal hospital bed. Twenty-five other coloured bundles cough and pray in their beds around her. A tube snakes from the abandoned glass cone beside her pillow to an oxygen tank under the bed. Satya's eyes are a dull ash-grey above the triangular gag that squeezes past her high cheekbones and ties behind her head. Henna-faded hair spreads across the pillow like dry grass. Shrunken bones roll within her kameez; flagpoles dressed in half-mast flags.

An old woman – Satya's Bebeji – sits by Satya's bed, wailing softly but accusingly all the same. Disinfectant and death smells fill the room. Satya's maidservant, Jorimon, frightened and forlorn, on her haunches at the foot of the bed, sits ready for Satya's slightest command.

Sardarji marches past Jorimon right to Satya's side, sits down on the side of her bed, scoops her into his arms, rocks her as if she were a baby.

He cries, 'Oh, Satya, Satya!'

Over his shoulder, Roop sees Satya's eyes close above the cloth mask. A dozen thin twenty-four-carat gold bangles slide back on an emaciated arm. Her hands clasp his neck at the base of his lemon turban.

Roop turns away from them, buries her nose in the baby's talcum scent. Sardarji clasps Satya to him, 'I'm here, don't worry. Nothing to worry, you'll see.'

This is a Satya Roop cannot help but pity, skin yellowed as old ivory, breath jagged, hoarse, her voice thick with unshed tears.

But still she is beautiful, even now.

A starched white cap leans close, the nurse touches Sardarji's arm. 'Her lungs are completely wasted, still she has been holding on. I've never seen a woman's body go so fast. She was not fighting at all until she knew you were coming.'

'I will move her immediately to the sanatorium in Murree,' Sardarji says, still clasping Satya to his breast. 'I will send her to a sanatorium in England. People get well now, modern medicines, decent doctors can do wonders.'

The nurse's gentle singsong says, 'Sir, only one lung is left, sir, she cannot be moved now, sir.'

'Go, call the doctor. Tell him I will move her to Murree.'

The nurse draws back with a sigh. Leaves.

Look at her, so shameless, she holds Sardarji in her arms before the curious eyes of strangers.

Even Jorimon draws her sari palloo forward, embarrassed at Satya's public display.

Sardarji holds Satya to his breast, crooning gently, as if holding a wounded bird and time folds back for Roop till she is sixteen, and locked away in Sardar Kushal Singh's storeroom again, looking through a tiny keyhole at the two of them. Oh, that she might fade away into nothingness before this sight.

The baby's smile lightens his weight in her arms. Why worry? Satya can no longer take her babies away.

Satya's difficulty has always been that she wanted love and marriage to go hand in hand. What a thing to want! It is the cause of all her troubles, even this.

Now Satya sees Roop standing at the door, and beckons. In a slow metallic rasp, pathetic shadow of her usual haughty tone, she says, 'Ethey aa.'

Come here.

Roop's eyes widen and dart to Satya, then to her baby. She backs away.

Again Satya's voice comes as if speaking through a veil of pain. 'Ethey aa.'

'Show me the baby,' she commands through the mask.

Roop moves to stand beside the bed. The women in the other beds turn their masked faces away from the newborn little boy, but Satya has raised herself on an elbow and holds out her arms for the bundle in Roop's arms. Grey eyes, hard as haematite above the triangle, impale Roop.

Satya should not ask this, should not ask to breathe upon my baby boy.

Sardarji says, 'Roop, see, she wants to hold the boy.'

Roop grips her baby a little tighter. She says, 'It's not good, Sardarji. Who knows what could happen?'

Sardarji raises his voice, 'Roop! Give her the baby!' He judges her unkind in showing the least hesitation before a dying woman's wish.

Every nerve in her body cries *No, not another, not this boy, too*, but Sardarji urges her with brows drawing closer and closer. Can she refuse? Before a dying woman, so needy and pale?

This is another test, like Sita's test. He tests me yet again. Before all, he asks me to prove I give no trouble.

So, before all, Roop places her third child in those cold proud arms and her tears begin anew.

Sardarji's brow clears. To Satya he says, 'See, your sister loves you so much, she cries to see you like this.'

The nub of her baby's dark downy head rests in the crook of Satya's emaciated arm, veiled by her white chunni.

Satya's eyes are closed, petals harbouring stones.

The hole at the base of Roop's tummy opens again.

Sardarji offers gallantly, 'This one will be a doctor – you'll see, he'll cure you.' The baby bares toothless gums. Sardarji laughs his big laugh. A few women turn to see who is it that can laugh like that?

Only a powerful man.

Satya looks down at the boy for a while, then her face contorts in a hideous smile.

'Too late, piara. Perhaps in the next life.'

Then slowly, as if reconsidering, she holds the small bundle out, offering the child back, back to Roop.

A cough snaps her shoulders forward. Before them all she whispers, 'Forgive me, Roop. I wish you had come to our house as my daughter instead of as my sister.' She is looking past Roop to her next life – Roop searches her face but can find no fear.

Satya lies back, exhausted. Sardarji is still holding her hand. Roop sits on the edge of the next masked woman's bed, wipes dribble from the baby's mouth.

Waits.

A small depression forms in the triangular mask; breath going in. The depression puffs outward. Again a small depression forms in the mask; breath going in. The depression lifts outward; breath going out.

Roop, Sardarji, Bebeji and Jorimon wait for another depression to form in the cotton mask, but now the mask is still. A death message spasms through the wasted body.

Satya's vaqt, her time, has come.

And now it is Sardarji who cries, holds Satya in his arms and cries loud and long as if his truth is gone from the world and only lies and pretences remain.

Roop moves to his side, but the baby weighs her down; she cannot comfort him. '*Shshshshsh*,' she whispers to him. '*Shshshsh*.'

Bebeji's hands are at Sardarji's shoulder now, pulling him away from Satya. She hisses with an anger held in these many years, and says right to his face, 'Look what you have done to her. Are you satisfied, now?'

Women lift masked heads to their elbows, twist necks and waists, pressing their morbid curiosity flat against the glass box that has risen about Satya's bed. Sardarji's turban hangs lower than Roop has ever seen it, silent.

The room fills with the masked women's silence. Accusing.

Sardarji dashes at his eyes, rises.

The steel gauze door slams behind him.

Bebeji shrieks after him, 'Even a tiger kills a kakar quickly, to eat the deer and survive, but you, you did it slowly, and your reasons were not reasons, but excuses!'

But Sardarji does not look back.

The nurse returns with the doctor.

Roop closes her eyes to pray a quick pauri of the Japji. When, strengthened, she opens her eyes, Satya's body lies covered in white on the hospital bed. Her head is the Himalayas, her feet are the Nilgiris. Her unused breasts are still.

Satya was Sardarji's tool, the instrument by which he tortured Roop, then stood back complaining how his women fought like cats, never giving him any peace. But so too was Roop the instrument by which he tortured Satya.

But is there any man who does not use another to distance himself from his torture?

The length of the TB ward spins about her, vision blurs as if her atma remembered deaths it died so many times. Roop tightens her hold on her nameless little boy, breathes in, a deep nasal ujjai-breath, a yogini filling two whole young lungs.

And in that breath, Satya joins the virulence of her unremitting anger to Roop's hope. For the one long moment that Roop feels the smoulder of Satya's anger the open wound of Satya's humiliation passes past flesh, past bone, past breath. For that moment, Satya's desires flame within Roop, and her times and Roop's grasp hands, dance forward, the balance between Word and Silence restored for just one instant.

No! Roop drags her thoughts back to her self. *Forget this!*

But because Roop felt that one, single moment, that single solitary empathetic moment, Satya will live on in Roop, the way every older woman who uses a younger one is reincarnated in a betrayed young woman's body. Sister and sister they will truly be, the way they could never be while Satya was alive. Roop will be Satya's vessel, bearing Satya's anger, pride and ambition forward from this minute. She will contain her, woman within woman, hold her within. Like the Gurus, they might be one spirit, different bodies. But for now . . .

Forget this! Roop tells herself.

Endure!

Outside on the dirt drive, Narain Singh holds the door of the Austin Princess open. Why is the sky still so painless a blue? Why do pippal and palm leaves still wave in the sunshine? The experience of the world will not be the same, ever again. Roop has changed, is more than her haumai, more than Roop. What Satya's body remembered has been felt for one long moment by Roop's and it will simmer, waiting some day to boil.

Sardarji waits in the car. He sits straight and solemn, both hands clasped above the handle of his walking stick. But the scent of sandalwood fixo and Brylcreem rises from his wet beard.

'Sir?' Narain Singh wants to know where he should drive.

'Nowhere,' says Sardarji, trying to hold his turban high.

When he is composed again, he heaves the door of the Austin open and goes back into the hospital to talk to the doctor. Roop waits in the motor car; the baby sleeps.

The nurse steps from the hospital's veranda and gives Roop a package tied in an old newspaper. She says, 'Sardarji says to give these to you. The Bari-Sardarni must be cremated right here in the oven on the grounds of the TB hospital tomorrow. Doctor-ji will send Sardarji her ashes and he can immerse them in the Ganga.'

Careful not to disturb the sleeping baby, Roop picks open the string around the newspaper, one-handed.

A dozen thin twenty-four-carat gold bangles and a gold Omega watch glint against the English script.

Roop slips them on, faces forward.

She cannot feel her body.

Soon, Sardarji returns with Jorimon and motions her into the front seat beside Narain Singh. Jorimon holds her sari palloo clenched between her teeth to hold it round her head, cries in jerky terrified sobs. '*Hai, Allah! Hai, Allah!*'

'Don't worry,' Sardarji says kindly to Jorimon, 'we will spend a few days at the haveli in 'Pindi; there should be prayer and giving to the poor. And then you can return with us to Lahore.'

That night the old haveli groans, bricks loosening further in their sockets as the banyan roots grow longer, stronger, squeeze tighter. Roop lies in the fevery heat on her fourposter canopy bed with the silk pukkha swaying above her, back and forth, back and forth, yearning for the clarity that hunger once brought.

She should remember Satya's contempt, how Satya took first baby Pavan, then little Timcu, how she put the evil eye on Pavan so she and Roop can see one another only in mirrors, how it is Satya's fault Pavan sees her mother as a man might see her, from the corner of her eye, how she made Roop fear poison, and then, how she asked to breathe on the little boy-baby Roop thought was not to be taken.

But Satya's emaciated body, invaded by agony long before the surgeon's knife, comes between memory and anger, that poor body covered with a white sheet so her head and feet were the Himalayas and the Nilgiri Hills.

If I had been born a few years earlier, I could have been Satya.

Satya's love for her Sardarji is working through Roop, teaching it new resolutions. As she falls into the black void, they crowd within her – *I'll learn more English. I'll be whatever Sardarji wants me to be.*

And with this, Satya's forgiveness settles within Roop like a parting blessing.

Across the courtyard, the fireplace in Satya's private sitting room is swept clean of ashes; only the scent of woodsmoke lingers.

Barefoot, Roop wanders into Satya's private sitting room with its short-legged furniture, its divan with Satya's dilruba leaning against the cushion rolls, strings stilled. And the cradle where first Pavan and then Timcu have lain. Before her, Jorimon is placing the boy-baby on his stomach in that same cradle.

She stops Jorimon, taking her baby back, 'Can you light a fire?' she asks. She still does not have the tone of command just right. Of course Jorimon can, as soon as she knows Roop's wishes.

'Hanji, Sardarniji.'

Jorimon returns soon, arms full of pine logs. Placing them in the fireplace, she fills the spaces between with newspaper.

Roop sits on Satya's divan with her baby in her own arms. Jorimon can't read, neither could Satya. But Roop can look over *The Statesman*, beside her, searching for simple paragraphs on which to practise her English. She picks out names she recognises – Master Tara Singh, Mahatma Gandhi, Pandit Jawaharlal Nehru, Quaid-e-Azam Jinnah. And the new name Sardarji's friends in Lahore are sure is coming, 'Pakistan.'

Beneath the tasselled skirt of the divan, her toes curl about a pair of sandals. She kicks them forward, into view. Kolhapuri sandals – Sardarji bought her an identical pair when he went to Bombay.

He was always just with his gifts.

She slips them on, but her feet do not fill them completely.

Roop shivers slightly, though the fire burns a burnished red-gold in the grate; pine scent fills the room. She returns the sandals to their place beneath the tasselled skirt of the divan; she shouldn't have tried them.

'Can you bring the cradle into my room?' she asks Jorimon. 'It's not good for the child to be in Bari-Sardarni's room.'

'Ah-ho, Sardarniji.'

The polished wood railing steadies her as she carries her tiny boy back to her room. Soon, with the cradle moved to Roop's apartments, Jorimon places the little boy in it, ties one end of a string to her big toe, the other to the cradle, sets it rocking.

Apricots will arrive from Sardarji's orchard in a few months. This year, Roop will supervise their sorting for the first time, as Satya once did.

'We will send fruit baskets to the higher-ups,' Sardarji will say.

And it will not be seemly for Roop to say, 'Oh, I can't!'

Shadow people tremble and whirl across the walls of Satya's empty sitting room, a new shadow in their midst.

32. Lahore, May 1943

Two toy trains cross a pinched loop track in the nursery, a green engine pulling a plain brown carriage past rows of English houses, motor cars and lorries, and a second, saffron, edged with blue, pulling beige wagons. Timcu turns the control knob, the trains race faster, faster.

In a moment, both lie on their backs, wheels turning.

Timcu looks surprised. Then the corners of his mouth turn down and he hiccups, threatening a storm of tears.

Roop drops her pencil immediately and though Miss Barlow's hand rises to stop her, rushes to comfort Timcu. She picks him up, holds him to her, precious little son who'll protect his mama always. She takes him over to the window to distract him.

Miss Barlow, poor unmarried thing, shakes her head, but busies herself at Pavan's side where Pavan will be sure to see her, clicking her tongue over the uneven strokes in the little girl's handwriting. She has noticed Pavan's different way of seeing. How could she not notice boys' things happening in a girl's body? And besides, English women are trained from birth to notice every Indian weakness and polish them almost to giving way.

'Take her to a doctor,' she says. 'My dear departed mother had such a malady, degeneration of the eyes. It's usually an affliction of old age. Mayo Hospital,' she recommends.

Roop remembers Mayo Hospital. Her ear sings a mosquito whine and her tummy tightens about her navel every time the Austin passes those brick-red walls, circles that roundabout. She was nine then, but it could have been yesterday. 'Perhaps,' she says, a new word that retains hope in its hearer.

Perhaps someday, but not now.

Outside, in the leaf-shadow of a papaya tree, Jorimon places Sardarji's younger son, Aman, in the perambulator. She straightens, begins pushing him around the lawn.

A lawn green as Lawrence Gardens – or like the Garden of Eden.

Miss Barlow says all women's pain began there, from Eve eating an apple herself instead of offering it to her husband, Adam, first, and asking his permission – such a selfish woman, Eve was. That garden was where the first seed was sowed in the first woman so that the first sons would be born.

If Satya were here, maybe *she* could have told Miss Barlow right to her face, 'Your Eve was also a colony, just like the rest of us.'

But Satya is not here and so Roop listens daily as Miss Barlow explains: women are descended from Eve and it has affected their karma ever since. Countering her words at whisky-soda time, Sardarji explains to Roop that men are descended from Hanuman, son of Vayu.

But, Satya would ask, what does Guru Nanak say? He says all men are born of women, that the lineage continues because of women. The Guru says all women are valuable as princesses and should be called Kaur to remind men of it. He says, 'Why should we talk ill of her, who gives birth to kings? . . . there is none without her.'

Then why should eating one apple without Adam's permission cause so much pain for so long?

Stories are not told for the telling, stories are told for the teaching. And so Roop knows, Miss Barlow is warning her, warning of the danger of aspiring to more knowledge than a husband needs in a wife.

So Roop has become careful to learn slowly. On after-dinner walks with Sardarji through Lawrence Gardens, night queen flowers scenting the dark, Roop makes her rehearsed mistakes so prettily, continually reassuring him.

But why does Satya still live in my mind? She comes in the fragrance of night queen flowers though it is I who should feel as if I spent a hundred Brahma-years in silence.

Now Satya is gone, why can I not speak? Jeevan said I should learn English, but he did not tell me what it means to know it. Now is the time to speak when Miss Barlow says to speak, but my own Punjabi words have turned to worthless coins, unspendable in her bazaar. They must be deposited at the door of her classroom and I must receive their equivalent, though not their equal.

She wants to empty herself of fear, the way she emptied herself of Pavan, then Timcu, then Aman. But fear lives in her constantly, fear for them. It listens at Miss Barlow's lessons. What is 'invincible ignorance' and why must Pavan know how that is spelled? What is 'little pagan baby' and why does Timcu need to know that he is one?

Roop turns away from the window.

Timcu twists in her arms, his braided head bringing the memory: his keshgundun ceremony last Sunday. Sardar Kushal Singh and Toshiji came all the way from 'Pindi for it, Sardarji's friends, British, Hindu, Sikh and Muslim, sat beneath a huge canopy on the lawn outside as the little boy was placed before the Guru Granth Sahib. And Sardarji held a frightened-quiet Timcu on his lap, the child's small braided topknot tucked under Sardarji's beard. Then four-year-old Pavan helped Roop wind a silk turban to a full-blown rose about the wide-eyed little boy's head for the first time, and Timcu was made ready to be a man. And Roop's hands have learned, as if repeating blood knowledge, how to tie a small turban in reverse. Every day she winds it about Timcu's head so that he is presentable in public.

Within the women's world of home tutoring, such as now, the boy needs no turban – time enough for him to know what courage is demanded of its wearers. Still, Roop thinks he carries himself a little straighter since the ceremony and no longer hides under the bed at Sardarji's shouted 'Ohai!' He is still a little scrawny, but even at three, like any Sikh boy of good blood, he is oblivious to physical pain.

'*Ho-oh, ooff-o!*' She wipes Timcu's tears with a corner of her chunni, holding his small body to her breast. She moves slower with him now; he is getting taller, heavier.

She walks taller though, since Timcu's keshgundun. For wasn't it Roop – not Satya – who braided Timcu's hair that day? Wasn't it Roop – not Satya – who sat beside Sardarji holding his son on his lap? The musicians sang the shabads with their eyes closed. Everyone sang with their eyes closed, but Roop knew a change had come with Satya's passing. That day, with Satya vanquished by her own kismat, the influence of Mangal vanquished by Sardarji's Mangal, her own wife-hood presented to the cream of Lahore society gathered beneath the red, green and yellow whorls of the canopy, her bad ear still, by Vaheguru's grace, undiscovered, the hole at the base of Roop's tummy began to mend.

Now no one can say let-her-be-alone.

And she looked at Sardarji, caressed his bearded face with her almond eyes, remembered the pressure of his full lips on her cheek, inhaled the scent of marigolds mixed with his sandalwood fixo and Brylcreem smell.

And while a silent shadow warned that this happiness was borrowed from her future, that a woman who feels so much happiness, all at once, is asking, begging, inviting her kismat to restore balance in the universe soon, very soon, Roop felt a great gratitude stir within her young heart.

This is what the English people's talkies call falling in love.

'Write your story,' Miss Barlow's voice breaks into her thoughts. 'Perhaps you can say you have come to Christ through me.'

Roop places a mollified Timcu back on the carpet, returns the trains to their tracks for him, then takes her seat at the desk again, dips her pen in the inkwell and writes. But her hand can only remember how to write about Sardarji, and it wants to tell the world only that Satya was beautiful as a rani. She writes: 'When a bird is released, the first song it sings is of the beauty of the cage it has lived in, and the birds that were in the cage with it.'

'I don't see the point you're trying to make, Roop,' says Miss Barlow. 'I really don't.'

Miss Barlow teaches English without knowing a single word of Punjabi – she says Punjabi sounds ugly, hard and rasping. Sardarji says Mr Jinnah called Punjabi a peasant language by contrast with Urdu. Roop wants to tell her Punjabi is the only language her mama knew, so it is beautiful. She wants to say it was the language of Guru Nanak and of land watered by five rivers and the Indus. But Miss Barlow is deaf to this with both ears. If Roop speaks in Punjabi, her face blanks as if Roop were a jackdaw calling.

Listen to me, you are a woman, like me. Learn my language, it will not harm you. Use the words I have and maybe we can say more than

> *This is a cat*
> *This is a bat*
> *This is a hat.*

I do not have a cat. I have never seen a bat. And I do not wear a hat; I wear a chunni.

Roop could be back in Bhai Takht Singh's school. 'A says ah, b says buh, c says cuh.' Every English letter has a name and a sound. If they spoke Punjabi she might explain to the governess, the letter and its sound are inseparable as blood and skin, one coursing within the other. The Guru knew this when he made Gurmukhi script; that without sound, one akhar – letter, she corrects herself – might be mistaken for another.

It is the difference in sound that makes each one special.

And then it is the umbrella lines that draw them close and give them meaning.

But Miss Barlow is the teacher-ni and Roop knows questions are not welcome.

33. Simla, May 1944

'Mr Gandhi has capitulated,' Sardarji says, thumb tucked in his waistcoat pocket, 'to Mr Jinnah's demand for Pakistan. Why discuss it at all, why elevate that unreasonable man by negotiating?'

Cunningham grunts approval. 'Yes, why indeed?'

Sardarji and Roop are guests in the green-slate-roofed summer cottage Rai Alam Khan rents from his British superior each summer. A cottage whose stone façade hides in the pine-scented bodice of a Simla hill, hedged with pale blue lantana and lavender hydrangea, built in the days when the British thought they were staying in perpetuity, thought the government would move to the cool of Simla every summer and back to Delhi after the monsoon, forever. One of Vayu's travelling winds might say it had sprung fully formed upon the hillside, transplanted from England.

Logs crackle in the fireplace. Sardarji leans against the grate, a four-inch peg of whisky-glow spreading within him. A bearer serves Roop, lace-sari-clad, displayed to optimum effect in the window seat, a crystal goblet of apple juice.

The British have released Mahatma Gandhi from prison. The war is going their way now and he can do no harm with his ideas of fighting the Japanese with folded hands or supplicating Hitler to be a man of morals. For all his unreasonableness, the British have proved they were indeed afraid Mahatma Gandhi might die in their custody and then a bloody revolution to dwarf any the Bolsheviks had visited upon Russia might come upon them.

'Oh, I believe you'll find the Quaid-e-Azam, Mr Jinnah, to be quite as reasonable a man as you find Mr Gandhi.' Rai Alam Khan's legs straddle a tapestry ottoman before his chair. 'I, for one, don't find Mr Gandhi reasonable at all – a man who says he is all religions, Hindu, Sikh, Muslim, Christian, is a man of no conviction. A shilly-shallying politician. And I don't think they are at the stage of negotiating, Sardarji. I think Mr Gandhi has finally understood that the Quaid-e-Azam exists and will not be subdued.'

'My dear sir, you *can't* be serious. Surely you don't . . . you can't possibly want this Pakistan of Jinnah's?'

'Why not?' says Rai Alam Khan. 'It will take us further than we are at present.'

'*Who is "us"?*' The expression on Sardarji's face frames the mute question.

'Muslims,' Rai Alam Khan says impatiently. Sardarji's thick black eyebrows rise toward the line of his turban. Would Rai Alam Khan speak so freely behind his Indian Civil Service accounting desk in Lahore? But they are off duty, here, vacationing in Simla, and the mountains hold a man closer to his God and encourage honesty.

Rai Alam Khan lifts one foot onto the tapestry ottoman, then the other. The soles of his European shoes are noticeably thin. He continues, 'Mr Gandhi makes one big mistake – he thinks we Muslims care only for our stomachs. The Quaid-e-Azam knows better.'

'My dear sir, if this Pakistan idea is allowed to happen, Muslims will begin to care only for their stomachs.'

'I think you may be surprised.'

'The British will never permit it.'

'Never,' says Cunningham, reassuringly.

Rai Alam Khan sounds faintly amused. 'They may not have a choice.' He becomes serious. 'Sardarji, look at the facts. Singapore and Burma fell to the Japanese, Hitler's giving them quite a run for their money in Europe, they have blood on their hands from the famine in Bengal all last year and if they're not careful, Subas Chandra Bose's Indian National Army is going to pour in from Burma and solve the independence issue with violence. When Gandhi said "leave India to God," he didn't specify how much of India was to be left to which God.'

'They should have accepted the Cripps mission's proposals two years ago. I never did understand Mr Gandhi's rejecting that. Indians were offered Dominion status and self-government as soon as Hitler is finished – and, with all due respect, I must mention there are enough Sikhs fighting him for me to believe he will be finished quite soon. If Indians had accepted Cripps's offer, they could write their own constitution as soon as the war is over. You and I – all minorities, even Christians – would have received the protection of the Crown, and Mr Jinnah would not have needed his Pakistan. But they rejected that!'

'The Sikhs rejected it too,' Rai Alam points out.

'Well, yes. Of course we did – because it assumed we would want whatever you Muslims want.' He waves a hand. 'The British could have been disabused of that notion. Naturally the Sikhs resisted any provision for separation of Punjab from an All-India Union. Still, perhaps we should all have accepted Dominion status. Actually, Mr Gandhi's rejection was what really did it.'

'We would have been the only non-whites in all the Dominions. Do you really think that would have been freedom? It would have been a travesty. Sardarji, understand, Britain now owes India more than a thousand million pounds. Sterling, sir, not rupees! They are trying to hold India hostage with their concern for minority rights. Concern! I tell you, sir,' Rai Alam Khan lowers his feet from the tapestry ottoman, 'we don't need their concern.' He gives a quizzical smile. 'Do we?'

Sardarji says, 'You and I may not, Alamji, but as for the

Sikhs, yes, the Sikhs *do* need their concern. If Gandhi gets his Hindustan and you Muslims get Jinnah's "Pakistan," will Master Tara Singh and his Akali Party get us a "Sikhistan?"'

Cunningham laughs – 'Sikhistan! What a preposterous idea!'

'Master Tara Singh swears he's going to ask for it, mind you. But asking doesn't mean receiving everything you ask for.'

'Really? I hadn't heard – and if Master Tara Singh asks for a Sikhistan, where will that be?'

'Punjab Province, naturally,' Sardarji says with certainty, Punjab being where the faith arose, Punjab where Sikhs once ruled, where almost all Sikhs live.

'But that will create yet another problem – how will you Sikhs guarantee the rights and safety of Muslims and Hindus who suddenly find themselves in your Sikhistan?'

'But of *course* we will, Alamji!'

'History does not inspire me with such confidence – you speak for yourself, for your intentions, which I have always found to be excellent. But, Sardarji, you are not exactly a typical Sikh. It is the Sikhs close to the land, men who run the gurdwaras and call on every Sikh to carry a longer and longer kirpan – it is they who speak loudest amongst your Sikh brethren.'

'Alamji, I hardly consider you typical of Muslims, yet you seem to have no hesitation in espousing a Muslim "nation." There are more Muslims who speak Bengali than those like you who speak Urdu; do you plan to move your people east, to Bengal? Will *you* move there?'

'No, no – I'm Punjabi head to toe.' Rai Alam laughs, shoots his cuffs under his navy blue blazer. 'I stay in Punjab. Can you imagine me learning Bengali? No, if the Quaid-e-Azam gets his new country, it will be right here.'

Sardarji leans forward. 'And how will you guarantee the rights and safety of Sikhs who suddenly find themselves living in your Pakistan?'

'But of *course* we will, Sardarji!'

A painful silence.

Rai Alam Khan sighs. 'You are right, I am not typical, even if we could say there is a typical Muslim, Sardarji. Even in

Punjab, some are Sunnis, some are Shias, Ismailis, Ahmadiyas, even Sufis, with whom your Guru Nanak found so much in common. But I do know that the alternative to Pakistan, life under Hindu rule, can bring no progress for any of us.'

'Progress comes slowly, Alamji, as more Indians climb to power . . .'

Rai Alam Khan interrupts, 'Those Indians will do very well. But I'm not talking about qualified men. I'm speaking of those I stand shoulder to shoulder with in the mosque. Islam has no high and low, you know. For true democracy, you have to go back to the Koran, you cannot go back to the Vedas and the *Ramayan*.'

'Sikhism, too, has no castes – equality is what we have in common with Islam.'

'Yes, that is what your Gurus *said*.'

Sardarji feels his posterior becoming a little too warm; he moves a little away from the fire, letting Rai Alam Khan's ironic tone pass.

'With all due respect, Sardarji, Sikhs are being given far more importance by the British in all these negotiations than the size of your population warrants, because the British need the Sikhs – and Muslims too, let us admit – in their war. Master Tara Singh can demand what he likes, I predict he cannot be victorious.'

'Let Tara Singh argue away!' Cunningham volunteers. 'Keeps the natives busy.'

'Anyway,' says Sardarji, as much to deflect Cunningham as Rai Alam Khan, 'will all of this replace any farmers' bullock carts with tractors? Not if Gandhi has his way . . . Nehru is more modern, but if Independence comes we'll all have to return to spinning.'

A chuckle escapes him at the thought of people like himself and Rai Alam Khan spinning.

'But you surely can't mean you want the bloody British to remain?' asks Rai Alam Khan.

Sardarji shakes his turban, thinking of Farquharson, who, if he returns, will want his position back and think *he* saved India from the Japanese. And of Cunningham, who is becoming quite a nuisance in the changing tide of things.

'No, not really.'

'Not much you *can* do, old boy,' says Cunningham.

'Tosh, Cunningham!' Sardarji says. 'A little statesmanship, that's all that's required. Negotiation – when the politicians really wish to work things out, they will.'

'Steady on, Sardarji. I'm above it all. Can't do a thing about it. So don't argue with *me* the way you always argued with Satya,' says Cunningham. 'It's simply not done.'

Satya.

A shadow passes through Sardarji's mind.

The isn't-ness of Satya has been rankling in him.

Satya lives in the thought realm, now.

Inaccessible.

And precisely because Satya is inaccessible, Sardarji mourns her, reaches for her in his sleep, sometimes.

If he were Shah Jahan, he would build her a marble Taj Mahal to show the world how much he loved her – a better constructed Taj Mahal, without an unsightly coffin as Muslims have everywhere. A samadhi, then, like the lotus-shaped ones in Lahore, commemorating the suttee deaths of four of Maharaj Ranjit Singh's wives.

If Satya had only given him a chance, he might have sent her here, to Simla, and she would have recovered. Here, away from all the responsibilities in Rawalpindi, she might have taken strength from these hills and realized he needed her good sense in these times. She was a well-constructed woman before her illness, every inch of her tuned to his needs. A functional woman, very functional. Whereas Roop – there she sits, at the corner of his eye, in the window seat – sometimes she is so silly, so ornamental, it irks him like an itch that he cannot quite reach.

But enough.

He has been warned. If Rai Alam Khan, a gentleman land-lord like himself, well travelled and well schooled, wants Pakistan, it is not merely the malcontents and the poor that Jinnah and the Muslim pirs, maulvis and mullahs have stirred into protest. It's irrational: Rai Alam Khan is a man who knows an asset from a liability – how does he think Mr Jinnah's Pakistan can survive? Give it a year or two, maximum.

Maximum! The Muslim-majority provinces straddle the Hindu and Sikh regions and most of the princely states in between, they lie west of the Indus and east of the central plateau – what does Mr Jinnah propose to do? Build a seven-hundred-mile fortified corridor between them?

He shudders involuntarily, spine tingling as warning messages surface within him from ages past.

Does Rai Alam Khan think the Sikhs can survive under the Muslims again – the same who slaughtered and martyred their Gurus? Sardarji's body remembers life-preserving fear, passed down centuries in lori rhymes his mother sang him, in paintings displayed in the Golden Temple Museum in Amritsar, in poem and in story – though his mind is open, he assures Cunningham, open to his old friends like Rai Alam Khan. But if fear of Muslims is what Sardarji's body remembers, though his ancestors were once Muslim, how much more piercingly will illiterate Sikh farmers feel its chill?

This visit to Simla, to Rai Alam Khan – far from providing respite from the fierce heat of Lahore, and his planning meetings for Bhakra Dam and its canals, has alarmed him more than *The Statesman*'s headlines of plots, conspiracies and battles have ever managed to do. Sometimes there is no need for violence, the threat of it will do just as well. He and his household – indeed the entire Sikh quom, only five million strong – will be guests at the mercy of their Muslim hosts if Pakistan is created in Punjab Province.

Guests.

In England he explained to Kitty that hospitality to a mehmaan, a guest, is the hallmark of nobility, that every man in India aspires to be known for it. That no friend in India need give warning of an intended arrival, but may just arrive. And may stay for as long as necessary and can expect the very best. But now he wonders how long and far hospitality can be stretched.

He has always been more comfortable giving than receiving it.

His starched collar feels suddenly tight. He swallows hard.

What's the worst one can do to a mehmaan?

A vague presence responds:

Make him want to leave, make him need to leave.

If Gandhi and Nehru barter the Muslim-majority provinces away as Pakistan, Sikhs and Hindus in places like 'Pindi, Lahore, Firozepur and the Punjab canal country will be permitted to leave only with Jinnah's permission, they will be allowed to enter only by Muslim invitation. And living in Jinnah's Pakistan, will, he is sure, require Sikhs and Hindus and even Christians to be always on their best behaviour, acutely aware of the religion and customs of their hosts.

Yes, like guests who can at any moment be made to leave.

What Rai Alam Khan's body remembers is a hundred years old, it comes from tales of domination by Sikhs. What his own body remembers comes from gory paintings of Gurus boiled and dismembered by order of Mughal emperors, the antique violence of Rai Alam Khan's forebears. These events, which are indelible, shape their karmic memory.

Speaking his fears before Rai Alam is weak whimpering, and Sikh men don't whine. They take action, *do* something, even if it turns out to be wrong, instead of sitting around like women wringing their hands.

But what action to take?

He is not accustomed to feeling helpless as a woman. Decisions and planning have always been his hallmark.

'I shall return to Lahore tomorrow,' he says to Rai Alam. 'The mountain air does not agree with me.'

Cunningham agrees. 'No point arguing further with a man whose mind is made up.'

Roop sits in the window seat, smiling brightly, sipping a goblet of apple juice, head turned just a little, trying to understand Sardarji and Rai Alam Khan's English conversation.

Beyond the window a sickle moon disperses stars as it struggles for rebirth into an indifferent sky. The stone path that brought her, the children, Mani Mai and Jorimon up this hill, in three rickshaws pulled by four wheezing men apiece, winds past this English house down the valley into night shadow.

A pye-dog barks, another answers; their debate echoes interminably across sleeping villages.

Roop smooths her new sea-green Belgian lace sari, she wiggles her toes in slightly heeled pink leather sandals and admires the silver lamé evening bag looped over her arm. She hopes Sardarji can smell the Evening in Paris cologne he bought her. Mama's sapphire ring flashes on a finger. Satya's gold Omega obscures the tattoo scrawled in Persian script on her wrist.

English words separate from marinades of sound for Roop; many carry meaning, now. Still Roop cannot yet converse at length. However, Miss Barlow says her 'comportment is vastly improved.' She has learned to tweeze her eyebrows, pour tea without spilling, skewer flowers into small beds of nails for flower arrangements, and play canasta with other second wives whose husbands are members of the Cosmopolitan Club. Satya's passing has brought no change in Roop's social standing in Lahore – there are plenty of families here who know Roop came second. Even so, no one would recognize Deputy Bachan Singh's youngest daughter, no one would think she once had too much Mangal in her stars and still has one bad ear.

A bearer stands by the French doors. 'Khana, sahib.'

'Dinner, Sardarji!' says Rai Alam Khan. Sardarji places his Scotch on a three-legged side table. To the bearer: 'Kya banaya?'

'Alamji, sir, the cook has made sell-ry soup, chik-ken Pitrograd, mush-rum om-late,' says the bearer, relishing each syllable before allowing it to roll off his tongue. Sardarji nods appreciatively. 'And he also has made quail Mughlai, Simla-mirch peppers stuffed with rice pilau. And chilled mango fool.'

'Vah! Wonderful!' says Rai Alam, raising the glass of apricot juice he is imbibing tonight instead of whisky-soda. His compliment is for the bearer, but his eyes are on Roop's face so her hand rises instinctively, to confirm her chunni covers her head.

To Sardarji he says, 'I have begun observing Ramazan again. Fasting, you know. I haven't done this for the full thirty days in years. I highly recommend it – cleanses the body. I'll join you at dinner, but I cannot partake.'

Anticipation fades in Sardarji's face. 'Oh, Alamji, I couldn't possibly eat if you are not eating.'

'That is friendship indeed,' says Rai Alam Khan, 'but you must not disappoint the cook, so you must eat – I insist. Whether you wish to or not.'

'Take the Choti-Sardarni to Begum Sahiba's rooms,' he tells the bearer, then turns to Roop with a silk-smooth smile, 'Begum Alam Khan is waiting for you – you must meet her.' He is speaking of his third wife, whom he still maintains in purdah, so the reputation of her beauty and his good taste will grow with the years. Sardarji and Rai Alam Khan took wives around the same time, Rai Alam Khan's first begum moving to Karachi to live with Rai Alam's eldest son. Even so, this is Rai Alam Khan's very first invitation to meet his most junior begum; a compliment afforded to very few.

Sardarji's hearty laugh fades in Roop's ear as the bearer opens the French doors before her and leads her through teak-floored rooms.

Gracious kidney-shaped love seats, damask fainting chairs and leather-bound books fill these rooms. Crystal leashes gather to shed light prisms upon the yellowed teeth of a grand piano. A telescope points from a corner of a greenhouse, in-viting her to read what afflicts the converging stars. Deodar-wood staircases recline against panelled walls, shouted English commands loiter in the recesses of vaulted ceilings. So many cummerbunded, topeed bearers have stooped here before their masters, whether English or English-speaking.

Silver photo frames on teak-wood Queen Anne tables dis-play pictures of English people.

Satya would say, *Everywhere they tramp across our land, they see and remember only themselves.*

Roop walks the length of a dining room adorned with still-life paintings of flowers and fruits in muted hues. The bearer bows and withdraws before the white-painted door of the Begum's private apartments, and Roop knocks as Miss Barlow has taught her. The door opens a crack.

Above a black veil sparkle unforgettable doe eyes.

Huma!

'*Hai-ni!* Roop-bi! Knocking, so here I thought it was some

stranger!' A black-lace-gloved hand closes about her wrist, pulls her into the inner sanctum. The voluminous folds of a maroon burqa envelop her in an odorous embrace. In a moment, the burqa is removed and a pepper-green lehnga edged with silver transforms Huma back into the girl who once played kikli in the tunnel at Pari Darvaza. She takes Roop's arm and leads her to sit cross-legged on a pastel blue-green Aubusson carpet, primroses of the chintz-upholstered love seats at their backs.

There she exclaims – 'Only three children?' Huma has four, all in boarding school now. About Roop's jewellery – 'Not nearly enough, you should ask him for more.' About her Belgian lace sari. Huma stretches out sock-clad feet in gold-embroidered jutis and sighs over the elegance of Roop's bare toes peeking from pink leather sandals.

She opens Roop's silver lamé evening bag and shakes its contents out on the carpet, unselfconsciously curious.

Satya would say she is simple, the way I once was, before Miss Barlow's lessons.

'How is Madani?' Huma's finger snaps Roop's oval compact mirror upright. She rings her lips with Roop's lipstick.

Roop lowers brown almond eyes. 'Theek-thaak – ' She corrects herself, 'All very well.'

'I know she has four children now, all boys, Allah is generous.'

'Yes, yes. Ah-ho, ah-ho,' says Roop, lapsing into Punjabi. She supposes Madani is all right; Roop writes infrequently to her. There is not much she can say about her life in Lahore that will not seem strange or boastful. Madani writes, occasionally, about her boys, how they attend the local gurdwara school, win prizes for recitation of the gurbani and love to play kabaddi and cricket. How they went on a pilgrimage to the Golden Temple in Amritsar and to the gurdwara at Nankana Sahib, birthplace of Guru Nanak.

But Roop writes to Madani now as if she travels through an indescribable country where the only words she and Madani still have in common are 'How do you do?' and 'Delighted to meet you.'

'And you?' she asks Huma, to change the subject. She

meets Huma's eyes in the eye of the compact.

A lace handkerchief abruptly smears Roop's lipstick firmly from the small red garland in the mirror. 'He says only the prostitutes in Hira Mandi and English women wear lipstick.'

A wave of shame washes over Roop immediately. Then she reminds herself that it is Sardarji who bought her the lipstick, and that she only does what he desires.

'But, as you see,' Huma gestures around the room, 'he is a generous man. I want for nothing.'

Roop says, a little on edge, 'How is it you're still in burqa? I thought Rai Alam Khan was quite modern – so many women are going unveiled now, in Lahore.'

Huma gives an exaggerated shudder. '*Haw!* I wouldn't want to go unveiled like you – you Sikh women are so *fast*. I see you sardarnis from my car in Lahore, you cycle everywhere on The Mall, even in Lawrence Gardens, so shamelessly, and your men don't even care. But I can go everywhere in my burqa without shame. Protest marches, meetings – it protects me. When I wear it no one knows I am a civil servant's wife.'

Roop remembers Mama, and how she never went beyond the walls of Papaji's home except in a palanquin, and how Roop might have been completely like her, full of that fear of her own body that rises from shame.

If she hadn't married Sardarji.

Roop shivers.

And in a strident voice that does not seem to be quite hers, she says, 'Why do so many women live their whole lives *afraid*, afraid to be free? Huh! I am a Sikh. I am not afraid.'

And just by hearing herself say this, she does feel more Sikh, less afraid.

'Don't worry, no one is forgetting you are Sikhs,' says Huma.

Even with the Aubusson, the floor is hard beneath Roop – it's been many years since she sat cross-legged on the floor except before the Guru Granth Sahib. She smooths her lace sari over her knees, changes the subject, 'What do you hear from Pari Darvaza?'

'My brother wrote to tell me he left North Africa with your brother Jeevan – I think they are somewhere in Assam now.'

Roop's hand reaches for Huma's, in a rush of joy to hear news of Jeevan. 'My abu is not happy with Ibrahim,' Huma says. 'He wants Ibrahim to leave the miltry and campaign for the Muslim League, now Pakistan is coming.'

Vayu sends a chill gust of wind through the pleasant room.

'Huma,' says Roop. '*Where* do you think Pakistan will be?'

'My abu says,' Huma is reciting now, 'wherever there is one Muslim village, there is Pakistan.'

'And Pari Darvaza? It is not a Muslim village.'

'It is a Muslim village except for tum-log.'

Tum-log. You people. A shudder passes through Roop; with one word, Huma has excluded her, Papaji, Jeevan, Revati Bhua, Gujri, Shyam Chacha and his family and all the other Hindus and Sikhs in Pari Darvaza neatly, so neatly.

'And where are hum-log – we people – to go?'

'You can go to Hindustan,' says Huma, as if it is all resolved. 'But you can't stay in Pakistan. We don't like Hindus here.' She looks at Roop's shocked expression and gives a high-pitched giggle.

Where in Hindustan does Huma think we will go? How far will it be?

Aloud, Roop says, 'Sikhs are not Hindus.'

Huma says, 'Do you join us to celebrate Id or do you join Hindus to celebrate Diwali?'

It's true. We join Hindus only, for their festivals – though the Guru says we are neither Hindu nor Muslim.

'But Huma,' says Roop, 'neither your abu nor Pandit Dinanath ever joined *us* in celebrating Gurpurb.'

And, Roop would like to tell her, there is more to being a Sikh than celebrating Gurpurbs. But she can see the memory in Huma's eyes – no need to remind one another – the memory of Gujri. *You shameless girl! Don't you ever come into my rasoi again.* Gujri, a hand raised high to slap, and Huma dodging away before her. *Chi! Dirty girl. Don't you let your shadow come near it! Huh!*

Huma says – hurt and anger from 'then' polishing itself, like sandpaper polishing shisham wood, to the sophisticated mask of 'now,' – 'Sikhs only marry Sikhs or Hindus. My abu says Sikhs are just Hindus who can't be disguised.'

'But it is also Muslims who do not marry Hindus or Sikhs unless we convert, Muslims who call us kafirs.'

'You *are* kafirs!'

A tense silence fills the room, pulls them in directions they cannot resist.

Roop's eyes fall to her tattoo, her name in Persian script. She rubs it, absently.

'It is late,' she says eventually. 'I must see if Sardarji or the children need me.'

She covers her head with her lace sari palloo and lets herself out by the white-painted door. She crosses the length of the dining room. The flowers and fruits are dejected, trapped within their frames.

She is reaching for the handles of the French doors when her lace sari snags on the floor, pulling her to a stop. She pulls at it to extricate herself and abruptly, the floorboard cracks, comes away in her hand.

White ants.

Slowly, patiently, doggedly, eating away the foundation of this house.

34

I am where there is no night, no day, no within, no without, no above, no below, no Indian, no English, no Sikh, no Hindu, no Muslim.

I occupy nothing.

No thing or body occupies me.

Cured and free of body, I am no longer woman.

I am not man.

But I am.

I am here, blinded by the beauty above me, on levels, planes, realms I cannot reach; here I wait, with all the other djinns, stunted, floundering in the cosmos, incapable of transcending our haumai, our self-ness.

Here I wait to roll the dice again, wait for a time when just being can bring izzat in return, when a woman shall be allowed to choose her owner, when a woman will not be owned, when love will be enough payment for marriage, children or no children, just because my shakti takes shape and walks the world again.

Just beyond me, tantalizingly beyond my grasp, are realms Guru

Nanak described: Dharam Khand, where I might feel satisfaction from having performed my duty — I find none; then Gian Khand, the level of knowledge, where I might learn why my arid womb never filled with children; Saram Khand, the level of beauty, where I might finally understand how an intellectual man like Sardarji could value Roop's vacuous beauty over my fine skills and mind; Karam Khand, where Vaheguru's grace might come to bridge the distance between my deeds and words. Then—

Distant, remote, I feel the pull of Sach Khand, apex plane of Sat, the truth I was named for, name I betrayed, lying to myself — confusing worship of a mere mortal, my husband, with devotion to the supreme — Vaheguru, forgive me.

But still I love.

These realms that could expand my being to vastness, to wholeness, are distant, ever receding. And I know why these realms are out of my reach: echoes of the world I departed in anger and pain impinge upon my djinn.

I am so far from where I might have been — I cannot ascend even to the first realm of realization.

Because I still love. Because I still watch the world unfold before my Sardarji, before Roop and his children.

How can I leave him? I see what is coming.

And Roop — I have amends to make to Roop, for my anger and actions, for the way I used her, made her join me in my pain.

I writhe at the junction of past and future, and because I am distant, I see more acutely than they. I see what is coming.

I have hollowed out my place in their minds.

Perhaps I can reach them. Say what I know: if you do not learn what you were meant to learn from your past lives, you are condemned to repeat them.

And tell Sardarji, the Gurus say sometimes a man can sow deeds and reap their consequences in the very same life.

I will speak from here, from this silence. Waiting, with other djinns and shadows also incapable of transcending their haumai, their self-ness. From the silence will I watch, wrest the meaning of my life from Sardarji's, from Roop's. Then perhaps my djinn can progress to atma and take human shape again.

Two years, I watch Sardarji as he moves Roop and his household south of Lahore to the princely state of Patiala.

The maharaja invited him there to modernize the canal system, and he does it well; he was always an excellent civil engineer.

35

Vayu the wind-god, God of all the northwest of India, bearer
of perfume, shuttles back and forth across the world, weaving
shifting winds, whimsical winds, devious winds into the fabric
of time, connecting cities and continents better than telegraph
lines.

In India, he ripples the pages of newspapers – *The
Statesman*, *Dawn*, *The Tribune* – then scatters them in rubbish
heaps where the ragpicking children make better use of them
as bags for roasted peanuts. Such children cannot read and so
they do not know that the newspapers say that Subas Chandra
Bose, the leader of the Indian National Army that tried to
invade India, is lost in a plane crash, that Mahatma Gandhi's
only reaction was not to raise the flag at his evening prayers.
The children cannot read and so they do not know that non-
violent Mahatma Gandhi helped recruit two and a half
million Indians to serve England in the war. The children
cannot read and so they do not know that they are still hungry
because their rice went to feed Allied soldiers fighting on the
front line against Japan. The children cannot read and so they

do not know that Vayu rode the wings of bombers to Japan, or that he saw death mushroom upon the ground. Vayu then comforted all of India with the thought that Indians, non-violent Indians, followers of Mahatma Gandhi, followers of Nehru and Jinnah, could never be so cruel.

Oh, foolish Vayu!

Vayu lifts the purple robe of the sky upon his shoulder and sees the brew moiling and roiling beneath and he grows fearful, releases changing winds, hoping to cool passion.

A Muslim, a Hindu and a Sikh, all soldiers in Subas Chandra Bose's Indian National Army, stand trial for treason in December, for having attempted to wrest India by force from the British with the help of the Japanese.

'Patriots,' say the newspapers, as boldly as they can.

'Ingrates and renegades,' say the British generals.

But though Vayu rushes across continents, blows hard and strong as he can, the wind-god only fans passion to flame, ignites the long fuse of memory till it sparks through the blood of men who fight for land.

Comes 1946, the year after the European war, and despite all their promises the British still rule India. Even Americans who came to fight in Burma have not departed; nor has their ammunition.

Vayu, that great pukkhawalla in the sky, leans into pulling rhythm. The breeze from his efforts fans his Hindu followers and the followers of the Prophet back and forth, back and forth, doing nothing to cool them.

India seethes with anger.

Hindus say the mounting violence is the fault of Muslims for supporting the British in their war. Muslims say it is the fault of Hindus for they cannot see that there is not one nation fighting for its freedom in India, but two – two nations married to one conqueror.

And each quom says they care not for themselves, but fight for their children.

Vayu swings this way and that bearing delegations, flying British Overseas Airways from Britain, sending a cabinet mission with new proposals. Perhaps a federation, with power-sharing for Muslim-majority provinces; perhaps the

Muslim-majority provinces of Punjab and Bengal could be given special rights. And when Vayu bears the cabinet mission homeward, the newspapers that the ragpicking children fold to bags say this: Everyone came to a conference table in Simla again, and everyone left it empty-handed.

India seethes.

Within Sardarji, living in Patiala with Roop, planning canals for the maharaja there, Mr Cunningham complains, 'The natives are restless, capable of anything!'

It is the year that changes nothing, then changes everything.

Comes August. Hot August when the sand-laden loo wind blows. Hot dry August, when Vayu rises as usual, bringing brains to boil as he sears the heart of India.

Comes the heat of August and Mr Jinnah turns away from words, calling for his Muslim followers to wreak violence upon Hindus, to break the stalemate on 'Direct Action Day.' Afterwards, when Vayu blows over Bengal Province in the East, he sees four thousand people dead or dying around Calcutta, sees ten thousand injured.

As Vayu weeps, the monsoon rains down.

In October, when Vayu believes the rains he brought have cooled the land and people, he counts fifty thousand people in relief camps in Bengal Province, then another thirty thousand dead, then a hundred and fifty thousand made refugees in their own land.

In November, another massacre, closer to Delhi, as if Dharmraj, green-skinned god of the netherworld, had slipped his noose about the country's neck, and drawn it tighter.

Vayu weeps again, extending the monsoon.

All men who can read newspapers now know that Mr Jinnah has broken the stalemate. Pakistan will come.

But in Punjab Province, miraculously, despite demonstrations, arrests and sporadic flares of naked rage, a frayed and fragile strand of peace still holds.

EIGHT

1947

36. Lahore, March 1947

A grim Sikh constable raises his arm to stop traffic on the
Mall Road; Sardarji's new black American Packard dodges a
procession of schoolchildren shouting, 'Leke rehenge
Pakistan!'

We will have Pakistan.

Sardarji's face shows no sign he has been inconvenienced by
the propaganda slogans at all as he alights before the
columned porticos of Faletti's. His grey flannel suit jacket is
too heavy for Lahore's March heat and his turquoise tie is
softening the starch of his white collar, but Sardarji wouldn't
dream of removing either.

Faletti's is a good hotel for Sikhs to dine at – they don't
serve halal meat from animals killed slowly as the Koran is
pronounced over them, and they believe in serving enough for
a hearty Sikh appetite. Afterwards, he will order pinni sweets;
he remembers their dry, salt-sweet taste the way Satya made
them – crumbly, bearing the imprint of being held in her fist.
Since her passing he's felt deprived of them, hungers for them

often, wishes they were ready at his fingertips even if they sat uneaten.

Sardarji raises his walking stick to the Muslim doorman employed in this Sikh-owned hotel.

A year ago I would never have noticed the doorman's religion.

Burhan-e-din, the six-foot-four blue-cummerbunded gold-braided doorman at Faletti's is a Pathan tribesman from the Northwest Frontier Province, who has learned to control his distaste for non-Pathans of all descriptions by learning to say 'Ji, huzoor' as he opens doors at Faletti's. Like the Prophet, he makes it a practice never to fill his stomach completely, so there is always a faraway look in his eyes as if he hears a rumbling and knows not from where it comes. It makes him look shifty-eyed, as if he were walking the narrow hill paths of Hunza expecting boulders to fall and bar his way. And while he knows his enemies are the grandsons of his grandfather's enemies, he is never sure they are not masquerading as Sikhs or Hindus or even Britishers. He became a master of the classificatory art before anyone gave the activity that name, being able to smell a man's faith at thirty paces. The only word in his vocabulary for men who are neither his friend nor his enemy is mehmaan – guest – and so the work at Faletti's suits him well. A rumour, tenacious as a thorn bur, follows him unchecked and undisputed, that his red-chili temper started at the age of seven when he slit a cousin-brother's throat. They say that at the age of twelve he throttled his first panther.

And that two days ago, under cover of the riots in the old city, he killed ten Sikh men single-handed.

Such exaggerated rumours. Still, there must be something to them.

Sardarji strides through the foyer into the comfortable teak-panelled dining room, abuzz with slightly less than its usual gaiety. He hooks his walking stick on a chair and moves around the starched cream tablecloth, greeting each member of the Tuesday Lunch Club.

'*Oy*, Sardarji, we are lucky indeed you were passing our way! We were beginning to think you had forgotten all your friends in Lahore!' jests Rai Alam Khan, embracing him.

'It's *your* unbridled desire for Pakistan that kept me from joining you – the Muslim League has to organize school-children to block the way of cars and fight their cause these days.' Sardarji's hearty laugh turns a few people's heads in the room.

'What can you expect? You Sikhs allow Master Tara Singh to brandish his sword in the street and shout "Death to Pakistan" – you know Mr Meher Chander, a fine advocate?'

A dark earnest man in a white Nehru jacket over a Delhi-style tung pyjama rises to his feet to greet Sardarji.

Sardarji brings his palms together, grateful for the diversion that allows him to gloss over the Sikh leader's rash demonstration. 'Of course, of course. Namaste, sir.' His greeting gives due regard to the advocate's Hindu name.

He knows the young advocate, having put in a good word for him once, since he could find no blood tie that would make it nepotism. Sardarji had written a to-whom-it-may-concern letter certifying Meher Chander was 'from a good family' – that most important predictor of competence.

'Jai Hind!' returns Meher Chander. Long live Hind or Hindustan, the name for Hindu India. The greeting is just a trifle too aggressive; Sardarji notices both Mr Farquharson and Rai Alam Khan wince.

'Simply not done,' agrees Cunningham.

Sardarji shakes hands with Mr Farquharson, takes a seat at the end of the cream-cloth-shrouded table. A bearer materializes; Sardarji orders mulligatawny soup and pomfret.

'I'll share his,' says Meher Chander, eyes bulging above his starched too-tight Nehru collar.

Sardarji has just returned to Lahore after a two-year courtesy posting to the court of the Sikh prince Maharaj Yadavindra Singh of Patiala, a posting that had removed him diplomatically so Mr Farquharson could resume his position as Superintending Engineer upon his return from the Burma campaign.

At Maharaj Yadavindra Singh's court everyone dressed well and ate well, no matter how low their salaries, and the riots in Bengal, Bihar and throughout India were faraway events. But many ancient canals through the maharaja's kingdom had deteriorated, the unlined ones soaking subsoil till evaporation spread salt everywhere, ruining acres of arable land. Supervising and planning canal improvements in the princely state was like living in some long-ago, faraway time, in a land of tiger shikars and durbars and all the jewelled paraphernalia of the past. Sardarji, aware that younger men might take advantage of his absence, is glad to now be back in Lahore with a silver-framed photo of the maharaja and an ivory slide rule as mementos of his service.

He peels open the intricate folds of a lace-edged cream serviette, drops it to his lap.

Roop was the right wife to present at the maharaja's court – beautiful, speaking a little English, thanks to her lessons with Miss Barlow and the children – and unlikely to outshine any of the maharaja's ranis. He enjoys watching Roop going about her duties, knowing she will never fight him the way Satya did, on every small issue, every inch of the way, but will meet him playfully, maintaining her innocent ways through the years. He has even promised to take her to see *The Merchant of Venice* on the Royal Shakespeare Company's next visit to Lahore, and has instructed Miss Barlow to ensure Roop reads the play and memorizes it.

On his return to Lahore, Mr Farquharson assigned him to the same whitewashed bungalow on Club Road, and allotted him a new Irrigation Department Rolls-Royce. A glow of satisfaction comes over him, remembering how he thanked Mr Farquharson – and instead bought himself the American-made black Packard sedan, imported to supplement Maharaj Patiala's fleet of luxury cars before the outbreak of the war.

And he'd bought it with money from his own jagir.

An excellent ride, awfully manoeuvrable.

He doesn't mind Mr Farquharson's stories quite as much now. Two years minus Mr Farquharson have brought description within his reach and he has discovered there are Punjabi words where English – yes, English, fails him.

Satya would approve.

The Club Road bungalow in Lahore has changed very little – its hibiscus bushes are taller, but its bougainvillaea white as ever, its garden still that ubiquitous insolent Muslim green, and Roop manages it quite as well as Satya would have. That mali persists in telling the children he is planting Prophet flowers in every earthen flowerpot – once these Muslims get an idea in their heads, no amount of education can dislodge it.

When Manager Abdul Aziz shouts questions about the management of the jagir or the flour mill in 'Pindi in his weekly trunk calls, Sardarji responds, as he has for the two years he has been in Patiala, 'What do you think the Bari-Sardarni would have told you to do?' and when Manager Abdul Aziz tells him, he says, 'Do the needful, then.'

It's quite amazing how sensible Satya was, for a woman.

And Sardarji has rejoined the Tuesday Lunch Club at Faletti's. He looks around the table; quite a few members are absent since the riots two days ago – a judge or two, the district commissioner. Usually the hotel owner joins them, but not today.

Sardarji notices absences more keenly since Satya's passing, absences not only of attendance at luncheons and banquets but the absence of manners, the general courtesies that smooth over difference among equals, the manners that begin from respect for other qualified men and only secondarily notice religions or languages. Absences at luncheons spell distrust – of what one might say, of what one might hear.

It's the riots.

Of course, there'd never be trouble around the government bungalows on Club Road, but just in case, Sardarji had hired an extra few stalwart young Sikhs as watchmen, and for the past three nights he had slept with his pistol beneath his pillow.

Mr Farquharson's Tuesday monologue is in full swing. 'The objective of each community – Hindu, Sikh, Muslim – should be to rise beyond their horrid animal urges. This was quite disgraceful – shops looted, innocent people killed. I'm leaving soon for England, thank heaven.' He pulls his serviette up, covering his old school tie.

But in fact, Mr Farquharson is losing face, pulling out after his return from Burma, with little idea of what he will do in England. He has been exposed to India's complexities without the convenience of Sardarji's mediation for the last two years, and Sardarji takes some satisfaction – no, actually he is

415

positively pleased – to find India's complexity, the real India, has taken its toll. In the company of Indians, Mr Farquharson no longer tries to hide the tipping of his hip flask; the brain-fever bird calls in his ear, *peoh! peoh!*

Drink, drink!

The man has lost his personal izzat, what Kitty called self-respect. All Mr Farquharson has left is pride in his quom. And that, Sardarji can see in his deadened eyes, is not sufficient. Necessary, yes, but never sufficient. Mr Farquharson sends Sardarji memoranda every day or so, forgetting or overlooking the small matter of signing his name. Even his initials are indecipherable. He hides behind the name of the Irrigation Department, seeks the anonymity of his quom. Then he runs for the shelter of his enclaved tribe, takes comfort from his cognac flask.

He will leave the Irrigation Department to God, just as Gandhi advocated back in '42.

Which God, Sardarji cannot guess.

'This,' predicts Mr Farquharson, slurring the words, 'will be the biggest bloodless handover in history.'

'Bloodless?' says Sardarji, blinking. 'Blood has been shed, sir. Just two days ago – is still being shed.'

'Don't be a fathead, Sardarji,' says Cunningham. 'He means English blood.'

Mr Farquharson surveys the table morosely. 'Spats between the bloody natives.'

'Well,' Rai Alam Khan winks at Sardarji, adopts a consoling tone. 'You're going home.' Sardarji notices Rai Alam Khan has ordered daal, cheese pakoras and chutney rather than eat meat killed without benefit of the Koran, forgoing his weekly favourite at Faletti's, brain curry. If they had been at a Muslim restaurant, and if Koranic meat had bothered him, Sardarji would simply have taken his steel kara off his wrist and touched it to the meat to purify it. But Rai Alam Khan has become so rigid these days – he steers clear of such compromises; he has become quite impractical.

Muslims. They think there is just one life to live and everything must happen within it.

Mr Farquharson is waving his hand in dismissal, '. . . the

Empire is magnanimous enough to bend, be flexible with the times.'

'Ah, but I don't think you would have been so magnanimous without Mahatma Gandhi or Mr Nehru – sir.' The advocate touches his collar, reassuring himself.

'We're magnanimous because we're just going to walk off and let you chaps have everything we've ever accomplished here.'

And who translated his every desire? A Punjabi.

Who dug the canals he designed?

Punjabis: Sikhs, Muslims, Hindus. Parsees, Christians. Jains, Buddhists . . . even animists.

Who laid the tracks of the railroads? Punjabis and other Indians.

Who paid for the post and telegraph, the railways and the canals? Punjabis and other Indians.

Punjabis and other Indians, all the way through India.

Cunningham says, 'Calling ourselves Indian today, are we?'

And Sardarji says simply, 'Yes. Though I'll have to find out what an Indian *is* and how to become one. But, yes.'

Mr Farquharson is saying, '. . . no matter how, but the date for the transfer of power has been set by Prime Minister Attlee. June 1948. The date for your "independence."' His words are small darts in the advocate's face. Spittle gathers at the corner of his mouth. He leans back, closes red-rimmed eyes.

That ass Attlee, Sardarji thinks. *That utter rotter, setting a date for independence without a constitution to protect minority rights.*

'It will be,' Mr Farquharson pauses, '. . . interesting to see if you Indians can cope with it. God knows we've protected you in two world wars, trained you long enough.'

How Mr Farquharson exaggerates. Two and a half million Indians just fought his war. The Statesman *says twenty-five thousand Indians died for England. And who trained him, I'd like to know? An Indian.*

But Mr Farquharson has a point – can India cope with independence? The country is moving rapidly toward anarchy. Prime Minister Attlee's announcement followed Hindu-Muslim riots in Bengal – four thousand dead in four days, fifty thousand refugees – and Hindu-Muslim riots in Bihar – thirty thousand dead, a hundred and fifty thousand refugees. Those two provinces are seven hundred miles east of Punjab, and anger carries faster than newsprint.

It can't happen in Punjab. Skirmishes, such as we had this week, but not like Bengal or Bihar.

Not here.

'Quite right,' says Cunningham.

But Gandhi's non-violence has taken so many lives, caused so much suffering. Surely violence might have been a faster, lower-loss route to independence.

'You Sikhs,' Cunningham says. 'Your blood boils so easily.'

Aloud, Sardarji says, 'Yes, but how will minorities like the Sikhs be protected? The date is set, but there is still no constitution. And the Akali Party has been insisting on a Sikhistan since its resolution last year. No one takes them seriously.'

Mr Farquharson flashes smoke-yellowed teeth. 'And what will be the new country's name? Hindustan? Hind? Bharat? India?'

He hasn't answered Sardarji's question.

'Pakistan,' says Rai Alam Khan, breathing in, whispering as though he will soon possess the crown jewels. 'Pakistan.'

He has ignored Sardarji's question, too.

'. . . this independence fight has taken so long,' Meher Chander is saying, 'because Gandhiji didn't want to use the very tactics we decry. When Dharmraj takes us to his netherworld to ask us, before our next lives, what are we guilty of, we Hindus should say, "Lord Dharmraj, we were the ones guilty of too much politeness, of speaking too softly, of hoping for greed to abate and true Christianity to seep from the heart of the British." But – even if Mr Jinnah takes half of Punjab and half of Bengal – Gandhiji has brought us independence.'

The advocate has also avoided Sardarji's question.

He wonders if it is of any use to discuss how minorities like the Sikhs might be protected if they are left in a hypothetical Pakistan. Pride forbids it, for even to ask the question is to acknowledge being afraid for his quom; historically, they have given as good as they got and don't require protection like – like defenceless women.

A single Sikh is like a force of 125,000 men.

'Quite so,' says Cunningham.

As the old saying walks his mind again, he remembers what Satya said one time he'd stated that axiom to her – she asked, How many Sikh men is a single Sikh woman worth? A nonsensical question, but that was Satya, quarrelling for the sake of quarrelling. Not that he didn't enjoy a robust debate, but it was so futile debating with Satya – nothing moved forward, she just went round and round the same old arguments, constantly questioning the natural order of things.

The scent of fried pomfret whiffs past him. Deboned, deep-fried, trying its best to approximate English fish and chips.

Serving tongs, clasped by the brown bearer's white-gloved hands, reach past Sardarji's chest. Just two pieces of pomfret and a few chips fall to his plate and the bearer moves on to serve Meher Chander. Sardarji is about to ask for more, but Cunningham whispers that it is simply not done. By the time he has remembered his appetite and overridden Cunningham, the bearer has returned to his place, hiding among all the other bearers behind the tall carved wood screen jutting from the kitchen door.

Sardarji shrugs, takes his fork and dips a piece of fish in tartar sauce. 'There really is no reason to be so worried,' he says, as much to himself as to Cunningham. 'Mr Jinnah is merely asking for Pakistan so that he can settle for less – it's a negotiating tactic worthy of the bazaar. He's concerned, as he should be, about the rights of Muslims scattered throughout India. Independence will come, yes. But Punjab will never be partitioned. Consider the planning impediments alone, sir – we do not have time to plan and negotiate such an event by June of 1948!

'There are other ideas and options than partition,' he adds, prompted by Cunningham's cushiony voice. 'Federations, tiered governments, shared power.'

But Rai Alam Khan says, 'Huh! Shared power! Partition will come; it is the only solution. Do you think we Muslims want to live under the Hindus or the Sikhs again?' He thrusts his cheese pakora in chutney.

He forgets to smile.

Sardarji finds he has lost his appetite for pinni sweets.

By the time he leaves Faletti's, with a generous baksheesh for Burhan-e-din for holding the Packard door open before him, the protesting schoolchildren and their shouts of 'Leke rehenge Pakistan' are gone. The usual hunger strikers mar the view of Queen Victoria's statue at Charing Cross as Narain Singh drives him back to the Department office.

But that evening, when he has taken a second bath of the day for coolness, and dressed to take his evening constitutional through Lawrence Gardens with Roop, Sardarji receives a telegram from Manager Abdul Aziz, delivered by Dehna Singh:

REGRET MUST INFORM STRIKE AT YOUR FLOUR MILL STOP RIOTING LOOTING STOP PLEASE RETURN TO RAWALPINDI POST HASTE STOP.

Tuesdays are inauspicious for beginning a journey, but what is to be done? He must leave for 'Pindi tonight.

The grooves of a cut glass bowl priceless beyond anything Papaji ever owned are sharp in my hands as I walk slowly on a metalled road in the soft light of a sickle moon. Crimson liquid fills that bowl, fills it to the brim, and I walk carefully, so carefully; not a drop must spill.

Red, colour of blood, colour of anguish. Auspicious red, colour of bad blood, lehnga red, colour of brides, vermilion red marking married women, blood-on-the-sheets red, red filling my womb, garnet-red eye of the white peacock, poppy red, clot red, red of aloneness, threatening red that says, 'Beware, young girl, stop before speaking.' That red.

Betel-juice red.

'Stop, don't love yet.' That red.

Men stand watching by the roadside, so many men. I feel their eyes follow me through the dark. They know whose wife I am, whose mother I am, whose sister I am, what religion I am, even if they do not know my name.

Now a woman stands in my path with a long sharp jade-hilted sword. Still I sleepwalk forward holding the cut glass bowl before me. I cannot turn back now, the road behind me is filled with shadows.

'Are you Satya?' I cry.

Where is that face, haughty and beautiful, that hair, black as a jackdaw's wing? That face that showed no fear as Death came?

'Bhainji!' I call to her, fear-filled, as if I were locked away again, alone in the godown below Sardarji's haveli. 'We are true sisters, now. I felt your smouldering anger that one long moment. Believe me, I felt the wound of your humiliation pass through my flesh, past bone, past breath. Bhainji, I hold you, woman within woman. Like the Gurus, we might be one spirit, different bodies. Satya, I felt all that your body remembered that one long moment and it simmers within me, waiting some day to boil.'

But no, it cannot be Satya, for now with swift relief, my body remembers Satya's forgiveness, settling in me like a parting blessing.

Then who is this woman with the jade-hilted sword?

She has sapphire eyes, a wasp waist and brown, shoulder-short curls.

Miss Barlow advances toward me, raises the sword high above her head.

The sickle moon, the woman's sword, shine as one.

The sword falls.

Crystal shatters to fragments . . .

There is red, everywhere crimson red.

Roop wakes, heart thudding.

'*Hai, Allah!*' says Mani Mai. 'You Sikhs and Hindus get so afraid.'

Rawalpindi, March 1947

The siren wails through Rawalpindi.

At nine a.m. the shops are usually stirring for the day, but this March morning doors of metal and doors of wood remain firmly locked. In the back seat of the Packard, the smell of panic comes to Sardarji's nostrils from the dusty street. The handle of his sturdiest Bond Street walking stick fills his right hand.

Manager Abdul Aziz, in the passenger seat beside Narain Singh, is getting old; henna-reddened hair shows past his furry karakuli cap. It must be too much for him, living with his family in the servants' wing of the haveli, with a skeleton staff of servants to help him manage the mill and the jagir . . . with Satya gone.

That Satya, such a competent woman she was.

Sardarji visited the local police commissioner in the early hours of the morning to report the strike at his mill and the damage through Rajah Bazaar, to demand the listing of the wounded, missing and dead – Manager Abdul Aziz was silent for a moment when Sardarji asked why had he not done so. 'I did call the police, Sardarji,' he says. 'I am ashamed to say they would not come.' It took Sardarji's personal visit for the superintendent of police to assure him there would be men from the local police station in place and ready at his mill today.

Satya, look at this, whoever you are now. India being left to God, Muslims fighting Sikhs and Hindus, my Muslim workers rising against me. You wanted the British gone, look, they're almost gone.

Narain Singh steers slowly and carefully around every vehicle known to the city – push-carts, tongas, bicycles and buggies – as turbaned men, chunni-clad women carrying babies and snot-nosed children walk away from Sikh and Hindu areas in 'Pindi with shocked, terrified eyes. They turn away from neighbours they had thought were friends first, Muslims second, going to blood relatives who will surely take them in.

Last night, Manager Abdul Aziz met Sardarji in the dark at the locked gate of his ancestral haveli and led him in. Anxious, and still loyal.

Sardarji had not returned here since Satya's death more than four years ago, and he had forgotten just how tightly the banyan squeezed his own half of the old haveli, and how ruined was his poet elder brother's half of the house. The terrace garden was still green, watering itself from the underground stream, but the white peacock no longer danced upon it, nor did the fountain arc for him in greeting.

In the heady whirl of the last few years in Patiala and Lahore he had all but forgotten the beauty of the old haveli's scalloped wooden archways, the scent of the old books in his study, the touch of his Underwood typewriter. Satya's shrill accusing voice seemed to echo in the marble-tiled centre courtyard still. She should be reclining on the sofa here, her imperious voice should still be ordering servants about in Punjabi and in Urdu. He tried to picture her face, but what he remembered best was her voice – that infernal, niggling voice. He wandered the rooms he'd furnished with stained-glass archways and European furniture for Roop and the children – he'd been so busy improving canals for India, they'd gone almost unused. On the third storey, dust clings to his fingers from the treasures collected from his travels. He had forgotten how dark was the spiral stone staircase, where he could walk up and up past the stone filigree window tossing its faded diamonds upon the stairs, forgotten how it felt to emerge into darkness, see the flat roofs of Rawalpindi reflect the moonlight like a child's toys flung in the lap of the Margalla Hills.

From the terrace he could see fires of the riots still smouldering in the distance, the smell of charring hair, beards and flesh carried on Vayu's winds.

The haveli, Manager Abdul Aziz reassured him as soon as he arrived, is safe. But the poor Sikh and Hindu shopkeepers in the mohalla surrounding it paid for their very existence with crushed skulls and slashed bodies two days ago. There Muslims singed the beards of easily identifiable Sikh men, tore off the turbans of young and old alike and, Manager Abdul Aziz told him, horror breaking his voice, pulled babies from mothers' arms, threw them to the ground and raped their mothers and sisters before all. Those who were known to be Hindus or Sikhs who displayed the slightest aversion were made to eat beef. Hindu temples were desecrated with cow's blood. Towards morning, fires ate the tinderbox home-shops in Saidpur Bazaar one by one, and their façades now lie crumpled and charred in the narrow streets.

There are reports from the village of Thoa Khalsa not far from 'Pindi that eighty-four – no, ninety – Sikh women jumped in a well, eldest last, rather than fall into the hands of

Muslims. No, not official reports – chatter, gossip, rumours – but still, like Pascal's wager, it is better to heed than to ignore.

How did we come to this?

The car inches past more walking, silent Sikhs and Hindus, traverses an open stretch of road past a monsoon drainage ditch, turns, comes to a stop.

Sardarji's flour mill stands in a walled compound dead-ending a residential street. The outer compound walls of the homes on this street have become billboards for pro-Pakistan slogans scrawled in Persian script.

Round-capped workers cluster before Sardarji's flour mill gate, raise fists, wooden sticks or cricket bats to the sky. Brown faces darkened by hate chant, '*Eent se eent baja denge, leke rehenge Pakistan!*' Though not a brick is left standing, we will not rest until we have Pakistan!

I gave you jobs, I put food in your children's mouths, my brother-in-law, a Sikh man, lent you money when the Koran said no Muslim could do so. I protected you from the demands of the British.

The mob presses closer – hoarse chanting rocks the motor car.

Abdul Aziz's shocked eyes turn to Sardarji:

'Sardarji, sir, we must go back.'

Go back? A Sikh does not go back.

'Where are the police?' Sardarji says. 'I must talk to the men. I will order them to disperse.'

The crowd has crushed the shiny chrome goddess of speed that was the Packard's hood ornament.

Where are the police?

'How do they dare?' says Sardarji, beginning to roll down his window.

A stone hits the side of the car.

Sardarji rolls up the window.

Where are the police?

'Go back,' counsels Cunningham. 'Rawalpindi police are mostly Muslims. There is no one to stop them.'

A wooden stick smashes into the passenger window.

'Go back,' Sardarji says to Narain Singh, keeping his voice even, unperturbed.

'Ji, huzoor!' Narain Singh cries.

'Juldee!' cries Manager Abdul Aziz, crimson drops welling from a cut on his temple.

Yes, hurry!

The Packard slowly backs away toward the monsoon drainage ditch, reverses gears and inches its way back to the haveli.

Sardarji gives Manager Abdul Aziz an old turban to use as bandage and orders tea from the bazaar for him. He sends Narain Singh to summon the police station house officer to the haveli.

Then he calls Sardar Kushal Singh and Toshi – they are well, by now fear has given birth to anger. Sardar Kushal Singh's godowns and cabinets were saved.

'No, no one dared to enter.'

Still, they should come and stay with him tonight in the old haveli – it will be safer.

And can Sardar Kushal Singh arrange four Bedford lorries? Sardarji will send all his valuables to Lahore since the police in Rawalpindi have been derelict in their duty.

Just till people have calmed down.

'No? Well, then, book a trunk call – I have a brother-in-law, Major Jeevan Singh – yes, he's a major. Try him in the cantonment at Amritsar, first. Ask if he can do the needful. I too, will try from this end.'

Narain Singh returns, turban slightly askew.

He says the police station house officer says if Sardarji wants to see him let him come to the police station himself.

The next morning, Narain Singh recruits labourers from the scorched bazaar and Sardarji and Manager Abdul Aziz supervise the wrapping and the packing of Chinese cabinets and grandfather clocks, the rolling of Tabriz and Kerman carpets, all the things Satya called 'useless,' things collected for their beauty through seven generations. All the books in his study, ancient manuscripts in Persian and Punjabi, even the pianoforte he once bought for Satya to play. These are to be loaded on the Bedford lorries Major Jeevan Singh asked his general to send for Sardarji.

Sardar Kushal Singh arrives in the front cab of a Bedford

lorry, three others spewing smoke behind. He climbs down the ladder from the cab and he walks through the charred remains of the mohalla to Sardarji's ancestral haveli shaking his white turban at the damage and calculating the interest on loans that will be required to rebuild it.

As the labourers load the Bedfords, Sardar Kushal Singh moves closer to Sardarji, now sitting at his Underwood writing a letter to the editor about the absence of the police. 'Sardarji,' he whispers in a diamond-studded ear. 'Perhaps this is not a good idea; some might think we Sikhs are afraid.'

'We're not afraid.' Sardarji's index fingers lunge and jab.

In the silver-framed photo on Sardarji's desk, Satya sits on the settee beside Roop, dressed in a lehnga of wedding red, hands folded in her lap. Her eyes speak, 'Really? Is that so?'

'I'm just saying . . . how will it look?' Sardar Kushal Singh believes most sincerely that jelsy is involved, but he is also careful to maintain the picture Sikhs have made ever since the quom began – the same picture Cunningham paints: the brave, the martial, the fearless Sikh, the one who often cannot tell where courage ends and foolhardiness begins.

He predicts, 'If you, a Sikh jagirdar, leave with all your valuables in these lorries, panic will spread through every Sikh and Hindu haveli in Rawalpindi. Can you imagine what will happen if every Sikh and Hindu tries to leave? You'll think the damage and the crowds you saw today were nothing. Nothing!'

The Underwood stops its clattering.

At night the labourers sweat to unload the Bedford lorries they loaded through the heat of the day. Now Chinese cabinets, grandfather clocks and trunks full of books and manuscripts from Sardarji's study return not to their places in the old haveli, but to the godowns used to store grain and gold below. When they are full, Sardarji locks every trunk and cabinet, even the pianoforte, orders the entrance to the godowns covered with the flagstone and, to Manager Abdul Aziz's visible relief, takes the keys.

Sardar Kushal Singh and Toshi will not move into the guest wing – against all his urging, Sardar Kushal Singh leaves for home. He must protect his own cabinets and godowns with hunting rifles and ammunition he has locked away.

When they have gone, Sardarji sits in his wicker chair on the terrace lawn, right ankle over left knee, stroking his beard. He knows now that in any demarcation of Jinnah's Pakistan, in any Muslim state that might be carved from India, his ancestral haveli sits in a Muslim-majority area like a loaded camel bound for Pakistan. So also do his villages, so does every apricot tree in his orchards, and his mill. And now he knows that Muslim policemen will not come to the assistance of any Sikh whose life or property are in trouble. In the chaos the British have created and are leaving behind, a man will no longer be measured by his achievement or contribution, but by his father's blood, whether he wears a round cap, a Gandhi cap or a turban, whether he is circumcised Muslim, or an un-circumcised Hindu or Sikh.

Cunningham says, 'Hold on, old boy, the British didn't divide Hindus and Muslims – one believes in many Gods and the other believes in just one. They won't even drink water from the same well. If you ask me, the Sikhs are just bloody unlucky to be in between.'

Divide et impera, he reminds Cunningham. *That was the policy, divide and rule. Separate electorates for Hindus, Muslims and Sikhs, remember? The Hindu and Muslim faiths were tools, the instruments by which you British divided us, then stood back complaining how we Indians fight, never giving you any peace.*

'You can't blame this on the British,' Cunningham says. 'It's simply not done.'

Cunningham, Sardarji explains, *if British law is no longer enforced, and a man is known only by his faith and the mohalla, the neighbourhood he lives in, none of us will remember the difference between what is done and what is simply not done.*

Tomorrow he will direct Manager Abdul Aziz, 'Do as you think best. I will return when Muslims have come to their senses and want their wheat milled to flour again.'

Walking through the scorched bazaar to the Packard, he feels anger rise red-hot within him, though he fights for distance, objectivity, analysis.

These are my people. What they believe is my belief. What they fight for is my fight.

'You Sikhs – always overreacting,' says Cunningham.

'For God's sake, Cunningham, shut *up*.'

Tomorrow he will return to Lahore and buy himself more ammunition for his pistol – he'll need to put a word in Mr Farquharson's ear to get a licence. And then he will donate to the Sikh Akali Party to buy guns smuggled past the checkpoint at Jamrud, for other Sikhs. And to gurdwaras, so that they will be able to feed the refugee Sikhs and Hindus he saw drifting aimlessly today. The Sikhs must organize or die – the choice is clear.

The banyan sighs as it extends its roots, squeezes the haveli just a little tighter.

Sardarji's letter to the editor rustles in his Underwood, unposted.

Lahore, March 1947

As Sardarji's Packard honks its horn on the Grand Trunk Road, returning from Rawalpindi to Lahore, Roop opens the door to the sleepy quiet of Miss Barlow's schoolroom, letting in a breeze that ruffles the pages of the children's exercise books. At his desk before Roop, Timcu bends his red turban over his lessons, tongue between his teeth, legs swinging under his chair. At the other desk, Pavan's plaits, doubled and held with white ribbons, curl like long dog ears about her bent sleek head, and a frilly frock drops past her white knee socks.

Placards dangle from their necks.

Pavan's says 'Joan.'

Timcu's says, 'Edward.'

Miss Barlow bends from her wasp waist to correct Timcu's letters, smiling wide as the lapels of her double-breasted jacket.

Roop's hand clenches.

Enough.

Miss Barlow has taught Roop to read English and understand it. She can say words she has been taught, the practised words, especially, 'How do you do?' and 'Delighted to meet you.' And Roop has listened and obeyed, knowing English is necessary for a woman who wants to keep her children, learning to talk about nothing with the greatest animation, to ask about relatives of Sardarji's friends and to express her great interest in their well-being.

But this?

If Miss Barlow has her way any longer, Roop's children will be hers – their minds, if not their bodies.

There are so many ways to take away children.

Timcu already had one English name – now she's hanging her own name for him around his neck. Can't she see that in the world that is coming, my children will need their Indian names, not new English ones.

Satya would say they will need their own ideas, not foreign ideas.

Perhaps the placards have helped Miss Barlow give her children the feeling not only that they belong to an important man, but that they are special, that they are not of many, but are the ones that many would like to be.

And I? Will I be the one they despise eventually? Lower born and raised past my father's station?

No matter.

She is Sardarji's wife; it makes her special too, though somehow less special than the children. She is the means by which his seed produced them – without her, they could not be. But then, she thinks, it was not she herself, Roop, who was required. Any other woman's womb would have been just as useful.

Am I blessed or cursed that it was my kismat?

A red-hot anger that does not seem to be her own moves Roop to 'Edward' first. She pulls the string of the placard over his turban. Then to 'Joan,' almost wrenching the cold stiff board off her daughter's soft neck. Pavan looks at Roop from the corner of her black eyes, like a man, so Roop feels like slapping her as well, but she doesn't.

She straightens, holds her head high as Satya would have done. Though her heart races as if a jade-hilted damascene sword is raised above her, she says with just a touch of Satya's arrogant tone, 'Their names are Pavan and Timcu.' Firmly, just as Satya would have, she adds, 'Remember them.'

The smile fades in the sapphire eyes. Miss Barlow says, 'They are too difficult to pronounce.'

'Not as difficult as Miss Henrietta Barlow.' Roop's heart is pounding now.

'My, we're not very grateful today, are we?' says Miss Barlow, sapphire eyes blazing. 'I really don't see the point you're trying to make, Roop, I really don't.'

Hurt and anger waltz together in Miss Barlow's deliberate incomprehension. She doesn't want Roop to graduate from her English lessons, any more than Satya ever wanted Roop to be her 'sister.'

The very next day, Miss Barlow is 'overcome by this terrible heat' and the day after that Atma Singh brings Roop her angular cursive on a flowered cutout card.

Miss Barlow has resigned; like all the English leaving Lahore in droves, she will go to Delhi, and then starboard home to England just as soon as she can get a berth.

Lahore, May 1947

'Not to worry, it is high time Timcu attended Chief's College,' says Sardarji, when Roop shows him Miss Barlow's flowered card.

Roop and Sardarji are taking their evening constitutional through Lawrence Gardens – a sporadic event since Sardarji returned from 'Pindi. He says exercise clears his mind after the day-long Irrigation Department planning and strategy meetings he has attended since his return. He is a member of the Planning Commission too; Narain Singh drives him back and forth to Delhi every week.

Tall Sikh men with flowing white beards and the royal-blue turbans of Akali Party leaders meet in conclave late into the night at the Club Road bungalow, and once Sardarji has completed Department work for the day, he joins them in the drawing room where they sit barefoot and cross-legged on his sofas, kirpan belts slung across chests or around waists. There he joins in the fierce thunder of their discussions.

So this evening when he said, 'Come, Roop, exercise is

good for you,' Roop knew he needed her for respite, and to ornament his arm.

City sound magically softens, in Lawrence Gardens. The gardens have changed little since Roop, in her parrot-green salwar-kameez, once balanced on the narrow divide between two reflecting pools, but today a border of woven gold slants across Roop's bare midriff, border to a lapis-blue silk sari. Heeled sandals kick the pleats of her sari a little at a time so she looks as if she glides, a little behind Sardarji, staying where he can see her.

'I had the foresight to register him for the college at birth, remember? Get a tailor to sew his uniform; let him begin attending next term.'

Arjan trees sway as Vayu sighs through their ranks. Night queen flowers scent the path.

'And Pavan?' Roop asks.

'Pavan can attend a convent school. Ask Dehna Singh to go and find out which one will take her.'

A clash of sticks and then the sound of galloping hooves in the distance.

A knot of horsemen follows the line of a white ball as it bounces across a summer-brown field tufted with patches of green – a game of polo is in full swing at Mr Farquharson's Gymkhana Club.

Sardarji is walking past the same Arjan tree where Roop made her bachan to her Papaji to listen as if she had two ears. Roop would like to stop and touch the bark of that tree, tell it she has kept her promise, but her place is at Sardarji's side.

'And I will continue your lessons myself,' he says, briskly. 'We can begin at once, with mathematics.'

His enthusiasm summons Roop's; she offers him a sweet-sweet smile.

'The Imperial system of measurement is elegant,' he instructs, 'because it is based on five factors – one, two, three, four, six – the way Singhs are based on the first five beloved Sikhs – do you see?'

Roop glances around to ensure no one is looking, then caresses his arm lightly. 'Hai, it's too difficult for me. All these factors, this counting-shounting.'

'Oh, do be sensible, Roop. Cogitate!'

'Achcha-ji, I don't know. But don't be annoyed.' Her hand touches his daringly, for just a moment and she gives him her pretty-pretty, sweet-sweet laugh. 'You try and explain it to me, na?' Roop knows just how much Sardarji loves explaining.

Sardarji continues, 'So, as I was saying, twelve has more factors than many numbers have ... so it's an extremely flexible system. It was developed with great planning and foresight.'

'Ah-hoji?' Roop's eyes are fastened upon Sardarji's lips. In an admiring tone, 'You must have developed it then?'

'No, no. It's very old.'

Roop veers away from mathematics. 'I'm *so-oo* happy Miss Barlow's gone.'

'You are?' An Englishman raises his hat to Sardarji, who raises his walking stick, bows his turban slightly.

'Hanji! I was beginning to notice her making eyes at you, I could tell she was thinking you would marry her, too! I was getting *so-oo* jealous,' and she adds mischievously, 'Hanji, I had jelsy just like Satya!'

'Now really, Roop!'

But Sardarji gives his moustache that well-pleased twirl.

Thock!

Tennis balls fly from Wilson rackets as they pass the grass courts at the Cosmopolitan Club. Roop's hip brushes against Sardarji, nudging him in the direction of the sound.

'One, two and three are prime factors,' he says, continuing her lesson as they enter the club for tea. 'Those that cannot be divided any further, except by themselves, and by one.'

38. Lahore, July 1947

Hoarse slogans pulsate in the hothouse of the city. Protesters, hordes of them. Indian National Congress marchers, men and women alike wearing their Gandhi caps, round-capped Muslim League protesters, all waving their fists and leaning from buses and lorries on The Mall Road. Horns toot and constables whistle ineffectually.

Sardarji's turban turns away from the third-storey window of his office in the red-brick Secretariat building. 'India, Hindustan, Sikhistan, Pakistan, representation, Quit India . . . who knows what they want this time!' He vents his spleen in the empty spaciousness, but ever since that March day in 'Pindi, he has known what they want.

Muslim men want Sardarji's land. They want Sardarji's home, the haveli in Rawalpindi, his mill, his orchards and every village his family has handed down seven generations. They want what he has, down to the books in his study, even if they cannot read them. It does not matter that he does not live in the 'Pindi haveli, that he stands at an office window far away across

Punjab, in Lahore while his body remembers each room in that haveli; it is his. The 'Pindi haveli is where his father and mother lived and died; the memory of that haveli sustained him all the lonely days in England. He has more right to that haveli and that jagir than many in his clan, being the younger son, the one who was never meant to inherit, yet negotiated creditor by creditor to save the family from debt. That haveli belongs to him, though he lives in government housing on each posting. He holds that haveli in trust for his sons and for future generations of his clan.

'Private property, quite so,' Cunningham allows.

Sardarji restrains his surge of anger by trying to quantify the problem. 'I judge there are the same number of protesters as yesterday.'

He touches his collar where he feels it turning up without its usual collar stay. His valet Dehna Singh spent two days searching Lahore for a chemist who might safely open his shop and sell medicines for a fever Timcu acquired at school.

A shout escapes him, 'Is this what we Punjabis in Lahore now call *normal*?' He strikes out, the arc of his arm sweeping a stack of brown paper files balanced on a nearby cabinet to the Bokhara carpet; papers of every size fall to the floor.

'The natives are restless,' soothes Cunningham. 'You are too.'

'*Don't* use that word, Cunningham!'

'Restless?' Cunningham plays innocent.

'Natives.'

'Ah, and why does it bother you, today?'

'Everything bothers me today, damn you! You, more than ever. I ask you, sir, what right do Muslims have? What right do they have that Sikhs do not have?'

'Numbers,' says Cunningham. 'There is great power in numbers.'

Sardarji nods. He has been in and out of the Irrigation Department library in the next room at least five times this morning to consult its maps and the census data from 1941.

'Yes, sir?' The door to his office opens a crack and the round-capped head of his steno appears. The steno and two personal assistants share a desk, a typewriter and the waxy smell of the cyclostyler in the cramped antechamber outside, entering only with tea or files or at his shout.

'Nothing,' says Sardarji. Then, 'Wait – pick up those papers.'

The steno begins bending and straightening, picking up the papers and filing them slowly. Sardarji turns to examine one of the survey maps thumbtacked to the walls above the level of the wainscotting as he waits, tapping a shoe impatiently. The overhead fan labours to stir the heaviness in the warm room.

Looking at the map, Sardarji's eye travels, coming to rest at the site of Bhakra Dam. He should be – India should be – building that dam right now. Mentally, he constructs coffer dams, relocates thousands of people, diverts rivers, generates power. Power and more power – all for Indians, and if Satya were here, he'd say that again. Electricity to drive factories, electricity to pump water from tube wells, power to the villagers, regardless of religion.

Maps lie.

Surprising. He has never realized this before, but maps lie.

Maps lie, for their colours can show nothing of what a man feels when he says 'I come home.' They say nothing of the distance a man will ride to avoid passing through areas inhabited by another's caste or quom, or the direction a man turns when he bows his head to pray. Maps lie, their scrupulous lines diminishing height to hair's breadth, contracting realms of the material to fit in the mind. Maps lie, the artful cartographer separating earth from sea with a simple line that refuses to tell that one does not end where the other begins, but continues, undergirding the sea.

They are an aesthetic achievement, that's all. Essential preparation for the next map that will be drawn, essential for discussions and negotiations, but in themselves mere approximations of the terrain, aids to dreams of conquest, marking familiar places in the roaming of the mind.

The steno places the papers back in their proper files and returns them to Sardarji's desk. Sardarji dismisses him with a nod.

He takes his seat now at Rai Alam Khan's envy, the large desk he commissioned from his own funds – carved mahogany, inlaid with mother-of-pearl.

He yawns, rubs his eyes. Oh, for a full night's sleep. Since he saw the March madness of 'Pindi – 'Pindi, of all places, 'Pindi where he grew up! – Sardarji's days are spent with government work and officials, and his nights with leaders of the Sikh Akali Party, religious men, straightforward people, entering politics as their followers look to them to forge a nation that can resist return to persecution under Islam. The Akali Party leaders – each man taller than Sardarji, with gentle eyes twinkling beneath their royal-blue turbans, men with flowing white beards, sharp kirpans strapped at their waists, like the one Sardarji's father, the Chaudhary, once wore – arrive unannounced, sure of his hospitality, as his guests and as leaders of his quom. They ask him for advice, as a jagirdar, as a Sikh, as an English-speaking qualified man. But what advice can he give? It is too late to demand the right of secession as the Muslims did. Partition will come to Punjab. And now Lord Mountbatten has hastened its date, as well.

The quom must defend itself, the leaders say. And since March, and his trip to Rawalpindi, Sardarji agrees. Not for Sikhs the passive resistance of Mahatma Gandhi, they say. There are too few Sikhs and though they do not – most certainly do not – hold their own lives precious, remember: what are the Gurus if there be no Sikhs left to follow them? A man needs land to feed his family, to hold his turban high. Gandhiji and the Hindus do not lose anything by giving Pakistan to Jinnah from Punjab because Pakistan will consume mostly Sikh-owned land. Remember: the Tenth Guru said that when survival of the quom is at stake, Sikhs can turn to the sword.

Sardarji donates money blindly to them – 'Do the needful.'

In his office now, Sardarji circles the problem placed before him, like a wrestler. Tension – knotty, dense – stands between him and his task.

His mahogany desk was once orderly, just so many files spread upon it as could be handled in one day, but now it is becoming impossible; two clerks, another personal assistant and cycle-messengers bring files and chits and letters faster and faster. The filing cabinets in his office overflow.

How can he think of issue upon issue, every canal, weir and

headwork, every generating station, every reservoir, every embankment, every barrage, their locations, their connections by road and rail, their history, and their dependants in the same moment? Because that is what he has to do to make his recommendation to the Sikh community's pleader before the Punjab Boundary Commission.

He has changed his mind four times already, like a field that passes four seasons in one day, each option leaving him hot, sweat-wet, cold and lukewarm in turn.

He remembers the Tuesday Lunch Club discussion in March over fish and chips at Faletti's. Mr Farquharson was griping over Prime Minister Clement Attlee's announcement that India would be given independence, and Sardarji was asking everyone: what about a constitution that will protect minority rights? At the time, Sardarji had thought March '47 to June 1948 would be too short a time to carry out any partition, and he'd said so.

Not that anyone was listening.

At the time, Prime Minister Clement Attlee had just sent Lord Mountbatten as the new Viceroy to India, charging him with the task of giving India independence by June 1948. But a few weeks ago, after the riots in Bengal, then Rawalpindi, Peshawar and Lahore – June 3rd, actually, will he ever forget that date? – Sardarji heard Mountbatten's cool clipped tones on the radio, changing the date for the British transfer of power to India.

The new Viceroy had hastened the date. No more round-table conferences, no more cabinet missions, no more discussions about constitutions, federations, power sharing, special rights for the Muslim-majority states of Punjab or Bengal. No more objections that the time is too short. Now it will be even shorter.

Now it will be August 15, 1947.

'August 15th!' Sardarji's eyes fall to the calendar on his desk. A date chosen arbitrarily, pulled out of that showman Lord Mountbatten's hat. With little consultation with the Indian National Congress or the Muslim League or the Akali Party, or even Prime Minister Attlee, Lord Mountbatten hastened the date. Brought it from its future greyness to overshadow the present.

And everyone, even the Akali Party's Sikh leaders, even the fiery Master Tara Singh, agreed! Agreed to a partition of India into India and Pakistan by August 15, 1947.

Seventy-three days!

Seventy-three days to cut a land in three, West Pakistan, India, and East Pakistan, like cutting arms from a body.

Seventy-three days, and already there are only thirty-two days left! Seventy-three days will leave no time for the luxury of justice. Two bodies of men have been set up, one for Punjab and one for Bengal. The chairman is an English man, Sir Cyril Radcliffe, imported from England for the job. The Punjab Boundary Commission has been set up and it has a terrible, impossible task before it – only ten days, to hear all arguments and recommend a border line to divide Punjab between India and Pakistan. The result will be a West Punjab that will go to Pakistan along with the other Muslim-majority provinces, and an East Punjab that will go to India.

Satya would say the Punjab Boundary Commission is another British sham.

Sham or no sham, Sardarji has to think of every snaking ditch and hand-placed lump of dirt in Punjab, the work of hundreds of years to be cut in half somewhere, in an instant. His recommendation will go to an eminent Sikh lawyer who will explain Sikh history and the Sikh perspective to the Commission. And in the same moment, he must think of himself and his quom.

The Muslims will never agree.

The commissions, one in Punjab, one in Bengal, will send daily reports of their proceedings, and all the maps and documents presented before it, including Sardarji's recommendation, to the Britisher who is to provide this madness with some method: Sir Cyril Radcliffe.

The ceiling fan slows, stops. A brown-out; Lahore's power supply has been capricious lately. Sardarji's turban is soaking up sweat; oh, to be enjoying the cool breezes of Simla at this time, like Sir Cyril!

Can he recommend that Sikh lands in Punjab go to either India or to Pakistan? No, and there is no way to separate them or cordon them off for safety from the Muslim villages around them. The British will surely give Lahore to India – they must! They cannot do otherwise; it was a Sikh city before they wrested it away, the capital of Maharaj Ranjit Singh's empire. If they no longer want it, let them hand it back to those who won it fairly as spoils of the last battle.

Fairly.

Satya would remind him that Jinnah, Rai Alam Khan – indeed all the Muslims he knows – would quarrel with that word. They think of Lahore as a Muslim city.

It is best not to speak one's thoughts about history too loud these days. Everyone's ears are tuned to take offence; they are deafened by their own concerns.

Punjabi Muslims will remain in West Pakistan, Bengali Muslims in East Pakistan and Indians in India.

But the Sikhs?

And the Hindus living in West Pakistan?

And the Hindus living in East Pakistan?

And Mr Jinnah, what can you do for millions of your Muslims who cannot see their future in your Pakistan? How will you represent them after the border lines are drawn?

The ceiling fan stirs, quickens, till a vortex of hot air swirls around Sardarji's desk.

The questions crowd in his mind as he shifts the files before him, bringing first one then another issue to the top – shuffling them, he might have described it, just a few weeks ago. But then he had not been tested, had not known the hesitation of a man, not Hindu and not Muslim, who must ask the one he fears less to be his neighbour. A massacre by Muslims or slow death under the rule of Hindus – like choosing between cancer and tuberculosis.

TB.

He shudders, remembering the bony lightness of that final embrace, Satya's still face, the slam of the oven under the palm trees behind the government TB hospital. Then her ashes, grey as her ever-accusing eyes, feather-light. His fingers still feel the trace of ash residue as he sprinkled her across the Ganga's waters at Hardwar. Sticky, those ashes clung the way Satya had clung to him, her last moments in their final embrace.

As if she could not bear to leave him.

Separation from Satya by his own command, with the knowledge that she was available to him just by booking a trunk call or driving a few hours across Punjab to the haveli in 'Pindi – that was one thing, but permanent separation from Satya is turning out to be something else entirely.

Those who never heard a dilruba cannot miss it. But a man who has heard it once, just once, never forgets its voice.

Now why would a thought like that enter his mind?

'Cunningham?'

'Not I,' says Cunningham.

He thinks of Satya so often, now that the British are leaving – this is what she wanted, hoped for so long. She should have been here to see her Independence Day come. She might have gloated, it's true – women do that whenever they can – but she would have been proud.

But no matter how often Satya comes to mind, he is not anxious to join her in the next life just yet. Death in a theoretical sense is mere transition, but Sardarji, being at the high end of karmic achievement, finds no need to hasten its unpleasantness – the next life could be substantially inferior in quality.

He is a Sikh. He tells himself that Sikhs have always been brave, can confront all dangers.

'I always said so,' agrees Cunningham.

Sardarji knows also that papers in government files can be as powerful as any steel kirpan dangling from a freedom fighter's waistband. And so he returns to public matters at hand.

Some say Mr Jinnah has assured the Sikhs many times they will be safe in Pakistan but Sardarji has not heard this personally, nor can he find it in any official documents or pronouncements of the Muslim League. And if Sardarji has not felt reassured, then men below his rank have not felt reassured either.

Destruction awaits, then – the Sikhs will be like the goats Muslims sacrifice at Sadqa. If not today, then tomorrow, when the British become just a memory. Self-appointed or newly hired watchmen sound the cry through Lahore, 'Jagte raho!' Stay awake, stay vigilant!

Analysing and re-analysing the situation points only to the same conclusion, again and again: Sardarji's treasured ambivalence must be forsaken. His greatest asset, his ability to straddle cultures and colours, an ability developed over years, must be curbed, must be restrained. For this he must set aside all knowledge of other perspectives and interests, for this he must prune back all the branches of his being, extended over the years; tear down all his mental bridges to other quoms, bridges built and maintained since returning to India. He must gather all the Sikh aspects of his being into one file, mark it top priority, then let it ride above the rest. He must view himself in one dimension, as just a Sikh, only a Sikh, with no affiliations past or present beyond religion, lower himself to see only as far on the horizon as the Sikh tenants he speaks for, votes for, can see.

'There is strength in numbers,' Sardarji growls at Cunningham.

'Not enough,' says Cunningham.

Then another explosion.

'Pakistan! What a name! What a strange idea. Then why not a Sikhistan, too?' Sardarji's bellow of rage galvanizes the ceiling fan; it makes a heroic attempt, succeeds in gusting a few papers into a corner.

'Now, now, sir!' says Cunningham.

But that third way, a Sikh homeland, has been rejected by Gandhi, the same who allowed Jinnah to have this – this 'Pakistan.'

Sardarji throws a few choice Punjabi swear words at the fan and marches to the corner, retrieves the papers. Pins them down securely beneath a glass paperweight.

He takes his seat behind the desk again.

And who would want to live behind the borders of some Sikhistan when the world is so much smaller today and just beginning to acknowledge the presence of brownness in the midst of white? No, a Sikhistan would be a playpen in which any Sikh leader like Master Tara Singh could make himself rigid as Jinnah; a prison, Sardarji thinks, for adventurous, modern Sikhs like himself.

It would stunt his sons' growth.

Make them extremely unreasonable.

If the Koran and the Vedas and the Bible do not speak of every choice a man must face in the world, then the Guru Granth Sahib does not either. Sometimes a man must take decisions, offer and stand by recommendations based on his own ideas, his own times, his own reason.

And his own instinct.

Cunningham raises an eyebrow.

'Yes, and instinct,' he says to Cunningham.

Satya, whoever she is now, will approve.

He moves all the files aside, glowers down at a map of Punjab spread across his desk. His forefinger traces all the pencil lines he's drawn around Sikh shrines, mosques, temples, headworks, weirs, dams and power stations.

Lifts, then traces the blue of the Indus all the way from the Hindu Kush.

Indus, for whom all of India may have been named.

Indus, lifeline in whom five tributaries, Jhelum, Chenab, Ravi, Sutlej and Beas, come together like the first five beloved Sikhs, till they join and flow south to the wrist of the sea.

He unscrews the cap of his Vacumatic and slowly, carefully draws a deep crimson line down the Chenab River – he demands all the land east of Chenab for the Sikhs, recommends that every field and canal east of the Chenab remain out of Pakistan. Demands that all the land east of Chenab should remain in Sikh hands and not go to Pakistan.

Including Lahore.

The line he draws takes hallowed ground, where Guru Nanak was born, where he travelled, where the other nine Gurus who carried his spirit preached and lived and died, out of reach of the Islamic state, into India. It takes ninety per cent of Sikh-owned land into India.

Surely the Commission will understand the necessity of that?

But the line Sardarji draws leaves his own haveli, that haveli in which his father the Chaudhary and his pious elder brother the poet lived and died, that haveli that Satya and he lifted from debt, the haveli where seven generations of his clan have lived and died, on the side of Pakistan. It leaves his mill, his villages, his orchards full of ripening apricots, leaves Punja Sahib Gurdwara, where he married his little brown koel, where Guru Nanak left his handprint, leaves gurdwaras, shrines, forts and jagirs of Sikhs going back to Maharaj Ranjit Singh, and before.

No one shall ever say I was not just.

His divider pricks the map, then the scale ensuring the red line curves about a weir, a dam, a village or two. He fans the ink a little, surveys his work. He will make his request and pen his argument even if the Punjab Boundary Commission is composed of men with their minds closed to Sikh rights, population and the all-important words that Sikh hopes have been pinned upon – 'Other Factors.' The pleader will show them this corner of the planet in two dimensions and the map will ask that the honourable judges imagine a third dimension and, more important, a fourth – memory.

What are the ten Gurus, if there be no Sikhs left to follow their path?

'Steno!'

And when the steno appears, he says, 'Write down . . .'

He feels no satisfaction. No matter where the dividing line is drawn or who draws it, the Punjab Boundary Commission or the British, there will be disputes.

Then India will need Sardarji to do what he does best: negotiate, make them agree. *Them* – he almost laughs. Punjabi Muslims like Rai Alam Khan, men he has known all his life. *Them.* Men who now want power so desperately they will sign anything. Men who have been listening to Iqbal's poetry when they should have been counting hectares of irrigated land and reviewing the plans for dams like Bhakra. He can see himself now, his hand on some future treaty, covering the small type, saying, 'Sign here.'

The details are everything, even if the British don't want to know the details. Executing the details of government is where one's skill and faith are really tested.

The annual summer heat rash under his woollen suit prickles. It is July, but like many other things this year, the monsoon is late. In other times, he might have rented a cottage in Simla for the summer and sent Roop and the children there, joined them for a week or a month when work became impossible. But this year too much is happening, too fast.

Too fast.

That ass Attlee, that utter rotter. That showman Mountbatten. That Gandhi – too old now, losing his grip. That Kashmiri pandit, Nehru. And wily, wily Mr Jinnah.

And, Sardarji thinks, what of Mr Tara Singh and all the Sikh elders in the Akali Party? They were so worried about who is a long-haired Sikh and who isn't that they didn't even demand Sikhistan officially till last year, six whole years after Jinnah's speech demanding Pakistan. Religious men, farmers, moneylenders, bureaucrats like himself – not a statesman among them.

The line is drawn, his recommendation made.

What do you have to say, Cunningham?

But Cunningham is, for once, watching Sardarji in silence. This situation is one that has no frequency of occurrence; it hasn't occurred in anyone's life before.

Cunningham has no theory that can help Sardarji formulate a policy that can establish a strategy for action.

Sardarji is alone.

Only his ten per cent – the untranslated, untranslatable residue of his being – can guide him now.

39. Lahore, August 14, 1947

Rail tracks squeeze the pebbled earth between them, narrowing in the distance, never meeting. The train has long passed, but lorries and cars wait on; the black-and-white barrier arm is down before them.

To the north crest the Himalayas, trails and roads scrawled across their bosoms, hill stations emptying of Britishers who took refuge from summer heat and protest in the plains.

Roop, with Sardarji's children, has turned her back to the Indus; she travels east from the Club Road bungalow in Lahore to 'India' – word, name, label, all shorn of meaning. The Boundary Commission for which Sardarji prepared his recommendations – one Sikh, two Muslims, and a Hindu, judges all – failed to reach consensus, and now somewhere ahead, Roop and her children will cross a line in the dirt, a boundary penned by Sir Cyril Radcliffe, an English man who has never met Roop, Sardarji or their children; who does not know this Punjab he carves, like a healer hoping too late to heal, creating the Dominion of 'India,' 'East

Pakistan' and 'West Pakistan,' empty names with no history.

But where will the borderline fall?

It has not yet been announced.

Meanwhile, everything is being divided – soil, power, water, army supplies, grain.

Families.

Everywhere, men are choosing to stay or choosing to leave. And where the men go, their women and children must also go.

In all the centuries since it was first incarnated in cobbled stone to carry the armies of Alexander the Great and Sher Shah, then Mughal, then Sikh armies, the two lanes of the Grand Trunk Road have never felt the press of so many sorrowing men and women as this day. On bullock carts and rickety ekkas, pushing three-wheeled redris, wheeling rusted bicycles, Sikhs and Hindus move east across Punjab, while Muslims from India pour north and west into the province, carrying their old, their sick, moving not in hope of freedom and independence, but from the fear their bodies remember from other ages.

And since they know not where the border will be, they know not where to stop.

When we return I will ask Sardarji to take the children to Murree instead of to Simla for the summer; I have always wanted to see Murree. I will ask Sardarji to take the children to Hunza or south to watch fishermen cast their delicate nets in the Indus.

Roop left Sardarji at Faletti's with not even his valet, but only Atma Singh to brush aside the assistance of that fierce-looking Pathan at the door and see to his needs. At least he will be with other Sikhs in the hotel until he can transfer command to a Muslim officer. He shook hands with Timcu – Timcu so handsome in his sky-blue turban, starched white shirt and khaki pants, tie and blazer – and then with four-year-old Aman, similarly dressed, except in a sky-blue underturban, when they parted this morning outside Faletti's. And he told them both, 'Remember you are Sikhs.' His big palm covered the crown of Pavan's chunni-covered head as he said, 'Be a sensible girl.' Then he put his arm about Roop's shoulders right before Narain Singh, Dehna Singh, Atma Singh and Burhan-e-din, the Pathan doorman, and said, 'Major Jeevan will send an army jeep to the Secretariat tonight at midnight, I told him I won't leave my office one minute before. Now, you listen, Roop – your sister would tell you to have courage now. Satya would say this is the cost of freedom.'

Now Roop, sitting in the Packard with the children and Jorimon, waiting before the barrier thinks,

Satya. What a strange time to remember Satya!

A woman with a bandage where her breasts should be staggers against the white-striped barrier arm.

She falls.

The crowd surges forward, around the fallen woman. Impatient, pressed from the rear. Bicycles and bullocks, tongas and pushcarts laden with the accumulation of each man's past and his women's ambitions for his future move slowly over the tracks.

The woman is left behind, where she lies.

Alone.

Beside Roop, Pavan's ribboned plaits bounce up and down as she tests the springs of the Packard's back seat, but as they join the mass of humanity walking from Lahore and hear cries and moans of loss and anger give way to dogged expressionless silence, she grows sober, sits with her small pointed chin pressed to the groove of the open window, black eyes glancing at Roop's in the rear-view mirror once in a while.

Perhaps it is a good thing she cannot see what lies directly before her.

At the other window, Jorimon wipes sweat beads from Timcu's upper lip with her sari palloo; his turban droops upon her shoulder. Jorimon could not be left in Lahore like Mani Mai – Sardarji said her village in Bengal will fall in East Pakistan; to reach it, she must travel four hundred miles further than Roop. There is a cousin-uncle, maybe a cousin-brother somewhere near Dacca. She will be protected travelling to Delhi with them, but Sardarji told Roop it would be prudent to 'let her go' to East Pakistan once they all reach Delhi.

There is 'no need' for his children to have a Muslim maidservant.

So wise he is.

The other Muslim, Mani Mai, watched them leave too cheerfully. Not that Mani Mai had not done her duty as any good maidservant would, but she had been too cheerful as they said goodbye for no one knew how long. She had promised to look after Roop's pretty clothes and any valuables in the Club Road bungalow, saying – was it with a certain satisfaction? – 'Go – you and your quom are those in danger, not I. Khuda hafiz.'

Khuda hafiz. Goodbye, Muslim style. God go with you – matter-of-fact, just like that.

Had Roop imagined it or in the last few days had Mani Mai not come immediately when she was called? She forgot Roop's orders more than once.

Roop asked Mani Mai what was the matter, was Mani Mai getting old, going deaf?

And it was then Mani Mai said, 'Nahinji. No, I hear you quite well – it is you who need always to sit with your ear towards me, you who can never hear me unless the room is well-lit and you are prepared.'

Roop had believed for the past ten years that Mani Mai did not know Roop's secret weakness. And now Mani Mai felt free to tell her that she had known all along, as if Mani Mai were sure her knowledge of Roop's secret would make no difference now.

At least Mani Mai was loyal enough to tell no one else.

Even so, Roop wept to leave her and feared for Mani Mai's safety left all alone in the bungalow. For, more than any woman, Mani Mai had, in the ten years since Roop came to Sardarji's haveli, become like a mother to her.

But Mani Mai's eyes were dry.

In the early morning, once Narain Singh and Dehna Singh had strapped bedding rolls and suitcases to the roof of the Packard and filled its dickey so full it needed to be roped to hold it closed, Dehna Singh held the back door of the Packard open for Roop. And Roop, standing on the front veranda, embraced Mani Mai as Sardarji and the children got in the car, and she gave Mani Mai the Kashmiri jamavar shawl Satya bought her so long ago, gave it on impulse – such an expensive shawl, to protect her till they meet again.

But still Mani Mai's eyes were dry.

But of course, of course – that was because we'll be back soon.

Narain Singh drives in first gear, inching his way. Sardarji has equipped Dehna Singh and Narain Singh with a .303 Enfield and a cricket bat besides the kirpans they always carry. Roop closes dust-caked eyelids, remembers the feeling of Sardarji's arm squeezing her shoulders, right before the eyes of three men-servants and that huge Pathan doorman.

'You remember, Roop, don't stop for anyone or any reason.'

The damned calm.

It is August 14th, and Sardarji has returned to his desk in the Lahore Secretariat to await the stroke of midnight. Today, a day before India gets her independence from the British, two wings of Pakistan, West and East, come into being from the partitions of Punjab and Bengal.

Two wings of Pakistan, separated by a thousand miles.

Two Punjabs, Hindu East Punjab and Muslim West Punjab and two Bengals, Muslim East Bengal and Hindu West Bengal, stand in the wings ready to take shape upon maps once the borders of India and Pakistan are declared.

At that moment, Sardarji will surrender his office in the red brick building to Rai Alam Khan, now appointed chief accountant to the Pakistan Service of Engineers.

But not a minute sooner.

Then he can leave.

He will not use the word the papers are using: *flee*. Trains out of Lahore – to anywhere – are so full people ride clinging to carriages, and it is becoming impossible to reach the railway station. Slaughter for slaughter continues across India. Muslims in Muslim-majority areas like Lahore are burning and looting Sikh and Hindu mohallas.

And in Amritsar and other Sikh- and Hindu-majority areas, Satya would remind him, Sikhs and Hindus are burning and looting Muslim homes and shops.

Newton's third law: for every action, there is an equal and opposite reaction.

Only money levitates over the coming border. Telephone and telegraph lines juggle it from one ledger to another, the journals of its travels chronicled in the calligraphy of legions of unfanned, unsung stenos and clerks. Sensible men, qualified high-up men like Sardarji, who see danger coming, move money to safer coffers – this Sardarji has done, visiting the bank manager at Lloyds Bank in Connaught Place on his last visit to Delhi. And, courtesy the connections of Major Jeevan Singh, he was able to send a lorryful of government ledgers and documents under army protection, to the Irrigation Department headquarters in Delhi.

To Delhi, eye of the storm, outside Punjab, safe from the looting and burning in Lahore.

Roop has gone ahead, south to the capital with his children; pray Vaheguru they reach it safely. He did not see any need to send the family until his neighbours on Club Road began painting sickle moons on their compound walls, sickle moons to alert hooligans that Muslims of their own quom resided in the bungalows within. The sickle moons made him want to leave, made him *need* to leave. Those sickle moons told him the situation in Lahore had become so unstable that hooligans of any persuasion could burn or loot even a government bungalow on Club Road, if a Hindu or Sikh might be found within.

And that even his neighbours expected the Muslim police of Lahore to look away.

But then, how many can the police arrest? Sardarji tells himself law and order will be restored only when people come to their senses.

Unless Lahore also goes to Pakistan.

If Lahore falls into Pakistan, every Hindu and Sikh in this city will be hostage for the well-being and safety of forty million Muslims who, the census figures tell him, will be left in the minority in India.

And so Sardarji chose Delhi. Sent his family to Delhi, because the eyes of all the world will be focused on the capital, because politicians of all religions cannot allow *Delhi* to turn nasty. He sent them in the Packard, because a motor car spells consequence; he cannot believe any man, Hindu or Muslim, will dare to stop it.

He shook hands with Timcu and Aman when they parted this morning outside Faletti's and told them, 'Remember you are Sikhs.' He rested his hand on his daughter's chunni-covered head and tried not to think of her falling into some Muslim man's dirty hands, tried not to think of his daughter's long hair meeting scissors, or worse. Pavan kept her eyes upon his shoes, and he said – rather lamely, to break the silence – 'Be a sensible girl.' He put his arm about his little brown koel right before Narain Singh, Dehna Singh, Atma Singh and Burhan-e-din, that scowling Pathan tribesman, and said, 'Major Jeevan will send an army jeep to the Secretariat tonight at midnight, I told him I won't leave my office one minute before. Now, you listen, Roop – your sister would tell you to have courage now. Satya would say this is the cost of freedom.'

Sardar Kushal Singh made an unusually extravagant six-minute trunk call a few days ago to say his second son, the one in government service now posted in Bengal, had 'pulled a few strings' to reserve seats for him and Toshi on a charter DC-3 to Delhi.

'You should have called me,' Sardarji remonstrated.

'It's done now,' Sardar Kushal Singh assured him. Knowing Sardarji's views on helping family, he had been considerate enough not to ask his brother-in-law.

But, his voice crackled down the line, they could take no baggage, so they had left the keys to their haveli with the Bishop of Rawalpindi.

'Better that some Christian live in our homes for a while than the Muslims,' Sardar Kushal Singh said. 'So much jelsy, Sardarji, what to tell you!'

But Sardarji could not, at this very last, leave his keys to his ancestral haveli and his mill in Christian or in Muslim hands – for him, the hands of both religions were tainted with the eviction of his quom. So he ordered Manager Abdul Aziz to take a bus from 'Pindi, come to his side in Lahore.

If a Muslim wants my property, let him use his bare hands

instead of words to break into my ancestral haveli, so his body remembers the cowardice of his thieving, his karma debt to be repaid some other lifetime.

If Satya were here she would say, 'It is not only Muslims who filch and thieve, it is we Sikhs too, we Sikhs and Hindus who turn them out of house and home and send them destitute into the arms of their Muslim brothers.'

And Cunningham, that hoary phantom remnant of his Oxford days who had saddled his mind so long, was either gone or silent.

Instead of giving Manager Abdul Aziz his keys, as other Sikhs and Hindus were doing, Sardarji embraced him when he arrived in Lahore, and signed a letter to him, a letter that says the manager and his family can live in his haveli rent-free and run Sardarji's flour mill as caretaker till Sardarji's return.

And Aziz embraced him in return and wept unashamedly. Said, 'I was at your wedding, I ate your salt. Allah has given me enough, I need no more.'

Forget this and all other unselfishness from that quom!
Survive!

Last month, Sardarji simply told the departing British settlement officer he had 'forgotten' to collect this year's grain revenue from the few Sikh lambardars of his villages.

And Sardarji's money has flowed into the war chests of the Akalis, to arm jathas of Defender Sikhs with kirpans, spears and unlicensed guns. And since the 'Pindi riots in March his money has bought ammunition for Sikh soldiers discharged and disbanded after the Burma campaign, residing in villages through Punjab. There is no shortage of guns for those who can pay for them; guns stolen from arsenals once intended for use by the British and Americans against the Japanese.

Sardarji is grateful to the Tenth Guru for asking every Sikh to carry a kirpan always, in defence of the wronged.

But Sardarji is not a soldier – he is an administrator, a qualified man, a civil engineer. What else can he do? There are too many Muslims and too few Sikhs all the way from Rawalpindi to Lahore.

The keys to the 'Pindi haveli lie before him on the mother-of-pearl-inlaid mahogany desk. A few pounds of iron, smoothed and moulded. Keys to every lock he ever had and never used, to the trunks in the underground godowns, keys to each suite of rooms, keys for sideboards and Chinese cabinets, chests and cupboards, grandfather clocks, keys to trunks full of books, the key to the pianoforte, keys to every gate and stable, so many unused keys. When Satya was alive, no one had never needed to lock away possessions. But here are ornately carved keys, long keys, short keys, thin keys, thick keys, all threaded through a strong cotton nallah.

His hands rise to the starched muslin of his turban, lift it away from his sweat-damp forehead. The keys mute their clinking as he places the heavy bundle in its hollow crown. Carefully, he bends his topknot to accept the load; he will carry his keys in his turban, to Delhi.

'I will take the train to the platform at Old Delhi railway station – meet me there,' he told Roop, as he closed the door of the Packard on her and the children. 'Go to the Imperial Hotel in Delhi,' he told Narain Singh. And to Roop he said, 'You will be safe with Mr Farquharson.'

This much at least he can claim from his long service with Farquharson (*to* Farquharson, Satya would say). Farquharson can be trusted to look upon Roop and be unmoved by her beauty.

Atma Singh's partridge-beige turban bobs below the ink-stained desktops of the stenos and personal assistants outside Sardarji's office door; he dozes, knees tucked beneath the silver luxuriance of his beard, waiting on his haunches like a faithful hound. A blanket, two starched shirts, several collars, two suitcoats, two pairs of trousers and a pistol are packed in the bedding roll beside him, along with all the maps of Punjab from the Irrigation Department library that could be folded or rolled within it. From the centre of the bedding roll peeks a large water bottle. Atma Singh, too, is ready to leave.

Sardarji rests his neatly rolled beard on the heels of his palms.

This silent waiting.

Since that March day in Rawalpindi he has asked himself often how he could plod through the daily files; why were these things important? Why should anyone be interested in new project proposals to irrigate fields around villages that could burn tomorrow? How could he continue building in the face of anger, violence, death – and why should he worry about building anything at all if the villages he builds for will go to Pakistan?

Because I am an engineer and an administrator – building and maintaining are what administrators do. We try to work within the handed-down rules of former times, inventing the future slowly, building on the past.

In due course, his office will be reassigned to a new type of man – a Pakistani. And given a chance, and a few years of education, that Pakistani Muslim will do Sardarji's duty just as well as he.

And if Satya were here, she would tell him that, right to his face, the way only she knew how. She never held such truths back, that wife of his. How he misses her bloody-minded rebelliousness now; he has need of her spirit, prickly as cactus.

He wonders at the temerity of Gandhi and Nehru and all those Hindu congressmen, that they do not understand: if you build dams between all religions, Sikhs, Hindus, Muslims, Christians, you create the emotional equivalent of hydrostatic pressure – water's pressure when dammed and raised to levels past its normal flow. Gandhi and Nehru are educated men, qualified men; they should realize that one fissure in any dam holding this pressure back is simply horrifying to consider. When catastrophe strikes, they will be the first to beg for reason from those who have passed it.

What Gandhi and Nehru and Jinnah have done! They have made going to jail a national occupation, raised law-breaking to a fine art, all in the name of 'Hindustan' – place for Hindus. And 'Pakistan' – place for pure Muslims. Is this a good example?

Sardarji snorts.

One should never trust a teetotalling Baniya or a Kashmiri pandit. Or anyone who builds a realm only from words.

He always believed improvement for the rich leads to improvement for the masses, being a man confident of his own generosity and the generosity of his friends. But Mr Jinnah was not prepared to wait for engineers to build more dams and canals and railroads and relocate more people to irrigated soil. Mr Jinnah was not patient – he incited the servant class, the untouchable converts – Sheikhs, as Muslims call them – to rebellion. Minds used only to rebel and destroy forget how to create, how to build, how to imagine a future unlike the past.

Can any good come of this?

He slips his new spectacles beneath the starched muslin edge of his turban to read his resignation letter again. Unsigned, waiting.

Satya's words, as she raged to him so many years ago, come back: *Let's stop pretending we know one another.*

'Cunningham,' he says, 'Lahore is no place to be Muslim if it goes to India. And Lahore is no place to be Hindu if it goes to Pakistan. A Muslim can pass for a Hindu, a Hindu for a Muslim. But we Sikhs with our turbans – we are such easy targets.'

Cunningham still has not a word to say.

But if Satya were here, she would say it aloud, because her very name was truth: at this moment, she would say that what Lahore and perhaps all of India needs is:

The relief of violence.

The thump of a hand steadying a body against the side of the car comes loud in Roop's ear. A grime-grey turban lifts the sun-weathered face of an old Sikh farmer; bewildered eyes behind a fall of greyed eyebrows peer into hers.

'Beti, do you know how far is Sikhistan?' he asks, calling her daughter.

Roop shakes her head sadly, 'I don't know, ji.'

The old Sikh farmer trudges on and Roop's hand is on the door handle, wanting to open the door and take the old villager in to rest his feet. Tell him no one has made any Sikhistan for him, find out where can he go.

But Sardarji said . . .

He looks so much like Papaji, only older.

But Sardarji said . . .

Oh, Papaji, Jeevan, Kusum, Revati Bhua, Gujri, where are you?

Vaheguru, have pity on us all.

On the outskirts of Lahore when the last bazaars gave way to fields, an army lorry of young Sikh soldiers had veered around a corner and crunched to a sudden stop beside two cringing burqa-clad women. A woman's ghostly hand lifted the edge of one burqa – could it have been the hand that held her own when it was small? And fully grown, was it not that woman's hand that ringed her lips with Roop's lipstick?

The veil falls.

Huma?

And Huma – if it was Huma – called to Roop – she thought she heard, 'Roopbi! Bachao!'

Help?

How?

Was it Huma?

What was she doing in the street, so far from home? The woman's face was dust-stained, tear drops channelled their way to her chin, too many to make wiping them worthwhile.

Compassion is weakness, disloyalty to the Sikhs.

Beware of pity. Pity charmed Sita, pity for an old beggar lured her out of her circle so Ravan could steal her away from Ram.

And Sardarji's orders were clear: 'Don't stop for anyone.'

A muezzin's unwavering call filled the sunny afternoon. In the midst of terror and blood, a Muslim called his quom to prayer.

His call invaded the car, divided Roop that moment from her childhood, hers and Huma's.

She could do nothing.

Every woman has her kismat.

A turbaned soldier leaned from the lorry and pulled Huma up like a black cloth sack and from that moment Huma and Roop were going in different directions.

Will those soldiers destroy her honour or protect it? How can I know the future? How can I know my own Sikh people's intentions?

From the window, Roop's eye caught a bloody white kurta in a mud puddle, its sleeves floating, empty of its owner. A woman in a cotton salwar-kameez, her head covered by a stark white chunni – was she Hindu, Sikh or Muslim? Impossible to tell, without a man beside her – walked to it, waded in to the ankle and stooped. She walked away as if in a stupor, pulling the kurta listlessly behind her.

Everyone is rescuing what they can.

A troop of monkeys swung hand over hand down telephone lines, jibbering and chattering with fear.

Black shapes of vultures circled in the sky.

The minarets and domes of Lahore diminished into the distance. Muslim war cries – *Allah ho Akbar! Allah ho Akbar!* – faded.

Now Roop sits in the Packard, on the Grand Trunk Road to Delhi. Unadorned. Like some neglected woman.

Like Satya, at the end.

Not a gold chain, not a diamond in sight. All her valuable things – gold no bank manager can freeze or seize for Pakistan, Mama's sapphire ring and the rest of Roop's wedding jewellery – are in a velvet pouch, hidden behind a slit in the back seat of the Packard. With them are the first gifts Sardarji gave her, the gold kantha, the three-tiered ruby earrings, the gold anklets, Satya's Omega watch and her dozen thin gold bangles, and all the jewellery Sardarji brought his wives from his travels over the years.

Roop's fingertips smooth the purple silk wrapped about the Guru Granth Sahib on the seat beside her. The Guru rests on Mama's phulkari-embroidered red shawl; she needs both for strength.

'It's so hot,' says Pavan.

'Go faster, Narain Singh!' says Timcu.

Can we not go any faster?

The temperature indicator needle creeps steadily towards the red.

At five minutes to midnight Rai Alam Khan, his old friend Rai Alam Khan, marches in, five accounting office clerks in his wake. He has exchanged his usual navy blue blazer for a kurta-pyjama. And a round cap.

Before him, Sardarji signs his resignation letter. His signature looks very small, spidery, bleak.

He rises to his feet and holds the letter out to Rai Alam Khan. 'It's all here,' he says. 'The contents of the office are listed with approximate values – even the desk and the carpet you want are here. Note here that I am taking some maps of equal book value. When I am reassigned to the Indian, West Punjab Irrigation Department office, we will make a full inventory and then we can exchange again.'

Rai Alam Khan reads the resignation letter through, then his fingers caress the mahogany surface of the desk. Clerks move around the office, taking inventory.

Sardarji moves to the other side of the desk and Rai Alam Khan takes his place behind it.

Alamji smiles a satisfied smile.

Surely he cannot want the desk and the carpets more than the maps in the Irrigation Department library? I have relied on those maps every day, inaccurate and inexact as they are, till this very last minute. For every discussion. Surely he cannot value my desk and the carpet above the data on those maps?

He moves to the window to let Rai Alam have a moment to think, looks down at the dark street. A jeep silhouette, bristling with guns and asserting the authority of khaki uniforms, should break the white edge of that sidewalk below.

But there is no jeep.

Perhaps it is late.

Sardarji pats the weight of extra bullets in his waistcoat pockets, checks his timepiece. Midnight.

He turns back to Rai Alam Khan.

Incredibly, Rai Alam Khan still seems unaware of his blunder, so anxious is he to take over, so intent is he on claiming the assets of Empire – so unschooled are accountants in civil engineering.

What can one expect of a Cambridge man?

Sardarji allows himself a brisk arm's-length parting embrace. Quick, embarrassed.

'Goodbye, brother. Sat Sri Akal.'

'Khuda hafiz,' Rai Alam Khan cannot permit himself any words of farewell but those of the Prophet, particularly in the presence of the clerks. 'Sardarji,' he says as they shake hands, 'send us the Taj Mahal.' For the Taj Mahal, like many Mughal monuments around Delhi and through India, lies outside Punjab and will not fall into Pakistan.

In the dark corridor, Atma Singh is on his feet, hoisting the bedding roll upon his turban. They descend to The Mall Road, which is filling with round-capped men swaying and dancing to the gulp-gulp beat of the dhol. Kerosene lanterns light the way of a celebrating procession.

'*Baley! Baley!*' they yell.

Muslims of the city are celebrating, though the Punjab Boundary Commission has not yet said where the border line of Pakistan begins, has not decided whether these men live within its boundaries or must travel to it. They celebrate Pakistan anyway, so sure are they that Lahore is theirs.

Sardarji congratulates himself on his foresight in sending Roop and his children with Narain Singh, to Delhi. But where is the army jeep and escort that Major Jeevan promised?

Sardarji grips his Bond Street walking stick tight. The two turbaned heads, his own and Atma Singh's, stay in the shadows of the Secretariat veranda columns, attempting to blend into the raucous night.

The army jeep should arrive any minute now.

Sten gun fire and the smell of smoke from petrol bombs tossed into Sikh and Hindu homes and shops in the old walled city ride the hot breath of Vayu's night winds, its pungent odour mingling with the fragrance of night queen flowers.

Evaluate, assess, analyse: is any way safe?

Sardarji squints into the darkness, searching. No jeep.

He turns back to Atma Singh, words of reassurance upon his lips.

And a huge figure looms before him.

It wears a round cap; a dagger blade glints from its right hand.

A grin flashes beneath a trimmed moustache in the dark.

'Ah-ho, Sardarji, kithey jason?'

Where is Sardarji going?

'To the railway station – out of my way.'

A match flares in the darkness and a jolt runs through Sardarji.

'*Burhan-e-din!*'

Sardarji remembers his own words outside Faletti's: 'Major Jeevan will send an army jeep to the Secretariat at midnight, I told him I won't leave my office one minute before.' Loud enough that Burhan-e-din must have heard them.

Atma Singh gives a small moan behind him.

Sardarji pulls himself up to his full height. 'You may kill me, but let my old servant go,' he says, his turban held high.

Another match flares. Teeth flash white in Burhan-e-din's beard.

'Sardarji, you were my mehmaan, my guest. Come with me.'

Where can Atma Singh and I run? How far can we go?

Every rumour he has heard about Burhan-e-din comes crowding back to his mind. *They say at the age of twelve he throttled his first panther. And that under cover of the riots in the old city, he killed ten strong Sikhs single-handed.*

He looks up at the Pathan. 'No, no, Burhan-e-din. We will not trouble you,' he says.

'No trouble, Sardarji. No trouble for my mehmaan.'

A guest, yes, he was Burhan-e-din's guest, just this morning. A guest is a sacred trust, surely no man can betray a guest. The worst you can do to a guest is make him want to leave, make him *need* to leave.

And Sardarji needs to leave.

War cries punctuate the thoughts clashing within him. '*Allah ho Akbar!*'

In answer, Sikh war cries. '*Raj karega Khalsa!*' The Sikhs shall rule again. '*Sat Sri Akal!*' God is great.

And Hindu. '*Jai Hind! Jai Hind!*'

Long live Hindu India.

How will he and Atma Singh reach the station safely without the army escort? Sardarji had requested the army specifically, because since the March riots in 'Pindi, he has known that the police all through Punjab cannot be trusted.

Can it be Burhan-e-din is his best option? Or is Burhan-e-din here to lead them away to die?

The din of a howling mob draws closer.

'Hurry!'

Sardarji takes a deep breath, says, 'Ah-ho, let's go.'

He and Atma Singh walk from dark into dark, following the hulking figure of Faletti's doorman, still dressed in his Sikh master's cummerbund and gold braid. Sardarji keeps his eye upon the blade of the khukri gripped in Burhan-e-din's right hand, and rues that his pistol is packed away in the bedding roll on Atma Singh's back – who would have thought he would need it so soon? He'd never imagined he could be accosted right near the Secretariat by Burhan-e-din.

In Burhan-e-din's footsteps, they walk, trot, walk again. Through the back streets off The Mall Road, and then further, winding their way through serpentine lanes in Muslim areas where no Sikh, certainly not Sardarji or Atma Singh, has ever been. They leave the yells and tumultuous noise of celebrating processions behind and pass the tent cities of Muslim refugees made newly destitute by their Sikh and Hindu neighbours in Amritsar, only thirty-five miles from Lahore. Then the even poorer leaning shacks of hundred-year-old slums. Sardarji feels a million Muslim eyes are fixed on their turbans; the two Sikhs shrink from every candle, every lantern, and the light from naked bulbs swinging this late at night in prostitute dens. But the Muslim areas Burhan-e-din leads them through are unusually deserted – he walks the areas inhabited by the most orthodox, areas whose inhabitants have gone to celebrate Pakistan, or to loot, kill and rape through Sikh and Hindu quarters.

Atma Singh's shoes are old. And I haven't walked this much in years. The train is our only hope. Where is this man taking us? There is no one of our quom here. What if he kills us – who will ever know?

They walk the dirt paths of yet another dark bazaar smelling of death, decayed vegetables and urine. They walk past dead ends and bifurcations, and wonder silent whys at paths the Pathan leaves untaken.

And now, suddenly, coming around a bend, the rank smell of nameless anger.

A maulvi, some Koran teacher tired of feeding the

Prophet's words to children, yells hate of infidels to adults standing before him, in a courtyard. And answering his spittled shout, the howls of a crowd being incited to loot, burn and kill.

Sardarji's upper arm feels the grip of Burhan-e-din's large hand through his coat sleeve. Beside him, Atma Singh recoils as Burhan-e-din seizes his arm, too. Burhan-e-din thrusts them first into a dark doorway, then swiftly leads them down smelly passages between havelis.

With each turn, the howl of the crowd fades behind them. Smoke from burning Hindu and Sikh homes and possessions obscures any star that could guide them.

By now, neither Atma Singh nor I would know our way back to The Mall Road.

A mosque's Mughal arch rising before them in the dark catches the breath in their throats, for fear Burhan-e-din spirited them past that crowd only because he planned to lead them here, deliver them to worse than death, to scissors and knives waiting to hack off their hair or beards or private parts . . . but still they walk, half run, and walk, dwarfed by the giant Pathan.

Suddenly, a brick wall looms in half light before him. The smell of burning coal, a puff and a whistle fill the torrid night air. Then a small, barred iron gate, a workers' entrance has swung open. Through it, by lanterns flickering in the station's smashed windows, Sardarji can smell panic, and see hundreds – no, thousands – of turbaned men, chunni-clad women, and their children, milling and clamouring before the train carriage at the platform, desperate to flee – yes, flee.

Burhan-e-din stops.

'Sardarji, be careful in the morning. Then you will meet Muslims.'

'But I did meet a Muslim.' Sardarji laughs a great laugh of relief. 'Shukriya, Burhan-e-din.' And he presses a gold mohur-coin into Burhan-e-din's hand.

'Khuda hafiz,' says Burhan-e-din, melting back into night.

Farewell, Muslim style.

Atma Singh exhales noisily.

'That man must be a carpet dealer's son – he raises his price just to make us feel grateful when he lowers it a little. *Huh!'*

Sardarji stares at the usually kindly old man in surprise.

He resents depending on Burhan-e-din's principles for even an instant. So did I – it made me feel like a woman.

If Satya were here, she'd say, 'See, now can you feel how any woman with any respect for herself feels?' That wife of his. So ziddi, she was. She must be troubling some new family with her uncomfortable truths somewhere, right now.

But this is no time to think of Satya.

'Old man,' says Sardarji. 'We're about to depend on the principles of many people, Hindu, Muslim and Sikh, all the way to Delhi.'

I saw what happened in 'Pindi – you did not. You're about to find out what people are capable of under cover of crowds. And we too will be tested and will find out if we learned much from our Gurus.

'Go on, hurry!' he orders.

Atma Singh holds the bedding roll to his chest to push his way through the crowd, then through gateposts in the high wall. With the bedding roll, he makes a space for his thin frame between men, women and children crowded on the platform.

Then he reserves space for Sardarji, by lowering the bedding roll and water bottle between the people crowded on the platform, inch by inch down the wall to the platform. Then he leans over the luggage and shouts over the wall to Sardarji.

Steam puffs, whistles shriek into night from the train's distant engine, even as its brown carriages rub like a protective snake against the platform.

Women scream children's names, fathers' names, brothers' names – even their husbands' names.

Men yell, babies cry.

Sardarji moves from the heat of night into the hotter press of sweating, panicked bodies. He clutches his walking stick at arm's length with both hands, making a railing, to hold away the crowd. This gets him through the gate posts and he searches the dark for Atma Singh's leathery face.

A raised elbow knocks him squarely, though unintentionally, on the jaw.

One step from the gate, but Sardarji has reached the bedding roll; he sinks down upon it; the maps crackle. Atma Singh leans over Sardarji's turban till his fingers rest on the wall, his torso and his turban shield Sardarji from the crowd. Sardarji's underturban clings to his wet forehead, both men panting as if they had just run a race, not moved three feet down a platform.

This is impossible – most undignified.

'Chalo, Sardarji!' Atma Singh urges.

A woman's head butts Sardarji's arm as he exchanges his seat on the bedding roll for a foothold on the platform, making it possible for Atma Singh to hoist the bedding roll up over his head again, till it rests upon his turban.

Sardarji needs to stop and loosen the laces on his pinching shoes, but there is no time. Keys press against Sardarji's scalp – a comforting weight.

'*Hut!*' Atma Singh tries to clear a path for Sardarji, understanding instinctively Sardarji has not taken a train in many years, nor been jostled and pushed this way by so many Sikh and Hindu men, women and children – each with such desperate, pleading eyes.

A shriek, and then a woman falls. Sardarji stops, reaches instinctively to give her his hand, then realizes Atma Singh has pressed ahead, passed him on a surge from behind.

'*Atma Singh!*' he yells, as men all around him are yelling.

The thought of being separated from old Atma Singh sends a shock to his core, and as he hesitates the woman is lost, disappearing beneath the press of kurtas and kameezes.

This is impossible – We will not be able to reach this train – and we must reach it!

Relief washes over him as he spies the bedding roll again, Atma Singh's silver beard beneath it.

'Atma Singh—'

A punch to his kidney; Sardarji grunts involuntarily, turns, hits some other refugee with the back of his hand. Is instantly sorry.

Sardarji feels Atma Singh's hand grip his shoulder; the bedding roll wobbles dangerously.

'Atma Singh,' shouts Sardarji, 'we must try a different way, there has to be another way, perhaps from the front of the station.'

Gripping Atma Singh's shoulder, he leads him back, one slow step at a time, back to the barred gate – so much easier when they do not need to push in the direction of the crowd. Even so, the two Sikh men almost fall out of the railway station compound, into the dark alley where Burhan-e-din left them only minutes before.

Sardarji leads now, and Atma Singh follows.

Shapes form from darkness in the alley. Amongst clusters of desperate people Sardarji can identify piles of discarded bicycles, carts, tongas, wheelbarrows, bedding rolls, suitcases.

Hope, dreams.

All the belongings that refugees cannot take onto trains.

Thieves slink from the shadows, clutching loot rummaged from open suitcases and unrolled bedding rolls.

The front entrance of the station must be choked with people too. Hurriedly, Sardarji leads Atma Singh down the alley, staying along the station's compound wall, in the direction of lamplight. His spine tingles; a knot clenches at its base.

Further down, the surprised eyes of oxen and bullocks freed from their traces.

Odour of dung.

An abandoned mare neighs, rears, catching a wave of hot fear from the despairing cries of the people on the platform over the wall.

A djinn watches, cloaking the two men as they move.

Another small barred gate, marked No Thoroughfare. The stationmaster's and other higher-ups' private entrance; Sardarji discerns an army jeep parked before the veranda of a small red-brick building, a Sikh sepoy on guard beside it.

A crack of light at the stationmaster's office, as if someone just entered.

'*Ohai!*' Sardarji taps on the gate with his walking stick. 'Open here!' in a voice of command.

The sepoy leaps from the jeep, his hand going to the pistol at his belt. The stationmaster's door opens at the same moment, and a tall Sikh man stands silhouetted in the doorway, the set of his shoulder straps proclaiming years of training.

Sardarji raises his voice and says in his best Oxonian accent – 'Irrigation Department officer, here. I wish to see the stationmaster *immediately*.'

The Sikh man silhouetted in the doorway calls 'Irrigation Department?'

'Yes, Irrigation Department. I say, open this gate immediately.'

The Sikh nods to the sepoy to open the gate. He jogs down the veranda steps and Sardarji can see he is wearing the uniform of a Punjab regiment subedar, a non-commissioned officer.

Still, an army man, and a Sikh. Sardarji feels the knot at the base of his spine unclench a little.

'Irrigation Department?' the subedar repeats. 'Do you know where is Sardar – ' and the subedar says Sardarji's name.

'This *is* Sardarji,' says Atma Singh, as if every man in India ought to know.

Sardarji touches Atma Singh's arm, restraining the old man's loyal affection.

'Sir, every-*wier* we have been looking for you – Major Jeevan Singh ordered us to take you to the station, but we were very much *de*-layed by the crowds. Then we made inquiries at the Secretariat . . .'

'Yes, yes, I understand,' Sardarji interrupts. 'Now, can you take us to that train?'

'Yes, sir! Imme-jately, sir!'

The subedar swings himself into the passenger seat as Sardarji and Atma Singh climb in the back. The sepoy drives through a larger gate marked No Thoroughfare, and instantly, Sardarji can feel the press and din of the refugees on the platform, scent their panic.

Back to the train, the train covered, like a long beehive, with refugees. This time, however, Sardarji and Atma Singh are safe in an army jeep bristling with rifles.

More and more refugees, shouting, 'Come, na! Come!' Men pull their wives and children behind them hand in hand.

'Go!' They push their young boys up carriage ladders to

cling precariously on the roof for the night-to-noon journey.

'Pull!' Sacks, bundles and bedding rolls move from hand to hand, through open windows. Men and women press shoulder to shoulder, almost cheek to cheek in the aisles of the train. Children of all ages scream for their parents.

The jeep beeps, ploughs away people, inches slowly, so slowly, across the platform, toward a brown carriage.

The subedar shouts over his shoulder, 'If this is a miltry special, there should be security guards, no? Very lax, the Baluch Regiment is getting.' He struggles halfway out of the jeep and fires his rifle into the air.

The army jeep ploughs a path through a few more people, then brakes before the terrified kohl-rimmed eyes of a Hindu toddler urinating on the platform.

'No security guards, that's why so many are blocking the carriage door.'

The subedar struggles halfway out of the jeep again, fires his rifle once more into the air.

Screams rend the night, but this time frightened refugees have nowhere to move. Young boys hang under carriages, dangerously close to the rails. Children perch on the couplings between the carriages.

Curses puff the subedar's rolled black beard and he sits back down in the jeep.

They have come as close to a carriage door as the wriggling mass of humanity will allow; the sepoy turns apologetically, 'Sir, this-much-only close I can get.'

The subedar descends from the jeep and holds his rifle across his khaki-clad chest, making space for Sardarji and Atma Singh to jump to the platform.

'Shukriya, bhai!' Sardarji thanks the subedar over his shoulder, calling him brother.

The sepoy switches the engine of the jeep off, saving petrol, for the jeep cannot reverse until the refugees have thinned on the platform.

The train whistles, giving warning – it is leaving.

'Atma Singh!' Sardarji yells. 'Hurry! We *must* get on the train now!' The door is only a few feet away, but there are so many people crowding between them and its mouth.

He looks up at the carriage windows – can he climb in?

Atma Singh begins using the bedding roll like a battering ram to move faster toward the door. Sardarji glances at the carriage, sees the wheels inching forward, slowly but surely.

Comes a yell, now, from one of the Gandhi-capped men crowded among the turbans in the window of the carriage. 'Sardarji!'

And then someone calls him by name.

Sardarji squints up. The voice is familiar, but the inky dark and the horde of people at his back jostle his vision. An elbow presses against his ribs, someone's breath is burning the back of his neck at the base of his turban. Glancing down, he finds the toe of his shoe is an inch from the edge of the platform. His body tenses, without need of instruction from his mind – now it tries to resist the pressing crowd, instead of pushing in the same direction.

'Sardarji!'

And again someone calls him by name.

Must be a qualified man.

The bedding roll swivels upon Atma Singh's turban as he, too, turns in search of the voice.

Now Sardarji sees two bulging eyes staring down from the carriage window, two bulging eyes above a starched, too-tight Nehru collar. It is the advocate, Meher Chander, for whom he once put in a good word.

'Give me your hand!' the advocate yells.

And a second after Sardarji drops his walking stick, he feels Meher Chander's pudgy fingers close about his wrists. The advocate's tug almost wrenches Sardarji's arms from their sockets. Then other strong hands are at his armpits. Air bursts from Sardarji's lungs as the rim of the carriage window catches him squarely in the stomach. He kicks, instinctively feeling for a toehold. His shoes scrape the side of the carriage, almost leave his feet. Then several strong hands pull his shoulders, and in another second, his turban is among those crowded in the train.

Immediately, he turns to look behind him –

'Atma Singh!' It is Meher Chander who shouts, picking up Atma Singh's name from Sardarji's earlier shout, for Sardarji has no breath left to speak.

Now Sardarji finds a foothold in the sweating mass of men at the window, and with Meher Chander holding him steady, leans from the carriage, reaching for Atma Singh's sinewy old arms.

But Atma Singh, putting loyalty before himself, thrusts the bedding roll up at the window before him.

The bedding roll, its maps and pistol secure within, passes through the turbaned men till it thumps to the floor of the train.

The train clangs and puffs harder. In desperation, Sardarji leans far out of the window – if the old man cannot come, Sardarji will rejoin him on the platform.

Again Sardarji reaches for the old man's hands, breath sobbing within him.

Vaheguru, help us!

Rough hands clasp his wrists.

Atma Singh's rough hands.

Atma Singh's wrists are in Sardarji's grasp; Sardarji grips tight as he can.

He feels the crowd, now, pulling Atma Singh from him. Other hands below claw at the sleeves of his suit. A jerk, and then a vibration begins beneath Sardarji's feet; the carriage is moving.

As the carriage begins to roll, falcon eyes promise the old man silently, that Sardarji is responsible for the frail bones in that body, that he will save his servant.

Will not let go!

Does not let go.

With help from strong arms and hands of Hindus and Sikhs behind him, Sardarji pulls Atma Singh through the window, and so pressed are they in the carriage that the old man's turban passes above all the other turbans till a space can be found for his feet on the floor.

By now every man, woman and child left on the platform can see that the train has begun to move.

Screams rend the air as Hindu and Sikh men, women and children on the platform realize the train can hold no more. A slanting forest of upraised arms rises piteously above turbans and Gandhi caps. Babies' and little children's bewildered brown faces appear at the open windows − women holding children up to the passengers from below. Tears stream down mothers' faces, beseeching a kind soul to take a precious child, save the little bodies wrapped in their mothers' sorrow.

But carriage wheels begin a thrum on the tracks; the train picks up speed.

Sardarji's throat fills, his breath comes even more ragged and thin. Muscles in his shoulders, his ribs, wrists, biceps all burn and scream a temporary pain. The station, then Lahore blur as his eyes cloud and star with unmanly tears.

Let's see what India brings − let's see if India will be grateful for our sacrifice.

The rolling orange of villages burning on the outskirts of Lahore is still imprinted on Roop's eyes; she cannot tell if the itching sweat that soaks her kameez began from the horror of those villages or from the burning sun that stalks the Packard's metal frame since it first brought dawn to the cloudless sky; Vayu has forgotten Punjab so far this year, forgotten to bring rain.

Dust clouds hang above the refugee columns, dust grits in Roop's teeth, fills each nostril, settles in her lungs.

The Packard's inching crawl is forced to a full stop where a side dirt path slopes upward to join the road; a pair of bullocks pull in front of it, in haste to add another Hindu family to the milling crowd on the Grand Trunk.

Narain Singh curses beneath his breath, jerks the stick shift to neutral.

Djinn wraiths rise, hissing, angry, ringing the chrome goddess of speed on the bonnet.

'No!' yells Narain Singh, but Dehna Singh, eager to help, has already leapt out and raised the black bonnet of the motor car. Before Narain Singh can stop him, Dehna Singh has unscrewed something in the engine.

A yelp, and Dehna Singh leaps aside.

A great angry djinn whooshes into the fiery air and is gone. The sound of the engine dies.

Dehna Singh is doubled over where the dirt road meets the Grand Trunk, teeth clenched, a scalded hand held to his solar chakra.

Beside Roop, sugar canes rise so high from the field, they are almost level with the Grand Trunk Road. Opposite, chinar trees crowd close to survey the forlorn opposing parades.

Jorimon snores a little through it all, even as Aman twists, wide-eyed, in her arms.

Roop cranes her neck to watch the two turbaned men confer behind the car.

'What is it, Mama?' asks Pavan.

'I don't know,' she says.

Dehna Singh wraps rags about both his hands as Narain Singh returns to the Packard, steering one-handed as he strains against the doorjamb. Dehna Singh's wrapped hands push against the scorching metal of the bulging dickey from behind, and between them, the two men wheel the motor car forward past the side road, then back, till its long black nose is clear of the Grand Trunk Road. The two men push again – '*Haisa!*' – and the big black motor car lumbers down the slope, coming to a stop at the base of the incline on the dirt path with its nose forty yards from the Grand Trunk Road.

Narain Singh pokes his turban back into the car, 'Choti-Sardarniji, this way Muslims will not know if we are driving to Lahore or away from it.'

But if Muslims do not know, neither will marauding bands of Hindus and Sikhs.

'We must get water,' Narain Singh says. 'The car will not move without it.' He edges his turban carefully out of the window.

Now Roop watches through the windshield as the two men walk into the middle of the cavalcade shuffling past the inter-section of the dirt path with the Trunk Road, in the direction away from Lahore.

There they simply hold the traces of the first bullock cart that happens to be passing.

The cart creaks to a halt, marigold-garlanded bullocks chewing placidly.

'*Ohai, bhai!*'

From the Packard, Roop sees the farmer's whip flick at the bullocks. But the two Sikh men have them by their curly horns. The farmer's eyes shine white in his dark face. His palms come together with an expression of abject pleading. She counts fourteen men and women – they must be Hindu, for they are moving away from Lahore – on haunches or knees perched on and among their belongings behind him in the cart. Two old women, veiled, three young women, arms weighed down with all the gold their families must have saved for their marriages. A bloody rag presses against a man's slashed cheek. A bullet wound gouges the arm of another clinging to the side.

They should not be asked to do more.

Narain Singh is folding his hands before the farmer: please take one of us to the nearest well or village or petrol station.

The farmer doesn't want to say yes, he doesn't want to say no.

Silence.

More humble pleading from Narain Singh. He must be mentioning three children, two women, duty, responsibility, Ram, Vaheguru.

Silence.

The motor car is skin-searing hot, as if all the plain cakes Atma Singh ever made were baking at once. Roop opens the door a crack, fans herself with a hand-pukkhi.

'Tell him to say yes, Mama,' says Pavan.

The farmer gestures reluctantly. Dehna Singh unwraps one oily rag, keeping the one on his blistered hand, and throws his cricket bat into the cart. He finds his footing precariously, on the back of the cart. Roop grips Timcu's belt tight as the boy leans out of the car, crying, 'I want to go with him!'

The bullocks strain forward. In a moment, Dehna Singh is gone.

Narain Singh runs back to Roop, 'Fikr na karo, Sardarniji.'

Don't worry?

How can she not worry?

'He will bring water from the closest well.'

Whose well? Will he find a Muslim well or a Hindu well?

More bullock carts, ekkas, buggies and bicycles move past Roop and her children. So many people in the world and they are all on the Grand Trunk Road, Hindus and Sikhs in one lane, Muslims in the other, going their opposite ways.

Three hours pass – a quarter of a day in English time, but only one peher of eight, by Indian fractions.

If they were back in Lahore and if this were a normal day, she might walk in Lawrence Gardens with Sardarji in the evening, walk in those gardens scented with night queen flowers, where she, in a parrot-green salwar-kameez, once balanced on the narrow divide between two reflecting pools. And if this were a normal day, Sardarji would walk under the same Arjan tree where she made her bachan to her Papaji to listen as if she had two ears, and continue teaching her about fractions and factors. The Imperial system of measurement is elegant, he instructed, because it is based on five factors – one, two, three, four, six – the way long-haired Singhs are based on the five beloved baptized Sikhs; twelve has more factors than many numbers have . . .

'Other factors,' Sardarji's worried voice said, recently, 'very important other factors, and unfortunately, there is no scientific basis for evaluating other factors.'

One, two and three are prime factors, he said. They cannot be divided any further, except by themselves, and by one.

Roop finds this difficult to understand, but somehow vital, now.

'There is strength in numbers,' Sardarji had said, walking ahead of her in Lawrence Gardens.

But Roop, waiting now in the car, can find no strength in numbers, even when she counts all the way from one to one hundred.

Thinking is impossible; the sun burns into her brain.

Narain Singh says there is no question of rolling up the windows in the sweltering heat but says to keep the doors closed and locked in case of Muslim hooligans. Jorimon draws her sari palloo forward; Roop cannot see her face to read what she may be thinking of his warning.

Timcu pulls Pavan's ribbons open. Roop ties them up again, one by each ear. She assigns them to searching the procession of Muslim refugees shuffling towards Lahore, search for a tall Sikh man.

How long can a Sikh walk towards Lahore in broad daylight?
How will that poor man return?

Skin settling on her bones. She forgets to move.

I think I left the tap trickling in the bathroom in the Club Road
bungalow. Wasting water. Tip-tip, tip-tip, I hear it still,
telegraphing its message to anyone with an ear open to hear.

Jorimon opens the door so the children can stand or squat
beside the motor car, one at a time, to do their pi-pi. The smell
enters through the open window, mixes with the sweat-
smelling leather.

Aman's face is flushed red.

'I feel like fainting, Mama,' says Pavan.

'Shut up,' says Timcu. 'Look for Dehna Singh.'

The same air has passed through her children's lungs too
often. Roop wraps her hand in her chunni to open the sun-
scorched door a little.

'You hydrostatic!' says Pavan.

'You reservoir!'

'You slidy slide-rule,' says Pavan, dissolving into tears.

How long has it been since Dehna Singh left?

Four hours, maybe five. Surely more than that.

We have sent him to his death.

Timcu takes his shoes off, then his socks. Pavan moves to
do the same, but Roop catches her eye in the rear-view mirror
so she stops. Jorimon opens the picnic basket; a chicken sandwich for Timcu, a cucumber one for Pavan.

'Choti-Sardarni?'

Roop shakes her head – what if the children need food
later? Her mouth is dry from fear or thirst, but she does not
ask Jorimon for the thermos flask.

Jorimon throws her head back, tilts her waterbottle.

'Mama, where are we?' says Pavan.

'I don't know.' It's her habitual answer to Pavan and Timcu's
questions ever since Miss Barlow left. Once Roop only said, 'I
don't know' in answer to Sardarji – 'I don't know,' said prettily,
lashes fluttering. Sardarji liked it, so Roop has acquired the
phrase as habit, and says it all the time, especially when she
does know. And she thinks, heat-irritable, what good will it do
Pavan to know?

'Pat-a-cake, pat-a-cake, baker's man,' Pavan sings a rhyme Miss Barlow taught her.

Roop's heart sinks a little further – her daughter doesn't know 'Mera vaid Guru Gobinda.' If she were dying like Mama, neither Pavan or Timcu could sing her that shabad to comfort her; their names might as well be Joan and Edward.

I am alone.

The old ache in her stomach opens again, begins its gnawing. Atma Singh would advise her to have milk, but . . .

Still no sign of Dehna Singh.

Pavan loops a nallah string about her sweaty palms, and lowers her middle fingers till her hands are two kakars facing one another. 'See, Timcu?' her left hand jabs its way under the white string looped about her right. 'It's simple.' Threads crisscross the cat's cradle till the two deer-shapes draw closer and closer, and only if the two shrug off the restraining threads together will they be free.

Timcu kicks Pavan's shins.

Pavan cries.

Roop smacks Pavan for being in Timcu's way.

Roop coaxes Timcu to sit in the driver's seat. Timcu's sky-blue turban slips below the seat as he tries to reach the pedals.

'Vrrroooom!'

He tries to pinch little Aman, but Aman wriggles away.

Little Amanjit – Aman – is one in whom harmony will triumph. This time it was Roop who suggested his name to Sardarji, suggested it for its meaning, gently whispering at Sardarji's diamond-studded earlobe till he believed it to be his own idea.

But Aman doesn't behave true to his name; he slips away from everyone's hands like a small greased monkey. It takes spinach saag and a makki roti from the picnic basket, then Jorimon's rhythmic patting, to make him succumb to another deep sweaty sleep, underturban resting on her shoulder.

Still no Dehna Singh.

Narain Singh's turban bends over the .303 to clean it, just as Jeevan's used to.

Where is Jeevan, now?

Time spreads before them again.

Shadows lengthen, bringing a slight respite from the heat. Clouds swirl, tourmaline blue-grey. A sickle moon claws its way into the sky above the plodding misery on the Grand Trunk Road. The cavalcade thins as people stop to fuel their bodies, tend to the old, the sick. Across the street a woman walking behind a cart going towards Lahore doubles over her distended belly. In a few minutes, Roop loses sight of her, pictures her squatting in the forest. She strains to hear that first cry so like the ones that came from her own children. Thinks of that poor woman, cleaning herself down-there, with leaves. Alone, with no mother or sister to help her. Something within her urges: open the door, go to the woman's help.

But at what cost, what cost?

Are there bands of Muslims waiting to pounce from that forest? Are there Muslims in the sugar cane field beside the car, waiting for dark?

We are all, all of us, alone with our kismats.

Still no Dehna Singh, no water.

The thermos flask is running low.

Jorimon wets a corner of her sari palloo from her water-bottle and wipes the children's flushed faces.

'Stay in the car, Timcuji,' says Narain Singh to Roop's little son in his sky-blue turban. Not one hair in Narain Singh's rolled beard trembles. He slaps away another mosquito that alights on Timcu's arm.

But now night is falling, falling. Night, when anything can happen. People on the Grand Trunk Road are stopping to rest. A few bonfires flicker from nearby ditches. A lantern swings from the branch of a kikar tree, turning men's sombre faces to burnished bronze.

Stars glow, multiplying the twenty red eyes of Ravan, Mangal sparkling brightest in their midst. Crickets sharpen dry wings, repeating the only two notes they know. Vayu holds his fevery breath. Across the Grand Trunk Road, the forest is ajibber with the fear of every monkey in Hanuman's army; though Hanuman may win, the monkeys know their slaughter is necessary for the battle to wage its course.

From ten directions, fear burrows its way into the stranded car.

Then, as if a thunderclap sounded in her ear, come the war cries '*Allah ho Akbar! Allah ho Akbar!*'

Roop stirs.

Fear rushes in her veins; her heart is pounding.

Dhak, dhak.

Yells, screams, in Punjabi, in Hindi: '*Chupo!* Take cover, Muslim hooligans are coming!'

It is a small section of sepoys whose bodies forgot all Koranic admonitions as they drank the contents of a bhang still in the last Sikh village they raided. Finding themselves free of officers, Indian or English, they felt themselves descending to disorder, a state more fear-filled than hell. And to stop that fear, though not their descent, they have named themselves teachers of lessons to unbelievers, the only pure followers of an only God. In a few short miles on the Grand Trunk Road their bodies have already learned that any man who kills, maims, hurts or rapes one of another religion finds his second and his third become easier, and easier. Led by a sometime-subedar, a non-commissioned officer, their tarp-covered lorry crunched gravel, moving twice as fast as the two refugee columns, angling along the verge of the Grand Trunk Road. But it stopped occasionally for these erstwhile soldiers to amuse themselves, dragging struggling Sikh and Hindu women into the lorry, shooting or maiming Sikhs and Hindus plodding to India, or at whim, converting men to Islam, simply, by tearing off salwars or dhotis, and slashing off foreskins.

A strident voice uncoils itself from the shadows, shrill, defiant, unbowed – and it says to Roop clearly: *Don't die – Sardarji still needs you. Don't die like this, like a dog smeared on a dirt road. If you die, let death have meaning, let it be for a reason.*

Roop taps Narain Singh's shoulder with her hand-pukkhi. He turns till he can see her from the corner of his eye.

Live, survive!

'Narain Singh,' orders Roop. 'Take the gun, and the children. We're going to hide behind the sugar cane.'

Pavan turns to look at Roop as if she has never seen her mother before.

Narain Singh gives her a highly affronted look. 'I will fight and die to protect you and the children, Choti-Sardarniji, I have my kirpan, I have a gun.'

'Don't talk to me about fighting or dying – we're going to *live*. You must save Sardarji's children from any harm.'

Narain Singh looks from her to the children. Then with no further protest, he takes the gun from beneath the seat and takes Timcu by the hand.

It's easy to give orders when people are trained to obey.

'Stay close together, han? Timcu, take your sister and brother. *Now!*'

No coaxing in her voice. Timcu looks surprised.

They scramble out of the car. Narain Singh helps the children down the dark roadside to the field. Before Roop, one small blue turban, one small blue underturban and a pair of doubled-plaits tied with ribbons disappear behind a tawny clump of sugar cane.

Roop and Jorimon follow until Roop stops at the edge of the dark field.

'*Hai, Vaheguru!* I left the Guru Granth Sahib in the car!'

Muslims might desecrate the Guru. They will not respect the book, they believe it to be beneath their Koran.

Should she go back?

'*Allah ho Akbar!*' The headlights of the lorry are slowing.

Surely it will not turn down the dirt path, with so many refugees still crowded on the Grand Trunk Road. Surely it will not see the big motor car at the bottom of the slope.

Yes?

No?

Supporting the Guru Granth Sahib, on the seat beneath the silk-wrapped book, lies Mama's red shawl.

With that thought, Roop is clambering back to the dirt road, back to the black shape of the Packard.

She pulls the door open, climbs in.

Just as she reaches for the Guru and Mama's shawl, twin headlamps shine from the tarp-covered lorry, filling the Packard's windshield, stabbing her eyes.

She lifts a hand to confirm her chunni covers her head. *It is time to die.* She cannot run back to the children now. Narain Singh cannot shoot any man who misbehaves with her without leading them to the children. She is alone with her kismat, and an open door.

No, not alone.

For behind Roop, a voice erupts out of silence.

It rises in a suppressed shriek. '*Allah ho Akbar! Allah ho Akbar!*'

It is Jorimon, who has followed Roop instead of staying with the children.

Jorimon, who now lays claim to the men's protection, as a Muslim woman.

A uniformed man descends from the cab, walks in the way of the light streaming from the lorry's headlamps.

Sugar cane rustles.

Roop reaches quickly, quietly, to the door handle of the Packard; she will try to melt into the dark shadows of its back seat. But instead of the handle, her fingers meet the worn cotton of Jorimon's sari, joining her in the Packard.

Dark contours of men descend from the back of the lorry, they saunter and lurch towards the Packard, laughing as if a cricket match were in the offing.

Jorimon will tell these Muslim men Roop is a Sikh. Why should she not? What has Jorimon in common with Roop, except that they are both women? And as soon as Jorimon tells them Roop is a Sikh, they will look for Sikh men and children to kill.

Now I die, die young as Mama, without ever having seen Delhi. Or I am about to be raped, mutilated like the woman whose breasts were cut off. Or my hair will be cut and I will be made to recite the Kalima and then . . .

But Jorimon is silent again. Sitting beside Roop, she reaches across the Guru Granth Sahib for Roop's hand, grips it tight, reassuring.

If Jorimon says no more, the men will believe the car belongs to some high-up Muslim. Then all Roop must do is let silence do the lying for her. No longer are they mistress and maidservant – for this moment, they are just two women, equally vulnerable.

She must trust Jorimon, unlucky Muslim orphan. But two women alone in public; it seems too strange.

Think of a story, keep it somewhat true, somewhat false, so they'll believe it.

Someone extinguishes the lorry's headlamps. The subedar lights a torch, elbows through gawking leering men admiring the car, speculating on the bodies of the women within. Roop rolls up her window as fast as she can, but before Jorimon can do the same –

'Salaam Aleikum.' Elbows rest on the window close to Jorimon.

'Walaikum salaam.' Jorimon quavers her response, shrinking away.

'We are on our way to meet my husband in Lahore,' Roop speaks Urdu as Satya did with Muslim servants, holding her chunni over her mouth, but with a voice imitating Satya's, surprising herself with its firmness. 'My driver has just gone to get water from a well he knows nearby – he will return in a minute.'

'I don't think you are Muslims. You seem Hindu,' he snarls. 'Faces open to any man's gaze!'

Jorimon answers, 'Her mia does not ask it.'

'Shameless women. Completely shameless.'

There is a long moment of silence.

Roop tries to look as haughty and commanding as Satya.

Then a hairy arm reaches through the window and opens the door.

Before Roop can stop him Jorimon's sari-clad body jerks to the dirt beside the car with a gasping cry. In a second, it disappears under a charged mass of men, grunting like animals in the dark.

'Teach her a lesson,' sniggers the subedar.

Roop finds herself out of the car, too, before she knows it. She finds herself pounding with clenched fists at the men, shouting into men's ears in the hot dark night, 'Jurrat kahan se aiee? How dare you?' They shrug her off. They do not see her.

Roop takes a huge gulp of hot night air.

'How do you dare?! What is your name? My brother is a very senior major. I will have you court-martialled for this.'

A spider hand squeezes her breast in the dark – she twists its fingers, balls her fist and boxes as hard as she can into the shadow man behind that hand, Jeevan's early training coming back as if he were saying again, 'Don't let me see your girly wrists!'

Knuckles sting against a beardless chin; the hand drops from her breast. Still she punches and pummels at the mass of panting men, a shrieking, spitting ball of nails and teeth.

'Where is your officer? *Ohai*, tumhara naam kya hai? What is *your* name? And *yours*? Baap ka naam? What is your father's name? And *yours*?!'

Fury rising like bile within her, she scratches at their shoulders and backs, she pulls at their hands, tries to pull them away from Jorimon. Still she has to stand behind and just to left or right so that each man sees her from the corner of his eye, sees her and knows this is no servant who speaks. Anger, pure heat of anger like molten steel within her. Does this anger violate rule number three? – 'Never feel angry, never never never. No matter what happens, never feel angry. You might be hurt, but never ever feel angry.'

No. This is the kind of anger Vaheguru knows is as pure as a steel kirpan; this anger is for another, not for herself.

If men treat a woman they know to be of their quom in this cruel way, can any woman be safe?

But though she demands his name in a rasping scream, demands it from each man, not one wishes to be known for the deed he intends today.

But slowly, agonizingly slowly, the demand for their names is startling them, taking effect, her daring to ask that question is bringing them back from bedlam, piercing the anonymity granted by the quom.

Roop's screamed threats – 'My brother is a very senior major, I'll have you court-martialled' – penetrate the fog in the subedar's brain. He halts his men with slaps, shouts, curses, threats they understand, promises of better woman flesh elsewhere.

Jorimon lies in the dirt sobbing, dust turning to mud streaks from sweat pouring down her neck, sari palloo in tatters, her round Bengali face streaked with tears, one eye swelling shut.

'I'm letting you go this time.' The subedar wags a finger at

Jorimon. 'Be grateful. Next time you may not be so lucky.'

'*Be grateful – da lagda tera chacha! Ooloo da patha!*' Roop finds Papaji's old swear-words. How weak they are to express the fury that still knots her fists and has loosened her long black hair!

Always we should be grateful that it was not worse! How dare you tell her she should be grateful?

Roop rushes to Jorimon, puts her arms about her and raises her, wipes Jorimon's tears on her chunni. She remembers Papaji, when he went to the aid of the Sikh boy whose hair was cut in Gujarkhan so long ago. This is how he must have felt that day, like a Sikh man whose duty it is to fight in defence of the wronged – but truly as the Guru bade Sikhs to do, for *all* who are wronged, not only for Sikhs.

Jorimon leans on Roop and the men shuffle their feet and spit into the fields as she helps Jorimon into the Packard, locks the door. In another minute Jorimon might have been raped, and despite herself, despite all her anger, Roop's knees are ready to fold beneath her with thankfulness it did not happen.

Thank Vaheguru, yes, but not that subedar!

She climbs in after Jorimon, rolls the window up.

A man's weight leans against the Packard. The subedar, leaning in the front window, panting his bhang-scented breath in Roop's face. 'This driver of yours – he has not come back yet. You were telling lies?'

'He is close by. Just gone for water.'

'There are only Hindu wells close by.'

Roop can feel the question; this subedar wants confirmation that the prey he leaves believes in his Allah. He wants Roop to tell him she is Muslim, too. But Roop cannot say that, not in the presence of the Guru Granth Sahib lying undiscovered on the back seat between Jorimon and herself. But to say she is Sikh is to ask for death, and if Narain Singh shoots his Enfield in her defence, death for her sons as well, and maybe worse for Pavan – in these few minutes of recent terror, Roop has learned, like simmer coming to boil, that there are so many things men can do to girls and women that are so much worse than death.

Roop is not yet ready to die.

Comes a thought from the fringe of awareness as if some other woman spoke from the wings, shaped the thoughts that speed across the theatre of Roop's mind:

Surrender is not the only option.

And then another.

Some men are not entitled to the truth.

And so Roop extends her unclean arm, her bared left arm, from the window till her upturned inner wrist falls in the spotlight from the torch. Her tattooed name, in Persian script, floats on the bronze of her skin.

'See?' Her almond eyes say, praying silence will save her; praying he will not ask to see her right wrist, circled as it is by her steel kara marking her as a Sikh; praying he will not take scissors and threaten her long dark hair, for death is preferable than to return to face Sardarji with even a single shorn strand.

The unaccustomed bhang has clouded the subedar's brain.

'Achcha,' he mumbles, satisfied.

Vaheguru will understand.

'Achcha*ji*,' she corrects the subedar, in guileful imitation of Satya's haughty tone.

'Achchaji,' says the subedar, her expectation of respect bringing respect in return. 'She's also one of ours,' he says to the men lurking in the shadows behind him. '*Hut!* Get away. A bad Muslim is still better than an unbeliever – she is under my protection.'

'*Ohai*, bhai,' says Roop, mustering her scanty Urdu, calling him brother as he turns to walk away. 'You have water?'

'Hanji,' he says, gesturing at the lorry. 'Lots of water.'

Muslim water.

Take it.

'Bring me a canister,' Roop orders.

He strides back to the window of the motor car and hiccups in her face. 'Nahin! Not for nothing. What do you have?'

Roop is ready, Satya's gold Omega watch out of its pouch, gleaming in her outstretched hand.

The subedar takes it in a callused palm. Then his head shakes. 'Too little.'

'It is not little,' she protests desperately. 'Take it, for the water.'

'Such a small watch,' he says.

Roop's fingers reach through the slit in the Packard's back seat and grasp tight, bringing one thin twenty-four-carat gold bangle into the torchlight.

'What is your name?' she asks, sweet as a koel. 'I will tell my brother how well your men protected us.'

Her question hangs between them till the threat of it penetrates the subedar's alcohol haze.

He takes the gold bangle from Roop, examines it, then grips it tight, again and again in his fist, till he has replaced its roundness with sharp angles. Then he turns abruptly, and walks back to the lorry. 'Pani!' he shouts to a shadow in the van.

Returning, he heaves a full canister to the ground.

'Shukriya, bhai,' says Roop, thanking him, calling him brother just as Satya would have.

'Khuda hafiz,' he says.

'Khuda hafiz,' she replies, and he turns to leave.

Grumbling men climb the back of the lorry. The odour of thwarted desire stains the dark. The lorry starts, reverses up the incline. Its headlamps swing slowly, lighting the sugar cane in a wide white arc. It turns and lumbers back onto the Grand Trunk Road.

They will find some other women, who cannot fight back or threaten, on whom to wreak their violence.

Narain Singh leads the children out of the sugar cane, back to the motor car. A little later, a little truth traded for a little water, the Packard fires to life, moves up the dirt path to turn onto the Grand Trunk Road. There it rejoins the stream of bullock carts and the footsore, weary refugee column.

When dawn vapour hovers over the sugar cane field again, the Packard is further on its way to the capital.

Delhi.

Indifferent Delhi.

A grey carpet undulates over a field, its whorls and ambi patterns shifting as if the hot still air were a full gusting wind.

Roop's almond eyes fix upon it, mesmerized. She waits for the motor car to inch closer. People trudging beside the Packard avert their eyes.

What strange food grows here?

She gags, her chunni lifts involuntarily to her nose. Timcu and Pavan stop their bickering to look. Even Aman wrinkles his nose in Jorimon's lap.

A metallic stench fills the car.

Vultures, feeding on the bodies from a Hindu or a Sikh village! Hai Ram!

Bodies, purple-black and bloated, show in patches where the satiated vultures cannot eat any more. Clawed feet tear and rip, featherless heads delve into flesh, strong beaks peck away eyes.

The Packard moves past and away.

Sweltering and balking as they are driven south, a herd of black-faced sheep and long-haired goats trot before a farmer's raised bamboo stick. Another farmer's Gandhi cap bobs over a ditch, as he tries frantically to extricate his oxen from the traces of an overturned cart. The poor man's belongings lie strewn across the Grand Trunk Road, detouring the procession of humanity. Bedding, bulging gunny sacks, brass pots, copper pans, a dancing Shiva.

Is this India we fought for God-chosen or Godforsaken? She is like a woman raped so many times she has lost all count of the trespassers across her body. Who will rescue and pyre the bodies of my quom? What use now to be Hindu, Sikh, Muslim or Christian, what use the quom, the biradari, the caste, the compartments that order our lives? What do they do for us now in time of chaos when person meets person and the question between us is only this: Can you feel as I feel? Do you agree to let me live if I let you live? And will you keep that promise even when no one watches, under cover of sandstorms, when the veil is snatched away, will you be kind?

Sun turns tar soft beneath bare feet, Peshawari sandals and jutis. A man clad only in a dhoti runs away in the wheat fields beyond the ditch, shoulders bowed beneath a looted gunny sack.

Tall stalks of wheat wave golden farewells; the men who sowed these seeds will not eat this harvest.

The wheels of the overturned cart continue their incorrigible turning.

Delhi, August 16, 1947

Two o'clock in the morning, still and dark. The black Packard draws up before the marble entrance to the Imperial Hotel, the load of luggage roped to its roof caked inches thick with dust. Although Narain Singh had driven Sardarji from Lahore to Delhi many times, he had to stop several times to ask for directions. With so many refugees on the streets it was difficult to find someone who knew the way.

Celebrities celebrating Independence are departing as Pavan and Timcu leap out and run up the stairs, into the red-carpeted lobby.

Then Aman slips away from Jorimon again, running to catch up. Jorimon hitches up her torn sari to chase him.

Roop hesitates, dazzled by bright silken saris, dinner jackets, hat stands festooned with hats, long mirrors and chandeliers; she has never before walked into a hotel alone for fear of what-people-might-say. Then she draws herself up, adjusts her chunni, smooths her crumpled kameez down over her thighs and follows her children.

Inside, the hotel clerk listens to her request, but then shakes his karakuli cap sorrowfully. She is too late, it is two in the morning and Mr Farquharson must be asleep. The clerk does not wish to be the one to disturb him.

It seems, Independence being only two days old, the hotel clerk does not have great confidence it will last.

'Madam-ji, what if Mr Farquharson doesn't leave after all, and he remembers that I woke him up at two in the morning? I have stayed here in Delhi while almost all the Muslims in this hotel left, because my pozeeshun is all I have. Please not to ask me this, this pozeeshun is not mine alone, it belongs to my son when I die.'

'But . . .' Roop's almond eyes plead.

But the clerk is obdurate; he is too small a man to wake Mr Farquharson.

'Madam-ji, Mr Jinnah and his Pakistan tried to deprive me of the satisfaction of passing this pozeeshun to my son, and *even* Mr Jinnah failed. Nahinji, I cannot call Mr Farquharson.'

Roop looks at the children, dusty, hungry and tired. At Jorimon, whose grazed elbows, torn sari and unravelling hair emphasize her lingering panic. And this hotel clerk? Small men have been given great power in the midst of chaos. Where else can Roop go, in a strange city, with three children?

'I want to see the manager,' says Roop, in an imperious voice quite unlike her own.

'The manager too, is asleep.'

'I said, call the manager!' Roop surprises herself with her vehemence.

And soon, apprised by the hotel manager, Mr Farquharson comes striding down the mirror-lined corridor in his silk dressing gown and slippers.

'Well, bless my soul,' sloshes Mr Farquharson. 'Yes, I did get a trunk call from Sardarji, but upon my word, I had almost forgotten.'

'Sardarji said I should bring Timcu to you.' And Roop pushes Timcu forward to shake hands with his namesake.

'My word, he *has* grown quite a lot, hasn't he?' Mr Timothy Farquharson chucks Timcu under his chin. 'Come along then, young man.'

He leads Roop and the children down the corridor to his suite, his bare white legs unexpectedly skinny and hairy beneath his dressing gown.

'These rooms,' says Mr Farquharson, unlocking the door to his apartments, 'were once converted for use by General Vinegar Joe.' Roop does not know he means the American General Stillwell. 'They are certainly better than any tent I slept in during the Burma campaign. You can take the smaller room, here. The General's orderly used that. I'll have the cooks wakened, you must have food.'

'I must go to the railway station,' Roop says, upon washing the dust from her face. 'Sardarji told me to meet him there.'

'Oh, not just yet, my dear. No place for a lady. Quite filthy, as a matter of fact.'

'Sardarji said,' Roop says, hint of steel in her voice.

So Roop leaves her children in Jorimon's care and goes back through the corridor, past the rule-bound hotel clerk, down the red-carpeted marble stairs to Narain Singh and the now unloaded motor car.

'To the railway station,' she says to Narain Singh. 'I will meet Sardarji there.'

40. Delhi, August 20, 1947

It is past sunrise but the unfinished moon tarries, astounded eye glued to the milling mass of human flotsam littering the railway platform. Some wait for trains to leave, some for trains to arrive. Some sit on their belongings, some are empty-handed, their eyes caves carved into skin. Dark bags of bones lying on spit-stained ground, many dead, and those alive breathing in heat and flies.

And germs. Sardarji would shudder.

Roop steps, unhindered and unrebuked, between people sitting, standing, sleeping on the platform at Delhi's railway station. She drops her chunni to her shoulders so she can hear better – no one taps her on the arm so she can remedy her immodesty. For the first time since her marriage she has no maidservant with her, just Narain Singh, left outside the station, with the Packard.

From the mudflats of Dacca, from Victoria Memorial in Calcutta to the red sandstone ramparts of the Old Fort in Delhi, through refugee camps, whitewashed cantonments and police stations where tortured political seditionists can now be hailed as freedom fighters, tales reeking of death and horror ride Vayu's wings, and fly. They murmur through the leaves of apricot and cherry orchards on hillsides near sleepy hill stations, through villages where they cause women to jump en masse into wells to save the izzat of a quom, down the winding alleys of old bazaars, past camel serais where the hookah passes, to the Storytellers' Bazaar in Peshawar. The stories Vayu carries filter and grow, infecting the memories of one family after another – Sikh, Muslim or Hindu.

Sir Cyril Radcliffe's boundary line has cut Punjab in two as a child might tear a newspaper, all the maps, data and plans placed before Radcliffe's Indian commissioner at Lahore, including Sardarji's, having been treated as lumber. Ignoring the natural watershed between Lahore and Amritsar, ignoring Sikh pleas and arguments for all the land up to the Chenab, Sir Cyril Radcliffe has drawn his boundary line through Punjab in equidistant points between the Ravi and the Sutlej rivers.

Lahore has fallen into West Punjab – Pakistan.

And the Radcliffe line has done more than break railway connections between cities, or tear headworks from canals – it has severed ties, severed all pretensions to culture, informed everyone of the savagery of which neighbours are capable.

When all the Union Jacks were lowered; when the tricolour of the Indian Union or the sickle moon on green of Pakistan were raised in every city; when all the banquets were banqueted, the fireworks fired, arms presented, and the parades paraded; then, only then, Mahatma Gandhi, Jawaharlal Nehru, Mr Jinnah and Master Tara Singh took to the airwaves to plead for reason.

Reason!

Somewhere, Satya laughs with the shadow people.

In times when the very earth turns to hot coals beneath her feet, a woman can only gather her babies about her and flee.

The odour of urine and faeces is overpowering Roop, and she is grateful she hears only half the pain of these poor wretches, that though Bengali and Hindi and Urdu rise around her, she understands only the Punjabi and English words. And she is glad she knows only one iota of their poverty, for it is too much, too much, and the fear fire in her belly feeds upon their tears.

'Cogitate!' Sardarji would say.

She must find Sardarji, Papaji, Revati Bhua, Kusum, Gujri, Jeevan, Madani, Sardar Kushal Singh, Toshiji – someone.

Anyone of my family, anyone of my blood.

If she does not see people she has seen before, how is she to know if she is not dead and already in the next life? She must smell them, come close to them, touch them, skin to skin.

An old pain lies heavy, caught in the sieve of her stomach.

A familiar voice says, clearly, in Roop's mind, 'We are each alone, though a crowd of our quom might mill about us, little sister. Always each woman is alone.'

Roop looks around, mystified; reminds herself she has one bad ear.

But even with only one ear Roop hears of women abducted, mutilated, always by *them* – never by *us*. Men etch their anger upon woman-skin, swallow their pride dissolved in women's blood.

'Hindu chai!' comes the call from a tea stall. 'Muslim chai!' comes from the tea stall beside it.

The chai sellers have set up small clay stoves on the platform and kettles of water sing upon them. Water rolls to a boil, the Hindu chai seller pours a milky brown stream from one brass tumbler to the other for Roop, juggling it back and forth to cool. She repents before her lips even meet the rim of the glass of spiced chai – the price of a cup of tea!

The tea reminds her – Miss Barlow came to tea at the Imperial the evening after Roop arrived in Delhi. Riding her bicycle from the Ladies' Hostel on Queensway, she came to say farewell to the children, and inquire whether Mr Farquharson had news of her brother, Dr Barlow.

And then Miss Barlow stayed to tea with Mr Farquharson, simpering a little, till Farquharson confessed he dreads the damp cold of England as much as he hates heat-glazed India, dreads the mewling of his wife.

Since arriving in Delhi about a month earlier, Farquharson said he has spent each day with unvarying routine, in a white-painted wicker chair on the terrace garden, ordering chicken-in-a-basket, cognac and whisky-soda from the few bearers who yet remain.

'There isn't a ticketed berth to be had,' Miss Barlow sighed. 'Even a little baksheesh won't buy anything certain. It's out-rageously inefficient. You see there's just no one left to set the *tone*.' Steamers out of Bombay are full to bursting, taking Muslim refugees from Bombay to Karachi, the closest port in Pakistan, now titled the new nation's capital.

Miss Barlow poured the tea, nibbled sugar toast and gave not a glance in Roop's direction as she passed the rapidly melting vanilla ice cream.

'Oh,' said she, 'there were massacres, yes. On my train. But I was titivating myself in my coupé and I didn't even know the train had been stopped and people slaughtered till I got to Delhi.'

'Well, I sincerely hope this teaches them a lesson. Now perhaps they'll stop their tiresome complaining,' said Mr Farquharson, quite sure Roop is still unable to understand English, she speaks it so slowly and softly.

'Would you believe,' said Miss Barlow, 'the bearer brought some frightful concoction called soup à la Gandhi – well, of course, I told him to take it out of my sight and I just rolled up my windows and stayed put until Delhi.'

Dramatic pause.

'It was quite awful.'

Now Roop at the railway station, looking, seeking family, finds a strange comfort in Miss Barlow's story; there *are* some who are surviving the massacres on trains to Delhi.

'Delhi is so crowded now,' Miss Barlow continued, wiping the tips of her fingers with a serviette. 'Too many Hindus – all they want to do is pinch my bottom. And they really won't hurry to get out of the way of my bicycle any more. I just don't see the point they're trying to make.'

Yes, Delhi is crowded, crowded with refugees. All-India Radio says half a million Hindu and Sikh refugees have poured into India this week alone from Punjab and Bengal Provinces and that millions more will arrive each week. And every day thousands of Muslims leave, some from fear, some from hope. More than ten million people will need to leave their homes and fields and a full two million men, women and children will die. But Roop has learned along the way that numbers are just numbers and do not have strength enough to hold each refugee's sorrow or story.

'What will you do in England?' Roop asked Mr Farquharson.

'Do?' Mr Farquharson started. In India, Farquharson always had England as zero degrees east or west. A beacon. But in England, he would have only the embroidered memories of his boyhood in exotic faraway India.

'When you go back to England, I mean.'

'Yes, do tell,' said Miss Barlow.

'My wife said her brother may have a job for me, he said it'll be just the ticket. Door to door, though. Lots of travel.'

'A boxwalla job?' slipped from Roop.

Miss Barlow frowned as if Roop were still her pupil, and Farquharson's affronted look brought Roop's instant contrition.

'My dear ladies, that's the way vacuum cleaners are sold in England. Door to door. Just the thing for an engineer, my brother-in-law says.'

Mr Farquharson dropped his head, clasped his hands, swung them between his knees as if he protected the crown jewels. Then he looked up at Roop and Miss Barlow, spoke as if making a confession: though he had left his mark upon dams and inundation canals through India, no man in England was ready to step aside for his benefit.

'But Mrs Farquharson will be overjoyed to see you,' says Roop, comfortingly. 'I have always felt so sorry for her, all alone in England except when you return for home leave.'

'She *likes* being alone,' Mr Farquharson assures her.

Roop was mystified, and has pondered it a few times since Farquharson's assurance.

What kind of woman is really unafraid of being alone, living alone, prey that beckons to any man who might mis-behave in an instant? Mr Farquharson simply does not see what lies in his wife's heart, or perhaps his wife is like Satya, full of anger accumulated through many lives.

'My, it will be good to taste a decent Yorkshire pudding!' he said to Miss Barlow.

As Roop rose to take her leave and return to the railway station, Farquharson hiccuped, 'I can't help thinking, though, who will put flowers on Mum's grave in Simla?'

But the possibility of staying fills him with panic. It's out of the question. He sleeps as soundly as the children, quite certain of his rights, even in times like these – when Hindus, Sikhs and Muslims are all too busy fighting one another to blame any English man for their loathing of one another.

A train screeches like a djinn in the distance, and Muslim men adjust their furry karakuli caps and shout in Urdu, reaching for women in burqas or saris. Some veiled, some unveiled, the women grip the small soft hands of crying, bewildered children. The Muslim families bound for Pakistan gather bundles, bedding rolls and tachey cases, pull their meagre savings from their pockets in hope that someone is amenable to a bribe, and join the surge of bodies pressing to the very edge of the platform.

The train slows, then stops.

Muslims trying to leave Delhi pull back around the doors, waiting for Sikhs and Hindus from Punjab to alight from the carriages so that they may take their place.

Roop climbs upon someone's abandoned crate, trying to discern the first class carriage of the train – if Sardarji is on this one, she will see Atma Singh first, clearing a path through the crowd. If Sardarji is alive.

But now a deadly hiss sidles like a cobra through the crowd. *Another one!*

Each carriage of this train, like so many others before it, comes smeared with blood, windows smashed. The silence of the slaughtered rises, palpable and accusing.

Roop sinks to her haunches on the crate; shards of ice seem to course through her veins.

Those waiting for family turn away from the carriage. Blood-curdling screams fill the air as they turn to wreak vengeance on the Muslim refugees waiting to leave.

Newton's third law: for every action there is an equal and opposite reaction.

Karakuli caps are torn off Muslim men, women lose their children's hands, children lose their parents. A young girl is whisked away over a man's broad shoulders, kicking and crying.

Roop backs away. A hand covers her ear, and when the station wall is steady against her spine, she closes her eyes and sobs dry, heaving sobs, *but what can anyone do?*

Everyone has their own kismat.

Afterwards, when the stench overtakes the crying and moaning, Roop models her voice on Satya's to ask questions the way Satya would have asked them. 'Where did this train start from?' 'Where did it stop on its way?' with that peremptory edge that says she has a right to their answers because of her high birth.

What would Mama have thought of her now? If she were alive, she would not know how to guide Roop in this new world either.

Shall I make my own rules, without husband or custom as consequence?

If Sardarji is dead, what is she? A widow with three small children seeking shelter in the navel of a strange and foreign land.

Alone.

She feels small again, so small, and Nani's wound is open before her, suppurating, maggoty pink. Widow-wound that would not heal.

A woman with no husband, with no one of her blood – hai, what kismat!

Roop's heart throws itself against the basket of her ribs. Poverty is all round her, decrepit, angry, smelly, ready to drag her back, lower than anything she's ever experienced. Poverty the way the real poor know it, live it. The only thing between her and them, between her and women who have begun crowding refugee camps and ashrams since the March massacres in 'Pindi, is Sardarji, his power, his wealth.

She must feel no fear, she must think only of the present.

Everywhere on the platform, as far as she can see, men and women like herself are turning bodies over to see if they recognize a dead face, or questioning these half-dead forms. *Have you seen my husband? – Did you see my son? – Did you pass through my city, my village, my land? – Do you know if my home still stands? – Did you see who took my cow? – Did you see who killed my brother? — Are we related, you and I, distant cousin-brothers, perhaps from the same village?*

Delhi, August 21, 1947

Roop must surely have met every bloodied sorrowful train from Lahore since August 17th when the border came down and Lahore was declared part of Pakistan.

A social worker in a cotton sari approaches Roop, huddled in the ladies' waiting lounge, asks her story. 'Who is your husband, what was your city or village? What are you, Hindu or Muslim?'

She says, 'I am a Sikh.'

And maybe Roop is, now, finally, a Sikh. For it's only when a fish is pulled from water that it truly understands it is not fowl.

'You have any father, brother, uncle?' asks the social worker, writing on a clipboard as fast as she can.

'They will come.'

But the fear-hole in her stomach has returned to gnaw upon itself. What is she but the things she has heard from the mouths of others, the bits and pieces of other people's expectations collected, shaped and moulded to woman form?

Nothing more to lose.

Is there?

There are stories, versions upon versions of the same stories from before the border was declared, from after the border came down.

'They threw a dead cow into the temple, they raped my daughters before my eyes.'

'They threw a pig into our mosque.'

'I made martyrs of seventeen women and children in my family before their izzat could be taken.'

'I made martyrs of fifty.'

The tales fly – naked Sikh women were forced by Muslims to dance before mosques. Naked Muslim women were forced by Sikhs to dance in the compound of the Golden Temple in Amritsar. Perhaps Huma was among them, who knows?

Everywhere on this platform, women pull the remnants of rags about their breasts – Satya would say they have learned shame, shame of their own bodies, from men of all faiths who cannot trust each other.

So much shame, so little izzat for girls and women.

Roop's very bones feel old, so old.

She can bear it no more; blood simmers to boil in her veins.

If Satya were here, she would shout from the top platform till everyone might hear – every man, woman and child should, just once in this lifetime, see a woman's body without shame. See her as no man's possession, *see* her, and not from the corners of your eyes!

Roop draws herself to her full height, crosses her arms about her kameez. In a minute it is gone.

A touch to the cord of her salwar; it drops about her ankles.

She wants to free her breasts, let her brassiere-bunyaan float away.

People are stopping to look.

She wants to free her body of its panty, step from its bonds, leaving it right there on the platform.

She wants to walk through the hushing crowd wearing nothing but her mama's sapphire ring. She wants to scream, *See me, I am human, though I am only a woman. See me, I did what women are for. See me not as a vessel, a plaything, a fantasy, a maidservant, an ornament, but as Vaheguru made me.*

A sepoy runs to her side, takes off his khaki shirt and covers her almost naked body. Scoops up her clothes, leads her away gently. Back to the ladies' waiting lounge.

If a man does not lay claim to my body, the country will send someone to do so.

Vayu, riding the sand-laden loo wind, abrades away tears.

Another day.

Smell of death seeping into her pores.

The rawness, the numbness, the coldness inside.

Roop waits still, afraid to leave the station at all now, in case she misses Sardarji's train. Waits till her eyes burn from

seeking and her back is stiff and sore from bending over any
body dressed in European clothing.

What else to do?

Tired, so tired. She massages her jaw, that aches from
gritting her teeth.

Night, again.

Her head nods forward; she is falling, falling.

*Somewhere, a brow furrows, a breath is held, a heart hardens, a
sigh is expelled, a slap is heard, a fist clenches, a welt reddens, a
tongue salivates for the kill, a noose tightens, a knife rasps against
bone, a child cries alone, an ear listens. Then an eye finds more tears.*

In her corner against the wall of the ladies' waiting lounge,
Roop stirs, raises her knees to her elbows, tucks her chin low,
and stays that way until a rooster struts from a refugee's basket
and crows he woke the sun.

On the eighth day of her waiting, climbing stairs of hope to
meet trains from Lahore and descending to platforms of death
and despair, a voice says, 'Bhainji.' A dilruba-sweet voice calling to Roop.

Sister.

She stops.

Madani? Who calls me sister? Is it Madani?

A small Sikh boy in a Peshawari kurta-pyjama with an
oversized red turban sits cross-legged beneath the railway
station's Ansonia clock. He props an elbow on a pile of black
umbrellas and his back against a stack of newspapers.

'Umbrella?'

Roop shakes her head.

'Akhbar? Newspipper?' he urges, trying his English on
Roop. '*Statesman*, very good, very good, English pipper?'

She does not wish to read *The Statesman*'s words about
Indians. She knows what they will say – that they are doomed,
that no European would have behaved as they have in the past
few months, that the years of British rule and British
authority kept the lid on the inborn savagery of Indians. That
India will never last.

Nowhere in their editorials will they acknowledge their own rape and plunder of India.

These thoughts come as if Satya were speaking.

'What is your name?' she asks him, buying time so she can refuse his long-lashed brown eyes.

'Zorawar,' he replies, as if surprised she should ask. He rolls a newspaper tight and gives the pile a whack to show he is giving her one with resilience, one with bounce, elasticity.

Zorawar.

The name of the Tenth Guru's youngest son, martyred by the Mughal ruler Aurangzeb, bricked up alive and breathing in a wall with his brother in full sight of his mother. Zorawar, the name of a young Sikh boy who died but would not recite the Kalima and convert to Islam.

'Where are you from?'

'Rawalpindi.' He is a refugee like herself, from beyond the border.

So small, so alone.

'And your father?'

A shadow passes across the boy's face. 'Killed.' Then his face sets again, determinedly.

'Where is your mother?'

'In the camp,' the rolled newspaper points vaguely. 'But I am here. I can look after her.'

Roop gives him a whole anna from her dwindling reserve, takes the newspaper roll for the sake of his optimism. He smiles a radiant smile like Timcu's, like Aman's, and hope stirs once more in Roop.

My people, Punjabi Sikhs, will survive; this Zorawar's spirit is in them. They will not beg, they will not die, they will work and build their lives again.

I will survive, even if Sardarji is gone – I made two sons.

But who was it that made the little boy call her 'Bhainji?'

Sister, my dead sister Satya, at last you come to my assistance in atonement, bringing me hope.

'Roop!'

She turns.

A middle-aged Sikh man, slightly rotund, in a soiled and

bloodstained woollen English suit opens his arms before her, falcon eyes hooded with fatigue.

No walking stick dangles from his right hand.

His beard, greyer than she remembers it, scratches her wet cheek. Her arms rise to link about his neck and his unique scent, past the scent of sandalwood fixo and Brylcreem, is with her. Euphoria rises, to the brink of tears. The pulse that throbs in Roop's wrists, clasped behind his head, matches his pulse against her cheek. His turban has loosened, the usually trailing safa cut off at the base of his turban, to serve as bandage about his forearm.

Sardarji kisses Roop on the cheek, as if they were screened from the eyes of all. Behind her, Atma Singh's turban turns away discreetly; he busies himself with the bedding roll and the waterbottle.

And when the three of them exchange the compressed despair of the train station for the clouded afternoon air, air that is sombre and still on their faces, there is Narain Singh, eyes glossing with joy as he spies Sardarji and behind him, Narain Singh's father, Atma Singh, walking towards him through the crowds.

Narain Singh relieves Atma Singh of the bedding roll, touches his father's feet, then Sardarji's.

Then Narain Singh's face crumples.

The car – Sardarji's Packard, the one he bought with money from his own jagir – is gone.

Just gone.

Narain Singh breaks down for the first time into unmanly sobs.

Atma Singh glares at his son, an eye on Sardarji's face.

'I went looking for a policeman, Sardarji, but there are none to be found.'

Who is interested in another report of loss and looting when there are so many who have lost so much more?

Sardarji puts a hand on Narain Singh's shoulder and says, 'Keep calm, Narain Singh.'

'Yes,' says Roop, with as much passion as if she were Satya. 'We must all keep our strength, keep our tears for bigger losses. Go, get Sardarji a tonga. This is only the beginning.'

In a minute, raindrops the size of four-anna coins sting the dust; the sky splinters, ushering in the monsoon. In five minutes, the street before the train station is aflood with muddy brown water, and black umbrellas bloom over chai stalls.

Sardarji hesitates; European shoes are not made for wading.

Roop hitches her salwar up over her ankles, returns to the train station, passes all those searching people again till she comes to the little newspaper boy.

'Zorawar, one umbrella,' she says.

She returns with a black umbrella for Sardarji; at least it will keep his blood-soaked turban dry.

By the time Rai Alam Khan realizes his blunder and sends a bald-pated clerk to Sardarji, they are all living – camping – in a dilapidated uncarpeted bungalow, quickly reallotted to Sardarji's use though its walls are still blackened inside and out by the torches of looters. At long last Sardarji is named Chief Engineer of Punjab, but with the western half of Punjab taken by Pakistan, he says it is a sorry title and does nothing for his loss.

As soon as he found a desk and a few chairs to place in the bungalow, Sardarji began recording and classifying water disputes that have arisen from the Radcliffe line. Main canals have been torn from their sources of supply, and the prospect of lowering the authorized full supply discharges of the canals looms before him.

Sardarji's bungalow lawn shrivels beneath the weight of refugee families, former tenants of his land in 'Pindi, or claimants upon his compassion by slightest vestige of his blood in their veins. Jeevan, a dull-eyed, grizzled Jeevan, fiercer, angrier than Roop has ever seen, barks orders alternately at his men and at the shell-shocked exhausted refugees. He arranges for tents, supervises the digging of latrines and drains to criss-cross the erstwhile garden, he assigns night watch duties to the men, badgers his superiors for flour and lentils, appoints a lambardar of the camp. Inside the bungalow, the Guru Granth Sahib has been placed upon someone's metal trunk at one end of the drawing room and some woman's treasured salvaged wedding chunni cut and hemmed to clothe it.

Roop tries to comfort the widows who kneel and rail before the Guru Granth Sahib, hush them, so Sardarji will not be disturbed in his office.

The silent women are the ones who were raped; even widows pity *their* kismat; families with any sense of izzat are not likely to take them back.

Each time Sardarji passes in or out of the bungalow, Rai Alam Khan's clerk is there, hanging his brown pate and fold-ing his hands before his sherwani coat, asking for the maps of Punjab Province that rode in Sardarji's bedroll all the way from Lahore, Pakistan, and presenting Sardarji with Rai Alam Khan's list. He said he was hired on the spot in August while coming out of Jama Masjid, the big mosque in the old area of Delhi, and says the new Pakistan Irrigation Department appointed him 'special peon,' though he has no uniform and has received no pay since he began.

The special peon sits in lotus position on the veranda each day, nodding his brown bullet head, and vowing he will not leave until he has persuaded Sardarji to let him copy the maps and all other documents about Punjab irrigation now sitting in the central government files in the Delhi office of the Irrigation Department.

But Sardarji says, 'He's a spy,' and refuses to let the clerk enter his office or even the bungalow. 'But,' he concedes, 'he is a brave man,' for the special peon is the only Muslim within Sardarji's bungalow compound, and Jeevan's sepoys have twice had to restrain distraught refugees from pulling him limb from limb.

Riots flare through Delhi; Hindus taking revenge on Muslims, whether they plan to leave India or to stay. More trains arrive from Pakistan, grotesquely silent, blood oozing beneath doors of closed carriages.

Shiva dances his tandav dance of destruction everywhere.

'Work', says Sardarji, 'is the best cure for all of us.'

Now Miss Barlow comes to Sardarji's bungalow to ask him to 'put in a good word' for her brother, Dr Barlow, who is 'positively *desperate*' to buy, pack and arrange shipping for a few objets d'art he would like to take home to England – 'Nothing very much – Mughal miniatures, some old paintings, a few carved ivory tusks, a couple of tiger skins, some mounted hunting trophies. Souvenirs. No, he's an armchair enthusiast when it comes to hunting, but he does like the trophies.'

And she says, 'Things are getting completely out of hand.'

Sitting alongside Roop in a rickety chair, Miss Barlow faces Sardarji across his government-issue wooden desk. Sapphire eyes ignore Roop as Miss Barlow tells Sardarji about her 'spot of trouble,' yesterday, when looting, killing mobs smashed into showrooms in the city's finest shopping centre, Connaught Place.

'I was attending a tea for the few of us who are departing just as soon as we jolly well can. By the time I came out onto the veranda, the whole circle of shops in Connaught Place was a deplorable shambles. The contents of showrooms littered the streets . . . a Sikh ran past me with his beard on fire. A fire started in the tack-and-saddle store – apparently it was owned by Muslims. It was all a jumble, everyone screaming and carrying on, you would have thought the world was about to end.'

'What did you do?' Roop asks, a shade too innocently.

'Well, I did the most sensible thing. Put on my hat, gloves and macintosh and just waited upstairs in the dining room till the natives calmed down. When it blew over, I went out onto the veranda and there was a hawker lying in wait to tempt me with a quite charming paisley stole, the kind you get from Kashmir. Well, you know I can never tell if these darkies in Delhi are Hindu or Muslim, and I didn't know where he got it till he had the cheek to start at a hundred. 'A hundred?' I said. 'I know you stole it, you cannot deceive Miss Barlow.'

'And sure enough, I got the stole right away for thirty. But the cheek of him, starting at a hundred! I mean, what was the point? Things are getting completely out of hand.'

Miss Barlow's silk stockings are turning clay-coloured at the ankle from perspiration in the early September heat.

'Indeed,' Sardarji agrees, gloomily, looking out of his office window at the mud-stained, sodden tents of refugees camped on his bungalow lawn. 'Things are completely out of hand.'

He rises, signalling the interview is over. 'You will forgive me, Miss Barlow, but I am now responsible to set the tone, you might say. And as you must know, I have always been philosophically opposed to "putting in a good word."'

He ushers her out of his office and escorts her to her bicycle. Returning from the bungalow's wrought iron gate, he stops at the side of the bald-pated clerk. The special peon looks up from his lotus position on the veranda floor, with beseeching eyes.

Sardarji sighs.

'All right. I will order that you be given the maps and the other items on Rai Alam Khan's list tomorrow.' The clerk's bald brown pate glows, he folds his hands before Sardarji.

'Perhaps the new Chief Engineer, my counterpart in the West Punjab Irrigation Department of Pakistan, and I can avert more bloodshed, see beyond what maps can tell us.'

After this, the special peon wears fountain pens to pinheads and pencils to stubs, copying laboriously, copying all day. The maps, Irrigation Department pay records, planning documents, survey reports and soil sample tests: he copies them all, and when they are completed, perhaps next year, he tells Sardarji he plans to leave Delhi for the first time in his life, take all twenty in his family to see the miracle of Pakistan.

But after that, he says, he will return to the city of his childhood, Delhi.

'Do you think, Sardarji, that when I return you could put in a good word? I am B.A.-failed, and as you see, Sardarji, a very good special peon.'

Jeevan and Papaji are the only ones Roop has left. Maybe Madani and her family. Maybe Lajo Bhua and her husband – Jeevan is still inquiring in camps and the gurdwaras that remain standing, and has not given up hope yet.

Papaji refuses to live with a married daughter's family, so Jeevan has rented a room for him in the Karol Bagh area of Delhi.

Instead of talking to Roop, Jeevan finds excuses in every task, avoiding her glance caressing his face. He brought This-one and That-one to leave in her care – his allotted bungalow in the cantonment area too, has become a camp for refugees from Punjab. But he would only shake his turbaned head when Roop asked, 'Kusum?'

Knowing comes to Roop from Jeevan's silence.

But how? But why? What happened?

Whenever Jeevan comes to the bungalow, he embraces Roop and pulls her plait mechanically, the old habit lingering past his awareness of it, sufficing between them till now.

Now, on the veranda, sitting knee to knee on reed stools pulled close to one another, sister and brother share a brass tumbler of tea, passing it back and forth between them, sipping its scalding comfort as Jeevan's story surfaces.

'In that time when everything was being divided, my commanding officer – a Pathan Muslim from Peshawar, you've heard me speak of him, na? – he informed us that the Two-eight Punjab Regiment, my regiment, would go to Pakistan. He passed around some forms asking us to choose if we would stay in Hindustan or go to Pakistan. Naturally I wrote down Pakistan, because Pari Darvaza would have to fall in Pakistan, Papaji and Kusum and my boys were there – she kept saying she would come and live in Firozepur in the house we were allotted by the army, but always she would think of Papaji and Revati Bhua left alone and say, 'Next year, not now, later' – but even if Kusum and the boys had been with me, tell me who would wish to leave his childhood home and the abundance of that land, and come here to live in this heat, among strangers?

'As I gave my form back to my CO, I saw him stop, look at mine carefully. "Major Jeevan Singh," he said, "I had heard that Sikhs are brave, but now I know it is because they have no brains."

'Much later, I understood.

'But by that time, the killing had begun.

'I could not bear the shots the Muslim soldiers fired into Firozepur's Sikh mohallas and gurdwaras, the fires they started, the looting they organized because they thought Firozepur would fall in Pakistan. When I volunteered to join the Punjab Border Defence Army, such as it was, my commanding officer would not give me permission to leave. He wanted me to watch as my quom burned. So I left without permission – it was chaos by then.' Early days of rebellion come to a man's help in times of need, and fear for Papaji, Kusum, his sons, Revati Bhua and Gujri pulled Jeevan back to Pari Darvaza at top speed, though the village lay in the area closed to social workers, rescuers and all turbaned men.

'I took a jeep I wasn't authorized to use and eight jerrycans of petrol I wasn't issued. Like other border rescue parties, we crossed at night. I drove, hot with purpose – like Ram setting off for Sri Lanka to bring his Sita home. My uniform protected me all the way to Pari Darvaza. Ibrahim bounced in the back seat holding his cap to his head yelling, 'Ahista, Jeevan-sir, ahista!' at intervals when he had enough breath to protest my speed. I thought when I had left Ibrahim in Pari Darvaza, I'd go – along with Papaji, Kusum, the boys and all if they hadn't gone already, and any Sikhs or Hindus I could accommodate – back across the border, to India.

'Just till all this uproar died down.'

Roop saw it as he described it:

The jeep lurched to a stop. Ibrahim and the jerrycans rolled together on the jeep floor. Jeevan didn't look back but bounded to the bright blue door of the post office.

'It was repainted green.'

He pounded at it, but there was no sound from the occupant he could sense was within.

'The postman we knew all our lives was hiding from the sight of my turban – turbans magnify us, you know, just as the Guru intended, so that every wrongdoing, every killing or looting by a Sikh is counted and recounted ten times for every Hindu or Muslim deed. There were armed jathas of Sikhs on the march through Punjab. Organized and purposeful, I thought their reputation must have walked before mine.'

Jeevan continues and his story enters Roop's body. This telling is not for Roop, this telling is for Roop to tell his sons, and her sons.

Jeevan raced up the packed-dirt footpath into the village, shouting, 'Papaji! Kusum!' Though the sun pulsing like the vein in his temple said it should be past midday, and Ibrahim had reminded him as they arrived it was almost time for zohr prayers, the mosque was empty, as if just vacated.

Abu Ibrahim was nowhere to be seen. But that didn't mean Ibrahim wouldn't find him in the mosque school. No need to worry there . . . whereas Kusum, his boys, Papaji, Gujri, Revati Bhua . . . perhaps they had already left.

The temple compound was locked. 'Pandit Dinanathji!' he shouted. No answer. A dry, flat dung patty fell from the side of a mud wall; he heard it crumble.

Soapy water ran in the centre drain of the streets, people must have been present in the walled compounds, but everywhere there was an eerie silence.

He came upon the gurdwara, a blackened shell, its plaster dome fallen. Perhaps there were still Sikhs inside?

'But,' Jeevan says, 'I told myself, "Don't stop!"'

In the bazaar Fazl Karim's brand-new black Singer sewing machine sat in his tiny stall, its large treadle stilled, and no Fazl Karim. A pattern lay strewn next to it. Arm shapes, the front panel of a jacket, the broad back panel.

'Khanma!' Jeevan called, boyhood authority in his voice again. No Khanma.

At the mouth of the tunnel, the blind man was gone.

'He always saw more than any of us, saw it coming,' says Jeevan.

The telling continues.

Jeevan drew his revolver from his holster and moved to the mouth of the darkness, slipped in. He felt his way, he had not forgotten a single brick in Papaji's haveli wall.

The door to Shyam Chacha's haveli was locked. He had never seen the carved shutters of the upstairs window – the one where Chachi's chunni-clad head usually appeared – closed.

Papaji's haveli door was unlocked.

The door creaked open, shut behind him.

In the rasoi, pots rolled past dried pools of their contents, like the severed heads of martyrs, a half-filled ladle left hurriedly on the clay surface of the stove. Gujri, Papaji, Kusum, his sons nowhere to be found. The air was warm, the smell of fear hanging thick and dense like a fog, catching within him, too.

The front room – Mama's room – yawned, a black and empty hole, its doors flung wide open to anyone, its contents for the taking. He moved to the niche in the wall near the door, took a candle and matches, lit one, held it at the level of his turban. By its wavering flame, he saw strange shapes backed up against the wall, Mama's and Kusum's dowry trunks thrown open, chunnis bordered with woven gold, lehngas, salwars, kameezes spilling over their sides, as if trying to flee.

A simple white-clad mound lay at his feet in the centre of the room. Jeevan shuddered, remembering how he shouldered Mama so many years ago – had she returned? Died again without taking rebirth?

He lifted the corner of the sheet closest to him. Took a deep breath, whipped the sheet away.

A woman's body lay beneath, each limb severed at the joint. This body was sliced into six parts, then arranged to look as if she were whole again. The candle guttered and dimmed, or perhaps it was that his eyes clouded to protect his heart from the sight.

He swallowed, moved closer to see her face.

'It was my Kusum.'

'No!' Roop recoils, a hand rising to cover her mouth.

Questions jump like trapped fish in the loose mesh of her mind.

Jeevan's shoulders tremble.

Roop touches her chunni to her brother's bearded cheek; it comes away damp.

510

'She looked accepting,' he says, after a moment. 'Almost as if she had been dismembered by her own hand. But that, I told myself, that is impossible. Can a woman ask for someone to do this to her? How can she actually desire it, move to her captor with a smile on her lips?

'Her hand was like this – unclenched. Her feet were like this – not poised to run. Her legs cut neatly at the thigh, why they must surely have used a sword or more than one! Why were her legs not bloody? To cut a woman apart without first raping – a waste, surely. Rape is one man's message to another: "I took your pawn. Your move."'

Even in death he can see Kusum only from the corners of his eyes. For how can he know, how does he know, if she was raped or not, when he has heard the same stories I have heard? But the cutting up, Jeevan continued, what message could this be?

This woman's body – he began to disbelieve his eyes, it could not be Kusum – was also cut just below the ribs. Looking closer, he realized that he, like her assailants, could put his hand into her very flesh the way a European surgeon might.

He did not. Could not.

Instead, he leaned over his wife and drew the sheet back over her body.

He received the message. Kusum's womb, the same from which his three sons came, had been delivered. Ripped out.

And the message, 'We will stamp your kind, your very species from existence. This is no longer merely about izzat or land. This is a war against your quom, for all time. Leave. We take the womb so there can be no Sikhs from it, we take the womb, leave you its shell.'

He drew himself slowly to his feet and placed the dwindling candle at her head. He whispered the first lines of the Kirtan Sohila over her, quickly, like an incantation, running the words together. In Papaji's sitting room, the loose bricks had been removed from the wall, his rupees taken. In the rasoi, This-one and That-one's waterbottles were not in their customary place on the shelf. Kusum was not yet odorous, and Jeevan realized this deed had been done but a few hours before.

'I became sure Papaji must have had a little time, even if Gujri had not. For only we,' referring to Papaji's family members, 'knew where Papaji kept his money. And you know how hot it was – I became sure the family had carried water.'

In the rasoi he found a large brass container of ghee, dipped his hand in it and smeared it on Kusum's shroud.

It would not be enough for a funeral pyre.

He left Kusum and ran all the way back through the silent village to the jeep. Dung patties would take too long. He would have to use the petrol from the jerrycans and hope he would have enough left to get to the border. He needed to work quickly. He would use the last sputtering candles to light Kusum's pyre in the centre of the courtyard.

'That message was one that should go no further. It must be ignored, so that no Sikh man show weakness or fear.'

But he does not feel so now, and so the telling continues.

The village was still so quiet, so quiet, as he ran through its streets, through the silent bazaar, past the temple, past the mosque, past the post office, back to Ibrahim, in the waiting jeep.

But there was no Ibrahim.

And two of the eight jerrycans were gone.

He turned, revolver in hand, left, right – no one in sight. Someone, someone who knew he would go to the largest, innermost havelis in the village, someone who knew he would go to the tunnel havelis, had taken the jerrycans.

It could only be Ibrahim.

Who else but Ibrahim knew he needed that petrol to get himself and his family out of Pakistan and into India?

Faithful Ibrahim. Boyhood friend, whom Jeevan had taken with him into the army, to stand behind his chair at the officers' mess.

Ibrahim, the pir's son. Abu Ibrahim's son. The man who'd just told him it was time for zohr prayers. No, surely it couldn't be Ibrahim. Jeevan turned to look at the mosque, straining to see Ibrahim's white kurta doubling, bending before his maker.

Then a plume of smoke appeared above the walled compounds, hanging low in the stale still air. A passing gust stirred the dust on the road, and Jeevan's eyes filled with a rolling black and orange-flecked cloud. Fire, low on the horizon, from the largest, innermost havelis in the village.

Ibrahim must have taken the jerrycans and set fire to the tunnel home. First ingratitude and thievery, and then betrayal!

'My training took charge of my body,' says Jeevan. Roop sees it as he tells:

He raced back into the village, keeping his back against the walls of each compound, keeping his revolver cocked.

He passed the mosque again – still empty.

The temple compound was still locked. The brand-new black Singer sewing machine sat in Fazl Karim's tiny stall – but no Fazl Karim. The blind man, had he been present, would of course have seen no one. He shouted for help – no one from the village, not the halwai or the goldsmith or Pandit Dinanath answered him.

Then he came upon it – a circlet of burning petrol poured before the flower-carved timber door of Papaji's haveli belched smoke and fire. Horses neighed and reared in the stable at the far end of the tunnel. Cows in the cowshed beside them lowed and jostled, cowbells ringing warnings. Which should he try to release first – the trapped atma in beings still alive or the trapped atma in one already dead? Duty provided the answer: a woman of his quom, alive or dead, came first.

But he could not enter the haveli again . . . the timber door was afire now and smoke billowed within, like the rain djinns that swirled in the courtyard so long ago.

'I thought: where is that dog, Ibrahim?'

He ran to the stable.

Quickly he removed his turban, tore off his underturban and bandaged his right hand with it. Turban back on his head, he opened the stables. Only two horses remained – Papaji must have hitched the others to the buggy and left for the border, for the buggy was gone. Their eyes rolled white, their mouths foamed, their flanks heaved in fear. Front hooves climbed invisible hills. They kicked and they bucked and he soothed them and lied to them, saying everything was all right, all right. They pulled away past him and were gone, hooves clattering down the brick-lined narrow street . . . 'so much valuable horseflesh, lost in a moment.'

The heat grew unbearable. Jeevan reeled a little as he moved to the cow compound – this was easier, and soon the cows milled and jostled past.

A rage came upon Jeevan, rage so strong it would tear Ibrahim limb from limb if he came upon him now – it was a matter of izzat. His shirt turned husk-stiff, hot beneath his fingers. If Ibrahim were still in there, he would have to come out soon; the smoke from the haveli was growing worse. It would spread to the weathered roof of the tunnel in a moment and then . . . the realization hit him . . . to Shyam Chacha's haveli.

It took but a moment.

Now the tunnel roof was a sheet of fire. Jeevan jumped back and away from its mouth, breath gasping from seared, labouring lungs. Though he sprawled on the red brick pavement, his turban was carved to his head.

As in a dream Jeevan saw a man run from the mouth of the tunnel. Expected to see a round-capped kurta-clad figure. But no, it was not Ibrahim who fell beside him, escaping his own handiwork.

It was Shyam Chacha who rose from the pavement, shedding his white Gandhi cap, Shyam Chacha who rose, fingering the black thread about his neck, Shyam Chacha who could not face Jeevan.

'I think he must have been well-hidden when the Muslims came – too craven to go to Papaji's help. Then when he thought it safe, he must have set the fire so Papaji would have nowhere to live if he ever came back, so that Papaji might need to borrow. Then maybe he thought we would sign away our tenant-right forever, blaming the Muslims for our woes. But he must not have realized he could not stop the fire from eating his own home as well. Maybe he thought he could stop the fire once he had started it. Who knows what was in his mind? Always he was greedy for our land.'

Realizing this fire went beyond a single Sikh man's ability to fight it, Jeevan did not stay to see what became of Shyam Chacha, but picked himself up and went back to the jeep, dazed, grazed at shin and elbow. There was a shout behind him and it was Ibrahim, who had just completed his prayers by the

Sufi tombs at the far end of the village, where once Jeevan and he played kabaddi with the other village boys.

But Jeevan swung himself up into the sun-baked seat of the jeep and reversed as fast as he could, to the tree-lined main road that would take him away, north to Sohawa and on to the border. Now his hand was steady on the ball of the gear-shift as he moved the sturdy vehicle into forward gear.

Behind him, the tiny village of Pari Darvaza burned and Abu Ibrahim and other Muslims smoked out of hiding would think Jeevan did it in revenge, for Kusum, for the fallen gurdwara.

And they would hate him for it as they rebuilt it and hate his sons, and his sons' sons and their sons.

It is a matter of izzat.

So Jeevan did not look back.

Because what would be the use?

Izzat has its own rules and does not stop for explanations.

'I wish now that I had embraced Ibrahim one last time. And that I had stayed to inquire what happened to the gurdwara and any Sikhs who must have perished within. This is my shame – that perhaps I could have taken a few Sikhs away with me. But at the time my heart was full of grief and anger from the message that came to me in my woman's body – Kusum's body. Whether Shyam Chacha sent that message or whether the Muslims we grew up with sent the message, it makes no difference. I used to tell Papaji we're all Punjabis and there is no difference. But now the only people I can feel trust for are other Sikhs.'

'Don't tell Papaji, when you see him,' Jeevan adds. 'He thinks we have something to go back to. Let him remember Pari Darvaza the way it was as long as he can.'

But I must remember, thinks Roop. *I must remember Kusum's body.*

Roop will remember Kusum's body, re-membered.

Roop climbs a rickety wooden staircase to see Papaji in his tiny cell, a rented room at the top of a leaning hovel in Old

Delhi. He cannot live with a married daughter; it is not customary. He cannot find enough energy to tie a turban, and without a turban he does not feel man enough to go out.

'Jeevan has been promoted!' It is the first time Papaji has shown interest in anything since his arrival. Like many Indian commissioned officers, Jeevan has taken the place of a British officer, speeding from senior major to lieutenant colonel. And now – his absence unnoticed or forgiven in the chaos of Partition – he has, to Papaji's delight, asked to be reassigned to the Sikh Regiment.

But he is being posted somewhere Northwest.

Again.

There is already talk of war with Pakistan, over who will possess the cherries of Kashmir.

Papaji says, as Roop swings her ankles up to join him on the rope manji, the only furniture in the room, 'I hope Abu Ibrahim arranged for labourers to harvest my fields. By this time perhaps he is sowing it for me, watering it well; the land should not think me unfaithful.'

Mindful of Jeevan's admonition, Roop is silent, holding Jeevan's tale of the fate of Pari Darvaza within her.

'And my partridges,' continues Papaji. 'Perhaps Abu Ibrahim will remember to feed them for me.'

'Tell, na. Speak, na,' Roop says today, as she has every day. 'I must know – where is Gujri, where is Revati Bhua?'

And today Papaji runs his sandalwood kanga through grey hair, winds his hair tight above his head. He holds the base of the knot tight with the small comb, so it doesn't unravel. He takes a deep, deep breath, and begins:

'We had begun to think Pari Darvaza would be spared the chaos,' he says. 'We said, no one will notice us – we have such a small village. Power has shifted so many times before, from raja to Mughal, from Mughal to Mughal, from maharaja to English man. Those rulers fought their battles with swords, face to face, looking their enemies in the eye, instead of voting and debating and making new maps to suit themselves better. But did anyone before these English tell the people *they* should move? No. So Independence Day came and went and we were still alive, still living – Muslims, Sikhs and Hindus together, all of us waiting for the rains. Even so, I was prepared for anything – Sant Puran Singh had stopped at our home on his way to Amritsar and he had told me enough terrible stories. It was he who suggested what I should do if Muslims came. So old as he was, he was on his way to organize jathas of armed Sikhs. He said they would have guns and ammunition and know how to use them. He planned retaliation against the Muslim quom in Amritsar, for what they had done all the way from 'Pindi to Lahore.'

Sant Puran Singh? thinks Roop. That kindly old man who performed my wedding to Sardarji at Punja Sahib Gurdwara? The one who became a sant after he shot a doe at the age of fourteen and realized he could not make a doe?

Papaji continues.

'I had that old .303 I bought in Peshawar, I had bullets, I sharpened my kirpan. Though Sant Puran Singh told me mullahs of mosques in Rawalpindi and around had issued fatwas and firmans calling for the death of Hindus and Sikhs, I couldn't believe there would be any disturbances in *our* village. I told myself I am the Deputy, I am lambardar, head man of the village council and no man, Sikh, Hindu or Muslim, wants to lose his livelihood. But then . . .' Bachan Singh's voice trails away.

'Then?' urges Roop.

Papaji swallows hard. 'The drums began at night,' he says. 'Soon the village was aglow, surrounded by torches. Abu Ibrahim went to talk with the mob leaders, tell them there were only a few Sikh and Hindu families in the village and that we were under his protection. He promised me he would protect our family, and reminded me that his own son, Ibrahim, was with Jeevan, that he was either Jeevan's hostage or under Jeevan's protection – sometimes, Abu Ibrahim said, the difference is very little.

'When I heard the drums, I took my gun and ammunition and ran to the gurdwara and I gave them to the other Sikh families who had gathered there. I thought Abu Ibrahim and the village council could protect my family, while just the sight of the .303 would protect the other Sikhs in the village, and the Guru Granth Sahib. They had sticks and stones, their kirpans and stout hearts – even the women were tying their chunnis around their waists, readying themselves for battle beside the men; the women were ready to kill, too, understand? Old women were giving opium to the younger women, first burying their gold jewellery beneath the Guru, preparing them for martyrdom.

'But after he came back from talking to that band of thugs – dacoits, robbers! – Abu Ibrahim came and begged me to let him convert me and my grandsons, Jeevan's sons, convert them to Islam!'

Bachan Singh pauses to confirm that Roop comprehends the complete unacceptability of such an alternative.

'He said the village council agreed that it would be for my own good. Huh! "*For-my-own-good*," *da lagda chacha!* It could be very quickly done, he said, and he had brought the barber behind him with his razor, brought a razor into my haveli to cut my grandsons' hair!

'Abu Ibrahim spoke quickly, "I came to warn you, my old friend. You must recite the Kalima now or I cannot help you."

'He kept his eyes lowered and I knew he, though he was pir of Pari Darvaza, could not stop his fellow Muslims and followers from putting into action what he'd preached in the mosque, what he'd read to his quom from their Urdu newspapers . . .'

Papaji's voice trails away.

'Then?' says Roop.

'Abu Ibrahim,' I said. 'Five-ten years of my life remain, if my kismat be good. I want only to die with izzat, understand?

'And I told him we could leave, but we could not cut a single strand of hair.

'Abu Ibrahim told me he found Pandit Dinanath near the temple and had warned him and any Hindus he could find, and he said he even went to Jyotshi Sundar Chand's home.

'"What did our astrologer say?" I asked, for I had been wanting to consult him for several days, but anyone I could have sent in was in hiding and if I had gone to the temple to consult him myself, your Shyam Chacha might have thought I was becoming a Hindu again. And many times I stopped myself because I didn't want to know his answer.

'Abu Ibrahim said, "The astrologer said everything has a vaqt." You know – a time,' Papaji translates for Roop, as if her learning English has wiped Punjabi from her mind. 'But the astrologer said the stars were saying it was not the right vaqt to go and the stars were also saying it was not the right vaqt to stay. So he had decided to stay until he could understand what had happened to the stars.

'"Did he understand," I asked Abu Ibrahim, "did the jyotshi understand that we could all travel together?"

'"I suggested it,' said Abu Ibrahim, "for I knew you would not convert. But the jyotshi said, 'Today is Tuesday and I cannot begin a journey on Tuesday – Mangal is too strong.' He is a superstitious man."

'I wanted to say to Abu Ibrahim – "And you? You're not superstitious? Giving amulets against the evil eye and camel blessings to people from miles around?" But it was not the right vaqt to say that; other people's beliefs, their principles and the things they hold dear, are always called superstition, when someone is manufacturing differences. I have *always* said that, you remember I always said that?'

Roop remembers Papaji once called Hindu beliefs 'superstitions,' when he was trying to become a better Sikh, but this is no time to remind him of that fact, either – though Satya would have.

'As we spoke,' Papaji continues, 'we heard the mob shouting, "Kafirs!"

'You know – unbelievers. As if their Allah and our Vaheguru had become separate instead of just different names for the same-same one thing.

'Abu Ibrahim said the mob was made up of Muslims from India, that Sikhs had killed their families and forced them to leave for Pakistan and so they wanted my haveli. Then he said they came looking for Sikhs "in self-defence," in case the Sikhs in Pari Darvaza began to kill Muslims. Huh! As if we could! So few of us, to so many Muslims. If there had been more of us they wouldn't have dared. So, who knows what kind of men they really were? Just men with no shame to stop them.

'Abu Ibrahim said to wait, he would go and talk to them

again. As he left the haveli, we could hear them yelling, "Come out and be saved by Islam! Come, we have beef for you to eat!"'

Papaji strokes his long beard, his hands shake a little.

'Revati Bhua almost fainted,' says Papaji, 'at the word beef. She climbed to the roof of the haveli and hid the boys behind the partridge cages. I had to think very quickly, quickly it became clear: Revati Bhua was old, if her izzat went, what man would feel dishonoured? Gujri was already a widow, long past childbearing age. But I had given your Nani my bachan, so long ago I gave her my word, that I would protect Gujri.

'If we left the tunnel now, to join the other Sikhs in the gurdwara, we could be caught by any Muslim in the village and given to the mob. The only direction that might be safe was the fields. So I told Gujri, "Leave everything and go! Understand? Run! Hide in the fields!" She ran, overturning pots and pans in her haste.

'But Kusum, she was my responsibility . . . I said to myself: Kusum was entrusted to me by Jeevan, she is young, still of childbearing age. I cannot endure even the possibility that some Muslim might put his hands upon her. Every day I had been hearing that the seeds of that foreign religion were being planted in Sikh women's wombs. No, I said: I must do my duty.'

An old wave of pain begins low in Roop's tummy, a fear-ache that burns from above her womb to her heart. 'Then?' she whispers, though she knows his answer. She knows it before Papaji speaks, because of all the tales that burdened Vayu as Vayu swept through the railway station. Roop knows because Papaji's story cannot be so very different from other men who see their women from the corners of their eyes, who know their women only as bearers of blood, to do what women are for. She knows this story, knows it like some long-forgotten, undeciphered dream.

But it must be spoken.

Roop wants her Papaji to say it, now. Tell this story, just one story of so many.

Say what he did.

'I called to Kusum – she was on the terrace, watching the

kerosene torches flame in the hands of the mob at the edge of the village. I took her into my sitting room and I told her what Sant Puran Singh said we Sikhs must do, and that I had to do it now. She understood. Always she made no trouble. She said I should take her into the front room, your mama's room, so her sons, on the terrace with Revati Bhua, should hear no cry from her lips.'

Revati Bhua was right – Papaji thinks that for good-good women, death should be preferable to dishonour.

'In your mama's room, I said the first lines of the Japji to give me strength, and to guide my kirpan. Then she turned her back so I should not see her face, took off her chunni to bare her neck before me. And then . . .'

Bachan Singh's telling falters. He doubles over the side of the manji suddenly, chest and stomach heaving. Roop puts her arm about him, rubbing his thin shoulders.

Nothing but sorrow, acid taste of sorrow rising.

After a moment, Papaji wipes his moustache on the sleeve of his kurta.

'I raised my kirpan high above her head. Vaheguru did not stop it; it came down. Her lips still moved, as mine did, murmuring, 'Vaheguru, Vaheguru,' as her head rolled from my stroke.'

One stroke?

Just one stroke.

'I felt the warm splatter of her wet blood here, through my kurta.' A cupped hand touches his breastbone. 'I didn't know one woman could have so much blood inside her. Blood arced, spouted, gushed everywhere. I opened the wedding trunks and pulled out clothes as fast as I could, my tears mingling with it.'

Jeevan's words repeat themselves within Roop as if he were sitting beside her, describing Kusum's body. 'Her hand was like this – unclenched. Her feet were like this – not poised to run.' Roop's shoulders hunch beneath the weight of Papaji's story, for his telling must be repeated to Jeevan, Roop knows. His telling is the telling that she will have to tell Jeevan's sons one day: that their mother went to her death just as she was offered it, baring her neck to Papaji's kirpan, willingly, Papaji says, for the izzat of her quom.

Vaheguru, send Kusum back to this family in her next life! Let her tell her story herself, remember this death herself, for I am not worthy to tell it! How will I tell This-one and That-one, but with Papaji's words? How will I ask her sons to know her pain when they learn to see as men see, like horses, blind to what lies directly before their eyes?

Tears are hot on Roop's cheeks.

'Then,' Papaji is saying, 'I wiped the stone floor myself instead of calling Khanma, ripped off my kurta and put on a fresh one.'

What is not even in Bachan Singh's silence, that Roop must fathom, to know this story?

How will she explain to This-one and That-one that Kusum – daughter-in-law who always followed rule number one, never saying 'nahinji' or 'no-ji,' who found her way around and under Papaji's directions and Jeevan's orders in her real home, who sometimes did not obey 'fut-a-fut,' at once – could not find the words *nahinji* and *no-ji* when the kirpan lifted above her bare neck? That those words could not get past her lips because her lips had no practice in speaking them, because those words drowned before they took shape or sound, in the blood she bore within.

Blood of the quom.

The rest – that must have been done by Muslims, later, the ripping out of Kusum's womb, that too. How deep an anger must they have felt in the bone to spend sword wounds on a poor body already dead.

Roop takes deep ujjai-breaths, suddenly grateful that her ear need only listen, that her own neck is spared the long blade of a sharpened kirpan.

'Then?' though her tears flow for Kusum, she must ask it all now.

'I covered Kusum with a sheet I found in the trunk,' says Papaji, 'and I ran up to the terrace, to Revati Bhua and the boys. I could hear the Muslims crowding into the tunnel, battering the door. When it gave way, they crowded into the courtyard. Even in the dark I could recognize labourers who had worked on my holding, helped harvest from Sikh land, and I saw Abu Ibrahim among them. I was so sickened by the sight of

Abu Ibrahim in the crawling mass of the crowd, I didn't even realize Revati Bhua had walked down the staircase to the court-yard, head held high, until I saw and heard her speak to the Muslims. She said, "When the family left two days ago, I told them to leave me. All the Muslims I know here have called me Bhua so many years. I am their aunt, so how can I be afraid? I am ready to eat beef and become a Muslim, but I cannot leave. I stayed behind – they will be back in a few days."'

Roop's brow wrinkles; it is difficult to imagine Revati Bhua acting quite so fearlessly. Revati Bhua, who never felt an emotion or took any action unless pre-approved by Papaji. And such bravery from that kindly but easily frightened old aunt is strange, stranger than Roop can imagine. But Papaji is the teller of Revati Bhua's tale and he tells it as he wishes it repeated.

'And then?'

'Abu Ibrahim turned to those men – those *goondas!* – and said, though he knew very well I was still there, for he had spoken with me but half an hour before. "Yeh correct hai, the fatty tells the truth – I saw them leave two days ago with my own eyes. But she is here and there is gold to take." Then he took Revati Bhua by the arm, pushed her into my sitting room. I heard him telling them, "Yes, behind that brick, and that one." He was showing them where I kept my rupees! He was the only person from outside the family I had told about those bricks, as a precaution, should anything terrible happen to me. And all this time, I was crouching on the terrace, my hands over the boys' mouths for fear they would make a sound.

'When they came out of my sitting room, the Muslim goondas were fighting over the gold and didn't bother to climb up to the terrace. They took Revati Bhua away with them. They must have made her a Muslim.'

He says it as if Revati Bhua is dead, because she agreed to be a Muslim, though she saved him and the boys. Perhaps she is dead, by now. But no, perhaps she is in some camp or ashram, somewhere. He tells her sacrifice as if it was only what he expected of her – that she owed him no less for all the years of hospitality.

'I told the boys I sent their mama to Delhi with another family that was leaving. That she could not say farewell, because that family was in such a hurry. That she would meet us on the way or in Delhi. How could I tell them I had just wiped their mother's blood from my kirpan, torn off my kurta stained with her blood, or how my heart swelled to bursting with tears for my son's Kusum, the daughter-in-law I loved as much as you or Madani?' Papaji moans.

'We left immediately: Gujri and I and the two boys.

'The boys were as excited as if we were going to the cattle fair, what did they know? We hitched two horses to the buggy, took two bullocks and loaded a cart with the tools,' he gestures at the twisted hunks of metal in the corner of the room, 'so I can plant again.'

Then why do you worry about whether your fields in Pari Darvaza are watered?

Bachan Singh does not seem aware of conflicting intentions. He purses his mouth, juts his yellowy beard past his chin. At fifty-one, he looks twenty years older than Sardarji, though they are so close in age. What he has survived has given him a belligerence Roop has never seen in him before.

Perhaps we need our enemies; they make us strong.

'We heard gunfire and screaming from the gurdwara as we crept our way through dark wheat fields sighing for rain, stopping only at the waterfall so the boys could fill their school waterbottles. Then north across Pothwar to the Grand Trunk Road.

'We joined a convoy of Sikhs and Hindus – there were some miltry men with them, like goatherds herding goats. Their subedar remembered Jeevan from when he was a beginning sepoy in training at Sialkot – Jeevan must have trained him, na? I had only three rupees in my kurta pocket and two gold mohurs that I'd left in my desk and here we were, going to travel I don't know how many miles across Punjab. I thought I must try to reach Delhi and ask the commanding officer at Indian Army headquarters, Where is my son, Major Jeevan Singh?

'Pandit Dinanath had loaded Lakshmi, all the other temple idols and all his family's gold on a bullock cart and left also – we caught up with him near Lahore; he said he had been robbed before he even got to Jhelum, all his idols smashed or broken.'

A long silence.

Then Roop presses a velvet pouch into Papaji's hand. He stares down at it.

'Open it, Papaji.'

His finger spreads the puckered mouth of the pouch, draws out Mama's hand ornaments, the ruby tikka first she, then Roop, wore upon her forehead, and the gold necklace that spiralled first on Mama's neck, then on Roop's at her wedding. All the jewellery Roop received at her wedding, except for Mama's sapphire ring. Papaji looks at them a long moment.

He sighs. His mouth trembles at the corner.

But he does not refuse to take them; they will melt in the goldsmith's shop near Connaught Place, but his izzat will be preserved.

Now Roop asks gently, 'Tell me – what about Gujri?'

Papaji's hands cover his face for a minute. He rocks forward, back. Beard trembling, he says at last, 'Gujri's feet hurt her so much, so much. They were swollen this big,' he gestures, 'by the time we got to Jhelum, not even halfway. I made her ride in the buggy with the boys, but she kept saying, every mile we walked, that we should never have started our journey on a Tuesday. Finally, she sat down on the side of the Grand Trunk Road and said, "Go to your India. What will this Independence do for a servant woman like me?" I stopped for three hours, till I grew afraid for the boys and determined to press on over the border, but no amount of coaxing and persuading would move her.'

Blood drains from Roop's heart just to think of it. Her Gujri, dear Gujri, who tended her when she had typhoid, Gujri whose solution to all the woes of life was to feed and cook for others. Where is her atma now?

Papaji's voice comes, thick with pain. 'Every night I see the vultures circling as I left her, for you know I promised your Nani I'd protect Gujri, even in her old age.' He puts an arm around Roop. 'Perhaps a maha-atma – what do you say in English? – a very great soul, will take care of her. There are refugee camps now – you never know, she may find her way back to us. We all have our own kismat.'

'How could you leave her?' Roop wants to ask Papaji.

But Papaji's face is that of a man who made a terrible choice, and will live with it till it solidifies within him, becomes a part of his being from life to life.

I, too, have done things I cannot recount with pride.

Each of us has betrayed something, someone, or a part of ourselves.

Could Gujri have passed for a Muslim? But for an easily discarded steel kara, no one would know the religion of a woman like Gujri, dressed in a salwar-kameez, if there were no turbaned men to claim her. She could sing 'Heer.' She knew parts of the Koran – but no, not enough.

No.

Why does a woman choose to die?

A shadow woman whispers in Roop's ear, 'Sometimes we choose to die because it is the only way to be both heard and seen, little sister.'

Sardar Kushal Singh called Roop 'Satya.'

'A slip of the tongue, no more,' said Toshi, and she hastens to say, in a complimenting way, that Roop walks like Satya, laughs like her, and that in a certain kind of light . . . She breaks off, pulling a chunni past her lips with still-bandaged hands.

Have I now become my saukan, my other-wife, my sister who hated me so long?

Leaf shadows applaud as if she gave thought-form to some grim cosmic joke.

Roop draws close to Toshi, standing at the bungalow window watching Sardar Kushal Singh under the gulmohar and jamun trees at the bungalow's wrought iron gate, trees so young and slight they can only have given fruit a few times.

White tents flare across the compound like giant birds. The slap-slap of women washing clothes under the hot sun in sewer-diverted water mutes the crying of children. Complaining is permitted only to those wounded in body, for, as Jeevan says firmly to This-one and That-one, 'Sikhs don't complain.'

Toshi helps Roop with the children as much as she can, now Jorimon has gone – children give hope that there is a future. There will be more children to look after soon, now that Jeevan has located Madani, her husband and their children in a refugee camp in Firozepur. Madani told Jeevan that when Sikhs and Hindus realized that Radcliffe's line curved around Firozepur, placing it not in Pakistan but within the borders of India, they avenged the earlier massacres Jeevan saw.

Madani's husband inquired through Firozepur day after day, but found no trace of Lajo Bhua or her husband. Even if they survived the horrors of Partition, their two-room home could not have escaped the Sutlej floods that tore through their bazaar, washing away the remains of the city to strew it over fields.

'That flood would never have risen if I'd been in charge of that weir,' Sardarji said, certainty ringing in his voice.

If Gujri were here, she would comfort them all, she would sing 'Heer' to the children, tell them stories of ancient times.

I should have listened more closely to Gujri.

Sardar Kushal Singh is standing at the gate as he has every day. He thrusts papers at the short, dark-skinned people in the streets of New Delhi and shouts at them as if they were all deaf – 'Read this, this is what I lost, feel this paper, it is all I have to build again, starting at the end of life as though ready to traverse its ashrams again, like a man of twenty.'

'Sardar Kushal Singh,' says Toshi, 'forgets many things now. Where we are, where we have come, what happened to others, who died and how. Only the terrible things the Muslims did to us. He remembers only that,' says Toshi, quietly marvelling. 'He weeds memories like a mali, ripping out the ones that mar the colours and textures of those he wishes to grow. He remembers we were abandoned by the Hindu leaders, he knows we are not wanted by Muslims, he does not trust the braying of our Sikh leaders either – so he has the fear he needs to protect him in the years ahead. But,' she holds out her hands, 'he says he does not remember how I came by this pain, trying to save his things. He says he does not remember our journey, how we left our home or what we saw as we walked through Rawalpindi to the airport to get on that DC-3. He remembers only what we lost.'

Sardar Kushal Singh sits rocking all day on an open bedding roll – ready to pack at a moment's notice, even though Sardarji has told him it is not and never will be safe to return. He makes lists in Gurmukhi script, in Persian script and in English, so he can explain to any official he meets. He knows the names of all the Muslim villagers who owe him money and calculates interest as if he will collect it someday. He knows each of his godowns and its contents as he left them – so many sacks of makki flour, so many maunds of wheat, so many sacks of almonds, so many of dried sweet apricots . . .

Sardar Kushal Singh notices Roop and Toshi and cries, 'Where have we come? These are not our people. These people don't have our blood, why should they care for us?'

Roop turns away – there are too many whose suffering is heavier than listening can cure. She wonders if Huma lives or died. Will Jorimon find her way clear across India to her cousin-uncle or cousin-brother in Dacca, now capital of East Pakistan? Little Aman gripped her sari palloo in one hand, Roop's chunni in the other when she left; he cries each night for her. Roop's fingers remember the last touch of Mama's phulkari-embroidered shawl slipping away to Jorimon in the hope it would protect her always.

She reaches, arms above her head, hands stretched out to sky. Thankfulness surges within her – she survived. She is in Delhi, with Sardarji. So many Sikh, Hindu and Muslim women did not survive that journey.

A touch, soft as muslin, an answering djinn-soft touch, brushes her fingertips.

Now there is no Bari-Sardarni, no Choti-Sardarni; no senior wife, no junior wife. Few people remain who remember Satya now. The wedding photo that could have reminded all of them of the how-they-got-there is left behind in 'Pindi. A bitter-almond taste rises on Roop's tongue as if it had seeped into her from all the years that have happened since.

Now there is only one Sardarni.

And Delhi too, is hallowed ground, although seven hundred Sikh shrines and the birthplace of Guru Nanak, from whom all Sikhs came, are left in Pakistan. In Delhi are Sisganj, and Rakabgunj, and many other gurdwaras Roop has never visited before. But she finds it comforting that the Gurus walked here before them and left their mark as they were martyred.

Roop is no longer like Sardar Kushal Singh who thinks this is temporary and that he might return to 'Pindi. She knows now her children will never see Pari Darvaza or 'Pindi, and when the Prophet flowers bloom in their earthen pots outside the bungalow in Lahore, Roop will not be there to see them. Nor will Roop ever walk The Mall Road in Murree. She will never see a fisherman cast his delicate net in the Indus, nor walk the mountain paths of Hunza.

Pakistan: land of the pure. A land purified of Sikhs, Hindus and maybe Christians, too.

Sardar Kushal Singh cries for things, he cries for work that must be done again, he mourns for the power he had and vows he will have it again. He, Sardarji and the Hindu and Sikh refugees around the bungalow compete in melancholy; it is becoming a way to tell the extent of their loss, could bereavement be measured. Sometimes he and his friends from 'Pindi shed tears loudly in public as if a great siapa were in progress everywhere. In private, they are wounded children and turn to their women for comfort.

Why do men love things so well and so dearly? – they are so easily lost.

Roop will never ride the banks of the Jhelum or ask the fairies at Pari Darvaza to help her. She will never touch her Guru's handprint again at Punja Sahib Gurdwara where she was married, walk beside the canals at Khanewal or balance on the narrow divide between two reflecting pools in Lawrence Gardens. That is what she has lost.

Not only things.

But a kind of calm is falling, after all the dislocation. Again everyone must worry who is higher-up and who is lower-down and what-will-people-say. Women and children are being sorted between the two countries like apricots brought in from the orchard. The sorting baskets are the old ones: religion, class, caste, quom.

Why can they not be like Kashmiri shawls and choose their owners?

Roop smiles involuntarily. No, Satya would go further today. She would scoff that no woman needs an owner unless she has been taught she does.

Hut! No wonder Satya died alone without a man to protect her. This is what happens to a disobedient woman.

And Roop?

Roop is becoming obedient again, so Sardarji will find no difference between her listening and obeying.

Now Sardarji says the Guru's words are important again. 'Kirat karo, vand chacko, naam japo.' Work hard, share with your neighbours, repeat the name of God.

He is doing kirat, assessing damage, planning everyone's affairs, filling out forms for those who cannot write in English, petitioning ministries for milk and fruit to be sent to refugee camps, poring over maps to pinpoint the location of village wells so army units can be sent to close them, seal their human skeletons within.

And Sardarji is doing vandana, giving almost all his salary to the gurdwaras to take care of those who have no relatives left.

But it is with the Guru's last admonition, 'Naam japo,' repeat the name of God, that Sardarji's duty falls to Roop.

Roop's hand touches her wrist, covering her name spelled in Persian script.

Just as Satya would have done, Roop organizes three-day Akhand Paath prayers at the bungalow and at the large gurdwaras in Delhi for those who have lost a son, a husband, a mother, sometimes a daughter. Just as Satya would have done, Roop supervises Atma Singh as he piles wheat rotis high on a tray and takes them to the gurdwara to feed all who come – maybe some Hindus and some Muslims among them; that they are not slow in taking does not mean Roop should be slow in giving. Mama always said – 'A beggar gives you an opportunity to be generous.'

'Maybe,' Roop says to Toshi now, 'Sardar Kushal Singh is the lucky one of all of us. He has been able to stop remembering.'

* * *

'Are you still asleep? It is almost noon,' Sardarji starts up at her touch, his eyes bulging with a fear that lights fear within Roop. 'Hush, it's nothing. So jao,' she says.

He looks about him uncomprehendingly.

'We are in Delhi,' she says helpfully.

A curtainless window faces a compound wall, where white-wash is rain-smirched to an ikkat print. From cracks in the plaster at its base, marigolds struggle from mud.

Sardarji groans and turns away, dragging a pillow over his face so only the back of his head appears, his topknot smaller now, shot with silver streaks. It has loosened in his sleep, exposing his bald spot. Another nightmare. He has never told her what happened on his train from Lahore, but over and over he repeats, 'Some things are best left undescribed.'

'Are you well?' Roop asks.

'Reney de.'

Leave him alone?

'You think I am so uncaring, I would leave you alone?' she teases. 'Uttho, na.'

'I cannot wake. There is so much to do, I do not know where to begin. There are so many of us, I don't know who to help first.'

'Ask Vaheguru where is your duty,' she advises, as Satya might have.

She has never seen him like this, childlike, in need. Sardarji, who always knows what must be done, how, when, and by whom. Sardarji, who guided her, raised her from Pari Darvaza to Rawalpindi, through Khanewal, Patiala and Lahore, gave her his protection like an umbrella in the monsoon. Yesterday he said science had lost all poetry for him, that he is no longer Sardarji, a qualified man, but just another Sardarji like all the turbaned men in Delhi trying to swallow grief and rebuild their shattered lives. Every kindness, all altruism, in this place he now calls Hindustan instead of India comes tarnished with self-interest.

Satya would tell him Hindus too, have suffered, many of them have lost just as much.

Today even when he was brought a letter signed by Prime Minister Jawaharlal Nehru authorizing him to begin construction of Bhakra Dam, he did not rejoice, but let the letter fall among all the forms and letters piled upon his desk.

A few days ago, Roop read him a letter from Manager Abdul Aziz:

Please not to worry – I have released a king and queen cobra into the godowns to guard your possessions by night. I give them milk each morning so, inshallah, they will sleep during the day and not harm the refugees who shelter in your haveli. Full four hundred people are living here now, both in your wing of the haveli and in your older brother's wing, but only till they can go back to their homes in India.

The banyan has thrown new roots around the haveli after these rains. It sucks so much nourishment from the underground stream, the walls are shifting inward as if a noose draws closer about our necks. We sleep on the terrace; if the haveli falls, it is best to be on the top, not the bottom.

But Sardarji only stroked his keys, sighed, said nothing.

He, who said he never dreamed while sleeping, now has ferocious nightmares that negate any Muslim deeds that may have helped to bring him through the slaughter. He shouts into the dark, 'Do you have no feeling, no feeling at all?'

He wants the books from his study, now sunken deep into soil, mourns for English books and five-hundred-year-old unbound manuscripts in Persian and Punjabi, buried till a reader worthy of conversing with the centuries can reach them to read again.

Roop leaves him, but only to go to the small kitchen. This sagging bungalow holds them in its inner dark till it seems they wander in it always, though their feet be motionless. The Muslim junior official's family it once sheltered before them must now be dead or in some Sikh or Hindu bungalow in the new Pakistan. Did a Muslim woman feel the fear that lives within Roop, and has she gone to Pakistan, carrying her fear within her? What stories will that woman tell her sons?

'Atma Singh,' Roop commands, 'go to the bazaar and buy

pinni sweets for tea. Like in 'Pindi, like the ones Bari-Sardarni used to make.'

The normally peaceful old man has been haggling to the point of quarrel with every shopkeeper; he cannot find his opium in Delhi at any price he can afford. And everything from fertile Punjab and Bengal is in short supply, wheat for rotis, tea, matches, eggs for Timcu and Aman, pinni sweets.

'Remember to speak Hindi, Atma Singh. Say "ji-han," in Hindi, not "hanji." And if you do speak Punjabi, say "hanji," not "ah-ho." Even Punjabi is different here. When you ask directions don't say "Kithey jason." Use Hindi! And get flour milled from Punjabi wheat – this rice is turning the children's stomachs to water.'

'You can't trust these Delhi people, Sardarniji,' Atma Singh says in a conspiratorial tone. 'They don't care that we lost everything for their independent Hindustan, they want to cheat us again.'

'Go, na,' Roop coaxes.

Roop returns to Sardarji's room, straightens his new moustache brush, manicuring set and silver kanga on the table serving as makeshift dresser, arranges his trousers and waistcoat as poor lost Dehna Singh would have. She notices Sardarji's turban on the night stand – he has begun to tie it Delhi style, smaller, without a trailing safa that says he is from Rawalpindi.

I will tell the new washerman to put more starch in Sardarji's turbans.

She covers the glass of water at his bedside with a beaded doily a Muslim woman must have crocheted and left behind here.

Delhi water tastes slightly bitter – it comes from the Jumna, instead of from the Indus or its five sweet tributaries.

Sardarji lies still; his closed eyes shut her out completely.

Something must be done or everyone will lose heart.

Madani, Madani's husband, Jeevan's sons, perhaps Papaji if she can persuade him, depend on Sardarji now. The refugees in their tents outside depend on him now. The people disputing canal water all through Punjab need him, India needs him to begin Bhakra Dam.

What would Satya do?

Satya would find a way to give him new heart now.

But how?

New hope, the strength of my youth for his second life in the new country.

Roop comes to Sardarji's side, takes his big square-fingered hand in her slender fingers.

This gift must be given so he never knows he was given it.

Something must be sacrificed for his haumai, his self-ness, to return, rise and move forward.

She says, 'Sardarji, I must tell you something.'

'Not now, Roop.'

'Now, because we are alone.'

'Say, then. What is it?'

He rolls away; his back is to her.

Roop crawls beneath the sheet with him and comes close, holding him from behind, smelling his unique scent past the scents of sandalwood and Brylcreem. She tells him her secret, carried so very many years. She tells him she has one bad ear, and only one good ear and assures him it is tuned to the message of his heart.

'How long is it since you cannot hear?' he asks, when she has finished.

'A few months only.'

'How did this happen?'

'Who can say?'

Vaheguru, forgive me, but a woman must choose the wisdom of lies over the dangers of truth.

They lie together like two spoons in a drawer, her knees tucked under his, her breath coming fast against his bare neck. If he spurns her now, she has nowhere to go. This life she sculpted from the pain of doing what a woman is for will vanish, and she will return to sitting cross-legged in some village or ashram on a dirt floor.

If he spurns her now, his children will be parted from her forever.

But will he do so?

There are so many women who have lost more than the use of one ear, so many maimed, so many defaced and violated –

what is one small ear that does not hear? Sardarji has lost so much – his ancestral haveli, his villages, his mill, his orchards, his sons' inheritance. What is one small ear that does not hear?

And surely he needs her now.

What will he make of her weakness?

Gift or burden?

Roop did not need to speak, she could have stayed silent.

But she *has* spoken now; there is no taking the words back. She will have to defend them, defend herself against their power. Silence has been wounded and will not spread itself about her again.

She did not need to speak, but she *has* spoken now. She has given him knowledge he can use against her, should he choose to do so.

But Roop has proven herself three times, before this, shown Sardarji three times she is good-good, sweet-sweet as Sita, shown him as Sardarji plucked her children, like apricot buds sprouting from between her legs, and gave them one by one, to Satya.

But remember, remember how Ram turned coward, became afraid of what-people-will-say and banished Sita just on suspicion that she was imperfect?

If he keeps me I will help him, give him the energy of my youth, turn my ambition for myself to ambition for him. I can do it now, I speak English.

She gives her weakness now, for him to take strength from his knowledge of it. Now, when he needs to be all his quom needs him to be.

We are Punjabis, we will rebuild – what other choices are there?

But if he spurns her now, sends her back to Papaji as damaged goods though she has done what women are for, she will have nowhere to be.

Her heart pounds in her ear. Every muscle cringes within her in anticipation of Sardarji's anger. The familiar fiery hole has returned to her belly.

Oh, foolish woman to venture past the protection of silence!

But now Sardarji turns to her, takes her in his arms so her face is buried in the silver-flecked hair lining his barrel chest and soon she feels his tears mingling with hers. He strokes her head as if she were his bride again, his small brown koel, and their limbs entwine through the sultry afternoon.

'I must take you to a doctor immediately – there are many in Delhi. Don't worry, I will do something.'

She says only, 'As you think best.'

And in the evening he is himself again, giving orders, his turban secure and proud upon his head, though tied a little smaller than before. He takes his new walking stick and Atma Singh brings his European shoes polished to elegance. After pinni sweets and tea he says, 'Call a tonga for me. I know several young fellows in the home ministry – I put in a good word for them years ago. They will remember me and I will remind them of their duty to their quom.'

Nothing more is said about Roop's bad ear until he is climbing into the tonga. With his foot on the step, he says, 'I will ask one of them to recommend a good doctor in Delhi, now the British ones are gone. Now remember, Roop, you leave things to me.'

He tests the step of the tonga, then commits his full weight to it, steps in. The tonga driver raises his whip. The wheels move forward, crushing night queen flowers, leaving purple-red stains from the fruit of jamun trees by the side of the road. As the skinny rubbed-raw tonga horse turns onto the broad avenue, so unlike the narrow lanes of Rawalpindi, and clip-clops away, Sardarji raises his hand, waves his walking stick, moving forward though still facing back.

Her gift is working within him, giving him the strength he needs.

Fear lifts, rises above the gulmohar trees.

Leaves Roop light, translucent as sky.

EPILOGUE

I, Satya, return from silence.
This life begins with a midwife bearded but turbanless, wearing
a white mask and a white coat. Lights above me shine painfully
white, the walls are white, the sheets are white, strange textures,
strange shapes. Medicinal scents assault my nose as I am severed
from the womb.

Too late, I remember: never open your eyes in a new life without
forgetting your past one.

Smack! On my small naked bottom. I kick, I kick!

Aaaaaiiiiiiiieeeeeeeeeeeeeee!

I open my new mouth and scream.

Aaaaaiiiiiiiieeeeeeeeeeeeeee!

All the visits I made to sants and all the offerings I gave at gurdwaras were not enough. All the suffering I endured, the wait-ing, the watching from the latent nothingness, all these were not enough.

Again am I born a woman, foolish girl-child who has entered the world with her eyes wide open and so will never lower them before a man. Foolish girl-child with two whole lungs to scream and a body that remembers, remembers the thought, remembers the un-thought, the good deeds and the bad, even as others remember only the bad.

This is my karma.

The man's voice comes deep, comes low, falling like a gramophone winding down.

I do not need to understand words to know he is disappointed I am not a boy. Some things need no translation. And I know, because my body remembers without benefit of words, that men who do not welcome girl-babies will not treasure me as I grow to woman — though he call me princess just because the Gurus told him to.

I have come so far, I have borne so much pain and emptiness!

But men have not yet changed.

Acknowledgments

Too many people gave of their time, knowledge and support as this book was written for any list of acknowledgments to be complete. Nevertheless, I especially thank: my grandmother Raminder Sarup Singh, Rani Singh Sodhi, G. B. Singh, Manjit Singh, and others in India who opened their hearts and memories to me. Also Vinay Oberoi and Ena Singh who helped with the research there.

In Pakistan, my thanks to Safia Awan, Shamim Anwar, filmmaker Shireen Pasha, Neelam Hussein of Simorgh, Lahore, Kakaji Sandhim, and the residents of Pari Darvaza, especially Moond-bi.

Grateful thanks to Sadhu Binning, I.J. Singh, Nighat Kokan, Dr Charu Malik, Dr Padmini Mongia and Pegi Taylor who read part or all of this book and gave valuable comments; to Judy Bridges at Redbird Studios, Elaine Bergstrom (Marie Kiraly) who leads my novel writers group, the librarians of Milwaukee Public Library and cyberfriends on SAWNET, SASIALIT and H-ASIA listservs. A grant from the Canada Council assisted me in visiting Pakistan.

Special thanks to my husband, David Baldwin, my resident reader and escort through Pakistan, and to my editors, Diane Martin, Louise Dennys, Nan Talese and Ursula Mackenzie whose questions and comments over many readings expanded and deepened this novel, and who asked for what was not yet on the page. Thanks to my agents, Jennifer Barclay and Bruce Westwood.

The following print sources were invaluable: Urvashi Butalia's articles and her book, *The Other Side of Silence; The Sikhs* by Owen Cole and Piara Singh Sambhi; Hew McLeod's books on Sikhism; J.S. Grewal's books on Sikh history; *Ethics of the Sikhs* by Avtar Singh; Ayesha Jalal and Sugata Bose's *Modern South Asia: History, Culture, Political Economy*; and Sardar Bahadur Sarup Singh's unpublished manuscript: *Note on the Canal Water Dispute between India and Pakistan*.